Alan D1609841

Alan Gibbons is a full-time writer and a visiting speaker and lecturer at schools, colleges and literary events nationwide, including the major book festivals. He lives in Liverpool with his wife and four children.

Alan Gibbons has twice been shortlisted for the Carnegie Medal ~~~ *Edge* a ~ *Shadow of the Minotaur*, wh ~~~ lue Peter Boo' Award in the ~~~ own' catego:

The Lost Souls Stories

THE DARKWING OMNIBUS

ALAN GIBBONS

Orion
Children's Books

This omnibus edition first published in Great Britain in 2007
by Orion Children's Books
a division of the Orion Publishing Group Ltd
Orion House
5 Upper St Martin's Lane
London WC2H 9EA
An Hachette Livre UK Company

1 3 5 7 9 10 8 6 4 2

Originally published as two separate volumes:
Rise of the Blood Moon
First published in Great Britain 2006
by Orion Children's Books
Setting of a Cruel Sun
First published in Great Britain 2006
by Orion Children's Books

ISBN 13 – 9781 84255 617 7

Printed in Great Britain by
Clays Ltd, St Ives plc

www.orionbooks.co.uk

Contents

The Lost Souls Stories Book 1

RISE OF THE BLOOD MOON

To the memory of Anthony Walker,
murdered by prejudice

CHAPTER I

The Black Tower

I

There is a dark tower at the end of the Earth. Perched high on the summit of a bare mountain, amid swirling winds and endless driving rain, it is a bleak, forbidding structure. There are no gates. There is no visible means of entry. There are no windows. No lights wink into the endless murk. Indeed, there isn't the slightest trace of a road, a path, even a foot-worn trail. There is no means of access at all. It clings precariously to a sheer rock face, the impossible creation of a lost civilisation of – who knows? Gods, demons, giants. Some say it was the work of one man. But how could that be? How could one pair of hands raise such a building?

For miles around you will not discover a single animal track or hear one note of birdsong. It is many years since even the scrape of insects has been heard. Neither provisions nor weapons nor armour have been carried through the dense, silent forests that carpet the lower slopes of the mountain. It is quite deserted. There are no sentries patrolling it. There has never been any need. Not once, in the recent life of this tower, has any living thing, other than its present owner, his minions and his captives, dared to approach its walls.

But, if you were somehow to penetrate the fortifications, if you were to climb its hundreds of barely worn steps, you would discover, on the tower's topmost floors, a series of echoing galleries, sealed from the outside world, but without lock or keyhole. There are no magic words that will gain you entrance. There is no abracadabra. But inside somebody stirs, a boy, in the high tide of adolescence.

The events in this story happened over a thousand years ago, so far in the past that history and legend mix. Only poets and singers have ever tried to guess what might have been. The year was 675. The dynasty of the Muzals had lasted six long centuries. Their coming ushered in a time of conquest and war. From the endless steppes of the west to the deserts of the east, the peoples of the known world lived under the sway of the Muzals' monstrous tyranny. The Empire was born in fire, tempered in the clash of steel on steel. Its reputation was painted in human blood. And, as the Muzals swept across the land, the stain of that blood polluted the world.

It was towards the end of the month of Samhair when it all began. In those days the Empire of all the Peoples observed the ancient calendar of the Vassyrian scholar Udmanesh. But, such was his notoriety among the rulers of the land, they refused to credit him with its invention. They were quick to acclaim his study of the moon and stars, his anatomy of the human body, the surgical skills their surgeons used on the battlefield, but anonymously. In

2

all other matters, they considered him the worst kind of heretic, one who did not think like them. Udmanesh's crime was to speak out against oppression, to tell the truth about the Muzals' reign. All his life he carried the torch of freedom until his enemies struck it from his hand.

It was the time of the Blood Moon, when the moon hung full, round and silver in the night sky. For as long as people could remember, in the lunar cycle of this land, on the sixtieth day, the demons had swarmed through the darkness and fed on human flesh. As if sensing their death-hunger, the boy who lived in the tower stirred. For the first time in many hours he wasn't alone. He didn't know what day it was. There had been a time he tried to keep count, but he'd long since abandoned the record he'd begun scratching on the wall in the first days of his imprisonment. Somewhere, in the furthest reaches of his memory, he had an image of happiness, of a home, parents, a sister. But in this awful place the memory of those days was disintegrating hour by hour.

Indeed, he could no longer even tell whether it was night or day, spring or summer, winter or autumn. In the absence of a window there was no way to judge. His only way of charting the passage of time was the pattern of the Darkwing's visits each Blood Moon. The only light, set at cubit-lengths around the circular walls, was provided by the tallow candles that guttered, casting a yellowish glow around the room. Where the breeze came from the boy had never discovered, but come it did, just as the Darkwing came to feed. Despair clouded the boy's mind. He lived in an endless present, with no prospect of rescue. So far as he was aware, nobody even knew he was here. Were it not for an astonishing ability, rare in one so young, to live within the precincts of his own mind, he would have gone mad.

A sliver of ice entered his heart. The Darkwing's shadow

was spreading across the wall like a vast obsidian bruise. His presence seemed to chill the air. He was the Prince of Darkness, Master of the Undead.

'Not tonight,' the boy begged. 'Please.'

But the Darkwing was not known for his mercy, only his appetite for blood. For him, blood was renewal, blood was life. The boy flinched. His tormentor's appearance was so grotesque as to turn your flesh to water. His entire body was encased in a black and scarlet carapace, a shell like a cockroach's. He was winged in the way of a huge bug or a bat. His fingers and toes ended in claws, scythe-sharp and obviously deadly. Many were his victims, their flesh hideously ripped by his slashing attacks. His head was similarly inhuman, almost insect-like. Fangs like needles glistened in his mouth. But it was his eyes that dominated his face. They were large, black and utterly emotionless. As he crossed the room a single maggot spilled like a tear from the corner of his right eye. The rancid perfume of decay escaped the demon lord. The boy shuddered.

'You must give me what is mine,' the Darkwing said, coming closer. 'You know I will take it anyway.' His hand gripped the boy's shoulder, the razor-like claws digging into his flesh. 'You do know that, don't you?'

The boy nodded wretchedly. He knew. Even then, weak as he was, his mind was sharp, his thinking clear. Seeing the Darkwing's hungry approach, the boy cowered but was unable to resist. He knew that he would survive the feeding. In the early weeks of his imprisonment he had wondered, each time the Darkwing came, whether he would wake up again. But death would have been a release, far less cruel than this enduring torment. The Darkwing did not take more than the boy could give. He never exhausted the scarlet fountain of warm blood, which had become his own life's elixir. Nor did he let the boy become infected by the

4

contagion of the undead. He needed the young man conscious, warm with the flickering flame of life. The Darkwing had fed on many victims but none had tasted so sweet. The blood in this boy was as pure as the first light of dawn.

'Come to me,' the Darkwing said.

The boy did as he was told. There was no alternative, this time or any other. Raising his eyes, he met the crow-black stare of the Darkwing.

'Will I ever leave this place?' he asked, trembling to the very marrow of his bones.

The Darkwing dismissed the question with a blink. The predator lord didn't waste words. He came. He fed. That was all.

Afterwards, the boy slept. He had never seen the Darkwing arrive in his windowless prison. He had never seen him leave. He seemed to be able to materialise from the walls the way mist gathers on a cold windowpane. This visit was no exception.

2

On that same sixtieth day of Samhair, at that same gathering of dusk, the evening bell tolled over the glittering city of Parcep. Known as the Gateway to the East, Parcep of the Tiger Gates was the main southern port of the Empire and the second city of the Muzals' vast domain. It sucked in metals, spices, jewels and silks from the many lands the Imperial armies had conquered. Most of all it drew in the Helati on whose labour the Empire's power was built. Along the port's quays trudged each new consignment of these slaves to be put to work to enrich the Children of Ra.

It was a tranquil summer's night. The heat clung to everything like resin. The waters of the southern ocean were as still and turquoise as one of the decorative pieces created by the Empire's master glassblowers to stand in pride of place upon some wealthy noble's table. Dhows and outriggers lay becalmed on the water's glassy surface. Galleys from far-off Lyria crossed the harbour, their oars churning the still ocean. They had loaded their amphorae with peppers and spices from the warehouses of Parcep in exchange for timber and ore.

In the thickening darkness two friends were walking down the processional Avenue of the Kings.

'Which room did you say was Julmira's?' the taller of the pair asked, staring across the wide avenue at a large, whitewashed villa.

'Well, well,' his companion said. 'It seems you don't know where your sweet betrothed lays her head each night.'

'Kulmat,' Gardep snapped, 'point out the room.'

He had had quite enough teasing since Commander Rishal had sprung his surprise: an arranged marriage between his daughter and his most skilled young warrior. As was the custom in old Parcep, the future bride and groom didn't meet formally until their engagement feast.

'That's it,' Kulmat said. 'The moment I heard the news, I got one of the house slaves to point it out.'

Gardep peered through the gloom. With three floors, the villa was one of the largest in the city. It stood next to the Temple of Ra. It was a rich man's house, with its own well, its own plumbing and many glittering rooms maintained by a veritable regiment of white-garbed house slaves. The roof gardens were sumptuously stocked. Rishal's bowers of wild roses were much admired. Indeed, Gardep could smell their scent from where he stood. The gardeners of Parcep were renowned throughout the Empire for their work and none more so than those employed by Rishal.

The courtyards of the villa, visible through the gates, were magnificent. Elaborate mosaics covered every inch of them. Statues of polished sandstone stood along every corridor, passage and walkway, illuminated by flaring braziers. Pride of place went to the statue of the sun god Ra, the deity in permanent conflict with his evil brother, the moon god Sangra. Gardep took in the sights and wondered why he was being offered a marriage that would give him all this. He had, after all, grown up not knowing his own roots, an orphan with only the haziest recollection of his past in one of the subject territories of the Empire. Solitary and shy of most of his fellows, with just the one close friend in which to confide, he felt ill-at-ease with the cream of Parcep society.

'Rishal-Ra must be the richest man in all Parcep,' Gardep said, marvelling at the ostentatious display of wealth.

'In the whole southern Empire, more like,' Kulmat said. 'Only the wealthiest families of golden Rinaghar itself live in greater luxury. Remember, your knight has another villa high in the hills, in the domain of the snow leopard. From there he goes hunting. It is rumoured that the preserved heads of hundreds of wild beasts decorate the villa's walls. Marry Julmira and you will inherit it all.'

Gardep was utterly in awe of his master, Rishal-ax-Sol. Rishal was the garrison commander, a seasoned warrior and hero of the Empire of all the Peoples. The gold-painted scars on his face and arms bore witness to that. Rishal was third in line to the Imperial Throne and its greatest general. He had conquered the Empire's greatest rival, proud Vassyria, taking its capital in spite of a grave wound to the shoulder. That day he earned himself the title Lion of Inbacus.

Two years Gardep had been Rishal's squire and, though he had hung on his master's every word, not once had he dared ask Rishal a personal question.

There wasn't another recruit to the academy who observed protocol as strictly as Gardep. The army was his life. He lived by its rules. He was certain that he would die by them, too. The truth is, he barely felt worthy to saddle Rishal's horse, never mind marry his noble daughter. Even now, all that time after he had been taken under Rishal's wing, he felt honoured merely to serve him. Was it any wonder that, when Rishal had told him of his intentions, to betroth Gardep to his daughter Julmira, Gardep had almost choked?

'Do you think her beautiful?' Gardep said.

'Who?' Kulmat asked, teasing as usual.

'Who do you think, Kulmat? I'm talking about Julmira, my betrothed.'

'You've seen her.'

It was true. Gardep had glimpsed her occasionally at some function but he hadn't paid her much attention.

'I want your opinion,' he said.

'Do you want the truth?' Kulmat asked.

'Of course I do.'

'Then, in all honesty,' Kulmat said, a mischievous twinkle in his eyes. 'I say she looks like a horse and brays like a mule. You've made a match with the ugliest crone in all Parcep.'

At that, Gardep turned his back on his friend and continued his vigil. The next time he looked at Julmira, it wasn't going to be as his master's daughter, but as a prospective bride. By now the twilight was deepening into the first indigo hours of night. Torches flared along Parcep's broad, palm-lined boulevards and lanterns swung on the balconies of villas. They weren't the only lights. From every villa, every workshop, every granary, warehouse and boatyard, the slaves were beginning their nightly exodus from the city. Torches and rush-lights guided their way, filling the air with their acrid fragrance.

It was the same every evening. As soon as the sun went down over the ocean the Helati, the Empire's slave caste, had to leave the city. It had ever been this way. There were many reasons, chief of which was the Empire's nagging fear of revolt. Throughout their rule, it had been the Muzals' enduring nightmare. Once, within the living memory of the city's elders, the slaves had come within a whisker of throwing off their chains and toppling the sun throne. There were, after all, ten Helati to every true child of the sun god Ra. Fear kept them captive. During daylight hours there were whips and chains, stocks and brandings, stonings and summary executions to break their spirit. With such an enormous apparatus of terror, nobody dreamed the Helati would ever rise again. At night, the Sol-ket put them outside the city walls in rough compounds and let them fend for themselves. Beyond the walls the Helati sheltered in mean mud-brick houses, crude wooden shelters or even out in the open, beneath the branches of the banyan tree.

Some said that among the Helati there were those who possessed the power to conquer death itself. Such tales often quietened the children of Parcep's wealthy elite.

The evening bell rang louder now, echoing across the bay. A pushing, jostling throng choked the streets. The Helati weren't in any hurry to leave. They knew what awaited them outside the city walls. But the Sol-ket drove the slave hordes out at swordpoint. It was the first night of the Blood Moon. The sooner the city gates were closed, the sooner the good citizens of Parcep could sleep easily in their beds. Let the slaves suffer; at least Parcep's free-born people would greet the dawn refreshed.

'Gardep,' Kulmat said. 'You're in luck. That's her now.'

Gardep followed his friend's pointing finger. Sure enough, on the third-floor balcony of Rishal's villa, beneath a saffron awning and framed by bowers of white and crimson blossom, there was a tall maiden in a flowing emerald sari. She had a *phuli*, a nose ring with an oval jewel hanging from it. Around her throat gold necklaces glittered in the light of the braziers. But, for all the magic of the spectacle, Gardep's eyes didn't linger long on her. He was no more attracted to her now than he was on the other occasions he had seen her. Even before his gaze left young mistress Julmira, anguish had begun to work into his heart, as if a thread was being pulled, ever so slowly, through it. His skin prickled and his throat went dry. A curious fire licked through every atom of his being. It was as if his entire life had been leading up to this moment.

The reason for his agitation? Below Julmira's balcony, at street level, the servant's entrance had just opened. It was a Helat, a slave girl. Seemingly oblivious to Gardep, she remained unveiled and breathed in the evening air. For a moment her face was caught in the light of a brazier. It was an unusual sight. It was forbidden for a Helat to be seen unveiled in public. But this girl seemed impervious to the Empire's laws. Everything about her flouted her lowly station in life. Though her salwar kameez was the plain white of the house slave, poorly cut, unembroidered and without finery, there was no disguising her poise and beauty. They were obvious in her every step as she seemed to glide across the ground in her bare feet. Every bob of her lustrous, plaited hair declared her natural grace. Gardep watched her progress, in turns enchanted and appalled. For a member of Parcep's military elite to look at a slave this way was taboo. But what better reason to die, Gardep thought, than in the adoration of beauty.

That's when he realised the risk she was taking. For any Helat, male or female, to be seen on the streets of Parcep wearing neither veil, nor hood, nor scarf, was an offence punishable by a beating. Were a slave to persist in this crime, disfigurement or death would surely follow. The message of the city's ruling order was simple: the slaves were as many pairs of calloused hands. The showing of their faces constituted an act of defiance. Their offending countenances must be hidden from the eyes of their masters.

The girl must have sensed Gardep's gaze upon her, felt his worshipping glance, because, without the slightest hint of shame or fear, she met it and faced it down.

Her features were darker than her mistress's. Gardep even fancied that the pride, so obvious in her features, was intentional. Could she be as drawn to him as he was to her?

Then and only then, when he had glanced away shame-faced, did she fasten her veil and join the crowds spilling out of the North Gate. Soon, she was just one more white shawl in the throng. Even so, long after she had gone Gardep continued to stare after her. He did not know that, in the girl's mind too, his features were indelibly printed.

'So what did you think of your lady?' Kulmat asked.

A sigh of yearning came from Gardep's lips. 'Beautiful,' he said, 'very beautiful.'

But he didn't mean Julmira.

3

Hundreds of miles to the west, under another sky, a man held a lonely battlement vigil. Here however, in a meaner, colder town than wealthy Parcep, there was no slave exodus.

Zindhar was the final fortress before the Demon Wall. No Helat was trusted to labour in this place. They had constructed it and then been evicted. Zindhar's existence was precarious enough without the added peril of a slave fifth column. The Demon Wall, massive in the distance, was an engineering marvel. This barrier, ten metres high and twice that distance wide, separated the Empire's lands from the vast wastes beyond, ruled by the Darkwing and his host of Lost Souls.

The Demon Wall stretched from the snow-peaked mountains of the northern territories to the sparkling ocean far to the south. It was conceived as a barrier to the swarming legions of the undead, the Lost Souls. They were composed of night-striders and dark-fliers. The night-striders walked the land, flesh rotting, eyes wild with a morbid hunger for human flesh. The dark-fliers roamed the skies, winged, scarlet demons desperate to slake their thirst for human blood. But the wall was more than a line of defence; it was a symbol of vigilance and power. So wide were its battlements that a dozen infantrymen could walk along them, marching abreast. The Muzals had begun its construction more than a hundred years before and it had cost thousands of Helat lives. Some Helati said, with a shudder, that any of the slave workers injured during construction were simply walled up, still alive. Their bones would provide insulation during the cold frontier nights. Such was the cruelty of the children of the sun god, Holy Ra.

Though still unfinished, the Demon Wall was already a formidable obstacle to the inhuman hordes that waited, ravenous eyes trained on the Empire, on the other side. There was a network of deep ditches, passages and wells reaching deep into the earth. The Sol-ket filled this labyrinth with thick, flammable oil, known as Lyrian fire. A single torch could set the defences ablaze, turning any night-strider who dared to tunnel beneath the wall into a walking torch. Nowhere else was there such a barrier to the night breed. Then there was the danger from the air. Archers, slingers and catapults were posted to bring down the dark-fliers, the feared dark-flier warriors. Huge ballistae, imported from Lyria, also faced the sky.

The watch that night was kept by Oled Lonetread, himself a mercenary drawn from the parched steppes, many leagues further north than most Imperial troops wished to journey. His fur cloak and his breastplate of leather and iron strips set him apart from the Sol-ket with their burnished armour, their helmets inlaid with gold and topped by horsehair tassels.

Oled was a full head and shoulders taller than the Easterners. His weapon was the battle-axe he carried strapped to his powerful back. It was Oled whom the garrison commander, Turayat, sought out when he needed advice about the world beyond the wall. Even though, like any Easterner, Turayat held the barbarian in contempt, he had learned to value his experience of this hostile western frontier.

'Well, Oled, what do you think?'

Oled looked along the wall. In the darkness the watchtowers rose like black storks, their spindly legs enveloped by clouds of steel-grey smoke from the campfires. Through the smoke drums sounded, like a heartbeat, and accompanying them there came the steady drone of the Lost Souls' voices. It was a chorus of the undead.

Oled was careful to use the respectful suffix 'Ra' when he spoke to one of the masters. If any of the Sol-ket showed disrespect they would have to endure a beating. Should a barbarian like Oled do the same he would be lucky to live.

13

'I don't like it, Turayat-Ra. The drums, the chanting, it's a bad sign. Death spills from the darkness.'

Turayat frowned. 'Don't you think you're exaggerating the danger, Oled? We are the Sol-ket, the Warriors of the Sun. Our arrows hiss on the wind, whispering their blood oath into the faces of our foes. Our blades sing with death. We have conquered all the nations from the arid desert wastes of Selessia to the saffron shores of Banshu. We have mastered the known world and created the Empire of all the Peoples. The demons will come and we will conquer them.'

Oled had heard all this before: the Sol-ket were a boastful bunch. They had good cause, that was true. They had fought hundreds of battles, often against seemingly insurmountable odds, but the Sun banners still flaunted the skies from the Demon Wall to the endless scrubland of Khut, from the frozen shores of the north all the way to the southern ocean, to palm-fringed Sharidasa and the thirty islands of Banshu. They ruled an empire of many million souls and hundreds of varied peoples. Nevertheless . . .

'Well, Oled, speak your mind.'

'They are preparing an attack, Turayat-Ra, and not just some small skirmish. Their legions are massing. They are as numerous as heads of wheat on the Plains of Jinghara. Just listen to their voices.'

Turayat listened. A veteran of so many fights with the Lost Souls, he couldn't, even in his worst nightmares, imagine them creating an army that could threaten the Empire's western boundary. Driven by their foul lusts, they lacked discipline. They were just one more gang of barbarians to be put to the sword, barbarians from beyond the grave.

'You've spent too many years looking at that wall, Oled. How long has it been?'

'Eight years,' Oled said.

'Yes,' Turayat said, gathering his scarlet cloak around his shoulders, 'and in all that time, have we ever been defeated? A few dozen dark-fliers might get through our defences. But a full-scale invasion? You talk of legions. You're dreaming, Oled. These creatures, they lack direction. We have always kept them at bay before. They are lower than the beasts of the field, without intelligence or culture. How could they ever create a command structure or develop strategy and tactics? They are an ignorant pestilence, not an army.'

Oled listened in silence. He knew Turayat was wrong. Things had changed. It was true that the night breed were normally chaotic and savage, as likely to devour each other as to attack human settlements. But events were moving fast. There was a method to their behaviour now. It had all begun with the Darkwing's most recent coming. He had started to transform them from a bestial throng into an army. But there was no point arguing with Turayat. He wouldn't pay any attention anyway. Still, Oled had heard the gargling voices of the undead beneath the Earth. He wasn't dreaming. He was having nightmares.

4

Gardep remained on the battlements long after the end of his watch. Kulmat had asked him over and over again to come into the barracks to play chess. But Gardep spurned the camaraderie of the dormitory. He was a lone wolf. He longed for a moment, a few fleeting seconds, in the company of the dark-eyed slave girl he had seen that night. Suddenly, though he was standing close to his comrades of eight years, he was a man alone, yearning for something his comrades would consider forbidden and wrong.

Sol-ket loyalty was legendary. Cadets joined the order as boys. During their years of training they would see their parents for only a few days a year, on visits home for the major festivals. Gardep didn't even have that to look forward to. He had no recollection of his parents' faces. His first memories were of siege, battle and death.

He did however remember every stage of his training as if it were yesterday. Raised in the furnace of war, he was a natural warrior.

More than any other experience in his early years Gardep remembered his Ket-Ra, the trial of manhood that took place on his fourteenth birthday. He had been summoned to stand before the other warriors. He had watched Rishal unsheathe his curved dagger. He had watched him sharpen it until the razor edge could cut floating silk. Then Rishal had told him to stand steady. There were many recruits who fell at this stage. The young cadet was expected to clasp his hands behind his back and accept the master's cuts without flinching. Instinctively some threw out their hands in self-defence and had to be restrained so they could complete the ritual.

Gardep did nothing of the kind. He stood expressionless under the blazing sun while Rishal had cut the Sun emblem into his chest, scoring the spreading rays outward across his flesh. Then, while the cuts were still fresh and the blood was still running, Gardep was taken to the Dragon Mountains. There, he had to survive on his wits and make his way home.

Many young men died out there in the arid thorn forests. Some were slaughtered during the long, hot nights by marauding bands of Lost Souls. Others simply lost their way and perished from hunger or thirst. There were rumours that dragons haunted the mountains that bore their name. Some survivors swore they had heard savage roars in the night. Those who survived their test had been steeled in the furnace of endurance.

Gardep refused to die. He was born to conquer. With bow and with sword he would serve his Emperor and his implacable god, almighty Ra. That was the determination that maintained him throughout his long trek. Hollow as his stomach became with hunger, cracked as his lips became with thirst, he defied the sun, the thorn bushes and the waiting vultures. He was ready for the dragons.

But even Gardep faced his moment of crisis. There was one dusty afternoon when he lay prostrate, the last of his strength gone. He truly believed he was dying. Then a voice came to him, carried on the wind. *You will not die here, na-Vassyrian*, it told him, *for you are descended from mighty warriors. You must live to fulfil your destiny, many years from now, on the tenth of Hoj.* He never knew where the voice came from or what the strange message meant, but he would never forget it. Fortified by the promise, he staggered to his feet and continued his long march.

Gardep's trial, at six days, was one of the shortest in the annals of the Sol-ket. Of all the Warriors of the Sun who had passed through the academy at Parcep, only Rishal had matched Gardep's astonishing achievement and he was one of the senior generals of the entire Empire, a man of whom ballads were sung. The orphan Gardep, a young man as serious and ascetic as a priest, immediately became a figure cast in Rishal's mould, looked upon in awe by all the other cadets, especially when the commander adopted him as his squire.

Thereafter he had bested mature Sol-ket in armed and unarmed combat on many occasions, marking himself out as a future general. Only Kulmat treated him with the old familiarity. His friend was incorrigible however, a rogue without respect for anyone. But the thrill of achievement is fleeting, Gardep thought as he looked out over the golden dome of the Temple of Ra. Life will always throw up another trial. And it had. How could he resist the feelings he had for this slave girl, feelings which, according to the code of the Sol-ket were taboo, punishable by death?

5

Once outside the Tiger Gates the Helati slowed their pace. This was the Blood Moon. They cast anxious looks into the darkened groves and thickets bordering the Great Western Road. Suddenly every shadow, every shape and outline harboured menace. The slightest moan of the wind was interpreted as a threat. Entirely pitiless, without conscience or mercy, these risen dead swarmed the Helat encampments. They attacked, they slaughtered, they fed. They created others like themselves.

Cusha, like every Helat in that throng, cast nervous glances at the night sky. Everything startled her now: the slightest rustle in the hedgerows, the snap of a twig, the scamper of a lizard. Added to her usual anxiety about the night breed, there was a new emotion, a curiosity about the young warrior who had stared at her so intently. It was as if his eyes had stared into the inner sanctum of her being. He'd seen her most private feelings, felt the stirring of her spirit within his own soul. They might not have spoken but they had communicated. Though there were hundreds of men, women and children around her on the Western Road she didn't see their faces or hear their voices. The warrior's proud handsomeness eclipsed them all.

'Cusha!'

It was Harad. This gaunt, hollow-cheeked boy of thirteen summers was her brother. They were not related by blood but some years ago Cusha had been found wandering the rice fields north of Parcep, frightened, alone and for many months made speechless by her experiences. Harad's mother Murima had adopted her. Yet, though there was no blood bond between them, Cusha loved Harad dearly. He was braver, more loyal, more devoted than any dog. She knew he would gladly lay down his life for her. He had shown that in a dozen demon incursions, watching over her with such selfless courage, with such intense protectiveness, that he scared her sometimes. Once, six months before, he had even torn a feeding dark-flier from Cusha's throat. He had got to her just in time. Murima had been able to burn out the contagion with a heated knife and save Cusha from a living death. It had left a scar on her flesh in the shape of the dagger. The hilt began at her collar bone. The blade crossed her throat. The point almost touched her chin. But she had lived to tell the tale.

'Where have you been?' Harad asked. 'We've been looking for you everywhere.'

'It was Mistress Julmira,' Cusha explained. 'She insisted that I take in her new sari. She wants to impress this soldier-boy of hers.'

Cusha imitated Julmira's exaggerated wiggle. 'How do I look, Cusha?' she cooed, copying Julmira's voice. 'Another henna tattoo on my fingers, perhaps?'

Harad looked aghast. 'You wouldn't dare do that around the villa,' he said. 'They'd have you flogged within an inch of your life. We are talking about the Sol-ket, butchers of the poor.'

Cusha remembered the warrior. There would be worse than a flogging in store if she were foolish enough to return his looks with favour.

'I know,' Cusha said. 'But here at least we are free to say what we think.'

'Yes,' he said, casting another fearful glance at the night sky, 'and free to die.'

'Poor Harad,' Cusha said. 'My gloomy little brother.'

She knew he had nightmares about the Blood Moon. He had been no more than seven years old when he lost two of his closest friends, taken one night by demons. Harad had good reason to be serious. At Cusha's words, he frowned.

'I'm almost fourteen,' he objected, 'and you're not fifteen until the first day of Murjin.'

That was typical of Harad. He remembered everyone's birthday, just as he remembered their favourite colour, food and flower. Cusha had never known a boy more thoughtful or more caring. Or more melancholy.

'So where are the others?' she asked.

Harad led her to a lemon grove. Murima rose and clasped Cusha's hands.

'My child,' she said. 'I was quite beside myself with worry.'

Cusha embraced her adoptive mother and stroked her greying hair. 'There was no need, *Mama-li*,' she said. 'I let one of those dark-fliers taste my blood once before. It will never happen again.'

Murima turned her face to the starlit sky. 'I pray to the Four Winds that you are right, my child,' she said.

Cusha hugged Murima hard, as if trying to shelter her from the approaching storm. 'I am.'

Ending the embrace, Cusha looked around. Qintu was there. Horror does different things to different people. The loss of his friends had made Harad anxious and gloomy. Qintu however seemed to have decided his life would in all likelihood be short and, most probably, brutal so he had to make light of its troubles. Even in the most extreme conditions of hardship he would come up smiling.

There were many more familiar faces but one was missing.

'Where is Shamana?' Cusha asked.

Harad shrugged. 'You know what she's like,' he said. 'She always has to be the mystery woman.'

Qintu mimicked Shamana, hobbling on a pretend stick. 'Older than the Dragon mountains I am,' he croaked, 'more weather-beaten than the distant mangroves.'

'Yes,' said Shamana, emerging from the lemon grove, accompanied by a younger woman, 'and tough as Vassyrian leather, you ignorant, disrespectful whelp.'

'Where have you been?' Harad asked.

Shamana fixed him with her green eyes. Though her skin was bronzed and weathered, the result of many years toiling in the fields, she stood out among the Helati. Her skin, if not burned by the eastern sun, would have reverted to its naturally yellowish hue. Her eyes had a Far Eastern fold and her flat cheeks were high. She was no natural-born inhabitant of Parcep.

Over the years there had been many rumours about Shamana. Some said she was from the far north-east, a Yakut or Manchutkan. Others said there was something dark and wild about her, something not quite human at all. But nobody said anything like that to her face and nobody challenged her right to be a counsellor, guide and healer to the suffering Helati people. She could coax a young mother through a difficult birth. She knew the herbs that could ease the rheumatism that plagued the rice pickers. She prepared the poultices that ended fevers. Her surgery saved lives and her words had settled many a quarrel. Yes, and with her stories she kept alive the memory of another time. Centuries before there had been no slaves, only the free peoples of the world.

'Where have I been?' Shamana said.

She exchanged glances with the younger woman next to her. 'Aaliya and I have been continuing the work of venerable Udmanesh, scourge of tyrants. What was I doing? I was balancing the Scales, of course.'

At the mention of the ancient rites of the Helati, Harad's face suddenly looked more gaunt than ever. To mention Udmanesh the scholar and the Scales in one breath was the greatest of heresies. Whole villages had been razed for less. Shamana was inviting death.

'Shamana!' Harad gasped, shocked at her boldness. 'Lower your voice. If the masters think you have anything to do with the Scales, come daylight they will butcher you on this very road. They will sacrifice you to their sun god.'

'And how would they know?' Shamana said. 'Who here will betray me to the Sol-ket?'

She seemed to meet every pair of eyes in the crowd. Some turned away. Others gave an embarrassed cough and bowed their heads. Satisfied that she had been shown due respect, Shamana nodded to Aaliya. She produced a tiny, intricately carved statuette, fashioned from rosewood, the kind that generations of rebel Helati had placed in secret altars away from the prying eyes of the Sol-ket. It was of a young woman in a salwar kameez, the traditional tunic of loose-fitting trousers and blouse, holding aloft a pair of scales, the ancient symbol of Helat resistance. The sight of the object drew gasps from the latecomers who were still making their way into the grove. Such a show of defiance was rare, even for Shamana. Any Helat caught in possession of the symbolic Scales would be put to death on the spot.

Cusha looked at the statuette and knew that, for Shamana to be so bold, something had to have changed in the fabric of the times. But what?

She held the attention of everyone there.

'We must never forget the teachings of venerable Udmanesh. He exposed the cruelty of the Muzals. He exposed their priesthood for what they are, meddlers in the underworld. Those priests, this Hotec-Ra, they're the reason the dead walk the Earth. Never forget that.'

She closed her eyes for a second and breathed in the night air. 'Should any of you have forgotten the teachings of Udmanesh, I will remind you. It is the way of the Scales to seek after peace and harmony, the laying down of the sword to free your strong arm to guide the plough. The divine purpose is the unity of all and the dominance of none.'

There was a hushed silence.

'But,' Shamana said, with heavy irony, 'in these unnatural times, even peace is a commodity to be fought for.'

She handed the statuette back to Aaliya. There had been rumours that she was Shamana's daughter but the priestess had always denied it. Aaliya was her apprentice, no more.

'Now, uncover your weapons.'

Primitive bamboo spears started to appear. Hoes, axes and hammers, stolen over many months, were dug up. It was forbidden for a Helat to bear arms under any conditions. Each Blood Moon the pitiless Children of Ra expected the Helati to go out of the city like so many sheep and offer their throats to the Darkwing's fangs. Shamana would have none of it. The concealed armouries she had organised throughout the countryside were the only defence the Helati had against the Lost Souls. To build forges and smithies to make metal weapons would have incurred the wrath of the masters and led to great suffering, so the Helati made do with farm implements and makeshift weaponry. For her doughty courage and strange, unworldly ways Shamana was respected and feared in equal measure.

'Arm yourself, Helati,' she said. 'Prepare to fight for the right to see another day.'

The words were no sooner out of her mouth when the night breed began their frenzied onslaught.

6

The ghosts came first. They were ever the stormy petrels who flew before the demon wind. Shadowy, translucent, like ribbons of fine, odourless smoke, they drifted through the groves.

'Ghosts,' Harad said, his nose wrinkling with disgust.

For some reason, Shamana was always trying to persuade the Helati that there was something sacred about the ghosts, that they were about death but somehow beyond death. Harad, like most people, thought that was an absurd superstition. Didn't they fly in with the dark-fliers? Weren't they the silent, ghoulish witnesses to the terror of every Lost Souls attack? To young men like him all the talk of the Book of Scales and its long-dead author Udmanesh was nonsense. The old ways were losing their hold on a generation whose memory of freedom was fading by the day.

'If they were solid I'd butcher the lot of them,' Harad said.

Oblivious to his feelings, the spectral forms swept through the crowd before finally fastening on Cusha. This was nothing new. It had been happening for months now. Cusha was always their first destination.

'What do they want?' Cusha said, unnerved by the attention of so many hazy forms crowding her.

She watched them swirling before her, their word-less mouths opening and closing, their infinitely sad eyes staring. Instinctively, she looked around for Shamana.

'Why do they do this?' Cusha asked. 'What do they want of me?'

'That I do not understand myself,' Shamana answered. 'But look at them. Somehow your destiny is entwined with theirs.'

'That's obvious,' Cusha said, 'but how?'

Shamana shook her head. 'I knew there was something special about you that first day I found you wandering in the fields. Just as it said in the Book of Scales, you arrived in the company of a ghost. Your coming was prophesied.'

Cusha found her words infuriating. Before she could interrogate Shamana further, Aaliya gave a warning cry from the edge of the crowd. 'Here they come!'

The swarm of ghosts dissolved before the advancing dark-fliers. Ranging from scarlet and crimson to a dull rust brown, these winged creatures were the advance guard, to be followed by the slower night-striders. The Helati prepared to defend themselves. Shamana rushed forward, hurling her bamboo javelin. The foremost flier thudded to the ground, spitting black blood. Inspired by Shamana's example, Helati fighters speared others, severing their heads. It was one of the surest ways of destroying the creatures. The others were fire and water.

But the fight wasn't over, far from it. The squadron swept skywards, wheeled overhead for a few moments, then came racing in once more. This time the creatures were met by axes, hoes, rakes, branches, even fists. The second attack was beaten off, the third too, but the fourth time the dark-fliers closed on the Helati their defensive perimeter started to crumble. Here and there, men, women and children were picked off. People started running forward, beating the dark-fliers as they sought out their victims' throats. Seeing one child dragged off her feet by a flier, Cusha ran forward and finished the beast with a scythe. Wiping the sweat from her brow, she returned the child to her mother.

'Good kill, sister,' said Harad, with a smile.

The smile vanished an instant later. It was the night-striders. These creatures, more human in appearance than the dark-fliers, made up the majority of the Lost Souls. They came at the run, like any living person. But there the similarity ended. Their grey-black skin was moist and oozing. Their eyes were expressionless. These creatures were the very backbone of the night terror.

Like the Helati many of the Lost Souls were armed with makeshift weapons: clubs, mallets and rocks. The fight now turned into a hideous mêlée. There were no battle lines, just a heaving, chaotic mass of struggling bodies. What made it worse was the fact that the Lost Souls didn't just attack on foot. Some of them would burrow beneath the feet of the Helati, seizing their ankles and trying to draw them down beneath the earth to be butchered in the darkness of the soil and clay.

Before the skirmish turned into a bloodbath however, Shamana's voice penetrated the murk. At the signal those Helati who were able tore themselves free and ran onto the open road.

The Lost Souls found themselves confronted by a solid line of fighters, hastily assembled by Shamana and Aaliya. Behind them cowered the children, the aged, the infirm. With the confrontation once more clearly demarcated, the Helati's superior organisation began to tell. A hail of throwing knives and slingshot, stashed over many weeks by the field slaves who tended the groves and tilled the fields, ripped through the demon ranks. At the first sign that the Lost Souls were wavering, the Helati rushed forward and completed the rout. Cusha, as ever, was in the vanguard, fighting alongside Shamana and Aaliya. The killing done, she touched the knife-edge scar on her throat and smiled. The fight was over until the Blood Moon rose again.

7

The seventh alarm bell sounded through the groves. Soon the dawn sunlight would begin to clear away the mist. The funeral pyres of the Lost Souls and the fallen Helati had burned down. Come the next rains ash from these bodies would fertilise the land. The toll of dead and wounded had been light. There were five dead, three seriously injured. Much as she hated losing anyone to the night breed, Shamana was satisfied. Five had been lost, but many hundreds had been saved.

The Children of the Sun wouldn't care how many had died, of course. Even the monthly incursions of the demons barely thinned their ranks. For one thing though, the Helati gave heartfelt thanks: there was no stench of roasting human flesh from the funeral pyres of the undead. The corrupted flesh of the Lost Souls was strangely odourless. Instead of the sickening sweetness expected from burning bodies, a different aroma filled the groves, a mixture of wood, earth and incense. The morning breeze woke Cusha. She looked around and saw Aaliya. Her eyes shot a question.

'Yes,' Aaliya said. 'It's over. The Lost Souls won't be back.'

Cusha sat up and rubbed her eyes. The dew was heavy on the trees and she washed her face in the clear water that she had shaken from the leaves. She looked around and marvelled at the normality of the scene. But for the row of funeral pyres, you would imagine that nothing had happened. The weapons had been systematically gathered and concealed until they were needed again.

Pulling a comb from her pocket, Cusha ran it through her tangled hair. It took time, but soon her hair was as straight and glossy as it had been when she had captivated the warrior. Though she didn't know his name, Cusha remembered the way the young Sol-ket had stared at her. She knew why men looked at her that way. Since her thirteenth year she had been attracting their attention. She remembered the way the warrior had stared and she shuddered.

'How much do you know about Shamana?' Cusha asked Aaliya.

'She is the greatest of all human souls,' was the answer.

'Every Helat is a witness to her greatness,' Cusha said. 'But where is she from? What is her nature?'

'You must ask Shamana herself,' Aaliya said. 'But she may not give you the answer you want. Secrets are kept for a reason.'

'But you know, don't you?'

Cusha's questions were making the priestess uncomfortable. Aaliya was relieved to hear a familiar voice.

'Did you get some sleep, Cusha?' Shamana asked.

'I did,' Cusha said. 'The question is, did you? I just realized. I have never seen you sleep.'

Shamana chuckled. 'When you are as old as I am, you don't need as much sleep. After all, one day you might not wake.' She patted Cusha's arm. 'Now, wouldn't it be a shame to miss another blue day?' She cocked her head. 'I heard you talking to Aaliya. I think you have some questions for me.'

'Last night you said I was special. Why?'

'You saw the way the ghosts gathered round you,' Shamana said. 'There is adoration in their eyes. They worship you, dear Cusha. Doesn't that mean anything to you?'

Cusha shrugged. 'Should it?'

'Do you remember what was written by the scholar Udmanesh in the Book of Scales?'

There will come two born of a single womb, Cusha recited, *'on the first day of Murjin, two Holy Children who will reunite dark and light, the living and the dead and end the hunger of the Lost Souls.* Yes, I know.'

'You are one of those children,' Shamana said.

'No,' Cusha said. 'Just because I was born on the first of Murjin, it doesn't mean I have magical powers. Shamana, you of all people should be able to distinguish between myth and real life. Look at me. I am a miserable Helat, one of the wretched of the Earth. I have no twin, no family. Can I turn lead into gold? Can I make the wild beasts talk? I am an orphan child. I have nothing. You found me without a name, without a family, without memories. What recollections I have, dearest Shamana, I got from you and my Mama-li.'

She meant Murima, cook to the household of Rishal-ax-Sol. Rishal was renowned as a brave knight and military commander of Parcep of the Tiger Gates. It was to Murima that Shamana had entrusted Cusha.

'One day,' Shamana insisted, 'you will know yourself, my child. Many children were born on the first day of Murjin, that is true. But the ghosts don't pursue them, Cusha. It is you they follow. I have often seen them watch over you from the moment you lay down your head until the first rays of dawn. A great destiny awaits you.'

Cusha tried to protest.

'No,' Shamana said. 'You are the one. Turn your back on

your true self if you wish. Your nature will find you out. I don't know why you can't remember your past. But you cannot escape your fate. It awaits you, as it does all of us. No matter how you twist and turn, you can never escape it. There is a dark fire within you. One day it will consume the demon throng.'

CHAPTER 2

The Two Maidens

I

As Cusha made her way back to Parcep, her head was full of Shamana's words. She was special, unique. Yet Cusha felt anything but. She stared down at her bare feet, grimed with dirt and couldn't help but feel ashamed of her poverty. *Special am I, Shamana? So why do I have to slave in that awful house? Why do I have to put up with the capricious temper of my mistress Julmira? Why have I never worn a beautiful sari or bathed in warm, scented water? Why don't I have the slightest idea where I come from?*

One thing was certain; her first task would be to help Mama-li bake flatbreads in the tandoor. That was a job she enjoyed.

Learning how to cook using the tandoor had been one of Cusha's earliest lessons after her adoption by Murima.

Though she had learned to cook in the kitchens of Rishal-ax-Sol's villa, the first flatbread Cusha had made had been produced in a large clay jar with an opening at the bottom for adding and removing fuel. Murima, like her son Harad, always seemed to fear the worst. She wanted Cusha to be equipped with the skills of survival should the family ever be evicted from the villa of the lord commander of Parcep. So quick-tempered were the great and good of Parcep of the Tiger Gates that even the most devoted servants could be thrown out on a whim. When she was young, Cusha used to watch Murima make the oven from good clay and shredded coir rope. She had watched her make a paste of mustard oil, jaggery, yoghurt and ground spinach and rub it on the inside of the tandoor to harden it. Remembering the smell of baking flatbreads, Cusha found her stomach grumbling hungrily. She glanced at Murima, waddling silently beside her.

'Mama-li,' she said, 'when I was little did I ever mention my life before I came to Parcep?'

'Your life before?' Murima said, surprised. 'No, never. It was as if you were born the day Shamana brought you to me. You knew your name and the date of your birth, but little else. All you had were the clothes you stood up in and a rag doll. To tell the truth, you were such a quiet child, almost mute, those first months. It was hard to get a single word out of you. There was something in your eyes, as if your heart had been broken and broken again. I have always thought that you must have seen something terrible. The memory of it was perhaps so painful you had erased it from your mind.'

Cusha bit her lip. What if that were true? What if, one day, whatever pain and anguish lay deep inside her were to all come to the surface? How would she ever cope with such memories? Murima slowed her pace.

'Why do you ask?'

'I was talking to Shamana,' Cusha said.

'Ah,' Murima said, a catch noticeable in her usually placid voice, 'that would explain it. She is a good woman, Cusha. She is brave and true, maybe the best of us all. The way she leads our people against the Lost Souls, that goes beyond courage.'

From the tone of Murima's voice, Cusha knew there was a but.

'But her mind is stuffed with dreams,' Murima said. 'She thinks the Helati can be free. She believes it is possible in our lifetime. Much as I wish it were true, dear child, I know better. Defiance is the act of those who do not understand consequences. She will go too far one of these days.'

She dropped her voice. 'All this talk of Udmanesh and the prophecies of the Scales. Someone is bound to tell the Sol-ket what she's doing. Udmanesh spent half his adult life in the Empire's prisons and died, who knows where. You'd think his example would have taught her something.'

Over to their left, Shamana was at the head of a column of slaves taking a fork in the road. Soon they would be toiling in the fields. Most were already adjusting their scarves and turbans against the cruel summer sun that would beat down upon them until dusk came to end their labours.

'She says my destiny is bound up with that of the Lost Souls,' Cusha said.

Murima sighed. 'The way the ghosts swirl around you at the time of the Blood Moon, you mean?'

Cusha nodded. The frown that Murima gave scored deep lines in her forehead. 'I have thought about that, too,' she said. 'I believe there's a simpler explanation, the one I gave you before. When you were little you suffered greatly. Like so many in this land you saw death. Couldn't that be it, the ghosts smell death around you?'

Cusha nodded. She felt so melancholy. She yearned for something that had been taken from her. Murima was right. She had witnessed something dreadful all those years ago and it had marked her. That had to be it.

'Thank you, Mama-li,' Cusha said.

'What for?' Murima asked.

'For being so sensible.' Cusha permitted herself a mischievous smile. 'And for the raisin and honey flatbreads you're going to make for breakfast.'

Together they walked. After a while, Murima paused. 'I remember the first time you spoke,' she said.

'What did I say?' Cusha asked.

'You didn't talk to start with,' Murima said. 'You sang.'

'Really?'

'Yes,' Murima said, 'it was such a strange little song. Now, how did it go?'

She thought for a while then continued walking. 'No,' she said, 'I really don't remember. Don't worry, it will come to me.'

2

Gardep had risen early. The other cadets were still snoring in their bunks when he slipped out of the dormitory, not forgetting to kiss his fingers and press them against the sun symbol embossed on the doorway. For the first time in his life he had felt something like pity for the poor wretches beyond the Tiger Gates. Their cries, and the memory of them, had haunted him long into the night. No, he thought, as he walked along the northern battlements, don't deceive yourself. There has been no sudden conversion. You don't

34

care for those miserable fools. There's only one Helat for whom you feel pity and that's the girl you saw at Rishal's villa. It is her face you saw before falling asleep, her lips you imagined this morning at first light.

Even then, her features remained as vivid as ever. He saw the smooth, brown skin and the still darker eyes. He had fancied she must paint them with kohl, but no Helat had money for make-up. There was night in her eyes, the intense darkness of tragedy. Though he had only seen her for a fleeting moment, he'd recognised something in those eyes. She knew loss and loneliness.

'Idiot,' Gardep groaned suddenly.

How could he know all this from the slightest glimpse of a girl through the hazy twilight? Love at first sight; was there such a thing? Not according to the priests of Ra. They spoke only of the struggle between light and dark, good and evil. Everything was reduced to one thing: obedience to holy Ra and his embodiment on Earth, the Emperor. In the established religion of the Empire there was no room for the complications of romantic love and affection, only duty, loyalty and conquest.

But Gardep had also read the love poems of the Selessians, which spoke of romance, of destinies forged by a single exchange of glances. Gardep sighed.

'Did you survive the night?' he murmured, gazing down onto the Avenue of the Kings. 'Do you live?'

The first of the Helati were already making their way back into the city. Gardep watched them. They were heavy-legged and silent. No Helat looked happy returning to a day's work in Parcep at the best of times. Their working day was long and hard, their punishments for slacking cruel. At the time of the Blood Moon it was worse. They returned to the city exhausted, sometimes mourning the loss of a child, a husband or wife, a mother or father, a lover or a friend. But still they had to toil. Refuse and you would have survived the onslaught of the Lost Souls only to die at the hands of your masters. The torments devised by the Children of the Sun to chastise their slaves were many, varied and of such an intense cruelty that the Helati no longer even dreamed of resistance. Gardep heard the eighth alarm bell toll and found himself searching the growing crowds. Where was she? Would he never see her face again? The thought gnawed at his heart.

'Where are you?'

Then there she was, walking beside a fat matron. Gardep's heart sang. All around this girl the Helati were covering their faces but she kept on walking, face bared, as if daring the guards to do their worst. Her eyes burned with a dark fire. Where did it come from, this fierce defiance, this self-destructive courage? Gardep wanted to ask the girl about herself. Who was she? He took a step forward and placed his hands on the battlement wall. The movement caught her eye as it was meant to and, for the second time, she returned his gaze with a studied indifference.

3

'Veil yourself!' Murima hissed. 'That Sol-ket is watching.'

Cusha continued to stare back at the warrior. She had cowered for years at the approach of the masters. Now nothing was as it had been before. A tiny part of her madly, inexplicably took pleasure in the Sol-ket's look and didn't want him to look away ever again.

'What's wrong with you, child?' Murima demanded. 'Wasn't there enough blood spilled last night? Do you want a flogging?'

Cusha continued to stare. At that moment, she would have walked through a regiment of Sol-ket bareheaded and proud. I am better than any of you, she wanted to declare. There was something else. Though she couldn't have explained why, she knew, actually *knew* that she need fear no flogging from the warrior. There was tenderness rather than cruelty in his eyes. She sensed an immense sadness in him, just like her own.

'Harad,' Murima said, 'tell your sister. She refuses to wear her veil.'

Harad placed a hand on Cusha's shoulder. 'Do as she says, Cusha. That soldier's got his eye on you. Don't provoke him.'

Harad's touch broke the spell. Lowering her eyes, Cusha veiled herself. Though Gardep's look stayed with her, she didn't raise her eyes again until she had reached the servants' entrance to the villa. Then she glanced back at the battlements. Silhouetted against the rising sun, there was the warrior, still watching her. She wondered what expression was on his face and what feelings were in his heart.

'Now,' Murima said gaily, 'let's prepare our breakfast before the masters start to howl for theirs.'

Cusha smiled. It was an unusually bold statement from the normally timid Murima. Cusha watched Mama-li as she started with lukewarm water. Into it she dissolved the yeast. Then she began adding flour, always stirring in the same direction. Cusha didn't do much. She just handed Murima the ingredients she needed. When the dough was stiff Murima turned it onto a floured board and started kneading. As she kneaded she kept the surface well dusted and continued to add flour. Finally she fed the shaped flatbread dough into the tandoor, laying it on the hot stone. Closing the door, she dusted her hands and said,

'Fetch some grape juice, Cusha. Oh, and don't forget the honey and raisins. You'll soon have your breakfast.'

Cusha crossed the courtyard to the thick-walled, windowless cold store and chose a jar of grape juice, newly imported from the banks of the Amputra where it entered the Lake of Coils. She measured out a couple of handfuls of raisins and emptied them into a paper cone. Finally she slipped a small bottle of honey into her pocket. As she carried everything back across the yard she could smell the baking bread. Another day had begun.

4

Far to the west there was no golden dawn, no blazing sun to burn away the early morning mist. Here, in the shadow of the Demon Wall, day could only be distinguished by a fragile lightening of the leaden skies. Just as the bitter winds had roared all through the hours of darkness, so they howled from hesitant dawn to murky dusk. As a result, there was no respite from the dismal chorus of the Lost Souls. In recent years, under the leadership of the Darkwing, they had learned to survive in daylight. So long as their withered flesh was not exposed to the naked rays of the sun, so long as they covered themselves somehow, they could now live, thrive, in its sacred light. They had started to raid as far as the Selessian Desert, robed all in black from head to toe, like the warriors of the dunes themselves.

Oled Lonetread, scout, mercenary, veteran of the western outposts of the Empire, a man who had walked alone most of his adult life, knew all about the Lost Souls. He had been fighting them for as long as he could remember. His arms and chest were criss-crossed with slash marks inflicted by the talons of the dark-fliers. He had even been bitten. He had had to burn away the venom that would have made him one of them. He still shuddered at the memory. Even as intense pain had wracked his body, monstrous nightmares had ravaged his mind, threatening to devour his sanity.

Never in his long military career had he seen such a gathering as this. The shrieks of dark-fliers and the monotonous groans of the night-striders boomed endlessly across the open, wind-scorched plains, relentless as winter rain. They had once been feral creatures, wild and uncontrolled, their frenzy reaching fever pitch during the Blood Moon. But the Darkwing had given them discipline. There was a new purpose in their behaviour. Steeling himself, Oled sought out Commander Turayat.

'Ah,' Turayat said, looking up from his breakfast of fish and lentil soup and flatbread, 'it's you, Oled.' He gave a sigh. 'You'll have more gloomy predictions, I warrant.'

'Great Commander,' Oled said, gritting his teeth as he forced himself to show due deference. 'Do I have permission to address you?'

'Speak your mind,' Turayat said.

'The demon host grows stronger and more numerous by the day,' Oled said. 'Listen to them. They rose from the earth many days before the Blood Moon. If I am right, the time they spend at large will last long after its waxing. Nothing is as it was. Everything we once believed about the night breed is blown away like dust. The threat has never been greater. Turayat-Ra, I entreat you to request reinforcements.'

Turayat listened. 'I hear the creatures,' he said. 'It isn't the way of the Sol-ket to cringe before them. Unlike you barbarians we face down our superstitions. We stare the demon in the eye.'

Oled struggled to disguise his feelings. 'I am not asking

you to cringe, Turayat-Ra, but simply to admit their numbers and their growing power. A reed must bend in the wind or it will break.'

Turayat tore off a chunk of flatbread and dipped it in his soup. 'Oled,' he said, waving the bread, 'you are getting old and cautious. Have you forgotten the channels of Lyrian fire? Do you have such disregard for the finest archers in the Empire? Even if the demons dare breach the wall they will be met by our sharp Imperial blades.' He saw Oled's expression. 'Look, they are growing stronger. I'll grant you that. But we have more than enough forces to repel them.'

Oled started to protest. 'Commander—'

'Enough!' Turayat barked.

Rising to his feet, he wiped his mouth with a napkin and jabbed a finger in Oled's direction. 'Listen to me, you unnatural half-breed. I am a decorated officer of the Sol-ket. I have fought campaigns the length and breadth of the Empire. I was with Rishal-ax-Sol when he stormed long-resisting Inbacus. My name is carved along with lion-hearted Rishal's on the walls of the Ziggurat in golden Rinaghar. I only allow you to live because your bestial talents serve the Empire. How dare you question my command!'

'I apologise, Turayat-Ra.'

Turayat watched him for a few moments. 'You are dismissed, Oled.'

Oled walked the battlements for some minutes, still burning from the Sol-ket's insults. How he longed to leave this place. It had never been his decision to come. But he had been entrusted with a mission. He must observe the Darkwing. No matter how long it took, he must find a way into the Black Tower. For many long years he had been unsuccessful. Maybe it was just not meant to be. Not then. But things were coming to a head. Now was the time for bold actions. Checking that he wasn't being watched, he threw wide his arms and flung himself from the highest point of the battlements.

As he launched himself into the swirling wind a transformation took place. The outstretched arms metamorphosed into wings. Oled's head became feathered and his eyes hardened until they assumed the steely glare of the predator. Instead of a nose and mouth there was now a fierce beak, fit to tear flesh. Oled's legs shortened and curved until they had been replaced by lethal talons. The shriek of an eagle pierced the chill wind. Oled Lonetread, scout, soldier, mercenary, had taken another role. A shapeshifter since birth, Oled was now a golden eagle, soaring high above the Demon Wall.

5

'I will not be a captive for ever,' said the boy in the Black Tower. He forced himself to stand. His legs were unsteady but, by clinging to the wall, he rose to his feet. 'I won't give in,' he murmured. 'I am Vishtar.'

He thought of what that meant and repeated it. 'For you, my sister, I will endure. I am Vishtar!'

His ancestors had given the twins a great power. One day, Vishtar told himself, they would be reunited. To that purpose, he would continue to defy the demon lord. For some time he paced up and down, forcing strength back into his rubbery legs. Soon he was running up and down the winding steps of the tower, exercising with an iron discipline rare in one so young. Shaking off the lassitude that always followed the Darkwing's visits, Vishtar forced himself to climb and descend, climb and descend. That done, he retired, heart pounding, to a corner. After a while his heartbeat returned to normal and he read, and read.

Then he read some more. Finally, he closed his book and smiled, encouraged by what lay between the covers. In spite of all his trials, he would not be a captive for ever.

6

Julmira didn't rise until ten o'clock.

'That mistress of yours,' Murima tutted under her breath, 'I swear she would lie in bed until the sun burned her eyes out.'

'If I had a bed with silk sheets,' Cusha retorted, 'then I too would sleep late.'

Unlike Murima, Cusha made little effort to speak softly. The blood of a lion beat through her veins. Harad and Qintu, who were sweeping the courtyard, raised their eyes in a gesture of despair. Qintu remarked that her mouth was wider than the Amputra Delta. He didn't mean it, of course. Like all who looked on Cusha, he was enchanted.

'Cusha,' Murima scolded. 'Lower your voice. The boys can hear you all the way over there. Imagine what would happen if the masters heard you.' She tutted. 'I don't know where you get your stubbornness. Haven't I tried to train you to be feminine and sweet?' She handed Cusha a tray. 'Here,' she said, 'take the young mistress's breakfast up to her.'

Cusha took the tray and headed for the stairs.

'And Cusha,' Murima said.

'Yes, Mama-li?'

'Try not to antagonise the mistress. Remember that time she took your doll?'

'Mama-li,' Cusha protested, 'that's history. I was only eight then.'

'Yes, only eight, and you flew into such a rage, I thought

you were going to tear the skin from her face. You were like a wild animal. Even when Mistress Serala took her whip to you, you carried on clawing like a tiger. It's the closest you ever came to being evicted from this house.'

'That doll was all I had to remember I once had another life,' Cusha said, her eyes suddenly far away.

'That may be,' Murima said, 'but you have a ferocious temper. We could all suffer for it. Remember that.'

Cusha smiled. Murima wasn't reassured. At the top of the stairs, Cusha knocked on the door. Julmira told her to enter.

'Oh, not sweetened bread again,' Julmira said, viewing the breakfast tray with distaste. 'Doesn't Murima ever vary her fare? Isn't there any fruit, a mango perhaps, or a kumquat? There are fresh shipments every day. Is a fruit salad too much to hope for?'

Cusha looked at the breakfast. 'Mama-li says you need a good breakfast inside you.' She was going to add that too much fruit gives you gas but she managed to bite her tongue. It wasn't the kind of thing you said to a lady.

'Cusha,' Julmira said, 'I'm not some slave girl, you know. I don't labour in the fields like an ox. What need do I have to stuff myself with bread?' She picked at a corner of the flatbread. 'Besides, I don't want to get fat like old Murima. Tonight I meet my betrothed for the first time. That sari has got to fit me like a second skin.' She lowered her voice. 'I want to inflame his passion.'

Cusha wrinkled her nose. 'You won't get fat by this evening, you know. You'll look fine.'

The way Julmira's eyes flashed, Cusha knew she had done it again. She was always causing a scandal by talking to the master's family with too much familiarity. In the same way, when she was little she was forever getting into trouble, thumbing her nose at her masters and provoking a beating. She'd learned to be more respectful, but only at the bidding of Mistress Serala's strap. Even then it was a most grudging obedience.

'Sorry mistress,' Cusha said hurriedly, 'what I meant to say—'

'I know what you meant,' Julmira said tetchily. 'Now stop this idle chatter. Bring me some perfume, a delicate fragrance. There is a new one. It comes from Lukshmir.'

Cusha stepped into the antechamber. She found the perfume immediately but tarried a while, looking at her old doll, sitting in pride of place among Julmira's childhood treasures.

'Oh, haven't you got it yet?' Julmira complained.

'Coming.'

'One more thing,' Julmira said. 'You shouldn't say Mama-li.'

'But I've always called Murima Mama-li,' Cusha said.

'I know you have,' Julmira said, 'but she isn't, is she? Cusha, you don't have a mother so it makes no sense to talk that way.'

Cusha wanted to dig the bristles of the brush right into Julmira's scalp until she drew blood but she restrained herself. She remembered what Murima had said about the doll incident.

'My betrothed is destined to be a magnificent warrior,' Julmira said. 'He goes by the clan name na-Vassyrian.'

Cusha frowned. Who cared?

'He is the finest cadet to pass through the academy in a generation,' Julmira said, oblivious to Cusha's rumpled brow. 'My father says he has never seen a finer soldier. Gardep is handsome and strong and prizes learning above earthly pleasures. He can recite Selessian love poetry by heart. We will make a good match, Gardep and me.'

'Na-Vassyrian?' Cusha said, unimpressed. 'What kind of name is that?'

'He is a descendant of the people of Vassyria,' Julmira said, 'an ancient and noble people, worthy opponents of the Sol-ket until my father conquered them. Don't you know anything?'

Determined to stay out of trouble for once, Cusha carried on combing.

'The Vassyrians fought a bitter war to defend their country, but nothing could deny the brave Sol-ket their inevitable triumph.'

Cusha looked away. If she had met her mistress's eyes then she would have betrayed her feelings. How she hated the Sol-ket with their swagger and cruelty. She had once seen one of the cadets hack a poor beggar to death. And for what? He had dared to touch the hem of the warrior's cloak to ask for a couple of dinar.

'My betrothed's past is shrouded in mystery,' Julmira said. 'Father says he is of noble blood. That will compensate for the fact that he isn't by birth a full-blooded Child of Ra. Perhaps our union will cement the Vassyrians' loyalty to the Empire.'

Cusha continued brushing. She hated the way Julmira called this man 'my betrothed'. The silly goose hadn't even met him yet. What if he was as ugly as a forest hog? Cusha knew that wasn't likely: physical perfection was one of the requirements of the academy.

'Lay out my new sari,' Julmira said. 'The gold one. I want to see myself from all angles.'

Cusha wanted to protest that she had seen herself from all angles every day that week but she thought better of it.

'Right away, mistress,' she said.

7

Across the broad Avenue of the Kings the cadets were practising swordplay in the courtyard of the academy. As usual, Gardep was paired with Kulmat. Though the fights were conducted with wooden swords there was no holding back. These contests often ended in injury. Broken fingers, even arms, weren't unusual. You weren't allowed to strike the face, however. The Sol-ket frowned upon facial imperfections. The only exception was when the scars were the result of battle and those they painted with a thin line of gold, to become a tattoo of honour. Incurring such a wound in a practice bout would be considered foolish.

'Are you ready for tonight?' Kulmat asked, parrying Gardep's thrust.

'It is my duty,' Gardep said.

'Duty?' Kulmat asked. 'I wish it was my duty to court the beautiful Julmira.'

'I thought you said she looked like a horse and brayed like a mule,' Gardep snorted.

Kulmat stole a glance at the watching Rishal, who was standing by Kulmat's own knight, Prakash. 'Not so loud, Gardep,' he hissed. 'That is her father, you know.'

Gardep grinned. 'I had *you* worried this time, didn't I?'

Kulmat pushed forward, striking Gardep's sword with three firm blows. Gardep parried them effortlessly. Rishal and Prakash looked on impassively while their squires fought to and fro across the training ground.

'I'll tell you something though,' Kulmat said. 'Your betrothed's got competition.'

'What do you mean?' Gardep asked.

'Didn't you see that handmaiden of hers?' Kulmat said. 'She was a beautiful little thing. I swear, she is a flower among weeds. How can she have survived the labours of her caste so completely unblemished? She's got spirit, too. Did you see how she went unveiled? She'll be dead before the year is out, flouting our laws as she does. If she weren't a Helat I'd have her myself. Maybe I should snatch her and sneak her into the barracks. By Ra, every man there would be burning with jealousy.'

Though Gardep knew it was all talk, Kulmat's words inflamed him. Content until that moment to defend, he suddenly drove forward, smashing blows into Kulmat's guard. Such was the ferocity of the attack that Kulmat couldn't keep his sword steady. Driven back across the yard, Kulmat stumbled and found himself kneeling, his shaking hand barely able to hold on to his weapon. Gardep's eyes were wild. A final crashing blow sent Kulmat's wooden sword spinning across the courtyard. Rishal and Prakash exchanged whispered observations.

'By Ra,' Kulmat panted. 'What possesses you today, my brother?'

Gardep blinked. He seemed to have surfaced from a trance. 'Kulmat,' he said, going to retrieve the sword. 'I'm sorry. I don't know what came over me.'

As he handed back the practice sword he noticed Rishal watching. The Commander seemed to be taking a greater interest in him than usual.

8

Oled Lonetread's journey across enemy lines confirmed his worst fears. Not half a mile from the wall he discovered the front ranks of the war host. With no will of their own, the foot soldiers seemed to drill endlessly, spurred on by an invisible general.

47

One thing struck Oled forcefully. Whereas in the early years of his time on the frontier the undead had attacked with their bare hands, striking at their victims in a frenzy of tearing and slashing, these creatures were armed. It was obvious to the winged observer that the Lost Souls were disciplined, drilled into companies and regiments. Stacked at intervals were swords, axes, and javelins. Only one form of arms was missing from the stockpiles and that was the shield. The Lost Souls had no interest in defending themselves. Commanded by the feared Darkwing, they hurled themselves at their enemy. After all, they had no life to lose.

This is bad, Oled thought. He swung lower, inspecting the ranks of this vast gathering. Though order and organisation were evident wherever he looked, Oled couldn't see a single officer of any description. He knew why. There was only one guiding intelligence in the entire army of the undead and that was the Darkwing himself. Oled continued to wheel in the skies above the demon throng. Still he saw no sign of the Darkwing. For a few moments Oled contemplated striking west, in search of the demon lord's lair. Then he noticed a small phalanx of dark-fliers spread their wings and look skywards. That was Oled's signal to return to the fortress of Zindhar.

9

As the day wore on the preparations in the villa became more frantic. Trestle tables were erected in the courtyard. Braziers were set up ready to be lit whenever the first guests arrived. Flowers were arranged in earthenware pots. There were orchids and anemones, rhododendrons and blue poppies. There were primula and clematis. Hastily erected bowers were dressed with musk rose and carnations, irises and peonies. Blossom petals were loaded into string nets and hoisted up to the third floor ready to cascade onto the heads of the engaged couple. Every room was dusted and polished until the surfaces shone. Even the grouting between the tiles in the entrance hall had been scrubbed white, a task that had taken half a dozen house-slaves the best part of two days. Vast, colourful wall hangings were lowered from the ceilings and balconies, inside and outside the villa. As the sea breeze picked up they started to billow across the courtyard, making loud snapping noises when the stronger gusts blew.

Musicians were tuning their instruments. There were sitars and surbahars, cymbals and lutes and bamboo flutes. There were the drums: tablas for rhythm and tanpuras to provide the drone. There were dancers too, practising their steps or having their fingers painted or henna tattoos applied to their skin. The tiny bells fastened round their ankles tinkled throughout the villa. Rishal-ax-Sol was sparing no expense. His only daughter's engagement feast was going to be the most lavish ever held in Tiger-gated Parcep, a symbol of his family's wealth and power.

Finally, there was food. From early morning, Murima's kitchen buzzed with activity. There was lamb and venison to be boned and cut into strips, shrimp and crab to be shelled, duck and chicken to be prepared for roasting. There were many species of fish. They needed filleting.

The smell of spices: ginger, cardamom, turmeric, chillies, tamarind and cumin filtered through the kitchens and out into the courtyard. Cloves of garlic hung over the ovens. There were fenugreek seeds, fennel and mint on the chopping boards. There were sacks of vegetables in the corner: okra, potato, chickpeas, lentils, onions, radishes, kidney beans and more. Cool yoghurt was ladled into dishes.

Crispy snacks were poured out. Chutney was prepared. It fairly made the mouth water to see it all.

Julmira's mother, Mistress Serala, whose own engagement feast in the Imperial capital Rinaghar had been talked about for years after, presided over all the preparations with an unforgiving eye. She saw the opulence of this engagement feast and the joining of her daughter to the most promising cadet to emerge from the academy in a generation as stepping stones to the court at Rinaghar, from whence she had gone sixteen years earlier to join her new husband at his first posting.

No matter how hard everyone worked it was never going to be good enough for the mistress.

'Murima,' she said as she entered the kitchens, 'how many varieties of rice are you going to offer the guests?'

Murima answered her mistress. There was saffron rice and pilau rice, mushroom rice, wild rice, Basmati and perfumed rice. She went on to name several more. Some, she knew very well, were unknown to the mistress. Mistress Serala nodded sagely then suggested that some sticky rice should be made available for the envoy from Banshu. This high-placed official from the Empire's most recent conquest should be shown due honour and respect. Murima told Mistress Serala that it would be done.

'But you made some and wrapped it in cloth to be steamed later,' Cusha said when the mistress had gone.

'I know that, child,' Murima said, 'but the Mistress has to believe she is contributing something, doesn't she?'

Cusha nodded and wondered how anyone could be as patient or as forgiving as dear Mama-li.

10

This time Oled observed the proprieties. The gravity of his report weighed heavily upon him. Even if he had to grovel to do it, he had to convince Turayat of the coming invasion's vast scale. Zindhar must be evacuated immediately. Running along the battlements Oled scanned the garrison. In the main courtyard troops were drilling. He had admired the iron discipline of the Sol-ket many times over the years. He'd seen them hack their way through armies twice their size then complete a five-mile march and dig a defensive ditch immediately afterwards. There had been times he had thought them invincible, but not now. They didn't understand the sheer magnitude of the approaching menace. They believed that, after a few days' raids, the Lost Souls would return to the earth. It was wishful thinking. On two separate occasions he had seen the creatures at large long after the fading of the Blood Moon. If he was right in his judgement, there would soon be no respite from the horror.

The once-impregnable formations of the Warriors of the Sun looked suddenly puny, no sturdier than the wood and paper houses of Banshu. Like coastal rocks that are engulfed by mighty waves, like a child's sandcastle broken by the high tide, they would surely be enveloped and destroyed by the demon host. What's more, while the Demon Wall was being constructed around the existing stone castles and keeps, the garrison had moved into a temporary fortress constructed of timber. It would not long resist the assault of the dark legions.

'By all the powers of the Four Winds,' Oled murmured, 'you are dead men.'

The words were still on his lips when he saw Turayat

striding across the square listening distractedly to the briefing of his three senior officers.

'Swallow your pride,' Oled told himself, as he hurried to the steps. 'No matter what insults he throws your way you have to get your story across.'

He hovered for a few moments at the edge of the group of officers. Eventually Turayat deigned to cast an enquiring glance his way.

'Great Commander,' Oled said, 'will you grant me leave to speak?'

'Granted,' Turayat said with a wave of the hand.

Look at you, you pompous fool, Oled thought. You are already sitting atop your own funeral pyre and still you want to look down on me. What will it matter who outranked whom if our bones lie bleached together on this storm-ravaged plain? Not for the first time, he considered abandoning the Sol-ket to their fate. But that would mean abandoning his mission of eight years and leaving the boy in the tower to rot.

'I have just flown west over the Demon Wall. It's worse than I thought.'

'You did what?' Turayat demanded. 'Are you telling me you undertook a mission without my authorisation?'

Oled realised he had acted rashly. 'I meant no offence—'

'You are a Tanjur,' Turayat said. 'Your unnatural race has a history of rebellion. I swear, you live only because I permit it. When I decided to recruit you, there were many voices raised against the idea. Until now, I have been content to use your shape-shifting skills. You are a good scout, but don't test my patience.'

'I apologise, Turayat-Ra.'

'Now let's have this report of yours.'

'Though I lost count of the minutes,' Oled said, 'I did not reach the end of the vast throng. I told you once before that the Lost Souls numbered many thousands. I can tell you now that I was wrong, Turayat-Ra. They are like the grains of sand on the beach. They have gathered in their hundreds of thousands.'

Turayat listened but said nothing.

'Something has changed,' Oled continued. 'The Darkwing has broken their traditional patterns. The Blood Moon ends tomorrow. I have a feeling they will not return to the earth.'

Turayat listened, unmoved.

'Great Commander,' Oled concluded, 'you must understand the scale of the problem. I was unable to conclude my scouting mission. In truth, there may be millions of the creatures. What's more, they have brought with them enough arms to cut an entire legion to ribbons. We are in the mouth of the dragon, Turayat-Ra, and the jaws are closing.'

All eyes turned in the direction of Turayat. 'Very well,' he said. 'I will alert Rinaghar. Until there is a reply, we maintain the defences with our present garrison.'

That's when Oled's patience ran out. 'No, you have to summon reinforcements immediately. Forget Rinaghar. It is too far. Call on Karangpur, Durbai, anywhere. Did you not listen? Don't you understand the danger?'

Hearing Oled's raised voice, Turayat's eyes hardened. 'That is my final word on the subject. We have the numbers to repel the enemy.'

'You must reconsider, Turayat-Ra,' Oled begged.

The plea fell on deaf ears. 'Who are you to tell me what to do?' Turayat demanded.

'You're an arrogant fool, Turayat,' Oled yelled, causing every head in the fort to turn.

It was a serious offence for any soldier to address a senior officer without the suffix Ra. But for a barbarian to do it, and to dare call him a fool – that was unheard of.

'Don't you understand? There is an army out there. It stretches as far as the eye can see. It is not going to simply turn around and resume its sleep in the soil. Like a dark tidal wave, the Lost Souls will fall upon this fort and smash it into toothpicks. If you don't fall back, and fall back now, every man here is going to die.'

Turayat glared for a moment. Just when Oled felt the commander was sure to order his arrest, Turayat threw back his head and roared with laughter. Within moments half his warriors had joined in. In the Imperial Army, if your commander laughed, you laughed too. Then, when the laughter was just beginning to subside, Turayat's smile drained from his face.

'Take this insubordinate dog,' he ordered, 'and throw him in the stockade.'

One of Turayat's officers protested. 'The man is a shape-shifter. What's to stop him changing into a mouse and scuttling away?'

'You're new to Zindhar, aren't you?' Turayat said. 'Let me tell you about these Tanjurs. Transforming themselves into creatures of a similar body weight is easy. But the greater the difference in size, the more difficult the metamorphosis. An inexperienced Tanjur can die trying to take the form of a mouse. Isn't that right, Oled? What's the smallest beast you can manage? A jackal, isn't it? And the largest? What was it? Oh yes, a buffalo. The gap between the bars is narrow. There will be no escape.' He thought for a moment. 'Just in case, chain him and post a guard.'

Turayat issued his final order. 'He is to be brought before the whole garrison at first light. The charge is gross insubordination. The penalty is death.'

11

'I swear to you, Kulmat,' Gardep said, 'all those hours I was in the thorn forests doing my Ket-Ra, not once did I feel such dread as I feel now.'

'Not even when you imagined the wing beats of dragons?'

'Not even then.'

'Is it any wonder?' Kulmat said. 'A month from now your freedom will be gone and Julmira will be sharing your bed.'

At that, Gardep blushed. The other cadets might engage in jokes about some slave girl, or tell tales of heavy drinking. Gardep didn't once join in their banter. He was as ascetic and tight-lipped as any saffron-robed priest of Ra. In truth, he knew nothing of women.

'I will miss you, my brother, when you leave the dormitory,' Kulmat said. 'Whatever will I do without that serious face of yours?'

Both cadets were wearing their dress uniforms. Their armour was finished with gold lacquer and embossed with the emblem of the risen sun. Scarlet horsehair tassels hung from the points of their helmets. In the scabbard that slapped by their sides there was a curved scimitar instead of the many-times-tempered steel blades they would carry into battle. Their shoes were made of red leather and curved at the toe. As they approached the villa's gates Harad and Qintu, both turbaned, bowed before garlanding the two warriors.

'Masters,' Harad said, 'if you will kindly follow me, I will take you to the Mistress Serala.'

Falling in behind the house-slave, Gardep and Kulmat pressed their fingers to the sun symbol at the front door. As they followed Harad, they exchanged glances.

'Courage, my warrior-brother,' Kulmat said.

Gardep took a shuddering breath and looked straight ahead. 'I wish to Ra that this were over,' he said.

Harad led them through an archway under a sapphire awning. In the crowded room beyond Mistress Serala greeted them. She was wearing a sari imprinted with motifs from her husband's campaign to subdue Vassyria.

'My dear Gardep,' she said, 'welcome to our home.'

Her gaze shifted to Kulmat. He would later confide to Gardep that, though her lips spoke sugared words, her eyes were like a cobra's, hooded and cold. Go against this Lady of Parcep and you would regret your actions.

'You know my husband, Commander Rishal, of course.'

The cadets bowed to their commanding officer. 'I am honoured by your hospitality, Rishal-Ra,' they said, observing strict rules of formality.

Serala then proceeded to introduce her entire family and every dignitary present. To Gardep, it took an age. By the time he had bowed to the last member of the Banshu delegation, he was beginning to realise what this match meant. His future would be punctuated by a hundred such tedious functions. Already he was choking on the formality of it all. He was a warrior, not a diplomat.

'Now,' Mistress Serala said, 'it is time to introduce you to your betrothed.'

Harad and Qintu walked before Mistress Julmira, scattering white and red blossom from wicker baskets while the guests clapped. Two female Helati followed, swinging copper pans loaded with burning incense. Julmira stood before Gardep, head bowed and eyes downcast as ritual demanded, though there was something about the set of her shoulders that was anything but shy. A white veil covered her head, face and shoulders. Through the translucent covering only her dark, glossy hair could be seen, dressed with golden chains. After due pause, Mistress Serala clapped her hands. At her signal, Cusha stepped from an alcove.

While she was approaching her mistress, Gardep found himself following her every step. Nothing had prepared him for this moment. Here, in the middle of a room thronged by people and resonating with music, it was as if Gardep had entered a silent temple. Transfixed by Cusha, he had forgotten all about his betrothed until, with a casual grace, the slave girl lifted the veil from Julmira's face.

Julmira was striking indeed in her golden sari, the silver border patterned with lions, symbols of her father's courage in battle. In addition to the jewellery with which her hair was dressed, Julmira wore a bulak, a dangling gold chain worn through her nose piercing. Some guests gasped, as protocol demanded, a public show of admiration of the future bride's beauty. Others applauded, those lower in status trying to outdo their more favoured neighbours. When the hubbub had died down, a priest in saffron robes called the couple together and asked them to stand face to face before him.

'Come forward, suitor,' he said, 'and declare your intentions.'

Gardep, stepping forward, placed a hundred dinar coin in Julmira's hand and said the words enshrined in custom: 'With this gold I declare my earnest intention to conclude our sacred bond. You will be mine and I yours as set down by the law of holy Ra.' Though the words tasted like ash in his mouth, he stumbled on. 'From this moment on,' he said, 'I shall have eyes only for thee, my legally betrothed.'

But, as the words fell from his lips, the ritual gasps of wonder at the beauty of the bride had turned to expressions of astonishment at Gardep's behaviour. The reason was simple: anyone who was standing anywhere near the young

Sol-ket and his betrothed could see who he was looking at as he took his vows. He had eyes only for the slave Cusha. What's more, in that crowded room, before all her mistress's guests, Cusha had the temerity to return Gardep's look.

12

Oled barely noticed the going down of the sun over the plains of Jinghara. He remembered his quarrel with Tur-ayat. The general thought Oled was the last of the Tanjurs. Well, not quite, Oled thought. Eight years before, the warrior-queen of his people had come to a decision. They must bring the Holy Children together. She would keep the girl safe until she was ready to fulfil her destiny. He must find the boy. So Oled set off for Zindhar and joined the army of the West. His purpose was to reach the Black Tower and free the boy-prisoner from the Darkwing's clutches. Many times he had tried to reach the tower. Many times he had been driven back by the Lost Souls. There were just too many of them. Now he was sitting in a Sol-ket cage, awaiting certain death at their hands. Soon, another stroke of Destiny's cruel whip was to cut his back. He could smell the thickening dusk and the rising menace at its heart.

All shape-shifters, by their nature, develop the instincts and abilities of the wild beasts whose form they take. Oled was in his fortieth year and his senses had never been more acute. He could hear a wild hare breathing at fifty paces. He could smell the pine resin oozing down the bark of a tree. So it was that he heard the distant tramping feet of the undead as a deafening chorus, swelling in the gloom. So it was that he heard the hissing wings of the dark-fliers. With each wing beat, with each footfall, with each panted breath, monstrous destruction was approaching.

'Guard,' Oled shouted, 'Guard!'

The sentry, a young Sol-ket of no more than twenty-five summers, scowled. 'What is it, barbarian?'

Is that what he'd come to? They didn't call him scout any more. They didn't even show him that much respect. No, it was the ancient insult of their kind: *barbarian.* So much for their Empire of all the Peoples under the Sun.

'You've got to let me out,' Oled said.

'Mm,' the warrior mused with heavy sarcasm, 'I've never heard a condemned prisoner say that before.'

'You don't understand,' Oled said. 'I've got news for Commander Turayat. It's the Lost Souls, they're coming.'

'Yes,' the warrior said, 'and you'd know about that, wouldn't you, locked up in this cage?'

'Listen to me,' Oled pleaded, 'if only because what I've got to tell your master may still save your hide.'

'Oh, so that's it,' the warrior said. 'You want to save my hide. Well, thank you but no thank you. I am quite capable of handling myself. Barbarian, there's nothing you've got to say that I want to hear.'

Oled crashed against the iron bars. 'Damn you, you young fool. Don't you see I'm telling the truth? I'm a shape-shifter. I can hear more acutely than you, see further, smell more keenly. They're coming. They're going to march over your skulls and crush them like egg shells.'

That was too much for the Sol-ket. Spinning round, he jabbed his spear into Oled's cage. The point pressed against the shape-shifter's throat, dimpling the flesh.

'One more word from you and I will pierce that yellow skin of yours. Are you in such a hurry to die?'

Oled knew better than to press the point further. With a low groan he slumped against the solid wall at the back of the cage, a failure twice over.

13

Gardep was halfway across the Avenue of the Kings when Kulmat grabbed him by the sleeve. 'What, in the name of Ra, do you think you're doing?'

Gardep pulled his arm away. 'I don't know what you mean.'

'Don't you?' Kulmat said. 'Well, Rishal does.'

Gardep's step faltered. 'What?'

'He's no fool. Gardep, at the moment of your betrothal vow, what did you do?'

Gardep's dark eyes met those of Kulmat. He didn't speak. Shame had him by the tongue.

'It's one thing to lust after some slave girl. Have her if you wish. Just do it in secret and tell nobody. By all that is holy, Gardep, Julmira raised her eyes to accept your betrothal vow and where were you looking, for Ra's sake? It would have been bad enough if you had just glanced at her handmaiden. Gardep, you were so taken with her, you failed to even acknowledge Julmira. There will be a scandal. Men have been cast out of the city for less. Couldn't you even disguise it?'

'I meant no offence,' Gardep said. 'It wasn't the girl I was looking at.'

'Don't lie, Gardep,' Kulmat said. 'Not to me. Since we were boys we have been blood brothers. We have stolen together. Yes, and we've been beaten for it together, too. Couldn't you at least try to make some pretence? There is no greater offence to a lady of the royal line than to have some Helat set above her. In the slums they put on plays telling lurid tales such as this. Do you want to know what happens to the lovers, Gardep? They die, my impetuous brother. They always die. You must apologise to Rishal and disown the girl.'

Gardep shook his head. 'If only it were that easy.'

Kulmat's eyes widened in horror. 'By Almighty Ra,' he whispered, 'it's worse than I thought. You're bewitched.'

'Don't be a fool, Kulmat,' he said.

'Fool, am I?' Kulmat retorted. 'You are innocent of the ways of the world, Gardep. I know these slave girls. They'll do anything to earn a crust of bread or a few dinar. They are worthless, every last one of them.'

'Shut your lying mouth, Kulmat,' Gardep snapped, rage clouding his face.

'What is this?' Kulmat said. 'Can you really love this girl? Is this more than mere infatuation?'

In a voice thick with emotion, Gardep finally confessed his feelings. 'Kulmat, you know me better than anyone else on Earth. Yes, my brother, it may be foolish, it may be utter madness, but I love her.'

Kulmat's face was etched with dismay. 'But you haven't even talked to her!'

'Sometimes looks can be more eloquent than words,' Gardep said. 'There is something in those dark eyes. I think about her every waking minute.'

'Oh Gardep,' Kulmat murmured, 'this is bad, very bad.'

'You have no need to fear,' Gardep reassured him. 'I will master these forbidden feelings. Though I love another, I will be a good husband to Julmira and a faithful servant to my Emperor and my God.'

Kulmat grimaced. 'If you get a chance.'

'Don't worry,' Gardep said, 'I'll make my peace with Rishal.'

'But are you sure you can keep any promise you make him?' Kulmat asked.

Gardep stared at his friend for a moment, then drew his scimitar.

'What are you doing?' Kulmat demanded, not a little afraid.

Gardep ran his thumb along the blade of the scimitar, opening the skin. A drop of blood oozed from it. Gardep caught the scarlet drop in his palm.

'You say that we are blood brothers, Kulmat.'

Kulmat nodded. 'Yes, until the end of time. You are my greatest friend. I would lay down my life to protect yours.'

Gardep took Kulmat's hand. 'And I would do the same. Do you believe that?'

Kulmat nodded. 'I know that.'

'Then mix your blood with mine,' Gardep said. 'Swear that you will never betray these forbidden feelings of mine.'

Kulmat hesitated. Centuries of Imperial taboos weighed down on him. 'Do you want me to betray the code of the Sol-ket,' he said, 'to place friendship above duty? You ask too much, Gardep.'

Gardep seized Kulmat's hand and pushed a piece of bloodied cloth into his palm. 'Remember this scrap of bandage? We were eight years old. I took a beating in your place because you were sick. It's my blood that stains it. We tore it in two, each keeping one half as a token of our comradeship.'

'Yes,' Kulmat said, pulling his own scrap of bloodied bandage from his tunic, 'and we have been true to that vow.'

'Today we have added more blood to our oath,' Gardep said. 'I swear that I will bury my love for the Helat deep in my soul. In return there is something you must do for me. Nobody must ever know how I feel.'

Kulmat returned the token to Gardep and duly slit his

thumb open. He mixed his blood with Gardep's. 'You are my brother. Nobody will know.'

'On pain of death?'

There were tears in Kulmat's eyes. 'Yes,' he said, 'on pain of death.'

Knowing that there was no more to say, Gardep and Kulmat returned to the barracks. They did not know that, across the broad Avenue of the Kings, from a second-floor balcony, still smarting from his daughter's humiliation, Commander Rishal was watching.

14

With the moon came the attack on Zindhar. The dark-fliers arrived in russet red squadrons, wave after wave of leather-winged demons sweeping down on the unprepared Sol-ket. At least a dozen warriors were carried off or simply dispatched where they stood. Their blood stained the earth and the faces of their shocked comrades.

'To arms!' the officers roared. 'To your posts, men.'

Horns brayed and drums beat, followed by the sound of hundreds of pairs of feet pounding on the courtyard and battlements of Zindhar. Three ranks of archers were quickly drawn up in the classic Sol-ket formation. Launching volley after volley of arrows as they moved forward, each row putting a new arrow to the bowstring as the next loosed theirs, they started to thin the ranks of the dark-fliers' advance party. When the dark-fliers finally wheeled away there was loud cheering. It didn't last long.

'By mighty Ra,' one sentinel groaned from the west watchtower as he saw what was still to come. 'That was but the first wave. More are coming. They cover the sky and the moon.'

There was no exaggeration in his words. Like a locust storm, thousands of dark-fliers were swarming towards Zindhar, enveloping the fort. The drums of war were beating more urgently now. More archers were supplemented by Vassyrian slingers. Two hundred Sol-ket swordsmen were ordered to unsheathe their blades. They were drawn up in a perimeter around the archers and slingers and ordered to point their long javelins skyward to protect them.

But while this unit was still waiting for the tidal wave of dark-fliers to break over them there was a loud pounding at the main gates. It was as if wild beasts were hurling themselves over and over again at the gates, but the creatures had no heartbeat, just the pulse of the night in their breasts. The timber shuddered with each blow, the wood yawning wider as the battering grew louder and more intense. Startled warriors exchanged glances of bewilderment. How could the invincible Sol-ket be overcome so easily? Had the barbarian been right after all? Was this more than a raid?

'Reinforce the gates,' Turayat roared, marching from his office to take command. 'Shore them up with those Lyrian timbers I ordered.'

Even as the timbers were being brought up to set against the gates another front was opened against the beleaguered garrison. Just when the soldiers were thanking Ra that the dark-fliers were relatively few in number, a second foe took the field. Beneath the feet of the archers and slingers the earth suddenly burst open. The roars and screeches of the Lost Souls erupted from the clay soil of Zindhar. Deep wells of Lyrian fire had always kept the night-striders back from the Demon Wall. Scores had been immolated in futile attacks. There were no such defences around the fort.

'They're here!' the soldiers yelled.

These cries of panic were their last. One after another they started to disappear into the gaping holes dug by the Lost Souls, dragged down by the slimy, decomposing hands of their subterranean attackers. Another terrible sound filled the air: that of men gargling soil.

'Get out of there!' Turayat bellowed. 'Climb onto the walls.'

No sooner had he issued the command than the second wave of dark-fliers rained down on the heads of the defenders. In one corner of the fortress Oled Lonetread was standing, clutching the bars of his cage. He cursed himself for his lack of discipline. He *had* neglected his powers. Train yourself, his warrior-queen had always told him, meditate every day and learn the ways of the Tanjur. But Oled had spent too many years in the company of the Sol-ket. He had put all his efforts into martial arts, training himself in the use of the bow and the axe rather than perfecting his abilities as a shape-shifter. While some of his kind had been able to shrink to the size of mice or swell until they possessed the girth of an elephant, Oled's abilities were restricted. What Turayat had said was true. He had never been able to shrink smaller than an eagle or grow larger than a water buffalo. Denied the company of his fellows, he had never perfected his abilities. Never had he felt the limitations of his powers more keenly.

'Let me out,' he cried, trying to get the attention of the young soldier guarding him. 'Listen to me,' he pleaded. 'I can help you defend the fort.'

But the warrior could only stare at the carnage all around him. Bewildered by the scale of the attack, he turned to look at Oled.

'The commander said—'

He never got to finish the sentence. At that moment

more night-striders broke through the gates. The first of them tore open the soldier's throat in an instant before moving on to charge the stairs leading to the battlements. Oled stared at the space between the bars of his cage. If he was to outlive the day, he had to complete a metamorphosis more challenging than he had ever done before. Closing his eyes, he summoned every ounce of strength and set about transforming.

The battle was a one-sided affair. Bravely as the Sol-ket defended, they were outnumbered many times over and, outside the gates of the fort, a much vaster throng was waiting to attack if it was needed.

'Draw swords,' Turayat shouted. 'If we have to die then, by Ra, we will go down fighting.'

He was true to his word. Gathering the remnants of the garrison around him, he drove a wedge into the night-striders, hurling them back from the stairs. It was only a temporary victory; at that moment, the wooden battlements started to sway.

'Those god-forsaken creatures are undermining the foundations of the fort,' Turayat groaned, knowing the die was now cast.

He stared down at the ground. He knew the fate that was awaiting his men, a tortured agony, suffocating as they were dragged down, through the clinging soil, to a murky death.

'Damn you,' he screamed at the demon host, 'at least let us die like men, standing on our two feet and breathing Ra's sacred air.'

In answer to his words, a shadow crossed the moon. It was the Darkwing, the living death made flesh. He swooped low over the killing ground. Seizing one unfortunate, he sank his fangs into the man's throat and drained him of his lifeblood before tossing his limp body aside.

'Very well,' he said, alighting on the roof of the north watchtower. 'I have every reason to be magnanimous in victory.' He gestured to the heaving ground. 'Hear me, children of the black earth. Face your foe in the open. Let the brave Sol-ket fight on firm ground.'

So Turayat led his men in a final charge, swords hacking, faces smeared with the black blood of the Lost Souls. Within minutes there were no more than fifty men fighting a rearguard action in the square. One by one they fell, carried off by dark-fliers or cut down by night-striders. Turayat was one of the last to fall. Still fighting with the shattered blade of his sword he was swallowed up in a snarling, writhing mass of frenzied creatures.

With one last roar of 'Victory or death!' Turayat succumbed. Oled despised the man but he couldn't help admiring the manner of his passing. There were many things you could question about the Sol-ket: their decency, their humanity, their compassion. Their courage, however, was beyond dispute.

With the last of the Sol-ket dead, the Darkwing ordered a search of the fort to make sure that nobody had survived. Oled chose his shape and transformed as a night-strider approached the cage. It didn't hear Oled's anguished cry as he completed his painful metamorphosis. It didn't see the python sliding through the empty gate of the fort.

15

Hundreds of miles away, on the road leading from the maize fields of Parcep, Shamana had just handed in her scythe to the overseer. She saw his eyes shift slightly as she offered him the blade. Even the overseers were wary of strange, wild Shamana, half-expecting her to launch herself at them with a wild scream. There was no show of defiance. Shamana smiled to herself as she handed over the scythe. If they only knew how many of these makeshift weapons lay hidden in concealed dumps around these same fields. No matter how many times they conducted raids they never found a single one.

Plodding home to the shack she shared with her apprentice Aaliya, Shamana pondered the prophecies. Still Cusha refused to face her destiny. Could I be wrong? Shamana wondered. No, that wasn't possible. Over the years she had come by many fragments of the work of Udmanesh. Fully one third mentioned the Holy Children, a boy and a girl. They would be Cusha's age. One line in particular had caught Shamana's eye: *a flower meant for us both*. It was as if she had heard it somewhere, yet she could not recall where or when. The flower, what could it be? In the middle of her thoughts, she reeled suddenly. The knowledge of what had happened at Zindhar burst into her brain like a searing knife slash. She could see the storming of the fort as if she had witnessed it in person.

'What is it?' Aaliya asked as she staggered with the savagery of the unseen blow.

'It's nothing,' Shamana told her. 'A slight pain, that's all.'

Shamana leaned on Aaliya for a second, then gave in to an overwhelming wave of nausea. She leaned over a ditch and was violently sick. It wasn't the images of death and destruction from Zindhar that had made the impact. She had no love for the Sol-ket. It was concern for the battle's sole survivor that had made her weak.

'Shamana?' Aaliya asked, concerned.

Shamana sniffed the night air. 'I told you, I'm all right.'

'Then what?'

'Danger,' Shamana said. 'There is death on this wind.'

CHAPTER 3

Council of War

I

It was Kulmat who broke the news. 'Rishal-Ra wants to see you,' he said.

Gardep was sitting on his bunk, sharpening his sword. He spent longer on this soldier's chore than any of the other cadets, easing the stone along the blade until it could cut a floating feather.

'Is it about last night?' he asked.

Kulmat shrugged. 'He didn't say. Gardep—'

'Yes?'

Kulmat frowned as if unable or unwilling to put his thoughts into words. 'Nothing. Just be careful what you say. This is serious, my brother. A Sol-ket who falls for a Helat; that's trouble.'

'I know, my brother, but all I did was look at her. All is not lost. Kulmat, I don't even know her name.'

'It's Cusha,' Kulmat said.

'Cusha,' Gardep said, as if intoning a verse from scripture.

'I made it my business to find out,' Kulmat said. 'Idiot that you are, you're still my closest comrade.'

Gardep nodded.

'And that's what you're going to tell Rishal?' Kulmat asked. 'That you don't know her?'

'Yes,' Gardep said. 'It's true. I have not expressed my love to her. I have never even spoken to her.'

'May the mighty Ra bless you with good fortune,' Kulmat sighed, 'that's all I say. Everyone saw the way you looked at her. The transgression is in the thought as much as the act. Tread carefully indeed, my brother. The commander's suspicions have been aroused.'

'There are no two men in the academy closer than us,' Gardep said. 'We have been best friends since we were eight years old. I am speaking the truth, Kulmat. Though it rips my soul apart to say it, I will obey the warrior code. She lives. That is enough. Somehow, I will force myself to forget her.'

'Can I believe you, Gardep?' Kulmat asked. 'Are you quite sure you can drive this madness from your mind?'

'I swear by Almighty Ra that I will put all thought of her aside. Before my Emperor and my God, the girl pales into insignificance.'

Only half convinced, Kulmat threw himself down on his bunk. 'You'd better go,' he said. 'Rishal-Ra won't like you being late.'

2

'I'm afraid,' Cusha said. 'I should never have returned the Sol-ket's look.'

Murima took her in her arms and embraced her. 'I will do everything in my power to protect you.'

Cusha still had her head buried in Murima's shoulder when someone spoke behind them.

'A touching scene,' she said. It was Serala.

Cusha moved away from her Mama-li. Ignoring Murima, Serala advanced on the girl. The mistress's eyes burned Cusha like a brand, reminding her of many childhood beatings. The mistress often punished the servants herself. She seemed to like it. Cusha was aware of the leather strap that hung from Serala's waist. She had felt its bite more than once.

'My daughter is distraught,' she said. 'Her reputation has been tarnished by last night's fiasco. Our family has been made to look a laughing stock.' Her voice fell into a venomous hiss. 'And I am an ax-Sol. I do not accept humiliation at the hands of a Helat.'

Serala spat out that last word. Then she fixed first Cusha, then Murima with a glare. All the while, she was tapping the strap.

'You do not know what this ungrateful wretch has done. Julmira has sobbed all night. The engagement may be salvaged but the suffering caused to my daughter may take many weeks to heal.'

Cusha was about to say something but Murima touched her arm. For once Cusha heeded the warning.

'What should have been one of the happiest days of dear Julmira's life has been reduced to ashes. My poor child is heartbroken.' Serala pinched the bridge of her nose as if trying to communicate the hurt Cusha had caused. 'I am careful who I accept into my household,' she said.

'I know, mistress,' Murima said, 'and we are all grateful for your bounty.'

Cusha wanted to protest. Bounty indeed! What were they supposed to be grateful for, a day's hard labour in this hateful house?

'But how do you repay me?' Serala snarled, pointing at Cusha with the strap. 'You bring her into my home.'

'Why do you hate me, mistress?' Cusha cried. 'What have I done wrong?'

She knew, the moment the words left her lips, that she had spoken too boldly and without due respect. Serala rounded on her.

'You dare talk back to me!' she screamed. 'To me you are little better than an animal. No, you are worse than an animal. You do not have a dumb beast's obedience.'

Cusha felt the tears start in her eyes.

'You run with the Sol-ket,' Serala said, her voice as cold as sword steel, 'just like some cheap field-slave earning favours by surreptitiously sharing a soldier's bed.'

Murima tried to restrain Cusha but her adopted daughter had always had a fiery temperament. 'Mistress, it isn't true,' she protested. 'I have never spoken to Gardep.'

This she would say again and again. It was her defence. But it hid a deeper truth. She could have looked away the moment his eyes met hers. She didn't want to.

'Yet you know his name,' Serala observed acidly.

'I heard it from the lips of your own daughter, gracious Julmira,' Cusha protested. For once she managed to observe protocol. 'Mistress,' she said, 'I swear, I am innocent. He looked at me, not the other way round. I did not mean to return the warrior's gaze. You have to believe me; I did not encourage him in any way.'

Serala's eyes blazed. Perhaps she sensed Cusha's confusion over these words. Without warning, she gave Cusha a backhanded slap across the face. With the strap in her other hand, she inflicted a searing lash that left Cusha reeling.

'You compound your crime with every word that comes from your lying mouth,' she shouted. 'I should have you stoned for your impertinence or burned in some public square for the education of your kind. I could have it done, too.'

Serala saw Murima's pleading gaze. 'You also have some responsibility, Murima,' she said. 'You should have raised this foundling with some sense of respect. If I discover you knew more about this outrage than I have been led to believe I will destroy your whole family.'

She struck Murima twice about the shoulders, glaring all the time at Cusha as if daring her to react. For once, Cusha kept a rein on her emotions and remained impassive. To do anything else would bring even worse reprisals down on her loved ones.

'Either you control those who work in my household, Murima,' Serala said, 'or every one of them – including you – will burn on the pyre of my daughter's misery.' She let this image sink in for several moments, then took out a cotton handkerchief and wiped her lips. 'You may stay, Murima, but you need reminding of the value of respect, then maybe you will be able to pass it on to your unruly charges. You will present yourself at the flogging post tomorrow.'

Cusha went to cry out but Murima flashed a warning look.

'There,' Serala continued, 'you will receive six lashes for failing to control this child.'

She continued to taunt Cusha with her stare. But Murima, too wise or too terrified, squeezed Cusha's hand, warning her not to protest further. The cook bent her head. The punishment was less severe than she had expected.

'I thank you for your mercy, my mistress,' she said. Her relief was premature.

'But her—' Serala began. She jabbed a finger at Cusha, who was still smarting. 'That foundling of unknown parentage, you will get her out of my sight this very day. Let her earn a living any way a street rat can. Let her fight for scraps with the other inhabitants of the gutter. Better still, let her return to whatever corner of Hell spawned her. She is banished for ever from my house.'

3

Taking a deep breath, Gardep knocked on Rishal's door.

'Come in.'

Gardep entered. His heart was throbbing inside his ribs. Rishal fixed his squire with a stare.

'What do you know of the lands beyond the Demon Wall?' Rishal asked.

Gardep didn't understand. This wasn't what he'd been expecting. 'The Demon Wall, Rishal-Ra?' he said.

Rishal nodded and leaned forward in expectation.

'It is the home of the Lost Souls, the dismal land to which they were expelled in the time of the Demon Wars.'

Rishal's face was expressionless. 'And?'

By now Gardep was utterly confused. What did this have to do with his behaviour at the engagement feast?

'It is the base from which they launch raids on the Empire. They attack small outposts. They prey on the Helati, waiting for them to leave the protection of our cities after dark. They find cemeteries from the old times. People used to bury their dead instead of cremating them.

It created an endless supply of recruits to the night breed.' His nose wrinkled with distaste. 'They violate the grave and raise the bodies from the earth. These undead they recruit into their ranks as fighters. Why do you ask me this, Rishal-Ra? It is common knowledge.'

'What you say might have been accurate just a few months ago,' Rishal said, ignoring his squire's questions. 'But the world has turned. Nothing is as it once was. The night breeds pose a greater threat than we imagined. Their attacks are increasing in frequency and intensity, Gardep. They continue outside the duration of the Blood Moon. Recent intelligence confirms that they are massing beyond the wall, possibly for some kind of invasion.'

'Master, does this mean I am to be sent to serve at the frontier?' Gardep asked.

That was it. They were sending him into exile. Rishal looked at Gardep for a moment then shook his head.

'We may both be sent to the western territories before long, Gardep. The talk is of an expedition to conquer the demon host for good and all. But that is not the purpose of our discussion. There is to be a council of war to plan their subjugation.'

'Why not their extermination?' Gardep asked.

Rishal snorted. 'Ask the Emperor's priests,' he said. 'They still think they can control the creatures and make some use of them. The Hotec-Ra dream of a Legion of the Dead under their command. If you ask me, the priests carry part of the blame for this state of affairs, with all the meddling they do in the sorcerer's arts.'

Gardep was shocked to hear his master criticise the Hotec-Ra. Were they not the earthly representatives of the Deity himself?

'Like you, I see no purpose in permitting the demons to exist. I would rather slaughter the lot of them. Still, it's these accursed priests who have the ear of His Imperial Highness.'

The young warrior's mind was racing. He had entered Rishal's office expecting to be interrogated about the slave girl, Cusha. Now here he was discussing the military situation in the west, and more dangerous matters still. Rishal pushed back his chair and stood behind his desk.

'Gardep,' he said, 'I have been summoned to Rinaghar to attend the Imperial War Council. We leave tomorrow. You will accompany me as my squire.'

Relief flooded through Gardep. 'Yes, Rishal-Ra,' he said. 'Thank you for the honour you bestow upon me.'

Rishal turned his back on Gardep and started to examine the map of the Empire on the wall opposite the door. 'That's all,' he said.

It was a few moments before Gardep reacted. 'Thank you, master,' he said. 'I will prepare my kit.'

There was no reply so Gardep let himself out, his head spinning.

4

Four days later the Darkwing looked around his war host.

'Fliers,' he declared in a voice that must have carried only a few yards, yet which echoed through the servile mind of each one of his creatures, 'which of you is the strongest and most audacious? Which of you can go unnoticed and unmolested to the Dragon Mountains and beyond?' He chuckled. 'Which of you wants to strike fear into the Children of the Sun?'

Several dark-fliers stood. In truth, the Darkwing had no need of spoken words. His thoughts sufficed to send the night breed on any mission, but his voice broke the solitude. Even a demon lord feels his own isolation in a hostile world. The Darkwing looked into each pair of black, expressionless eyes. Sometimes he despaired of their utter stupidity, but then he prized their unthinking obedience, too. If only these poor, mindless creatures understood what they had been and what they were now. The Darkwing chuckled at the irony of it all. Once he had savoured the moment, he called forward the most promising candidates, laying his hands on their heads. Probing with his fingers and his mind, he peeled back the madness of the living death and explored the life the creatures had had before succumbing to their present condition. He weighed the prowess of each one.

'I have made my choice,' he said. 'You were a Sol-ket master in life, a war hero no less.'

The dark-flier looked back, uncomprehending, even then not knowing that he had once ridden into battle with his helmet's scarlet horsehair tassle streaming in the wind, the scourge of all barbarians.

'I have a duty for you to perform,' the Darkwing said. 'Discharge it with honour.'

The creature simply stood before his master, waiting to be told his mission. Like the rest of the Lost Souls, he had no will of his own, just the bleak, instinctive understanding of a hawk on a falconer's arm. Unthinking, unquestioning, he would obey the Darkwing's command even if it meant his own destruction.

The Darkwing handed his minion a hessian sack, weighted by something heavy. As the dark-flier rose into the turbulent, blue-black sky, the Darkwing permitted himself a smile.

'Golden Rinaghar,' he said, 'city of cities, light of the Sol-ket, I am sending you a present.' His opaque, sable eyes blinked just once. 'I'm sure you will enjoy it.'

77

5

Nearby, a lone tiger padded through the cedar-carpeted slopes of the Jinghara Hills. Jinghara was the heart of the Empire, a vast and varied peninsula that jutted into a warm, sparkling ocean. The hilly north was barren. The centre consisted of vast, fertile plains. The south yielded rice, fish and spices. No matter which road Oled took to escape the war host, he had a long journey ahead of him. Solitude was nothing new to Oled. His very name meant: walk alone.

He examined his surroundings. Soon these undulating uplands would give way to mile upon mile of rolling plains, the breadbasket of the whole Empire, rich in wheat, barley and maize. Oled, for safety still assuming animal form, thought of all the garrisons, cities, towns and villages between here and Rinaghar and started to lope through the gloomy woods. Much as he resented his treatment at the hands of the Sol-ket, his mind was continually filled with the images of all the innocent men, women and children in the path of the Lost Souls.

The Book of Scales taught the unity of mankind. Oled imagined the night breed's victims drained of life and taken into the ranks of the living dead. Though the Empire's peoples were led by tyrants, they were by no means all as bad as each other. Often, over the years, some soldier or other had performed some small kindness for him. Whatever the crimes ordered by their officers and priests, there were women and men who did not deserve to die at the hands of the demons. Oled could not allow them to go about their everyday lives ignorant of the coming storm. Then, of course, there was his sacred mission.

'Why didn't you listen to me, Turayat, you fool?' he said. 'You could have saved thousands of lives.'

The words came out as a throaty animal growl. Moments later Oled had cause to regret expressing his thoughts out loud. In a clearing ahead he saw a small mud-brick house. The demons had got there first and were feasting on a family: a man, a woman and their young son. The moment they heard him growl their heads snapped round. Shifting shape, Oled was once again the warrior-giant who had served at lonely Zindhar. Detaching his battle-axe from the criss-crossed leather straps on his back, Oled rushed the dark-fliers. The first two he beheaded before they could tear themselves away from their victims. The third gave a shriek and started to climb into the air. It slashed defensively at Oled but he brushed away the talons with the padded sleeve of his tunic before hacking open its chest with the axe. The creature fell to the earth writhing and lashing out with its clawed hands. Steeling himself for the final act, Oled put his boot on the dark-flier's stomach. Holding the squirming demon down, he severed its head as he had the others.

Then came the task he always dreaded. The dark-flier's victims, their flesh still warm, lay torn and twisted on the ground. No matter how many times he had done this, Oled could never release a human being from the contagion of the Lost Souls without shedding a tear. Leave it just a few days though and this family would have begun their transformation into demons of the inhuman dark. The Darkwing would have three more recruits to his legions.

Oled wiped the axe blade then set a fire. He found oil and salt. Cleansing the steel in the flames, he sprinkled it with the oil and salt as an offering to the Four Winds. He took ash from the fire and placed it in both hands, turning his palms to the sky to make the sign of the Scales. He marked the foreheads of the man, woman and child with ash, making the spiral symbol of the Four Winds. Finally, he raised his axe and removed their heads. Only then did he douse the fire. It had been a risk to build a fire, even a small one, but Oled wanted to honour them with some ritual, however rudimentary. Erecting a funeral pyre, however, would have been folly indeed, attracting the attention of the night breed, so Oled buried the corpses, their severed heads set at right angles to their bodies.

'Sleep well in the earth my brothers, my sister,' he said.

Then, for a long time, he sat watching the smouldering ashes. Dusk gathered around him. Darkness fell. Finally, from the shadows, an owl came. The bird became a woman and the woman spoke. 'Our warrior-queen has instructions for you, Oled Lonetread,' she said.

'I have failed,' he told her.

'How so?'

'I have been driven further from the Black Tower than ever.'

'There is nothing you could have done to stem the demon tide,' the figure in the shadows told him. 'The destiny of the oppressed, dormant so long, is stirring. For now you must stay with the Sol-ket. You will receive further instructions presently.'

After that she did not tarry. Oled watched the owl vanish into the dark. Rising to his feet, he embarked on a night journey towards the Sol-ket.

6

Gardep checked the saddlebags. He examined the hooves of his own mount and Rishal's. He inspected his weapons: the bow, the quiver of arrows, the sword, the throwing knives, the shield. Finally, he tightened the buckles that secured his scarlet cloak to his shoulders. Satisfied that everything was in order, he took down his helmet with the horsehair tassels and set it on his head.

'I wish I was going with you,' Kulmat said.

'You will see golden Rinaghar one day,' Gardep told him.

'Yes,' Kulmat said, 'but you will see it first.'

'I can't help thinking it's strange,' Gardep said. 'I walked into Rishal's quarters expecting to face his fury for the way I insulted Julmira and here I am preparing to accompany him to Rinaghar to be part of the council of war.'

'You're in luck,' Kulmat said. 'He's going to overlook your fit of madness.'

Doing his best to drive Cusha's face from his mind, Gardep smiled. 'You're right. I'll miss you.'

'You won't be gone long,' Kulmat said. 'You never know, I might get to join the march west alongside you.' He clasped Gardep's arms. 'I thought you had thrown it all away over that slave girl,' he said. 'I should have known better. One day, Gardep-na-Vassyrian, poets will sing songs about you, the greatest warrior of them all.'

'Yes,' Gardep answered, 'and you, Kulmat-na-Zamir, will be by my side in all my victories.'

With that, he led his and Rishal's horses out into the square. He steadied Rishal's mount, allowing his master to climb into the saddle. Gardep sprang effortlessly into his own saddle. He looked back. Rishal was taking fifty warriors with him. Their armour flashed in the morning sun. We are invincible, Gardep thought, the sons of Almighty Ra. Let the Darkwing tremble.

7

The next few nights Cusha slept in a granary store in the Parcep slums. Murima ordered the villa's flour from a freeman merchant called Babur, and Serala entrusted Murima with the management of the kitchens and allowed her to pay him. A little arrangement over the payment for his services convinced Babur to overlook the presence of a Helat in his store. The arrangement was, after all, worth fifty dinar a month. Murima didn't tell Babur why the girl needed a roof over her head. Any mention of what had happened at Julmira's engagement feast and Babur would have thrown the pair of them out on the street. Even a freeman didn't dare incur the wrath of the Children of the Sun.

For the first four nights Harad and Qintu took it in turns to bring Cusha food. After the flogging Murima had to lie on her stomach to let the lashes heal. But on the fifth night there she was.

'You shouldn't have come, Mama-li,' Cusha said. 'You're taking a great risk.'

'The overseer went easy on me,' Murima said. 'I'm in pain but I've taken worse beatings.'

'What's going to happen to us, Mama-li?'

Cusha's face was grimed with the dust of the street and her tears had cut tracks down her cheeks. Guilt burned into her soul. It was her fault Murima had been flogged. Serala had chosen the punishment well. More than ten lashes and Murima wouldn't have been able to cook for weeks. Six had left her in agony but still just about fit to toil in the kitchens. The mistress knew how to inflict searing pain without losing a day's work. If she had been a man, she would have been an asset to the Hotec-Ra. But even now,

Murima was risking everything for Cusha, slipping away from the villa to visit the granary.

'I don't know, darling child,' Murima said. 'I will think of something.'

'You must regret the day you took me in,' Cusha said.

'Never, my child,' Murima said. 'Through no fault of your own you find your throat laid against the master's blade. At worst, you have acted the way any girl would when subjected to a young man's gaze. So it has been always. If we dare show our human frailties, we find ourselves teetering over the very mouth of Hell. It is our destiny to toil and suffer and die.'

'Well, I refuse to live like that,' Cusha said. 'When all this is over I am going to join Shamana. She wants to fight the Sol-ket. I will serve the Scales alongside her and Aaliya. If the masters seek my blood, I will spill theirs in return.'

Murima placed a finger on Cusha's lips. 'Hush, daughter,' she said. 'You don't know what you're saying. This affair has cost you your home and earned me the overseer's whip. I won't have any more blood spilled because of it. The Helati have fought before. They have risen against the Sol-ket but they have always been crushed. When I was a child there was a man called Shinar, greatest and best loved of all the Helati. He read the scriptures as told by Udmanesh. He believed the prophecy of the Scales; that we could once again walk free. That was what led him to his death.'

'Yes,' Cusha said. 'I know the story.'

'You still need to hear it again,' Murima said. 'It has a moral of which you may be unaware.'

Cusha resigned herself to listening to Murima's tale. Truth was, ablaze as she was with indignation at her treatment, she would have preferred Shamana's prophecies of a republic of the free.

'With thirty others bold Shinar broke out of the slave stockade up-country at Gussorah.'

'Mama-li, I know all this,' Cusha said. 'Ask any child and they will relate the adventures of Shinar.'

'You think you know the story,' Murima said. She sounded angry and Murima never got angry.

'Shinar went to war with the Sol-ket, the first man since venerable Udmanesh to resist the Muzals' evil rule. At first the Empire dismissed him as a bandit but his strength grew. He liberated slaves from the estates all over northern Parcep province. He trained them and bound them together into a brotherhood of fighters. Soon he threatened Tiger-gated Parcep itself. He did something no man before had done. As directed by the Book of Scales, he started to unite the oppressed peoples of the Empire. He made an alliance with the shape-shifting people of the north, under their warrior queen, the She-Wolf of Tanjuristan. In golden Rinaghar the masters trembled. Were Parcep to fall they would be next to face the just fury of the risen Helati.'

Cusha tried to interrupt but Murima silenced her with a look. 'Hear me out. Together the freed slaves and their Tanjur allies became a beacon for all those who wanted to end the tyranny of the Empire. All who had suffered under the lash of the Sol-ket rallied to their banner. Five times the Sol-ket marched against the Army of the Free. Five times bold Shinar threw them back.'

Murima clenched her fists as if reliving the events in her mind. 'It was a time of great hope. A new world seemed to be dawning when the Helati could throw off their shackles. The ancient struggle against the demon host seemed to be over. The Muzals had won the Demon Wars and driven most of the Lost Souls to the west. It was not the night breed the Empire feared but its abused, resentful slaves.'

'Mama-li, I have heard this a hundred times. Harad has told me the stories.'

Murima shook her head. 'Harad has told you the myths. He doesn't know the truth. He wasn't there.' She broke off. There was grief in her voice.

'Mama-li?'

Murima rubbed her eyes with her sleeve and sobbed until the tears dripped from her nose and chin. She gave out a cry of misery.

'Mama-li! What's wrong?'

'I witnessed it,' Murima said. 'Five years the rebellion lasted. Shinar created a haven of peace and security for the Helati. We made our own laws, dispensed our own justice. I was born in the weeks after the revolt broke out. I was raised free, Cusha. Do you understand what that means, child? I know a different, better world than this one. Every single day of my life I ache for its return. I was raised believing it was my birthright. My mother nursed me as she walked with the baggage train of the Army of the Free. Still a tiny child, I clutched my doll and prayed for victory every time bold Shinar rode into battle. I was there, Cusha. I saw it all.'

'But you have never spoken of it in all these years,' Cusha said wonderingly.

'No,' Murima said. 'I have never spoken of it.'

'But why?'

'Why do you think?' Murima said. 'Because we lost, Cusha. I was only six years old when Shinar and the She-Wolf faced the Armies of the Sun at Dullah. There were widespread expectations of a final, crushing victory. The taste of freedom was on our tongues, like honey. But Shinar made a terrible mistake. He put his trust in a man who did not merit it. The Selessians had been wavering, unsure which side to support. A rebel prince, Uhmet

Haraddin, had promised to come over to us. Still somewhat unsure of his new ally, Shinar decided to keep the Selessians in reserve. The old guard, veterans of five years of revolt, would do the bulk of the fighting. The Selessians would only be called upon to complete the rout. The omens were good. The Empire seemed to be crumbling. So grave was the situation of the Sol-ket that the Imperial troops had to be led by the Emperor himself, Muzal-ax-Sol, twenty-fifth monarch of a cruel dynasty, and its cruellest son. He commanded the centre. His son Sabray, a boy-prince of sixteen, led the cavalry on the right. The battle went on all day. We watched from a hill, my mother and I.'

Again, she wiped away her tears. 'Finally, as dusk started to fall, the Sol-ket began to waver. Shinar called up his reserve to complete the victory. With a glad heart, I watched the Selessians galloping down the hill to join the attack. That's when it happened.'

Murima looked deep into Cusha's eyes. 'Do you know this part of the story, my rebel tigress?'

'I think so,' Cusha said. 'The Selessians betrayed the Army of the Free. That's right, isn't it?'

'Yes,' Murima said. 'Led by their Sultan, the scorpion Uhmet Haraddin, they betrayed us. The Selessian charge crashed into our right flank. Surprised by this knife in their back, the Helati and their allies were thrown into confusion. The Emperor was able to rally his troops and win the day. Caught between the Selessians and the Sol-ket the Great Alliance was destroyed. Within weeks, ten thousand rebel warriors had been caught. Every few paces along the Great Western Road, they were subjected to the most appalling cruelties. Some were left to starve to death in cages. Others were strung up by their ankles and speared. Still others were staked to the earth and trampled by elephants. These were the best of men, Cusha, and the Empire served them up as food for the crows and vultures. Every day the Helati had to trudge to work past the decaying bodies of their heroes.'

'But why are you telling me this now?' Cusha asked.

'Darling child,' Murima said, 'I am going to tell you something I have never even told Harad.' She hesitated. 'If I tell you my secret you must swear never to say a word to another living soul, not even Harad. Swear!'

'I so swear, Mama-li. But what is it?'

Murima took Cusha's hands. 'Bold Shinar was my father.'

Cusha's eyes widened. 'You're Shinar's daughter!'

Murima nodded. 'That is my burden.'

'But you should be proud,' Cusha said.

Murima put her palm to Cusha's cheek. 'I am proud, daughter. I am so proud of my brave father.'

'And yet you disown everything he stood for,' Cusha said. 'You tell me to have nothing to do with the Scales.'

'I do it to spare you the pain I have suffered all my life. You see, Cusha, I have only told you half my story.' She steadied herself before continuing. 'It is what came after the battle that made me what I am today. I know what happens when you take on the Masters and lose. Most of our men the Sol-ket butchered that night. Then, for weeks after, they hunted down the remnants of the army. The women and the children they put to work in the fields and in their homes.'

There was no protest from Cusha now. She was hanging on Murima's every word.

'For many months there was no word of Shinar. We still dreamed that he would return for us. We dared hope he had escaped and lived to fight another day. One day, when I was six years old, mother and I were sent to the market to buy fruit for our master's table. We heard a lot of noise coming from the Avenue of the Kings.'

Cusha suddenly realised that she didn't want to hear the rest.

'In the middle of the processional road the Sol-ket had built a funeral pyre,' Murima said. 'We wondered who it was they were cremating. It must be someone of renown to set their pyres in the middle of the Avenue of the Kings. Then we saw a man in chains being dragged down the middle of the road.' Two huge tears spilled down her cheeks. 'It was my father. He had finally been hunted down, a year after the defeat at Dullah.'

'Oh, Murima,' Cusha said. 'Poor Mama-li.'

Murima was determined to finish her story. 'My father saw mother and me. He smiled and cried out in anguish. He couldn't even tell us he loved us one last time. Nobody among the Helati had given us away, you see. The masters didn't imagine they had the wife and child of Shinar in their grasp. Who knows what they would have done to us if they had understood the prize they held in their hands. The Sol-ket burned Shinar that very day, the way they had burned the books of Udmanesh many generations earlier. Cusha, they burned the rebel leader alive. I heard my father's dying screams.'

She crushed her fingers into Cusha's until it hurt. 'That's why I won't let you serve the Scales, Cusha. My father did and it led our people to disaster. Thousands were put to the sword or sold back into slavery. The worst punishment of all was reserved for the Tanjuri people. The Sol-ket thought the shape-shifters inhuman, barbarians, an abomination. Every man, woman and child found by the Sol-ket was butchered on the spot. The queen, the She-wolf of Tanjuristan, disappeared. Some say she died of grief. Others believe she lives on in a cave somewhere, impaled on the spear of her own loneliness. Her people were all slaughtered. Tanjuristan ceased to exist as a nation.'

Murima allowed a few moments for the tale to sink in. 'We can never defeat the masters,' she said by way of conclusion. 'They break our backs by day; the Lost Souls tear our flesh by night. All we can do is endure and survive. Somewhere, amid all that horror, we have to find what fleeting moments of joy we can.' She threw up her arms in despair. 'I have you and Harad. You are my joy. After all that I have suffered, I can't lose you too. Please, do as I do. Bow your sweet head and endure. Learn to find the tiny pleasures of this life amid the suffering. Even a life yoked to oppression is better than torture and death. Don't throw your life away in pursuit of an impossible dream.'

8

Rinaghar was five days' ride from Parcep. Dusty and saddle-weary, Rishal's column stopped by a mountain stream to drink. Some of the men were refreshing themselves with a powerful brew called kinthi. The wiser ones were fortifying themselves with water and a potato-filled flatbread. Once the first hot rush of the kinthi wore off it left a man with a raging thirst and a thumping headache. Gardep was sitting alone, munching a piece of bread, when Rishal called to him.

'Gardep,' he said, 'go up to that rise. We should be able to pick up the trail down to Rinaghar.'

Gardep nodded and jogged to the top of the slope. The sight that confronted him took his breath away. Below him stretched a vast city of domes, towers, minarets and temples. The wall that encircled the city was decorated with glazed golden tiles. Many of the domes also glittered gold in the strong sunlight. From the battlements, palaces, castles and temples scarlet banners and pennants flew. Statues of Ra lined the broad boulevards. Finally, at the heart of the city, there it was: the enormous step pyramid, the Ziggurat of the Sun, the shrine at its top blazing scarlet in the sunlight. If Parcep was a tribute to the gods, this was surely their home.

'That's it,' a voice said behind him, 'golden Rinaghar.'

Gardep turned to look at Rishal. 'You knew what was over the rise, didn't you?'

Rishal smiled. 'Of course I did.'

'Is that why you sent me?' he said. 'To give me my first sight of the holy city?'

Rishal nodded. 'This is where I was raised, Gardep. When the Emperor told me he was sending me to command the garrison at Parcep, I thought my heart was going to break. To rot in some provincial backwater after the splendour of Rinaghar was a terrible punishment for a young man. This is truly the greatest of cities, the heart of civilisation. It is for this that man descended from the sun.'

Gardep stood a long time watching the city. Rishal observed his wonderment and smiled. For years they had been almost like father and son.

'There is greatness in you, Gardep,' the commander said, his fondness for the boy obvious to anyone who cared to watch them. 'I saw it in you when you were a small boy. Even when you were only eight you could outfight boys two or three years older. You proved your skill and courage again during your Ket-Ra. Be single-minded in pursuing your destiny as a warrior and you can return here in triumph.' He gripped Gardep's arms. 'Do you want glory, Gardep? Do you want to ride into golden Rinaghar and have the crowds rush forward to garland you?'

'Of course,' Gardep said, unsure what Rishal was asking him. 'It is the dream of any Sol-ket to enter the sacred city of Ra in triumph.'

Rishal released his arms and walked away, shaking his head. Somehow Gardep had disappointed him. 'But you are not any Sol-ket,' the commander cried, spinning on his heel. 'Do you have no ambition? Do you have no sense of who you are or what you can be?'

Gardep threw out his arms in bewilderment. 'What do you want of me, Rishal-Ra?'

'I want you to recognise your destiny,' Rishal told him. 'What do you want to be, Gardep, just one more victorious general? Why settle for that? You can have so much more.'

Gardep frowned.

'The Emperor is an old man,' Rishal said. 'He has no heir.'

Gardep's heart lurched. What was the Commander proposing?

'The imperial family is riven with conspiracies and squabbles,' Rishal continued. 'None of them is either worthy or strong enough to inherit the Sun throne. Are you so blind?'

All kinds of ideas were racing through Gardep's mind. Was this some test of loyalty? Had the incident at the betrothal party made Rishal suspect him?

'I don't understand, Rishal-Ra,' he said.

'Oh, I think you understand me very well,' Rishal said. 'Some day soon, His Imperial Highness will be dead. Without a strong leader, the Empire will descend into civil war. Gardep, we can provide such leadership. I am the First General of the Empire. You are its greatest young warrior. Together we can forge the greatest dynasty the world has ever known.'

The commander met Gardep's stare. 'Join me in this undertaking,' he said, 'and you can inherit the entire world. But first I have to be sure that I have not made a mistake in choosing you. It is not enough to possess a strong right arm. You must be single-minded and true. Gardep, you have embarrassed me in front of the most powerful men in Parcep. You must never show such weakness again. That would not just cost you the throne. It would also cost you your life. Do you understand?'

'Yes, Rishal-Ra.'

'Then you must prove yourself true to Julmira. I will give you a month to make amends for your actions. Then we will speak again.'

Even then, even at the moment Rishal was offering him the Sun throne, in his mind's eye Gardep saw a slight figure shimmering in the heat of a Parcep twilight. She wore a white salwar kameez and looked at him with night-dark eyes. In his heart of hearts, he knew he would have given up golden Rinaghar itself for the press of her lips against his.

9

Oled's journey was an arduous one. Judging by the cloud of dust on the far horizon and the shuddering vibrations in the earth, the Lost Souls were still half a day's march ahead of him. With these overcast skies there was no need to shelter from the rays of the sun. They were making good time. But how am I to warn the people of the Jingharan plain, Oled wondered. His options were limited. Changing shape would be no help to him. The dark-fliers would spot and intercept a bird. Any wild beast of the plains would be hunted down for food and torn to shreds. No, he might as well continue as he was, in human form. Exhausted, haunted by the terrors of Zindhar, Oled secured his battle-axe to the strapping on his back and started to run.

He felt the wind in his face and squinted against the cold and the dust. He had been waiting so long for this moment, when the prophecies would come true and the Army of the Free would rise again. But, now the waiting was over, he had failed in his mission. He had devoted most of his adult life to it and he was further from success than ever before. For a moment he allowed his despair to fly up. Then there were other thoughts in his head, unspoken words that nourished him.

Outrun the host, Oled, and we may still win the prize. Once the Holy Children are united, our long agony will have been worth it. Run, brave Lonetread. Follow your destiny.

Suddenly the tread of many thousand feet was not a warning but a challenge. With the fire of conviction burning in his veins, Oled picked up the pace.

10

The sight in the Square of Ra was breathtaking. Gardep had never seen so great a throng. There were representatives from every corner of the Empire. Hooded, masked and dressed from head to foot in flowing black robes, there were the Selessians, desert fighters with a fierce reputation, both as soldiers and as hired assassins. It was their change of heart that had turned the final battle at Dullah against the so-called Army of the Free, which had turned it the Empire's way. The Vassyrians were there too in great numbers. Distinctive in their chequered scarves, they stood a little apart from the rest. Subjected to Imperial

Rule less than ten years before, these warriors still seemed unsure of their standing in the army.

Statues of polished sandstone, depictions of mighty Ra, looked down upon the delegates to the war council. Gardep found himself at the foot of one of these representations. It showed the dual character of the Sun God. The front of the head was Ra's, the back his mortal enemy, the evil Moon God, Sangra. This image of the Empire's savage god was everywhere, two spirits in one body, forever fighting with the other, opposing side of his character. Ra stabbed at his foe with golden knives, Sangra with silver ones. In cutting his enemy, each representation of the god slashed his own flesh. Gardep looked up at the statue and, though he venerated mighty Ra, he shuddered at the eternal violence for which the statue stood.

Then trumpets blared and all eyes were on the Ziggurat that dominated the centre of golden Rinaghar. It was from the top of this vast edifice, a testament to Imperial power, that the Emperor would speak. His Imperial Highness, Light of the Sun, Conqueror of Shinar, Muzal the Great, twenty-fifth monarch in the six-hundred-year dynasty, was absolute ruler of millions of souls. Now in his seventy-third year he had had no heir since the downfall of his son, Sabray the traitor. Some said that, since Sabray's revolt, Muzal had not dared trust anyone, not even members of his close family, not even his wife who was said to grieve secretly for her renegade son. That, they observed, was the reason there was no heir. Already Muzal's nephews were jockeying for position. All had their eyes on the Sun throne. Many expected a bloody civil war to break out the day Muzal died. But nobody was thinking of civil war at this moment. Their thoughts were dominated by the prospect of an expedition to annihilate the Lost Souls.

The person of Muzal was protected by the Priesthood of

Ra. They and only they were permitted to climb the Ziggurat and attend Muzal. Even the Sol-ket were not allowed that close to the Emperor. The priesthood formed his palace guard. Dressed in their traditional saffron robes, the Priests of Ra fanned out from the summit of the Ziggurat, armed with bows and sabres.

'That's Linem-hotec,' Rishal told Gardep.

Gardep stared in wonderment. He had heard the name. Now here he was in person, the man who was said to be the second most powerful figure in the Empire. Linem-hotec was in his sixties but still tall, slim and striking. His father had served the Emperor and passed on his mantle to Linem. So feared was Linem-hotec that mothers used his name to silence their children at bedtime. He had a network of spies and assassins to enforce his wishes.

'Who's that one step below him?' Gardep asked.

'That's Shirep-hotec, Linem's adopted son,' Rishal said. 'The priesthood, as you know, are forbidden to marry. They are permitted, however, to adopt an orphan child as their own and raise them to continue their line. Linem advises the Emperor what needs to be done. Shirep makes sure it is carried out. He is head of the Hotec-Ra.'

This needed no explanation. The Hotec-Ra was the Emperor's secret police. They had spies everywhere. Even a member of the royal family like Rishal had good cause to fear the Hotec-Ra. This body of men, utterly fanatical in their devotion to the Emperor, had the power over life and death even among junior members of the royal family. They answered to one man and one man only, Muzal himself.

Gardep was about to ask Rishal something else when a gong was struck. Hundreds of white doves were released into the skies and many braziers were lit on the steps of the Ziggurat, casting swirls of black smoke towards the azure sky. Simultaneously, every man in the square fell to his knees and bowed his head. The Emperor was about to appear.

A second gong sounded and, as a man, the warriors raised their faces from the ground. A third gong sounded and, again perfectly orchestrated, they rose to their feet and roared their loyalty to the Emperor. Gardep fought to get a glimpse of the man who was ruler of the known world. He saw an elderly but still robust and powerful man, dressed in white and gold, the Imperial crown on his head.

'Children of Holy Ra,' the Emperor said, 'you are my strong right arms, my bold hearts, my defence against the demon host. Sad tidings I have to bring you. A message was put into my hands this very day. Brave Zindhar has fallen to a cowardly surprise attack.'

A murmur ran through the crowd. Zindhar fallen! It was many years since the Empire had suffered such a grave loss. Had their implacable march from victory to victory come to a halt?

'Warriors,' the Emperor continued, silencing the hub-bub, 'this was expected. This is the third major challenge to my rule. The Helat vermin rose and I defeated them.'

This drew a huge roar from the assembled warriors.

'The traitor Sabray, an unnatural son and foul usurper, rose and I defeated him too.'

Another roar filled the air.

'Forewarned of the gathering of the Lost Souls I had already ordered this council of war. The Darkwing's murderous incursions have been becoming ever more audacious. The news from Zindhar only strengthens my resolve. With Ra's blessing I will defeat the demon menace.'

Before the roars of approval had faded, Muzal raised both fists. 'Let the word go out. One month from now my armies will gather to defeat the Darkwing. From there, we will march to face the night breed. Many years ago my ancestors drove the Lost Souls west in the Demon Wars. Warriors, it is time to go a step further and break the demons' power for ever. We will destroy the Darkwing and bend the Lost Souls to our will.'

There followed a thunderous roar. Gardep shouted with the rest of them, overjoyed at the prospect of winning glory in battle. His entire life had been a preparation for this moment. The chorus of voices was still rolling across the city when it happened. A lone dark-flier, heavily swathed in black robes to protect it from the sun, appeared in the cloudless sky above. There were pointed fingers and shouts of alarm. Then the flier emptied something from a hessian bag. The object fell and landed not ten paces from the Emperor. The thing rolled down the Ziggurat's steps and came to rest halfway. Gardep craned to see what it was.

'It's a head,' he shouted to Rishal.

Rishal recognised it. It belonged to his old comrade, Turayat, Commander of Zindhar.

CHAPTER 4

Kidnap

1

'Vishtar.'

The boy stirred. Somewhere in the Black Tower his name had been spoken.

'Vishtar. Wake up.'

Vishtar sat up, rubbing his eyes. 'Is that you, Aurun-Kai?' he asked.

On cue, Aurun-Kai appeared from the shadows. 'Now tell me,' he said, 'who else would it be?'

Even now, after so many days in his presence, Vishtar couldn't help staring at Aurun-Kai, the twisted, reptilian figure who acted as his jailer. Though his face, for all its disfigurements, remained human, his body was a scaly carapace, his hands twisted, deformed, his eyes desolate with lost humanity. Aurun-Kai caught Vishtar's eye and the boy looked away.

'Have you recovered your strength?'

'Yes.' Vishtar stood up to stretch his legs. He marvelled at his own resilience. Mere days since the last visit of the Darkwing and he was feeling better.

'Lord Darkwing is wondering if you have anything to tell him,' Aurun-Kai said.

'No,' Vishtar said, 'nothing.'

'So you still don't know where she is?'

Vishtar shook his head. 'No.'

'Did you study the records?' Aurun-Kai asked, pointing to a pile of ledgers.

'Of course I did,' Vishtar said. 'I told you. I found the record of my sister's sale, then her re-sale in a small town on the Plains of Jinghara. After that . . .' He shrugged. 'There is nothing.'

Aurun-Kai scowled and made his way painfully across the stone floor. 'Are you sure you have searched every entry?' he said. 'All the Helati are logged and the record of their movements passed to the central office in Rinaghar. She must be there somewhere.'

'You forget,' Vishtar said, 'my sister and I were free-born.'

'Yes,' Aurun-Kai said, interrupting, 'and the day she was given into slavery she became a Helat. Her name may be a common one but, I tell you, the girl is in there somewhere.'

'Aurun-Kai,' Vishtar groaned, 'I have gone through the books with a fine-tooth comb. I swear, her name is not there.'

Aurun-Kai shook his head and turned to go. Only when he was gone did Vishtar permit himself a smile. There was nothing that either the Darkwing or Aurun-Kai could do to make him betray his sister. What options did they have? Torture him? Kill him? Then the Darkwing would be unable to feed on holy blood. The Darkwing had tried to probe Vishtar's mind many times but the intelligence he found there was strong. The demon lord could find no way into his thoughts.

He had found her name early in his search but it wasn't the entry in Jinghara. That was a different girl by the same name. Indeed, he had known where she was for over a year. He had hidden the volume that contained the information, replacing it with a meticulously copied facsimile. This second volume differed from the original in only one detail. Cusha. That way, no matter how Aurun-Kai checked his work, he would never find her. Aurun-Kai could bribe him as much as he liked with sweets and books. The Darkwing could torture him every day until the end of time. Vishtar would never betray her.

Never.

2

The Parcep delegation was going to return the next morning at first light. Rishal had granted the cadets a few hours to wander the city and most of the Sol-ket headed for the taverns. Gardep didn't follow. Perhaps because of his Vassyrian parentage, he didn't drink alcohol and he still couldn't get Cusha out of his head. He had barely looked at a girl but his attraction to this one Helat was becoming an obsession. Foregoing the pleasures of the taverns, Gardep decided to visit the Temple of Ra. He wanted to pray for the strength to put Cusha out of his mind.

A statue of Ra engaged in permanent struggle with his evil twin, Sangra, dominated the entrance hall. Walking the temple's marble floors, Gardep made his way into the inner sanctum to make an offering to Ra. As he knelt before the shrine, incense from the prayer sticks wove dreamy patterns in his mind. He heard the rhythmic, droning chants of the Hotec-Ra and bowed his head. He was about to offer up his prayers when he felt something on his hand. Looking down, he saw an asp slither over the skin. Startled, he recoiled. By the time he had recovered from his surprise, the creature had vanished behind the shrine. He was staring at the spot where it had disappeared, wondering if he had taken leave of his senses when he heard movement behind him.

'Who's there?' he asked, spinning round.

There was no reply. For a few moments he held his breath, listening. He glanced back at the shrine. Immediately, from overhead, he heard the sound again. It was wing beats. Not the serpent, then. Instinctively, though he knew not why, his hand closed round his dagger. He was still searching the vaulted ceiling when he sensed a presence behind him. For the second time, he spun on his heel, his dagger drawn. By now his heart was pounding.

'Who's there?' he said.

Out of the corner of his eye, he glimpsed a white blur. His head snapped round. Whatever was moving round the temple, it was taunting him, circling like a hungry predator.

'I demand to know,' Gardep cried. 'Who's there?'

'Another such as you,' came the answer. It was a woman's voice.

'What do you mean?' Gardep demanded.

'We are outlanders, barbarians.'

'Barbarian?' Gardep retorted. 'You are mistaken. I am of the Sol-ket.'

'Yes, but you are Vassyrian by birth.'

A sensation like a crawling insect stole over Gardep's neck. How did she know this?

'It is only because you were placed under the tutelage

of Commander Rishal that you were admitted to the Academy at all. You may not know this, but Rishal's peers were bitterly opposed to your enrolment.'

The tickling sensation continued, spreading like goose-flesh. He looked around. 'Who are you? How do you know so much about me?'

Though he searched high and low he couldn't see who was talking to him.

'You try so hard to be one of them, don't you?' the voice asked. 'You never will be. You know that. The Empire of all the Peoples is a sham. The Sol-ket rule. Their allies may not be slaves, but they are not equals. Rishal tempts you with the Sun throne. Do you really believe that's for you?'

Gardep felt a deep chill in his soul. How did she know this?

'Face the truth. Deep inside, you are aware that you are different.'

'I am Sol-ket,' Gardep yelled.

'Tell yourself whatever lies you will,' the voice drawled, 'but here is something that may change your mind about serving the Empire, yes, or even possessing it. Your beloved is in danger.'

'My beloved?'

'Don't play games, Gardep. You know who I mean. Her name is Cusha-ul-Parcep, though Parcep is not the place of her birth.'

With each new rebuttal of his protestations, rivulets of icy fear ate through his flesh.

'What do you know about Cusha and me?' Gardep asked.

'Only that your master has not forgiven you for the slight to his daughter.'

Gardep's skin crawled. *Not forgiven.* 'But the fault was mine, and mine alone,' he said. 'Cusha is innocent.'

'True, but when in this world did innocence get any reward? Do the Sol-ket not march over a mountain of innocent skulls?'

There was a moment's silence.

'In that case,' the voice said, 'if the fault was indeed yours, then maybe the solution should be yours too.'

'What do you mean?' Gardep said.

'I will show you.'

A white dove, like the ones he had seen released at the council of war, appeared before him. Then, while he looked on transfixed, the bird transformed into an elderly woman. The shape-shifter's green eyes flashed.

'Because of what you did at the betrothal ceremony,' she said, 'Cusha's life hangs by a thread. She is in hiding. I have to get her out of Parcep.'

Then came the final, brutal statement, like a nail through his flesh.

'You must come with us.'

'Are you mad?' Gardep cried.

'It is your destiny,' the shape-shifter said.

'Then I refuse it,' Gardep retorted. 'You are asking me to betray my order. That I will never do.'

'Your precious order of warriors is a fraud,' the shape-shifter said. 'Your destiny is fixed. You can't escape it.'

With that, she assumed the form of a dove once more and flew across the room, down the long corridor that led to the Ziggurat, and out into the blazing sunlight.

3

Three days after Gardep's encounter with the shape-shifter, Serala-ax-Sol had a visitor. It was the merchant Babur.

'You wanted to see me, mistress Serala,' he said.

His face was covered with a sheen of nervous perspiration. Unscheduled interviews with the ax-Sols were not to be recommended. They rarely ended happily.

'Sit down, Babur,' she said.

Babur did as he was told and sat uneasily on the edge of the chair. 'Is something wrong?' he asked.

'That's for you to tell me,' Serala said.

'I don't understand,' Babur stammered.

Serala's patience snapped. 'You understand perfectly well, you ungrateful scoundrel!'

'Mistress, I . . .'

'I don't want your pathetic excuses,' Serala snapped. 'I want to know where you are harbouring the Helat girl.'

Babur's eyes widened in horror. She knew! 'How did you find out?' he gasped.

There was a moment's silence. 'I didn't,' Serala said, her lips twisting into a triumphant smile. 'I have been interviewing everyone Murima deals with.'

Babur mopped his face with a handkerchief. She had tricked him. 'Please accept my apologies, mistress,' he babbled. 'I meant no disrespect.'

'Of course not,' Serala said, 'your greed got the better of you, didn't it? Now tell me where the girl is and I may go easy on you.'

'She is in my granary,' he said, 'the one on the Alley of Nails.'

Serala nodded, then summoned her bodyguards. 'Get him out of my sight,' she said. 'Give him a sound thrashing and send him on his way.'

Babur did not protest. He was relieved to escape with a beating. The moment Serala was on her own, she took out the message that had arrived that morning from her husband in Rinaghar.

I have spoken to Gardep about our plan, it read. *There is a problem. He still has feelings for the girl. I am certain of it. We will not have his loyalty until this Helat is out of the way. You know what you have to do.*

Serala folded the note and slipped it into her sari. She knew what to do all right.

4

Kulmat was feeding his horse when he heard the stable door swing open. 'Prakash-Ra,' he said, 'you startled me.'

'I have a job for you, Kulmat.'

'What is it?'

'Do you remember a Helat? She was the chief hand-maiden at Mistress Julmira's engagement.'

Kulmat's mouth went dry. What is this? he wondered.

'The girl has absconded from Commander Rishal's household. Mistress Serala is very angry. I want you to go after her.'

'Why me, Prakash-Ra?'

Prakash frowned. 'Because I have asked you, Kulmat. Is it your custom to question a superior officer's orders?'

'No, Prakash-Ra, of course not.'

'Good,' Prakash said. 'Have I not been a father to you since you came to the academy? Have I not defended your interests as if you were my own son?' He smiled. 'Even when you stole or climbed over the barrack walls on some adventure?'

Kulmat lowered his eyes. It was indeed true that Prakash had been his father-protector all these years, just as Gardep had been his brother. They were the two poles of his world.

'This matter requires discretion,' Prakash said. 'A master

Sol-ket can't be seen skulking around after some slave girl. That's why I'm entrusting you with this task.'

Kulmat would have done anything to wriggle out of his mission, but Prakash wasn't the type to negotiate.

'The girl is in a granary off the Alley of Nails,' he said. 'Do you know it?'

'It's a bad quarter,' Kulmat said.

'But you know it?'

'Yes.'

'Go now,' Prakash said, 'and bring her back unharmed. Commander Rishal will want to interrogate her on his return.'

At the word *unharmed*, Kulmat breathed a sigh of relief.

'May I ask a question, Prakash-Ra?' Kulmat said.

Prakash nodded.

'After interrogation, Prakash-Ra, what will happen to her?'

Prakash smiled. 'Just get the girl. The rest is up to Commander Rishal.'

5

The sun had begun to sink over the battlements of Parcep when Cusha heard a noise. 'Mama-li?' she called.

But there was no answer.

'Harad, is that you?'

Still, there was no answer. Cusha felt the rustle of fear.

'Who's there?' she asked. 'What do you want?'

The crimson light of the setting sun barely relieved the gloom inside the granary. Cusha searched in the long shadows for some sign of the intruder. Then she heard it again, a movement in the long corridor that led from the store to the street. Her blood pumped more strongly. Her heart was slamming against her rib cage. She wasn't imagining it. Somebody was there. Looking round frantically, Cusha saw something. Scrambling across the grain in her bare feet, she started to dig. Using her hands like shovels to make a gap, she peered through. A shaft of light was lancing across a second store. Squirming through the archway, Cusha rolled down to the stone floor, jarring her elbow. She didn't cry out. Instead she bit her lip.

She listened for a moment. There were no footsteps. Padding barefoot across the cold tiles, Cusha looked around the store. She was looking for a way out when a door slammed. There, on the far side of the room was a tall figure.

'What do you want?' she asked, fighting in vain to control the shake in her voice.

'I was sent here by my master,' Kulmat said.

'Who's your master?' Cusha asked.

At first, Kulmat didn't answer. 'Come with me,' he said. 'You have nothing to fear.' He held out his hand.

'I have everything to fear,' Cusha said. 'You are Sol-ket.'

'I swear,' Kulmat said. 'You will suffer no harm at my hand.'

It was an easy promise. It might be a different matter after he handed her over to Prakash.

'You have no choice but to accompany me,' Kulmat said. 'You know you can't escape.'

That didn't stop Cusha trying. Sprinting across the room, she tried to squirm back through the gap she had found into the other store. She had only managed to force her head and shoulders through when Kulmat grabbed her ankle. Struggle as she might, he was much stronger than her. Something was pulled down over her head. Was it the musky aroma of the sacking or the smell of her own fear that made her gag? She didn't know. Of one thing she was sure: any hope of escape had gone. She felt herself being hooded and bound. Then a knife blade touched her throat. Terror bit deep into her heart.

6

Gardep saw the domes and minarets of Tiger-gated Parcep with mixed feelings. Though the elation he had felt at being part of the council of war had yet to fade, he felt apprehension too. He couldn't get the strange experience in the temple out of his mind. Cusha was imprisoned, the voice had told him. Could it be true? And if she was, how could he help her escape without endangering both their lives? How could he save her without betraying his warrior code? His head was spinning.

'Stable the horses,' Rishal ordered. 'I have something to do.'

Gardep bowed. 'Do you want me to report to you when I've finished, Rishal-Ra?' he asked.

'No,' Rishal said, 'get some rest.'

For some reason, this order filled him with foreboding. Taking his time stabling the horses, he watched Rishal cross the training ground. The commander didn't go to his office but instead headed for the far side of the academy grounds. Gardep unsaddled and fed the horses. He brushed them down and settled them. He cleaned and stowed his and Rishal's equipment. He was seated on a low bench by the stalls when he heard something behind him. Turning, he saw a white dove. His skin crawled.

'Is it you?' he asked.

Unknown to him, another cadet was in the stables. The Sol-ket gave Gardep a questioning look, then continued his chores. For a few moments the dove sat perched on one of the roof timbers. Then it spread its wings and flew through the open door. Gardep followed it out, away from the curious cadet's eavesdropping. The bird had flown in the same direction Rishal had gone. Hurrying to the corner of the cadet dormitories, Gardep searched for the dove. Am I crazy? he thought. There must be thousands of doves in the city. Then he saw her. The green-eyed shape-shifter was watching him from the shadows.

'Do you have news of Cusha?' he asked.

The shape-shifter pointed to a window. Gardep un-buckled his sword and dagger and slipped off his sandals before stowing them under one of the dormitories. Checking there was nothing else that could jingle and give him away, he jogged lightly over to the window and peered through it.

Cusha was crouching in a corner while Rishal stood over her. Prakash was there too. Though he couldn't hear what they were saying, he feared for Cusha. Much as he revered the commander and his deputy, Gardep knew how ruthless they could be with enemies of the Sol-ket. He returned to the shape-shifter.

'What do you want from me?' he asked.

'You must help me to free her. Will you?'

Gardep didn't hesitate. 'Yes.'

7

'What are you to Gardep?' Rishal demanded.

'Nothing.'

'Do you expect me to believe that?'

'I swear,' Cusha answered, 'I don't know him.'

Her dark eyes were ablaze with fear. Did the commander know the truth? Towards the warrior Gardep she had felt

109

deep attraction but, more recently, resentment for her family's suffering.

'I saw the way he looked at you,' Rishal said. 'Do you really expect me to believe he would affront Julmira that way just because he had seen a stranger?'

Cusha looked imploringly at the commander. 'Lord Rishal, I served for eight years in your household. Did I ever give you cause to distrust me?'

'You are a Helat,' Rishal said. 'What makes you think I ever trusted you in the first place? You presume too much. You are nothing to me.' He gestured towards a scurrying cockroach. 'Your life is equal to that bug's.'

A needle of ice penetrated Cusha's heart. Rishal exchanged glances with Prakash. Prakash shook his head. 'All these Helati are liars. It is in their nature.'

Rishal dropped to one knee and grabbed Cusha by the throat, his fingers biting like steel tongs, almost choking her. Tears spilled over her cheeks.

'Gardep is going to be my son-in-law. I need to be certain he has no secrets. Is there anything I should know?'

Cusha shook her head.

Rishal seemed satisfied. He left the room with Prakash and locked the door.

'Do you think she's telling the truth?' Prakash said.

'Of course she is,' Rishal said. 'She's too terrified to lie.'

'What do you want me to do with her?' Prakash asked.

'Do with her?' Rishal said. 'Nothing has changed. Kill her, of course.'

8

Oled had finally managed to get round the demon lines. By transforming into a pike, a large one of course, given his limited powers, he had swum down a tributary of the Amputra before continuing his journey as a buzzard to make up time. Excited by his triumph as a python, he had begun to experiment. Some miles into the grasslands of western Jinghara he discovered an Imperial patrol of about sixty men. Their scarlet standards told him they weren't from a local fort.

'Warriors of the Sun,' he hailed them. 'Brave Sol-ket, I am Scout Oled Lonetread, newly arrived from Zindhar.'

'You were at Zindhar?' the officer said suspiciously. 'We heard the entire garrison had perished.'

Oled couldn't help wondering who had broken the news. 'It is true that the garrison was destroyed,' he said. 'The Lost Souls were vast in number. They overwhelmed Commander Turayat's force. I am the sole survivor.'

The Sol-ket looked unimpressed. 'Why didn't you fight to the last and lay down your life alongside your commanding officer?' one asked.

'I am a shape-shifter,' Oled answered. 'I thought I could make my way through the lines and raise the alarm.'

He didn't say that he had a greater mission than fighting alongside Turayat, and a lot more sense than to die beside him.

'We know all about Zindhar,' the officer said. 'We know about the Darkwing's army too.'

Oled thought he sounded very calm about the approach of such a war host. He noticed fires in the distance. The Sol-ket were engaged in the age-old practice of burning the graveyards.

'Can you take me to your commander?' Oled said. 'I have intelligence that may be of use.'

One of the Sol-ket glanced enquiringly at the officer. He nodded. 'We'll take you to General Barath. I hear you shape-shifters can keep pace with a horse,' the officer said. 'Is that true?'

Oled confined himself to a simple answer. 'Ride,' he said. 'I'll keep up.'

9

'Tell me about Rinaghar,' Kulmat said the moment Gardep walked into the dormitory. 'Did you see the Emperor?'

He wanted to tell Gardep what he'd done, how he had handed Cusha over to Prakash. But how?

'Rinaghar is everything they say,' Gardep told him wearily, 'the greatest city of the world.' He sighed. 'And yes, I did see the Emperor.'

'What's wrong?' Kulmat said. 'You sound strange.'

'Do you remember the girl, Cusha?' Gardep said.

Kulmat winced. He knew she might already be dead. 'Yes, I remember her.'

'She is being held in the barracks. I saw Rishal interrogating her. If anything happens, her blood will be on my hands.'

Kulmat went quiet.

'What do I do, Kulmat?'

Kulmat didn't answer. Gardep gave a humourless chuckle. 'Forgive me. I shouldn't be burdening you with my troubles. What could you know of this?'

Kulmat wanted to tell Gardep exactly what he knew but he didn't dare. Gardep would never understand his actions. Their friendship was in enough danger as it was.

'All I know,' Gardep said, 'is, I have felt desire for an innocent young girl and now, through my thoughtlessness and weakness, I have put her life in danger.'

He felt Kulmat staring at him. 'I know what you're going to say. It is forbidden. She is just a Helat. But I can't help it. I just keep thinking about her.'

Kulmat shook his head. 'This is madness. You know the unbreakable laws of Ra. If you dare fall in love with a Helat then, by Ra, that road will lead to both your deaths.'

'I know,' Gardep said, rubbing his temple in despair. 'I know.'

'Forget her,' Kulmat said, 'as you promised to. Once Commander Rishal knows she poses no danger, he will send her to work in the fields or to some slum workshop to sew garments.' He hated himself for the lies he was telling Gardep. 'Put her out of your mind, my brother,' he said. 'How can you love her when you have never even spoken?'

Gardep didn't answer.

'Listen,' Kulmat said, 'you will probably never see her again.' He felt deep shame. He knew exactly why Gardep would never see Cusha again.

10

Gardep's four-hour vigil was rewarded. He saw the dove. He was about to slip out of the dormitory when he heard footsteps. It was Kulmat.

'In the name of Ra, Gardep,' Kulmat whispered, 'what are you doing?'

'I've got to go,' Gardep told him.

'Is this about the girl?'

'You know it is.'

'Will nothing dissuade you from this course?' Kulmat asked.

Gardep shook his head. 'Then I'm coming with you.'

Out in the night air, Gardep looked around for some sign of the dove. 'Stay here,' he told Kulmat. 'From the corner of the dormitory you can see the sentry posts. If there's any activity, warn me.'

'You can rely on me.'

Though apprehension twisted in his gut, though he was betraying his god and his code, Kulmat kept watch. Gardep made his way through the hot night.

'If it's that bird you're looking for, think again,' a familiar voice whispered.

Gardep looked round and saw a black panther lurking in a dark corner. Though he knew the creature posed no danger to him, the very sight of it made his throat tighten.

'What did you expect?' the shape-shifter said. 'What could a dove do against the guards?'

'What do you want me to do?' Gardep asked.

'Rishal's keys,' the panther said, its human voice mingling with the feline rumble in its throat, 'where are they kept?'

'In his office,' Gardep answered.

'Get them for me,' the panther told him.

Gardep hesitated. He was being asked to break every rule in the Sol-ket code.

'What, you're thinking of yourself?' the panther said. 'Have you forgotten that Cusha's life is in danger? If it had been up to your knight, she would be dead already.'

'This way,' Gardep said, chastened.

He and the panther raced through the shadows, always on the lookout for a night sentry who might raise the alarm. Sure enough, at the door to Commander Rishal's office there was a guard, a cadet by the name of Janil.

'I will attract his attention,' the panther said, 'while you deal with him.'

There was a moment of startled surprise as Janil saw something emerging from the shadows. Then Gardep, coming from behind, clubbed him senseless. Stepping over Janil, Gardep got the keys.

'Good,' the panther said. 'You have just crossed an important line. Now keep watch.'

With that, the panther began to metamorphose. Gardep saw a human hand take the keys and a shadowy female form mingling with the darkness. His heart was in his mouth as he waited. Could Janil have seen who attacked him? By Ra, Gardep thought, I'm a dead man if he did. Several minutes passed then the shape-shifter appeared with Cusha running crouched, lithe as a cat herself, by her side. When she saw Gardep, she looked startled. The shape-shifter whispered something and she nodded. Gardep wanted to speak to her too, but there was no time. Just for a moment Cusha met his look then followed the shape-shifter. Once they had gone, there was nothing to do but return to the dormitory. Without a word, Kulmat followed Gardep inside.

11

'She is safe?' Murima said. 'You are sure my precious daughter is safe?'

'She is with Shamana,' Harad said, leading the way. 'Now please, Mama-li, think about yourself for once. We have to flee this very hour. If we delay for just a minute, we may be sealing our fates. They flogged you on account of the betrothal ceremony. The next time they will kill you.'

Murima hesitated.

'Please,' Harad said, 'you must hurry.'

For the first time in his life Harad was grateful for the law that placed the Helati outside the city gates after dark. It would give them a chance to escape among the crowds being evicted from the villas and workshops of Parcep.

'The coast's clear,' Qintu said. 'There are no Sol-ket patrols on the road.' He looked into the night sky. 'There are no fliers, either.'

It was a good night to flee the city. In the days immediately after the Blood Moon, the skies usually emptied of dark-fliers. This was just such a night. Taking advantage of the lull, the three Helati ran towards the barn Shamana had indicated.

'Will Cusha be there?' Murima said.

Harad shook his head. 'Shamana had to get Cusha as far away as she could. She is the one in the greatest danger.'

He pushed open the door. There were three horses waiting for them. There was food and even some money in the saddlebags.

'How does the old witch do this?' Qintu gasped.

Harad shared his amazement. 'These are fine horses,' he said, examining the animals. 'She is truly a sorceress.'

'When will I see Cusha again?' Murima asked, her chin trembling.

'Soon,' Harad said. 'Shamana promised to find us.'

'But how?' Murima asked. 'How, in all this vast land?

'We must hope Shamana knows what she's doing,' Harad said.

Though Murima still looked troubled, she allowed Harad to help her on to her horse. As she cantered after Harad and Qintu, Murima allowed herself one last look at Parcep. She wondered if she would ever see its terracotta-coloured walls again.

CHAPTER 5

Brothers No More

1

'Wake up!'

Prakash's voice roused Gardep's dormitory. His voice was hard, like the beat of metal in a blacksmith's shop. Outside it was still dark.

'They've discovered Janil,' he murmured. 'What have you done, Gardep?'

'Out of bed,' Prakash barked, ripping off sheets and slapping bare feet against the floor. 'A prisoner has escaped. You are to form a pursuit group.'

The other cadets exchanged glances. Prisoner, what prisoner? Since when did the academy act as a jail? Gardep and Kulmat had no need to ask such questions but did their best to look bewildered along with the rest. By dawn a column of twenty Sol-ket was riding through the West Gate. Prakash led them. Three gold-painted lines on his cheeks testified to his battle scars. Rishal watched from the battlements. At the fork in the road, where the maize fields began, the column split in two, one going north and one west. No escapee in their right mind would go east towards Rinaghar where the swords of the Sol-ket were as numerous as stars in the night sky. To the south was the ocean. There were only two escape routes that made sense. Gardep's heart sank when Prakash chose to lead his group west. If there was one thing Gardep knew about the deputy commander, he was a shrewd tracker. If he had taken this fork then he had a good idea where to find the fugitive.

2

'Are you a witch, Shamana?' Cusha asked.

'Witch?' Shamana said. 'No, I am just a very old woman with certain . . . talents.'

'You took the form of a panther,' Cusha said, her respect for the priestess transformed into wonder. 'Mama-li has told me of the shape-shifting people. She said they were all dead. Tanjuristan was no more than a memory.'

'She has good reason to think us extinct,' Shamana said. 'The Sol-ket have been merciless in the persecution of my people.'

'It is strange,' Cusha said. 'Even she did not recognise your true nature and she has known you a long time.'

'Yes,' Shamana said, a far-off look in her green eyes, 'a very long time.' Then she snapped out of the daydream. 'Some things you are better off not knowing. I have chosen to lie low waiting for the winds of freedom to blow again.'

'Is this the time?' Cusha asked excitedly. 'Are our people going to fight back?'

'That,' Shamana said, 'is for the future. The question you

should ask is much simpler. Can we escape our pursuers?' For the first time anxiety was showing in Shamana's green eyes.

'Are they coming?' Cusha asked.

'Yes,' Shamana said. 'They are behind us.'

'How far?'

Shamana gave this some thought. 'Soon the earth will shake with the beat of their horses' hooves. Their mounts are superior to ours. We can't outrun them.'

Cusha's startled eyes widened in horror. She could almost hear the hiss of Sol-ket swords. 'What will we do?' she asked.

Shamana answered with actions. Dismounting, she tethered the horses and unfastened her blanket roll. From it she produced a bow and arrows, a belt of throwing knives and a sword. The sword astounded Cusha. It was a formidable weapon of a quality rivalling a Sol-ket blade. Never, during all those long nights of struggle against the Lost Souls, had such a weapon been brandished.

'Where did you get all that?' she gasped.

Shamana ignored Cusha's question. Quickly, she slipped the sword into its scabbard and buckled it to her waist. The belt of throwing knives she slung over her shoulder. These too were superb weapons, complete with lapis lazuli handles. Having set out her hand weapons, Shamana planted her arrows point down in the earth and strung her bow. It had the double bend of the Vassyrian archers. Finally, she thrust a second, shorter, sword into Cusha's hand.

'Use it if you have to.'

Though she knew that a Sol-ket would prove a more formidable opponent than some crazed night-strider, Cusha nodded.

'Quickly, into the swamp.'

'Not without you,' Cusha said.

'Don't be a fool, girl,' Shamana snapped. 'This is no time for heroics. I will hold them up. You have to hide. I will defeat these Sol-ket and follow.'

Again, Cusha tried to protest.

'Do it!' Shamana commanded. 'You are the important one, the Holy Child. You are the key to the downfall of the oppressors. Now go.'

Cusha's head was spinning. Her, the key to freedom! How could that be?

'Go!' Shamana repeated.

Cusha could hear the approaching patrol.

'Take care, Shamana,' she said, before plunging into the mangrove swamp.

3

Prakash pulled on the reins and raised his right arm. Immediately, the ten warriors under his command came to a halt. Prakash slipped out of his saddle and examined the ground. He didn't speak. Instead, he raised two fingers before pointing out the direction the fugitives had gone. Gardep and Kulmat exchanged glances. Prakash stood and gave his orders in a few well-rehearsed gestures. He instructed three warriors to fan out to the right. Three more he sent straight ahead. Prakash, Gardep, Kulmat and the scout Niraj went left. Prakash's choice worried Gardep. Usually the deputy commander would have put him in charge of a group of Sol-ket. A thought flashed through his mind: *you're watching me.*

Prakash's final unspoken command was simple: approach slowly. At that, several of the Sol-ket frowned. All this for a single Helat? What was going on? Prakash saw the question in their eyes and shook his head. Two fugitives, he reminded them. Whoever had sprung Cusha, the gesture told them, was dangerous. Putting his foot in the stirrup, Prakash swung himself silently into the saddle and started moving forward through the trees. Following, Gardep noticed the spongy ground under his mount's hooves. They were going into the mangroves.

4

Cusha was wading calf deep in the swamp. She could hear the wavelets against the mangroves' exposed roots. Startled, a blue heron rose into the sky. Cusha watched it rise above the treetops. If the Sol-ket had seen the bird they would know who had disturbed it. Taking care not to fall over the prop roots that arched out of the water at intervals, she moved forward, listening for the warriors or for Shamana. Her trousers were stained almost up to her knees by the brackish salt water. From time to time she hesitated, alert to the slightest sound. But there was no splashing, no beat of hooves.

Where are you?

After eight years in the household of Rishal-ax-Sol, Cusha was a city girl. She hated the lapping water and the rotting plants and swamp material that slid between her toes and clung to her skin.

Where are you?

She was about to move on when she glimpsed movement out of the corner of her eye. Her head snapped round. There! A shadow fell across the eddying surface of the water. It was a single horseman, half-hidden in the trees. Then there was a splash. Over to her left a second rider had appeared, younger than the first. Even as she was sliding the sword from her belt a third rider emerged from the woods, then a fourth. She was surrounded.

5

Shamana too could see her pursuers. Two Sol-ket were making their way down a slope. A third mounted warrior was moving in to her left. They didn't seem to have spotted her yet. Shrinking back against the largest tree trunk she could find, Shamana scanned the woods for any more riders. Three, she thought, but I heard six at least. Unease chilled her skin.

You've split up.

But how many had gone after Cusha? This narrowed Shamana's options. She couldn't simply hide or wait for the Sol-ket to ride past. If she did that, Cusha could be dead within minutes, and with her the hopes of the entire Helat people. Cursing low under her breath, Shamana put an arrow to the bowstring. One of the horses snorted. She was discovered.

That was the signal for Shamana to attack. She fired three arrows in succession, scampering across the clearing as she did so. Two found their mark. The third, released hastily on the turn, whistled past the next warrior and thudded into a tree. The last Sol-ket standing was brave. He dismounted with one spring and raced towards her. The young cadet's courage was not matched by his skill, however. Shamana's arrow found the tender flesh beneath his Adam's apple, a spot unguarded by his breastplate or helmet. He was dead by the time his body hit the ground.

Shamana looked at the dead boy and shook her head. His face was unshaven and the downy whiskers of early manhood clung to his chin. The other two cadets were groaning. One had an arrow in his shoulder. The other was bleeding profusely from a thigh wound. The artery was severed. He was dying. Shamana's thoughts were beginning to turn again to Cusha when a twig snapped behind her. Hurling herself into a thicket she felt the hiss of an arrow past her left ear.

Damn me for getting old!

The second attack party had outflanked her. Rolling over, Shamana saw the rider bearing down on her. Snatching a throwing knife from her belt, she sent it singing on its way. Her attacker fell without a sound. There was no time for celebration. Where there was one warrior there were bound to be more. Shamana listened.

Yes, there's one. He was behind her. *And another. To my right.*

Shamana sucked in her breath. Slowly, willing the scabbard not to creak as her blade left it, Shamana unsheathed her weapon. With a wild scream she engaged the first warrior. He was strong. Aware of his comrade approaching behind her, Shamana considered transforming. No, she thought, there are more Sol-ket out there. I must keep something in reserve. Unable to best the lad at a trial of strength, she used the wiles of an experienced swordswoman. Feinting left, she thrust under his guard. The cadet gasped and sank to his knees. Turning, Shamana braced herself for the final cadet's attack. That's when she heard Cusha scream.

6

Cusha crouched, sword in hand. Her heart was hammering. Four warriors, she thought, three cadets and an experienced Sol-ket.

123

I'm dead already.

The Sol-ket moved forward. Cusha felt the hilt slide against her clammy palm. Now the second and third warriors had begun their advance. Why were they showing her so much respect? Her, a fourteen-year-old girl, a mere child. Cusha started to back away, crouching, confused by their caution. The last fighter hadn't even moved. Cusha glanced from one to the other. While her eyes were flitting between them she recognised the leader and one of the cadets. One she didn't recognise at all. The other was hidden by the twisted branches of the trees. The leader had been present at her interrogation. The cadet had been at Julmira's engagement feast, a friend of the idiot Sol-ket who had started all this. Gardep. Cusha willed them to make their move.

If I must die here, then get it over with.

Cusha noticed a lizard on a branch. It was quite, quite still. Then the leader of the Sol-ket spurred his horse forward through the glade. The lizard ran. So did Cusha. Plunging through a dense webbing of branches, she glanced behind. The Sol-ket leader was almost on her. He was standing in his stirrups, sword raised. Cusha swung her own blade to meet it. Her defensive move proved feeble against the downward sweep of the warrior's sword. Such was the force of his attack that Cusha cried out in pain at the impact of steel against steel.

Even that wasn't the worst thing. All the time she was struggling to defend herself from the slashing onslaught, the cadet was moving to prevent her retreat. As a second thrust sliced through a branch above her head, Cusha realised she didn't have the strength to fend off her more experienced and stronger opponent. With a scream of hatred and terror, she slashed at him and flung herself into the water, splashing and kicking through a narrow channel.

7

Prakash could smell the Helat's fear. He enjoyed the sour fragrance. It told him the kill was near. Urging his mount forward, he hacked at the latticework of roots and reeds that were screening the girl. Gripping his reins, Prakash leaned forward, over the neck of his horse, and chopped at the twisted stems.

'Damn you to fiery Hell,' he roared. 'Get out of there. Niraj, go round the other side.'

Niraj tried but, in an act of desperate self-defence, Cusha drove her sword into his foot. Niraj screamed and fell into the latticework of roots, clutching the wound. Prakash showed little concern for the injured cadet.

'Kulmat, Gardep!' he yelled. 'Don't just watch. Help me flush her out.' To his surprise, they didn't move. 'What in Ra's name is wrong with you?'

There was no answer. Instead, his horse stumbled against something and pitched him into the water. Coming up spluttering and rubbing at his eyes, Prakash looked around to identify the cause of his fall. When he found it, his mouth sagged open and his insides turned to water. It was a full-grown crocodile. Venting his horror in a throaty, watery roar, Prakash scrambled backwards, cracking his head against an overhanging branch. With a curse, he started kicking. Once, twice, three times he aimed his foot at the monster's head. Each time its jaws snapped, narrowly missing his toes. By now, Prakash's cries for help had turned to animal screams.

'Come to my aid. For Ra's sake!'

The mangrove water was churning. The warrior was kicking and scrambling but nothing he did slowed the crocodile's measured advance. As the world reeled around him he saw the horrified stares of Niraj and Kulmat.

'Please,' Prakash shrieked. 'For Ra's sake, help me!'

But nobody helped. Within seconds the mangrove channels were running scarlet with his blood.

8

'What are you doing?' Kulmat cried, seeing the peril his master was in. Kulmat's bow was strung, the arrow nocked, but he could not take aim. Gardep was blocking his path. 'You're mad,' Kulmat said. 'The Helat girl has bewitched you.'

He could hear Prakash's desperate cries in the air.

'Gardep, you can't let that thing kill Prakash-Ra. For ten years he has been a father to me.' He tried to push past but Gardep restrained him.

'If he has to die to save Cusha,' Gardep said grimly, 'so be it.'

'Are you mad?' Niraj roared, voicing Kulmat's thoughts.

A scream that ended in a gurgle of blood announced Prakash's death. Kulmat threw his arms wide. 'She's a slave,' he yelled, 'a Helat. Gardep!'

Aware of the bewildered Niraj watching their every move, Kulmat drew Gardep closer and whispered the next words. 'By the holy face of Ra, I helped you get her out of the barracks but this is a step too far.'

Kulmat looked down at Prakash's lifeless, bloodied corpse that was floating face down in the swamp. From his tunic, he pulled the scrap of bloodied bandage that he'd kept since childhood. Flinging the token of friendship at Gardep, he drew his sword.

'You have allowed that monster to butcher my master,'

Kulmat said. 'It wasn't the wild beast that killed Prakash-Ra. It was you.'

'Traitor!' Niraj yelled, still nursing the injury to his foot. 'Draw your sword, Kulmat. Kill him.'

'You have betrayed your order and your faith,' Kulmat told Gardep. 'You have shamed me in my master's dying eyes. His ghost will haunt me. I will have to answer to him through all eternity.'

Gardep retrieved the piece of bandage.

'Keep the token,' Kulmat said.

'He is a traitor,' Niraj cried. 'Kill him.'

In an agony of indecision, Kulmat gripped the hilt of his sword.

9

Cusha didn't move. Prakash's body was floating less than a yard from where she was sitting, arms wrapped round her knees. In spite of the heat of the mangrove swamp, she was shivering. The reptile that had snapped Prakash's rib cage like a walnut shell and torn out his heart was lying very still in the bloodstained water. Now it was watching her.

Watching me. That's when Cusha understood. She was looking at a crocodile, but a crocodile with human eyes.

'Shamana!'

The priestess transformed and stroked Cusha's tear-stained cheek. 'I was in time,' she said. 'Oh Cusha, thanks be to all the stars in the heavens. You are safe.'

But Cusha's eyes had strayed from Shamana's green eyes to the confrontation just a few yards away. Kulmat was standing with his back to her. For the first time she saw Gardep. She found herself screaming at him.

'You! Do you know what you've done?'

Cusha saw the eyes that had run over her skin with a young man's hunger and plunged her family into mortal danger. The thought that she had actually been flattered by his attention shamed her. Though he had helped her escape from the barracks, she could not forgive him. With a contemptuous flick of her hair, Cusha looked away. 'Send him away, Shamana. The Sol-ket is to blame for all this. He has turned our world upside down.'

'No,' Shamana said. 'You must not blame Gardep. He is not your enemy.'

Cusha searched Shamana's face for an explanation. 'He's to blame for all this,' she retorted.

Shamana slowly shook her head. 'He has helped us twice,' she said. 'But for him, you might be dead. Does that not count for something? He is as much a plaything of Destiny as you.'

'Do you hear that?' Kulmat demanded, seizing on the exchange. 'This precious Helat of yours despises you. I could have saved Prakash-Ra, but you stopped me. You have killed the man who has guided me to manhood.' He glared at Cusha, then at Shamana, now returned to human form. 'A shape-shifter!' he gasped. For a moment he did nothing but stare, unable to believe his own eyes. Then he turned on Gardep.

'You sided with them,' he snarled, 'with the wretched Helati against your own kind. You broke the greatest taboo of your faith. You even lied to me, your blood brother. How could you do that, Gardep? What possessed you?'

By now, the wounded Niraj was beside himself.

'Kill the traitor, Kulmat,' he cried. 'Do it or I will report your actions to Commander Rishal.'

Reluctantly, Kulmat started to draw his sword. Then he saw something that stopped him in his tracks. Shamana had an arrow pointed at his heart.

'Drop your sword,' she said.

'Do as she says,' came a second voice.

Kulmat turned. Qintu and Harad were on the far side of the glade. Both had arrows aimed at the young warrior

'Drop it!' Shamana ordered.

Kulmat looked into Gardep's eyes. Reluctantly, he dropped his sword.

'And the rest,' Shamana said.

Harad ran forward and gathered Kulmat's weapons.

'Your comrades are all wounded or dead,' Shamana said. 'We will leave you one horse to carry the wounded back to Parcep. See to them.'

Kulmat stared at Gardep for a moment. Despair crossed his face.

'Go,' Shamana repeated, 'or you and this wounded cadet will die where you stand.'

Kulmat lifted the groaning Niraj into the saddle. He led the horse out of the clearing. Shamana looked at Gardep. There were tears welling in his eyes but he made no attempt to follow Kulmat. With Niraj as a witness to what had happened, he dare not return to Parcep. He would be a dead man if he did. Shamana spoke softly.

'This is the moment I have seen in my dreams. A Sol-ket who was born to rule turns from Ra because he loves a Helat. The journey has begun.'

CHAPTER 6

The Doll

1

Rishal hurled Kulmat across the table on his back, making the cadet's skull thud against the wooden surface. 'Say that again!' he roared.

It took a moment for the dazed cadet to reply, so ferocious had been Rishal's assault.

'They are all dead,' Kulmat sobbed. 'Before I returned to Parcep, I searched for our comrades. I found them all. Most died in battle. Two must have bled to death where they lay. Only Niraj survived the attack.'

As an afterthought, he added: 'Niraj and me.'

Truth is, it was as if he had died himself out there in the mangrove swamp. Two things had kept him going on the way back to Parcep. He'd had to get the wounded Niraj to a surgeon. It was a matter of duty. The cadet had lost a lot of blood. But, more importantly, there was the stew of emotions Kulmat now felt for his traitor comrade Gardep. Some day, though he knew not how, they would have to settle this score. Kulmat's sense of despair and betrayal were all the stronger because of the love and friendship he had felt for his blood brother throughout his childhood years.

'How could this happen?' Rishal demanded. 'Our brother Prakash survived ten campaigns against the toughest of enemies. He was with me at the storming of Vassyria. Why, after conquering the most seasoned barbarian foes, would he succumb so wretchedly to a couple of runaway slaves, an old woman and a girl? I don't understand.'

Kulmat was searching for the form of words least likely to enrage the commander further. 'The one who killed Prakash-Ra,' he panted. 'There's something you should know, Rishal-Ra. She is not a Helat but a barbarian creature. She is a shape-shifter.'

The commander reeled as if struck by a heavy object. 'A shape-shifter!'

Kulmat nodded. 'I know. I too believed them extermin-ated. But I swear by the holy face of Ra, at least one of the creatures lives. She took the form of a crocodile. Prakash-Ra had no chance.' He had succeeded in staunching the commander's fury. 'In addition to the shape-shifter,' Kul-mat explained, 'there were at least three more fugitives and they were well-armed.' He did not say that they were a girl and two boys. 'How many more of their band lurked in the mangrove I can't say.'

Rishal let him up. 'It doesn't make any sense,' he said. His expression grew thoughtful, as if something had suddenly become clear. 'A shape-shifter, you say?'

Kulmat nodded.

'And Gardep, did he die along with the others?'

Kulmat searched his heart but, on this occasion, there

was no easy way to tell Rishal. 'No, Rishal-Ra, Gardep lives.'

A brooding intensity came over Rishal's features. There was the threat of violence in his stare.

'You said Niraj was the only survivor. What has happened to Gardep?'

Kulmat averted his eyes.

'Explain yourself.'

'I tried to help Prakash-Ra,' Kulmat said. 'The crocodile was almost upon him so I ran towards it, preparing my bow.'

'And?'

Kulmat forced out the words. Even then, after Gardep's bitter betrayal, he felt tempted to protect him. 'It was Gardep. He blocked my path.'

'What!'

Looking at the set of Rishal's features, the swollen veins in his temple, the eyes bulging with fury, Kulmat understood how he had led his armies to conquest. Who would ignore an order from such a man?

'Are you trying to tell me that my own squire chose to let Prakash die?'

'Commander,' Kulmat said, 'Gardep was suffering from a kind of insanity. He was protecting the Helat girl, the one you questioned here, in these barracks.'

Rishal placed his palms on the table. 'He could have been a great warrior,' he said, 'a leader of heroes.'

Like Gardep, Rishal chose not to mention the promise of the sun throne to Kulmat.

'Well,' Rishal asked, 'what happened next?'

'The Helati surrounded me,' he explained. 'Their bows were drawn. Their arrows were pointed at my heart.'

'Yet you chose to live?' Rishal said. 'Why did you not take the way of the Sol-ket? Why did you not fight to the death?'

'Niraj asked me the same question, Rishal-Ra.'

Rishal's stare did not leave Kulmat's face. 'And what answer did you give?'

Kulmat said nothing. Frustrated by the cadet's silence, Rishal overturned the table. It fell with a crash.

'Why didn't you fight to the death? Answer me, you craven coward!'

'Rishal-Ra,' Kulmat croaked, fearing that he was about to be put to the sword. 'Gardep was my blood brother. I drew my sword. You know that I have never broken my Sol-ket code. I wanted to fight him . . .'

Rishal waited for him to finish.

'How can I explain?' Kulmat said, overwhelmed by helplessness. 'For eight years he has been my closest friend and comrade. It was not cowardice. I did not fear for my skin. Master, I was overcome with despair. During all those years of training I never once thought that I would have to fight a fellow Sol-ket, let alone my dearest friend.' Tears spilled down his cheeks. 'Commander, I have shamed my order. I am ready to accept my fate.'

With that, Kulmat knelt and lowered his head, offering his neck to Rishal's sword. He squeezed his eyes shut and awaited the blow. He would die a warrior's death. Yet the blow never came. A moment later he heard the door slam. When he looked up he was alone in the room.

2

Shamana walked over to Gardep. 'You must eat,' she said, offering him a plate of carp.

Gardep was sitting alone, some distance from the others. He shook his head.

'Your heart is heavy,' Shamana said.

'What do you know of my feelings?' Gardep said bitterly. 'I am a fugitive from my brother Sol-ket. I did what I thought was right. But Prakash died.' He remembered the way he had looked down on golden Rinaghar and been promised the Empire.

'He would have killed Cusha,' Shamana answered. 'What choice did you have? It was your destiny.'

'What destiny?' Gardep cried. 'I am an outcast.'

'What you leave behind is an illusion,' Shamana said. 'All your life you have craved the glory the Sol-ket can give you. Know this, Gardep: all the glory, all the gold, all the renown the Empire could have bestowed upon you, will pale into insignificance compared to the cause you have been called to serve.'

'Cause,' Gardep said, 'what cause?'

'The cause of the Scales.'

Gardep stared. 'You say that to me!'

'It is your future,' Shamana told him.

'You are not Sol-ket,' Gardep cried. 'You do not understand how great an insult that is.'

'Gardep,' Shamana said, 'forget the Children of Ra. That time of your life is over. Now you must serve a greater cause. At the far ends of the earth, there lies the explanation of everything that has happened.'

'Enough!' Gardep cried, drawing suspicious looks from the three Helati. 'Do you really think I will take up arms against everything I hold dear? Let me be, witch. Go back to your friends.'

'What will it take to reconcile you to your destiny?' Shamana asked.

'I am already aware of my destiny,' Gardep said. 'I must return to my kind.'

'The Sol-ket are not your kind and never will be,' Shamana insisted.

Gardep stayed silent but his eyes were hard with suppressed rage.

'Do you not love Cusha?' Shamana demanded.

Gardep resented her for trying to use his softer feelings against him. 'She does not love me,' he retorted.

'So much has happened,' Shamana said. 'Her head is spinning. Give her time.'

'Time won't make her contempt go away,' Gardep said. 'I tell you, I am going.'

'The Sol-ket will condemn you as a traitor,' Shamana protested. 'You will be killed.'

'I would have death before dishonour,' Gardep said.

'Don't be a fool!' Shamana snapped. 'Why do young men want to throw their lives away on futile gestures?'

'Do you call serving your god and your Emperor futile?' Gardep demanded. 'Save your breath. No matter what you say, I will act according to my conscience. I will find my own road back to Parcep. I will redeem myself. I used my wits to survive the thorn forests. I can do it again.'

'Gardep, please,' Shamana pleaded, softening her tone. 'Come with us. You will never return to the Sol-ket. There is greater work for you to do.'

'And what's that?' Gardep demanded. 'Don't mention the heresy of the Scales again. Do you want me to turn against my faith? Do you want me to fight my brothers?'

'Gardep—'

'Silence!' Gardep cried. 'I'm going.'

Shamana understood that she was wasting her breath. Reluctantly, she accepted defeat. 'Go if you must,' she said. 'Just promise that you will return.'

Gardep started saddling his horse. 'I promise you nothing, witch.'

Shamana shook her head. Leaving Gardep to his preparations, she accepted a serving of the carp.

3

In the next week Oled saw more standards come fluttering over the horizon to join General Barath's army. High-cheeked Khuts arrived, several hundred of them, thundering across the grassland on their sturdy, barrel-bodied ponies. Selessians came too. Dark-robed and silent, they settled on the far side of the camp, oblivious to the welcoming hails of the other troops.

Judging by the already varied composition of the encampment, it was obvious that this was but the first contingent of a much greater force. The baggage train too was growing. Ox and bullock carts carried provisions.

Oled viewed the growing multitude with mixed feelings. He had good cause to hate the Sol-ket. Once, when he was no more than a baby, they had butchered his people. He had only enlisted in their army to watch over the Dark-wing and discover his lair, the fabled Black Tower, where he held the Holy Child. But the Sol-ket, in spite of their cruelty, in spite of their arrogance, were men like him. He would do as his warrior-queen had commanded. He would stand with them against the demon contagion. For now at least.

'This is officer Murak,' General Barath said, interrupting Oled's thoughts. 'You will be assigned to him.'

Oled glanced at the officer. He looked young and inexperienced.

'Well,' Barath asked Oled, proudly surveying his force of more than ten thousand men, 'are you still worried about the Lost Souls?'

Oled surveyed the growing band. As a matter of form he shook his head, causing Barath to chuckle. But Oled had lied. Strong as this initial gathering looked, it faded into insignificance compared with the demon horde. Dusk was gathering over the long day of mankind. Night was coming.

4

For all the promise of glory in the coming war in the west, Kulmat greeted each new day with a heavy heart. His friendship with Gardep was dead and he mourned its passing. There was nobody with whom he could share his innermost feelings, nobody he trusted like Gardep. Sometimes he no longer felt bitterness at all, just loss. Within days of the skirmish in the mangrove swamp, Kulmat was ready to ride out of Parcep as part of a column of ten thousand Sol-ket, Rishal-Ra's personal command. It was as though Rishal had completely forgotten his squire's betrayal. Indeed, Rishal had just conferred upon Kulmat the honour of becoming his new squire in Gardep's place. If Gardep had been far and away the most talented recruit to the academy, Kulmat was the most able of those who were left. Truly, it made the young cadet's head spin. Three days before, he had knelt expecting Rishal's sword to fall upon his neck and now, here he was, the commander's squire. Yet his heart was heavy.

'Kulmat,' came a voice. It was Janil, recovered from the blow that had rendered him senseless the night of Cusha's escape.

'Yes?'

'The commander wishes to see you in his quarters.'

Kulmat looked at the regiment waiting impatiently for the order to ride. He wondered what was so important it could postpone their departure. He made his way to the commander's door and knocked.

'Ah, Kulmat,' Rishal said. 'Let me introduce His Holiness, Shirep-hotec.'

Kulmat felt a rivulet of terror steal down his back. Shirep, second lord of the Hotec-Ra, here! What did the warrior-priest, third most powerful man in the Empire, want with him?

'Don't look so worried, Kulmat,' Shirep said. He stretched out a hand. 'Take a seat.'

Feeling more uncomfortable than ever, knowing that the Hotec-Ra were the ears and eyes of the Emperor, and quite often his torture instruments too, Kulmat took the offered chair.

'Tell me about the shape-shifter who rescued the girl,' Shirep said.

'I'm not sure I can tell you much,' Kulmat said, anxious that his actions that day had dishonoured him.

Shirep's eyes flared. 'Cadet,' he snapped, 'that is for me to decide.' Thinking better of his show of anger, Shirep lowered his voice. 'Just the facts, Kulmat.'

Kulmat gave a brief bow to indicate submission. 'Your Holiness,' he said, 'she took the form of a crocodile when she killed Prakash-Ra, but I also saw her in human form.'

'Describe her,' Shirep said, his voice dropping to an excited, conspiratorial whisper. 'I want every detail.'

Kulmat did as he was told. 'She was old, sixty or seventy I would say, judging by her appearance, but somehow more ancient still.'

Shirep nodded. That seemed to make sense to him. 'Continue, Kulmat.'

'Her hair was grey,' Kulmat said. 'And yet . . .'

'Yes.'

'She didn't move like an old woman. There was a grace about her. It's hard to explain.'

Shirep gave an encouraging smile. 'You seem quite taken with her.'

'No,' Kulmat said, 'it's not that. But she was like nobody I have ever seen.'

'Say what comes into your mind. I will decide what is to be considered important and what is to be discarded.'

Kulmat thought for a moment. 'There was something of the infinite about her. She seemed both ancient and youthful.' He hesitated. 'I'm not making much sense, am I?'

Shirep waved the comment away. 'You are making perfect sense, Kulmat. Go on.'

'She was practised in the martial arts,' Kulmat continued. 'She overcame six of our fighters. We discovered their bodies. Your Holiness, I believe she would represent a most formidable foe.'

This time Shirep's face was expressionless. He had one last question. 'Tell me about her eyes,' he said.

'What?'

'Her eyes, cadet; what colour were they?'

Kulmat shook his head. 'I don't know.'

Rishal pounded the desk. 'Answer His Holiness!' he roared.

But Shirep held up a hand. 'There is no need for that, commander. The lad has forgotten. Let me use the ways of Ra to stir his memories.'

Shirep leaned forward. 'Close your eyes, Kulmat,' he said.

Kulmat allowed his lids to droop. He felt Shirep's hands on his face. Despite the heat of the day, they were cool.

'Now,' Shirep said. 'Look upon the woman's face.'

Shamana's features exploded into Kulmat's mind with such force he gasped.

'Green,' he said, 'her eyes were green, like those of the northern tribes.'

Shirep nodded with satisfaction. 'It's her.'

5

Something woke Cusha, a curious whimper. She sat up and looked around. The fire had burned down and cast only the faintest light. On the fringe of the camp, the ghosts were still maintaining their silent vigil. Though they had been there for hours, there was no sign of the night breed. Curiously, Cusha wasn't afraid, or disgusted. Shamana had hinted once that the ghosts were not part of the demon host. For the first time, Cusha was beginning to see the truth of her words. The whimper came again. To Cusha's surprise, she saw Shamana tossing and turning in her sleep.

'Shamana,' Cusha said, 'what is it?'

Still Shamana moaned.

'Mama-li,' Cusha cried. 'It's Shamana. I think she's ill.'

Murima came over and placed a hand on the priestess's forehead. 'This isn't fever, Cusha my child. She is in a trance.'

'I don't understand.'

'I have seen this before,' Murima said, 'when I was a child. The shape-shifters of Tanjuristan sometimes slip into this state when they have a premonition. The dragon-people are dream-readers. Until a few days ago I truly believed they were all dead and that I would never see this dream-state again.'

'Premonition?' Cusha said. 'Premonition of what?'

'Of death,' Murima said. 'Either that or some terrible danger. The instincts of the Tanjurs are finely tuned. They see glimpses of the future.'

140

'Should we wake her?'

Murima shook her head. 'No need for that. She will come round when she is ready.'

Together the two women kept watch over Shamana. Just before dawn the old woman's eyes at last flickered open.

'Shamana!' Cusha cried. 'Thank the Four Winds for your safety.'

Shamana looked exhausted. 'What time is it?' she asked.

'The first light of dawn is beginning to show,' Murima said.

'That time already,' Shamana said, sitting up. She felt in her pocket for something.

'What are you doing?' Cusha asked.

By way of answer, Shamana sprinkled some black powder into the last glowing embers of the fire. With a loud hiss a single blue flame rose, at least a cubit high, waking Qintu and Harad.

'What witchcraft is this, old woman?' Qintu demanded.

'Less of the *old woman*,' Shamana scolded, 'and less of the witch. I've listened to enough of that nonsense from the Sol-ket.' She turned to Cusha. 'Look into the flames,' she said. 'Tell me who you see.'

Cusha recognised Rishal and Kulmat. The third man was unknown to her. 'Who is that?' Cusha said, indicating the shaven-headed man.

Shamana's face had pulled tight over her cheekbones. For once, she looked genuinely afraid. 'He is Shirep-hotec,' she said, concern in her voice.

'Second Lord of the Hotec-Ra!' Murima whispered. 'What brings that monster to Parcep?'

'Me, by the sound of it,' Shamana said as she read Shirep's lips, 'and Cusha.'

6

Four miles out of Parcep, Rishal turned to Kulmat and said, 'You keep looking round. Why?'

It was true. Kulmat was riding beside his master at the head of ten thousand horsemen. He had been searching for Shirep-hotec among their ranks.

'I haven't seen His Holiness since we left the Tiger Gates.'

'That,' Rishal told him, 'is because His Holiness is not coming with us.'

Kulmat nodded and said no more. He knew better than to enquire further without permission.

'Is something bothering you, Kulmat?' Rishal asked.

'A little,' Kulmat admitted.

'Tell me.'

'His Holiness is a most powerful man,' Kulmat said.

'Yes,' Rishal agreed, 'that is true. With the stroke of a pen he can snuff out a man's life, decide the fate of a nation or launch a war.'

'That is what has been nagging away at my mind,' Kulmat said. 'I was wondering, master, why he is so interested in a slave girl and an old woman.'

Rishal gave his squire a stern look. 'Ours is not to question the priesthood of Ra,' he said.

'No, Rishal-Ra,' Kulmat mumbled, regretting his temerity in speaking out so boldly.

'I will, however, put your mind at rest on this matter,' Rishal said. 'The girl is a most unusual slave. It is said she possesses a gift. As for the old woman, she is a danger to the Empire.'

'One old woman?' Kulmat said. 'But why?'

'It seems she has been fanning the flames of rebellion for

many years. She is the one who has been organising the Helati to resist the Lost Souls . . . and us. I thought we'd all but stamped out this Udmanesh conspiracy, but this shape-shifter has kept it alive against all the odds. I only wish I had been aware of her importance. She's a devil-woman, Kulmat.'

That Kulmat could believe. He and his fellow cadets had had a taste of her power. 'So why didn't we pursue the runaways,' he said, 'especially after what happened to Prakash-Ra? It is a question that has been torturing me for days.'

Rishal smiled. 'Strategy, my boy,' he said. 'Vengeance isn't everything. Sometimes you offer your enemy enough rope to hang himself. But don't worry, my young friend, hunters have been dispatched this very day to find the fugitives.'

7

In Commander Rishal's office, Shirep-hotec was expecting a visitor. Sure enough, there was a knock at the door.

'Come in.'

Shirep looked at the black-robed figure who had entered and smiled. 'Atrakon,' he said. 'It's been a long time.'

The newcomer didn't return the smile.

Atrakon Ebrahin, a Selessian, was a paid assassin. He was a man who killed without sentiment. He had never failed in any of his missions.

'Who is my quarry?'

'There are three targets,' Shirep told him. He cupped his palms and blew on them. A flickering image appeared of their faces. Atrakon feigned indifference. Inwardly, he feared the Hotec-Ra and their sorcery.

'I extracted these pictures from the memory of a witness. The first is the traitor cadet Gardep-na-Vassyrian.'

'A cadet?' Atrakon said. 'Why do you require my services to kill a mere boy?'

'The boy has the makings of a magnificent warrior,' Shirep said. 'The mark of Destiny is upon him. Don't underestimate him.'

Atrakon looked unimpressed. 'The second?'

Shirep held out his hands. 'Commit this face to memory, Atrakon. She is a slave girl by the name of Cusha.'

'Slave girl!' Atrakon exclaimed. 'First a boy, now a low-caste child. You insult me, Lord Shirep. Can nobody else undertake this mission?'

'I want you to do it,' Shirep told him. 'Well, what's your answer, Atrakon? Will you take the commission?'

'I will,' Atrakon said, after a few moments' hesitation, 'but on one condition. It will be my last. I have served you well, Lord Shirep, but I tire of this bloody trade. I want to return to my homeland.'

'Oh, complete this mission successfully, Atrakon,' Shirep said, 'and it will settle all your debts.'

Atrakon seemed satisfied. 'So why the slave girl?' he asked, looking at the image of the beautiful young woman as it danced in the priest's hands.

'We don't yet know why this Helat is important, Atrakon. Kill the Sol-ket by all means. He is of no importance. But the girl is mine. I intend to use the sweet arts of persuasion to unlock the secrets of her mind.'

Atrakon nodded. He knew all about the sweet arts of the Hotec-Ra. 'And the third? I trust this one will be more of a challenge than a slave girl and a cadet.'

'Her name is Shamana-ul-Parcep,' Shirep said, sharpening her picture with his breath. 'She is a Scaline priestess.'

There was a spark of interest in Atrakon's eyes. He

inspected Shamana's face. 'I assume there is more to it than that, Lord Shirep,' he said. Being of the Selessian faith, he didn't call Shirep *Your Holiness.*

'Oh, there is more, all right,' Shirep said. 'The woman is a shape-shifter.'

The moment he spoke the word, the head of a crocodile replaced Shamana's face.

'A shape-shifter!' Atrakon said. 'I thought the creatures were extinct.'

'No,' Shirep said, 'there are one or two in our service at the front as scouts. There could possibly be others concealing themselves amongst the slave population.'

'I thought the Hotec-Ra had ordered their extermination,' Atrakon said.

'We did. The campaign was most successful. But even the fiercest desire for revenge burns out in the end. The beasts have their uses. After all, what commander wouldn't want a scout who can fly over enemy lines?'

'There is something you are not telling me,' Atrakon said. 'What is it?'

Shirep clapped his hands, dismissing the pictures he had conjured. 'Her real name,' he said. 'Here.' He pushed a scrap of parchment across the desk. Atrakon took it. For the first time the Selessian looked impressed.

'Now this,' he said, 'is a mission worthy of my talents.'

8

'We had better move on,' Shamana said. 'Put out the fire, Qintu.'

Qintu tossed soil over the embers. All the while he was mimicking her: 'Put out the fire, Qintu. Fetch the horses, Qintu.'

'And less of that grumbling.'

Qintu pulled a face. Shamana chose to ignore him. She went over to Cusha, who was helping Murima pack her saddlebags. 'Now do you believe you have a great destiny?' she asked.

Cusha looked at the priestess. 'I don't know what to think, Shamana. Do you know any more than you have told me already?'

Shamana shrugged. 'Prophecy is an imperfect art. I have to confess, the signs that seemed so clear have proved most unreliable.'

'So what *do* you know?' Murima asked.

'I know that Cusha holds the key to defeating the Sol-ket,' Shamana said. 'I know that her destiny is bound up with that of the warrior Gardep. More than that I cannot tell you for sure.'

This time neither Cusha nor Murima tried to dismiss the prophecy. Instead they climbed into their saddles.

'What about Gardep?' Harad asked. 'Shouldn't we rouse him?'

'He has gone,' Shamana said.

In spite of herself, Cusha felt her heart lurch at the news, but it was Qintu who spoke. 'Gone?' he repeated. 'But I thought he was part of the prophecy.'

'He is,' Shamana said, 'but there was nothing I could do to keep him here. He is not yet free of his allegiance to the Sol-ket. I just pray he does what he must and returns to us.'

Harad thought it was odd that Shamana had allowed Gardep to leave so easily. He didn't know that Shamana had summoned her apprentice Aaliya to follow him.

9

Gardep had left the fugitives' camp as soon as he had finished his conversation with Shamana, and it was noon before he stopped to feed and water his horse at a roadside tavern. His presence drew a lot of interest.

'Are you joining your regiment?' the innkeeper asked, bringing Gardep a beaker of water and a dish of spiced okra, beans and rice.

The innkeeper was a man of fifty years. He was wearing a soiled leather apron. Gardep didn't like the look of him.

'Why do you ask?' Gardep said, dipping a chunk of flatbread into the sauce.

'You may have missed them,' the innkeeper said. 'The rear of the column passed this way two hours ago.'

Gardep continued to eat, determined not to let his surprise show. 'How many horse?' he asked.

'There must have been five thousand at least,' the innkeeper said, 'maybe more.'

Gardep finished his food and downed the water. 'Then I have tarried too long.'

He tossed a few dinar on the table and left. As he galloped off, the innkeeper earned another ten dinar. This time, the money came from Atrakon Ebrahin.

10

Atrakon knelt, studying the tracks. He counted five riders going due west. Gardep, he already knew, was heading across country, taking a route that would cross that of Commander Rishal. Atrakon frowned, wondering why the lone Sol-ket had taken such a suicidal course. The Lion of Inbacus would surely be ready with a summary end for his errant squire. Atrakon's course of action was simple, however. He would send his apprentice Zahar after Gardep and continue alone to pursue the others, the shape-shifter and the girl.

'Zahar,' he said. 'Take the Sol-ket. Kill him quickly. He is of little importance so there is no need for interrogation. Rejoin me as soon as you can.'

Without a word, Zahar turned his horse north-west and rode off. Atrakon watched him go. Let the Sol-ket have their code, he thought. It would never match the power of Selessian obedience. He had great hopes for Zahar. Once you're fully trained, Atrakon thought, I can retire from this bitter trade. That's when the Selessian master noticed the innkeeper watching.

'Do you have something to say?' he asked.

'I was wondering,' the innkeeper said. 'What if anyone else comes this way asking about a Sol-ket and a bunch of slaves the way you did, my Lord?'

Atrakon knew right away what the man meant. He wanted a few more dinar to keep his mouth shut. 'Now who else would be interested in the slaves?' he asked.

The innkeeper smiled. 'You paid me ten dinar,' he said. 'That is a high price for news of a few Helati. I thought there might be other parties involved.'

Atrakon stood up and put a hand inside his robes. The innkeeper's eyes sparkled in expectation of gold. A moment later the same eyes widened in horror. Atrakon had drawn a dagger.

'My Lord, no,' the innkeeper cried, falling to his knees and holding out his hands in supplication.

Atrakon was about to strike when he saw a woman appear at the inn door and clasp a hand to her mouth. A small girl whimpered and clung to her mother's salwar kameez.

'It's your lucky day, innkeeper,' Atrakon said, sheathing his weapon. 'It is not my custom to slay a man in front of his child.' He gripped the man's tunic. 'But understand this, my greedy friend: if it were not for the woman and the child, I would have slit you open from throat to navel. Mention my passing to anyone and I will return to settle accounts. Believe me, I know how to prolong a man's death agony.'

11

Swathed in darkness, Gardep watched the campfires of Rishal's column blinking on the hills two miles away and brooded over the danger to his former comrades. They had chosen to stop for the night on the Durbai road. He had no idea what he was going to do but he knew he had to talk to Kulmat, just as he had to beg Rishal for forgiveness. Gardep wondered if he could have done anything differently. But in defending Cusha, he had acted out of love, a noble emotion. Though his actions had cost the life of a decorated Sol-ket officer, he truly felt little remorse. Prakash had chosen his own fate, as all men do. He had not been engaged in a fair fight with a warrior who was his equal in skill and strength, but in the pursuit of an innocent girl. No, Gardep's sorrow was for the rift with his friend Kulmat and for his exile from the Warriors of Ra. His heart already ached with loss. Now it stuttered with anxiety.

'No matter what I did,' Gardep murmured, 'I am no traitor. This I will prove to you, Kulmat my brother.'

He was about to lay his head on his bedroll when he saw something, an owl in one of the trees. It fluttered down, perching on the scabbard of his sword.

'How did you find me, witch?' He scowled. 'I don't care what you say, I'm not returning with you. Leave me alone.'

The owl spoke softly, barely making words at all. 'You mistake me for my mistress,' Aaliya said. 'She guards the Holy Child. I was summoned to warn you.'

Gardep stared. *Two* shape-shifters.

'Beware, Gardep,' Aaliya said, 'you are being followed. Close by, there is one, a Selessian assassin, who plots your destruction.'

Following Aaliya's example, Gardep too spoke in a whisper. He listened to the sighing darkness and detected a presence.

'Thank you,' he said, swallowing his pride. 'I owe you my life.'

The owl stretched her wings. 'My mistress Shamana sends you this message. When you have completed your mission, you will return to her. She is wise, Gardep. She knows the hearts of men, Sol-ket. No matter how far you journey, no matter what trials you endure, Cusha's face will always be on your mind. There is one more thing before I go. My mistress wishes you to remember this, Gardep. Far to the west, your life will take a decisive turn. It will unfold on the tenth day of Hoj.'

The words rocked Gardep back on his heels. It was not the fact that Hoj followed Murjin, giving him less than sixty days until the predicted crossroads. It was a childhood memory.

'What!' Gardep gasped, remembering a day in the scrubland of the Dragon Mountains when he had heard the self-same prophecy before. 'What did you say?'

'I see that this prediction is not new to you,' Aaliya said, 'but there is little more I can tell you. You can no longer ignore the prophecies, Gardep. Be it many days from now, you must return to Cusha. Do what you will in the meantime. Face the danger that lurks in those bushes. Redeem yourself with your friend. But, when all that is done, you must turn west and fulfil your destiny.'

Without another word, she was gone. His thoughts and feelings still in tumult, Gardep reluctantly bent his mind to the small matter of his own survival. He knew he must do nothing to alarm the Selessian. As a result, he did everything the assassin would expect of a Sol-ket. He kept his sword, bow and quiver within easy reach. Crouching forward however to disguise his movements, he slid his dagger belt under his bedroll, then placed his bedroll between his horse and a bamboo grove to prevent the assassin using his bow. Gardep finally slipped two of the throwing knives onto hooks in his sleeves. Satisfied with his preparations, Gardep lay down and pretended to sleep.

12

After leaving Gardep, Aaliya went looking for any more Selessians. She spotted Atrakon in a clearing.

'If he is alone,' she murmured, 'then he is sure of his powers. He must be a most dangerous man.'

Alighting on a branch, she took the form of a python and slid down the tree trunk. She watched him checking his weapons. She noted the black clothing, the fine knives, the meticulously tempered sword. She watched his preparations. This assassin knew his trade. Aaliya remembered what Shamana had taught her. She knew, contrary to the teachings of the Sol-ket, that there was no glory in combat. She knew that blood doesn't cleanse. It stains the hearts and minds of those who live on.

When should you die? Aaliya thought, repeating the Scaline scriptures, written long ago by wise Udmanesh.

When you are old and grey and your children stand as proud and strong as a mountain ash.

How should you die? Free as the Four Winds, with the least pain, and in full knowledge of the good you have done.

Where should you die? In your own bed, surrounded by those you love and have loved you.

13

The shadow of a shadow, that's all Gardep saw of the Selessian Zahar. What came to Gardep's senses was something only the greatest warriors can know. Alerted to the menace in the woods, Gardep could hear Zahar's shadow breathe.

Attack by sword or by dagger. I will kill you anyway.

Zahar had left his shoes in his saddlebags, half a mile away, and was approaching barefoot, testing every inch of ground with the utmost care, so as not to give himself away. Seeing Gardep's defensive position, Zahar laid his bow on the ground. A clean shot was clearly out of the question. Inwardly, he cursed. This could mean combat at close quarters. Even a Sol-ket cadet was a formidable adversary. Still, the young warrior was sleeping. With the grace of Almighty God, Zahar thought, I will dispatch the enemy before he even wakes.

In the clearing, Gardep slipped one of his daggers off its hook. His whole body was tense. The assassin had put down his bow. That's good, Gardep thought; I got my defences right. Now he has to move in closer. Keeping his breath shallow, Gardep laid his cheek flat on the ground. Through slitted eyes he watched the Selessian's bare feet flexing and stepping over the earth.

For the kill, Zahar too chose the dagger. A sword might

hiss through the air and warn the Sol-ket. Throwing stars suffered from the same disadvantage as arrows. They might miss the target and strike the horse or one of the trees, thereby provoking a long and unnecessary struggle whose outcome was uncertain. No, it had to be the dagger. Zahar was just a few yards from his prey. Still, he didn't rush his attack. If one twig were to snap, if one leaf were to crunch, the Sol-ket might still be able to resist.

Years of training had taught Zahar never to rush a kill.

This is it, Gardep thought. Choose the moment. Choose the direction you are going to run. Make the throw quick and accurate. He shifted, as if in his sleep, giving a loud yawn to cover the drawing of the dagger. He saw Zahar stiffen, then relax.

Now!

Springing forward, Gardep twisted and turned, throwing his dagger back-hand. He saw the startled look in Zahar's eyes, saw the astonished O made by his mouth, heard the exhalation as the blade sank into his heart. Like a young tree, supple and falling before its time, Zahar fell forward, hitting the ground with a thump. Even then, Gardep knew better than to turn his foe over. The man might, by some miracle, still be alive and able to stab with his knife. Trained for just such a moment, Gardep took his sword in a two-handed grip and beheaded Zahar. The kill was clean. Death would be instantaneous. Only when he had wiped his sword and covered the body to show due respect for his fallen foe did Gardep check the black robes for some clue to his identity. There were no papers. Gardep never knew the name of the man he had killed.

14

Aaliya stayed until morning. 'Let me come with you,' she said.

Shamana shook her head. 'You are needed elsewhere,' she said. 'I want you to watch over Gardep. Without him, our quest will fail.'

Aaliya nodded sadly and flew off to find him. Shamana returned to the others.

Harad was wishing Cusha a happy birthday. 'A song,' he said. 'Who will sing a song for the birthday girl, this first day of Murjin?'

'I have one,' the priestess said. 'It's a kenning.'

'More of your northern nonsense,' said Qintu, not entirely seriously.

'Let's have your poem, Shamana,' Harad said.

Shamana recited her poem:

'*Mistress server,*
Julmira teaser,
Quick of temper,
Foot stamper,
Rebel heart,
Eyes like coal,
Sweetest daughter,
Guess who?'

'That's easy,' Harad said, 'my beautiful sister of fifteen summers, Cusha.'

'It was an easy one, wasn't it?' Shamana said. 'But this is your day, young jewel of Parcep. You deserve a poem of your own.'

'*One* poem,' Harad said. 'She deserves a whole book of them.'

'Even that is too little,' Qintu said, in an extravagant

show of one-upmanship. 'An epic is what she needs. Let's call it "The Song of Cusha".'

'Hush now,' Murima said, 'you'll embarrass her.'

Cusha didn't look embarrassed. She clapped her hands, demanding attention. 'My turn,' she said. 'This is a song I remember from long ago.'

Shamana and Murima exchanged glances. From long ago? From a past Cusha didn't have? What was this?

Cusha closed her eyes and accompanied the song with slow, graceful hand gestures, flaring her fingers. Her voice rose without faltering:

'In the forest
there is a clearing
where the sun picks out new growth.
And from the earth,
kissed by the wind
is a flower meant for us both.'

Cusha concluded the poem by holding out the imaginary flower in her palm. She looked round with a smile. Then, seeing the expression on Murima's face and especially on Shamana's – one that bordered on horror – the smile began to fade.

'What's wrong?' Cusha asked.

'That song,' Murima said, 'it's the one I was trying to remember. You haven't sung it since you were a little girl.'

Shamana was now staring at Murima with the same intensity she had fixed on Cusha. 'Since she was a little girl!' Shamana exclaimed disbelievingly. 'You mean to say you've heard the song before? Why did you never tell me about it?'

'It is but a song,' Murima said, her voice beginning to falter under the priestess's furious glare. 'Cusha would sing it back in the early days, soon after you brought her to me, Shamana. Once Cusha knew she could trust me, she would sing it all the time. Then, after Julmira took her doll, Cusha never sang it again.'

'It's true,' Cusha said. 'That's when I knew I was worth nothing in my new life, the day that spoiled brat snatched away the only possession I had.'

'It didn't matter what Julmira did,' Murima said. 'You were worth the world to me, my dearest child.'

Cusha smiled. 'I know, Mama-li.'

'Why didn't you tell me about this song?' Shamana demanded again. 'This is the sign for which I have been waiting these many years. Do you know what sacrifices I have made in search of a clue like this? And now you tell me it was here all the time, right under my nose!'

'But it's only a song,' Murima said, taken aback by Shamana's seriousness. 'It is a child's rhyme.'

'You don't understand,' Shamana said. 'What do you think it means?'

'I don't know,' Murima said. 'It's an old love song, isn't it?'

'No, no,' cried Shamana. 'Why do you not understand? It's the key.'

She groaned for all the wasted years when the prize she had sought was so close at hand. Eyes burning, she seized Cusha's hands.

'This means it's true,' she said, 'you *are* the chosen child.'

'But I have no twin!' Cusha cried. 'How many times do I have to tell you?'

'You do have a twin,' Shamana said, 'though, for some reason, it is erased from your memory. It is there in the lyrics: *a flower meant for us both.*'

Four pairs of questioning eyes fastened on the priestess.

'I have it now. It was there in the prophecies all the time: a flower representing the balance of things, a flower that was white and black. The message recurs throughout the

Book of Scales.' Her face was flushed with excitement. 'It is the night orchid, rarest of flowers. It grows only in the hills of northern Jinghara, close by the Demon Wall. It is sacred to the Scales and represents light in darkness, the survival of beauty, the conquest of death. It was Udmanesh himself who discovered its properties. It opened the door to the House of the Dead. Cusha, did you ever see a black flower with a white bloom? Maybe there was a note about your person, a tiny scroll perhaps.'

Murima was about to protest but Cusha interrupted her. 'A black flower?' she said. 'Yes, there was such a thing.'

'Where?'

'On my doll's dress. I remember. There was a single black flower.'

'The doll!' Shamana cried. Now the secret of the Black Tower seemed further away than ever. 'Is that why you clung to it so, because somebody told you it was important?'

'I don't know, Shamana,' Cusha said, still bewildered by the turn of events. 'I was a little girl. It was my doll.'

Turning towards Murima, Shamana demanded information. 'What happened to the doll, after Julmira took it?'

Murima shook her head. 'I don't know.'

'I do,' Cusha said. 'I know exactly where it is. I saw it only recently.'

'What?'

'The mistress throws nothing away,' Cusha explained. 'She has kept all her dolls, much as she has kept all the other treasures of her childhood. They are on a shelf in her changing room, mine amongst them. How could I ever forget? It was the one thing I had to remind me of a time when I was not a slave, and she could take it, just because she was high caste and I low.'

'That's it, then,' Shamana said. 'I have to return to Parcep.'

CHAPTER 7

The Memory Lamp

1

Many miles to the north-west, close by the hills where the Night Orchid bloomed, Oled Lonetread was watching the Sol-ket making preparations to ride out of camp. Seeing the barbarian watching, Murak called to him.

'Hurry, Oled. Saddle up.'

Oled simply shook his head. 'We're going nowhere.'

Murak stared in disbelief. 'What did you say? Is this insubordination?'

'No,' Oled said. 'It is a fact.' He pointed to the eastern horizon. Dark shapes, like ash swirling above a fire, were rising into the dawn sky. 'Do you know what they are?'

Murak knew, though he couldn't believe his eyes. 'Dark-fliers.'

'Very good,' Oled said, 'and here's me thinking you're new to the frontier.'

Murak ignored the last comment. 'But it is dawn,' he said. 'The sun is coming out.'

'That won't stop the creatures now,' Oled said. 'The rules of the game have changed, my friend. They are stronger at night and stronger still during the time of the Blood Moon, but the Darkwing has taught his dark-fliers well. These days, they will wrap themselves in dark clothing against the sun and come out in daylight. The Darkwing has added strategy to the savage power of the night breed. I have even seen them cake their skin with mud to prevent the blistering of the sun. Guided by the demon lord, they have learned to fight night or day. Believe me, they know we're here. It won't be long before they attack. We'd better hope they are well in advance of the Darkwing's main army. If he is close by with all his troops, then we are truly doomed.'

Murak stared for a moment at the distant swarm, then called a trumpeter. 'Sound the alarm,' he ordered. 'Prepare for battle.'

The signal brayed across the camp. Inexperienced he might be, but Murak hadn't forgotten his training. He wasted no time in setting up a perimeter manned by archers. Within this circle, he organised slingers, spearmen and swordsmen. He was prepared for a battle on two fronts. The demons would come from both sky and earth.

'We are ready,' Murak said, looking apprehensively to the west.

'Almost,' Oled said.

'Explain.'

'Your battle plan is good,' Oled said, 'but you need to move the entire formation up onto that ridge. Your main threat comes not from above, but from below.'

His gaze indicated the brown earth beneath their feet.

Understanding immediately, Murak gave the order to move the perimeter. 'How long?' he said.

Oled indicated a shape in the distance. It looked like a flock of crows. 'A matter of minutes,' he said. 'Are you ready for your first encounter with the undead?'

'Yes,' Murak said. But his face told a different story.

2

Come the dawn, the Sol-ket of Rishal-ax-Sol saddled up and continued their north-western expedition, blissfully ignorant of the danger their comrades faced in the distant Jinghara hills. Gardep followed. None of his old comrades in the academy would have recognised him now. He was dressed in the black robes he had stripped from his Selessian attacker's body. His face was masked. He even carried the assassin's weapons, his traditional Sol-ket arms concealed in his bedroll. Zahar's body was buried in the woods.

Though Gardep was riding the assassin's stallion, a fine animal, he had kept his own horse and was leading it, tethered to his saddle. Who knows when he might need a fresh mount? Gardep kept a steady pace, following the Sol-ket column at a distance, awaiting the opportunity to redeem himself. Some men keep their eyes on the horizon and allow themselves to be lulled into a kind of trance by the hoof beats of their horse. Not Gardep. His mind was filled with swirling images. The latest of them gnawed at him most. No matter how he tried, Gardep couldn't get Aaliya's words out of his mind, the ones he had heard two years earlier during his Ket-Ra, the prophecy about his future:

Your destiny will unfold on the tenth day of Hoj.

3

The dove crossed southern Parcep in a few hours. Seeing the Tiger Gates and terracotta-coloured walls, she wheeled several times over the Avenue of the Kings before swooping down to the balcony outside Julmira's room. Only when she had assured herself that the young mistress was not in her chamber did Shamana assume her human form and enter.

Barefoot, she padded across the carpeted floors. Shamana ran her eyes over the many saris that hung in Julmira's antechamber; examined the pots and dishes of face paint and perfume; ran her fingers over necklaces, bracelets, anklets and jewellery. There were chokers, toe rings, nose rings and shawls made from pashmina wool. She breathed the perfume and remembered her one true love, the man who had made her heart sing and who died in a Sol-ket cage. Then, snapping out of her reverie, she got down to business. One or two small objects she tucked in her pockets. Julmira, after all, would scarcely miss these trinkets. She wanted for nothing.

Finally, Shamana found what she was looking for. In the middle of a carefully arranged row of dolls, there was the one the young mistress had taken, as a child, from Cusha. Picking it up, Shamana examined the Night Orchid symbol. She squeezed the toy. There didn't seem to be any hidden object inside. It was a cheap rag doll, nothing special about it at all. For a moment, Shamana's heart lurched. What if Julmira had found the toy's secret? How could the original message have survived after all these years? Her thoughts were interrupted by a voice.

'Who are you?' It was Julmira. 'What are you doing in my chamber? Mother!'

Her cry echoed throughout the villa. Over Julmira's shoulder, Shamana saw the girl's mother, the lady Serala. It was Serala who raised the alarm.

'Guards,' she screamed, 'an intruder!'

Shamana heard running feet. She thanked the Four Winds that the homes of the wealthy citizens of Parcep were guarded by armed freemen and not by the Sol-ket. Had the Warriors of Ra been present, Shamana might have found them a greater challenge than the two household guards with their short swords.

'Stop!' they yelled.

Shamana did no such thing. Shoving Julmira out of the way so that the young mistress landed on her rump on the floor, the priestess crossed the bedchamber in five strides and hurled herself into the air. Transforming immediately into the dove that had arrived on the villa's balcony a few short minutes earlier, she rose quickly into the sky. Turning north-west, she looked down at the helpless guards. She was relieved to see that neither of them was in possession of a bow.

4

The drums of war were beating over the plains of Jinghara. Trumpets called the Sol-ket to their battle stations. Veterans looked east without outward emotion. The less experienced warriors shifted uneasily, wondering what to expect. Oled had accompanied Murak to an advanced position. For a man in command of his first engagement, the young officer seemed very assured. These Sol-ket train their soldiers well, Oled thought.

'Don't waste your arrows and shot,' Oled advised the officer, though it hardly seemed necessary. 'The creatures will come in fast and exploit the air currents to their advantage. No wild shooting.'

Murak passed the order down the line. His men were to wait until they were sure to hit their target. 'How many times have you fought the Lost Souls, Oled?' he asked.

'I was eight years in Zindhar,' Oled told him. 'I've lost count of the battles I've fought.'

He pointed out the fliers, sweeping in low over the wheat fields. Unbuckling his battle-axe, he weighed the monstrous weapon in his huge hands.

'For his Imperial Majesty,' Murak shouted.

The Sol-ket roared their response. 'And for Almighty Ra.'

They roared again, this time accompanying their shouts with the drumming of spears and swords on their shield. From hundreds of throats the Sol-ket issued their war cry: 'Victory or death!'

Only Oled remained silent. As the first wave of dark-fliers hurtled towards the Sol-ket line, the ranks of warriors loosed a hail of spears, arrows and shot. Crimson rain fell from the sky and dozens of writhing fliers slammed into the earth to be dispatched by the eager soldiers. Fortified by this initial success, the Sol-ket raised their voices in a victory hail. It was premature. A second wave of fliers was coming in.

'Hand-held javelins,' Murak ordered.

He no longer deferred to Oled. He sent forward a phalanx of spearmen to break the dark-flier wave. Though there were casualties, the phalanx held its ground.

'Archers,' Murak cried. 'Loose your arrows.'

A hail of arrows hissed through the air, thinning the dark-flier ranks.

'Again.'

More fliers tumbled, twisting and snarling, to the ground.

'Remove the heads,' Murak ordered.

Immediately, the swordsmen went about their gruesome task. That's when Oled saw the looming forms of the undead, silhouetted against the rising sun.

'Get your men back on the high ground.'

Murak saw the danger. The spawn of the underworld were emerging from the hazy dawn mist. Others were bursting through the earth, clawing at the warriors' ankles. Murak ordered the trumpeters to sound the retreat. His swordsmen streamed back up the slope. Catching the advancing undead in the open, the Sol-ket cut them to ribbons with arrows and shot, once more rushing forward to remove the heads. They didn't want the night-striders recovering to fight again. From start to finish, the entire skirmish lasted no longer than ten minutes.

'We did it,' Murak panted.

'Yes,' Oled said, 'you beat their scouts.' He pointed in the direction the first wave had come from. 'But can you beat that?'

From his vantage point on the higher ground, Murak could at last see the enemy. 'By the golden face of Ra!' he gasped.

Strung out along the horizon, for as far as the eye could see, seemingly untroubled by the now blazing sun, were the legions of the Lost Souls.

5

Serala-ax-Sol greeted her visitor with clasped hands and a bow.

'It is an honour to have you in my home, Your Holiness. My husband has spoken of you often.'

The warrior priest Shirep-hotec took a seat. He didn't

respond to Serala's flattery, but instead got down to business.

'I was intrigued by your message to the acting garrison commander, mistress Serala,' he said. 'You spoke of an intruder.'

'I did, Your Holiness,' Serala said. 'Before he left, my husband told me to alert the authorities of any strange events. Though I can't imagine how, he must have anticipated something like this.'

Shirep refused a drink offered by one of the house slaves. When the Helat had left the room, he leaned forward. 'Perhaps you would like to tell me exactly what happened,' he said.

Serala nodded. 'My daughter went up to her room to find a sari for a function. We have been invited to formally open a new terrace of the Hanging Gardens.'

Shirep nodded, though only to get her to cut her story short.

'That's how she disturbed the intruder,' Serala said.

'An intruder who escaped, I hear.'

Serala read criticism into Shirep's words. 'There was a good reason for her escape,' she said. 'The woman was a shape-shifter.'

Suddenly she had Shirep's undivided attention. 'The witch was here!'

Serala nodded, taking satisfaction in Shirep's sudden interest. 'So I was right. It's important.'

Shirep gave the matter some thought. 'Is anything missing?' he asked.

'Just one item,' Serala said. 'It is most curious.'

Shirep appeared tense. 'What was it?' he asked, urgency crackling in his voice.

Normally, the warrior-priest affected an attitude of aloof boredom. At the mention of a missing item, however, he had moved forward, gripping his seat until his knuckles whitened. His reaction caused Serala some anxiety.

'It is something of no value whatsoever,' she told him, 'one of my Julmira's dolls.'

To Serala's surprise, Shirep shot out of his seat. 'A doll, you say? Might I speak to your daughter?'

Serala smiled, though rather thinly given Lord Shirep's obvious agitation. 'I anticipated your request, Your Holiness,' she said. 'Julmira is waiting outside.'

6

Cusha had been watching the skies to the east for over an hour, desperate for some sign of Shamana. To her growing dismay, she had seen nothing but rose-ringed parakeets, squabbling in the trees.

'You don't think she's been captured, do you?' she asked.

'Shamana?' Qintu said, by way of reassurance. 'Anyone who caught as strange a fish as that would have to throw it back.' But his ready humour cheered nobody.

'She'll be back,' Murima said, but she too looked eastwards.

'If the masters have taken her,' Cusha said, 'I will never forgive myself. I'm to blame for all this.'

'Don't say that,' Harad told her. 'Shamana took the decision to go, nobody else. She's the one who believes the prophecy of the Scales.'

'What made you sing that song, anyway?' Qintu asked.

'I don't know,' Cusha said. 'I haven't thought about it in years. Maybe it's got something to do with my birthday.'

Harad nodded. 'Maybe.'

That's when Qintu started hopping up and down. 'Is this her?'

It wasn't the dove winging its way towards them. A tiger had just broken cover not a hundred yards away.

'Shamana,' Harad shouted, 'is it you?'

The tiger advanced through the long grass, muscles rippling, paws spreading as it walked.

'Shamana?'

The beast gave a low grumble. Murima's eyes widened. 'It isn't her,' she said. 'It's a wild beast. Draw your bows.'

Harad went for his. Qintu managed to pull his sword from its scabbard. That's when the tiger started to run. Harad managed to nock his arrow to the string. Qintu raised his sword.

'Oh, put your weapons away, you silly boys,' a familiar voice said.

The tiger melted away before their eyes, to be replaced by the priestess.

'Don't do that,' Qintu said, a definite shake in his voice. 'You scared the life out of me.'

'I know,' Shamana said with a grin, 'that was the idea.'

Qintu scowled. 'You think you're so superior, don't you?' he snapped.

But Cusha wasn't interested in their bickering. 'Did you get it?' she asked.

Shamana produced the doll and handed it to her. 'Though I haven't examined it properly,' she said, 'I have to admit I can't see anything.'

Cusha looked at the doll.

'Is there anything different?' Shamana said. 'I thought that there might be something in the stuffing. Did you ever notice anything, a solid object perhaps?'

Cusha shook her head. 'It was an ordinary doll,' she said.

She turned the toy over, squeezing it and examining it this way and that.

'Do you see anything?' Shamana said hopefully.

Cusha shook her head. 'Nothing.'

7

It was Murak who broke the news to Barath, his commanding officer. 'We engaged an advance party in combat, Barath-Ra,' he said.

'I see you were victorious,' Barath said, picking at his food.

'We were, Barath-Ra, but that is not my news. The victory is of little importance.'

Murak exchanged glances with Oled. 'It was overshadowed by another development.'

'And what is that?' Barath asked.

'I have seen the Darkwing's army,' Murak said. 'Oled was telling the truth. The Lost Souls are as numerous as the grains of sand in the Selessian Desert. They cover the entire plain from south to north. What I witnessed was not a rabble of mindless demons but a disciplined army. Barath-Ra, they carried clubs, javelins, swords, axes. The Empire is in peril.'

Barath put down his dish and looked at Murak's junior officers. 'Do you all confirm this report?'

The officers nodded. Every one of them appeared to be still reeling from the shock of seeing the sheer magnitude of the demon horde.

'You truly believe that we will not be able to hold them?' Barath asked.

'Commander,' Murak said, 'if you had seen the Darkwing's war host, you would not ask such a question. It will take every sword, spear and bow in the Empire to halt the demon lord. He has been preparing his revenge. He has done his work well.'

Barath conferred for a moment with his deputies. They were all of the same opinion. 'We accept your report, Murak. You have our thanks.' He consulted a map. 'We will fall back to the banks of the Amputra. There is a defensible fort at Karangpur. We will shelter there and wait for the rest of the Grand Army. To sacrifice ourselves to no purpose would be folly.'

Oled grunted. If only Turayat had come to the same conclusion.

8

'Give me the doll,' Murima said.

'What are you going to do?' Shamana asked.

Murima ignored her. She held up the doll to the light of the sun, peering at the fabric of the dress. Convinced that there was nothing in the patterning of the material, she picked at the stitches down the doll's back. A little sawdust fell out. There was nothing else.

'Stir the fire,' she told Harad.

'You're not going to burn her!' Cusha cried. Though a young woman now, she still had a child's fondness for her lost and recovered doll.

'Of course not,' Murima said. 'I want to try something.'

Shamana looked interested, as if she had just realised what Murima was up to.

'Mama-li,' Cusha asked, 'what are you doing?'

'If I'm not mistaken,' Shamana said, 'Murima has re-membered a child's trick we all used to play. I don't know why I didn't think of it myself.'

Murima held the doll over the flames, not close enough to singe it but close enough to let the heat of the fire act upon the material.

'There,' she said, 'do you see that?'

There was the faintest outline on the cloth. Shamana leaned forward and copied down the symbols in the soil with a stick.

'When we were children we used to make invisible messages with a concoction,' Murima explained. 'I have to say, I didn't hold much hope when I brought the doll close to the flames. The messages we made would never last longer than a few minutes.'

'The base of your mixture was onions, wasn't it?' Shamana asked.

Murima nodded. 'That's right. What is this one made of, to last so many years and still produce a bold image?'

'I suspect,' Shamana said, 'that the clue is in the pattern on the dress. The juice comes from the Night Orchid.'

'What do the symbols mean?' Cusha asked.

'They are a form of ancient Vassyrian script,' Shamana said. 'These characters were among the first ever drawn to communicate language. They were cut into clay tablets.'

'But what do they mean?' Cusha repeated.

'This character indicates a temple near the town of Sangrabad,' Shamana replied.

'Surely there is no such town,' Murima said. 'Why would the Sol-ket name a place after the god of evil?'

'It is abandoned,' Shamana said. 'The name belongs to a distant time.' She inspected the writing. 'Look,' she said, 'this one speaks of a memory lamp.' She turned to look at Cusha. 'You see, darling girl, if they thought a captured warrior might yield under torture and betray his comrades, the Vassyrians would creep up to the bars of his cell and, by burning a special oil for him to inhale, remove any of the man's memories that might endanger his people.'

Small fires leaped in Cusha's eyes. 'I see, by the look in your eyes, that you understand,' Shamana said. 'Your long ignorance is almost over, my child. Your lost memories are stored in just such a lamp.'

'We must go to this town of Sangrabad,' Cusha said, her heart beating like a tabla drum.

Murima read the priestess's eyes. 'There is a problem, isn't there?'

'Yes.' Shamana nodded. 'The temple of Sangrabad is in the foothills where the plains of Jinghara give way to its snow-peaked mountains.'

Now everyone understood. To get the lamp, they would have to enter the lands presently being contested by the armies of the Darkwing and the Empire.

CHAPTER 8

Vishtar's Dream

I

In the forest
there is a clearing . . .

Mist was tumbling down the weathered hills of northern Jinghara. Flocks of cranes drifted across the gradually darkening sky. On the plain, jackals set up their blood-curdling chorus of screams. Meanwhile, downriver, through the silvery haze, a lone boatman was poling his way home-ward, his boat-light twinkling. With the night breed sweep-ing across the land, the fisher may have been one of the few men left alive in this part of the province. Shadows were lengthening across the ruined walls of the temple of Sangrabad. Twilight trickled down the well-worn stone reliefs.

. . . *where the sun picks out new growth.*

The haunting melody, sung by a single female voice,

whispered through the small copses of trees that clung to the bare hills. Presently the ancient song began to echo mournfully through the deserted precincts of the temple, resounding around the sandstone and brick dome and humming into the inner sanctum where a single lizard crouched, still as eternity. Statues made of stucco, once brilliantly painted but now faded to a dull grey, seemed to be listening to the girl's singing.

And from the earth,
kissed by the wind . . .

The tall stone galleries, filled with rows of scarred and damaged pillars began to resonate with the sound of a human voice for the first time in a generation.

. . . is a flower meant for us both.

On his mean pallet, high in the Black Tower, Vishtar woke, stirred by the same singing. He murmured the words he had dreamed.

'A flower made for us both.'

He said it over and over again, savouring the words, allowing their taste to linger on his tongue. Suddenly, for the first time in years, he knew the date. It was the first of Murjin.

'My birthday.'

2

Gardep continued to follow Commander Rishal's column. Occasionally he noticed a bird fluttering above him and wondered if it was Shamana's apprentice, Aaliya. He tried to keep his mind on the problem of returning somehow to the Sol-ket fold but, try as he might, he couldn't drive Cusha from his mind. Her eyes haunted him. Maybe Aaliya was right, after all. Could it be that, once accounts were settled with Kulmat and Rishal, he would turn his horse west and return to her? But what would be the point, if she still despised him so? How could the tenth of Hoj bring him anything but pain?

The regiment was joined by another contingent of the Grand Army, a hundred war elephants from the rose-coloured fort in the town. Heavily armoured, the elephants carried reinforced howdahs, designed to protect the driver and warrior inside. Here, working as a pair, were the mahout, an experienced driver, and a spearman or archer. Sick of the dust stinging his eyes, Gardep rode out wide of the growing force. He could see Commander Rishal travelling at the head of his troops, accompanied by his new squire, Kulmat.

'You think that the paths of our lives have diverged,' Gardep murmured. 'You are wrong, my brother. Not until I have gained your forgiveness will I give up my vigil. Not until I have fought side by side with you against the demon war host and triumphed against the Darkwing will I leave.'

Once more, Cusha's face burst into his mind. Preoccupied as he was by his determination to rejoin his brother Sol-ket, Gardep could not help but regret leaving Cusha behind. To him, she was the very picture of perfection. It was as if a mirage were shimmering before him. He could see her eyes, shaped like lotus petals, her expression gentle as a fawn's, her lips a deep russet-red like the wild roses that grew in Rishal-Ra's bowers, her skin like coffee and her hair as dark and shiny as the coat of a black panther. To him, she represented the very essence of beauty. What did it matter that she had been raised a Helat? Her lack of finery did not make her plain. Her stained salwar kameez did not render her graceless. To him, she was in every way a princess. Shamana had been right. Cusha would be impossible to forget.

'But haunt me as you do,' Gardep murmured, 'my future lies here, with my comrades, not with you.'

3

The five fugitive Helati were also making their way northwest, though by a very different route from Gardep's. Hour after hour they plodded through woods and splashed along streams, doing everything they could to evade capture. It was just after noon when Shamana came to a decision.

'This is no use,' she said. 'If we continue to avoid the main roads we will add many days to our journey.' Instinctively, she glanced behind her. 'Don't forget we've got that Selessian on our tail. If we carry on at this pace, he will kill us all.'

'But he's just one man,' Qintu said.

Shamana shook her head at his naivety. 'He is one man whose trade is death. We can never drop our guard while he is following us.'

'So why don't you turn into a tiger?' Qintu said. 'Yes, you could eat him.'

'He is skilled with bow and spear, sword and knife. I am old, Qintu. I hesitate to face him in mortal combat. That I will do only as a last resort.'

Qintu's suggestion had been mainly in jest. Hearing the apprehension in Shamana's voice, he fell silent.

'We can't take the merchant roads,' Murima protested. 'We'd be spotted immediately. Five Helati travelling openly through the towns, why, it would be like putting our heads in a noose.'

'But one of us will not be a Helat,' Shamana said. There was a twinkle in her eye.

'Oh dear,' Qintu said, 'I always said this was bound to happen. She's gone crazy as a temple monkey.'

'There's nothing crazy about my plan,' Shamana said. 'Who among us is graceful in spite of her trials? Who among us has the poise to pass herself off as a Child of the Sun?'

All eyes turned towards Cusha.

'Oh no,' she said. 'I won't do it. Shamana, this is lunacy. I can't pass myself off as one of the masters.'

'Cusha,' Shamana said, 'believe me, you can and you will.'

4

Aurun-Kai discovered Vishtar running along one of the galleries. At first he couldn't understand what the boy was doing. Then he saw what he had in his hand.

'Where did you get that ball?' Aurun-Kai demanded.

'I made it,' Vishtar told him, 'from scraps of leather I found.'

'Leather?' Aurun-Kai said, frowning. 'Ah, they will have been left by the bookbinders. Many of the books you see on these shelves were bound here, in this very building, the greatest library outside Inbacus or Rinaghar. The master expelled the last custodians when he made this place his sanctuary. In its day, of course, it was so much more.'

Vishtar waited for him to finish, but Aurun-Kai wasn't about to give away the Black Tower's secrets as easily as that.

'Don't go, Aurun-Kai,' he said.

'Why should I stay?'

'You can tell me about Lord Sabray's campaign against the Army of the Free. I've read several accounts but you were there. What was it like?'

Aurun-Kai stopped in his tracks. 'That interests you, does it?'

Vishtar nodded. 'It was the moment when the world could have been made anew,' he said.

'But the world stayed old,' Aurun-Kai said. 'Men dream of heroes. They long for paradise on Earth. They deceive themselves. This is the time of the Muzals. It is the final age of humankind.'

He drew up a seat and gestured to Vishtar to join him. 'I'll tell you a better story. I'll tell you the tale of how the master became the Darkwing.'

5

Oled shaded his eyes with his hand. The fort of Karangpur soared abruptly before him, clinging to a sheer cliff that made up one side of a huge outcrop. The hill looked out on one side over the northern hills and, on the other, across the rolling Jingharan plains. The fort itself was a formidable monument constructed of dun-coloured masonry. It had crenellated bastions and, rising high above them, a many-tiered governor's block, punctuated with pillared balconies and fretted stone lattices. All in all, it presented a stern façade to any would-be besiegers.

Unfortunately, Oled thought, this was no ordinary siege. The demon host commanded the skies and the deep, dark soil. After a long climb through many walls and many gates the ten thousand men in Barath's command reached the fort's inner defences.

Barath's first order was that a thorough inventory be

taken of Karangpur's food stocks. Oled was present when Murak arrived with the news. After reading the report, Barath smiled with satisfaction.

'Excellent,' he said. 'We can withstand a siege for two months. At most, it will take the Grand Army half that to assemble.' He glanced at Oled. 'Do you agree, scout?'

'The gates can withstand the night-striders,' Oled said. 'The fliers can be held off by archers. Yes, Barath, I would say you are in a strong position.'

'Do I detect a but, scout Lonetread?' Barath asked.

'Barath-Ra,' Oled said, 'the Darkwing has turned the night breed into an army. Don't underestimate your enemy.'

'I don't,' Barath said. 'Did I not order a tactical retreat? But let's not exaggerate the threat. There are more of them, I'll give you that, but the Lost Souls are creatures without intelligence or purpose. It takes civilisation to display the kind of organisation of which you speak. Giving the beasts weapons is one thing. Teaching them to use them properly is another. We will sit tight. It won't be long before the Grand Army relieves us.'

Oled shrugged and exchanged glances with Murak.

'Now, gentlemen,' Barath said, looking around his senior officers, 'a round of kinthi for you, and a flagon of rice wine for our barbarian friend. It's the best, imported from Banshu.'

The drinking was well underway when there was a knock at the door. A man at arms, looking wide-eyed and utterly terrified, whispered something in Barath's ear. Oled saw the General's eyes go glassy with astonishment.

'What is it, Barath-Ra?' Oled asked.

Barath didn't answer. Instead, he threw open the doors that led onto a balcony. From this vantage point it was possible to look down on the western approaches to the fort. This time even Oled was taken aback by what he saw. Far below, huge siege engines were being pulled into place before Karangpur's outer gates. The first projectiles were already crashing into the walls.

6

This is the tale Aurun-Kai told Vishtar, the prisoner of the Black Tower:

'Bold Sabray was one of the heroes of the Battle of Dullah, when the Empire faced the insurgent wrath of its risen slaves. Again and again, without any thought for his own safety, this prince of just sixteen summers attacked the Helat lines. His men were astonished by the maturity and reckless courage the youthful prince showed in battle. But his father, the Emperor of the Sun and King of Kings, Muzal-ax-Sol, was a mean-hearted man. With each generation, the Muzals had become more ruthless and bloodthirsty. Great wealth and even greater power had begun to blind them to the things that mattered in life. Intrigue and power struggles were tearing the court apart. Murder by poisoning and stabbing was commonplace. The clan had begun to devour its own. In his growing son Muzal didn't see cause for pride, but an emerging rival. He was jealous of Sabray's success and accorded him no honours. Instead he fêted the Selessian satraps whose belated charge helped win the day, ignoring the battle's greatest hero.

'This caused much muttering among the veterans who had been dazzled by the boy-prince's dashing show of courage. Though the Selessians were now their allies, the Sol-ket still considered the men in black utterly treacherous. How could they ever trust these desert shadows? To elevate a barbarian above one's own son in this way was seen as an act of madness. It was this snub that first set a wedge between father and son.

'Worse was to come. In the months that followed the victory at Dullah, many nations whose rulers had stayed neutral in the struggle rushed to pledge their loyalty to the Empire. One such nation was the Island Kingdom of Banshu. Now, the Shogun of that land was quick to realise that, if he didn't conclude an alliance with the Empire, he would see his kingdom invaded and his cities razed to the ground. He duly sent his daughter Kewara to golden Rinaghar to make a match and conclude a pact of friendship with the Empire.

'The Shogun naturally thought that this union would be with the Emperor's son, Sabray, who was the same age as Kewara. All seemed to be going well. Sabray was enchanted with the Princess of Banshu and courted the lovely Kewara. She looked favourably on Sabray in return. She exchanged many sweet words and amorous looks with the young prince.

'But Sabray's father, Emperor Muzal, was besotted with power and was used to getting his own way. In his turn he fell under the spell of Princess Kewara. He began to covet her beauty for himself, wishing to add her to his harem. One night, inflamed by kinthi, he burst into the lady's chamber. Appalled by the Emperor's advances and determined to defend her honour at any price, Princess Kewara flung herself to her death from the palace window. Sabray was inconsolable. Driven mad with grief he left golden Rinaghar and raised an army to challenge the Emperor.

'Father and son met with their armies in the shadow of the Dragon Mountains. It was the first time the Empire had been torn asunder by civil war. For many hours the outcome was in the balance but eventually Sabray's lines broke and the boy-prince fled. After long months hiding out in the provinces, Sabray was betrayed by one of his own advisors and brought to the Great Ziggurat of Rinaghar where his fate would be decided by the Priests of Ra. It was Linem-hotec who designed Sabray's punishment. Linem, an expert in the dark arts, a man to whom softer feelings such as mercy and compassion are alien, delighted in his task.

'He devised an elixir that could condemn Sabray's soul to dwell for ever in his tortured, dying body. In this way Linem forced the young prince to endure a horrifying fate for all eternity. Sabray would experience a living hell as his flesh became corrupted and started to rot on his tortured bones. Yet his mind would be undimmed, subjected to endless torment and eternal humiliation. Year after year he would see his own flesh melt away. He would smell its decay, feel the maggots feeding on it. It was a punishment drawn from the furthest reaches of Hell.

'After some months a group of veteran warriors, loyal to Sabray, staged a daring rescue attempt. Sabray was indeed spirited away, but the leader of the prince's followers was captured. Even under torture he didn't betray his master. He was eventually to rejoin his master, but only after suffering the cruellest punishment for his loyalty. A once handsome man was transformed into a creature so grotesque none would look upon him without disgust. As I have told you, Lord Linem delights in his cruel schemes.

'But, thanks to his supporters' actions, Sabray would live. By applying various potions to Sabray's body and protecting it with a carapace of reptile skin, the corruption of his flesh was halted. Sabray even drank the tainted blood of a dark-flier in order to draw its essence into him and make himself more than a mortal man. Still, this proud warrior was reduced to a mockery of his former self. He could only be sustained in this half-dead form by the consumption of human blood, and very special human blood at that. Eventually, such was the rage and despair in his soul that all his supporters abandoned him, all save one loyal, old friend.

'Now he searches the Earth for the secret of rebirth in the hope that he can regain his former life. That, young Vishtar, is the story of how Sabray-ax-Sol became the Darkwing, lord of demons. For so many years he has been gathering his forces, learning to control their chaotic energies by the power of his mind. He is ready to take his revenge.'

Vishtar listened to the end without interrupting. He had three questions.

'Ask them,' Aurun-Kai said.

'Are you the loyal warrior who was captured?' Vishtar asked.

Aurun-Kai nodded. 'That is my burden. Everyone else has abandoned Sabray, but I never will. He is my master until the end of time. Like you, I will never leave this tower. Charged with taking care of you, I share your imprisonment.'

'And is this, your present condition, your punishment?'

Aurun-Kai answered yes.

'Finally,' Vishtar said, 'are you ready to tell me what makes my blood so unique and special to your master? He drinks the blood of others but he always returns to me. There seems to be some special bond. I know I possess some power. My mother told me before she died. But why, when I am at his mercy, does the Darkwing fear me so? Why does he want my sister? After all these years, surely I deserve to know the full story. Tell me, please.'

Aurun-Kai shook his head. 'No, Vishtar,' he said. 'That, on penalty of death, I can not do.'

7

'Shamana,' Cusha protested. 'This is a step too far.'

'My dear, it is the only way. We need protection from the Selessian. He is a professional assassin. A man like him will be feared throughout the Empire for his skill and ruthlessness. Even I hesitate to face him sword against sword. By now, he may well have us in his sights. We can't out-distance him for long.'

Out in the open, with no idea of the Selessian's where-abouts, the Helati were like grazing deer awaiting the tiger's claws. Shamana had been relying on Gardep's strong right arm to repel their enemies, but he was gone. They would need to rely on stealth instead of force. Cusha was shifting her feet self-consciously. Shamana had dressed her in a sumptuous crimson sari and a matching choli, the cropped bodice worn beneath it.

'You can't expect me to impersonate mistress Julmira,' she protested.

'That's exactly what you're going to do,' Shamana said. 'Soon we will come to the village. The elder's name is Anjit. Stick to the story I've told you and he will take us in.'

'And we will be safe there?' Harad asked.

'These district elders maintain small garrisons,' Shamana said. 'They're hardly Sol-ket, but they can fight.'

'But what if this Anjit has been to Parcep?' Cusha demanded. 'What if he knows what Julmira looks like?'

'He doesn't,' Murima said. 'Believe me, I have spent enough years preparing banquets for Rishal. I know the kind of guests that get invited to his villa. As highly as these provincial officials think of themselves, they are of little importance to the great and good of Parcep. Shamana's right. We must seek shelter before nightfall. If we don't, then none of us will live to greet the dawn.'

'But what if Anjit asks me about Rishal?' Cusha said.

'Answer him,' Shamana said. 'You have lived in his household long enough. You will be able to convince him.'

Shamana told Harad and Qintu to wear their bows and swords openly. 'You look a bit young to be bodyguards,' she said, frowning. 'Pages, if you are asked; you are Julmira's pages.'

Half an hour down the road, Shamana reviewed her band. 'You know what you have to do?' she said.

The others nodded.

'Remember to put on a show.'

With that, she spurred her horse. The five Helati galloped along the banks of the Amputra River and into the courtyard of district elder Anjit's house, thundering past a pair of startled guards. By the time they arrived in front of the veranda they were surrounded by half a dozen spearmen.

'Pray announce the arrival of Mistress Julmira-ax-Sol,' Shamana declared, her words and her manner stopping one of the guards in his track. 'Tell Master Anjit to prepare to receive Commander Rishal-ax-Sol's daughter to his household.'

The priestess watched the guard's reaction. He seemed duly impressed and scampered away to alert the master to his illustrious visitor. Within minutes, Anjit came running, pulling on an embroidered waistcoat.

'Mistress Julmira,' he said, eyes wide, 'to what do I owe this honour?'

'I am travelling to discuss an important matter with my father,' Cusha said.

'Isn't he marching to meet the demon host?' Anjit said.

'Indeed,' Cusha said, 'but I have urgent news.' She

leaned forward conspiratorially in her saddle. 'Master Anjit,' she said, 'is there somewhere we can confer in private?'

'Of course,' Anjit said. 'Come with me, mistress.'

Shamana exchanged glances with Murima and the boys. Cusha was doing just fine.

8

Commander Rishal chose, for that night's camp, a palm-fringed lake. Narrow, shady canals radiated from its waters. A temple on the far bank seemed to float gently on the eddying surface while scarlet ibises waded languidly in the shallows. In better times, Kulmat thought, this would be the perfect place to bring your beloved. He watched the ark-shaped rice barges making their way down the backwaters and sighed.

'Is something making you sad, Kulmat?' somebody asked.

It was Janil, the cadet whom Gardep had clubbed unconscious the night he and Shamana sprang Cusha from captivity.

'No,' Kulmat said, 'nothing in particular. I was just admiring the beauty of this place.'

Janil nodded. 'It is for this we fight, brother cadet, to preserve the sacred land of Ra.'

Kulmat wasn't sure about Janil. He was extremely ambitious and was suspected of spying on the other cadets.

'You do sound melancholy this evening,' Janil said. 'Why so? Soon we will win glory in battle.'

'You forget,' Kulmat said. 'I have lost my closest friend.'

Janil seated himself beside Kulmat. 'Who would have thought it? Gardep a traitor. Is it true that he has run away with a Helat girl?'

Kulmat nodded miserably.

'I bet Commander Rishal isn't happy,' Janil said. 'Just imagine. You lead a regiment and your own squire does that. The reputation of the Lion of the Inbacus has been damaged by this affair. Does Rishal-Ra speak of it?'

Kulmat shook his head. 'Not a word.'

'No wonder,' Janil said. 'It must be a huge embarrassment.' He looked across the lake. The setting sun was painting it gold. 'I would like to thank you, Kulmat. You saved my cousin Niraj.'

'Niraj is your cousin?' Kulmat said. 'I didn't know that.'

Janil nodded. 'He would have perished without your help. If I can ever do you a favour, just say.'

Kulmat smiled, though at that moment he wanted only to be alone with his thoughts, his regrets.

'I tell you,' Janil said, 'if I ever catch up with Gardep I will slay him myself.'

Kulmat said nothing. A moment later Janil shielded his eyes. 'That's odd.'

'What is?'

'A single Selessian rider. I wonder what he's doing here?'

Kulmat saw the rider, silhouetted against the sun. 'Maybe there's a contingent of desert warriors on its way,' he said. 'He could be a scout.'

But there was something about the lone Selessian that gave Kulmat cause to wonder.

9

It hadn't taken Oled long to convince General Barath of his plan. Given the huge numbers at their disposal, the Lost Souls had already smashed through the outer gate and poured into the open ground between the first lines of defence. No matter how many missiles the garrison rained down on their heads, no matter how many of the demons' bodies littered the earth, the legions of the undead just kept coming. There were only six more barriers separating the demon host from the garrison. At this rate of advance, the Lost Souls would be inside Karangpur in just a few days.

'This is your last chance to withdraw,' Oled said, reviewing the unit under his command. 'Do you understand the nature of this mission and accept it freely?'

The Sol-ket, Lyrians and Khuts before him nodded. As was their way, the Selessians looked straight ahead.

'Do any of you wish to walk away?' Oled asked.

Not one of the assembled men stepped back.

'Very well,' Oled said. 'Open up the tunnel.'

Karangpur had a number of secret tunnels, used to infiltrate troops behind enemy lines in case of a siege. Most of these Barath had ordered blocked. Just one had been left open for Oled's mission. It had an advantage over the other tunnels: a double wall of Jingharan stone, enough to keep out the night-striders. The men in Oled's command were all dressed in black, making them almost indistinguishable from the Selessians. Their faces were daubed with charcoal. With them they carried large barrels. As they penetrated silently into the stone tunnel, the pounding of the siege engines grew louder.

By the time the warriors were halfway along its length, soil was beginning to trickle down on their heads and the floor was shaking underfoot. The battering rams were crashing remorselessly into the gate above their head. One of the Khuts glanced at Oled. He chose to ignore the man's look. Leaders don't show fear, or acknowledge it in their men. After a few minutes they had reached the end of the tunnel, where a heavy block of stone covered the opening. A concealed system of pulleys and levers was used to slide it open. Oled looked around as if asking the men whether they were ready. Some nodded. Others merely drew their weapons.

With a sound like a stone giant clearing its throat, the slab covering the tunnel slid back. Oled was first out. He ran straight into a night-strider and split its skull with his axe. Black blood spurted from its ruined face. As the rest of his band spilled out behind him his axe cleared a path through the mass of the Lost Souls.

'Bring up the barrels,' he ordered.

The Khuts were in charge of this task. Sturdy, heavily muscled men, they had little difficulty hoisting the heavy barrels of pitch out of the tunnel. The last of the Khuts could already hear the tunnel being filled with rock and cement behind them. There would be no way back through these underground passages. Oled organised the Sol-ket and the Selessians into a defensive ring around the Khuts as they stumbled forward carrying the pitch. A team of Lyrian torchbearers brought up the rear. They understood better than most the properties of the pitch, known across the Empire as Lyrian Fire. The fighting was heavy but, so far, the Lost Souls hadn't understood Oled's plan. This situation ended suddenly when the Darkwing appeared on the battlement walls. He grasped the situation at a glance.

'Protect the siege engines,' he ordered.

But the command came too late. Already Oled was cutting a path to the battering rams.

'Light the barrels!' he roared.

Immediately blazing barrels were rolling into the siege engines. Within moments the night was being illuminated by at least a dozen fierce fires. Dark-fliers were detonating into the blackness, already on fire and screeching in their death throes. Though the mission was a success, none of the warriors were celebrating. They had to face the wrath of the night-striders.

10

'An assassination attempt!' Anjit gasped.

He paused to let his servants bring in the meal. It was simple fare, noodle soup, roti and green tea. The village was anything but poor, but Anjit's visitors had caught him by surprise.

'But who would dare move against Lion-hearted Rishal, hero of Inbacus?'

Cusha almost laughed out loud at Anjit's eagerness to ingratiate himself with her. To have a freeman grovelling at her feet was a strange experience.

'That I cannot say,' she said, sipping her soup, 'but you must know that the Emperor is in his seventy-third year and without an heir. The court is full of conspiracies. Even now there is a Selessian assassin approaching this place.'

Anjit's eyes betrayed fear.

'Master Anjit,' Cusha said, warming to her task, 'as you must already know, I am betrothed to the bravest young Sol-ket in the Empire. If our marriage produces an heir, it threatens the claim of some at the court to the Imperial throne. This assassin intends to kill me then go on to cut my father's throat. I need your help.'

Anjit looked more scared than ever. Year in, year out,

the people of Parcep province trembled before the Sol-ket and their tax demands. To find themselves between their traditional oppressors, the Warriors of the Sun, and this new Selessian menace was cause for concern. As for the talk of conspiracy, frankly he was terrified. No matter how things worked out in the struggle for power, the farmers were bound to lose. But, briefed by Shamana, Cusha knew what to say to stiffen Anjit's backbone.

'My father will be very grateful if you can offer me protection,' she said. 'You should know, Master Anjit, that the commander's gratitude can be measured in gold dinar.'

At this promise of a reward Anjit actually licked his lips. Cusha could barely prevent herself from laughing now.

'I have but twenty men at my disposal, mistress,' Anjit said, 'thirty at most. Out in the dark they would stand no chance against the Selessian. These men of the desert are professionals. Unlike my brave boys, your pursuer has been trained to kill.'

'Are you telling me you are going to throw me to the wolves?' Cusha asked indignantly. 'My father will be most displeased.'

Anjit fell over himself to deny this. 'We can certainly give you protection, mistress, but only if you remain in my house. For generations we have resisted the incursions of the Lost Souls. But protection *within* the village, that is all I can offer. Even then, the Selessian may be able to penetrate our defences. This is a most precarious situation, mistress.'

Cusha smiled. Anjit had been deceived by Shamana's ruse, just as she had said he would be. 'Maybe not,' she said, emptying a bag of gold dinar on the table in front of Anjit. 'I have an idea.'

What she meant was, Shamana had an idea.

'A triumph!' General Barath declared to his senior officers. 'A palpable and complete triumph.'

Men who had, a few hours before, looked out upon the war host of the Lost Souls with bleak despair in their hearts, were now bright-eyed with optimism. They had the food and the arms to withstand the demon throng until the Grand Army relieved them. The kinthi had already been broken out, again.

'A toast,' Barath shouted. 'Raise your glasses to Scout Oled Lonetread, hero of Karangpur.'

Oled raised his eyes and looked around the council of officers.

'What?' Barath chuckled. 'No smile, Oled? Come on, man. Join us. Our good cheer is because of your actions, after all.'

Oled rose, knocking his chair over, and strode towards the door. His face was as dark as an ocean storm. The horror of the fight with the Lost Souls still swam through his mind. Barath's eyes hardened. Nobody turned his back on a senior officer. What was the barbarian doing?

'Oled,' Murak said, responding to General Barath's steely glare, 'where are you going?' He caught Oled by the sleeve. 'At least acknowledge Barath-Ra's congratulations,' he whispered. 'You don't want to make an enemy of him.'

Oled stopped.

'Please, Oled,' Murak continued, taking care to keep his voice low. 'Listen to me. Even speaking to you this way, I am committing treason against the Sol-ket code.'

Oled finally met Barath's eyes. He stared at the general for a few moments then, on impulse, he marched over to the table where a beaker of rice wine had been poured for him.

'I'll give you a toast,' Oled said. 'Here's to fifty brave men who died to save the fort of Karangpur. That's right, Barath-Ra, you are ready to celebrate the exploits of the mission's sole survivor. You seem to forget, there were others with me and they could not change form to save their skin. What of the men alongside whom I fought?' He drained his beaker of its contents. 'What of them?'

Barath shifted uneasily in his chair. He didn't like the direction Oled's speech was taking.

'Do you want to know why I'm not celebrating?' Oled asked. He approached the window and threw it open. 'You think the Grand Army is going to triumph, don't you, warriors?'

His question set off a round of raucous cheering. But they didn't know what was in Oled's heart. 'You think you're going to cover yourself in glory? I'm right, aren't I?'

More cheering followed. Every man there was relishing Oled's rhetoric.

'But let me ask you this,' he said, his voice descending to a growl. 'Even if you triumph, how many bodies will we have to throw on our funeral pyres? How many of you will have been reduced to ash before this campaign is over?'

The officers exchanged glances. This was insolence, compounded by the fact that Scout Lonetread was a barbarian. One fact was saving him from an immediate court martial: Lonetread was a hero and the saviour of Karangpur.

'Enjoy your success,' Oled said bitterly. 'I go to mourn our comrades who will rise again before long, recruits to the legions of the undead.'

Without another word, he left the hall. General Barath stared after Oled long after he had closed the door behind him. He couldn't act against a hero but he wasn't about to forget this affront.

12

Atrakon Ebrahin reined in his mount.

'Is this the best the witch can come up with?' he said out loud. 'A walled village in the middle of nowhere? She is playing into my hands.'

He approached the walls. From his vantage point among the banyan trees, he heard excited chatter. 'What's all that about, I wonder?' he said.

He saw village men in dhotis hurrying from the elder's gates. Somehow, the witch had persuaded the villagers to take in the Helati. But how? He soon found out. Creeping closer to the gates, he overheard the villagers talking about an important visitor from Parcep.

'They say it is Commander Rishal's daughter.'

Atrakon frowned. Rishal's daughter! Then he understood. It was the girl, Cusha, impersonating her mistress. Climbing a tree that overlooked the walls, he pulled out his spyglass. Sure enough, on the veranda of master Anjit's house, he spotted the Helati. Atrakon identified Cusha immediately. She was wearing an expensive sari and her hair was dressed like a princess's. He could hardly believe the transformation.

During the next hour, he gleaned more information from the local people's gossip. According to their chatter, the great lady from Parcep had given the village two hundred dinar. It was in restitution of taxes so they could celebrate her father's expedition to destroy the Lost Souls. There was going to be a feast the following evening.

'Now that explains it,' Atrakon said. 'A few dinar will

convince the most sceptical of men. I'll give Shamana this: she never fails to surprise.' Exasperation showed in his voice. 'But where did a fugitive slave get two hundred dinar?'

He retired to the banyan trees. It made no difference. As soon as it went dark he would take her.

13

Vishtar was excited that night, the first of Murjin, his birthday. In his dream, he had heard his beloved sister's voice. All these years and she was alive and well. Judging by the way she sang the Song of the Night Orchid, her spirit was unbroken. Maybe, at long last, after all his trials, his ordeal was nearing its end. For long minutes he listened. Had Aurun-Kai retired to his apartments?

Vishtar heard the howl of the wind and the lash of the rain against the outer walls of the Black Tower. But no other sound did he hear. Pushing back his blankets, he slipped his legs out of bed and padded across the stone floor. At the staircase leading to the upper galleries he paused again. For a few moments he rejected what he was going to do as utterly reckless. He even took a few steps back towards his bed. But the memory of his sister's eyes was too much. The sad refrain of the Night Orchid filtered through the back alleys of his mind. Taking a deep breath, he retraced his steps and slowly climbed. Tiptoeing along the gallery, he knelt by a bookcase. Finally, crouching and reaching behind, his fingers closed around the package.

Darting looks around the silent galleries, Vishtar unwrapped the cloth that contained his treasures. He examined the likeness of his sister. 'Cusha,' he murmured. 'Thank the Four Winds that you are safe.'

He then unfolded the pages he had eased so carefully from the binding of the ledger. He read the entry: 'Cusha-ul-Parcep, house slave in service to the household of Rishal-ax-Sol, Commander of the Military academy. Female.'

Vishtar was about to return the package to its hiding place when he heard a voice that chilled his blood: 'Parcep, eh? So that's where the master will find her.'

Vishtar spun round. 'Aurun-Kai!'

The fallen warrior turned his back.

'Please,' Vishtar cried, 'don't tell him.'

But Aurun-Kai had vanished. In despair, Vishtar fell to his knees and screamed, his voice echoing around the walls.

'Please,' he cried, 'don't let him hurt her.'

CHAPTER 9

Abducted

1

Vishtar felt the draught of the demon lord's coming even before he saw his shadow spreading across the walls of the Black Tower.

'So,' the Darkwing said, 'it seems you've been lying to me all this time.'

'Who wouldn't lie to save his sister?' Vishtar said, his defiance only tempered by the slight shake of his voice.

The Darkwing paid Vishtar little attention. Instead, he turned to Aurun-Kai. 'You have done well, old friend. Your vigilance will be the key to our liberty. Soon we may both be free of the grotesque shells that imprison our spirits.'

Aurun-Kai nodded.

'Where is the girl?' the Darkwing demanded.

'Her name is Cusha-ul-Parcep,' Aurun-Kai explained. 'She lives in the town that gives her her name.'

'So,' the Darkwing said, 'I am to renew my acquaintance with Tiger-gated Parcep, second city of the Empire. I was there many years ago, I remember, raising a regiment to crush the Shinar rebellion.'

'Yes, Master,' Aurun-Kai said. 'I was with you.'

The Darkwing breathed in deeply, as if sucking in his memories, dredging them up from some corner of his mind. Maybe he remembered the Sun standards, banners of scarlet and gold. More likely, he remembered the sunlight on his face, the brush of the breeze on his skin, pleasures denied him for so many years.

'It was a long time ago.' Then, recovering himself, he spoke to Aurun-Kai. 'Remind me, who is governor there now?'

Vishtar looked from demon lord to underling. As he did so, despair filled him.

'His name is Rishal-ax-Sol,' Aurun-Kai said. 'It is in his house that the girl Cusha resides.'

'She is in the governor's household?' the Darkwing said. 'She serves a member of the Emperor's family? Whoever has been sheltering the girl chose well.'

'There is certainly a strong intelligence at work here,' Aurun-Kai said. 'I wonder who it could be.'

The Darkwing didn't answer. Perhaps he had an inkling as to the owner of that intelligence.

'Snatching her shouldn't be as difficult as it may seem,' Aurun-Kai said. 'Even as we speak, Commander Rishal is riding westwards to engage Your Royal Highness. He leaves his home and his garrison exposed.'

The Darkwing's impenetrable eyes seemed to grow moist with anticipation.

'You are right,' he said. 'I will strike at the Empire's underbelly. I will seize her this very night.'

'You are going yourself!' Aurun-Kai exclaimed.

'Do you seriously think I would entrust this task to anyone else?' the Darkwing asked. With that, he turned to go.

Vishtar immediately threw himself at the demon lord. 'I won't let you!' he cried. 'You shan't have her.'

But the Darkwing cuffed the boy away without so much as looking in his direction. Vishtar landed in a heap against the opposite wall.

'My long exile is almost over,' the Darkwing said. 'I can taste my freedom.'

By the time Vishtar had recovered his senses the Darkwing had gone.

2

Kulmat and Janil rode ahead of the column, galloping to the top of a rise. Before them they saw the rolling plains of Jinghara, mile upon mile of wheat fields. Kulmat turned and waved. Soon Commander Rishal had joined them.

'The heartland of Jinghara,' Rishal said with satisfaction. 'It is but a matter of days before the other columns converge from every corner of the Empire. No longer will our people fear the Darkwing.'

'We cadets are eager to cover ourselves with glory, Rishal-Ra,' Janil said.

'Of course you are,' Rishal said.

Rishal's response seemed to disappoint the cadet. Seemingly oblivious, the commander turned to his squire. 'What, no brave words from you, Kulmat?'

'I too am looking forward to combat,' Kulmat said, but he was unable to conceal the flatness in his voice. He was angry with himself for letting Janil speak first. He, as squire to the commander himself, should have said something.

'Look!' Janil said.

Another column had appeared on the far horizon, heading their way. Preceding the main force, there were war elephants and Vassyrian chariots.

'The Grand Army is gathering,' Rishal said with obvious pride. 'Ride over and pass on my greetings, cadets.'

Kulmat and Rishal spurred their horses and rode through the wheat fields, scattering crows and buzzards. They hailed the column's commander. He it was who gave them the news that Karangpur was under siege. On their return, they saw the grim determination in Rishal's eyes.

'We will relieve Karangpur,' he said, 'then we will smash the Lost Souls. Victory or death, cadets.'

'Yes, Rishal-Ra,' Kulmat said, this time seizing the opportunity to speak first. 'Victory or death.'

3

Atrakon waited patiently for the festivities to end. From his vantage point in a banyan tree, he watched cobras sway before a snake charmer's flute, wasp-waisted dancers with swirling skirts and skilled puppeteers delighting the crowd with their performance. Word of Julmira's generosity had spread to all the neighbouring villages. At long last, in the early hours of the morning, he saw his opportunity. Slipping down from the tree, he padded almost silently to the wall and climbed over. Even when he dropped down on the other side, the inexperienced guards noticed nothing. Satisfied that none of these poorly trained provincial fighters would give him any trouble, he made his way to Anjit's house.

There, he explored the outer walls. The front door was guarded by half a dozen men, too many to take without raising the entire garrison. The back door was equally well guarded. Finally, reconnoitring the house a second time, he noticed a window that was slightly shaded by an over-hanging tree. Though the branches that tapped against the open window were too frail to carry his weight, they would give him enough protection to make his climb without being discovered. Using a grappling hook, he scampered up the wall, a fast, lithe, deadly figure in black. Inside he discovered one sentry. The man died from a single dagger thrust without ever seeing the face of his attacker. Dragging the body out of sight, Atrakon penetrated deeper into the house.

It was larger than he had thought, with many rooms. He had to make somebody talk. Moments later he found what he had been looking for. Using a ligature, Atrakon strangled a second sentry and entered a large chamber. There, master Anjit was asleep next to his wife. Without a moment's hesitation, Atrakon seized the woman and held his dagger to her throat. When Anjit woke, his eyes widened.

'Make a single murmur,' Atrakon hissed, 'and you will watch your wife die before I kill you too. I will do it. I assure you.' He remembered what he had said to the inn-keeper. It had worked then and it would work now. 'I can make your end long and agonising.'

Anjit nodded, his face a picture of utter terror.

'Where is the girl?' Atrakon demanded. He remembered the fabrication the Helati had used to trick Anjit. 'Where is Julmira-ax-Sol?'

'I will take you,' Anjit whispered.

Atrakon shook his head. 'No,' he said, pressing the dagger into the wife's flesh, 'she will.'

Tying Anjit's arms and legs, Atrakon gagged him. All the while he kept an eye on Anjit's wife, lest she cry out.

Leaning forward, Atrakon pressed the dagger just under Anjit's eye.

'Try to raise the alarm in any way and I will come back to fillet you like a fish.'

Secure in the knowledge that Anjit would remain as still as any stone; he followed the wife to a chamber.

'Here?' Atrakon asked.

She nodded.

'You go first,' Atrakon ordered. Inside the room he saw a sleeping girl. 'Wake her,' he said. 'Cover her mouth with your hand. Let her make a sound and I will kill you.'

But when Anjit's wife woke the girl, Atrakon's heart started thudding with anger. 'Who's this?' he demanded.

Immediately the girl started to babble. 'Mistress Julmira made me exchange clothes with her. She paid me to watch the entertainment in her place. I was to keep my face hidden throughout.'

'Where are they all?' Atrakon demanded.

The girl hesitated. The sight of the Selessian's dagger loosened her tongue.

'Where?'

'They left some hours ago. They took a boat down the backwaters.'

Without another word, Atrakon ran from the house. Two men tried to bar his way. They both died.

4

Much as Cusha regretted the loss of the beautiful sari, in many ways she was more comfortable in her old salwar kameez. She had, after all, been wearing one her whole life. She was sitting at the prow of the boat, trailing her fingers in the still waters, when Shamana came to sit by her.

'There is something on your mind, Cusha,' the old woman said.

Cusha waited a beat before answering. 'I was wondering how much time our ruse has bought us,' she said.

'Really?' Shamana said. 'And there was me thinking you were wondering what had happened to the young Sol-ket!'

Cusha shook her head ruefully. 'I sometimes think you know me better than I know myself,' she said.

Shamana smiled. 'I wouldn't go that far,' she said, 'but I do occasionally see into people's hearts.' She squeezed Cusha's hands. 'So you do still think of Gardep?'

Cusha sighed. 'Yes, I do. I think I feel sorry for him, Shamana. He has betrayed his people and broken his code of honour. No roof the length and breadth of the Empire would willingly give him shelter. He is a man alone.'

'My dear child,' Shamana said. 'He is not alone. Your face is always before his eyes.' She noticed Cusha's flustered expression. 'No,' she said. 'Don't look away. The shadow of the warrior's destiny follows him. We will see him again. You, my dear, will see him again. Don't forget, I have Aaliya watching over him.'

'There is a time I would have resented talking about him this way,' Cusha said, 'but no longer. I am curious. Why was he so taken with me?'

Shamana chuckled. 'You should look in the mirror more often, dear child.'

'That's no explanation, Shamana,' Cusha said. 'Men look at women. Women return their gaze. Such things don't always change the world. There must be more to it than that.'

'Oh, there is,' Shamana said. 'Believe me, there is.'

'Then tell me.'

Shamana sighed. 'I'm not hiding anything from you, Cusha. The picture, like all images of the future, is hazy.

All I know is this, when the time comes for us to understand the truth of your destiny, we will all be there: you and I, Murima, Harad and Qintu . . .'

'And Gardep?' Cusha interrupted. 'Do you think he will follow?'

'Yes. He will be there too.'

'How long will it take to reach Sangrabad?' Cusha asked, changing the subject.

'Not long,' Shamana said, 'though, by taking these backwaters, it will take us longer than I had expected.'

Cusha nodded. 'And will I really find my past there?'

'Yes. Your past is waiting for you in that memory lamp. More importantly, once you understand your past, you will be able to change the course of your future.'

Cusha shivered. 'That's what frightens me.'

Shamana put an arm round the girl she loved so much. 'There is much to fear,' she said, 'but there is cause for hope, too.'

5

It was many long years since the Darkwing had last seen Tiger-gated Parcep. As he approached the terracotta-coloured walls, flanked by dozens of dark-fliers, his eyes fixed the streets greedily. He saw the broad Avenue of the Kings, where he had once ridden in triumph, newly arrived from Rinaghar to raise troops to crush the Helat rising. He had been young then, the Empire's golden prince. He remembered a night in golden Rinaghar, not long after his return from the slave wars, when he had fallen in love with the princess Kewara. Had his ruined face not prevented it, he would have shed a tear over her.

From his vantage point, gliding on the air currents, he

saw the Hanging Gardens, fabled across the Empire. Most of all he saw life and beauty, bustle and warmth, things that had no part in his present existence, trapped decaying in his hideous carapace. Had his life not taken a different path he might be part of it even now, walking with his beloved Kewara, watching their children and even grandchildren, accepting the acclamation of the crowd. In the loneliness of his cold, corrupted shell of a body, he yearned to be part of that vibrant hubbub, to live again. Most of all, he dreamed of rescuing his beloved Kewara from the House of the Dead and making her his queen. Was it possible? The Holy Child had the answer.

'This,' the Darkwing murmured, gazing down at the busy streets, 'will all be mine.'

Spotting Commander Rishal's villa, the Darkwing ordered a diversionary attack on the Temple of the Sun. The right flank of his fliers broke off, sweeping down on the saffron-robed Priests of Ra. The first assault carried off a dozen priests, hurling their bodies against the battlements and rousing the Sol-ket from their slumbers. Shrieking their war cries, the dark-fliers dragged a statue of Ra down from its pedestal, smashing it to pieces. In response to the onslaught, drums were soon beating and trumpets were sounding. Fifty cadets and half as many seasoned warriors, part of the skeleton garrison left behind by Commander Rishal, came running along the battlements. Seeing the broken bodies of the priests and outraged by the violation of the temple, they unleashed a hail of arrows on the dark-fliers. Soon they were hacking off the fallen creatures' heads with triumphant roars. Their celebration was premature. Unbeknown to them, the Darkwing's main objective wasn't the temple.

Leaving dozens of fliers wheeling about the roof of the villa to protect their master, the Darkwing and a handful of bodyguards entered the house. Soon they came across Mistress Serala. Seeing the monstrous intruder, she screamed and tried to run, but the Darkwing seized her.

'Where is she?' he snarled. 'Where is the girl Cusha?'

'Cusha,' the trembling Serala said, 'whatever can you want with that ungrateful wretch?'

The Darkwing's clawed hands squeezed her fleshy jaw. 'I ask the questions, old woman,' he said. 'Now, where is the girl?'

'Gone,' Serala stammered. 'I threw her out.'

The Darkwing placed a razor-sharp claw to her throat. 'You lie,' he hissed. 'Now tell me of her whereabouts or die.'

Serala's eyes were as wide as the Tiger Gates themselves. 'I swear by Almighty Ra,' she said. 'I am telling the truth. Why would I protect one of those cursed Helati?'

The Darkwing looked deep into her eyes, then released her in disgust. 'Where did she go? Why did you cast her out?'

Serala had crumpled to the tiled floor. 'She got involved with a Sol-ket, my daughter's betrothed.'

The Darkwing leaned forward. 'So your daughter knows something of this affair?'

Serala suddenly understood the way his thoughts were turning. 'No,' she said, 'by Ra, no, that is not what I meant.'

The Darkwing climbed the stairs.

'No!' Serala screamed.

But the Darkwing was already in Julmira's chamber. The young mistress tried to cry out for help but, by the time the scream was rising in her throat, the Darkwing had covered her mouth with his clawed hand. Satisfied that he had something to bargain with at least, he rose into the night sky clutching his prize.

6

Julmira carried on screaming all the way across the rice delta. In the end, the Darkwing had had enough of her protests. Opening his claws, he let her fall. Feeling herself tumbling free and seeing the green earth rushing towards her, Julmira redoubled her cries, yelping and shrieking like a bickering seagull. Cold, naked fear cascaded through her. She was going to die. Then, as quickly as her fall had begun, it stopped. She looked up to see a pair of dark-fliers holding her up by her sari. She begged the material to hold. As she hung forlornly beneath the inhuman creatures, the Darkwing approached.

'Now, will you stop your whining?' he said.

Julmira nodded frantically.

'Good,' the Darkwing said. 'Let's set you down.'

The moment Julmira's feet touched solid earth, her legs gave way and she crumpled to the ground. Struggling into a sitting position, she clutched her knees to her chest for comfort.

'What am I doing here?' she panted. 'What do you want?'

The Darkwing watched the sun going down and loosened his heavy robes to reveal his face. Julmira shuddered with revulsion.

'What I want,' he said, 'is information. Tell me about the girl Cusha.'

'Cusha?' Julmira said.

'Yes.'

'She is lazy and insolent, just one more Helat girl, no different from any other.'

The Darkwing listened, unimpressed. 'Was that the last time you saw her?' he asked. 'When your mother threw her out of the house?'

'Yes.'

The Darkwing seemed intent. 'There is something else,' he said. 'Tell me.'

'I thought she was dead,' Julmira said. 'My mother ordered her killed. It seems she escaped from the barracks. Deputy Commander Prakash pursued her towards the west. He took many men. How can she have survived?'

'How indeed?' the Darkwing said thoughtfully. 'And you haven't seen her since?'

Julmira shook her head.

'Has anything else happened?' the Darkwing asked.

Julmira thought for a moment. 'There was something,' she said. 'A shape-shifter came to my room.'

'A shape-shifter?'

'Yes,' Julmira said. 'She was disguised as a field-slave but she was a shape-shifter all right. She left in the form of a bird.'

'Then there's more to this than meets the eye,' the Darkwing murmured.

He paced the earth. Julmira watched him, silhouetted against the dying light.

'Do you know where the shape-shifter is now?' the Darkwing said.

'No.'

The Darkwing nodded. 'I believe you.'

'Does that mean you will let me go?' Julmira asked.

The Darkwing seemed to consider this. 'No,' he said. 'You are the daughter of an ax-Sol. I may yet find a purpose for you.'

At that, Julmira's heart turned to stone.

7

Two days later, Commander Rishal received a message. The saddle-weary envoy seemed to slow his pace as he came closer.

'Well,' Rishal demanded, 'what's the news?'

He was handed a piece of paper. The fingers that pressed it into his were trembling.

Kulmat searched the rider's face for some clue to the message's contents. He saw only fear. On reading the note, Rishal cried out.

'What is it, master?'

Rishal handed him the message. It was simple: *Your daughter has been abducted. She is in the hands of the Darkwing.*

Rishal rested a hand on Kulmat's shoulder. 'Julmira.'

8

Vishtar would have torn out his own tongue if he could. How could I have been so stupid? he thought. How could I have been so careless with my sister's life? He stared into the gloom of the tower and felt more wretched than he had for many months. 'Cusha,' he said out loud, imagining her already in the Darkwing's clutches.

No sooner had he uttered the word than he heard something. 'Aurun-Kai?' he said. 'Is that you?'

There was no answer. He had heard something an hour or so earlier, a rush of wind maybe, similar to the sound that accompanied the Darkwing's visit. He had been too miserable to pay it any attention. Now that he thought about it, it might have been the demon lord. But he only came to feed. He strained to hear. There it was again. It was a voice, a human voice, a *girl's* voice.

'Help me,' she cried, her voice echoing through the passages and winding staircases of the tower, resonating from the lower galleries.

'Cusha!' Vishtar raced down the steps. 'Don't be afraid. I'm coming.'

He made his way to the lower floor with mixed feelings. He so wanted to see his sister again. But if Cusha were here, they would both die. Vishtar reached a wall, another doorless chamber in this sealed tower.

'Who's there?' he asked.

'My name is Julmira,' the proud, angry voice replied. 'But you must know that.'

Vishtar realised what she meant. She thought he was in league with the Darkwing. 'I'm not your jailer,' he said. 'I'm a prisoner just like you.'

'And I'm supposed to believe that?'

'Whether you believe it or not,' Vishtar said, 'it's true.'

'Oh, go away,' Julmira said.

'When I first heard you,' Vishtar said, 'you were calling for help.'

'It was a moment of weakness,' Julmira said, her voice as bitter as myrrh. 'Hearing you coming, I realised how foolish it was to expect a rescuer in this desolate place. Whatever game you or your master are playing, I'm not interested. If you're going to kill me, just get on with it. I am my father's daughter. I will die with honour.'

Brave as her words were, Julmira couldn't hide the shake in her voice.

'I don't serve the Darkwing,' Vishtar said. 'I swear by the Four Winds, I've languished here for many years. Believe me, I *am* a prisoner.'

There was no answer.

'I'll leave if you wish,' Vishtar said.

Still no answer.

'I know you're suspicious and afraid,' Vishtar said. 'I once felt exactly as you do now. I was alone. I cried myself to sleep. Believe me though. I'm not your enemy.'

The silence continued. Shaking his head, Vishtar walked away. By the time he reached his own quarters, the girl was sobbing uncontrollably.

9

The Darkwing stood in the mangrove swamp, attracted by the smell of the recently slaughtered Sol-ket. Finding the place where Shamana had fought Prakash's band and saved Cusha's life wasn't difficult. In his years in exile in the land beyond the Great Wall, he had developed an instinct for the newly dead. He had been able to smell them from the walls of Parcep.

'Well, my brother,' the Darkwing said, discovering the creature that Prakash had become stumbling through the swamp, bewildered by his new incarnation, 'what tale do you have to tell me?'

The torn and mangled figure was barely recognisable but his robes distinguished him as a Sol-ket officer. He looked at the Darkwing. Struck by a ray of the sun as it filtered through the treetops, he screamed.

'Take care to shield your flesh,' the Darkwing commanded. 'The sun has not yet fully set.' The living corpse drew its tattered cloak over its face. 'That's it,' the Darkwing said.

Prakash's undead form jerked with a monstrous second life. Slowly, he finished protecting himself and approached his master.

'Welcome,' the Darkwing said. 'This is my universe of rage, of dark anguish – ' he hesitated for a moment, and then hissed ' – and revenge. Now, let's peel open what's left of your mind and see what happened here.' The Darkwing laid his palm on Prakash's ripped, blood-caked forehead. 'Give me your secrets.'

So the pair stood. For long moments the only sounds were the lapping of the salt water and the shriek of the night birds. Then the Darkwing stepped back, satisfied with the knowledge he had drawn from the creature. 'So that's what I'm looking for: a girl, two boys, a lowly cook.' The images from Prakash's murky consciousness flooded through his mind. A smile formed on his black, leathery lips. 'Ah yes, and the little matter of a shape-shifter.'

The Darkwing took Prakash's skull in his two hands. 'You have done well, my desolate child,' he said.

The Darkwing pressed his hands hard, like a vice. Immediately, Prakash's grotesque transformation was complete. His torn flesh turned a livid crimson hue. His eyes became obsidian. His fingers lengthened into razor-sharp claws. Next, his mouth opened to reveal a set of curved, deadly fangs. Finally, two huge, leathery wings sprouted from his back.

'You shouldn't cower in this mangrove,' the Darkwing said. 'Embrace your new, higher condition. Follow me and I will reward you with fresh blood.' He chuckled. 'You will gorge yourself on death.'

CHAPTER 10

The Caves of Suravan

I

The Helat fugitives had rowed all night through the maze of sometimes-uncharted channels that made up the backwaters of northern Parcep and southern Jinghara. This intricate latticework of waterways would present the assassin with a formidable puzzle to solve. They had taken it in turns to nap fitfully, rocked by the lazy rhythms of the shaded waterway. Nobody truly rested, however. Nobody lost sight of the quest. Grave risks seemed to lurk in every shadow. Strangely, in spite of their unheeded progress, Shamana was becoming more agitated and anxious with every oar stroke.

'What is it?' Cusha asked. 'What do you fear? Is it the Selessian?'

'It's the Darkwing,' Shamana explained. 'I see his eyes peering through the trees. I didn't expect him to be on our tail so quickly. Somehow, he has discovered your whereabouts, child.'

'The Darkwing?' Cusha asked. 'The lord of all demons is following us too?'

Shamana nodded. 'I hear the wing beats of his minions. They are far away but they are coming.'

Cusha searched in vain for some sign of the Darkwing's eyes as if, at any moment, their piercing glare would fix on her. 'You say he knows where I am,' she said. 'When will he come?'

'He knows where you *were*,' Shamana said, correcting her. 'There is a disturbance in Parcep. The demon lord has violated the household of Rishal-ax-Sol and taken Julmira hostage. For what purpose, nobody knows.'

'How do you know all this?' Qintu asked. 'Are you truly a witch?'

Shamana raised an eyebrow. 'If you didn't sleep so soundly, young Qintu, snoring like an over-fed hog, you might have seen a falcon come early this morning.'

The falcon was the form taken that day by her apprentice Aaliya.

'But if the Darkwing is truly searching for me,' Cusha said, 'then how can we shelter from his gaze? If the stories are true, he controls all the Lost Souls. Now we are pursued by both assassins and demons.'

'All that is true,' Shamana said. 'But that may work to our advantage.'

'How?' Harad asked.

'Because they may fight over us. The hunters, being in competition, could miss their prey.'

'So all is not lost?' Cusha asked.

'No,' Shamana said, 'all is not lost. We may yet avoid the Darkwing and his legions. With luck, these waterways will take us to the Land of the Four Rivers. From there it is but a few days' journey to Sangrabad.'

'What do you mean, *with luck*?' Qintu asked.

'There is one obstacle I wish to avoid,' Shamana said.

'And that is?'

'Have you heard of the caves of Suravan?' Shamana asked.

Qintu shook his head, as did Cusha and Harad.

'What about you, Murima?'

'Only that it is a place of evil repute.'

'What, worse than this?' Harad asked.

Shamana nodded. 'We face a terrible choice. Here, in the open, we are exposed. Yet I hesitate to enter Suravan. It is a place of death.'

'Then we avoid it,' Qintu said.

Shamana looked away. 'I wish it were that simple,' she murmured. 'So far, all things seem to have conspired to drive us towards Suravan. I feel the shadow of fate upon us. But who knows, we may yet steer clear of its gates. That depends on our pursuers.'

2

Many miles to the north-west, Barath was standing with his commanders on the battlements of Karangpur. 'What's happening?' he demanded.

The Darkwing's war host, until recently a dense, menacing tide, had begun to dissolve into a chaotic, disorganised mass. Fights were breaking out as the creatures' discipline dissolved before the eyes of the Imperial troops.

'Well, do any of you have the slightest idea what's going on?'

The most visible sign of change was the departure of

hundreds of dark-fliers, silhouetted against the setting sun.

'They're leaving,' Murak said, astonished.

'No,' another officer said, 'the mass of the beasts remains. But why are the fliers going? With their bombardment from the air and their numbers on the ground, they have us in a vice.'

Oled was the first to offer an explanation. 'It can only mean one thing,' he said. 'What unites the Lost Souls?'

Barath refused to venture an answer. He didn't want to hand the barbarian any more credibility.

'Let me tell you,' Oled said. 'It is the intelligence of their master, the demon lord. Something has distracted him. That's why the things are returning to their old ways.'

Barath considered his suggestion. 'For how long?' he asked.

Oled shrugged. 'I wish I knew. For as long as the Dark-wing has something else to think about, that's all I can say.' He was concerned. What could be more important than the assault on Karangpur? There was only one possibility. 'If you want to break the siege and survive with your men, Barath-Ra,' he said, 'then I would make preparations to attack their lines at first dawn.'

Barath's eyes met Oled's. There was no doubting the Sol-ket's hatred. He knew however, from personal experience, that the shape-shifter was no fool. He had saved the regiment once. Who was to say he couldn't do it again?

'Very well,' Barath said. 'Split the men into two watches. One sleeps while the other prepares. All warriors are to be at their posts an hour before first light. If the creatures are still without direction at break of day, we will break out.'

He did not even acknowledge Oled's contribution. Instead, he swept past and entered his quarters. Murak caught Oled's look and shook his head.

3

Gardep's long pursuit of Rishal's column had taken its toll. He was hot and weary. The Selessian robes chafed his skin and made him uncomfortable. Looking around warily, he unmasked himself and mopped the sweat from his face. It was to prove a costly error. For the last hour he had been watched by a priest of the Hotec Ra. The priesthood were the eyes and ears of Imperial rule. They struck fear into every living soul within the Empire's borders. The priestly secret police operated beyond the reach of the law.

Indeed, not even the martial code of the Sol-ket restrained these shaven-headed men in their saffron robes. With the Emperor's blessing, they were permitted to imprison, torture and kill as they wished. They were accountable to no man but the high priests Shirep and Linem and, finally, to all-powerful Muzal-ax-Sol himself. Being watched by any priest would have been dangerous. But this wasn't just any priest. The man concealed among the banyan trees had served in Parcep. He had recognised the Sol-ket officer masquerading as a Selessian. While Gardep took his rest, the priest stole away to report his discovery.

Several hundred yards beyond the camp's perimeter, Gardep stole a glance behind. He gave a deep sigh. There was nobody following him. Happy to have left the camp behind, he urged his horse up a steep rise. From the brow of the hill he could see the camp laid out before him. Banners snapped in the wind: scarlet and gold for the Sol-ket, black for the Selessians and white for the Vassyrians. The other, less well-represented nationalities had their own banners rippling gaily against the sky. An elephant trumpeted loudly, making men laugh and horses whinny. The rising night breeze made the sand on the more barren open ground away from the river stir like a giant corkscrew. Gardep, trained since childhood in the arts of war, felt his heart swell with pride. Then, knowing he would never be part of this expedition, he felt very alone.

'Let's get some rest,' Gardep said to his horse, kicking its flanks and raising a canter.

Back at the perimeter of the camp, one of the most feared men in the Empire lowered his spyglass.

'Send a message to Atrakon,' he ordered. 'Find out from the assassin why he has lost track of the Sol-ket.'

The priest, the one who had first spotted Gardep, hurried away to send a messenger pigeon. The others turned to receive orders from their master, Shirep-hotec.

'Wait until sundown,' he said. 'Once he has slipped into a deep sleep we will do what the heathen Selessians failed to do. We will take Gardep.'

4

Reassured that Aurun-Kai was not around, Vishtar made his way from the upper gallery where he slept and studied Julmira's cell. 'Are you awake?' he whispered. He pressed his lips to an air vent set in the wall. 'Julmira?'

There was no answer.

'Julmira, are you there?'

'I'm here.'

'So why didn't you answer?'

'Maybe,' Julmira answered, 'I don't care to walk so eagerly into your master's trap.'

Vishtar felt the first stirrings of exasperation. 'I told you,' he said, 'I don't serve the Darkwing. I loathe him. I am his captive just as you are.'

'Yes,' Julmira said, 'so you say.'

'Look,' Vishtar said, making a show of leaving, 'if you want to sit here and go mad with loneliness, that's your choice.' He took a few steps towards the stone steps that would lead him back to his quarters. He made sure Julmira could hear.

'Wait!' she said. There was panic in her voice.

'Are you sure?'

'Yes,' she said. 'I'm sure. What's your name? Why are you here?'

'I'm Vishtar,' he told her. 'I have been held here since I was a small boy.'

'But why would that monster take a child? It doesn't make sense.'

Vishtar smiled to himself. 'That depends on the child.'

'What's that supposed to mean?'

'I will explain when I know you better,' Vishtar said.

Julmira snorted. 'I'm not that interested in this precious identity of yours anyway.'

'How did you get here?' Vishtar said. 'The full story, I mean.'

Julmira embarked on her story, but when she reached Cusha's part in her tale, Vishtar gasped out loud.

'Cusha!' he cried. 'You know my sister!'

It was Julmira's turn to be taken aback. 'This has to be a trick,' she said after a moment's hesitation. 'By what co-incidence would I meet my maid's brother here, at the end of the Earth?'

'It's no coincidence,' Vishtar said. 'Think about it. United, my sister and I pose a danger to the demon lord . . .'

He pulled up short, realising he had said too much. Then, drawn on by the thought that this girl knew Cusha, Vishtar continued:

'Somehow, the Darkwing fears us and needs us at the same time. He went to your villa in the expectation of finding Cusha there. Discovering you instead, he took you as . . . I don't know . . . a bargaining counter.'

'Don't talk about me as if I were a trinket on a market stall,' Julmira protested.

'I didn't mean any disrespect,' Vishtar said.

There was a long silence.

'Have I offended you?' Vishtar asked.

'No,' Julmira said, 'not at all. Yours is the first kind voice I have heard since that thing abducted me.'

'The Darkwing isn't a thing,' Vishtar said.

'Then what?'

Vishtar explained about Prince Sabray and the creation of the monster from his ruined flesh.

'Is this true?' she asked. 'The creature that abducted me was once a prince of the court, our great Emperor's son?'

'Yes,' Vishtar said. 'But you are high born. How could you not know?'

'I am also a woman,' Julmira said, 'and not privy to such knowledge. As a general of the Empire, my father must know of the Darkwing's origins. He has never shared the information with me.'

After a few moments' silence she spoke again. 'But how do you know your sister's whereabouts?' she asked. 'And after all this time, too.'

'There is a bond between us,' Vishtar said. He told Julmira nothing else. Though he enjoyed her company, he was not ready to trust an ax-Sol.

5

Still listening for the approaching dark-fliers, Shamana led her companions towards the Suravan caverns. The heat of the day soon fell away and inside the stone walls something like eternal night was waiting.

'Why are people so afraid of Suravan?' Cusha asked, gazing at the cliffs, somehow massively silent and massively threatening.

'Once this complex was riddled with traps and fortifications to protect it from invaders,' Shamana answered. 'In truth, I know little of Suravan. Centuries ago, long before the Muzals, our world was very different. My hope is, within the precincts of these temples, we should have more chance of survival than out on those waterways.'

'You don't sound too sure,' Qintu said.

'I'm not,' Shamana agreed. 'In all honesty, I have thought of taking my chances in the open.'

'Then why don't we?' Harad demanded.

'Whether it is the Selessian we face,' Shamana said, 'or the Lost Souls, we are more vulnerable out here. We have to take our chances in the depths of the caverns.'

'So what *do* you know of these buildings?' Cusha asked, peering into its depths.

'Very little,' Shamana said. 'The Book of Scales issues dark warnings, but there are few details. There has to be a reason why nobody dares enter these portals.'

The boat started to glide down the narrowing channel into the enormous stone complex of Suravan. Dozens of closely set octagonal columns flanked the first vault that greeted them.

'Such craftsmanship,' Murima marvelled.

'Yes,' Shamana said, 'the detail on the demon heads is very fine indeed.'

'Demon heads!' Qintu exclaimed.

'Yes, there.'

Shamana was right. Carved into the columns at regular

intervals were recesses containing finely detailed marble heads. Their eyes popped and their tongues protruded.

'Lost Souls?' Harad asked.

'No,' Shamana said. 'These carvings commemorate a time before the age of the undead. They represent the children of the moon god Sangra.'

'That proves it then. It's true what you told us. The Sol-ket built Suravan.'

'It would seem so,' Shamana said. 'At least, their ancestors did, the people of ancient Jinghara. According to the rumours, for centuries, Suravan was one of their holiest shrines.'

'So what happened?'

Shamana scowled. 'Muzal's miserable dynasty happened. The first Muzal made Rinaghar his capital. All the religious artefacts he could have transported, he brought there. The wealth of the golden city was built on this pillage. The ancient temples were allowed to fall into disrepair, and with them the values that had inspired them.'

'But why destroy all this?' Cusha asked. 'This was their faith.'

'It was once,' Shamana said. 'Long ago, the people who became the Sol-ket shared a faith much like ours. Ra, the sun god and Sangra, the moon god, were seen as two sides of the same deity. The grotesque faces you see here don't represent evil but an attempt to ward it off. It is all about day and night, light and dark, balance.'

'The Sol-ket,' Cusha said, 'worshipping the Scales? I don't believe it.'

'It's true,' Shamana said. 'In some ways, in times gone by, we and they held similar ideas of how the world works. Then they decided that they must separate themselves from the other peoples of the world and conquer them. They introduced another idea, that the moon god Sangra was pure evil and Ra pure good. No longer would they see the world as unity and harmony, but as endless war. The age of conflict would only end with their conquest of the entire world. It was the tinkering of their foul priesthood that unleashed the Lost Souls on the world.'

'Shamana,' Harad said, 'surely you're not trying to tell us that we come from the same stock as the Sol-ket.'

'Of course,' Shamana said. 'All mankind traces itself back to the first woman, and the first man.'

'All mankind?' Qintu teased. 'Even you shape-shifters?'

'Especially we shape-shifters,' Shamana said, 'for we are closest to our true nature, when mankind understood that they were but superior beasts.'

'Look,' Cusha said, pointing up at the intricately carved ceiling.

Shamana spoke: 'Just as I said, you can see light and dark, line and relief in perfect balance. It makes you wonder, doesn't it? How did the craftsmen and priests who built this place become the cruel Sol-ket?'

They moved on past images of black basalt stone. There was Ra and there was Sangra. What shocked Shamana's four companions was the sight of the two gods standing arm-in-arm, like brothers. The only statues of the two gods they had seen in Parcep represented them as implacable enemies, constantly at war. The deeper the Helati penetrated into the complex, the more monumental the silence. They spoke only in whispers.

'What about the traps?' Harad asked. 'How do we know where they are?'

Shamana lit a makeshift torch to guide the way. 'I don't know,' she said. 'But our only hope is to find them and turn them to our own advantage.'

'And if we don't?' Qintu asked.

'If we don't,' Shamana answered, 'then the dark-fliers will corner us here. We will be caught like rats in a trap.'

6

Just before dawn Barath surveyed the wild throng outside the gates of Karangpur and came to his decision.

'The creatures are in disarray,' he said. 'For whatever reason, the Darkwing's attention is elsewhere. Give the order. On my signal, open the gates.'

Archers and spearmen moved silently to their positions on the battlements. Kneeling, backs to the battlement walls, they remained out of sight and braced themselves for action. By the first hazy light of dawn, Oled made his way past them and found Murak.

'Stay close by me,' he said under his breath. 'I will watch your back. You do the same for me.'

Murak instinctively glanced across at Barath and nodded. The hostility of a Sol-ket was for life, and this man was his superior officer. That meant his life was hanging by a thread.

'Our friendship has offended the general. All you can do now is prevent his anger destroying you.'

They were interrupted by the jangle of harness. Barath and his senior officers had mounted their horses. Another sound, low and gruff like a giant clearing his throat, vibrated through the earth beneath the garrison's feet. It was the gates. Their gears were beginning to move. Soon the warriors would see the ocean of demons awaiting them.

'Mount up!' The order ran down the line. The horsemen slid into their saddles. The infantry prepared to follow at jogging pace. 'Archers and spearmen.'

Javelins rattled. Arrows whispered from quivers. 'Open the gates!'

In unison, the three barriers that had been protecting the garrison swung open and the Imperial cavalry swept down the steep gradient towards the swarming night breed. With a roar, the horsemen smashed into the demon ranks. Oled, on foot, kept pace with the cavalry and started to lay about him with his battle-axe. Disorganised, uncoordinated, the demons fought as individuals, driven only by their primal blood lust. Without the Darkwing to direct them, they were hurled back by the Imperial onslaught. Even as the cavalry carved a wedge through the heart of the Lost Souls, the infantry swept in behind, reinforcing the bridgehead.

'Call up the remainder of the garrison,' Barath ordered. 'With their numbers behind us, we can finish this.'

Sure enough, within minutes the demon ranks had thinned sufficiently for the first horsemen to break through. Wheeling round, as only the most disciplined of cavalry can, the Sol-ket kept open the gap for their comrades to pour through.

'We've done it,' Murak shouted in triumph.

'The Lost Souls are broken,' Oled said. 'Just keep an eye on Barath. In the press of battle, he may yet move against us.'

Side by side, Oled and Murak hacked through the mass of the undead, leaving dozens beheaded and released from the demon contagion. With dust stinging his eyes and the roar of conflict in his ears, Oled searched for Barath. His every instinct told him to beware. That's when, through the fog of combat, he saw the glint of a spear point. Then another.

'Murak!'

Oled hurled himself at the young Sol-ket. He was relieved to see the two spears whistle overhead and bury themselves in a pair of advancing night-striders. Few survived a Sol-ket javelin attack. As the warriors crashed to the ground, Murak's mount fell with them, kicking wildly with fright. Oled saw Barath turn away and curse. His plan to kill Oled and his Sol-ket comrade under cover of battle had failed. When Oled finally emerged from the din of war, he turned to Murak, now back in the saddle.

'Didn't I tell you?' he said. 'Barath wants us both dead.'

Murak nodded. 'If I had any doubts, Oled, they're gone now.'

7

Something woke Gardep: the cry of a bird. Cusha haunted his dreams but the sound banished her face like a stone breaking the reflection on a lake. A bird, Gardep thought. Aaliya? He glanced at the horses. They were still. In spite of the animals' lack of reaction, Gardep was worried. There it was again, the whisper of grass against booted legs. Men were coming. There were two of them. No, three. Maybe more. Curling his fingers round the hilt of his sword, Gardep searched the dark for some sign of them. He felt for his throwing knives and eased himself up onto his elbows. In the blue-black gloom he glimpsed a shadow, then something else. There was an arrowhead pointing directly at him. With a cry, Gardep hurled the knife and scrambled across the clearing, drawing his sword. His victim was sobbing with pain and kneeling, the knife embedded in his thigh.

'Give yourself up!' a guttural voice ordered.

'Show yourself,' Gardep responded.

But there was to be no negotiation. Three shadows detached themselves from the darkness and charged him. Gardep planted his feet and prepared for battle. He cut down the first attacker with a single sword thrust. Aaliya, hiding in among the trees, killed the second with a single arrow. Already the third man was closing on Gardep. He was a better swordsman than the first, skilled in attack and defence. Gardep's opponent was at a disadvantage, however. It soon became apparent that he was holding back. His aim was clearly to incapacitate Gardep, not to kill him. This gave Gardep pause for thought. Even as he was bracing himself for a new attack, a sharp pain stung his throat. He clawed at his neck and felt the dart sticking out of his flesh. For a moment he was alert enough to try to dislodge it. More men were approaching.

'Aaliya,' he groaned. 'Go before they get you, too.'

Then the world swam and fell away from him. He crashed to the ground.

8

Leaderless, the Lost Souls did not follow Barath's troops across the Jingharan plain. Instead they wrought havoc on the now-deserted fort of Karangpur. Soon flames were licking its walls and towers. Acrid smoke stung the eyes of Barath's warriors as they made their escape.

'Mindless destruction,' Murak said. 'I can't believe these wild beasts are the same ones who attacked us with such purpose and order a few days ago.'

'The Darkwing's armies are growing,' Oled said. 'Every ancient cemetery offers them new recruits. Every body left on the battlefield is a new foot soldier. Believe me, it won't be long before his war host resumes its march towards the heart of the Empire.'

'And will you weep for us, Oled?' Murak asked. 'If Tiger-gated Parcep falls or even golden Rinaghar itself, will you regret the passing of the Children of the Sun?'

'I would mourn the deaths of the people,' Oled said.

'There are millions of men, women and children in the path of the demon army.'

'You are not answering the question I asked,' Murak said. 'What of the Empire, Oled? What of that?'

Oled checked that nobody was listening. 'Your Empire, my friend, is a curse on all mankind. Had I the power I would grind it to dust tomorrow.'

Murak looked back at the burning walls of Karangpur.

'Yet you fought with heroism to save us. Why?'

'You are men, not demons.'

'No,' Murak said, 'there is more than that.'

'You're right,' Oled admitted. 'I have a mission. It is something that will move the gears of time into motion.'

Murak questioned him with his eyes. 'I'm intrigued.'

'I'm sorry, Murak,' Oled said, 'but you surely don't expect me to tell you more. You are Sol-ket and I am one of the last surviving Tanjurs. There can be friendship between us, but trust . . .' He stretched out his hands in a non-committal gesture. 'Who knows? Suffice it to say, my interests and yours came together at a point in time. That is all I can say.'

'And our friendship,' Murak said, 'was that mere calculation?'

Oled shook his head. 'Don't confuse me with a man like Barath,' he said. 'I fight not to crush people under my heel, but for the good of all. I could not eat a hearty dinner after seeing a commando of one hundred men butchered. If I grasp a man's hand in friendship, there is no deceit in the act.'

His eyes met Murak's. 'One day soon I will find a way to complete my mission,' he said. 'The moment I see the sign, I will leave. Then I will be unable to protect you. Promise me you will never lower your guard. Because of our friendship, Barath is out to destroy you.'

'I promise,' Murak said. 'When we come across the Imperial Army I will ask to be reassigned. After my victory in the hills of Rinaghar, my commanders will not refuse my request.'

Oled smiled, but sadly. Soon he would have to leave all human company behind.

9

The first face Gardep saw when he recovered his senses was Shirep's. He recognised the priest from his visit to Rinaghar.

'Did you sleep well, my brave Sol-ket?' Shirep asked.

Gardep tried to reply but a bitter taste filled his mouth. He wanted to vomit.

'Yes, the effects of the drug will take some time to fade,' Shirep said.

Gardep found it painful to move but, by slowly turning his head, he ascertained that he was bound spread-eagled against one of the trees in the clearing. At least they hadn't taken him back to the camp. He did not want to face Rishal.

'I was most surprised when I discovered you were following Commander Rishal's column,' Shirep said. 'It seems a suicidal course for you to take, Gardep.'

Gardep met the priest's gaze.

'Yes, I know your name, Sol-ket,' Shirep said, 'but that is all I know.' He picked an iron brand from the camp fire. It was glowing red. 'Maybe you would like to answer a few questions.'

Gardep said nothing.

'Why did you break your Sol-ket code?'

Gardep watched the brand.

'Where were you going with those Helat scum?'

Shirep brought the glowing point close to Gardep's face. 'How did you give Atrakon the slip?' Shirep traced Gardep's features with the brand, almost brushing the surface of his skin. 'Why, when it might endanger your life, did you return?'

Gardep clamped his lips shut and shook his head. Shirep returned the brand to the fire. 'Oh, don't tell me you're going to resist,' he said. 'Courageous refusal is the stuff of melodrama, not real life. All men break. Why delay the inevitable? You are forcing me to act against my true nature. Gardep, I am a man of peace, a priest. I would rather sit in the Temple of Ra reading the scriptures than hurt a man.'

Gardep stared back with disbelieving eyes. He knew the reputation of the Hotec-Ra. The Sol-ket killed in order to conquer. The Hotec-Ra killed out of religious conviction. Either way, there was no mercy for their foe.

'I do hate torture,' Shirep said, the smile on his lips belying his words. 'The smell of burning flesh, the screams, the final confession, it is all so predictable. Why, proud Gardep, do you want to subject yourself to it?'

Horns echoed in the distance. Gardep turned towards the camp.

'Yes, that's Rishal rousing his column,' Shirep said. 'You'd like to go with them, wouldn't you, Gardep? I wonder, do you hope, through some feat of arms, to rejoin the Sol-ket?'

Again, he toyed with the brand. 'But why return? That's what I don't understand. You must know there is no way back into the ranks of the Sol-ket. Remove this feeble Selessian disguise and Rishal will have you executed and fed to the vultures. Your actions perplex me.'

Still Gardep maintained his silence.

'Very well,' Shirep said, handing the brand to one of his men. 'You have forced my hand.' He turned to the man. 'See if you can loosen his tongue.'

10

'We are deep inside the rock,' Shamana said. 'I feel it, as monumental as death, weighing down on me.'

'There she goes again,' Qintu said. Then he lurched forward. 'What a place to put an iron bar,' he said, rubbing his leg.

'What did you say?' Shamana demanded, her green eyes flashing with fear.

'There was an iron bar on the floor,' Qintu answered.

Shamana listened for a moment, then screamed a warning. 'Down!' she cried. 'Flatten yourself on the ground.'

No sooner were the words out of her mouth than the rock groaned and opened and a huge pendulum, in the shape of a scythe, swung across the passage, missing Qintu by inches.

'By the Four Winds!' he gasped, feeling the brush of wind caused by the deadly instrument.

The pendulum swung back, cutting a channel in the ground between Qintu and Harad, sending shards of rock arrowing.

'Stay where you are,' Shamana ordered. 'Don't move.'

But the danger wasn't over. Now it wasn't just Shamana who could hear long-unused mechanisms grinding into motion. Moments after the pendulum had been released sharpened bolts hissed through the air, cracking against the opposite wall. Then something fell from the ceiling.

'Now,' Shamana yelled. 'Run. Follow in my footsteps.'

They did their best to keep up. As they reached the narrow passage ahead a heavy net, weighted by metal shot, fell to the floor. Seconds later, javelins thudded down from above, intended to spear any caught intruder. Qintu only survived because Shamana hurled him bodily out of harm's way. This time there were no jokes.

'Maybe we should backtrack,' Harad said. 'Even the night breed couldn't be worse than this. In this hell-hole we don't even know where the danger is coming from.'

Shamana stopped dead.

'What now?' Harad asked, his voice full of dread.

Everyone clustered round the silent Shamana. They saw what she was looking at. Even the priestess of the Scales was shocked by what she had discovered.

'It can't be,' Murima said.

But there it was. A vast relief was carved into the rock, giant stone figures emerging from the wall as if they were alive. There was a battle scene in which warriors fought and died. Horses reared and battle-elephants raised their trunks. Arrows fell like rain. Nor were the ranks of the fighters made up solely of humans. The demons made their appearance too: dark-fliers and night-striders. But there was more, much more. Rising abruptly in the distance, but dominating the entire wall somehow, was the Black Tower of myth. Doorless, windowless, unmanned, the vast structure appeared to point, at one and the same time, upwards to the heavens and downwards to four figures that dominated the foreground.

'Gardep,' Cusha breathed.

The warrior was unmistakeably the young Sol-ket whose actions had led her to this place. Only one thing was different. A long scar ran from the corner of his eye to his jaw. He looked older than the raw cadet who had stared at her at Julmira's betrothal, haunted somehow.

'And you, my sister,' Harad murmured.

Sure enough, the startled young woman caught fleeing from the battle was Cusha herself. The features were hers. The doll with its Night Orchid symbol was hers. The scarred throat was hers. Level with her face was the representation of the object they were seeking, a stone replica of the memory lamp of Sangrabad.

'And the wolf?' Cusha asked, recovering her voice. 'Why is there a wolf?'

'Show them, Shamana,' Murima asked. She met the priestess's stare. 'Yes, Shamana, I have known your true identity for some time.'

Shamana returned the look. Yes, it seemed to be saying, just as I know yours. Gathering all her strength, she became a form she had not assumed in many a long year, a grey wolf.

'The She-Wolf of Tanjur,' Murima said, 'the rebel leader I watched in awe all those years ago.' To everyone's surprise, she put her palms together and bowed. 'All hail, sole surviving leader of the Army of the Free.'

Returning to her human form, Shamana smiled and stroked Cusha's face. 'There is so much for you to take in, my child,' she said. 'But there is one more piece of news I must give you.'

In the relief Cusha was holding the hand of an adolescent boy, the fourth character in the central group. Shamana ran her hand over the boy's features.

'This, dearest Cusha, is your brother.'

Cusha stood before the statue and a single tear ran down her cheek.

CHAPTER 11

The Demons Rally

1

As Atrakon Ebrahin stood before the entrance to Suravan, he didn't realise that death was approaching in a crimson swarm that would soon block out the sun. He found fresh footprints in the soil and a boat, recently abandoned to judge by the scraps of food left inside. There was no sign of staleness or mould. He stared into the dark of the tunnels. Though he didn't know why, the hairs rose on the back of his neck. 'Are you man or child?' Atrakon demanded of himself. 'Do you sleep with a candle by your bed to ward off evil spirits? Look around. Architecture, that's all there is. They're blocks of stone, lifeless, inert and utterly harmless. The statues do not move. There is no heart beating inside those marble breasts.'

He started to move forward. 'It is time to complete your mission, Ebrahin.'

He was still standing at the entrance to the complex when he heard a sound, like the whisper of a southern wind through the coastal palm trees. At first it was a single sound, like a strong breeze or the rush of water. Soon, however, it was possible to distinguish many smaller notes that made up its constituent parts. It was like the patter of many feet or the beating of thin drumsticks on stretched animal skin.

'What is that?' Atrakon asked out loud.

It reminded him of the sound of the night breed. But it was broad daylight. He turned to the west, switching his unease from the gloom of the caves to the vivid blue skies. That's when he saw it, a dark pattern almost like a bruise or blemish spreading across pale skin. It appeared black at first but soon it lightened into brown, then a dark crimson.

'By the Almighty!' he gasped. 'Dark-fliers.'

He stared disbelievingly at the blazing sun. What were they doing hunting in broad daylight and in such great numbers? Didn't the things usually maraud under the cover of darkness? It wasn't even the time of the Blood Moon – that was still many days away. But there was no dismissing the evidence of his eyes. Recovering his composure, Atrakon shot his first arrow and slew his first flier. Soon the Selessian's quiver was emptying and, though the crimson demons fell from the sky in large numbers, it barely seemed to have any effect on the vast swarm. As the blizzard of dark-fliers swirled around him snapping and slashing, Atrakon drew his sword.

The weapon seemed to blur in the air as he used all his arts to cut the fliers down, but still they came, in ever-increasing numbers, their hissing and shrieking exploding in his brain. He felt a hot pain sear his flesh. Clutching his throat and seeing blood spurting between his fingers, he toppled, face first, into the river.

2

Vishtar visited Julmira at least twice a day. Each time he had to spend a few minutes reassuring her that she wasn't going to die. There were occasions when he wanted to shake her.

'Has Aurun-Kai been to see you?' he asked on his latest visit.

'He came with my food,' Julmira said.

'Doesn't his appearance scare you?' Vishtar asked.

'No.'

'You must be very brave.'

'No,' Julmira explained. 'You don't understand, Vishtar. I have never seen him.'

'But you must have,' Vishtar said. 'He brings your food, doesn't he?'

'Yes,' Julmira said, 'but he passes it through a hatch in the wall.'

'A hatch?' Vishtar said, looking along the brickwork. 'But how can that be? These walls are solid. I thought the Darkwing and Aurun-Kai used magic to pass through them.'

'Maybe it isn't magic,' Julmira said.

'If there is a mechanism to open the hatch, then there might be one to open the door,' Vishtar said. 'I'm going to get you out, Julmira.'

'You have been very kind,' she answered.

'It is out of pure selfishness that I come,' Vishtar said. 'You are the first human being I have spoken to in so many years.' He pressed his face close to the vent. 'Julmira,' he said, 'think back to the night you came. Do you remember *how* the Darkwing opened your cell?'

'No,' she said. 'I was terrified. I kept slipping in and out of consciousness. I woke up lying on this floor, with no door or window.'

'Can you show me where the hatch is?' Vishtar asked. For the first time he believed, really believed, that escape might be possible. 'Tap the wall so I can look for it, maybe.'

'So you really think we can escape?' For the first time since she had come to the Black Tower, Julmira sounded excited.

'Yes.'

'Oh Vishtar, if only that were true. My father would reward you with many dinar.'

Vishtar was disgusted at the thought of accepting money from a Sol-ket. 'I don't want money,' he said.

For hours they sat talking, until Aurun-Kai's footsteps rang on the steps from the upper galleries. Slipping away from Julmira, Vishtar climbed the stairs and met Aurun-Kai. He was in an open area where a pile of illustrated Lyrian works was stored.

'You are awake early,' Aurun-Kai said.

Vishtar smiled. That meant it was daylight outside. It also meant he must have sat up most of the night talking to Julmira.

3

That night, as the campfires burned low, Oled raised his head. Somebody was coming, one such as he. He glanced at Murak, then stole away. Once he had found a quiet spot Oled transformed into a vulture and flew to a nearby ridge. There, a sea eagle joined him. Secure in the knowledge that they were alone, they each returned to their human form. It was the same visitor he had received after the fall of Zindhar.

'You bring news, Aaliya,' Oled said.

Shamana's apprentice drew close. 'On your mother's instructions I have been following a traitor Sol-ket, Gardep. The Hotec-Ra have him. This warrior is important to our mission but it is beyond my strength to liberate him alone. He needs our help, brother Oled.'

Aaliya related what she knew. Oled was packing his belongings when he heard Murak stir.

'You're going, aren't you?' Murak asked.

Oled reached out his right hand. 'I told you that this time would come,' he said. 'Remember what I said, Murak; watch Barath. He means you harm. He sees any Sol-ket who befriends a shape-shifter as a traitor.'

Murak clasped Oled's hand. 'Yes, I understand. Will I ever see you again?'

'One day, maybe,' Oled said, 'at the end of the time.'

'Do all you shape-shifters talk in riddles?' Murak asked.

'Yes,' Oled said, smiling, thinking of a greater riddle-maker than he would ever be, 'every single one.'

Sadness came over him for a second. Every single one? But there were only a handful of shape-shifters alive in the whole world, just a few grains of sand floating in the ocean of humanity.

'Farewell, brother Murak,' he said.

'Yes, farewell to you, Oled Lonetread. May Ra watch over you.'

Oled shook his head at the Sol-ket blessing. 'And may the Four Winds grace you with a good life,' he answered.

'Wait,' Murak said. He slipped a dagger from his belt. 'Take this,' he said. 'It will remind you of our brief friendship.'

Oled took the knife. 'Thank you.'

With that, Oled ran crouching between the sleeping men. Murak watched until he vanished into the hot, scented night. Then he smiled and looked towards the east. Moments later, he saw a bird cross the sky, followed by a giant fruit bat. Oled pursued Aaliya, keeping low over the trees lest some marauding dark-flier band should see him. He was in luck. Not a soul stirred that night, even a lost one. Hour after hour he flew until, at last, he saw Commander Rishal's campfires. But that wasn't his destination. Some miles further on, as the dawn light filtered through the trees, he saw what he had been looking for: a single doused fire and four figures. Two were sleeping. One kept watch. The last was strung up, the stench of his burned flesh filling Oled's nostrils.

4

For two evenings running, Vishtar concealed himself in a recess at the bottom of the stone steps leading to Julmira's cell. Each night he watched the same strange spectacle. Aurun-Kai would make his painfully slow descent and look around before crossing the stone floor and inserting a hand into the brickwork. Vishtar watched keenly. He counted the rows of bricks and memorised the spot. Julmira had tapped on the wall as he had told her but it was an inexact science. He needed to be sure. Squashing himself into the recess, he watched a section of wall slide open, just wide enough and tall enough to insert a tray with Julmira's meal on it. Aurun-Kai would then close the hatch and wait patiently until Julmira announced that she had finished. Then he would gather the tray and make his way back up the steps.

'Well,' Julmira asked, the moment Vishtar assured her the coast was clear, 'did you see how he did it?'

'Yes, let me try.'

'Are you sure he isn't watching?'

'I'm sure,' Vishtar said, before remembering that Aurun-Kai had surprised him once before.

He crept over to the foot of the stone steps and listened. Eventually, convinced that Aurun-Kai had retired to his quarters, Vishtar felt for the crevice. His fingers slid between the bricks.

'It's an optical illusion of some sort,' he said. 'The bricks are not flat and regular as I'd thought, but overlaid in such a way the opening lies in shadow. You'd swear the mortar was solid but there is a gap wide enough to get my hand inside.'

He felt around for a moment.

'Can you open it?' Julmira asked.

'No. Oh, where is it?'

Then he felt it, a small lever. The moment he pressed it, he heard something roll back inside the wall and the section of brick swung open.

'Could it be the same with the door?' Julmira asked excitedly.

'Yes,' Vishtar said, 'and the entrance to the tower itself. Julmira, I will search every inch of the place until I find both doors. We're going to get out.'

5

Directed by Aaliya, Oled stole through the undergrowth leading to the camp. He recognised the saffron robes of the Hotec-Ra. He had seen them when they came to interrogate Turayat about the situation at Zindhar. Even the arrogant Turayat had trembled in his shoes at their approach. How Oled despised their casual cruelty. Peering through the gloom he could see their handiwork already.

Their prisoner, a youth, barely more than a boy, was tied to a tree. His head was drooping. But it was his face that drew Oled's attention. A livid burn ran the length of one side of his face.

Poor lad.

Then he shifted his gaze to the Hotec-Ra. One was keeping watch. Lazily. It was obvious he wasn't expecting trouble, not here, still close to the heart of the Empire and with Rishal's column close by. The others appeared to be asleep. Oled loosened the straps that held his battle-axe. He would show no mercy to these torturers. With a loud roar, Oled burst from the undergrowth. Aaliya covered him with her arrows. The sentry tried to resist but Oled beheaded him with one blow. The first of the sleeping men died without opening his eyes, an arrow through the throat. His companion was a different kettle of fish. His eyes snapped open. Appraising the situation immediately, he scrambled to his knees and started begging.

'Please,' he stammered. 'Don't kill me. I am worth more to you alive than dead.'

'I'm not a bandit,' Oled snarled. 'I don't take hostages.'

But the Hotec-Ra wasn't done. 'Do you know who I am? My name is Shirep-hotec, son of the most reverend Linem. My father has the ear of the Emperor himself. You want gold? I can get you gold. What do you want? Land? Women? Name your price.'

Oled continued to watch the kneeling man.

'I can offer you ten thousand dinar.'

Oled's face was expressionless.

'Not enough? Very well, I'll make it twenty thousand. I will throw in a villa and a harem of many maidens. Please, just name your price.'

The longer Oled listened to Shirep's pathetic begging, the more he suspected that it was an act. The priest hadn't got to be second-in-command in the feared Hotec-Ra by being a craven coward.

'Still your damned tongue!' Oled yelled.

That single moment of anger almost cost him his life. While his voice was still echoing through the night, Shirep made his move, drawing a tiny dagger from his robes and slashing at Oled. The blade cut Oled's padded jacket open.

'Now die, barbarian!' Shirep howled, throwing himself at Oled.

But Aaliya's bow protected the giant. An arrow pierced Shirep's hand and he dropped the knife.

'I suppose you're going to start begging again,' Oled said.

Shirep sneered. 'What's the point?' he said. 'It's obvious I'm not going to change your mind. Finish it.' Shirep exposed his throat. 'Make the kill quick, barbarian.'

With a single cut, Oled dispatched the warrior-priest. After checking that all three had been cleanly beheaded and would not return as Lost Souls, he untied the prisoner's bonds and lifted him down.

'Can you hear me, boy?'

Oled laid the youth down on the grass. 'Aaliya.'

She came over and examined Gardep. 'I will treat the wound,' she said. 'He is strong. He will recover quickly.'

Oled stared at the Sun tattoos of a Sol-ket. 'So why the Selessian robes?' he wondered out loud.

Aaliya smiled. 'I'll explain,' she said.

6

'No, my children,' the Darkwing commanded as they gathered hungrily around the senseless Atrakon. 'Leave him!'

The fliers cowered before their master's approach. The Darkwing drew Atrakon up onto the riverbank and ran a hand over his forehead, much as a surgeon examines his patient, teasing out his memories.

'What is your purpose here?' he said. 'Why do you pursue the Holy Child?'

He continued to probe into the Selessian's mind. Interest sparked in his black eyes. For several moments, he observed the bounty hunter, a plan forming in his mind.

'Let him live,' he told the dark-fliers, and they retreated to await his orders.

Sensing that the black-robed warrior would soon be stirring, the demon lord withdrew but, from a discreet distance, continued to observe. Atrakon recovered from the attack soon after. Once he was fully conscious, he bathed his face and started to explore his surroundings.

Suravan is dangerous, Atrakon thought, possibly deadly. But he would never be able to track the Helati if he didn't enter the caves. Even a man as versed in the arts of the hunt as he would be unable to find them by any other means. Deciding to forego the delights of Jinghara's backwaters, Atrakon knelt, preparing himself for the secrets of Suravan.

'You didn't let me in on this little secret, did you, Shirep?' he murmured. 'No wonder you were prepared to offer me my freedom in exchange for this mission.' It was indeed the greatest test of his murderous career. 'But I will find the girl,' he announced to nobody in particular.

'Yes,' the Darkwing murmured, watching Atrakon from far away, 'perhaps you will find the girl.'

Where Atrakon went, the Darkwing reasoned, the Holy Child could not be far. With the assassin's skills as a tracker, he might be of use in locating Cushā. The demon lord issued his final orders to his fliers: enter Suravan and find the fugitives. Bring the Holy Child to the Black

Tower. Alive. Warm. Once she was reunited with Vishtar the entire world would be his. For her companions had no purpose. They must die. The Darkwing smiled, sure that this time he would have the girl. But, if his demon children failed again, he might yet turn to this Selessian.

7

'Who are you?' Gardep asked the moment his eyelids flickered open.

'My name is Oled. This is Aaliya.'

Gardep's gaze seemed to clear. 'Where are the Hotec-Ra?'

'Dead,' Oled said simply.

Gardep sat up. 'All of them?'

Oled pointed out the fresh graves. 'Every one.'

'Did you complete the kill?' Gardep asked.

'I severed the heads and laid them at right angles to the bodies,' Oled said. 'They won't rise again, if that is what you're thinking.'

Remembering his torture, Gardep raised his hand to his face. He discovered that the wound had been covered with a poultice and bandaged. He opened his shirt and found that the wounds on his chest had also been treated.

'Why did you help me?' he asked, looking from Oled to Aaliya. 'Don't you realise what you have done? That was Shirep-hotec, warrior-priest and hunter of heretics. If the Hotec-Ra discover you did it, they will pursue you for all time.'

Oled chuckled. 'What's new about that?'

'How can you laugh?' Gardep cried. 'Listen to me. You are obviously barbarians. Perhaps you are unfamiliar with our ways. You don't know what you have done.'

'We know exactly what we've done,' Oled said. 'We

killed your tormentors. Now, I'm going to tell you what I know about you, Gardep. You fill in the rest.'

8

Atrakon Ebrahin ate alone that night as he would for many days to come, nibbling his meagre rations in the echoing chambers of Suravan. His neck was bound with a piece of torn cloth. Atrakon prayed that the contagion couldn't be passed on through a claw slash, of which he had several on his skin. He didn't know that the feared Shirep-hotec, the man who had given him his mission to kill, was dead. How was he to know? He was many days' ride from the camp where Oled was tending Gardep's wounds.

Atrakon sat brooding. The mission had cost him dear. His intended successor Zahar was dead and the demons had very nearly done for him too. For a moment he felt a tremor of suspicion. Why had they let him live? But he was unable to find an answer. How had all this come to pass? It had seemed such a simple mission when he accepted it from Shirep. Only the mention of the She-Wolf had seemed unusual and she was old. But he had clearly underestimated the witch.

Many a man might have turned back after suffering as Atrakon had, but he had good cause to go on. He took a small keepsake from his cloak, a love poem he had written to his wife Leila years before. She was long dead, the victim of a local warlord. He had tried to entice her to his house. When she resisted, he had simply cut her. Their unborn child had died with her. At a stroke, Leila's murderer had destroyed an entire family.

'But I avenged you, my love,' Atrakon murmured, pressing the paper to his lips.

It was true. He had avenged her, but at a price. The warlord, discovering the identity of the woman's husband, had gone into hiding in the governor's castle. Atrakon, driven half-mad with grief and the desire for vengeance, had sought audience with the governor, a greedy, good-for-nothing Sol-ket who had retired from warfare and run to fat, making his fortune from bribes.

'Name your price,' Atrakon had said. 'Tell me what you want. I will pay it gladly. Just give me a few minutes with the man who murdered my wife and take no retribution for what I do to him.'

But the price had been beyond Atrakon's imagining. He would have to sell himself into the governor's service for ten years and do his bidding without question. He could buy himself out, but at the price of five thousand dinar a year. So choked by despair had Atrakon been by the loss of his wife however, that he accepted the bargain gladly. He slew his wife's killer that night, making him kneel and beg for his worthless life before finishing him, but that act had begun a long nightmare.

Atrakon, once as good and noble a man as had ever donned the Selessian black, a true believer renowned for his honour, had become an assassin, a paid butcher. He had killed many men, some bad, some no doubt good. He tried not to think about it, but the faces of the innocent dead haunted his dreams. After some years Shirep had heard of Atrakon's expertise and purchased his debt from the governor. The day he had taken Shirep's latest commission, to capture Shamana and Cusha, Atrakon had believed it would be his last. He had accepted the mission to pursue the Helati in the expectation that he could finally return to Selessia a free citizen. The debt would be discharged. Yes, at long last he would be free.

9

The Helati picked their way along miles of gloomy passages, illuminating them with torches. They were more cautious now, fearful about triggering some deadly device. Here and there, Shamana's flickering torch would pick out a statue, a relief and wall painting. They were now in the most remote, ancient reaches of Suravan. One image dominated everything, the Black Tower.

'Why is the tower so important?' Cusha asked, examining the latest representation of it.

'It holds your brother. I have had someone looking for it for many years. They say it lies beyond the Demon Wall, in a place where none dare venture lest they unleash the wrath of the Lost Souls. Udmanesh fled there to keep alive the Scaline faith.'

'You're sure Vishtar's there?' Cusha asked.

'I believe so,' Shamana replied. 'I have had someone watching it. We will find out for sure when we reach Sangrabad.'

'*If* we reach Sangrabad,' Qintu grumbled. 'Do you even know where we're going?'

'There has to be a way through,' Shamana said. 'Why would there be all these carvings of the Black Tower if it led nowhere?'

Qintu was about to say something when Shamana held up her hand.

'What's wrong?' he asked, but by the time the words had left his lips he could hear it himself.

First there was a sound like a rushing torrent. Then he heard something like a thousand running footsteps. Finally, in a chilling moment, he realised what it was: wing beats.

'Run!' Shamana screamed, drawing her bow.

'We can't leave you like this,' Cusha cried. 'There are too many of them.'

'Just go,' Shamana said. 'The passage is narrow. I can hold them off until you have made your escape.' She didn't even convince herself. 'Go!' she screamed, seeing the crimson fliers sweeping towards her.

'I won't leave you,' Cusha said, drawing her sword.

'Damn you, child,' Shamana cried, the tears blurring her eyes, 'this is no time for futile gestures.'

'It's no gesture,' Harad said, drawing his own sword.

'We live together or die together,' Murima said, availing herself of her son's bow and arrows.

The screams and shrieks of the dark-fliers echoed through the passages of Suravan, mingling with the shouts of the five companions. Arrows hissed and swords slashed through corrupted flesh. At one point Cusha tripped over an obstacle and cursed. Harad offered a hand.

'Look out!' Cusha yelled.

But the dark-flier slammed into Harad, throwing him to the ground. Gripping the obstacle over which Cusha had stumbled, he smashed it into the creature's distorted face.

'We can't hold them off,' Murima panted.

That's when Harad saw what he had used to strike the flier. It was a metal grid covering an opening. 'Down here!'

Murima hesitated. 'Do you have any idea where it leads?'

Harad shook his head, striking down another dark-flier. 'Does it matter?' With that, he led the way into the shaft.

10

Having observed Atrakon's progress, the Darkwing returned to Karangpur. He saw the bickering war host and the smoking remains of the fortress and he scowled. His plan had been to leave the fortifications strewn with enemy dead. He'd wanted the officers' heads impaled on spikes above the gates to strike fear into any armies the Empire might send against him. He was angry with himself for neglecting his troops.

'Silence, my children,' he said, standing high on the battlements of Karangpur. In moments he had quelled their rage. 'The Warriors of the Sun have slipped through our lines but they should not celebrate too soon.'

He turned his eyes towards another sunset. 'Blessed night approaches,' he said. 'It is the end of Murjin. The Blood Moon rises once more. Soon your bodies will burn with a furious power.' He spread his wings and raised his arms wide. 'I have thrown you against the foe at his strongest. Now is the time to fight on our own terms.'

The moon rose behind him, its scarlet-tinged silvery light illuminating the faces of the undead.

'By the time this moon sets,' he promised, 'the men in Barath's column will be food for the vultures.'

The air filled with a hideous chorus that could be heard not only by Barath's soldiers, but in the camp of the Lion of Inbacus, brave Rishal himself.

11

The same sound even reverberated as far as the lonely spot where Gardep and the Tanjurs, Aaliya and Oled, were talking.

'Lost Souls!' Gardep gasped. 'Here.'

Oled looked north. 'It is the Blood Moon,' he said. 'The Darkwing has returned.' He thought of Murak. 'By the Four Winds, Gardep,' he murmured. 'He means to attack tonight.'

'How far away are they?' Gardep demanded. 'Can he reach Rishal's column?'

Oled still had his eyes trained on the distant plains. 'By the sound of those roars, I'd say yes. Even we are not safe.'

'I don't care for my safety,' Gardep said, rising to his feet and approaching his horse. 'I care about my duty.'

'Duty?' Oled gasped. 'You've just been tortured by your Imperial masters. What, in the name of all that is holy, do you owe them?'

Gardep continued his preparations.

'What are you doing?' Oled asked.

'I am going to fight.'

'Don't be a fool,' Aaliya said. 'You have suffered a terrible ordeal. You are weak and your wounds are still open and angry.'

'I will stand shoulder to shoulder with my brother Sol-ket,' Gardep insisted.

'Even though they have disowned you?' Oled said. 'Even though they would have killed the girl you love?' He seized Gardep's shoulders and shook him. 'Even though they have just tortured you?'

'Yes,' Gardep said, shrugging the shape-shifter away, 'even so. A senior officer died because of my actions. My blood brother thinks me a traitor. My heart is heavy with shame. I must recover my honour.'

Oled rolled his eyes. 'I don't understand you Sol-ket.'

'I don't need you to understand,' Gardep said. 'I need you to fight. Will you ride with me, Oled Lonetread?'

Oled watched Gardep climbing painfully into his saddle, masking himself with his Selessian headdress.

'There is a condition,' Oled said.

'Name it.'

'After the battle we ride west. You're needed there.'

Gardep sensed that there was truth in Oled's words. He had tried to deny his destiny too long. 'If that is where Cusha is, then yes, you have my promise.'

Oled smiled and glanced at Aaliya. 'Let's fight.'

CHAPTER 12

The Bloody Bandage

1

Murak stirred. What was that? Rubbing his eyes, he rolled over and looked through the light cast by the dying embers of the camp fire. He saw nothing. He listened. There was the croak of frogs and the chirping of crickets. Had he been mistaken? Had he imagined that unearthly scream? Then he saw other men's eyes searching the darkness. Apprehension stirred inside him.

'Did you hear something?' Murak asked.

There were anxious nods.

Murak rose to his feet and drew his sword. 'Sentries,' he said, 'what reports?'

'There was a noise,' one said, 'over there.'

'What kind of noise?'

Then there was no need for questions. Staccato shrieks pierced the air followed by a chorus of blood-chilling roars.

'It's the Lost Souls,' Murak said. 'They're on the move. Rouse Barath-Ra.'

'There's no need,' Barath said, emerging from the blackness. 'I heard them myself.' He gave his orders. 'Bank up those fires. If it is to be a night attack, then we need light or it could turn into a massacre. Paint the perimeter with Lyrian oil and light it.'

Teams of infantry set to work. They had barely begun when another chorus of roars and howls echoed across the plains, this time accompanied by the beat of war drums.

'It's the Darkwing,' Murak said.

'Of course it's the Darkwing,' Barath snarled. 'It's the night of the Blood Moon. By Ra, now you'll all understand what it's like to be a Helat. Well, we Sol-ket are made of sterner stuff than the wretched slaves. Archers, spearmen, look to the sky.'

But it was from the earth beneath his feet that the first attack came. Not five yards from where Murak was standing a young Sol-ket screamed in terror. Blackened fingers, bones barely covered by the rotting flesh, were clawing at his legs. The night-striders had infiltrated the camp and buried themselves in shallow graves. Murak ran to the soldier's aid, but even as he started hacking at the creature that had him by the ankle, more erupted from beneath the ground.

'To arms!' roared Barath, joining his men in the desperate attempt to keep the night-striders at bay. 'They draw renewed strength from the Blood Moon. Victory or death!'

Even as the hand-to-hand fighting flared around the camp, the dark-fliers were beginning their onslaught from the sky. In the light of the fires the archers and spearmen started their work. With Barath preoccupied fighting the undead as they tunnelled from below, Murak took charge of the ring of archers and spearmen. He displayed a cool assurance that might have surprised Oled, if he had been present.

'You are shooting wildly,' he said. 'Kneel in a row behind the spearmen. Wait until you are certain of your target, then shoot.'

The archers' work became more organised and effective. Murak had them working in unison with the spearmen, not acting as isolated individuals. Even then, the Lost Souls' attack was still gathering pace. Sheer weight of numbers had begun to neutralise the Sol-ket's organisation.

'Look to your left,' came the warning cry.

What Murak saw next confirmed the Darkwing's hand in the attack. Thousands of perfectly drilled night-striders were swarming through the night, leaping over the line of fire Barath had established.

'Swordsmen,' Murak cried. 'To the perimeter.'

He watched the fighters racing forward. There were not enough of them. There were huge gaps in their line. The night-breed were breaking through everywhere.

'Barath-Ra,' Murak yelled. 'Our lines are failing.'

At Murak's warning shout, Barath turned and saw the danger. 'Pull the men back!' he roared. 'Overturn the carts in the baggage train. We have to set up a new defensive line.'

But Murak could see the night-striders doing their work. Even this second defensive line could do nothing about the attack from below. He remembered another fight in the open against the Lost Souls and feared for the outcome of the battle.

2

Miles away, Rishal's men were also awake. They could hear the war trumpets in the distance. A Sol-ket column was clearly in trouble. By the time Kulmat found him, Rishal was already buckling his sword belt.

'Shall we go to their aid, Rishal-Ra?' he asked.

'Of course we go to their aid,' Rishal snapped. 'What kind of question is that, Kulmat? I just wish I knew why they decided to leave the security of Karangpur and what forces they had at their disposal.'

Kulmat had nothing to say.

'The elephants and cavalry will leave immediately,' Rishal said, fastening the chinstraps of his helmet. 'The infantry will wait here for further orders.'

The camp was alive with preparations. Mahouts were stirring their elephants. The cavalry were saddling their steeds. Still, from far off in the dark, the din of battle was rising.

'Selessians!' Rishal bellowed.

Their commander stepped forward.

'Ride to the north-west,' Rishal ordered. 'Bring me news of what you discover.' He strode through the camp, followed by Kulmat.

'This is chaos,' he snarled. 'Where is the rest of the army? This is not the way of the Sol-ket, to fight defensive skirmishes on the enemy's ground.'

Kulmat had never seen Commander Rishal like this. Maybe it had something to do with the disappearance of his daughter, Julmira.

'Bring my horse, Kulmat,' he ordered.

Within minutes, Rishal's hastily assembled force was making its way north. The soldiers at his disposal were grim-faced. They felt the same as their commander. The Sol-ket usually chose their terrain well and avoided battle until all their regiments were assembled. It was a sign of the Darkwing's success that he was choosing where and when to fight. After an hour, the Selessian scouts returned.

'What news?' Rishal demanded.

'I saw about three thousand men holding a line against a vast throng of Lost Souls,' the chief scout answered. 'Some hundreds of their comrades already lie dead.'

Rishal's veterans exchanged glances. This was bad.

3

On their way towards the sounds of battle, Gardep, Oled and Aaliya skirted Rishal's camp.

'The only standards I see belong to the infantry,' Gardep said.

There wasn't a single horse or elephant to be seen.

'You're right,' Oled said, surveying the scene. 'Your former master is on the move. He aims to relieve Barath.' He pointed out a cloud of white dust hanging in the moonlight. 'This Rishal of yours doesn't know fear, I'll give him that; riding into Hell to save his comrades.'

'In matters of courage,' Gardep said, 'the Sol-ket are never found wanting.'

Oled remembered Turayat's last stand. 'Do you still want to do this, Gardep?'

Gardep nodded. Don't die, Kulmat, he thought. Don't you dare die before I get to you. Live long enough, my brother, and you will see that I am still a man of honour. He looked at the Tanjurs. 'I have told you my story,' he said, 'but why are you here? You are not Sol-ket.'

'Our destiny is bound up with that of the Darkwing,' Oled said, 'as is yours. That is why we came to your aid.'

'You say *my* destiny is bound up with the Darkwing?' Gardep said. 'How so?'

'As you know,' Aaliya answered, 'the demon lord rules the land beyond the Great Wall. That is your beloved's destination.'

'Cusha is going there, into the very lair of evil!' In his mind's eye he saw Shamana's face. 'This is the old witch's doing, I'll wager.'

At the word *witch* the faces of both Oled and Aaliya clouded. Gardep didn't notice. His mind was full of Cusha.

'Look,' Aaliya said suddenly.

The sky overhead had filled with ghosts. Like ink spreading over parchment, they were sweeping northward. Oled's eyes were hard.

'Many men will die tonight, Gardep.'

4

Deep in the caves of Suravan, Shamana sensed the battle taking place many miles distant.

'What is it?' Murima asked apprehensively. 'Is there some new danger?'

Shamana followed her bedraggled companions out of the underground stream into which they had plunged to escape the dark-fliers.

'Yes,' she said. 'There is danger. But not to us.'

'There she goes again,' Qintu said, 'more riddles.'

'They are only riddles to the stupid,' Shamana snapped.

'Yes,' Qintu said bitterly, 'I'm stupid all right, stupid enough to follow you. I'm wet, I'm hungry and I'm . . . here.'

Shamana looked around. 'I'm sorry,' she said. 'We are all tired. Let's rest and have something to eat. With any luck the fliers have been deterred by the water.'

Murima produced some flatbreads and cold mutton from her backpack. 'We will have to go easy on the food,' she said, 'if we are to ever reach Sangrabad.'

'So who *is* in danger?' Qintu demanded, returning to the original question.

'Gardep, for one,' Shamana said, though the Sol-ket wasn't her first concern.

Cusha looked interested but said nothing.

'A battle is raging,' Shamana said. 'The Darkwing leads his troops against Rishal's column.'

'How do you know all this?' Qintu asked.

'I am a Tanjur,' Shamana said. 'My kind do not communicate by speech alone.'

'At least we're safe,' Harad said, cautious as ever. 'Aren't we?'

'I wouldn't go that far,' Shamana told him. 'The Darkwing is able to travel fast and we have many miles to go. You can be sure the pursuit will resume when we emerge from these caves.'

'Cheerful as ever,' Qintu observed.

'Truthful as ever,' Cusha corrected.

Murima interrupted her. 'Eat your food,' she said. 'There's a long journey ahead of us.'

5

Kulmat watched Rishal fight. He understood the frenzy of the commander's assault. Somewhere in this vast throng was the Darkwing, Julmira's abductor. But fury was soon replaced by concern. The impetus of the cavalry charge had drained away. The Sol-ket were now embroiled in bitter hand-to-hand fighting. Ghosts hovered overhead, drawn by the prospect of many deaths.

'By Ra,' Rishal said out loud, staring at the massed ranks of the night-striders. 'Never have I seen so many.' There was dismay in his voice. He raised himself in his stirrups and looked around. 'The Lost Souls are moving in behind us,' he said. 'Kulmat, take a unit. It is essential you keep open a line of retreat.'

This was the first time Kulmat had ever heard the commander mention the word retreat. It was a sign that things were not going well.

'Turn about,' Kulmat ordered the men under his command. 'We must stop the demons closing ranks behind us.'

The flanking manoeuvre was not yet complete. By hurling themselves against the night breed, the Sol-ket were able to drive a wedge into their ranks.

'Dismount,' Kulmat ordered. 'We hold this position no matter what the cost.'

It was easier said than done. Wave after wave of demons swept in, a few dropping from the sky, many thousands more racing across the plain. Defending the break in the Lost Souls' encirclement was exhausting, demoralising work. It was as if the warriors were caught in a double pincer movement. Kulmat was beginning to fear for the outcome.

6

Beyond the Demon Wall, within the walls of the Black Tower, there was no din of battle. Men did not cry, horses did not whinny, elephants did not trumpet. There was no clash of steel, no hiss of arrows, no thud of spear shaft against shield. It was as silent as the grave. Yet, in some strange, unfathomable way, another manoeuvre was taking place in a wider war. Cautiously, hardly daring to breathe, Vishtar made his way down the stone steps to Julmira's cell.

'Who is that?' came her voice.

'Me.'

'Vishtar. Thank Ra. Have you been there long?'

'No, I just arrived. I am going to search for the mechanism to open the door.'

Julmira sounded excited. 'So you're sure it's there?'

'It's there.'

Vishtar worked systematically, running his fingers over every inch of the brickwork from top to bottom, right to left, prising them into the mortar, easing them over the rough surface of each individual brick.

'Anything?'

'No, not yet.'

He could hear Julmira's impatience seeping out of her with each breath. He understood it. For so many years, she had wanted for nothing. She was the daughter of a high-born Sol-ket. Snap her fingers and a slave would scurry to attend to her needs. She was pampered and spoiled. But here, in the Black Tower, they were equal.

'Just give me a few minutes,' he urged.

He was about halfway round the curved wall of the cell when it happened. As he slid his fingers under a deceptive lip of brickwork, he felt them sink into a crevice just like the one that worked the food hatch.

'I've found it!' Working his way round he eventually sprung the lever and the door opened.

'Vishtar, you did it!'

Triumphant as he felt, Vishtar hadn't forgotten about Aurun-Kai. In the few days since Julmira came, he had come closer to escaping from this terrible place than he had in all the years of his imprisonment. But one moment's carelessness could destroy it all.

'You must return to the cell,' Vishtar said.

'Oh, how can I?' Julmira said.

'You must. If Aurun-Kai discovers the door open, we will never leave this place. Julmira, consider it. I have been here half my life. Imagine that sentence repeated many times over. Imagine a lifetime within these walls. What point would there be escaping from the cell, only to remain entombed for ever in the tower?'

Julmira looked at him for several moments before nodding. 'You're right. But Vishtar, before you close the door, tell me you will find the way out. Promise me.'

Here she was, the daughter of a general. Yet she didn't speak like one. In the Black Tower they were two young people, imprisoned at the end of the world.

'I promise.'

'I believe in you, Vishtar,' Julmira said.

He smiled and reluctantly led her back to the cell. Taking one last look at her, he closed the door. The moment he heard the mechanism snap into place the smile drained from his face. He considered the vastness of the tower's walls. Finding the door through which the Dark-wing entered was going to be harder, much harder, than finding the door to one small cell.

7

Kulmat's muscles were screaming. He had no idea how long he had been fighting but it seemed like hours. Men were falling about him, devoured by the night tribe. Their blood slaked the demons' hideous thirst. Nothing slowed the Lost Souls' assault. Fear did not grip their hearts. Despair did not weaken their resolve. Blind instinct drove them, and an insatiable lust for blood.

'We have to hold on,' he cried. 'Don't despair, warriors of Ra, victory or death.'

'Victory or death,' came the answering cry.

But it was a weak, disheartened response. The Sol-ket no longer felt invincible. Too many of their number had perished. Kulmat saw the cadet who had asked whether they would see the dawn. He was on his knees, still clinging to his splintered sword. It was obvious he could not fight. Two dark-fliers fell on him. Their claws stroked his throat. They were about to feed.

'No!' Kulmat roared.

He would not see his comrade butchered before his eyes. Rushing forward, he struck out, severing the first creature's head. The second slashed at him, its razor sharp claws scraping against his breastplate. Hacking and sawing, his movements driven by disgust and rage, Kulmat dispatched this demon as ruthlessly as he had the first. He was in his blood rage.

'Get to your feet,' Kulmat ordered.

The cadet was sobbing. 'I can't.'

Kulmat spun him round and dragged him to his feet. The cadet's face was smeared with the demons' black blood. His eyes were wild with the killing. 'You can. You will! Stand or you die here.' Kulmat picked up a sword from the bloodstained ground and forced it into the cadet's hand. 'Take it.'

'Kulmat . . .'

'No whining,' Kulmat said. 'Just fight.'

The cadet looked bewildered.

'Fight, damn you, fight for the Emperor and fight for holy Ra himself.'

The fire in Kulmat's eyes seemed to burn pride back into the cadet. With a cry that was as much shame as courage, the Sol-ket returned to the fight. But still the demons came, wave after wave. Their reserves seemed endless.

'Kulmat!'

Somebody had shouted a warning. Kulmat spun on his heels but too late. The night-strider was already upon him. It hurled Kulmat to the ground. The impact drove the air from his lungs. For a moment he barely knew where he was. Then a night-strider's hateful, rotting, snarling face filled his vision. Kulmat could feel its bloody spittle on his face, rancid with corruption. An instant later he was struggling in the dirt, trying desperately to hold its head away from his face. Its jaws opened and closed, strings of bloody saliva dripping onto his face. Kulmat felt its sour breath too and saw the blackened teeth just inches from his throat. He saw the ghosts moving in. Then the creature drove a dagger into his shoulder. Kulmat screamed and the world seemed to slip away in a scarlet haze. It was over.

'Kulmat!'

He recognised the voice. No, it couldn't be. Another ghost? Kulmat's eyes fastened on a curious sight. A Selessian rider had appeared, sword raised, followed by an axe-wielding barbarian and a female archer. They burst through a sheet of flame like spectral warriors. Where had they come from?

'Kulmat, hold him off.'

It was him. It was Gardep.

'Is that really you?'

'Hold him off!'

From somewhere, Kulmat found the strength to grip the strider's skull. The thing roared in frustration. It was threshing from side to side, trying to break loose.

'Now let go!' the Selessian yelled.

Kulmat understood. The moment he released the night-strider, the Selessian's sword blade hissed through the air and beheaded it. The body slumped over him, black blood pumping like pitch from a tar pit. Disgusted, Kulmat pushed it away. He gulped down a few tortured breaths.

'Gardep,' Kulmat asked, searching for his saviour in the murk, 'am I dreaming? Is that really you?'

Then he felt something pressed into his hand. When he opened his fingers and looked at the object he saw a familiar scrap of bandage, marked with an old bloodstain. Tears of recognition spilled from his eyes.

8

'What *do* you know of the Black Tower?' Harad asked Shamana. 'It is the Holy Child's prison, but who built it? I know the legend.'

She saw expectation in her friend's eyes. 'Udmanesh gathered all the knowledge he had drawn from his travels to the four corners of the known world. He accumulated histories, manuscripts, maps, encyclopaedias, and dictionaries.' She looked around, as if sensing imminent danger. 'He sought to enlighten all mankind. His philosophy was that the tower could not belong to any one people. The very remoteness of the tower was its protection against misuse.'

Her eyes darted about the blackness. 'The Black Tower would become a place of pilgrimage for only the most pure of heart, a symbol of knowledge and truth. The dream of Udmanesh was simple but ambitious beyond belief. He wanted to find some common ground between people of all creeds and faiths, to unite all the ideas of the working of man and of nature, into one philosophy. There would be no false gods, no demons driving men to kill and wound, no spirits demanding blood sacrifice, nothing to poison the human heart. Udmanesh believed that, brought together this way, all mankind would one day be reconciled and at peace.'

'What happened?'

Shamana gave a weary sigh. 'What always happens? The hearts of men were poisoned by greed and fanaticism. The Muzals launched their campaign of domination. In order to strengthen their rule, they successfully exploited every human failing. They pitted nation against nation. They set about destroying every faith, every subject people who might stand in their way. The imperial castle and their foul priesthood wanted to use the knowledge accumulated in the Tower for themselves alone. They unleashed a war of terror against the followers of the Scales. They hunted Udmanesh as if he was a wild beast. In hiding, the great scholar was rarely seen. Indeed, few knew whether he was alive or dead. After that, war followed upon war. Soon the Black Tower was not a place of pilgrimage but a distant dream.'

'So that's where we are going,' Cusha said. 'We are in pursuit of a dream.'

'You could be right,' Shamana said. 'But what a dream!'

After that, the companions snatched a few hours' sleep. When they awoke, Shamana was gone.

9

On the battlefield, Gardep was propping up Kulmat and pouring the contents of his water canteen down his friend's throat. Kulmat was holding a strip of Selessian robe to his wounded shoulder. Soon after he had cut down the attacking night-strider, Gardep had seen the dawn light reddening the tops of the acacia trees. There was a lull in the fighting.

'You saved me,' Kulmat said.

'You said I was a traitor,' Gardep answered. 'This is my answer.' He felt Oled's hand on his shoulder. The shape-shifter was looking around nervously.

'We have to go,' Oled said, 'or we're dead men.'

Aaliya nodded. 'There are many Sol-ket,' she said.

Gardep knew the Tanjurs were right. 'You're going to be all right, Kulmat,' he said. 'I must take my leave. I have much to do.'

'May Ra go with you,' Kulmat said. 'I was a fool. I allowed rage and despair to poison my mind.'

'So we are still friends?' Gardep asked.

Kulmat grasped his hand. 'For all time, brother.'

Gardep looked at the Sol-ket picking their way through the battle. 'Come with us,' he said.

Kulmat shook his head. 'My place is here.'

'Are you mad?' Gardep cried. 'What can the Sol-ket offer you but horror and death? Come with me, Kulmat.'

But Kulmat shook his head. 'What else do I know, Gardep?' he asked. 'I wish Ra's blessing upon your quest, but I can't join you.'

Gardep pleaded but Kulmat would not be swayed.

'He has made his choice,' Oled said.

Gardep shook his head. 'I pray that you don't live to regret your decision,' he said.

With that, he followed Oled and Aaliya across the battlefield. They were climbing a rise when Oled reined in his horse.

'See over there,' he said. 'The Darkwing.'

Gardep looked in the direction Oled had pointed. Sure enough, surveying the carnage was the Darkwing.

'He must be feeling a deep contentment,' Oled said.

Gardep knew the truth of the barbarian's observation. From the high ground, he could see the survivors of the battle, including the commander. Rishal had come riding out of the dark like an avenging angel.

'Look at his face,' Gardep said.

'The night breed have not won a total victory,' Oled said. 'Already the Imperial army is approaching. I can hear the vibration of its hoof beats in the earth. The first outriders will be here by noon. Maybe, one day, the Darkwing will triumph, but it will not be today.'

The three riders spurred their horses and galloped west.

CHAPTER 13

The Holy Man of Anahastra

I

The army was counting the cost of the struggle the night before. Between them Barath and Rishal had lost more than a thousand men, several hundred horses and two dozen elephants. Suddenly nobody was talking about the destruction of the Lost Souls. Instead, the army was digging in for a defensive campaign. All that was left for the commander was to count the cost of the disaster. Even the most seasoned generals were shaken by the reports of the Darkwing's strength and organisation. The night breed was a pestilence, but a chaotic and disparate one. Now they hung like so many daggers over the Empire's throat.

Though the High Command didn't criticise Barath or Rishal openly, rumours were eddying through the camp like riptides. Die-hard veterans of the Parcep barracks would insist stubbornly that Rishal was about to be elevated to the

High Command for his heroic relief of Barath's belea-guered unit. They were in the minority, however. More common was the verdict that it had been reckless behav-iour. Some even said that Rishal's judgement had been coloured by his daughter's disappearance. Kulmat had spent the hours after the battle being tended by a field surgeon. As his wounds were cleaned and treated, he was wrapped in his own thoughts. Just after dawn he was lying on an operating table, gritting his teeth as the surgeon did his work. While the stitching went on, Kulmat pulled out the scrap of bloodied bandage, a symbol of brotherhood and loyalty. Gardep had torn a gaping wound in their friendship. But he had returned to heal it. Suddenly Kulmat's thoughts were scattered like birds.

'What's that in your hand?'

Kulmat's neck prickled. It was Rishal's voice. 'Nothing, Rishal-Ra.'

Rishal dismissed the surgeon. 'You don't fool me, Kulmat. It's a token of brotherhood. It is a common prac-tice, part of our lore. Prakash and I were blood brothers. In our youth, we carried just such things. So it's true. He was there.'

'He saved my life, Rishal-Ra. I . . .' Kulmat didn't finish the sentence.

'Did he say anything to you?'

Kulmat propped himself up on one elbow. 'I have lost a lot of blood,' he said. 'The climax of the battle passed in a haze. I saw him. Commander, beyond that, I can't help you.'

'Swear on the holy face of Ra that what you have told me is true,' Rishal boomed. 'Swear it!'

Kulmat touched the Sun scar on his chest. 'I swear.' It was hard to tell whether Rishal believed him or not.

'I wish I had never set eyes on him,' the commander

snarled. 'The day I come face to face with the traitor, I will water the earth with his blood. Tell me, what are your feelings towards him? I have to know that there are no divided loyalties.'

Kulmat forced the answer the commander wanted to hear. He prayed that his voice wouldn't betray him. 'I broke with him the day Prakash died. Nothing has changed.'

Rishal was suspicious. 'Yet you keep the token,' he said.

Kulmat looked at his hand. Seeing the scrap of bandage nestling in his palm, he cast it away. 'When I am stronger, Rishal-Ra,' he said, 'I will help you hunt him down.'

Rishal nodded. 'I will hold you to your word.'

2

Atrakon sensed Shamana's presence the moment the owl-form entered the chamber.

'Show yourself, witch,' he said.

Shamana appeared on a stone causeway high above him. She was armed with a Vassyrian bow. 'Turn back, assassin,' she ordered. 'Refuse and I will kill you where you stand.'

'I will complete my mission,' he said.

Shamana loosed her arrow. Atrakon anticipated its flight. He tucked his head into his chest and rolled out of danger, picking up his own bow on the way. Evading the second, he dropped to one knee. He then shot three arrows in the time Shamana managed just one.

'Damn me for growing old,' she growled. 'If I was younger, he'd be dead by now.'

Atrakon was running towards her, taking the stone steps two at a time. Transforming back into the owl she swooped across the roof of the cavern. To her disgust, another of Atrakon's arrows clipped her tail wings.

'Give up, old woman. You can't defeat me.'

Shamana dropped to the ground at the foot of the steps. Two of her arrows clattered against the stone at his feet.

'Close,' Atrakon said, 'but not close enough.'

His next shots had her scampering for cover. She was breathing heavily. It was all she could do to keep out of harm's way. How was she ever going to stop him? This Selessian was a great warrior. He was fast and strong. Most of all, he never acted out of anger. He was as merciless as a hunting falcon. He was the right hand of death.

'Show yourself, She-wolf,' Atrakon said. 'You've led me a merry chase. It's time I completed the kill.'

Drawing her sword, Shamana broke cover. 'You will not pass,' she said.

'You know that's not true, witch,' Atrakon said. 'You're breathing heavily. It's only a matter of time before I finish the job. What's it to be? Will you change into tiger or elephant? Either way, my arrows will pierce your heart. You've met your match. I'll bring Shirep your head.'

Shamana was about to tell him the priest was dead when the dark-fliers came again. Her brief duel with Atrakon was over. Faced with the demon threat, he was running one way. She was flying the other.

3

Vishtar left Julmira's cell. He closed the secret door behind him. He was about to climb the steps to his quarters when he paused to look at the curved walls of the tower itself. Vishtar was still wondering about the mechanism that would finally free them from their incarceration when he heard Aurun-Kai's footsteps. Cursing, Vishtar fled into one of the many recesses and watched from the shadows.

'I have your food, Julmira,' Aurun-Kai said. He knelt and sprang the lever to open the food hatch. 'Take it,' he said. 'Why starve yourself? What will it accomplish?'

'I don't want your slop,' Julmira yelled. 'Take it away.'

'You must eat,' Aurun-Kai said, 'or you will be no use to my master.'

Vishtar wondered if maybe Julmira wasn't more than a hostage. Was her blood going to slake the Darkwing's thirst too?

'Your master can go to Hell,' Julmira cried, proud and spirited as ever, 'and you with him. Leave me. I eat when I choose.'

'Julmira,' Aurun-Kai said, 'please take the food.'

'Why should I?' Julmira asked. 'What's the point of being alive just to languish here?'

Aurun-Kai crouched by the hatch. 'The master means you no harm.' His words were met by mocking laughter.

'Really?'

'Really,' Aurun-Kai said.

'Well, I don't believe you,' Julmira snapped.

Aurun-Kai rose to his feet and started to go. 'I will leave the food,' he said. 'Perhaps you will change your mind.'

Julmira hurled her plate after him. It clattered on the floor. Aurun-Kai shook his head and slowly climbed the steps. Once Vishtar was convinced he had gone, he crept over to the cell. He noticed that there was no food on the plate or the floor. He found himself smiling.

'Julmira,' he said, 'it's me.'

She answered through a mouthful of food. 'I thought you'd gone.'

'No,' Vishtar said, 'I was hiding. Anyway, I thought you were refusing to eat.'

'I was just putting on a show,' Julmira said, still eating. 'I don't want that monster thinking I'm easy to control.'

271

Vishtar remembered Aurun-Kai's weary climb back up the stairs. 'Oh, believe me, he doesn't think you're easy to manage.'

Julmira chuckled. 'Good.'

4

Just before nightfall the following day the four remaining Helati reached the exit from Suravan. Dusk was beginning to gather but the light was harsh after the murky tunnels. Blinking and shading their eyes, they emerged onto a harsh, windswept plateau. The immediate landscape was rocky and arid, but far below a different world opened up. Green, fertile and criss-crossed by streams, rivers and lakes, the Land of the Four Rivers was a veritable garden, ringed by the white-capped mountains of northern Jinghara. They had no sense of triumph, however. They had arrived without Shamana. Nobody spoke. Instead they slumped to the ground, weary arms hugging equally tired legs. Finally, a voice interrupted their thoughts.

'There's no time to rest.'

'Shamana!'

The priestess had just concluded her transformation from osprey to human. 'Why the wide eyes?' she said. 'Didn't you expect me?'

Cusha ran forward and embraced the priestess. 'Thank the Four Winds you're safe,' she said.

Shamana returned the embrace, then released Cusha. 'Anyway,' Shamana said. 'Do you want to know what I've found?'

*

Half an hour later they were approaching an unremarkable dome-like structure, barely visible in the thickening murk. There were no lights to be seen and no life except for a few bickering buzzards and the odd deer barking in the forest. The building looked deserted.

'It's a temple,' Shamana explained. 'They dotted the landscape before the Muzals launched the cult of Ra. Now they are deserted and in disrepair.' She hesitated. 'Do you smell that?' she asked.

The others sniffed and shook their heads.

'We don't all have your keen sense of smell, shape-shifter,' Qintu said.

'That's jasmine,' Shamana said. 'Yes, and there's wild rose and marigold, too.'

'So?' Qintu said. 'You can smell flowers. So what?'

'The fragrance is coming from inside the temple,' Shamana said. 'The flowers are fresh. Maybe I was wrong to think it deserted.' She snapped her fingers. 'We would be wise to approach this place armed.'

Swords drawn, the companions walked through the main gate of the temple. As Shamana had predicted, flower petals carpeted the floor. The priestess pointed out the figures of Ra and Sangra, picked out in fretwork. They looked serene. It was a far cry from the hideous, warring statues that lined the avenues of Parcep and Rinaghar. The stupa obviously belonged to the distant past. Ahead of them, leading deeper into the building, was an unlit colonnade. Shamana gestured to the others to let her go first. Without a sound, she entered. She was back a few moments later.

'It looks like we have found shelter for the night,' she said.

The moment Cusha entered she noticed the line of scent sticks on the plain altar. They were still smoking.

'Someone *is* here,' she said.

Right on cue, a curious figure entered. Long-haired and bearded, the man was stick-thin and dressed in rags. His eyes were sunken and dark. He didn't so much as acknowledge his visitors.

'Who's he?' Cusha whispered.

Shamana breathed a sigh of relief. 'He's a holy man,' she said. 'He lives without belongings and relies upon donations from travellers to eke out an existence.'

'So he's like you?' Qintu suggested. 'You know, holy woman, holy man.'

'No,' Shamana said, 'he is very unlike me. I struggle to make sense of the ways of men. The holy man has withdrawn from the world. He wishes to interpret the world, not to change it. He seeks only enlightenment.'

'He's no danger to us, then?' Harad asked.

'None at all,' Shamana said. 'He won't object to us staying.'

Up to that point, the holy man had not spoken. That all changed when a gust of night wind entered the temple.

'Ghosts,' he murmured, following the haunted breeze.

The spectral forms swept across the stone floor and gathered round Cusha as they had done many times before. They peered into her face and stretched out their translucent fingers as if trying to stroke her face. Their mouths opened and closed, wordless and sad. The holy man stopped and stared. For the first time he focused on Cusha. His mouth sagged open. He seemed transfixed. Cusha felt his stare burning into her.

'Damn the things!' Qintu said. 'They will bring the dark-fliers down on our heads.'

The holy man shook his head, still unable to take his eyes off Cusha. 'No,' he said. 'They exist according to their own devices. They do not serve the Lost Souls. Far from it.'

'But they gather round the dead and those who are about to die,' Harad said.

The holy man held out his hands. 'Of course, they are the spirits of lives that have been extinguished. They are the memory of what once was.'

Qintu frowned. 'They're the same as the Lost Souls, if you ask me. Grave rats, the lot of them.'

'No, no, no,' the holy man said, urgency in his thin voice. 'You don't understand at all. The ghosts are quite the opposite of the demons that prey upon the flesh of men. They are the soul, the thinking, feeling part of those who have died. These Lost Souls of which you speak, they are wretched creatures. They are but decaying flesh infested with a monstrous hunger. They have no consciousness. Others bring that to them. The Lost Souls are captive to their hellish instincts.'

Harad ventured a question. 'So, in the absence of their spirits, the Darkwing does the thinking for them?'

'Indeed,' the holy man said. 'The demon lord alone directs the creatures. Now the ghosts, they are altogether different. Within these spectral forms you will find thought, feeling, regret. Their insubstantial hearts still feel emotion. They are the very essence of humanity.'

'But what do they want of me?' Cusha asked.

It was as if her voice stirred something inside the holy man. He approached her and examined her face. The way he gazed at her, haunted, fascinated, he reminded Cusha of the ghosts.

'You do not understand them?' he asked.

'No.'

'They want you to give them rest,' he said. 'If they can invest the demon host with consciousness of what they are and end the monstrous contagion that blights the land, then the ghosts will pass from the Earth. Like mist, they will fade and their tormented spirits will rest. They look to you for peace.'

'But how can I do that?'

The holy man reached for her throat. 'Do you mind?' he asked.

Cusha exchanged glances with Shamana. Shamana nodded. 'Do what you have to,' Cusha said, turning her neck.

She had become accustomed to people's curiosity, but his was more than inquisitiveness. The holy man inspected Cusha's throat and sighed. He passed a hand over her face, as if engraving every feature on his memory, though he didn't once touch her. 'It *is* you,' he said.

He put his palms together and bowed. Cusha questioned Shamana with her eyes. This time the priestess had no explanation.

'You honour me with your presence,' the holy man said.

'Honour you?'

'Of course,' he said. 'You have restored meaning to my life. I have waited for this moment. The Holy Child is here, in the temple of Anahastra. It has been a bleak, barren time during which I have sought life's meaning in the smallest of things. Truly, I feared you were dead.'

'Do you know me?' Cusha asked.

The holy man seemed not to hear. 'Your arrival means that the long tyranny is coming to an end,' he continued, heedless of her question. 'Take your rest, child. Tomorrow you must turn your steps towards Sangrabad.'

'But how do you know where we're going?' Cusha asked.

'I have known for many years that one day you would embark upon this quest,' he said. 'There was a time I thought the monsters must have found you.' He patted her hand. 'My heart is full,' he said. 'I have awaited your coming for so long.'

'But how?' Cusha asked. 'How?'

The holy man turned to go but Cusha intercepted him.

'How?' she repeated.

'Not now,' the holy man said. 'I must give this some thought, my child. Your coming has come as a great shock.' He smiled. 'Though not an unpleasant one.' Before he left the inner sanctum, he spoke briefly. 'Tomorrow you will have the answers to your questions.'

CHAPTER 14

The Tomb of Udmanesh

1

'I'm not going in there,' Qintu protested.

The holy man didn't so much as smile though he did continue, as he had since the previous evening, to stare at Cusha. 'Access to the mausoleum is through there,' he said simply.

Murima's eyes widened. 'Did you say mausoleum?'

'Of course,' the holy man said. 'That is the purpose of the temple.'

Without another word he ushered his guests down a flight of worn stone steps to a water drain. They peered through the gloom, Murima doing so from over Harad's protective shoulder. The holy man stood behind them, watching. Cusha couldn't help glancing in his direction. It was as if he was judging them. Nobody else paid him any attention. They were too intent on discovering the entrance to the mausoleum. All they could see was an underground stream cutting a channel beneath Anahastra. The holy man gestured towards the limpid water.

'The holy water is a powerful barrier against the demon contagion,' he said. 'Its purity protects the secret of this place.'

Qintu and Harad exchanged glances. Qintu couldn't help screwing a finger to his temple, a sign that he didn't trust the holy man's sanity. Shamana put an end to that with a sharp glance. Satisfied that he was going to show more respect, she waded into the water, leading the others. Several yards into the tunnel, the water rose to its stone roof.

'More water,' Qintu said. 'Just what we need after Suravan.'

'There's no way through,' Cusha said.

'There is always a way through,' the holy man said from behind them. 'Now leave aside your doubts. There is a slight current. Let it take you.'

Everyone looked at Shamana. Sucking in a deep breath, she vanished into the water, her long, matted hair floating to the surface for a second like so much weed. Taking the form of an otter, she plunged into the still water. Within moments she was back.

'You don't have to go far,' she said. 'Four or five strokes and you emerge in a large chamber. This is the only entrance. It really is cleverly disguised.'

'But why all the secrecy?' Harad wondered out loud. 'There were several tombs in the upper chamber too. The whole building's a mausoleum. It isn't as if the dead are going to . . .' His voice petered out.

'What were you going to say next?' Qintu chuckled. 'The dead aren't going to walk, something like that? Harad, that's exactly what they do.'

'The tomb belongs to a great man,' Shamana said, cutting the exchange short. The way she said it lent great import to the words she spoke next. 'You are the most privileged of the sons and daughters of the Earth. The scholar Udmanesh himself is interred here.'

Nobody said a word. Until this moment, to most of them, Udmanesh had been a legend, a symbol of freedom rather than a real man. Now, it seemed, they were standing at the threshold of his tomb.

'But what can a dead man's resting place tell us?' Harad asked.

'No ordinary man lies here,' Shamana said. 'So special a voice is not easily silenced, even by death.'

She looked around. 'Now, who's first?'

'I'll go,' Cusha said.

Anxiety paled into insignificance compared with the promise of the hidden sanctum. All she had to do was penetrate the water's cold embrace for a moment or two and she would discover a treasure few had ever seen: the resting place of Udmanesh, a man whose name was usually spoken only in whispers. There, she secretly wished, she would encounter another signpost to her destiny. The holy man had promised as much.

'Very well,' Shamana said. 'Take a deep breath.'

Cusha did as she was told. Shamana waited for Cusha's signal that she was ready, then guided her under the water. Cusha kicked hard and swam forward. It was as Shamana had said. A little way down the flooded passage, she broke the surface and looked with wonder at a perfectly constructed dome. Directly beneath the highest part of the ceiling lay a stone sarcophagus. Around it, like inhuman guards, there rose four iron pillars, each as tall as a full-grown man. Atop the pillars stood representations of the Scales.

'Come and see,' the holy man said.

Cusha frowned. 'How did you get here?' she asked. 'Surely you were behind us.'

But he ignored her. 'Come.'

Cusha examined the script that ran, carefully etched into the surface, from top to bottom in a long spiral. The holy man's eyes caught hers. Just for a moment she felt a flicker of recognition as if, in another life, she had known him.

'It is the story of Udmanesh,' he said, 'from his humble origins to . . .' He permitted himself a smile. 'Well, to his equally humble end.'

Looking at the pillars and the sarcophagus, Cusha thought his end was anything but humble. In the narrative, she discovered what the holy man meant. This is what the first pillar said:

> Of Udmanesh I sing,
> Born a poor flower-seller's son
> In the city of Inbacus,
> Who rose in three score years
> To become the greatest man
> Of all antiquity.

This, to Cusha, seemed a preposterous claim. In Parcep his name had rarely been spoken. But she remembered what Shamana had told her: it is the victors who write our history. It made sense. Why, if that were not true, was it a crime to utter the scholar's name in public? The masters had to be afraid of something. Cusha read on:

> Come close, wanderer,
> And listen to my story,
> How this poor man became acquainted
> With the meaning held in
> The music of the stars,

The lament of the wind,
The need to journey
To the furthest reaches
Of the known world
In search of truth.

The pillar recounted how the young Udmanesh excelled in
music and letters and became the custodian of the Library
of Inbacus. It related how he decided to travel and learn the
ways of the world. The second pillar began this story.

Walk with him, stranger,
Keep step with venerable Udmanesh
As he takes the road
To Selessia, Lyria and savage Khut
And finally, fatefully,
On to Tiger-gated Parcep
Then to the eye of Ra,
Golden Rinaghar.

For the first time, Cusha noticed that Shamana, Qintu and
Harad had joined her. 'Where's Mama-li?' she asked.

'She decided to wait back there,' Harad said.

Cusha nodded and looked at the holy man. 'It says
fatefully,' she said. 'Why was his journey to the founding
cities of the Empire fateful?'

'You will find the story in the third column,' the holy
man answered.

A few minutes later, there it was:

Look now through the scholar's eyes,
Reader, listen with his ears,
For this is the age of the Muzals,
The greatest but the cruellest of men,

In whose reign all the children of the Earth
Were made to tremble in Death's long shadow.

'Remember those lines, Cusha,' the holy man said. 'They
are meant quite literally.'

The pillar told its tale. Udmanesh watched the relentless
rise of the cult of Ra. He denounced it, then was declared a
heretic and thrown into prison.

Suffer with him,
Weep with him,
Yearn, as he did, for your freedom.
Listen to his thoughts, reader,
And imagine his dismay,
That this man who spoke
Of peace, of harmony,
Of the balance of light and dark,
Of a Republic of all the Peoples,
United and equal,
Should languish so much of his life
In cold and dark Muzal dungeons.

'It's the prophecy of the Scales again,' Cusha murmured,
glancing at the images that stood at the top of the
story-columns.

'It is,' Shamana said. 'As I have told you before, our faith
is not the property of one race or one nation but of all
mankind. Indeed, its roots lie not among the Helati, but
in ancient Vassyria, among its poor and suffering masses. It
was from their literature that Udmanesh learned of it.
From there it spread to the oppressed of every part of the
land.'

The fourth column described the rise of the Empire and
the enslavement of the Helati.

But there was another, more intriguing tale:

Draw closer now, listener,
If you wish to bend an ear
And listen either to life's rustle,
Or to death's uneasy slide.
It was in this time of the Empire's rise
That a great struggle got underway
Between the followers of venerable Udmanesh
And the rising Hotec-Ra.
For both temples learned the secret
In those days of how to draw back the curtain
Between the land of living men and women
And the regions of the dead.

'I don't understand,' Cusha asked, searching the pillars for more. 'Drew back the curtain – what does that mean?'

The holy man answered her. 'This all happened in the time of the first Muzals,' he said, 'distant ancestors of the present tyrant. In their reign, the greatest wrong ever to befall mankind was done. Driven by a savage thirst for power, the Hotec-Ra meddled in the dark arts. Not content with ruling the greater part of the known world, they wanted to harness the powers of the House of the Dead. We all know the result. It was the priests' doing, you see. They violated the most sacred law of nature and caused the undead to walk. Their dearest wish was to use them as obedient, unthinking slave-masters to control the Helati. For that, the power-hungry fools unleashed the contagion of the Lost Souls on the world. But once released from the sleep of death, the Hotec-Ra were unable to bend the Lost Souls to their will. The night breed turned on those who had summoned them.'

The old man shook his head. 'The followers of Udmanesh went into every market place to denounce this abomination. For this they were declared heretics and hunted like dogs.'

Cusha stared at the column. It told, finally, of the escape of Udmanesh and his trek westward, harried by his pursuers, to the most inhospitable wastes of the known world, of the building of the Black Tower, a repository of the world's knowledge.

> Of Udmanesh I sing,
> Who lies beneath this stone.
>
> Know this, if you seek after truth
> And hunger for freedom,
> Though his body lies here
> His spirit dwells to the west,
> In a dark tower, at the end of the Earth.

Cusha's eyes were immediately drawn to the sarcophagus and a carved representation of the Black Tower, just like the one they had seen in Suravan. There were lines of an ancient script, unintelligible to Cusha, and finally a carved night orchid. 'What do the letters say?' she asked.

'It's ancient Vassyrian, isn't it?' Shamana said, inspecting the inscription.

The holy man looked on impassively. Qintu enjoyed seeing the look on her face. For once it was Shamana who was the disciple, not the master. And how the holy man's tranquil superiority irritated her! 'What do you expect them to say?'

'It's to do with me, isn't it?' Cusha said.

'It predicts that two will come,' the holy man said. 'There will be twin children, a boy and a girl, born of the same womb and separated since early childhood. It is the old balance: light and dark, male and female. The girl can summon the dead. She can speak to them. The boy can lay them to rest. Reunited, the twins will have the power to repair the torn curtain between life and death. They will end the contagion of the night breed. This was the final work of Udmanesh, to pass on to new generations the power to undo the Hotec-Ra's terrible crime.'

'There,' Shamana said. 'Didn't I tell you? You can restore the world to what it was before the demon host stalked the land.'

'But I don't understand,' Cusha said. 'How was this knowledge passed on?'

'Udmanesh trained a new priesthood,' the holy man said. 'You have inherited the venerable scholar's knowledge. But there is a warning. Reunited, the holy children can bring the age of the demons to an end. But, should the Darkwing capture you and drink the blood of both of you while it is still warm, he will become the Angel of Death, a creature of unstoppable power.'

'But that is too cruel!' Harad exclaimed. 'We have come so far and endured so much.'

'Cruel it may be,' the holy man said, 'but true nonetheless. I will explain.'

2

'Vishtar!' Aurun-Kai's voice rang out through the Black Tower. 'Vishtar, where are you?'

At that moment Vishtar was sitting talking to Julmira. 'Get back inside,' he hissed. 'Quick.'

Vishtar scurried to the steps and climbed quickly, taking care to make as little noise as possible.

'Vishtar!'

'I'm here, Aurun-Kai.'

'Where were you?' Aurun-Kai asked, suspicion fairly crackling in his voice.

'I was reading.'

'Reading?' Aurun-Kai said. 'What were you reading?'

It was evident that Aurun-Kai saw the knowledge that lined the tower's walls as a dangerous thing, perhaps more menacing than an equal number of sword blades.

'A ballad,' Vishtar said, thinking quickly, 'from . . . Tanjuristan.'

Aurun-Kai snorted. 'Those good-for-nothing rebels. We put that rabble to flight at Dullah. What do you want with their worthless chatter?'

'I find it interesting,' Vishtar said.

'Interesting?' Aurun-Kai said. 'What, the prattling of gutless barbarians? What's interesting about that?'

Vishtar didn't answer. He was satisfied that he had successfully diverted Aurun-Kai's curiosity. 'What did you want me for, Aurun-Kai?' he asked.

'Prepare yourself,' Aurun-Kai said. 'The master is coming.'

Vishtar's flesh turned cold. 'You don't mean that he is coming to feed?' Vishtar gasped. 'Not that. It can't be a month.'

'You are wrong,' Aurun-Kai said. 'Tomorrow is the first day of Hoj. The master has been preoccupied. The Blood Moon is already on the wane. He must not be denied nourishment. He craves your life blood.'

Vishtar's mind reeled at the news that the Darkwing was coming. What of the escape plan? What of Julmira?

'Please,' Vishtar said, 'not now. Not now.'

There was no mistaking the urgency in his voice, the desperation as he searched for a way out of the blood-letting. Aurun-Kai's face clouded with renewed suspicion.

'Why not now?' he demanded. 'Why is this month different from any other? Why these protests, Vishtar?'

'It is fear,' Vishtar said, 'pure and simple. You know how I dread your master's visits.'

'Then cease your babble and go to your chamber. The Master will come to you presently.'

Vishtar nodded, but he had other ideas. When the Dark-wing came to Vishtar's chamber, the boy would be gone. So would Julmira.

3

Gardep consigned the Selessian robes to the flames. They had served their purpose.

'Why would you want to wear that uniform again?' Oled asked, looking at the armour with distaste.

'In spite of all that has happened,' Gardep said, 'I am still a Warrior of Ra. My boyhood was spent in the service of the Sun god. You do not put aside the beliefs and practices of a lifetime on a whim.'

'But put it aside you must,' Oled said. 'Whether you do it today, or whether you do it tomorrow, you must leave the Empire and its tyranny behind you. This worship of endless war, you must pull its claws from your flesh. Do you not see, Gardep? The worship of Ra is a contagion. For generations it has done nothing but suppress the people. It is not just the slaves and the subject races that suffer. Even the lives of the Sol-ket are twisted by this wretched faith. They put all their efforts into crushing those they enslave. It corrupts their hearts and makes them cruel.'

Gardep didn't argue.

'You started something back in Parcep,' Oled said. 'By

falling in love with Cusha you set in motion events that will one day bring the Empire crashing down.'

'Do you really believe that?' Gardep asked.

'I wouldn't have spent all those years at Zindhar if I didn't,' Oled told him. 'I have sacrificed all my adult years to finding the Black Tower and releasing the Holy Child. I did it because I believe what is written in the Book of Scales. By ending the time of the demon dead, we can usher in the time of freedom.'

'But Oled, the Empire grows stronger all the time. How can you think to topple it with a mere handful of desperate fugitives?'

'Soon,' Aaliya interrupted, 'that handful will become millions.'

Gardep shook his head. 'I am ready to leave behind the cruelty of the Sol-ket,' he said, 'but I would be mad to fall for the fantasies of half a dozen slaves and shape-shifters.'

'You'll learn,' Oled said. He sniffed the breeze. 'We're not going to change the world on an empty stomach,' he said. 'Rabbit or venison?'

Gardep laughed. He liked this barbarian. 'Venison.'

Oled nodded and transformed into a wolf.

'What's he hunting?' Gardep asked.

Aaliya pointed out a stag on a distant hill. The creature had just become Oled's quarry.

'He'll make the kill,' Aaliya said. 'I hope you like your meat fresh.'

'I do,' Gardep said, 'just so long as you don't expect me to eat it raw.'

4

In the hidden mausoleum beneath Anahastra, the holy man continued his tale.

'The Darkwing has the boy,' he said. 'The blood of the Holy Child nourishes the demon lord. But the demon lord wants more than mere survival.'

Cusha placed an encouraging hand on his forearm. 'Go on,' she said.

'This concerns you,' he said.

'I know.'

'You may not like what you hear.'

'After all these years,' Cusha said, 'I am ready for the truth.'

'The Darkwing's purpose is simple,' the holy man told her. 'He was condemned to a living death. All these years he has lived in a foul, decomposing corpse. He craves rebirth.'

Cusha bit her lip. 'And I can make that possible?'

'You can, you and the boy, but only at the cost of your lives. If he and his beloved Kewara are to live again, if Prince Sabray is to rise from the twisted, tormented creature he has become, you and Vishtar must die. The demon lord must drink from you while you both live; drain your warm blood from your veins. Then he will conquer death.'

Cusha nodded.

'Now you understand,' the holy man said. 'The fate of the world will be decided in the Black Tower. That is the irony of fate. Because the Darkwing must drink the blood of both of you while it is still warm, it forces him to do the very thing that threatens to destroy his power. He has to bring you together. That is your window of opportunity. Find your brother and join hands with him, allow your sacred flesh to touch, and you will harness all the power the House of the Dead contains. You can end the terror that has stalked the Earth for so long. But should you fall into the demon lord's hands . . .'

He framed her face with his hands, though strangely he did not touch her once. To her surprise, tears spilled down his cheeks.

'Should you succumb to him,' he said, 'he will feed on you both. If he can harness your joint powers by feeding on your lifeblood, he will surely become master of the entire world.'

With that, he released her and walked away. He started to cross the floor, as if ready to go. For a few moments nobody spoke, then Cusha approached him.

'You know so much about me,' she said, 'yet I know nothing about you. Tell me, holy man, who are you?'

He turned. 'All night long I turned one question over in my mind,' he said. 'Is it right for me to reveal what is hidden in the lamp?'

'Please,' Cusha begged. 'You must.'

The holy man hesitated then gave a brief nod of acquiescence. 'Your memories are stored in the lamp at Sangrabad,' he said. 'When you breathe in the vapours you will remember where you are from and who raised you. You will also understand how to use the powers that have lain dormant inside you these many years.'

'Why will you not tell me now?' Cusha asked.

'Both of us have dangerous paths to tread,' the holy man said. 'It will have to wait.'

Judging by the holy man's expression, it was pointless arguing.

'I have done what I can to help you,' he said. 'I wish you well in your quest. Farewell.'

5

Vishtar shook Julmira awake.

'Everything has changed,' Vishtar whispered. 'We must make our bid for freedom now.'

'Do you know where the door is?' Julmira asked excitedly.

'I spent all last night searching for it,' Vishtar said. 'I have eliminated every gallery but one. If we both put our minds to it, we can find our escape route.'

Doubt crept into Julmira's eyes. 'What if we are discovered?'

'We won't be,' Vishtar assured her. 'Aurun-Kai has retired. We have several hours.'

Vishtar crept to the door and peered out. Satisfied that Aurun-Kai was fast asleep, he waved to Julmira to follow him. Moments later they were climbing to the topmost gallery.

'Vishtar,' Julmira whispered, seizing his sleeve, 'I don't understand. You were so cautious. You said we had to be sure we knew how to get out before we took a risk like this. What's changed?'

Vishtar hesitated before answering. 'You remember I told you about the Darkwing,' he said, 'and how he comes monthly to renew himself by draining my lifeblood?'

Julmira nodded. 'The time has come again.'

'I can't suffer it again,' he said. 'I can't.'

'I understand,' she said.

'No,' Vishtar said. 'It isn't just the loss of blood. In my weakened state, I can feel my spirit entering the House of the Dead. I have walked there, Julmira. You can't imagine what I have seen.'

'If we escape,' Julmira said, 'you will never see such things again.'

Without another word they hurried to the gallery and started feverishly exploring the walls. Hour after hour they ran their fingers over every crevice. Time after time, they exchanged hopeful glances. Still they didn't find the mechanism to release the secret door.

'It's hopeless,' Julmira said, throwing up her arms in frustration.

'Are you sure you have searched every inch?' Vishtar asked.

'Of course,' Julmira snapped. 'Do you think I'm stupid?'

'No,' Vishtar said, 'but I'm sure it's here. You check the parts I searched. I'll do the same for yours.'

Grudgingly, she agreed. It was about forty minutes later when Vishtar found it. 'Oh Vishtar,' Julmira said, 'I'm sorry. I should have been more careful.'

'Forget it, Julmira,' Vishtar replied. 'It doesn't matter. We're free.'

But when he released the mechanism, he discovered two reasons for despair. He was standing on the edge of a dizzy precipice without a handhold to be seen. Worse still, coming closer to the Tower with each wing beat was the demon lord.

6

It was with some sadness that the five companions left Anahastra. There had been a striking peace about the temple, as if the laws and manners of a distant, better age still prevailed there. The secret mausoleum had strengthened their belief that their quest was sanctioned by fate. Even Murima, who had not seen the resting place of Udmanesh with her own eyes, had long since stopped doubting Shamana.

'I am afraid,' Cusha said as they skirted the banks of the Amputra, the greatest of the four rivers that gave this part of Jinghara its name.

Shamana cocked her head. 'We are all afraid,' she said. 'That is the third deserted village we have passed. The Lost Souls have been here, that's for sure.'

'No,' Cusha said, 'it's not that kind of fear. I'm afraid that I am not the person you all need.'

'Can it be true?' Shamana said. 'After everything the holy man told you, you still have doubts?'

'Yes,' Cusha said. 'You have all invested such hope in me, but I am just an ordinary girl. I cry at the slightest thing. I have all sorts of moods. I lose my temper over nothing. I am not great or grand. No words of wisdom fall from my lips. I am not special in any way. How can I be the key to freedom?'

'It is foretold,' Shamana said. 'Didn't you listen to the words of the holy man?'

'And that's it?' Cusha said. 'My face is carved in a wall somewhere. My name is written on a stone column.' She pressed her hand to her heart. 'None of that changes the way I feel in here. It doesn't make me any different from the rest of mankind.'

'Is that it?' Shamana asked. 'You think you are unworthy?'

Cusha nodded. 'Yes,' she said. 'Exactly that. Here, in my heart, I feel no destiny, no greatness. What if I let you down?'

Shamana reached over and patted Cusha's knee. 'Do you think great people are born that way?' she asked. 'Consider Shinar. He was the bravest of them all, yet I saw his sword hand shake before he went into battle. I dare say Udmanesh, when he was wandering the desert trails of Selessia, would sometimes ask himself where he was bound and what his purpose was. It is the way of all mortal souls, Cusha. We are not *born* good or great. Life makes us so.'

'And you, Shamana,' Cusha asked, 'you who are the She-wolf, the only leader of the Army of the Free to survive the horror of Dullah, do you have doubts?'

'Every day,' Shamana said, 'every single day.'

'But you don't doubt me. You never have.'

'Cusha,' Shamana said, 'that is because I know you will be the greatest of us all.'

CHAPTER 15

Sangrabad

1

Julmira watched in revulsion as the Darkwing drained Vishtar's precious blood. Daughter of the legendary Rishal-ax-Sol she might be, but Julmira had never witnessed the blood and suffering on which her family's wealth and power was built. As she looked on, Vishtar's head rolled and his eyelids started to close. For a moment, she thought the boy was dying. Then the demon lord leaned forward. He lowered the semi-conscious body to the floor and drank his fill. That's when the Darkwing said:

'Sleep well. The next time I drink from you, it will be the last.'

'Do you mean it?' Julmira cried, looking at Vishtar and seeing his eyes still flickering. 'His ordeal is over?'

The Darkwing's eyes fixed on her. The intoxication of

the warm blood cleared from his eyes. It was as if he had forgotten her presence completely until that moment.

'You could say that,' he replied. 'Yes.'

Julmira's face shone with naïve joy. 'Are you truly going to set us free?' she asked.

'Free?'

The Darkwing seemed to taste the word, allow its sweetness to dissolve on his tongue. As the delicious taste spread through him, its dark irony caused him to smile.

'Yes, that's right,' he said after a few moments' consideration. 'I'm going to set you free.'

Aurun-Kai had been listening. As if in shame, he lowered his head and shuffled from the room. But he did not question his master.

'It's so far from home,' Julmira said. 'And the Lost Souls stand between here and Parcep. You cannot just set me on the road and expect me to survive.'

'Believe me,' the Darkwing said, 'neither you nor Vishtar will have any reason to fear my legions.'

But for his nightmarish appearance and the way he had fed on the boy, Julmira might have felt grateful to the Darkwing.

'Which of you discovered how to open the doors?' the demon lord asked. 'Was it you or the boy?'

'It was Vishtar,' Julmira said.

'Of course it was,' the Darkwing said. 'Wonderful, bookish, ingenious Vishtar, the Holy Child. Come closer.'

Julmira hesitated, but he raised his voice.

'I said: come here.' The Darkwing reached out a clawed hand. 'I won't hurt you.'

Heart slamming in her chest, Julmira edged forward. It was as if she were dragging feet made of lead. That's when the Darkwing seized her. Effortlessly he lifted her feet from the floor and carried her to the open door.

'Do you remember the last time you were in my arms?' he said.

'Oh no,' Julmira begged, understanding his meaning. 'Please.'

'Would you like to see the tower's exit?' he asked.

'For Ra's sake, don't!' Julmira screamed. The sound left her throat like a wild bird fleeing a thicket. 'No, please no!'

But the Darkwing wasn't listening. Standing on the very brink of the dizzying precipice, he reached out so that Julmira's legs pedalled in thin air, kicking over the drop.

'I showed you once before what would happen if you defied my will,' he said.

Julmira glimpsed the dizzying fall to the rocks below. 'Don't,' she stammered. 'Oh no, don't!'

He shook her the way a jackal shakes a wild duck. 'Do you think you can escape?' he asked.

Julmira shook her head until her teeth rattled. 'No,' she screamed. 'Vishtar was foolish. It can't be done.'

'Say it again.'

'We tried,' she screamed. 'Please. We understand now. It's impossible.'

'That's right,' the Darkwing said. 'Quite, quite impossible.'

'Don't drop me,' Julmira cried. 'By almighty Ra, I swear I will never try to escape again. Please, I beg of you.'

'Do you know my story, Julmira?' he asked.

Julmira could feel the wind howling around her. 'Yes, Vishtar told me.'

'And do you think my father, Muzal the Great, Emperor of the Sun, was merciful when he handed me over to the Hotec-Ra?' Something like anguish throbbed in his inhuman face. 'It was beyond punishment,' he said, a groan of regret and horror welling up from deep within. 'They made me suffer a living death. Was that a father's love? Was that merciful?'

Julmira shook her head, eyes so wide they seemed to take up half her face. 'No!'

'But this was done by your own family, Julmira, the *ax-Sol*.'

'Then I disown them,' she cried.

'All of them?' the Darkwing asked. 'Do you disown them all, even your mother and your father?'

'Yes.'

'Louder.'

'Yes!'

'So they were not merciful?' he asked again, relishing her tortured answers.

'No. It was terrible what he did to you, an outrage. Please.'

The Darkwing seemed to like the word *outrage*. 'Julmira,' he said, 'I couldn't have chosen a better word to describe my treatment at his hands. The day the Hotec-Ra consigned me to this living death, I learned that mercy is a myth, the whim of fools. Only one thing matters in this life, and that is power. There is only one real question a man must ask: who wields the whip and who feels it on his back? All else pales before that simple question. Those in power may surround themselves with poets and musicians who sing of love and beauty . . . yes, and mercy too. But their stage is built upon a mountain of skulls. That is the true picture of man.'

With that, he returned a trembling Julmira to solid ground. 'Do you care for this boy?' he said, indicating the senseless Vishtar.

She hesitated. 'He was kind to me.'

'Is there anything else?'

Julmira lowered her eyes. 'How could there be? He is not my equal.'

'That's good,' the Darkwing said. 'Not your equal. Here you are, at the end of the world, and still you cling to your status. Love can be weighed in golden dinar and in power, can it not? If you were to die tomorrow, I swear, your corpse would refuse to be burned on a Helat pyre. Do you love anyone but yourself?'

Julmira sobbed miserably. 'I don't know.'

The Darkwing spread his wings. 'Soon,' he said, 'mankind will pass from the face of the Earth. I for one will not mourn.'

2

'Shamana!'

The She-wolf turned in the direction of Qintu's voice, expecting to see dark-fliers. Many times they had had to hide from the scouts of the Lost Souls. But it wasn't demons Qintu had seen.

'This is it,' he said, 'the Night Orchid.'

Shamana knelt next to him and examined the flower. It was just as the prophecies described, a black flower with a white bloom, the most perfect whiteness emerging from the purest black. She touched the petals gently then waved the others over.

'The boy's right,' she said. 'Well done, Qintu. Your eyes are as sharp as a buzzard's.'

Qintu looked shocked. Of all people, Shamana had praised him!

'Does that mean we're close?' Harad asked.

'Very,' Shamana told him.

'Look,' Harad said. 'There are more. Yes, there are four, five with the one you found, Qintu.'

'Fancy that,' Murima said. 'Five companions. Five flowers.'

Harad picked the flowers and gave them to Cusha. 'Wear them,' he said. 'They belong to you.'

Cusha smiled and accepted his gift.

Less than an hour later the companions came across Sangrabad. They had just forded a shallow stream when they happened upon an orchard of lemon and pomegranate trees. It was overgrown and neglected. Further on, framed by ancient, snow-peaked hills a temple stood, its ruined walls and reliefs overgrown with bushes and creepers.

'I see it,' she said, her voice little more than a whisper.

Then, more strongly, excitement mingling with apprehension, even dread, she repeated the words. It appalled her that soon her mind would be flooded with the memories the holy man had described. Murima was the first to join her. She rested a hand on Cusha's shoulder.

'Are you ready for this?'

Cusha nodded. 'Yes, Mama-li, I'm ready.'

They picked their way down the gentle slope to the temple.

'Look there,' Shamana said, 'Ra and Sangra are depicted as brothers, not enemies. In place of conflict, there is harmony. This temple was built long before the Muzal dynasty perverted the old ways.'

As they came closer it was easy to see the truth of her words. Many of the stucco statues had been defaced.

'That's the work of the Hotec-Ra, I shouldn't wonder,' Shamana said.

Inside the temple, it was the same story. The walls had once been covered in beautiful paintings. These had almost all been chipped away and replaced by crude graffiti, mostly of the Sun symbol of Ra. Statues lay broken on the floor, the detritus of an ancient faith.

'But where is the memory lamp?' Harad asked. 'You don't think it's been destroyed, do you?'

'There you go again,' Qintu said. 'Always the gloomy one.'

'It is here somewhere,' Shamana said. 'The ancients always kept the old ways alive. Remember the underwater sanctum at Anahastra.'

They searched for over an hour for the lamp. There was no sign of it, not even a painting on the wall. Soon their search was being hindered by the thickening dusk.

'We may as well get some sleep,' Murima said. 'We can continue the search at first light.'

Soon the fugitive Helati were curled up in their blankets, their breathing seeming to sigh around the walls of Sangra-bad. For one of their number however, sleep would not come. Cusha, haunted by the promise that her memory would be restored, rose from her makeshift bed. Taking care not to wake the others, she started to walk around the temple walls, running her hands over the defaced murals, imagining them as they once were when the world was new and the Helati were free. Absent-mindedly, she began to sing. It was the same song that had alerted Shamana, the one fragment of Cusha's childhood memories to survive intact.

'*In the forest
there is a clearing,
where the sun picks out new growth.*'

Harad looked across for a moment and smiled. Qintu stuffed his hands over his ears. Cusha continued her walk.

'*And from the earth*

kissed by the wind
is a flower meant for us both.'

Then, even as the last word left her lips, Cusha heard something. It was faint, little more than a whisper. No, that wasn't it. This wasn't made by a human voice. It was a rustling sound. Stepping between two columns, Cusha found herself in a murky gallery. Here, there was hardly any light at all, nothing to help her pick out the interior of the room. Feeling something on her face, Cusha started. But it was sand. She reached out her hand. Sure enough, it was spiralling down from above. Stepping back, Cusha looked up. She could just make out a fine trickle of the sand. Reaching out her palm, she watched it gather. But where was it coming from? Instinctively, she started to sing again.

'In the forest
there is a clearing
where the sun picks out . . .'

The sand was falling more quickly and that wasn't all. As it gathered in a small pile on the floor, she heard a grating sound, like bricks rubbing together.

'And from the earth,
kissed by the wind
is a flower meant for us both.'

At that, the sand began to gush and the sound of rock scraping against rock became louder and louder still. Finally, Cusha saw where it was coming from. A section of the floor had begun to roll back.

'Shamana,' she called excitedly. 'Shamana, I think I've found it.'

3

'Vishtar,' Julmira said, 'thank Ra your strength is returning.'

She helped Vishtar to sit up and offered him some water. He drank for a moment, life flickering back into his eyes, then pulled away. 'How long is it since the Darkwing fed?' he asked. 'How long have I been sleeping?'

'Two days,' Julmira said. 'At least, that's what Aurun-Kai tells me. How am I supposed to know how long it is in this dungeon?'

Vishtar blinked away the stupor of blood loss. 'Two days!' He was wide-awake now. 'Where is he?'

'The Darkwing?' Julmira said. 'Gone.'

'And Aurun-Kai?'

'He brought food and water a few hours ago,' Julmira replied. 'Since that time, I haven't seen him.'

Vishtar's mind filled with memories of their botched attempt to escape. 'I failed,' he said.

'It doesn't matter,' she said soothingly. 'Everything's going to be all right.'

Vishtar stared at her as if she had taken leave of her senses. 'Are you mad?' Vishtar was completely alert, his face a picture of bewilderment. 'What did he tell you?'

'He's going to let us go,' Julmira explained.

'Listen to me,' he said. 'Whatever you think it is you heard, believe me, that monster is never going to let us go. Either we escape, or we languish here until the end of time.'

'No,' Julmira said. 'No, listen to me. I remember what he said word for word.'

Vishtar waited to hear. 'Then tell me,' he said, 'word for word.'

Joy lit Julmira's eyes. 'He said he was going to set us free.'

'That's it?' Vishtar asked. 'There was nothing else?'

'Yes,' Julmira said. 'He looked at you and said: *the next time I drink from you it will be the last.*'

At that, Vishtar buried his head in his hands.

'What's wrong?' Julmira said. 'I thought you'd be pleased.'

'Pleased?' Vishtar shook his head. 'Julmira, are all daughters of the Sol-ket as empty-headed as you? Are you so desperate to get out of this awful place that you're prepared to convince yourself of the impossible? I swear, you are willing to believe anything, just so long as it holds out the promise of escape.'

Julmira's brow furrowed. She resented Vishtar's words. How dare a Helat think himself superior to her, a member of the Imperial family?

'Did he say anything else?' Vishtar said. 'How did he act?'

Julmira's eyes flicked away from his face, just for a second.

'What is it?' Vishtar said. 'What did he do?'

She led Vishtar to the still open door and pointed outside before explaining how the demon lord suspended her over the sheer drop.

'This is no happy ending,' Vishtar said. 'The next time he feeds, I am going to die.'

4

Alerted by Cusha's cry, her companions crowded round the large hole that had opened in the floor.

'Light your torches,' Shamana said.

'What about the Lost Souls?' Harad asked, casting an anxious glance at the temple door. 'Won't the light draw them in?'

'We must take that chance,' Shamana said. 'Without the memory lamp, we are lost anyway. Cusha must recover her identity. She must learn the nature of her powers. There's no point trying to hide now. We must find the lamp quickly and flee.'

Qintu lit a torch and held it over the hole. Shamana took a second from Harad. 'I don't see any stairs.'

Cusha didn't wait for them to be discovered. Without warning, she snatched Qintu's torch and jumped into space.

'Cusha!' Shamana used the light of her torch to search for her.

'It's all right,' Cusha said. 'I'm not hurt.'

'Do you see anything?' Murima asked.

'Give the child a chance,' Shamana said. 'String your bows and keep your eyes peeled. The demons may yet come.'

Cusha explored the underground room, padding across the sandy floor in her bare feet. 'It's here,' she said, with a cry of delight.

Sure enough, right in front of her, hanging from an iron bracket, was the lamp. It was made of glass and decorated in enamel and gold. Metal chains were attached to the handles and there were inscriptions in the same ancient script she had seen in the mausoleum of Udmanesh. Within it glowed a silvery light. Cusha explained what she could see.

'That's your memory,' Shamana said. 'Is there any oil in the lamp? It is the oil that will release it.'

'Oil? I don't know.'

Cusha held the torch closer. The lamp was empty. There

was nothing but a handful of dried white petals, clearly very old, and a crust of yellow wax.

'No!' she cried, desolation in her heart. 'It can't be. My memory is here before me but I can't release it.'

'Cusha,' Shamana said. 'Speak to me.'

'The lamp,' Cusha said. 'It's empty.'

'It's not possible,' Shamana said.

Cusha sank to her knees. As she did so, she let fall the night orchids Harad had picked for her. One white bloom fell into the lamp. Cusha frowned for a moment then slowly stroked her torch against the lamp. The heat released a pungent odour. Immediately a vision entered her mind. It was the holy man. He was much younger, but it was unmistakeably him.

'The Night Orchid!' she cried.

'What's she saying?' Murima asked.

'It's the Night Orchid,' Cusha repeated excitedly.

'Of course,' Shamana said. 'That's what the song's about. Cusha, don't burn the petals. The smoke will be dissipated too quickly. Crush the petals to produce the oil then warm it in the lamp.'

Cusha did as she was told. Soon, inside the lamp, there was a layer of filmy white oil.

'Now warm it,' Shamana said. 'Hurry, the night breed are close by. I can sense them.'

The flames were already doing their work. Soon Cusha's nostrils were filling with the oil's perfume.

5

The Grand Army had a visitor. When the caravan of the Lord-priest Linem-hotec reached the army encampment, it was as if a shudder ran through the assembled warriors. As the camels and horses made their way forward, seasoned warriors moved out of the caravan's path. Few men were brave enough to make eye contact with the saffron-robed priests. Even the cream of the Sol-ket averted their gaze. General Barath met Linem with all due honours, but Linem dismissed the formalities with a wave of the hand. Within minutes of his arrival, he was addressing the senior officers.

'My lords,' he said, after reviewing all the available intelligence, 'it is obvious that we are in the midst of a grave crisis.'

There wasn't a single dissenting voice.

'I was still mourning the loss of my son, Shirep-hotec,' Linem said, 'when bad news and dire omens started gathering like buzzards. Even as I speak, within earshot of this council, the Lost Souls face our lines. They have overrun much of northern Jinghara, slaughtering thousands of villagers and putting the rest to flight. Refugees have begun to swell the towns of central Jinghara. If we do not halt the Darkwing's army then the road to Parcep and then to golden Rinaghar itself will be open.'

He paused to take a sip of water.

'It must be obvious to you all that the Darkwing has embarked on a campaign of extermination.'

His words attracted a murmur of assent.

'Events at Karangpur prove that the night breed are a demon rabble no more, but a potent threat to the Empire. They are organised. They wield weapons. They possess war machines.'

His eyes swept the members of the council. 'What's more, the Darkwing has already struck once at Tiger-gated Parcep, violating the Temple of Ra and abducting Commander Rishal's daughter.'

Rishal showed no emotion. 'Generals, warriors, priests of Ra, there is worse still to relate.'

Those assembled exchanged looks of apprehension.

'One of our greatest foes, a woman we believed to be long dead, has emerged from hiding. I refer to the She-wolf of Tanjuristan. She leads a criminal band.'

A murmur ran through the room. It was a name even the youngest warriors knew. For years, mothers had used it to discipline their children.

'The She-wolf, Shamana as she calls herself now, may evade our justice nine hundred times and ninety-nine, but on the thousandth time she meets our swords she will die. That, brother Sol-ket, brother Hotec-Ra, is my prophecy, my promise to you. We will destroy this threat. We will overcome all our obstacles. We will defend the Empire to the last drop of our blood.'

He rose to his feet. 'We will prevail no matter what.' He drew his sword and roared the Imperial battle cry. 'Victory or death!'

His cry was greeted with thunderous acclamation.

'Victory or death!'

6

For a long time there wasn't a murmur from the underground chamber where Cusha had breathed the vapours of the memory lamp.

'Is she all right?' Murima asked.

'I'll go down,' Harad said.

'No,' Shamana said. 'Leave her. Imagine what thoughts and feelings are assailing her. Break in on them and you may cause Cusha great pain, even harm. Let her absorb her memories and face her destiny. She must do it in her own way and in her own time. The child may have many tears to shed before she is ready to come back to us.'

The four settled down to wait. They remained vigilant, looking out for fliers, but all the time their thoughts were with Cusha. Then, as the first rays of the morning sun started to break over the eastern horizon, Cusha's voice could be heard at last, though it was almost inaudible.

'Shamana,' she said. 'I did it. I breathed the vapours. I know who I am.'

Seeing Cusha climbing back up, Harad and Qintu reached down to help her.

'Did you suffer?' Murima asked anxiously.

Cusha hugged her adoptive mother. 'I'm fine, Mama-li. I feel . . . whole.' She turned and grasped Shamana's calloused hands. 'I saw them all: mother, father, Vishtar. Finally . . .' She bit her lip. 'I remember hearing my parents die. The Sol-ket hunted them down as heretics. But Vishtar and I escaped. We had a guide. Then the Darkwing came for my brother and we were separated.'

Tears glistened on her cheeks. 'It hurts. Knowing who I am; it hurts so much.'

Shamana took Cusha's face in her hands and kissed her forehead. 'I know. Things are once more in balance. You have sensed the joy of regaining your memory. You now remember your mother's kisses, your father's embraces. But you also know the pain of memory. They come hand in hand, these two, just like the boy and the girl who will renew the world. Such is the life of mortal women and men. The sweetest pleasure is often laced with sadness.'

'There is another memory,' Cusha said.

Shamana gave her a questioning look.

'The holy man,' Cusha said. 'He came to our house many times. I remember what my mother called him.'

'And what was that?'

'Udmanesh.'

'By the Four Winds!' Shamana said. 'He lives.' The news

310

shook her to the core of her being. 'But how can that be? He would have survived many centuries.' She thought for a moment. 'Did he ever touch you?' she asked.

Cusha shook her head. 'You think he is a ghost?'

'Perhaps.'

Finally, Shamana brushed back Cusha's hair. 'Are you ready to face the Darkwing?' she asked.

Cusha breathed the warm morning air. 'I am ready.'

CHAPTER 16

The Great Wall

I

The Darkwing's mind was made up. The fliers were a sledgehammer, too crude an instrument for the task of securing Cusha. Atrakon, on the other hand, was a scalpel, much more effective. Yes, the Selessian would deliver the Holy Child to him. That one man should prove so much more efficient than all his russet minions irritated the Darkwing. It seemed to call into question his belief in a new, superior, demon race. Nevertheless, everything was falling into place. Cusha was making her way ever closer to his lair, doggedly tracked up the rugged hills by the single-minded Atrakon. She believed she was doing it of her own volition. She believed that she had free will.

'How delicious,' the Darkwing sighed. 'The Holy Child rushes to rescue her brother. But all she will succeed in doing is offering me eternal life.' He stretched his wings.

'And this Selessian is equally eager to detach her from her companions.'

He gave the matter a little more thought then chuckled with satisfaction. At the right time, he would instruct his fliers to give Atrakon a little help to separate the Holy Child from her allies.

'Then, at a convenient moment,' the Darkwing said, 'I will pluck her away from you, my Selessian friend. Yes, it is all going according to plan.'

2

In the Darkwing's absence, Aurun-Kai had relaxed the restrictions on Julmira's movement. She couldn't escape from the tower, after all.

'Does that creature feel no pity?' Julmira asked.

'Many times over the last eight years I have tried to shake his attachment to the Darkwing. Sad to say, his obedience to his master is absolute.'

'I think he's contemptible,' Julmira said.

Vishtar laughed out loud. 'I'll wager you have a fierce temper, Julmira-ax-Sol.'

Julmira pouted a protest. 'What makes you say that?'

'I saw you throw your plate at him,' Vishtar answered.

Julmira allowed herself a smile. 'You liked that, didn't you?'

'Of course,' Vishtar said. 'Can I tell you something?'

Julmira inclined her head. 'You are the first ax-Sol I have met. I did not dream we would get on so well. We could almost be friends.'

Julmira looked at him. 'Almost,' she said. 'But when all this is over, things will be as they were. I will remember our time in the Black Tower, Vishtar.' She sighed. 'You must know friendship between us is impossible.'

Vishtar nodded. 'I know.'

'I'm glad you understand.'

With that, she was gone. Vishtar stared after her, his heart heavy. He sat a while then returned to his own room. On his way he passed the open door where the Darkwing had dangled Julmira over the dizzy precipice. He listened to the roar of the wind. He couldn't help but wonder why neither the Darkwing nor Aurun-Kai had closed it. Something had indeed changed in the tower. The very fabric of the place felt different, yet, for all the new relaxation in its rules, Vishtar was more than troubled. For eight years there had been a routine. Every day Aurun-Kai had delivered his meals. Every month the Darkwing had come to drain the lifeblood from his veins. Suddenly, things were changing.

'What's happening?' he murmured. 'Why is everything different?'

The more he asked the question, the more the dark shadows of unease and apprehension started to rise from the corners of his mind. This was no accident, no act of forgetfulness.

'You're coming, aren't you, Cusha?'

How could he have been so blind? After all these years his beloved sister would be here. That's why the Darkwing had left the entrance to the tower open wide, to entice her, to draw her ever nearer. Vishtar walked to the door and looked out. Darkness seeped into every fibre of his being. Even now, the demon lord was approaching the Black Tower to wait for her. Vishtar watched the monster coming from the east, fresh from launching his war host against the Grand Army.

'By the Four Winds,' said Vishtar, watching his return. 'How could I have been such a fool? It's a trap.'

3

The monsoon broke that day, the ninth of Hoj. Through the thunder and the endless, drumming rain, Kulmat watched for some sign of the demon offensive. Like the storm, the demon presence had become ever more oppressive. The assault came in the early hours, when mortals are at their weakest and least alert. He even saw the Darkwing give the order to attack. The demon lord hovered over the battle lines, wings outstretched, and unleashed the night breed on the Sol-ket trenches and picket lines. Strangely, once he had given the command, he wheeled away to the west and left the field. It was a sight that gave Kulmat not the slightest encouragement. Already, the night breed were hurling themselves again and again at the Grand Army's lines. Creatures of the night that they were, they had no interest whatsoever in their own self-preservation. The Imperial soldiers, many knuckling the sleep from their eyes, hurried to their posts.

They soon understood that this was no skirmish. The Battle of Jinghara Plain, an event that would live long in the annals of historians, had begun. Dark-fliers swept down in their thousands, hurling throwing knives, axes and balls of Lyrian fire. The effect on the Sol-ket and their allies was devastating. The screams of the dead and the dying soon mingled with the roar of the rain and the growl of the thunder. Those still alive after that first murderous onslaught slithered and skidded on the earth, rendered slimy by the pounding rainstorm. The officers' guttural commands failed to put a stop to the confusion. Each time the battle-hardened veterans managed to restore some semblance of order, a new menace would erupt. The latest shock came in the form of catapults and ballistae, hauled into place by seemingly endless columns of night-striders. Maybe this was the reason for the brief interregnum between the Lost Souls' attacks. They had been repairing their engines of war. Rocks, blazing oil and dozens of baskets of hissing cobras crashed among the soldiers, injecting yet more terror into the soul of the army. Finally, just as the advance ranks were beginning to waver, Rishal arrived on his black steed.

'Don't crowd together,' he roared, physically driving some of the terrified soldiers back to their positions. 'You are making it easier for the projectiles to cause maximum damage. If you want to save your skins, for Ra's sake thin your lines.'

His presence had an immediate effect. The soldiers shuffled into their assigned places. 'That's it,' Rishal said, approving the return of order, 'pull back at the rear. Give the front ranks a chance to take evasive action. Pass the word along.'

Spurring his horse, he galloped between the newly organised rows of soldiers. This time, instead of the threats with which he had assailed the first soldiers, he brought encouragement to bear.

'That's it, my brave lads. Use your heads. Battles aren't just won by muscles and blades, you know, but by our wits.'

In spite of the shrieks of the dark-fliers and the relentless drone of the night-striders, Rishal's voice seemed to carry the length and breadth of the Imperial cohorts.

'Now, plant your feet and draw your weapons. You are the sons of fine and honourable women, the future of mankind, the beating heart of the Empire of all the Peoples. Choose your targets and strike well. Tonight, if you hold fast, you will win immortal fame.'

His horse reared, gleaming and magnificent in the

streaming downpour. Erect in the saddle, Rishal raised his sword. 'Present your standards, my brothers.'

'Victory or death!'

Rishal stood in the stirrups. 'For your Emperor.'

'Victory or death!'

He threw both arms high above his head, a mace in one, a sword in the other, a sign that he had tossed aside his shield and cared nothing for his own safety. 'For your families, victory or death!'

'Victory or death!'

With that, Rishal swung his horse round towards the oncoming night-striders. The other generals joined him. Seeing the army on the verge of breaking and running, they had summoned their leadership in the centre, where the elite troops of the whole Empire were concentrated.

'As one man, charge!'

Their nerves steadied by their commander's words, the Grand Army rose like a tidal wave and hurtled towards the oncoming night breed. With a huge crash the two titanic forces came together in the mist and the rain and the blood. The earth shuddered. It was as if Hell itself flinched at the impact.

4

Far off, the five companions were poling across the swollen confluence of the two mountain streams. They had long since left the rolling plains behind and had been climbing steep slopes for hours. Their cloaks were useless against the driving rain and were clinging to their skin like tissue. The rain had been beating down for an age, enveloping the entire landscape and what few living creatures moved there in a grey fug, occasionally illuminated by crackling lightning. In truth, it was impossible to tell if it was day or night. Only the Demon Wall could be distinguished in the seemingly endless gloom, a lowering, monumental presence that promised only further trials. Soon every one of the struggling Helat band was drenched to the skin, their hair plastered to their glistening faces. From their vantage point, where the storm raked the wooded mountain slopes overlooking the open grassland, they could hear the unmistakeable sounds of battle.

'It's begun,' Shamana said, 'the Battle of Jinghara Plain. Man and demon locked in mutual slaughter.'

'Then we must make haste,' Cusha said.

'Why?' Harad asked, shouting over the howl of the wind. 'What can we do to change the course of the battle? We're going in the opposite direction.'

'And why would we want to try to do anything?' Qintu demanded. 'Let the butchers of our people perish.'

'Yes,' Shamana said, 'and see an army of Lost Souls twice, even three times its present size fall upon the land and the cities like hungry wolves. Have you forgotten that the Helati live alongside their masters? Do you imagine that the demons would discriminate between master and slave? They never have before. Whatever our hatreds and divisions, we are one human race. We will not die as master or slave, but as human beings.'

Chastened, Qintu stabbed his pole into the streambed and heaved.

'Do you want me to divulge to them what we face at the Black Tower?' Shamana asked under her breath. 'Do you want them to know how thin the dividing line between victory and defeat is?'

Cusha shook her head. 'It would be better to protect them from the rising darkness,' she said. 'What could I tell them, after all? That I could soon be dead, drained of my

living blood, or more alive than at any time in my existence, mistress of all the ghosts of the world? I do not fully
understand the dangers that await us, myself. I know that
light and dark will be in perfect balance there. I also know
that either great good or great evil will emerge from within
its walls.'

Shamana closed her eyes and sniffed the air. 'So it is
written in the Book of Scales.' She took Cusha's hand. 'So
it will be.'

5

The going was hard. Atrakon's mount snorted with the effort
of climbing the slope after the fugitives. The stallion bowed
his head, as if the heavy skies were weighing down on him.
Thunder grumbled through the sparkling rain, cascading
round him like shards of broken glass. Whipping and stabbing, the droplets coursed over his face and through his hair.
His clothes were clinging to him like a second skin.

'By the Almighty!' he gasped. 'Rarely have I seen such a
storm.'

As he urged his reluctant mount forward through the
screaming darkness, Atrakon continued to find his mind
filling with a starburst of images. He remembered Shirep
and Linem and the promise of freedom. He remembered
Shamana. She posed the greatest threat to his mission. He
was still brooding on the events of his journey west when he
caught sight of his quarry crossing a clearing in the forest.

They were making their way towards a cave where they
might shelter. This was no Suravan, but a mere recess in a
rock face. Once they were inside, there would be no escape.
Atrakon dismounted and led his horse through the dense
woods that carpeted the slopes. From there, he began his

vigil. He had to find a way to overcome the She-wolf. With her out of the way, he would have little trouble dealing with the others.

He could almost taste his freedom.

6

Gardep, Oled and Aaliya were also pushing on through the storm. Since picking up the five fugitives' trail, they hadn't spoken for almost an hour. There was little point. The storm was howling around them, the thunder and the drumbeat of the rain combining to overwhelm all other sounds. The monsoon, so different from the gentler version that broke over Parcep and Rinaghar, had entered every atom of this strange, increasingly desolate world. Here, it was harder, more extreme, like the terrain. The three riders no longer looked for dark-fliers or night-striders. The creatures had ignored them so many times; it was obvious they had more pressing concerns. They were absorbed in the Darkwing's thoughts.

Aaliya was excited at the prospect of rejoining her mistress. Oled was looking forward to the end of his exile. But the road ahead promised to be littered with broken bodies and the innocent usually died along with the guilty. All these years Oled had been preparing for this challenge and now his hands trembled at the thought of what was waiting for him.

Gardep's mind was in turmoil. Cusha, as ever, was in his thoughts. Much as he yearned to see her face again, he dreaded her contempt. Then there was the prophecy. Twice it had been foretold that he would meet his destiny on the tenth of Hoj. He had heard it first as he stumbled through the foothills of the Dragon mountains as a boy.

Eight long years later, Shamana had spoken of it. Gardep longed for day to dawn, yet he dreaded its consequences.

Finally, Aaliya spoke. 'There is something you should know,' she said.

Something in the shape-shifter's voice caused Gardep concern. 'What is it? What's wrong?'

'They are being followed.'

Gardep digested the news. 'Then we must make haste.'

7

No matter how many of the Darkwing's followers the Sol-ket and their allies cut down, still more swept in to take their place, and all this without the direction of their curiously absent master. Rishal was having a minor wound dressed before returning to the battle.

'Is there no end to it?' he said under his breath.

From his place among the wounded, Kulmat heard the question and trembled. If even Rishal was having doubts, how could the army endure? Kulmat peered into the gloom. Man and demon were mired in filth, spattered with mud and gore, almost indistinguishable from one another in the grim, brown swamp that was the battlefield. And still the grinding conflict continued.

'Hold them!' Barath was roaring. He dismounted and set about the surging mass of night-striders with his sword. 'Stand firm, Sol-ket,' he bellowed. 'Know this, warriors: if you yield now the road to Parcep is open.'

The fighters had heard this appeal before. What had been stirring when first uttered now sounded desperate. Their sense of doom was reinforced by the presence of the ghosts. The sky was boiling with them. For the second time the Sol-ket were on the verge of breaking.

CHAPTER 17

The Black Tower Revisited

I

The fugitive band passed beyond the Demon Wall and entered the lands to the west. Soon they would see the Black Tower. They trudged silently through the driving rain, slipping and sliding on the increasingly treacherous ground.

'Your parents were priests?' Shamana said at last.

Cusha nodded. 'Like you, they kept alive the ways of the past. Somebody betrayed them to the Sol-ket.'

'It must hurt to know the truth.'

'It does,' Cusha said, 'but it is better this way. Nothing will ever be worse than the darkness in which I lived my life until now.' She wiped the rain from her face. 'This way I can complete the work they began.'

'I always knew you were strong,' Shamana said.

'Is it true what you have always said? Will Gardep be there with us at the Black Tower?'

'Why?' Shamana said. 'Is that what you want?'

Cusha seemed uncertain. 'I think so. I . . . I don't know how I feel. But how will he ever find us?'

'He is on his way,' Shamana said. 'You can be sure of that. Believe me, there is no power on Earth or in Hell that will keep him from you.'

2

In a final throw of the dice, Rishal, Barath and the other commanders called up their reserves.

'Charge the demon centre,' Rishal bawled. 'Do it now!'

The approach of the heavy cavalry caused the earth to rumble beneath the feet of the struggling fighters. Rain glistened on their hides, turning them into blurred juggernauts. Even the night-striders paused for a moment at the sound of the charge. Spears and arrows flew. So dark, so curtained in rain, so mired in filth was the battlefield, nobody could be sure if it was friend or foe who fell beneath the murderous shafts. Before the charge the front lines convulsed, the bodies of the living and the dead being sent spinning through the air by the ocean crash of the impact.

But even the elite Sol-ket were of limited value against the limitless multitude put on the field by the Darkwing. Though they had shaken the Lost Souls at first, the press of the night breed soon hemmed them in. The last hope of the Imperial Army was being bogged down in the mud and surrounded.

'By Ra,' Barath groaned. 'We're finished.'

3

Shamana advised that they take shelter in a cave. Murima was gathering what food they had left: a few scraps of flatbread, some meat, some paste made from spiced chickpeas. They were all exhausted after the climb. She wished she could offer them more.

'This is the last,' she said. 'I pray we reach journey's end soon.'

'It's not far,' Shamana said.

Then she stopped. Turning her head, she raised her hand. Instinctively, everyone looked out into the drumming rain, gleaming on the rocks. A thin dawn light was making its way through the greyness of the monsoon. Pointing to the weapons stacked against the cave wall, Shamana silently urged her companions to arm themselves. Inching forward to the mouth, she peered outside. Something was moving.

'Shamana,' Murima asked, 'what do you hear?'

Easing her sword from its scabbard, Shamana crept forward, feeling the splash of the rain on her face. Behind her, Cusha had started to move. Shamana stopped her with a pointed finger. Sure that the Holy Child was in the safest place possible, Shamana weighed the drawn sword in her hand.

'They're here,' she said. 'Dark-fliers!'

The fliers exploded from the gloom, fighting one another to reach the Helati.

Swinging her blade in a lethal arc, Shamana cut a swathe through the nearest demons. 'Draw your bows,' she yelled. 'I can't stop them all.'

Soon the hail of arrows was thinning the crowd of hissing fliers. In the confusion, what nobody saw was a dark figure stealing towards Cusha.

4

The Darkwing approached Vishtar.

'Well,' Vishtar said, offering his throat defiantly, 'what are you waiting for?'

The demon lord set Vishtar down on the far side of the room and manacled him to a set of chains hanging from the wall.

'There is no hurry,' he said. 'I am going to feed on you presently. I will not touch you until I have your sister. Your blood and Cusha's must mingle while warm and fresh or I will not be made anew. When she arrives I will take her. Then I will return to finish you.'

Vishtar set his jaw. He stared back at the Darkwing, hatred in his eyes. But he didn't say a word.

'Soon,' the Darkwing said, 'the Holy Child will be mine. My victory is at hand. Do you understand what is about to happen? All this corruption of flesh will fall away. I will be as I was, young and alive, but with this one difference. I will have all the powers of the risen dead. A new world will replace this domain of suffering. I shall be all.' He turned. 'I must leave you for a little while, Vishtar, to get my prize. On my return, you and your beloved sister will open the gates of eternity for me.'

5

With a roar, Shamana transformed. A raging elephant shook off the attacking fliers. Her tusks speared a pair of them and sent them tumbling down the mountainside towards the abandoned terraces carved from the lower slopes. Shaking her great head back and forth, the shape-shifter scattered her attackers. As they came again, the fliers plunged into another volley of arrows. Their shrieks echoed across the mountaintops.

'How are your quivers?' Shamana demanded.

'Maybe a dozen arrows between us,' Harad answered.

Shamana cursed and charged the night breed again, but they were coming from every direction, slashing and biting. Drops of blood beaded the grey elephant hide. Cuts and gashes criss-crossed its back. The press of the demons was becoming intolerable. Any moment, Shamana thought, they will overwhelm me. She tried one last, desperate stratagem. Transforming into a mouse she scurried under their frenzied attack and returned to human form behind them, this time hurling a succession of daggers and throwing stars. The fliers wheeled round and attacked again. This was it, Shamana thought, the final stand. But, as the night breed came on, a volley of arrows cut them down one after the other. Shamana recognised the archer.

'Aaliya. Thank the Four Winds.'

The words were barely out of her mouth when Gardep burst through the gloom, cutting down the demons. Oled was at his side, swinging his battle-axe at the remaining fliers. Caught between Aaliya's arrows and the charge of Gardep and Oled, the last of the dark-fliers vanished into the night. Oled leaped from his horse and threw his arms round Shamana.

'Mother. You're safe.'

Murima, Harad and Qintu stumbled forward, exhausted but safe. They exchanged glances.

'Yes,' Shamana said, 'this is my son Oled. We and the priestess Aaliya are the last of the Tanjurs.'

Then the joy in her eyes dimmed. Something was wrong. Gardep was riding back and forth. He looked distraught.

'Where's Cusha?' he cried.

Shamana's gaze swept the scene. 'Cusha!'

'She was right by my side,' Harad said.

But she was gone.

6

Four men conducted themselves with the greatest courage during the Battle of Jinghara Plain. They were the Generals Rishal and Barath, and their junior officers Murak and Kulmat. Kulmat led the wounded men from the field hospital. At the head of this regiment of walking wounded, he went forward into the furnace of battle. His hastily donned armour ran red from his wounds. Standing shoulder to shoulder, they stiffened the ordinary soldiers' resolve and plugged each gap that opened in the Sol-ket ranks. If anything, Murak was even more prominent. This one learns fast, Rishal thought. Murak went to the left flank, where many senior officers had fallen. He surprised everyone with his ability to take command. Here was a junior officer rallying leaderless men and forging them into a fighting unit. Yet, no matter how courageously they fought, no matter how tenaciously they rallied to the Sun standard, they knew the day was lost. They would perish with honour.

'Look,' Kulmat said, 'on the eastern horizon, the face of holy Ra.'

Sure enough, the sun was beginning to rise. Then the din of battle started to fade.

'What's happening?'

The night breed were drawing back.

'Is it over?' Kulmat asked.

'No,' said Rishal. 'Quite the opposite. They sense that our strength is broken. They are bracing themselves for the final onslaught. There is no other explanation.'

As if to confirm his prediction, every surviving night-strider moved into line. Overhead, the first faltering rays of dawn were quickly obscured by the gathering dark-fliers. The drumbeats and roars of the Lost Souls rose to a crescendo. The death blow was about to fall.

'Farewell, my brothers,' Rishal said. 'Acquit yourselves with courage. Do not lay down your lives cheaply.' He shouted against the rapidly swelling clamour. 'If the time of man is ending, let it pass in glory. Victory or death!'

Seemingly for the last time the Sol-ket summoned their age-old battle-cry: 'Victory or death!'

7

Atrakon spurred his horse down the mountain slope. Ahead the going would be easier.

'At last my debt will be discharged. I will be free.'

Cusha stared at him. Atrakon was leading her mount. Her hands were bound behind her back. 'How did you turn into the creature you have become?' she asked. 'I sense honour in you but you will not embrace it. How can you win freedom for yourself but deny it to me?'

Atrakon set his face.

'How can you let yourself be used by the Sol-ket?' she demanded.

'You know nothing of me,' Atrakon said.

'But I will,' Cusha retorted.

'You think so?' Atrakon snorted. 'I doubt it. I will soon have you delivered to Lord Linem.'

'Shamana will stop you,' Cusha said.

'Oh, I think not,' Atrakon said. 'I know all about the She-wolf and her kind. What I just saw was a very old, exhausted shape-shifter. By the time she recovers her strength, we will be long gone.'

'You think I'm helpless, don't you?' Cusha said.

Atrakon shook his head. 'Save your breath. I'm not going to listen.'

'No?' Cusha asked.

'No,' Atrakon said. 'There's nothing you can say or do that will make any difference. Your fate is sealed.'

Cusha started to struggle with her bonds. 'If that's what you think,' she cried, 'then you don't know me.'

Without another word, she twisted her body and recklessly hurled herself from the saddle, crashing to the earth. She was lucky not to land on one of the rocks that jutted through the thin soil. Lucky, or favoured by providence.

'By the Almighty!' Atrakon said. 'Do you want to kill yourself?'

He reined in his horse. Cusha was lying, apparently senseless. She had fallen awkwardly, her face hidden from him. Brushing back her hair, he turned her head.

'Cusha?'

Her eyes snapped open, but they were not the eyes of a fifteen-year-old girl. In place of the pupil, the iris, the whites, her eyes were the purest obsidian black.

'No!' Atrakon cried. 'What sorcery is this?'

Cusha raised herself on one elbow. Gritting her teeth, she struggled for a few moments before easing her hands from her bonds. Cusha pointed at her captor.

'You are afraid, Atrakon,' she said. 'Tell me why.'

Atrakon was scrambling backwards, kicking with his legs.

'You know I am not a demon,' Cusha said. 'A demon you could fight. There is courage in your soul. I know what you are experiencing. It is . . . shame.'

Springing forward, she gripped his shoulders and stared

deep inside him. 'You fear your past. You dread judgement.' She dug her fingers into his flesh. 'I see her. I have found the one you dare not face.' Then a sigh welled up from within. 'Come forth, Leila Ebrahin,' she said.

At the name of his wife, Atrakon flinched.

'I summon the shade of Leila Ebrahin,' Cusha intoned. 'Rise from the House of the Dead, sister. Give your verdict on this man.'

Atrakon watched in appalled fascination as something made its hissing approach through the earth.

'Rise!'

In the time it takes a heart to give a single beat, the ghost of Atrakon's wife stood before him.

'Why?' she said, in a voice as deep and mournful as the soughing of the night wind. 'Why do you do it, my beloved? Why do you serve the oppressors?'

Sobbing like a child, Atrakon tried to hide his face, but Cusha tore his hands away. 'Look into her face, Atrakon Ebrahin,' she commanded.

'What good is vengeance,' the ghost of Leila Ebrahin demanded, 'when you sell your very soul? What good is retribution when you kneel at the feet of evil?'

Atrakon cried in pain, his arms outstretched. 'I loved you so,' he groaned.

'And I you,' Leila answered. 'But how can I love the man you have been these many years: a killer, a mercenary?'

Atrakon clamped his hands to his ears in a vain attempt to block out her accusations.

'Now, by delivering this girl to the oppressors, you would become a child-killer too. This is an abomination, husband. Do this and you deserve to rot in the deepest pit of Hell.'

'I don't want to deliver her to the Hotec-Ra,' Atrakon cried. 'But how else can I win my freedom?'

'You cannot take the road to freedom if the way there is through the dismal vale of tyranny,' Leila said. 'Though you would shrug off your own burdens, every day your conscience would remind you that you had only passed them on to others.'

'Let me have your forgiveness, Leila,' Atrakon cried.

'If you want absolution, husband, there is only one way to attain it. You must make yourself anew and be the man you can.'

'But how?' Atrakon said.

He looked at Cusha and repeated the question.

'You must find that answer for yourself, Atrakon Ebrahin,' she said. 'Go. The ghost of your wife will not leave until you have completed your journey. Then you will know what to do.'

Atrakon stared at her. 'You do not condemn me,' he said, 'though I was going to turn you over to the Hotec-Ra.'

'I have no more to say to you, Atrakon,' Cusha said. 'I must go my way and you must go yours. Discover your destiny as I have discovered mine. Who knows? We may meet again some day.'

'You humble me, Holy Child,' Atrakon said.

Cusha saw two riders in the distance and a pair of golden eagles flying overhead.

'That's my friends,' she said. 'Go now, Atrakon. They may not be as forgiving as me.'

8

Cusha started to walk unsteadily towards her companions. The eagles had to be Shamana and Aaliya. There was also a rider unknown to her. But one figure she recognised immediately. It was Gardep. He was waving. Her heart lifted to see him and she waved back. But Gardep wasn't just waving. He was shouting and pointing at something in the sky. Suddenly, Cusha felt a cold shadow fall over her. Spinning round, she gazed upward, right into the face of the Darkwing as he swooped upon her. Before Gardep could reach her or Atrakon could react to her screams, the demon lord had swept her off her feet and up into the sky.

'Cusha!' Gardep cried.

He wheeled his horse round and set off in pursuit. Even as he followed, the unknown warrior took the form of an eagle, just as Shamana and Aaliya had. The shape-shifters attacked the Darkwing, slashing with their talons, but were forced to retreat by the demon-lord's superior power.

'Eagles,' the Darkwing scoffed. 'Is that the best you can do? Call yourself shape-shifters!' With that, he turned in the direction of the Black Tower.

Shamana issued her orders. 'Aaliya, I will pursue them to the tower in our present form,' she cried. 'Oled, follow with Gardep.'

Obeying her order, Oled dropped into the saddle, a man once more.

'We are almost there,' he said, 'the place where both our destinies lead.'

'Then let's not delay,' Gardep said. 'On to the Black Tower.'

9

Cusha was struggling wildly, clawing at the Darkwing with her outstretched hand. He saw her eyes turn obsidian, like his own. But the Darkwing was familiar with the dark spaces of the world.

'What?' he snarled. 'Did you think to use your newly

discovered tricks on me, the demon lord? Do you imagine that there is some shade you can raise from the House of the Dead to shame me?' He thrust his monstrous face into hers, chilling her soul. 'Believe me, after all my trials I am quite, quite shameless.'

He stroked Cusha's throat. 'I see one of my children has fed on you already. That's good. You know what to expect.'

Cusha flinched, remembering the steely fangs that had sunk into her flesh.

At that moment they flew low over a menacing-looking crag. Beyond the spur, the plainest, simplest, most monumental of buildings loomed. They had reached the Black Tower. Through the open door, Cusha saw a boy chained to the wall.

'Vishtar,' she said. 'My brother.'

'Cusha.'

'How touching,' the Darkwing said, setting her down. 'Now, which of you wants to watch the other die first?' He chained Cusha to the wall opposite her brother, out of his reach.

'The time has come,' the demon lord said. 'Never will your hands touch. Never will you repair the damage wrought by the Hotec-Ra. Forget the futile prophecies you have heard. The past belongs to mankind, the future to a far superior race. There will be a brief moment of pain, then you will be able to sleep for all eternity, secure in the knowledge that you have served a greater purpose. By mingling your blood and his' – he indicated the struggling Vishtar – 'with mine, I will repair the damage to this wretched body. I will be made anew.'

Behind the Darkwing, sweeping back and forth, darkflier guards protected the approaches to the tower. Nothing could stop the creature.

10

Gardep reached the tower. 'There is no entrance,' he cried.
'Up here!'

It was Shamana's voice. Sure enough, high above their
heads, near the top of the tower, a door was open. There
was no cause for celebration. A dozen dark-fliers protected
it.

'But how, in the name of Ra, do we reach it?' Gardep
demanded. 'Can you help, Oled?'

Oled shook his head. 'An eagle would never be able
to carry you,' he said, 'and how would we get past the
dark-fliers?'

They stared at the impossible task until Shamana and
Aaliya appeared, back in human form.

'Forget the open door,' Shamana said. 'It is too well
protected. The Darkwing wants us to launch an all-out
assault and be torn to shreds by his guards. Mortal men
built this tower in times gone by and you can't build from
top down. No, there has to be another way in.'

She stared at the stone walls. 'This will take great
concentration.'

'What are you going to do?' Oled asked, concerned.

'Something you obviously haven't, my son. I will take
the form of an insect and probe every nook and cranny.'

Shamana joined her palms and closed her eyes. Oled
knew this was the most dangerous of the shape-shifter's
arts, to metamorphose into a creature so dissimilar in size
and weight to oneself. Nobody spoke. Then it began. Slowly
Shamana shrank. Her body became encrusted in a black
carapace. Six spindly legs emerged from her body. Within
moments a tiny beetle was scurrying over the surface of the
building.

'Gardep,' Oled said, looking upwards, 'look.'

Half the dark-fliers were moving towards them.

'It looks like Shamana was right,' Gardep said. 'Why would they attack if there wasn't an entry here?'

11

'No more arrows!' Gardep shouted, inspecting his quiver. 'We have to fight them at close quarters.'

It was exactly what Oled wanted. He was master of the axe and brought down two of the creatures as they hurtled towards him. Gardep drove his sword through a third but it continued to hiss and slash at him until Oled beheaded the creature. The remaining dark-fliers wheeled away to prepare for another assault.

'I just wish I had some arrows,' Aaliya said. 'Hand to hand fighting with the night-fliers is a dangerous business. One slash, one bite and we could be finished.'

'Would these do?' came a familiar voice.

It was Harad. He was running towards the warriors with a full quiver. Gardep saw one dark-flier's head turn. It was about to attack.

'Throw the quiver,' Aaliya yelled. 'Now!'

Seeing the creature coming straight at him, Harad froze. This was his nightmare. He had seen two of his best friends killed by the night breed.

'Harad,' Gardep shouted again. 'If you want to live, give her the quiver.'

Harad threw the quiver with all his might. It didn't stop the dark-flier crashing into him. Screaming, Harad clung to his assailant, desperately trying to keep its fangs from his face. Instantly, the creature was being set upon from two different directions. Murima was beating it with a primitive staff while Qintu jabbed with a shattered sword blade. The dark-flier shrieked and clawed at them. The clumsy assault gave Gardep the time he needed. He didn't dare use his sword, for fear of striking Harad. So he ran forward, tearing the creature away from the boy.

'Stand back!' Aaliya cried.

Gardep pushed the dark-flier away from him. Aaliya's arrow flew straight and true, piercing the dark-flier's throat. Immediately Oled strode forward and removed its head. With two more arrows, Aaliya shot the last of the dark-fliers and Gardep finished them with his sword. He turned to see Oled raising the trembling Harad to his feet.

'Up you get,' the giant said. 'You did well. Where did these arrows come from?'

'We gathered them from the bodies of the demons,' Murima said. 'It was a messy business.'

'But not messy enough to put you off completing your journey.'

Murima shook her head. 'Did you find Cusha?' she asked. 'We hoped . . .'

'She's in there,' Gardep said.

Murima's hands flew to her face. 'By the Four Winds,' she said. 'Tell me it isn't true.'

Shamana, returned to human form, interrupted them. 'We can still save her,' she said. 'There's a mechanism. Strike here, my son.'

Oled accepted the task with relish. He spat on his hands and wielded his axe against the spot Shamana had indicated. Each time he struck, the sparks flew. At the third blow the mechanism was sprung. They had gained access to the tower.

12

'I will take you first,' the Darkwing said, bending over Cusha. 'I have tasted your brother's blood often enough.'

Cusha fought, stubbornly but without hope, twisting her head from side to side. The Darkwing seemed to enjoy her struggles. He peered at Vishtar.

'Just imagine, boy,' he said. 'There I was, desperate to drain you of every last drop of your lifeblood, but I couldn't. I had to measure it out. But now' – he raised Cusha from the floor so that her legs kicked frantically – 'I will tear open your throat with my teeth and drain you in a single gulp. Oh, to slake my thirst at last!'

Cusha could feel the demon lord's rancid breath, the stipple of his saliva. His mouth opened, revealing two rows of deadly, barbed fangs. He drew her closer, breathing in the scent of her blood through her flesh. Then she saw him blink. He looked across at the winding steps that led down to the lower floors. What had he heard? Then Cusha heard it. Blows, as if from a hammer, followed by running feet. Grunting with frustration, the Darkwing turned away from Cusha and rushed towards the stone steps.

'Guards!' he yelled. 'You are defending the wrong entrance. To the stairs.'

The remaining six dark-fliers flashed across the room and hurtled down the steps.

'I must finish this quickly,' the Darkwing said. 'In the confines of the staircase, your friends will not find it easy to get past my fliers.' He reached towards Cusha. But as he did so, he saw a reflection in her dark eyes. It was a fluttering bird.

'Maybe you should have left one guard here,' a woman's voice said.

The Darkwing spun round. 'The She-wolf,' he said. 'I remember you from Dullah. How old you have grown!'

'I have fared better than you, demon,' Shamana said, drawing her sword.

The insult seemed to sting the Darkwing. With a shriek of hatred, he came at her, steely claws slashing. Shamana defended herself well, but it was an unequal contest.

She watched in horror as the demon lord forced her back, finally driving his claws through her shoulder.

'Shamana!' Cusha cried.

But the fight wasn't over. Somebody else had entered the room. Peering round, Cusha caught sight of the newcomer. It was Gardep. Her heart turned over at the sight of his scarred face. It was exactly as the frieze of Suravan had predicted. He was racing towards her, sword unsheathed and dripping with the black blood of the Darkwing's dark-fliers. Cusha could hear the fight continuing on the stairs; the others must be covering his ascent. Gardep's chest was heaving violently with the exertion of the climb.

'Face me, Hell-fiend,' Gardep roared.

The Darkwing opened his mouth. A swarm of flies emerged. They blinded Gardep for a moment, their wings stinging his eyes, their buzzing filling his ears, forcing him to recoil. Taking advantage of the warrior's surprise, the Darkwing slashed at Gardep, but the warrior evaded the sweep of the talons, each as honed and deadly as any Sol-ket blade. Sword clashed against claw in a desperate fight. Gasping for breath, sucking each gulp into his tortured lungs, Gardep crouched, hoping Oled would overcome the dark-fliers and come to his aid.

'Do you know who I am?' the Darkwing snarled. 'From your uniform I see you are a cadet. Before you stands the greatest, most powerful Sol-ket who ever lived, renowned Sabray.'

Gardep threw the boast back at his foe. 'Sabray is dead,' he retorted. 'He was murdered by the foul tyrant who now rules in Rinaghar.'

'*I* am Sabray-ax-Sol,' the Darkwing shrieked, 'future lord of all the world.'

Gardep shook his head. 'No, you are nothing but a frame of corrupted flesh. There is not an ounce of the prince left in you.'

At that, the Darkwing hurled himself at Gardep. 'I smell blood,' he screamed, crushing Gardep beneath him. 'You have fresh wounds.'

A single claw traced the scar on Gardep's face.

'You have this brand, too,' the Darkwing said, 'the work of the Hotec-Ra, I believe.' He pressed the scorched, tender flesh. 'Does it hurt?'

Though determined to remain defiant, Gardep could not contain the scream that boiled in his throat.

'That's nothing to what you will suffer next.'

His lethal claws closed round Gardep's throat. But, much to the demon lord's consternation, a smile spread across the warrior's lips. Then the reason became clear. Having overcome the dark-fliers, Oled had entered the room. With a single blow, he scythed through Cusha's chains. The Darkwing's grip tightened and Gardep's blood oozed between the claws. But still Gardep held on, though the pain was excruciating. No matter what it took, the Holy Children must be reunited.

Seeing her chance, Cusha flung herself across the floor and reached for Vishtar's hand. Even then, the battle wasn't over. Aurun-Kai appeared and thrust a spear at Cusha. Two desperate struggles ensued, one between Aurun-Kai and Oled, determined to defend Cusha, the other between

Gardep and the Darkwing. That's when the decisive blood was shed. With a low moan, Aurun-Kai slumped to the floor, the axe-head sticking from his chest.

'Finish it!' Oled shouted.

Cusha clasped Vishtar's hand. At their touch the very fabric of the air seemed to resonate with a dark power. The doorway was filled with a raging maelstrom of spectral figures. Ghosts. Hundreds of them filled the chamber. Many thousands more swirled outside. All sound fell away and concentric circles of energy rippled out from the twins. In a pathetic attempt to claw back the ghosts, the Darkwing grabbed at their intangible forms. Despair was written into his features.

'Look!' Oled said.

Like a spreading whirlwind, the ripples eddied across the landscape. Countless multitudes of ghosts rode the translucent waves. On and on, the silent storm swept.

Then Oled saw Shamana. 'Mother?' he asked anxiously.

Shamana pushed herself up into a sitting position. Aaliya tended to her, pressing a bandage to her wound.

'I'll be all right,' she said. 'The wound is slight.'

'But is it over?' Vishtar asked. 'Have we won?'

Cusha squeezed his hand and smiled. 'Soon,' she said, turning to the Darkwing, 'your dread reign will be over. By the time the sun has set upon this day, none shall serve you. Go, lord of nothing, go into exile.'

Emitting one last shriek of venomous hatred, the Darkwing fled. Soon, he was no more than a blemish on the flesh of the sky. Staggering unsteadily to his feet, Gardep pressed a hand to his bleeding flesh. With the other, he struck off Vishtar's manacles. 'I have faced my destiny,' he said.

'Yes,' Cusha said. 'Your servitude to the throne of Ra is over. When the next sun rises you will take the first steps towards freedom.' She embraced Vishtar, then turned his face toward the door. 'Look,' she said, 'these are our comrades. Without them, we would never have got this far.'

Murima, Harad and Qintu had appeared at the top of the steps. Shortly afterwards Julmira, who had been hiding during the course of the fight, emerged from the shadows.

'What about me?' she asked, her voice trembling.

'You have nothing to fear from us,' Shamana said. 'We will set you on the road back to your own people.'

Julmira looked grateful.

'Just try to remember,' Shamana added, 'you owe your freedom to slaves.'

Even then, Julmira's expression registered distaste. She, the same as a Helat? Never!

Cusha barely heard the exchange. She had gone over to Gardep. Her face was full of joy.

'Come, Vishtar,' Oled said.

Vishtar frowned.

'Don't worry about your sister,' Oled told him. 'She will be along presently.'

With those words, he led Vishtar down the tower's many stone steps. The warrior and the Holy Child were left alone. Gardep had his back to Cusha, struggling with his emotions. He no longer knew what he believed or where he belonged. Then something happened, something that meant it hardly mattered any more. He felt Cusha's hand pressing his palm.

'I don't understand,' he said. 'You felt nothing but contempt for me.'

'I despised the man the Sol-ket had made you,' she said, remembering the way Leila had spoken to Atrakon. 'I believe that one day I can love the man you have chosen to become.'

Gardep looked at her, his heart full. 'When will that day be?' he asked.

By way of reply, Cusha reached up and took his face in her hands. In the heat of a Jingharan morning she pressed her lips to his and felt an immeasurable joy.

13

The impact of the twins' touch was seen most dramatically at the Battle of Jinghara Plain. Lying prone in the mud, his face being held by a night-strider's skeletal hands, Kulmat was coughing and spluttering, desperately trying to force the thick, brown ooze from his nostrils and mouth. Lungs bursting, he expected the end at any moment. Then, as quickly as the night-strider's steely hands had applied the agonising pressure, it relaxed. Gratefully gulping down delicious breaths of air and spluttering gouts of oily sludge, Kulmat rolled over and propped himself up on his elbows. He continued to spit the filth from his mouth until at last he recovered his senses. When he did so, he couldn't believe what he saw.

The length and breadth of the killing field, the demons were reeling, clutching their heads and emitting plaintive, tortured groans. The swirling ghosts were descending from the skies and entering the Lost Souls by way of their mouths. Once reunited with their ghosts, their conscious spirits, these soldiers of the dead, until moments before seemingly invincible, were now stumbling around the battlefield like frightened children. As if appalled by their own condition, and by the new knowledge of what they had done in the Darkwing's name, the night-striders were staggering drunkenly, clawing at their faces. One or two even seized swords from the appalled Sol-ket and fell on them, so ending their torment. The dark-fliers, the most savage and merciless of the Darkwing's minions, had also broken off their assault. Some were tumbling from the air and lying in crumpled heaps in the mud, whimpering like beaten dogs. Others were flying recklessly, out of control, through the heat of a Jingharan morning, broken kites spiralling in a high wind. Still others simply continued to fly in lazy circles, keening helplessly, trying to fathom what had happened to them. Kulmat mirrored their confusion.

'What's happened?' he wondered out loud.

Rishal, as thoroughly caked by mud and gore as Kulmat, shook his head in utter bewilderment.

'By the holy face of Ra, this is . . . a miracle.' He searched for the words. 'The Sun god has saved us.'

He could feel the morning sun beginning to dry his soaked uniform. Barely daring to believe the battle was over, his fellow fighters watched the night breed as they reeled across the battlefield, completely oblivious to the attentions of their human opponents.

'I don't understand,' Kulmat said.

Nobody attempted a reply. In truth, after so long a slaughter, even the Sol-ket had lost their taste for war. But not Rishal. Gathering his senses, he issued a command.

'Seize the time,' he cried. 'Slaughter the vermin.'

Nobody moved.

'Well, do I have to repeat the command? Behead them, every one.'

A few Sol-ket did as they were bid. Most just stared. 'My Lord,' one man said. 'There is no need to kill them.'

In the light of the civil war that had erupted among the Lost Souls, Rishal's order made little sense. Soon even the most obedient warriors sheathed their swords. Beheading the night breed had been like hacking at mannequins. They

343

offered no resistance. They were either stumbling about like sleepwalkers or crumpled on the ground, shrieking in horror. In normal times sheathing your sword when ordered to complete a kill would have been an act of insubordination, punishable by death. These were not normal times. The men stared at their commander, pleading. Rishal met their look and nodded.

'You are right,' he murmured. 'The demons are broken. We will do no more fighting this day.' He threw his hands into the air. 'We have won. Rejoice!'

At these words, the Sol-ket started to celebrate. Some embraced. Others capered wildly, despite the bodies of their comrades littering the battlefield. Still others broke out the kinthi and started to pour great quantities of the fiery liquid down their throats.

'Victory,' Rishal cried. 'A great and memorable victory.'

Barath joined in the shouts of triumph. 'The threat to the Empire has been lifted.'

In the middle of the increasingly wild celebrations, a figure in saffron robes appeared. It was Linem-hotec. But for once his presence went virtually unnoticed. The dancing went on. Casting a scornful look at the show of vainglory, Linem drew the two generals aside.

'Did you sanction this?' he asked. His voice was low, but menacing.

'Of course,' Barath said, a certain nervousness evident in his speech. 'We are victorious, are we not?'

Out of earshot of the men, Linem turned his quiet fury on their leaders. 'Call yourself commanders?' he hissed. 'Call yourselves Sons of Ra? We have not won, you fools.'

'Look around you,' Rishal retorted. 'The creatures have been put to flight.'

'Don't lie to yourselves, generals,' Linem growled. 'We lost.'

Bewildered, Rishal and Barath turned in his direction.

'Do you not understand why the demons have broken off the attack?' Linem said. 'It is the work of the Holy Children. They have conquered the demon lord.'

Seeing the continuing looks of confusion, Linem sighed.

'The Darkwing is banished. The Holy Children have returned the ghosts to their former bodies. The Lost Souls know what they were and what they are now. They have discovered conscience. The realisation tortures them.' He pointed toward the Great Wall. 'The Darkwing sought to end the rule of men and bring a new race to dominance. For now his great scheme has been thwarted. He may rise again but not this day. For now the danger comes, not from the west, but from within the Empire itself.'

'Then should we not celebrate?' Barath asked.

'The legions of the Lost Souls are disintegrating as we talk,' Linem said. 'But a far greater threat may yet rise in the east, at the heart of the Empire. All these years, the Blood Moon has cowed our slaves and made them obedient. Ask yourselves this, gentlemen: what will hold them down now?'

He looked at the dancing warriors. 'The Helati will not rise this day or tomorrow. They have neither the leadership nor the organisation. Indeed, the servile masses do not even know what has happened here. But understand this, we must track down the Darkwing's conquerors. Though they are few, they may soon become thousands. We must find them and exterminate them before they can spread their message.'

He shook his head at the mayhem around him. 'Let your soldiers have their fun, if you wish. I dare say it is good for morale.' He wrinkled his nose in distaste.

'Then, once they have slept off their headaches, have them give the dead a respectful funeral. Send your men to the nearest town. Tell them to take their rest and heal their wounds. We may even engage in the farce of a victory parade. Yes, make it Parcep or even golden Rinaghar. It pleases the crowds and puts some backbone into the men. But once restored to battle-fitness, the Sol-ket must return to serious business. They will scour the land for some sign of the Holy Children and their allies. If we allow this pestilence to spread, we may soon become the Lost Souls ourselves. In the coming weeks, months and years we will face a desperate fight for the survival of our kind.'

Subdued, Rishal and Barath nodded. They understood the truth of the Lord-priest's admonishment. Linem reached for the Sun symbol of Ra on a fluttering standard and pressed it to his lips. After a moment's silent meditation he delivered his final words.

'The story does not end this day. It has only just begun.'

The Lost Souls Stories Book 2

SETTING OF A CRUEL SUN

To Paul Foot —
rise like lions from your slumbers.

CHAPTER 1

The Nine

I

It was the day the sun began to die, the tenth day of Hoj, in the year 675. After that day, nothing would ever be the same again. On Jinghara Plain two mighty armies clashed. Hour after hour, in thunder and pounding rain, man and demon fought their pitched battle. The carnage was terrible to behold. War elephants fell with piteous roars. Horses screamed as their riders tumbled from the saddle, dead by the time they struck the ground. In return the hands of men struck down the demon predators. Black blood sprayed through the murk and chaos of battle. But nothing slowed the assault of the night breed. Millions strong, they fought without concern for their own safety. Without conscience, without thought, they were mere tools of a superior, but hate-swollen intelligence. These legions of the undead, minds swirling with blood lust, attacked and attacked, then attacked again. Mired in mud, slithering through the blood and filth of battle, the two sides wore each other down.

But it wasn't the ocean crash of war that changed history. Just as the great Sol-ket army, pride of the Muzal Empire, started to waver, just as the oceanic press of the undead threatened to engulf the beleaguered ranks of their foe, the battle ended. At the moment of their triumph, for no apparent reason, the demons dropped their weapons. Some fell to the ground, wailing and gnashing their yellow, rotting teeth. Others chose self-slaughter. Before the astonished eyes of the Grand Army of the Empire, their ferocious enemy dissolved into a wretched, despairing rabble. There was no breakthrough, no final rally, no heroic charge to break their ranks. There appeared to be no reason for their collapse. Strange to say, the demon host just stopped fighting.

The cause of the battle's unexpected end was not to be found among the struggling combatants, but on a desolate crag miles away. In a dark tower, high on a bare mountain, an unlikely band of nine travellers severed the bond between the demon lord and his night breed. The Nine overcame him through courage, wisdom and faith. They did what many thousands of soldiers had failed to do by force of arms: they ended the demon plague that had terrorised the land for many generations.

As dawn broke over Jinghara, two of the Nine appeared in the doorway of the Black Tower, barely able to believe that the fight was at an end. The first to step out into the morning light was Gardep, a boy of sixteen summers. Though he was a warrior Sol-ket, he had not fought at Jinghara Plain. Losing faith in his god and his code, he had given up allegiance to the Empire of the Sun. Inspired by strange new ideas, he had fought in the Black Tower. His opponent was the general of the demon masses. It had been a savage struggle. There was fresh blood on his tunic and a scar on his face, evidence of the arduous journey he had undertaken to reach this place.

A young woman followed him out onto the mountain-side. She was Cusha, the slave-girl who had set these events in motion. Though, by law, Gardep could have purchased a slave-girl like her any time he wanted, she would never be his property. She was unique. She was the woman he loved. Gardep had given up all his privileges, everything he had ever known, to protect her from evil. He had fought battles, suffered torture, all to be by her side.

'Is it really over?' Gardep asked, lifting his face to feel the sun's rays.

'Yes, it's over,' Cusha said, darting a look towards the top floor of the tower where they had fought the demon lord. 'We have conquered the Darkwing and broken his power over the Lost Souls. Their long servitude is over. We have liberated them from the horror of living death.'

Hope was in the air. By dusk however, the joy of victory would have been replaced by bitter despair.

'This is a strange kind of freedom,' Gardep observed, pointing across the bare mountainside that led to the Black Tower.

The demon lord was defeated. Now the aftermath was unfolding before their eyes. Ghosts were circling the tower like a stream of Lyrian fire. They were prising open the mouths of the undead. The translucent phantoms then forced the Lost Souls to swallow them whole. Immediately the faces of the night-striders, the foot soldiers of the undead, changed. For centuries, these monstrous predators had terrorised the land. No longer.

They had become bewildered men and women, appalled by their own condition. Against their will they had been raised from the grave and trapped in the slimy, decomposing shells of the night breed. The bestial hunger that normally lingered in their eyes faded, replaced by something that was recognisably human. First, they registered confusion. Then came a fearful understanding.

'Look at them,' Cusha said. 'They have recovered their consciousness. They know that they were once mortal men and women, like us. I pity them.'

She was right to feel pity. Rational thought did not bring joy to the night-striders. Out of the fog of primal blood-lust came the bright, searing light of shame. One turned his own sword on himself. Driving in the blade, he slashed open his belly. His entrails spilled like so many wriggling eels on the stony ground.

'Poor creature,' Cusha said. 'He can remember what the Darkwing made him. He can remember how he was resurrected from the cold clay to kill and maim the innocent.'

The night-strider's fading eyes met hers.

'Imagine his feelings,' she said. 'All those years, his mind was shrouded in ignorance. He obeyed the demon lord, becoming the monster's unthinking tool. By breaking the Darkwing's power, we have brought it all flooding back. We have shown him the full horror of what he has done.'

All around them, the night breed were wailing and moaning, clutching their faces, beating their heads and chests. Cusha and Gardep had heard them moan before, but not like this. It wasn't the dismal chorus that had filled the night hours, promising the living a wretched, agonising end. This was a piteous whine. The once merciless creatures were begging for an end to the thoughts that had begun to torture their newly-conscious minds. One of them fell to his knees, palms flat, forehead thumping the floor. That's when it happened. The night-strider lifted his head and met Gardep's eye.

'End my suffering,' the creature begged. 'I can't bear this any longer.'

Gardep recoiled in horror. 'You spoke!'

Gardep had never heard the creatures formulate human speech. A snarl, a screech, yes, but not intelligent communication. Ignoring Gardep's cry of astonishment, the night-strider grabbed for his ankle. 'Please, Lord. End my torment.'

Gardep shot Cusha a querying glance. She nodded. Gardep then unsheathed his sword and beheaded the tortured soul kneeling before him.

'He spoke to me,' Gardep said.

Cusha didn't answer. It wasn't clear to Gardep whether she understood what was happening. He was wiping the black blood from the blade when he saw one of his comrades, a giant by the name of Oled Lonetread.

'Oled,' he said, calling him over, 'where is everyone?'

Oled was a full head and shoulders taller than any man Gardep had ever met. He was powerfully built, like a lumbering mountain bear. Little wonder. Oled was one of the last of his kind, a Tanjur. The Tanjurs were known as the people of the dragon, shape-shifters who could assume the form of wild beasts. Sometimes their beast-form was reflected in their human gait. Once they had been nomads, wandering the length and breadth of the Jingharan Plain. Now there were just three remaining survivors of this once mighty race.

'They are employed in the same grim task as yourself, Gardep,' Oled answered. 'The night-striders want to die. We decided to give a merciful end to those that asked.'

Cusha's eyes glistened with tears. 'To think, they have suffered the fate of the living dead. Now this.'

Oled shrugged. 'Nobody said the world was fair, Holy Child.'

Cusha knew the truth of Oled's words. 'Take us to the others,' she said.

The Tanjur led the short walk to the cave where the others were taking what rest they could get. It wasn't easy. For as far as the eye could see, hundreds of demons were exposing their flesh to the sun, allowing themselves to be consumed by fire. Such was the multitude of the risen dead that the whole world seemed to be ablaze.

'Here they are!' Harad shouted gleefully.

He came running, his eyes flashing a joyful greeting. Harad was Cusha's adoptive brother, a boy of almost fourteen summers. Cusha was a year older.

'You've finished then?' he asked.

Cusha smiled at Gardep. 'We haven't even begun.'

Harad frowned then turned to watch the Lost Souls. 'Did you ever see anything like it?'

Cusha shook her head. 'It's terrible.'

'Terrible?' The word was spoken by Qintu, Harad's best friend. 'I don't see what's so terrible about demons killing themselves,' he grumbled. 'They've killed enough of us in their time.' He scowled, remembering one such day of blood. 'Good riddance, I say.'

Cusha listened. Yes, good riddance to the Lost Souls. A shadow crossed her mind. It was the Darkwing. Yes, and good riddance to him, too.

2

But Cusha had dismissed her nemesis too easily. The Darkwing did not die in the Black Tower. He fled. Leaving the ancient building far behind, he flew far and wide across Jinghara, alone in defeat, desolate in exile. As the sun rose in the cloudless sky, burning away the few wisps of morning mist, he saw roving bands of his Lost Souls, utterly disoriented by their new condition. Once or twice he called to them, just as he had for many years, summoning them to implacable war on mankind. But they did not obey. If they looked at him at all, it was with eyes full of hatred, loathing their former master for the countless crimes he had made them commit. There they were, the unthinking, obedient creatures he had once formed into an army of many millions. But they had understanding. They had consciousness. Damn them, they had free will. In their new condition, they rejected him, spitting their contempt, glaring their hatred.

The Darkwing saw the Demon Wall. The Muzals had erected it as a barrier against his hordes. It was abandoned now. He had driven the defenders from its battlements and keeps, slaying most, driving the rest into the arms of their comrades, gibbering with nerve-shredding tales of butchery and horror. There, a little way beyond, was the fortress of Zindhar. He had triumphed there too, killing the garrison to the last man before torching it. He almost smiled at the memory. But smiles don't come easily to ruined faces such as his.

Once, so many years ago, he had been a prince of the Muzal Empire, a darling of the court. Possessed of charm and courage, dashing good looks and a ready wit, it was only a matter of time before he ascended to the Imperial throne in his father's place. But he had fallen from grace.

An evil priesthood had summoned the dark arts, subjecting him to an ordeal that cocooned his body and soul in a shroud of torture and decay. That made him what he was today, a monster. The Darkwing closed his eyes for a moment, conjuring his own form in his mind's eye. His body was encased in a scarlet and black carapace, a giant insect shell. Vast, leathery wings gave him the power of flight. Lethal claws tipped his fingers and toes. His head was repulsive to all living things, a bare, raven-black skull from which a pair of merciless eyes stared, inky with vengeance. Surrounding him, no matter where he went, no matter whose company he sought, there was the putrid aroma of decomposing flesh. He was the distillation of death, cruelly denied the escape of oblivion. His only succour was revenge.

Revenge. He slowed the beat of his wings. Of course. Defeated I might be for now. Exiled too. But I will not be destroyed. He circled, pondering his next move. He imagined the Holy Children, reunited, swapping stories of the lives they had led while apart.

'Enjoy your triumph,' he snarled. 'It will not last long.'

3

Atrakon Ebrahin sat apart from the others. He had fought alongside them against the Darkwing. But they did not trust him. Why should they? He was a late convert to their cause. Atrakon was an assassin by trade. But for the Holy Child, he would be a mercenary still, taking lives at the behest of the Imperial priesthood. He gave Cusha a sideways glance. She had rescued him from his former life. His brown eyes welled with gratitude.

'Will you eat with us?' Cusha asked, catching his eye.

'Will your comrades accept me into their company?'
Atrakon asked.

Oled speared him with a suspicious glare. He'd cast his
vote already.

'Come and join us, Atrakon,' Shamana said, ignoring
her son's hostility. 'Cusha vouches for you. That is good
enough for me.'

Shamana was old. Atrakon didn't know how old. But
she had the agility and power of a predatory beast. She was
a shape-shifter like her son.

'Thank you.'

Atrakon sat as far as he could from Oled. The cook,
Murima, Cusha's adopted mother, was serving what food
they had. Atrakon found himself staring at the small band.
It was a long time since he had broken bread with a
family (for that's what adversity had made this strange
group). He watched Murima fussing over everyone. She
was Harad's natural mother. She had also taken Qintu
under her wing. Cusha, the orphan brought to her by
Shamana, also called her Mama-li. The shape-shifters ate
in silence. Besides the priestess Shamana and her son Oled,
there was Aaliya, third and last survivor of a proud race.
Finally, there was the boy-warrior, Gardep.

'Can I ask you something, Gardep na-Vassyrian?'
Atrakon asked.

Gardep turned his head. 'Ask your question, Selessian.'

'When I look around those assembled here, I understand their motives. They are slaves, shape-shifters. They
have no stake in this Empire. For years, the Sol-ket has
treated them as beasts of burden. They have a reason for
fighting for their freedom. But why you? You are Sol-ket.
You were raised to serve the Imperial cause.' He turned in
the direction of the great battle. 'Why are you not over
there, fighting alongside your brother Sol-ket?'

Gardep chose to answer simply. 'I have chosen to act according to my conscience.'

'Or your heart,' Shamana said, a mischievous glint in her eye.

Gardep felt Cusha's hand steal into his. 'What Shamana says is true,' he admitted. 'It has been my love for a woman that has changed me. I have served the Empire all my life. Until just a few months ago, I was Sol-ket, raised as a member of the warrior caste and content to remain part of it until I died. The garrison barracks was my home, the prosecution of war my sole horizon. The Sol-ket put a sword in my hand and taught me to cut throats and break bones. They made me a man. Cusha has done something more important. She has made me a man with a soul.'

Gardep thought of his great friend Kulmat, still serving in the Imperial Army. When would he too take the first step to freedom?

'What now?' Atrakon asked.

There was a brief silence.

'You have conquered the Darkwing,' Atrakon said. 'But the job is only half done. The Empire still stands.' He could feel everyone's eyes on him.

'The Selessian is right,' somebody said behind him. It was the final member of the group, Vishtar, the boy they had come so far to free. 'I have been eight years in this prison,' he said. 'Young as I am, I have a right to speak. The Darkwing is broken, but the Muzals still rule. Have you forgotten so soon that the Helat masses have two enemies, not one?'

'Nobody has forgotten,' Shamana said. 'We have come far, Vishtar. We have fought many battles. Soon we will resume our quest. What Atrakon says is true. For freedom to endure, the Empire must fall. But that is for the future. Now it is time to rest.'

Atrakon shook his head. 'The Empire will not rest. Within days the Sol-ket will be scouring the countryside for you.' He hesitated, aware that he had said *you*, not *us*. Oled would surely have noticed the slip of the tongue. 'Already the Hotec-Ra will be drawing up plans to destroy you.'

At the mention of the Imperial priesthood, Oled spoke. 'You should know, Selessian. You served those saffron-robed thugs.'

Atrakon did his best not to react. 'You're right, Oled Lonetread. I served them. But I did not do it for money. A great injustice was done to me and my family. I sold my soul to avenge the wrong.'

Judging by his face, Oled was far from convinced. Atrakon was in no mood to appease him.

'I will not plead with you to accept me,' Atrakon said. 'Ask me to go and I will leave this minute.' He indicated Cusha with an outstretched palm. 'This Holy Child redeemed me. I accept criticism from her and no other. She made me see what I had become. The night-striders are not the only Lost Souls.'

With a fierce stare, Shamana prevented Oled interrupting. 'You are welcome among us, Atrakon Ebrahin. You turned from the Hotec-Ra when you could have bought your freedom from them and returned to your own land. You chose to turn your back on the oppressor and bring our dear Cusha back to us. In my eyes, you are a man of honour.'

Gratitude showed in Atrakon's face. He knew Oled didn't trust him. Changing the giant's mind would take time.

'Then I will stay,' Atrakon said. 'Until your quest is at an end, my sword will be at your service.'

4

At the site of the battle of Jinghara Plain, the council of war was about to end. Linem-hotec, Lord-priest of Rinaghar, the second most powerful man in the Empire after Muzal himself, was speaking. At his side stood Timu-hotec, his new deputy. Linem indicated the demons that were staggering aimlessly across the battlefield.

'The legions of the Lost Souls are disintegrating as we speak. But a far greater threat may yet rise in the east, at the heart of the Empire. All these years, the Blood Moon has cowed our slaves and made them obedient. Ask yourselves this, gentlemen: what will hold them down now?'

He fixed the officers around him with a stare. 'The Helati will not rise this day or tomorrow. They have neither the leadership nor the organisation. Indeed, the servile masses do not even know what has happened here. But understand this, we must track down the Darkwing's conquerors. Though they are few, they may soon become thousands. We must find them and exterminate them before they can spread their message.'

He finished his speech and dismissed the Council. The senior generals, Rishal and Barath, were about to go when Linem called them back.

'Would you accompany me to my quarters?' he asked. 'There is somebody I want you to meet.'

Rishal and Barath followed Linem to his tent. There, they found a junior officer, Murak.

'What's this all about?' Rishal demanded. 'As General of the Grand Army, I am a busy man.'

Linem gave him a superior smile. 'You are keen to capture the rebels, are you not?'

'You know I am.'

'Then this is the man to help you do it.'

Rishal eyed Murak with suspicion. 'I don't understand.'

Linem savoured the moment. 'Meet priest Murak of the Hotec-Ra.'

'Priest!' Rishal exclaimed. 'But I've seen you before. You were at our side during the battle. You're just a cavalry captain.'

'That's what you were meant to think,' Linem said. 'My apologies for the deception, commander.'

'Do you want to tell us what this is all about?' Barath demanded.

'I have been following the Helat plot for many years,' Linem said. 'We in the Hotec-Ra have not been idle. We employed Atrakon to track Shamana and the Holy Children. We rather hoped he would deal with this traitor Sol-ket of yours. Unfortunately, the Selessian has proved a great disappointment to us.'

Rishal scowled. He didn't like being reminded about Gardep. Before he went over to the enemy, the young warrior had been Rishal's own squire.

Linem watched the effect of Gardep's name on the commander before continuing. 'Murak here was our second line of attack. The Hotec-Ra always have several irons in the fire. He was assigned to follow Oled Lonetread's every move.'

'Why was I not informed?' Rishal wanted to know.

'The Hotec-Ra can't afford to be too transparent, General Rishal,' Linem replied. 'One of our roles is to gather intelligence. That requires secrecy.'

'Go on,' Rishal said. He was developing a grudging respect for this priest. A strong right arm wasn't enough to rule an empire. You needed cunning and ruthlessness too.

'I have had my eye on Oled Lonetread for some time,' Linem said. 'I hoped he would lead us to his mother, the

She-wolf of Tanjur. This Shamana has been a burr under our saddle for some time. Sadly, the son is as incorruptible as the mother. During his time as a scout at Zindhar, my agents attempted many times to sway him to the Imperial side. He refused every time. We had to find a different way to draw him into our web. We decided to use his soft heart against him. I employed Murak to gain scout Lonetread's trust.' He glanced at Barath. 'You, General, were an unwitting pawn in the game. When you took such an obvious dislike to Oled at Karangpur, Murak saw his chance. He pretended to take Oled's side.'

'By Ra, you're devious!' Barath exclaimed.

'Thank you,' Linem said, revelling in the compliment. 'Trust me, Murak will deliver the heads of the Helat plotters.' He then explained his plan. 'We could move against the Nine. But why rush? We are in a strong position. We can insert Murak into their ranks. Then every time some Helat malcontent rushes to their banner, we will have his name. Why settle for crushing one rebellion when we can behead all future rebellions?'

Rishal and Barath swapped glances. The idea of weeding out potential rebels appealed to them. This priest was a master strategist.

'You have our support,' Rishal said.

'Thank you,' Linem said. 'I will set events in motion.'

Rishal and Barath left satisfied. Linem watched them go then turned to Murak. 'They are pleased.'

'So they should be, Your Holiness,' Murak said.

'You understand what I must do?' Linem asked. 'This has to look convincing or the rebels will not accept you.'

Murak nodded. 'I understand.'

'And you subject yourself to this trial of your own free will?'

'I do, Your Holiness.'

'Before we begin,' Linem said, 'let me give you this.'

He passed Murak a ring. It was embossed with the symbol of the Hotec-Ra. Timu's eyes flashed. This he hadn't expected.

'Your Holiness?' Murak said, allowing it to nestle in his palm.

'Oh, no false modesty, please,' Linem said. 'You understand the significance. It is the seal of the Hotec-Ra, the eyes and ears of the Sun God. My adopted son Shirep wore this ring until his untimely death. Oled murdered him. I want you to take Shirep's place at my right hand. I am making you second lord-priest of the Hotec-Ra. If anything happens to me, you will take my place.'

Timu was staring in horror. So soon after taking the dead Shirep's place at Linem's side, he was being usurped, tossed aside like a discarded garment.

'This is a great honour,' Murak said, his heart pounding with joy at his sudden advancement. He noticed Timu standing just behind Linem's right shoulder. As attendant to the lord-priest, Timu clearly believed he should have received Shirep's ring next.

'You will not be able to wear it until your mission is completed,' Linem said, taking the ring back and handing it to Timu. 'It will be kept for you at the Ziggurat of Ra.'

Timu put the ring away. His resentment was obvious. Murak made a mental note. His rival would not forgive this slight.

Linem snapped his fingers. A dozen saffron-robed Hotec-Ra, led by Timu, lined up to their right and left. Timu passed Murak a phial of green liquid.

'Drain it to the dregs, Murak,' Linem said. 'It will lessen the pain.'

Murak drank the potion. He showed little emotion.

Linem admired him for that.

'You will give me the Helat plotters,' Linem said. 'In return, I will give you a place at my side.' He drew Murak to one side, leaving Timu to seethe with impotent rage. 'Now that you are my adopted son, I wish to share something in confidence.'

Murak waited, barely breathing.

'The Emperor is in his seventy-third year,' Linem said. 'He will not live for ever.'

Still Murak didn't speak but his throat was dry with excitement.

'The army is the Empire's strong right arm, Murak. We, the Hotec-Ra, are its brain. I assume you know which is the more important.'

'Obviously it is the head, Your Holiness.'

'It is. We are taking our first steps towards the Sun Throne, Murak. The defeat of the Darkwing and the Helat conspiracy have given us our chance. We must seize the opportunity before Muzal throws the Empire away.'

He guided Murak back to the waiting priests. He didn't stay to see them give Murak his beating, a beating in which Timu took special, almost sadistic, pleasure. Instead, he slipped out of the tent.

He didn't notice the bat-like shadow that was sweeping towards him.

5

Cusha and Vishtar were sitting side by side, watching the knots of night-striders in the distance. Though they were brother and sister, they had been separated for eight years. They had been talking for an hour, maybe more, rediscovering this or that childhood memory.

'I was the lucky one,' Cusha said. 'Unlike you, I didn't have any memories of a happier time to torture me. But for the memory lamp, I would still be in ignorance.'

'What was it like,' Vishtar asked, 'living without a past?'

'Every waking moment I ached to know who I was,' Cusha told him. 'The day I breathed the vapours of the memory lamp, my heart sang for joy.'

'My memories caused me no pain,' Vishtar said. 'Thinking about you, knowing one day we might be reunited, was the one thing that kept me alive.'

'You must have been so afraid.'

Vishtar nodded.

Cusha hugged her knees. 'We conquered him. We defeated the demon lord.'

Vishtar smiled. For someone who had changed the entire world, his beautiful sister sounded so much like a child.

'All those years in that prison,' Cusha said, 'it must have been terrible.'

Vishtar agreed. 'But I had my books. Just imagine the things I learned during all those hours of study. I can speak ten languages: Khut, Miridan, Selessian, Obir, many more.'

Cusha noticed that he was blinking continually and his eyes were streaming. 'Does the sun hurt them?' she asked.

'I am not used to it,' Vishtar admitted. 'For eight years I have lived in a perpetual twilight. The only source of illumination was a line of flickering candles. Sitting here, beneath the golden sun, it is as if a fire has been lit inside my brain.' He squeezed Cusha's hand. 'For all that, I would not want to return to my cell. Listen.'

Birdsong was welling up from the lower slopes. Together, the Holy Children listened to the chorus of finches.

'Up there!' Vishtar cried excitedly.

A crane was drifting across the sky. To Vishtar, after eight years in a windowless cell, it was impossibly beautiful.

'But for Shamana,' Cusha said, 'none of this could have happened.'

'She is a great sorceress,' Vishtar agreed.

'She wouldn't thank you for saying that,' Cusha told him. 'She is a priestess of the Scales. Sorcery, she says, is for the dark forces of this world.'

Vishtar nodded. Sorcery had given the world the Lost Souls. Who knows what future horrors the dark arts were preparing. The twins talked this way for a long time. Suddenly, without any warning, Vishtar's body went rigid. He convulsed, a glassy stare in his eyes.

'Vishtar!' She took his hand. It was clammy with fear. 'What is it, my brother?'

Then she felt it herself. Though it was not yet noon, she could feel tendrils of darkness coiling around her, constricting her throat, invading her soul. A sliver of ice entered her heart. Vishtar's eyes cleared. Slowly, he straightened his back.

'You sense him too, don't you?' he asked. He didn't need to speak the demon lord's name. 'I can feel his shadow advancing across the land.'

'But we defeated him,' Cusha cried.

'Maybe not,' Vishtar said. 'He has no army. That does not mean he is finished.'

In a gesture of panic, Cusha wound her fingers through her hair. 'Tell me it's not true!'

Vishtar shook his head. 'I am not going to tell you lies, sister. We both sense him. We see the shadow world behind this one, you and I. We hear the chorus of the dead. We feel the pulse of hell throbbing beneath our feet. You must accept the inevitable, Cusha. The monster is not done with us yet.'

Cusha turned away, as if willing the evil presence to fade and die.

'Our companions talk as if the Darkwing's time is over,' Vishtar said, refusing to let her avert her eyes from the truth. 'It is as if they believe there is one less player in the game. We know that to be false, don't we, sister?'

Cusha nodded grimly. 'In spite of all we have done,' she said, 'still his shadow is everywhere. Though his demon army is destroyed and only scattered fragments wander the land, he haunts us still. Somewhere, far from here, he is plotting his revenge.'

They sat there for a long time, imagining the Darkwing.
Vengeful.
Waiting.

6

Linem had two groups of priests to see. The first were the spies. He listened to the reports. It was true. Everywhere, the Lost Souls had become aware of their true nature. They realised that they had once been human, that they had died and risen again to commit countless evil acts. Their memories had reduced them to pathetic wretches, whimpering helplessly as their memories haunted them.

'Have the messenger pigeons returned?' he asked.

'Yes, Your Holiness.'

As yet, there hadn't been a single sighting of the rebels. They hadn't moved from the Black Tower.

'Instruct your men,' Linem said. 'They are to keep watch. The moment the rebels start to move, I am to be informed.'

'Yes, Your Holiness.'

Linem watched the smoke from the funeral pyres climbing to the sky. A battle was over. The war was about to begin. He had been expecting something like this. With each year that passed without news of the Holy Children, he had sensed disaster approaching. The Sol-ket were fools. They thought everything could be resolved by the sword. He knew that knowledge, magic and faith were more powerful tools than any weapon. He turned to a second group of priests.

'I hear you have something to show me,' he said.

'We have,' they confirmed, excitement in their voices.

'Continue,' Linem said.

One of the priests carried a terracotta pot towards him. Linem noticed the way the man walked. He seemed nervous of the pot's contents.

'What is it?'

'Fire Dust. This simple red dust may one day change the world, especially on the field of battle.'

'What does it do?'

'Let me demonstrate.'

The priests dragged in a struggling Helat. Gingerly, the head priest scooped a spoonful of the dust. Then, with a deferential smile in Linem's direction, he showered the dust over the slave. The moment it touched his flesh, the man burst into flames. Within moments he was reduced to a charred corpse.

'Excellent,' Linem said. 'How much of this material do you have?'

'Very little,' the priest admitted. 'It is important to get the mixture right. We have lost ten men during our experiments, all roasted like this poor wretch.'

'Speed up its production,' Linem said. 'This concoction of yours will give us an enormous advantage over our enemies.'

370

'Yes, Your Holiness.'

The business of the day concluded, Linem set off in the direction of his quarters. On the way, he reviewed progress. Murak would fulfil his mission. Of that he was sure. Not since Shirep had he seen so much promise in a young priest. Linem knew how Timu felt, of course. This was part of a Hotec-Ra's training. Your loyalty wasn't to the priesthood but to holy Ra himself. To become lord-priest, you had to kill your rivals. Either Murak would slay Timu, or Timu would slay Murak. It didn't matter which. The fittest would survive. The victor would come out of the experience stronger, more equipped for high office. What was one dead priest when the entire order would be strengthened by sacrifice?

He thought of the Nine. All the rebels were together now. There were no loose ends. He would use them as bait to catch all the Empire's enemies. Yes, he had good cause to feel satisfied. He was halfway back to his tent when he heard something. He paused and looked around. The bodies had been cleared from this part of the battlefield. It was deserted. Dismissing the noise as an old man's imagination, he continued towards his tent. That's when the noise came again.

'Who's there?' he asked. He turned all the way round. He saw nothing. 'Who's there?'

Before the words were out of his mouth, he felt the rush of wind, glimpsed the shadow looming over him. Instinctively, he shot a look skywards.

'You!'

A moment later the priest was gone.

7

The Holy Children reported their fears to Shamana. In spite of the heat of a Jingharan afternoon, they were both possessed by a deep, numbing cold. Sensing their fear and their almost physical misery, Shamana immediately took them seriously.

'I didn't expect him to move so quickly,' she said.

'So you knew it wasn't over?'

'We are talking about the Darkwing,' Shamana said. 'He is a creature who has ruled the entire western world. Did you really think he would quietly accept defeat then simply fade? No, somehow he will pursue you. His heart has space only for vengeance. It will go on until either you or he is dead.' She hesitated. 'There is a verse in the Book of Scales. I did not understand it until now.'

Cusha's teeth were chattering. Instinctively, though he too felt the primal bite of an impossible winter in his bones, Vishtar slipped an arm round her shoulders.

'This is what it says,' Shamana told them.

> 'From one arid land to another,
> the final struggle will spill.
> There, in the dying light,
> an innocent and generous heart
> must learn to redeem the irredeemable,
> or perish in the attempt.'

'Is there no end to this?' Cusha cried. 'Did we cross the Empire from Parcep to the western lands for nothing?'

'For nothing?' Shamana said. 'What a short memory you have. The demon lord's army is broken. Your brother is restored to you. Is that nothing?' There was anger in her voice.

Cusha regretted her outburst. 'I'm sorry, Shamana. I spoke out of turn.'

'There is no need to apologise,' Shamana said. 'You reported your fears to me right away, that is the main thing. We must inform the others.'

The Nine were soon discussing the unexpected development.

'But what does it mean?' Gardep asked. 'What can he do, one against the world?'

'If he were a mortal man,' Shamana answered, 'I would say very little but I am disturbed by the prophecy of the Scales. It is this reference to the dying light.' She looked at the Holy Children and sensed the bleak, glacial shadow that still had them both in its grip.

'You're right,' Murima said, picking up Shamana's thread. 'He is inhuman. The danger is real. We must watch over the Holy Children night and day.'

Oled frowned. 'I agree that we should guard Cusha and Vishtar. Somehow, that is not sufficient. I don't believe that mere vengeance is enough for the Darkwing. He very nearly won the world. Why would he now settle for revenge against these two? Surely he has greater ambitions.'

'You're right,' Shamana said, deep concern veiling her green eyes. 'Yes, you're right.' She pointed at the Holy Children. 'Just look at these two. Look how they tremble. There is some larger scheme. There has to be.'

'But what *can* he do?' Atrakon said. 'When he still commanded the Lost Souls, all Jinghara trembled before him. He broke bodies like bread and drank blood like wine. He was the consumer of men. But he is alone. I say we put him to the back of our minds and concentrate on raising an army against the Sons of Ra. It is the Sol-ket who crush the peoples of the world under the heel of their boot. They are our first concern, not one solitary, broken creature of the night.'

Oled bristled. 'Since when did the assassin have a voice here? Only yesterday, he was our enemy. Have you forgotten so soon? He kidnapped Cusha. Mere days before that he would have slit your throat without a thought, mother.'

Shamana listened to her son. 'This is true. Atrakon and I crossed swords in the caves of Suravan. But let me ask you this, Oled, is any man beyond redemption? He did everything you say. He also brought Cusha back to us. He fought courageously at our side against the demon lord. Cusha is the Holy Child. I trust her instincts in this.'

Cusha spoke next. 'Don't let suspicion poison you, Oled. I have seen into this Selessian's heart. Atrakon is a changed man.'

'I've said my piece,' Oled concluded gruffly, turning to Shamana. 'Make your Selessian first among men if you wish. I remember what he was. I also remember an infamous day forty years ago. Slave and Tanjur combined to fight their common oppressor. Great Shinar led a revolt that made the Empire tremble. Who changed sides and betrayed the Army of the Free, Selessian? Tell me if you dare. The Empire could have fallen that day but you stabbed our people in the back. That one act gave us forty years of oppression.'

Atrakon reacted angrily. 'You don't need to quote history to me, Oled Lonetread. I know all too well what happened at the Battle of Dullah. The name of Ehut Haraddin, leader of the Selessians that day, is cursed among the great mass of our people. It is the great shame of the desert kingdom that we fought for the Muzals. The clans of Selessia have been regretting it ever since, wishing there was a way to right the wrong.'

'A pretty speech,' Oled retorted. 'There is just one thing wrong with it, Atrakon. After Dullah, your people got to live in peace, their pockets jingling with imperial coin, their mouths stuffed with gold. It's a lucrative business, treachery. You were able to trade and build houses. You were able to have families and break bread with your kinsmen. What happened to the peoples represented here? The Helati have groaned ever since under the yoke of slavery. The Sol-ket beat them, sell their children, kill them. We Tanjurs have been all but exterminated. Three, that's how many survived the manhunt. Talk until the sun grows cold if you want, Selessian, I'll never trust a single one of your kind. Damn you to hell, desert rat!'

With that, Oled stalked away. Aaliya watched him go, then rose and followed.

'I apologise for my son,' Shamana said. 'He grew up suffering for the terrible consequences of Dullah.'

'He spoke his mind,' Atrakon said. 'I hold no grudge against him.'

Murima shook her head sadly. 'We are nine against a cruel monster and an Empire of millions of souls. If we are not united, how can we hope to win?'

Nobody tried to answer her question.

8

Linem opened his eyes and screamed in terror.

'Scream all you like,' the Darkwing said. 'Nobody can hear you.'

Linem looked around. He was in a temple carved out of solid rock. 'Where am I?'

'Don't you recognise it?' the Darkwing said. 'Your priesthood ordered that the monks be evicted from this sacred ground. If I remember correctly, they were all murdered for heresy.'

Linem groaned. 'Nandraghiri.'

'Yes, this is the temple of Nandraghiri. Ironic, don't you think? When your foul priesthood destroyed the old ways and created the cult of Ra, there were two great sites of resistance. There was the Black Tower.' He waved his arm. 'Then there was Nandraghiri.'

In the land of Khut there is a range of colossal mountains. Each peak is like a column supporting the vault of heaven. They are the Mountains of the Moon. High on one such peak, Mount Sangra, there is a long-abandoned monastery. The ancient building is perched just below the summit. It is as bleak as it is remote. The only access to it is by a flight of thirty vertiginous steps, similarly carved into the sheer face. These exposed, slippery steps lead to a hoist. The ropes have long since decayed or been swept away. Once they lowered the monks and visitors hundreds of feet to a broad granite shelf below. But the monks are long gone.

'What do you want?'

'What does any demon lord want?' the Darkwing said, indulging in sour humour. 'World domination, vengeance, perhaps the end of all things?'

Linem rephrased his question. 'What do you want *from me*?'

The Darkwing chuckled. 'I want your magic.'

'I don't understand,' Linem said.

'You have immersed your arms in the vapours of living death,' the Darkwing said. 'Only a score of men have entered the shadow world between life and death. Your power is great. There is something I want you to destroy.'

Linem wondered at his captor's words.

'Cast your mind back forty years,' the Darkwing continued. 'You were a young priest and I a rebel prince.'

'I remember,' Linem said. He could smell the rank odour of his own fear.

'They called me Sabray then,' the Darkwing reminded the priest. 'I adored a woman, a princess of Banshu. But my father . . .' He shook his head. 'Father, is that the word for him?' He leered, his black eyes boring into Linem's brain. 'Lord Muzal, Emperor of all the Peoples, coveted my sweet Kewara. He wanted her for himself. Imagine that, Linem, a father who takes his own son's betrothed. But he did not take her. Princess Kewara defended her honour. She leapt from her window. She died.'

'For Ra's sake!' Linem cried. 'I know the story. I know my part in it, too.'

The Darkwing seized the priest's face with his steely claws. Linem's protest died in his throat. 'If it entertains me to tell my story, then I will tell it.'

Linem held his tongue.

'I raised an army against my father,' the Darkwing said, 'but I lost. So he gave me to you. You used all your arts, didn't you, Linem? I was . . . an experiment. You turned me into this.'

Linem saw his handiwork and his heart stopped for a moment. 'What are you going to do to me?'

The Darkwing seemed genuinely confused. 'Do to you?' He considered Linem's words for a moment then chuckled. 'I understand. You think this is about the way you tortured me.'

'Isn't it?'

'Do you think my ambitions are so limited, priest?' the Darkwing asked. 'Do you think I care about your miserable fate?'

'Then what?' Linem croaked.

The Darkwing started to explain. 'You Hotec-Ra have a great understanding of life and death. You can harness

377

dark magic from the House of the Dead. You used it to make me what I am. But that is such a trifling project. I have powers too. Together we can do something truly . . . final.'

In spite of the mountain cold, Linem's face was covered in a sheen of sweat. 'I don't understand.'

The Darkwing drew closer. 'Then let me explain. The purpose of your order is to serve the Sun God, holy Ra, is it not?'

'You know it is.'

'And you use sorcery to protect your god?'

'Some call it that.'

The Darkwing nodded. 'What I am asking is that you turn those powers inside out. You are going to reverse your life's work.'

Linem shook his head. 'What are you saying?'

'You will endow me with power over your god. I will be the dark lord of eclipse.'

The Darkwing explained his momentous scheme. Linem listened for a few moments then twisted his head round to meet his tormentor's eyes. 'You're insane!'

'Only because you made me so,' the Darkwing said.

'You want me to give you power over the light of the world!' Linem cried. 'It's blasphemy.'

The Darkwing sneered. 'Look at what you did to me, priest. You are no stranger to blasphemy.'

'But every living creature on Earth will die.'

'You're wrong,' the Darkwing said. 'The lord of darkness will survive. Night is my true home. I will have an eternity to spend in its black realm.'

Linem sensed the Darkwing's murderous thoughts.

'You can help me of your own free will,' the demon lord said, 'or you can force me to torture you.' He stroked the lord-priest's throat with a steely claw. 'Believe me, I am good at torture, even better than the Hotec-Ra. Now stop talking. We are about to begin.'

9

The Nine waited in the Jingharan twilight. They were expecting news of the Darkwing.

'How do you know he will speak?' Murima asked Shamana.

'There is a bond between this monster and the Holy Children,' Shamana said. She looked at them. 'Are you ready?'

Cusha and Vishtar nodded.

'Open your minds to him,' Shamana said. 'He is one of the half-dead. You can summon that part of him which is ghost. He will not resist you. Already this day he has teased you with his presence. He is eager to speak.'

'No!' Harad protested. 'You can't ask Cusha to face him again. Hasn't she suffered enough?'

Shamana stood in his way. 'It must be done.'

Murima supported her son. 'Do you want to put them in danger again?' she asked.

'If we do not act,' Shamana said, 'all mankind will be in peril.' She glanced from Murima to Harad. Qintu lingered in the background.

'It isn't fair,' Harad said. 'They have only just escaped from his clutches.'

'I agree with Harad,' Qintu said. 'Let them at least rest.'

'There are three votes against the course of action you propose, Shamana,' Murima said. 'It is too dangerous. Don't make the Holy Children open their minds to him. It could destroy them.'

'Very well,' Shamana said. 'Murima demands your opinions. Oled?'

'We must listen to what the Darkwing has to say.'

'Aaliya?'

'I agree. Do it.'

'That makes three for summoning the demon lord's voice, three against. What about you Atrakon?'

Ignoring Oled's scowling face, Atrakon turned to Cusha and read the message in her eyes. 'We have to know.'

She nodded. 'We do this of our own free will.' She held out her hand to Murima. 'I'm sorry, Mama-li.'

Without another word, she took Vishtar's hands. They stood facing one another and closed their eyes. After a few moments a polar wind rose. It started to gust and whip around them, throwing up stinging dust. Strangely, despite the warmth of the day, everyone felt the arid howl of the wind. It swirled and growled around them, gathering speed, until it was roaring into their faces. That's when the Holy Children reopened their eyes. They resembled the pure obsidian of the Darkwing's.

'Show yourself, demon,' Cusha intoned. 'Your spirit speaks to us. Tell me what you want.'

Gradually a translucent form emerged from the writhing column of wind. Cocooned in the spiralling currents of air, the Darkwing's image floated, initially oblivious to the watching rebels.

'We summon you,' the twins said, 'you who were lord of Lost Souls.'

Reacting to her voice, the Darkwing turned. 'So you wish to speak to me,' he said. 'I am almost flattered.'

'We have both felt your presence,' the Holy Children said. 'You have something to tell us.'

'I have something to tell all mankind,' the Darkwing said. 'I could have been all. So many years I have watched this mortal race of yours as it plundered, tortured and murdered. Mankind is not worthy of its pre-eminent place in creation. You foiled me in this. For that I can never forgive you.'

Murima edged protectively towards Cusha. She had been a mother to her for eight years, ever since the child was found wandering in the fields north of Parcep. It was her deepest instinct.

'If I can never rule the land,' the Darkwing continued, 'if I can never be restored to the man I was, if I can never hold my dear Kewara ever again, then there is only one course of action left to me. There must be atonement. All are fallen; all are corrupt; all must die.'

Shamana stepped forward. His words were like a sliver of ice in her heart. 'What have you done?'

The Darkwing turned lazily. 'Ah, the She-wolf,' he said. 'We are a pair, you and I. I am a lord of Lost Souls and yet I am lord of nothing. You are a queen without a people. What does that make us, Shamana? I'll tell you, it makes us the loneliest creatures in this cold, heartless world.'

'But what have you done?' Shamana cried.

A second image appeared beside the Darkwing's. 'Do you recognise him, She-wolf?'

Though his eyes had been torn from his sockets, Shamana knew Linem-hotec immediately. For half a century he had been the spiritual leader of the Children of Ra. He it was who had ordered the extermination of her people. He had very nearly succeeded in his mission.

'I see you do,' the Darkwing continued. 'I asked Linem to help. It took a little persuasion, but he has been more than generous. He has given his eyes, his blood . . .' The Darkwing squeezed the priest's jaw, making his mouth gape open. 'He has even given his tongue.'

'But to what end?' Shamana cried.

'You disappoint me, She-wolf,' the Darkwing said. 'I thought you would have worked it out by now. The demon lord, sick of life, weary of mankind, abducts the lord-priest of Ra. Put them together, the lord of Lost Souls and the Sun's representative on Earth. What do you have, Shamana?'

Dense grey clouds started to boil behind the Darkwing. Membranes of ice crawled down the granite walls behind him. Tortured faces floated behind the translucent sheets, mouths wide with horror. A blazing, golden orb bobbed amid the raging tide of cloud before sinking into an ocean of whiteness. Finally, all that was left was a black, starless night. Shamana's eyes widened. Now she understood.

'What is it?' Oled demanded. 'What has he done?'

But Shamana ignored her son's question. She had one of her own. She addressed it to the demon lord. 'How long?'

'Such work as this,' the Darkwing said, 'will not be achieved overnight.'

Shamana repeated her question. 'How long?'

The Darkwing's image started to fade.

'How long?' Shamana screamed.

Finally, the Darkwing gave her his answer. 'You have until the first day of Kukhala-Ra. I think it's a good choice, don't you? It gives you a hundred days. On the first day of the month of the sun, the day the Empire was founded, this cursed world will perish.'

Shamana sank to her knees.

'He can't do it, can he?' Oled asked. He turned to the Holy Children. 'Well?' They were recovering from their trance but they did not answer him. He tried one last time. 'Is this possible?'

'It begins from this moment,' Cusha said. 'The Darkwing has drawn upon all the powers of the Hotec-Ra to destroy the thing they venerate and worship most. In the next two months, the sun's power will wane. Its warmth will fade, abandoning the world to a cruel, barren winter. On the first of Kukhala-Ra, the sun will set for the last time. Yes, Oled, it is possible. On that day the world will die.'

CHAPTER 2

The Nine Become Ten

I

'I see them,' Atrakon said.

'So do I,' Gardep confirmed. He noticed Atrakon watching him.

Both of them were gazing through an identical Selessian spyglass. Atrakon recognised the instrument Gardep had in his hand. It had belonged to Atrakon's apprentice Zahar, whom Gardep had killed. Atrakon's eyes remained fixed on the spyglass. If you had killed him for the spyglass, the Selessian thought, I would have had to settle accounts with you. But Zahar had been on a mission to slay the boy-warrior. There would be no more killing. Sensing the tension between them, Shamana made a hasty intervention.

'How many do you see?' she demanded.

It was noon on the eleventh day of Hoj. Already, Commander Rishal ax-Sol had his men out scouring the lands of the west for some sign of the Nine.

'Twenty horsemen,' Gardep replied.

'Twenty-five,' Atrakon said, correcting him.

'We would be foolish to engage them,' Shamana said. 'Even if we won the skirmish, we might sustain disastrous losses. No, we must skirt round them to the south.'

Oled grunted. 'We'll have to fight sometime.'

'Yes,' Shamana said, 'but not yet.' She gestured to Aaliya. 'Take bird form. See if there are any more patrols.'

Without a word, Aaliya transformed. Instantly, a hawk fluttered away through the cloudless sky.

'Where did you find her?' Oled asked, watching the bird vanish into the distance.

At his mother's bidding, he had lived apart from her for eight years, acting as a scout for the Sol-ket. He found this disciple of hers a fascinating creature, and a beautiful one.

'She was with a band of travelling entertainers,' Shamana told him, 'a circus. They kept her in a cage and made her transform to please the rich noblemen and their ladies. When I discovered her, she was filthy and illiterate. Over the years I have trained her in the ways of the Scales.'

'Then you have taught her well,' Oled said. 'She is a graceful and intelligent young woman.'

Shamana had little trouble reading the true meaning behind the words. 'Yes, my son, and of marriageable age.'

Oled gave another of his characteristic grunts. 'I hadn't noticed.'

'Then you're a fool, Oled my boy. I've seen the way she looks at you.'

Oled looked away for a moment. When he did speak, he could only manage this clumsy observation. 'She transforms easily.'

'Yes,' Shamana noted, before adding an acid rejoinder, 'rather more easily than you. I have taught her self-discipline. She hones her arts every day. She can take the form of the tiniest mouse or a rampaging elephant.' She gave him a long, hard look. 'I suspect that, while you have been away, you have been less devoted to the ways of the Tanjurs.'

'I was living among the Sol-ket,' Oled protested. 'They despise shape-shifters. I would have been a fool to risk my life.'

'All the same,' Shamana said, not entirely satisfied, 'you have a lot of catching up to do.'

As they went south all that day, Cusha asked the obvious question. 'Why this way?'

'First,' Shamana said, 'we must evade the Sol-ket. No doubt Rishal will be keen to nip our revolt in the bud. When Aaliya returns we will know the scale of our task.'

'Can the Darkwing really kill the sun?' Harad asked.

'Yes,' Shamana answered, 'with the help of Linemhotec, I believe he can. I have witnessed the power of the Hotec-Ra at first hand. They are well practised in their unnatural arts.'

Gardep touched the scar on the side of his face. He remembered them well.

'But to kill the sun,' Murima said, 'to plunge the land into eternal night? How can that be possible?'

'You must remember the nature of the Hotec-Ra,' Shamana said. 'They save Lord Ra, god of the sun. Their devotions ensure his life-giving rays. But they know the deity's weaknesses. The darkness of the underworld can extinguish his golden light.'

'There has to be a way to stop this happening,' Murima said.

'There are two ways,' Shamana said. 'We could try convincing the Darkwing to spare the world.'

Gardep shook his head. 'Surely you're not serious. We have seen the demon lord at close quarters. He is without mercy.'

Shamana seemed to agree. 'The second option is simple. We destroy him.'

'Then we should already be looking for the creature,' Oled said, 'not wandering the land, hiding from Sol-ket patrols.'

'If only the world were as simple as you make it sound, Oled,' Shamana said. 'You can't sort out every problem with that battle-axe of yours. There are nine of us, nine against millions. We are not in a position of strength. Our task was difficult enough when we thought we only had the Sol-ket to contend with. Now that we know the Darkwing's plan, it will take a miracle to achieve our aims.'

'We have achieved miracles before,' Cusha said.

Vishtar supported her. 'We will achieve them again.'

2

The patrol the Nine had spotted did not belong to the Sol-ket. Concealed beneath the army uniforms were the saffron robes of the Hotec-Ra.

'Did they see us?' Timu asked his scouts.

'Yes, Your Holiness. They did as you expected. They turned south. We couldn't stay on their tail. The She-wolf has despatched her apprentice to reconnoitre the area. She would have sensed the trap.'

'Where is she now?' Timu asked.

'She flew east, towards the Grand Army.'

'That makes sense,' Timu said. 'They will be expecting

Rishal to hunt them down. Let's get this done quickly. If your reports are correct they will come this way within the hour.'

Four of the warrior-priests lifted Murak from the litter on which he was being carried. At the first movement, he groaned. His face was puffy and covered in blood. Both eyes were completely closed. Timu looked down at him and remembered the way Linem had given him the ring. It would have been so easy to remove the upstart. But Linem would have known. No, Timu thought, I will bide my time. It is between me and Murak now. One of us will succeed His Holiness. I must ensure it is me.

'Bind him to the tree,' Timu ordered.

The priests reached for Murak's wrists.

'Not like that. Hang him by the ankles.'

The priests registered shock at his words.

'A man's legs are stronger than his arms,' Timu said. 'If this plan is to succeed, he must survive.'

It wasn't the only reason for hanging Murak upside down. Timu wanted to see him that way. The upstart deserved this moment of humiliation. Soon, Murak was hanging suspended from the tree, tied by the ankles to a sturdy branch. He had lost consciousness again.

'Check that he's still alive,' Timu ordered.

The nearest priest pressed a finger to Murak's pulse and nodded. Suppressing his disappointment, Timu mounted his horse.

'Let's go,' he said. 'There is no more we can do here.'

3

Aaliya was returning from Commander Rishal's camp. In spite of the losses they had suffered, the Sol-ket remained a formidable force. Worryingly, they showed no sign of returning to Karangpur or Parcep. It looked as if they were going to remain in the field. By way of confirmation, their patrols were already ranging far and wide across the endless Jingharan Plain. She rode the warm air currents and found it hard to believe that what the Darkwing had said was true. How could the sun die? Yet Shamana was concerned and she, more than any living soul, understood the extent of the Hotec-Ra's power. Sweeping westward, Aaliya allowed her thoughts to fill with Oled. Did he notice her at all? She was still wondering about him when she saw something.

'What is that?'

Like a dark fruit hanging from a tree, there was the body of a man. Aaliya immediately feared a trap. But she had been brought up on the Book of Scales. It was her duty to aid her fellow man. Circling the area several times, she made sure there were no lurking assassins. Finally, still darting her eyes left and right, she settled on the branch of a neighbouring tree. After a further inspection of the terrain, she transformed and dropped agilely to the ground.

'Are you alive?' she asked, as she approached with care. There was no answer. 'Tell me,' she whispered in the bloodied man's ear, 'do you live?'

That's when she heard a low moan. Supporting his weight, she cut his bonds and lowered him to the ground. For the first time, she could see the extent of his injuries. He had been beaten senseless. Judging by the extensive bruising, more than one man had been involved in the vicious assault.

'By the Four Winds!' she gasped. 'Who did this to you?'

The man gave no answer. Aaliya produced a mixture of herbs from her belt. It would ease the pain. Knowing that her companions would soon be passing this way, she stayed with him until they arrived.

'He's in a bad way,' Shamana said, examining the victim.

'Is there anything you can do for him?' Cusha asked.

'It's hard to say. He's lost a lot of blood. Is this the way we treat our poor, suffering brothers?'

For all the horrors she had seen, Shamana had never got used to mankind's appetite for cruelty. Beside her, Aaliya was unbuttoning the man's tunic to examine him. She stopped abruptly.

'What is it?' Shamana asked.

Aaliya pointed out a scar in the shape of the rising sun. 'He bears the mark of the Ket-Ra. This man is a Warrior of the Sun, a Sol-ket.'

Her words raised a disturbing thought in the minds of two of those present. Simultaneously, Gardep and Oled leaned forward to take a closer look. Gardep, thinking for a moment it might be his childhood friend, Kulmat, was relieved to discover that he was wrong. It was Oled who saw something familiar in the battered features.

'Can you clean some of the blood away?' he asked.

Aaliya did as he had asked, gently cleaning the face before her.

Oled gasped. 'I know this man. We fought battles together. When I was a man alone, he befriended me. He is a Sol-ket officer.'

Aaliya wiped more blood from the man's face. 'Are you sure?'

'Yes, it's him,' Oled confirmed. 'His name is Murak.'

4

Timu hadn't even dismounted when he saw a cadet running towards him. He recognised Kulmat, Commander

Rishal's new squire.

'Your Holiness,' Kulmat panted. 'The commander requests your presence. Rishal-Ra has some terrible news.'

Timu followed without a word. When he entered Rishal's tent, he saw that General Barath was also in attendance. Two generals, Timu thought: this has to be important. His gaze settled on a third man, a young soldier from the ranks.

'Tell His Holiness what you saw,' Rishal ordered.

The Sol-ket hesitated.

'You have nothing to worry about,' Barath reassured him.

'I was in a cremation party,' the warrior explained. 'We were gathering the dead. We had just built our third funeral pyre. That's when I saw His Holiness, Linem-hotec.'

He had Timu's attention. 'This is about Linem?'

The Sol-ket started to babble. 'I tried to help him. I really did. But I was too far away.'

'Just tell your story,' Rishal said. 'I've already promised you immunity. You won't be punished.'

'I don't think Linem saw us,' the Sol-ket said. 'We were about to light the pyre. Linem was a hundred paces from me. I noticed him turning round as if somebody had spoken to him. Then I saw the reason. It was the Darkwing.'

'The demon lord,' Timu said. 'He was here?'

The Sol-ket nodded. 'I know I should have shouted a warning. I should have got my bow. But it happened so fast. I failed, Your Holiness. I just watched.'

Timu grabbed the warrior by the jaw. 'I don't want your excuses. All I want is the facts. Did the Darkwing take Linem-hotec?'

Frightened, bulging eyes stared back at him. 'Yes.'

'Get this fool out of my sight,' he barked. 'Is this how you train your men, Rishal-Ra, to gape uselessly while the first priest of the Empire is spirited away?'

Ignoring Timu's sleight, Rishal dismissed the Sol-ket. Relieved, the warrior scurried away.

'Now you know why I had to see you,' Rishal said.

Timu frowned. 'What could the Darkwing possibly want with Lord Linem?'

Something in his tone made Rishal wonder whether he knew more than he was saying.

'Who can read a demon's mind?' the Commander said. 'He abducted my own daughter, Julmira. She has only just been restored to me, after an ordeal that could have taken away her sanity.'

Timu wanted to tell Rishal that, compared with Linem, his daughter was of no importance whatsoever. But he knew it would have been a foolish, possibly fatal, thing to do. Rishal was the greatest warrior in the land. He also had a famously foul temper.

'I know the priesthood has certain tricks up its sleeve,' Rishal said. 'Is there anything you can do? We need to know why he took Linem.'

'It will be done,' Timu said. 'Come to Lord Linem's quarters tonight.'

5

Only Atrakon was against establishing camp.

'Are you mad?' he demanded. 'You are taking on an entire Empire and fighting for the survival of the world, yet you stop for one man.'

'The ways of Fate are complex,' Shamana said. 'This

event may be important in the wider scheme of things. If you want to care for all mankind, you must start with one suffering soul.'

Atrakon shook his head. 'I'll never understand you, She-wolf. Sometimes I think you are the wiliest creature on this Earth. Other times you seem both innocent and gullible.'

'Maybe it is good that we are so different,' Shamana said.

A few paces away, Aaliya was tending to Murak. Beside her patient there were the tools of the surgeon's trade: needles, a mortar and pestle, turmeric to heal wounds and garlic to kill bacteria.

'Is he any stronger?' Oled asked, looking down at his sleeping friend.

'It is too soon to say,' Aaliya answered. 'None of the wounds is fatal. He is young and strong. His body must be given time to return to harmony and balance. He needs rest.'

Oled nodded. 'Tell me when he wakes.'

He was about to go when he heard Murak's voice. 'Oled,' he croaked through blistered lips, 'is that you?'

'It is.'

'Thank Ra.'

'Did Barath do this to you?' Oled demanded, remembering the way the general had looked at them together.

'He ordered it,' Murak said. 'The Hotec-Ra carried out the punishment.'

Oled's green eyes flashed. 'Why would they torture one of their own?'

'You've just answered your own question,' Murak said. 'You knew I had doubts. I no longer serve the Empire of the Sun.' Aaliya offered him a cup of water. He paused to take a sip. 'You know how I feel about the cruelty of the Sol-ket. That's why we became friends.'

A frown creased Oled's forehead. It was a long journey from doubt to rebellion. What had brought about the sudden conversion? Oled had served as a scout in the Imperial Army. In all that time he had only known one man to break from the Sol-ket. That was Gardep. But he was a most exceptional case. A warrior like him only emerged once in many generations.

'But you chose your path, Murak. You could have come with me when I left Karangpur. You had only to ask.'

Murak took another sip of water. 'What do you want me to say, Oled?'

Oled came straight to the point. 'I want you to tell me the truth.'

Murak nodded. 'I owe you that. I thought I could continue in the service of Ra. I fought the demon host at the battle of Jinghara Plain, though it meant standing shoulder to shoulder with a man like Barath. But our friendship opened my eyes, Oled. I found your words running through my mind. I envied you your faith in the future, the strength of your conviction. You made me believe that there could be another, better world where no man held another as a slave. You made me question every belief I ever held.'

Still Oled was wary. 'You chose to remain with the Children of Ra,' he observed. 'You did that of your own free will, even though I had offered you an alternative. You could have come with me. What changed your mind?'

'It was Barath. The man is a monster.'

'Yes,' Oled murmured. 'Barath.'

Like all the Sol-ket elite, Barath detested shape-shifters like Oled more than any living creature. Maybe he detested those who befriended the dragon-people just as much.

'Do you remember Karangpur?' Murak asked. 'He tried

to kill us – you for daring to stand up to him, me for being your friend.'

'Even so, you remained Sol-ket.'

'I did,' Murak said. 'At first I thought I had made the right choice. Barath acted as if we were reconciled. Then, after the Battle of Jinghara Plain, came the reckoning. The moment the threat of the Lost Souls was lifted he denounced me as a traitor and handed me over to the Hotec-Ra for interrogation. He told them that I would have important information regarding your whereabouts and those of the other rebels.'

'What did you tell them?'

'Nothing,' Murak said. 'There was nothing to tell. I didn't know where you were.'

Oled turned the story over in his mind. He wanted to believe Murak. 'The Hotec-Ra rarely let their prisoners live,' he said, still cautious.

'Do you really think they intended me to live?' Murak cried. The effort caused him to cough and double up in agony. 'Look at my wounds, Oled. They hung me from a tree in the middle of nowhere. They meant me to die.'

Aaliya caught Oled's eye. 'Oled, he is still weak.'

Murak waved her away. 'Say you believe me. We are friends. Surely you know I am telling the truth.'

'Are you done with the Warriors of Ra?' Oled asked.

'I despise them,' Murak said. 'Give me the chance and I will devote myself to the cause of freedom. You must believe me.'

Oled hesitated for a moment then seized Murak's outstretched hand.

'I believe you.' He glanced at Aaliya. 'Now we are ten.'

6

The order to retire to bed sounded over the camp as Rishal and Barath entered Linem's quarters. Timu greeted them by pressing his palms together and giving a little bow. There was incense in the air and one of Linem's robes was hanging outstretched above a flaring brazier.

'What's that for?' Rishal asked.

'Watch,' Timu said.

He sprinkled a fine powder on the fire. Immediately the flames leaped and started to consume the saffron robe. As they burned away the thin material, purple wreaths of smoke started to curl towards the roof of the large tent. Within these ribbons an image formed. Barath was the first to spot Linem.

'By Ra, the creature has mutilated the Lord-priest! See his bloodied features.'

Seemingly unmoved, Timu peered into the flickering picture of a place far away. He saw the columns that helped support the roof, the painted frescoes on the walls. 'I know this place,' he murmured.

Rishal opened his mouth to ask a question. Timu silenced him with a raised hand. 'The frescoes are damaged,' he said. 'See, there is Lord Ra. But a second figure has been chiselled away. It is the moon god, Sangra. Yes, I can name this place. It is the monastery of Nandraghiri, one of the main sites of the Scaline heresy.'

'Explain,' Rishal ordered, nettled by the impudent way Timu had treated him. It was the second time this priest had offended in this manner.

'Many generations ago,' Timu began, 'there was a strong Scaline strand in our faith, blathering about peace and a community of equals. While the dominant Hotec-

Ra proclaimed that there was only one true deity, the Sun god himself, the followers of Udmanesh preached a different view. They set it down in the Book of Scales. In their eyes, all must be in balance, light and dark, sun and moon, male and female. My predecessors all those centuries ago responded to heresy in the only way possible. The blasphemers would have weakened our stock and condemned us to inferiority among the peoples of the world. So our ancestors rooted out the false prophets, putting the heretics to the sword.'

'This monastery of Nandraghiri,' Rishal said, tiring of the lesson in theology, 'where is it?'

'It is in the Mountains of the Moon,' Timu told him. 'It was built high on Sangra Peak. The followers of Udmanesh thought that they would be safe there.' He smiled. 'They were wrong, of course.'

Barath saw movement. 'Look,' he said, 'somebody's coming.'

A shadowy figure stepped over Linem's bloodied corpse. A scream tore through the gloom of the monastery.

'It's the demon lord,' Timu said.

The priest and the two generals watched the Darkwing stalk across the chamber, folding his leathery wings. He carried two struggling figures, one under each arm. The first was a young man of about twenty summers. The Darkwing shackled him to a wall. The second was a Khut maiden in her eighteenth year, recognisable by her patterned woollen dress. The Darkwing inspected her for a few moments before adding her to his collection. A dozen men and women, some near to death, others untouched, sat manacled to the wall.

'You know what he does with his captives,' Barath said. 'He feeds on their blood.'

Rishal clenched his fists. His own daughter was very

nearly added to the list of the monster's victims. But Timu wasn't interested in the Darkwing's menu. He had seen something.

'Look there,' he said. He peered into the fading image. 'No!' he said, as the smoke thinned and danced away through the roof vents.

'What did you see?' Barath asked.

'Something was painted on the wall. It vanished before I could make it out.'

'I can tell you what that was,' Rishal said.

The other two men turned towards him.

'It was the sun symbol of the Hotec-Ra.'

Timu's eyes widened. 'Was there anything else?'

'Yes,' Rishal said. 'I saw a hieroglyph.'

Timu pushed a sheet of parchment towards him. 'Draw it!'

Though he resented Timu's tone, Rishal did as he was told. He drew a crude house with twin towers and a large door. There were no windows.

'By the holy face of Ra!' Timu groaned. 'No. No. Lord Linem, why did you succumb?'

'What is it?' Rishal asked. 'Why are you so frightened?'

'Don't you recognise the symbol of the House of the Dead?' Timu asked. 'By terror, the Darkwing forced His Holiness to invoke the Spell of Eternal Darkness.'

Rishal was growing impatient. 'Meaning?'

'It is the greatest magic known to our order,' Timu explained. 'Nobody outside the Hotec-Ra is meant to know of its existence. From the day of its invocation, the spell will drain the strength of the sun's rays. One day soon, the sun will set, never to rise again. Life on Earth will perish.'

'Can this be true?' Barath asked.

Rishal had seen the priest's face. He knew the answer to Barath's question.

'Do we have long?'

'I must consult the holy texts.'

'Make it quick, priest,' Rishal said. Suddenly he felt very cold.

7

The Khut maiden was called Jinghirza Ghun, daughter of a Khut hammer-lord. The Darkwing had seized her and one of her father's attendants from their village that very day. She watched him, a shadowy, gliding figure, without mercy or humanity. Still naively unaware of what he wanted from her, she spoke innocently, thinking that she could appeal to his conscience.

'No,' she pleaded, 'please don't hurt me. I have done no wrong.'

The Darkwing examined her face. His prey did not usually speak. This one had spirit. 'Who said you've done anything wrong?'

'Then why am I here?' Jinghirza asked. 'My father is chieftain of our clan. We are poor but we have animal pelts and some gold. My family will pay a ransom for me.'

'Ransom!' the Darkwing snarled. 'Is that what you think? I am not some bandit to be bought off with ransom.' He leaned closer, his rancid breath making Jinghirza turn away in revulsion. 'I'll tell you what I want from you, my child.' He whispered into her ear before watching with pleasure as her face started to twist in horror.

'My blood! Please no!'

'Oh, don't plead,' the Darkwing said, disappointed. 'I thought you had courage. I thought you, unlike these spineless wretches, were worthy of my intentions.'

Grasping at any shred of hope, Jinghirza answered. 'Do you respect courage, my lord?'

She had his attention. 'It . . . interests me.'

'Then I will be brave.'

The Darkwing blinked, intrigued by the new strength in her voice. 'What are you saying?'

'Set me some challenge,' Jinghirza said. 'Put my courage to the test. Give me a chance to win the right to live.'

'You remind me of someone,' the demon lord said. 'She had courage.'

Jinghirza didn't know what to make of this, but at least he was speaking to her. Maybe, so long as she entertained him, she could delay the date of her execution.

8

Shamana waved away Oled's protests.

'We have to go,' she said. 'The sun has already risen. Soon the Sol-ket will be on our trail. We have cleaned and sewn Murak's wounds. There is no infection. He has a few broken ribs. They are bound and will mend by themselves.'

'Do you really think he is ready to be moved?' Aaliya asked, torn between her loyalty to Shamana and Oled.

'Normally I would say no,' Shamana answered. 'But we have no choice.'

Oled made a decision. He transformed into a water buffalo. Seeing what a struggle it was for him to manage even this beast, Shamana wrinkled her nose.

'Put him on my back,' Oled said. 'Aaliya, you will ride with him. Do what you can to ease his pain.'

Aaliya nodded. 'I have already mixed the herbs.'

Atrakon shielded his eyes against the rising sun. 'So we're going east now?'

Shamana nodded. 'It is dangerous, but the Darkwing is the first priority. We strike east, then north to the Mountains of the Moon. If the sun dies, there will be no world to win.'

Oled was still unhappy. 'And why did you need to strip him?'

'Do you remember nothing I taught you as a child?' she grumbled. 'There is an old Hotec-Ra trick. I have even employed it myself. They can trace their men through the pigment they dye into their robes.'

'So you think Murak's a spy?' Oled asked, accusation in his words.

'I didn't say that,' Shamana replied, 'but, in the Hotec-Ral, we face a cruel and brilliant opponent. I'm not going to take chances.'

'I don't know what you're complaining about,' Qintu said. 'You got the spare clothes for this Sol-ket from me and Harad. Why does he get our best things?'

'Oh, do stop complaining,' Shamana told him.

The exchange over, the group of companions, now numbering ten, set off.

'This is madness,' Gardep said.

'Why is it?' Cusha asked him.

'Are you serious?' Gardep demanded. 'On that plain, just beyond the Demon Wall, there will be tens of thousands of Sol-ket, every one of them looking for us.'

'What would you do?' Vishtar asked.

Gardep shrugged. 'I have been trained to command regiments of warriors. I would build an army.'

Slowed down to ease Murak's suffering, the band made only gradual progress but, by evening, they were within sight of the Demon Wall.

'Once we are through those gates,' Shamana said, 'we will turn north-east.'

'What about Sol-ket patrols?' Gardep asked.

'If they come,' Shamana answered simply, 'we will fight them.' The words were no sooner out of her mouth when a sword hissed from its scabbard. 'What are you doing, Atrakon?' she demanded.

Atrakon pointed with the point of his sabre. 'Over there,' he said, rummaging for his spyglass, 'on that ridge. Somebody's spying on us.'

Shamana trained her hawk's eyes on the silhouetted figure. 'You need have no worries about him,' she said. 'The watcher is a night-strider.'

9

Vishtar rose in the early hours of the night. He had only gone a step when Shamana stepped out of the gloom. She had taken first watch.

'Where are you going?' she hissed.

Vishtar's whispered answer held no surprises. 'I have to talk to that night-strider. It's me he wants. Shamana, I can hear his voice in the wind. He is calling me.'

'I heard nothing,' Shamana said.

'He talks only to the Holy Children.'

Shamana nodded. 'It makes sense. You have the power to end his suffering. What will you say to him?'

'I will ask why he continues to walk the Earth,' Vishtar replied.

'It is a good question,' Shamana said. 'I have been asking myself the same thing. Tell me his answer.'

'You expected me to do this,' Vishtar said. 'How did you know?'

'You and your sister are the Holy Children. You live in the regions between the living and the dead. If anyone should speak to the Lost Souls, it is you.'

'So should I wake Cusha?' Vishtar asked.

'No, let her sleep,' Shamana said. 'I sense that you are the one he wants. You can lay the Lost Souls to rest. Go to him.'

Without another word, Vishtar walked off into the night. He followed a trail of trampled grass all the way to the ridge where Atrakon had spotted the night-strider.

'You prepared a trail for me,' Vishtar murmured.

He continued along the makeshift path until he saw movement ahead. For a moment, aware of his own vulnerability, Vishtar glanced back at the camp where Cusha and the others were sleeping. That's when a skeletal figure stepped out in front of him, his haunted eyes flashing in the dark. When the creature emerged into the moonlight, Vishtar noticed that his exposed bones were blackened, as if by fire.

'Why did you take so long?' the night-strider asked. 'I have been waiting for you since sunset.'

'I was afraid,' Vishtar replied honestly.

'I am not the one you should fear.'

Vishtar felt an icy ripple down his spine. 'What do you want from me? Why did you not destroy yourself like so many others of your kind?'

'You tread the empty lands between life and death,' the night-strider said, echoing Shamana. 'You released us from our monstrous contagion. Because of you, the pollution of hell has cleared from our minds. You and your sister freed us from the demon night. We owe you a great debt.'

'But you have chosen to continue walking the land. Why?'

The night-strider touched the decomposing flesh on his face. 'Many of my kind chose self-slaughter. They could not live with their memories, the consequences of what they had done. I could not follow them. How could I leave a world blighted by horror and oppression? I have to put right my wrongs. I am not the only one of the night breed to think this way.'

To Vishtar's surprise, the creature bent his knee and held out a pair of beseeching hands. 'You must not leave a job half done. Help us compensate for our crimes. Lead us to redemption, I beg of you.'

'How do I do that?'

'Search your soul, Vishtar,' the night-strider said. 'You are the Holy Child. It is your destiny to lead the Lost Souls. United with your sister, you exercise great powers. You must find a way to lift the burden of guilt from our shoulders.'

'Do you know what the demon lord has planned?' Vishtar asked.

'I do.' The night-strider's suppurating lips formed something approaching a smile. 'I was in his service. When he invoked the spell, I felt the world shudder.'

'You say you want redemption,' Vishtar said.

'More than anything.'

'Then help us prevent this evil happening,' Vishtar said. 'Defeat your former master; save this world from eternal night; and I will give you peace.' The night was thick round them, like swamp water. It was as if streams of darkness were flowing out of the underworld and spreading through the silent land. 'How many of you are there?'

'So far,' the night strider replied, 'we are but a few score. But there are many more out there waiting to join us. Our tormented brothers and sisters are scattered far and wide.'

'Then these are my orders to you,' Vishtar said. 'Gather your forces. Return in your hundreds, in your thousands. When that is done, come and find me. Will you do this?'

'Of course,' the night-strider said. 'You are the Holy Child, my redeemer.' He turned to go. Vishtar could make out a line of shadowy figures waiting for him.

'Wait,' Vishtar said. 'I don't know your name.'

'There will be no names,' the night-strider said. 'Names belong to a man's mortal life. For me, all that ended many years ago.'

'I have to call you something,' Vishtar insisted.

The night-strider thought for a moment. 'I will take the name of the king of scavengers,' he answered. 'Call me Jackal.'

10

Far to the north, in the Mountains of the Moon, the Darkwing sat brooding in his lonely monastery. He wandered its echoing corridors, gazing at the broken statues of the god Sangra. He hated these moments of lucid thought. They filled him with humiliation, rage, bitterness, a mixture as corrosive as acid. How he loathed to be reminded of what he had been. The thought of what he could have become, the greatest of souls, the ruler of the entire world, tortured him. Even the world of nightmare was preferable to memory. He remembered his youth. He remembered falling in love. The scent of his loved one's hair was in his nostrils. Her voice sighed on the wind. Then he recalled the fall.

'Kewara.'

She had been so young, so wonderful and alive. He had adored her. He ached to remember the moment he had seen her body, broken on the stone square beneath her window. Once more, the demon lord saw the halo of scarlet blood, the still open, startled eyes. He had taken her in his arms, marvelling at how small she was, fragile as a baby bird fallen from its nest. Even now, he could not believe that the life had gone out of her. Then the torment of memory got too much for him. With his steely claws he slashed the walls, scoring deep gouges into the rock.

'No! No! No!'

His voice reverberated through the monastery, sending ripples of horror down the spines of Jinghirza and the other prospective victims. The madness of regret and loss seared through his veins. He saw it all: his rising against his Imperial father; his defeat; his ordeal in the torture chambers of the Hotec-Ra and finally his reincarnation as the Darkwing. In that moment he despised himself for what he had become, a creature so foul that he was abhorred throughout the land. But he despised the world more. He staggered towards the monastery's entrance and gazed out at the mist-hung mountain world. Turning, he fixed his eyes on the image of the sun, painted on Nandraghiri's walls in Linem's blood. For a moment, in his madness, he fancied he saw it sinking into the House of the Dead.

'I see you, Holy Child,' he screamed, imagining the girl with death in her eyes. Cusha's face danced in his imagination. 'You denied me,' he snarled, 'you and your whining whelp of a brother. You're what stood in my way, a pair of adolescents. Well, enjoy the moment of your triumph. It will be short-lived. Who can live without the sun? Only I. We are marching towards the day of reckoning, Holy Child. This will be my revenge. One by one, I will watch the death-throes of my enemies. I will walk between their funeral pyres. Then, when the last of them has perished, I will be master of the world.' Cusha's eyes filled his mind. 'I will be the thing you called me.' He roared it through the precincts of Nandraghiri. 'I will be lord of nothing!'

CHAPTER 3

First Blood

I

The goblet that Rishal hurled across the tent almost struck
Kulmat in the face. The twelfth day of Hoj had begun
badly for the commander of His Imperial Majesty's
frontline troops.

'Say that again, priest!' he roared.

The supercilious smirk that most high-ranking Hotec-
Ra usually wore had vanished from Timu's face.

'General Rishal,' he protested. 'There is no need for
violence.'

'There's every need for violence!' Rishal bellowed. 'You
tell me the world is going to end in a mere two months,
you tell me the sun is dying, and you whine about a

thrown cup? I should pull out your fool tongue and nail it to my battle standard.'

Timu did his best to reassure the commander. 'All is not lost, Rishal-Ra.'

Kulmat succeeded in reaching Rishal without injury. 'Please listen to what he has to say, Master.'

Rishal planted his hands on the table in front of him. 'Spell it out, priest. I'm a soldier. I need an enemy to kill, an objective to take. Tell me there is something we can do to stop the creature.'

'I spent the whole of last night reading Linem's notes,' Timu began.

Always the man of action, Rishal growled his frustration. 'The world ends on the first day of Kukhala-Ra and you sit up reading! Am I surrounded by lunatics?'

He glimpsed Kulmat's pleading eyes and made an effort to restrain himself.

'Very well,' he said. 'Continue, Your Holiness.'

'Again and again, Lord Linem stressed the importance of the Holy Children,' Timu explained, 'in destroying the Darkwing's hold over the Lost Souls. According to the journal, their power stems from their relationship to the House of the Dead. The female can call to the undead. She can summon their spirits from the House. The male has the power to redeem them and to give them rest. We have no choice. We must harness their power.'

Rishal's eyes bored into the priest. 'Are you going to get to the point?'

Timu gave a sigh. 'We need the girl Cusha. Her brother too. They alone can destroy the Darkwing.'

Rishal stared back in disbelief. It was a few moments before he said anything. 'We are talking about the same Cusha we left out there on the Jingharan plain?'

'That was before we knew what the Darkwing had

408

planned,' Timu said, a bead of perspiration working itself down his brow.

'Nonetheless,' Rishal said, with menacing calculation. 'What I say is true, is it not? We allowed the key player in the game to wander the plain. Though we need her to stop the Darkwing, we managed to let her wriggle out of our grasp.'

'You agreed to Lord Linem's plan,' Timu objected. 'We would insert Murak into the Helat conspiracy and tease out any prospective rebels. That way we would behead any future rebellions. It was a brilliant plan.'

'Oh yes,' Rishal said, his voice little more than a whisper, 'it was very clever, too clever in fact.'

'Commander . . .'

Rishal was in no mood to listen. 'Can you trace Murak?' he demanded. 'Maybe we could get to her through him. Is it possible to use that trick you used to find Linem?'

Timu shook his head. 'I tried. They seem to have destroyed his tunic. Nevertheless—'

Rishal held up a hand. 'I have heard enough from the Hotec-Ra for one day,' he said. 'Get out.'

Timu saw this as an affront to his dignity as a senior member of the priesthood. 'I really must protest!'

Rishal gripped the hilt of his sword.

'General Rishal,' Timu cried, 'you cannot draw your sword against a representative of the Hotec-Ra.'

'Then do as I say,' Rishal told him, beginning to slide the blade out of the scabbard. 'Get out of my sight.' He hurled a final comment at Timu's back. 'And don't come back until you have used your infernal tricks to contact His Imperial Highness. I need his permission to abort our original plan. We have two months to avert catastrophe. To hell with clever stratagems. I want the Holy Children and I want them now.'

Once Timu was gone, Rishal turned to his squire. 'How did it come to this, Kulmat? Why do all the threads of this tale coil around me? This Cusha once worked in my kitchens. She cut the onions and ground the cumin. I barely gave her a second glance. How did a mere slave-girl come to hold our destiny in her hands?'

2

The girl of whom Rishal spoke was standing on the Demon Wall, looking back towards the Black Tower, remembering the desperate struggle there. She sensed Gardep behind her. He lifted her plaited hair and stroked the nape of her neck.

'Don't,' Cusha giggled. 'Somebody might see us.'

'You amaze me,' Gardep said. 'Shamana tells us the world is dying and you are worried about a little thing like this.' His fingertips lingered on her back, marvelling at the softness of her skin. 'I want to be with you every moment of every day. Weeks may be all we have.'

'This is all so new,' Cusha said. 'It's . . . frightening.'

Gardep laughed. 'Can it be true? You face the demon lord with invincible courage yet you flinch at my touch.'

'I barely understand my own feelings,' Cusha admitted. She looked at him. The padded cavalry jacket he usually wore was spread over the battlements. He was wearing a light, armless, white tunic.

'Do I sound stupid?' Cusha asked.

'Not at all,' Gardep said. 'It is the same for me. We will unravel this mystery together.'

Cusha turned to look at him. 'Can that really be true? Am I more than a despised Helat to you? I used to hear the Sol-ket boasting about their conquests. You soldiers, you think you can do what you like with us.'

Earnest as ever, Gardep sought to reassure her. 'I am not like them. To me, you are every woman on Earth. This I swear: I will protect you till my dying day.'

Cusha looked around to make sure they were alone. Then, heart beating fast, she reached up and laid her palm against his face.

'No,' she said, 'you are not like them at all.' She ran her hands over his arms and paused. 'What's that?' There was a tattoo on his upper arm.

'Oh that,' Gardep said. 'I have had it since I was a child.'

'Let me see.' The tattoo was of a lion with a bull's head. 'Do you know what it means?'

Gardep shook his head. 'It is from my childhood in Vassyria, a time I can barely remember.'

Cusha was about to enquire further when Gardep's eyes hardened. His attention had been drawn to something behind her.

'What is it?' she asked, beginning to turn.

Before she could get halfway round she heard the jangle of harness. A Sol-ket patrol had just topped the rise and was galloping towards them. Already, arrows were clattering against the battlements of the Demon Wall. Stringing his bow, Gardep killed two of the riders. Simultaneously, Cusha ran to raise the alarm. Even as she reached the keep, her companions were already responding to the drumming hooves. Aaliya shot her bow with great skill, adding to Gardep's deadly volleys. Another Sol-ket thudded to the earth, lifeless. As one, Oled and Atrakon hurled themselves from the walls, toppling two of the enemy from their mounts.

'Draw your bows!' Shamana yelled at Murima, Harad and Qintu. 'Cover us.'

With that, she joined Oled and Atrakon in taking the

411

fight to the enemy. Cusha raced back to Gardep.

'Train your arrows on the rearmost riders,' Gardep told her, before vaulting from the walls after Shamana. 'You must prevent them surrounding us.'

The fight under the wall was a fierce one. Though, in the initial skirmish, they were just four against three times that number, Gardep and Atrakon, Oled and Shamana had halted the Sol-ket charge, clashing with the lead riders. The hail of arrows from the Demon Wall split the patrol in two, forcing the following cavalry to slow. Gardep killed his man and raced to engage the next. Oled and Atrakon had similar successes. Shamana alone was in a vulnerable position. Wedged between two horsemen, she was parrying their blows desperately. She succeeded in cutting one of them down but, as she spun round, the second was slashing downwards.

'No!' she screamed.

Even as the blade sliced through the air towards her, the attacking Sol-ket sagged in his saddle before tumbling to the ground.

'Whose arrow was that?' Shamana gasped. 'Who saved me?'

Oled pointed to the battlements. There, Murak was reeling backwards, exhausted by the effort of drawing the bow. In spite of his injuries, he had rescued the She-wolf with a single arrow.

'Do you trust him now?' Oled asked.

Shamana said nothing. She was troubled by the slowness of her reactions. Even a year ago, she would have transformed into some small creature and scurried out of danger. By the Four Winds, she thought, I'm getting old. She didn't dwell on the moment long. Her sword arm was needed. Soon the tide of battle was turning the way of the rebels. As the front riders fell, those at the rear swung their mounts round and started to retreat. Instinctively, the Tanjurs and their Helat allies lowered their weapons.

'What are you doing?' Gardep roared. 'Don't let a single one get away.'

He shot his arrows quickly, one after the other, killing three of the fleeing Sol-ket.

'Shoot,' he yelled, 'or they will be back.' He met Atrakon's eye. 'You understand, don't you?' he demanded.

Atrakon nodded and raised his bow. Reluctantly, their companions followed suit. Soon all the enemy lay dead. Without pause, Gardep gathered the horses. Some marvelled at the businesslike way he handled death. Others found him merciless, a dog of war.

'We must move the bodies out of sight,' he said. 'There must be no evidence of this fight.'

It was only when he had finished dragging the last body into the nearest keep that he noticed the way the others were looking at him.

'What's wrong?' he asked. 'It is first blood to us. We have fresh horses and there are no survivors to reveal our position.'

Oled shook his head. 'You may be right, Gardep. But you are more bloodthirsty than the assassin Atrakon. I just wonder whether you don't enjoy your work too much.'

3

As his troops engaged the rebel band far away, in golden Rinaghar, capital of the Empire, His Imperial Majesty Muzal ax-Sol was eating a light lunch of spiced lamb. Every mouthful was a trial. The Emperor, who was still robust for an old man, had bad teeth, the legacy of too many sumptuous banquets, too many sugary sweetmeats. Though his cooks were the finest in the land, even they couldn't make it so tender his gums didn't ache.

He downed a glass of *kinthi*, the strong Sol-ket brew, before pushing the plate away in disgust.

'Is there a problem with the food, Your Imperial Majesty?' his personal slave Sanjay enquired.

'Yes, there's a problem,' Muzal grumbled. 'The meat is tough and the spices haven't been fried properly.'

'Should I order the guard to execute the cook?' Sanjay asked.

'Yes,' Muzal said, 'make it slow. Pull out his teeth. Have the dog suffer as I suffer.'

Then, as Sanjay hurried away to give the command, Muzal called him back. 'No, let him be. He's the best of a bad lot. I've lost three cooks this month.'

Sanjay was still wavering when a page scurried past him across the marble floor.

'What now?' Muzal groaned. 'Will the demands of State never leave me in peace?'

The page flung himself to the floor, prostrating himself before the Empire's absolute monarch.

'Imperial Majesty,' he began, averting his eyes from Muzal's face, 'I have news.'

'It will be bad, I expect,' Muzal said.

'I am not privy to the contents of the communication,' the man said, continuing to grovel at Muzal's feet. 'It is from His Holiness, Lord Timu of the Hotec-Ra. Lord Asun took the message.'

'Then I want to hear from Asun.'

It was as if the page was trying to bury himself in the marble. 'To that end, Priest Asun respectfully requests your presence at the Great Ziggurat. He says the message is for your ears only.'

'Tell Asun to come here,' Muzal told him.

'Lord Asun fears that, outside the precincts of the Ziggurat of Ra, there may be spies. This communication must not fall into their hands.'

At this, Muzal relented. He was in his seventy-third year. The twenty-fifth monarch in the six-hundred-year-old dynasty had no heir. As a result, a virtual army of princes, priests and generals were eager to succeed him. They circled the Sun Throne like so many sharks and barracudas. Muzal knew that, should there be any news that reflected badly on his rule, he might succumb to the poisoner's phial or the assassin's dagger. Rinaghar had become a nest of cobras. With each year that passed, his rule was becoming more fragile, more vulnerable to their venom.

'Sanjay,' Muzal said. 'Send the Eternals to me.'

The Eternals were his palace guard, elite Hotec-Ra. They were sworn to give up their own lives to keep him safe. Once they were assembled, he crossed the elevated walkway which connected the Imperial Palace with the Ziggurat of Ra. Resplendent in white and gold robes, the Imperial crown on his head, Muzal entered the inner sanctum of the Ziggurat. There, Asun-hotec was waiting for him.

'Your Imperial Majesty,' he said, bowing, 'I apologise for the inconvenience. There was no other way to give you the news in confidence.'

'Come,' Muzal said. 'Walk with me.'

He wasn't altogether happy that he had to discuss such matters with a man who was only the third most senior man in the priesthood. They stepped out onto the steps of the Ziggurat. From their vantage point they could see all Rinaghar, the jewel of the Empire.

'Here is a transcription of Lord Timu's communication,' Asun said, handing Muzal the parchment.

Muzal started reading it. 'There must be some mistake,' he said. 'Linem abducted? I don't believe it.'

'You must read on, Majesty,' Asun said. He saw Muzal's eyes widen. His jaw went slack. 'Is this possible?' he asked. 'Can the sun burn out?'

Asun was silent.

'Well, speak, damn you!'

'When the priests of Ra opened the gates of the House of the Dead, we stared into the face of eternal night.' He hesitated. 'We had a great dilemma. What do you do with the knowledge that you can end all human life? Nobody ever dreamed it would come to this.'

Muzal felt like tearing out Asun's throat. 'Cut to the chase, priest!'

'This is the essential law of the universe, Majesty: all things will pass, even the sacred light that warms our world.'

'Blasphemy!' Muzal roared. 'The sun is the holy face of Ra. It will last for all time. Isn't that what your priesthood teaches in every temple throughout the land?'

'The Spell of Eternal Darkness had to remain secret,' Asun whispered, 'lest some enemy, your son for example, were to discover its existence.'

Muzal detested being reminded of his son, the foul traitor Sabray, now the Darkwing. 'My damnable son *has* discovered the secret!' he bellowed. He was beside himself with fury and terror. For long moments, he paced the Ziggurat. Finally, he spoke. 'Can nothing be done?'

'There is but one fragile ray of hope.'

'Tell me.'

'The Holy Children were able to tame the blood lust of the Lost Souls. They broke the Darkwing's power over his minions. Perhaps they can prevail against him one more

416

time.' Asun gave Muzal an enquiring look. 'Lord Timu awaits your orders, Imperial Majesty.'

'Find these Holy Children,' Muzal said. 'Harness whatever power they have. Send my miserable son to Hell.'

Asun bowed. 'It will be done, Imperial Highness.'

4

Kulmat waited until Rishal's lamp was extinguished. A short while later, sure that his knight was asleep, the cadet quietly made his way across the camp. He wanted to find a quiet spot where he could think. Soon he reached a spreading acacia tree. Sitting beneath its branches, he pulled out a scrap of bloodied bandage.

'Are you with her, Gardep?' he murmured.

The bandage was a memento of their childhood friendship, a bond of which he dared not speak, lest Rishal fly into a rage. Kulmat leaned back against the tree trunk and gazed up at the star-studded sky. He felt a sudden chill. Was that the first sigh of the dying sun? Kulmat remembered Rishal's question that same evening: how did a mere girl come to hold their destiny in her hands? It made him recall a sunset months ago in Tiger-gated Parcep. That night, Gardep had fallen in love with Cusha.

'Soon,' Kulmat said, with only the stars and the moon to hear him, 'the order will come to hunt you down, my brother. Flee, flee with all your cunning and all your strength. It would break my heart to face you on the field of battle.'

He pressed his hand to the sun symbol tattooed above his heart and prayed that they would never draw swords against one another. That's when he realised the futility of his wish. He was praying to a dying god.

5

Jinghirza Ghun was woken by a curious sound, a kind of wet mumble. For a few moments she peered into the darkness, trying to see what it was. Then she made sense of the crumpled figure chained to the far wall. A moonbeam caught his face. It made her shudder. The Darkwing had torn out his eyes and drained copious amounts of blood from his veins. By some miracle the saffron-robed priest was still alive.

'Why did he do this to you?' Jinghirza whispered, fearing for her own fate.

The priest tried to speak. Then Jinghirza understood how the sound had been made. The monster had cut out his tongue.

'By the gods of the sky!' she croaked, overwhelmed with the horror of the priest's tormented features.

'Don't speak to him!' a familiar voice hissed behind her.

The Darkwing stalked across the temple. His gaze swept the room, making his captives cower.

'If a single one of you dares address this priest or offer him succour,' the demon lord told them, 'you will pay the ultimate price.'

Some nodded, others simply hid their faces in shadow. Jinghirza alone found her voice. 'What has he done to be treated so?'

'You again,' the Darkwing said.

'Do you have no mercy?' Jinghirza asked.

The Darkwing gave a desolate chuckle. 'You are not the first mortal to ask me that question. The answer is no.'

Turning his back on Jinghirza, the Darkwing hauled Linem to his feet. The priest uttered a gurgling scream.

'Have you reconsidered your answer?'

Linem nodded.

'Then I will let you live another day.'

Jinghirza watched as the monster dragged his pathetic, broken captive away. She did not know what the Darkwing had asked him. She did know it could only lead to evil.

6

At dusk the Tanjurs sat together, breaking bread. There was precious little and nothing to accompany it. Hunger was becoming a major problem. Gardep was busy in the keep, aided by Atrakon. He had some plan.

'The boy-warrior is the most natural fighter I have seen,' Oled said. 'For all that, he has faults.'

Shamana chewed a spiced flatbread. 'We all have faults, my son. There are even some Tanjurs who struggle to take the form of a buffalo.'

Ignoring his mother's chiding, Oled persisted with his argument. 'Gardep's faults are great. When he fights, the blood lust takes him. He is not content with defeating his enemies. He wishes to annihilate them. This is not the way of the Scales. He lacks the quality of mercy.'

Shamana patted Oled's arm. 'Don't judge him too severely. He is young. All his life he has been immersed in the brutal ways of the Sol-ket. For all that, he has a great heart. He knows the ways of our enemy. His destiny is mentioned in the Book of Scales. He will be our general.'

'I will not oppose you,' Oled said. 'He is a leader of men, that is clear. He is loyal and true. I believe he has grown to love the cause of freedom. But he does not understand our ways. For there to be peace, all things must be in balance, light and dark, male and female. Do you think he can ever walk the path of reconciliation? Can he learn to live alongside his former foe?'

'We will teach him,' Shamana said. 'You are quiet, Aaliya. What is your view?'

'I understand what Oled says,' Aaliya replied. 'In battle, the gentler side of Gardep's character is lost. But look at him with Cusha.'

The lovers were sitting side by side, their heads together, sharing some secret.

'He loves her dearly,' Aaliya said. 'Surely his adoration for her will soften him.'

'It is a gamble we must take,' Shamana said. 'There has not been a rebel leader since Shinar with his qualities of generalship. Do you agree, Oled?'

'So long as we are ready to temper his excesses, yes.'

'Aaliya?'

'He will give us steel. We will give him heart.'

'Then it is agreed,' said Shamana. 'On the shoulders of this boy we will build the new Army of the Free.'

7

The Darkwing laid the semi-conscious priest on the stone floor, deep inside one of the caves that honeycombed Sangra peak. He gazed into the depths of a well. Here, the monks of Nandraghiri had drawn their water.

'It is time to do me one more service,' the demon lord said.

Broken, humiliated, Linem offered no resistance. The Darkwing dipped his claws into the well and watched the water trickle between them. Next, he upended a basket of cobras and watched them swarming in the black water. In the next few moments he deposited the contents of half a dozen more baskets into the well.

'Now the Lyrian fire.'

Linem craned to hear what he was doing. The Darkwing poured a thick stream of the pitch-like substance on the water's surface until it was entirely covered by a thick membrane of the stuff.

'One last ingredient,' he hissed.

He seized the priest, holding his head in a vice-like grip. At last understanding the direction of the Darkwing's thoughts, Linem gave a wet scream of despair, but the demon lord slashed his throat and deposited him into the vile soup. Then, with a razor-sharp claw, he sliced a vein and watched his own black blood ooze from the opening and spill into the well. The water immediately boiled and roared. Then he lit the Lyrian fire and watched. The bubbling mixture popped and hissed like a spitted bull. Clouds of scarlet and black smoke billowed across the chamber. Eventually, the flames burned down and the Darkwing could see the results of his experiment. He bathed in the foul concoction. When he surfaced, he roared across the mountains.

'Hitherto, there has been too much of the human in me,' he declared to the desolate peaks. 'I allowed the vestiges of the boy I was to cloud my judgement. Now I am made anew. I will not make the same mistake again.'

8

When Rishal's scouts reported the disappearance of one of his patrols, he marched them to the map that dominated his quarters. He tapped the line that symbolised the Demon Wall. 'Show me where they were last seen.'

'They broke camp here and turned north-west.'

Rishal examined the map. With his finger he drew a

triangle. 'Send every available man,' he said. 'Flood this area with light cavalry. We want soldiers who are mobile and quick. What trackers do we have?'

'There are the Khut mercenaries.'

'What about Selessians? They are the best at this kind of work.'

At this point General Barath interrupted. 'I hear that a fresh unit of Selessian cavalry was recently ordered to Karangpur. They are supporting the new garrison.'

Rishal nodded. 'I want them here as soon as possible.'

'Are you sure that's a good idea?' Barath asked. 'The Hotec-Ra tried to use the assassin Atrakon Ebrahin. They gave him good gold to capture the Holy Child. He repaid them by murdering Lord Shirep-hotec.'

'You can't judge all Selessians by the actions of one renegade desert rat,' Rishal said. 'He had the misfortune to meet the slave-girl Cusha. She has an uncanny ability to twist men's minds. No, the Selessians have served us well. Have you forgotten their role in our greatest victory? They turned the tide at Dullah.'

'That was forty years ago,' Barath answered. 'These are not the same men.'

Rishal was not swayed. 'Forget Atrakon,' he said. 'The warriors of the desert kingdom have been a mainstay of Imperial rule. We need them, Barath-Ra.'

Barath succumbed. 'As you wish.'

Having won the argument, Rishal strode out of the tent towards the horses. 'Tell the men to saddle up,' he shouted to Kulmat. 'We're going hunting.'

'At night?'

'That's right,' Rishal said. 'We're going after the rebels. When the Holy Children go to face the demon lord, it will be in our company.'

'What about their companions?'

'Why, they will die, of course.'

Kulmat ordered that the muster be sounded. As he watched the Sol-ket strapping on their armour and saddling their mounts, he could feel his heart kicking against his ribs. It was the moment he'd been dreading.

9

A dozen companies of Sol-ket horse were scouring the territory Rishal had marked out on the map. They rode together as far as the razed fort of Zindhar before splitting into separate units. It was Kulmat's northernmost patrol that discovered the bodies Gardep had had hidden.

'Cadet Kulmat,' one of his men shouted. 'You must see this.'

Kulmat followed him into the keep. By a shaft of moonlight, he saw the bodies. Though there had been an attempt to burn them, he recognised Gardep's hand in their destruction.

'Bring me a lamp,' he said.

Yellowish light bathed the room, illuminating the macabre scene. He discovered a Selessian sword-cut on one man, the effects of a Tanjur axe on another.

'It's them, for certain,' he said.

He made a search of the room. Once, fastening on some detail, he paused.

'What is it?' the soldier asked.

'Nothing,' Kulmat lied. 'I recognised one of the dead. He was in my dormitory at the Academy.'

The soldier didn't see him move one of the corpses with the toe of his boot, obscuring something. Returning the light to its owner, he climbed to the roof of the keep and surveyed the darkened plain. He had been scanning the area to the north and east when he saw a light. It was a faint glow, like dancing fireflies.

'Is that the best you can do, Gardep?' he wondered out loud. He heard the jangle of harness. Keen to keep Rishal out of the keep, he called to him. 'Commander, what do you make of this?'

Rishal raced up the steps to join him. 'It could be a campfire.' His brow furrowed. 'I thought I taught Gardep better.'

'The same thought occurred to me, Rishal-Ra.'

Rishal pondered for a while. 'What about the keep?'

'Nothing.'

'This fire,' Rishal said, 'it's got to be a ruse of some kind. Investigate the lights, Kulmat. The rest of our troops will ride in a line from the Great Wall to Zindhar. If we travel due north-east, we are bound to discover them.'

Kulmat nodded. Once Rishal's back was turned, he permitted himself a smile. Ten minutes after the Sol-ket left the keep, one of the bodies moved. It was covering a disguised hatch. Gardep was the first to emerge. Crouching low, he padded over to the door. After that, he checked the walkways and the bleak terrain either side of the Demon Wall. Was that really Kulmat's voice he had heard? Could it be his friend had protected him? Satisfied that the Sol-ket had gone, Gardep returned to the hatch.

'You can come out,' he hissed.

At that, one by one, his companions climbed out of the underground storage cellar. Oled appeared last, carrying Murak on his back. They then recovered the horses from a ravine on the far side of the Great Wall and rode due east, behind the Sol-ket lines.

10

It was mid-morning the next day when Rishal called off the pursuit. The light had been made by a flock of goats with lighted tapers attached to their horns. None of the companies had discovered any trace of the fleeing rebels.

'Somehow,' he said, 'they have outwitted us.' He scowled. 'These Khut trackers weren't much use, Kulmat. We need the Selessians.'

'I agree, Rishal-Ra.'

Rishal looked at his squire. For somebody who had been awake the whole night, he was surprisingly bright and cheerful.

'If I didn't know better,' he said, 'I'd think you were relieved that we've missed Gardep. I hope there are no divided loyalties.'

'My friendship for the traitor is over,' Kulmat said, a little too hurriedly for Rishal's liking.

'We will track him down, Kulmat,' Rishal said. 'When we do, I want to know you will do your duty. Would you have any hesitation in executing him?'

'None, Rishal-Ra.'

The prompt response seemed to appease the general, for now.

'Do you think there is a chill in the air this morning?' Rishal asked.

Kulmat thought for a moment, then nodded. 'I noticed it last night too, Rishal-Ra. Could this be the beginning? Is the sun's light starting to fade?'

The question hung. Neither of them had an answer.

'We will return to camp,' Rishal said. 'Before you take your rest, Kulmat, organise more search parties. The manhunt continues night and day until we find them.'

'Of course, Rishal-Ra.'

Again, Rishal noticed the cadence of happiness in his squire's voice. 'There's a spring in your step, Kulmat,' he observed.

'Do you think so, Rishal-Ra?' Kulmat asked.

Without another word, he fell in behind the general. In his mind's eye he recalled the search he had conducted in the keep. Step by step, he went through the events. He had seen the bodies and asked for the lamp. He had stopped suddenly, noticing a trickle of blood between the floor tiles. The soldier accompanying him had asked if there was anything wrong. Kulmat had dismissed the question, of course. There was nothing wrong, nothing at all. By overlooking the tell-tale trickle of blood between the tiles, he had just saved the lives of Gardep and his friends.

11

That same morning, through his window, General Ghushan ax-Sol, nephew of the Emperor and the new commander of Karangpur, saw one of his cadets climbing the steep flight of stone steps towards him. He closed the ledger in which he was writing.

'The signallers have just received this message by relay from the Grand Army,' the soldier said.

'Let's see it,' said Ghushan. He read the communication. 'Who commands the new Selessian regiment?'

Omar arrived ten minutes later. 'You sent for me, Ghushan-Ra.'

'Your presence is required at the front.'

Omar frowned. 'But we have barely installed ourselves at Karangpur. It is only four months since we left Juttah. My men are exhausted.'

'The order comes from General Rishal ax-Sol.'

'What is this about?'

'You're new to this land, aren't you, Selessian?'

'Yes.'

'Let me give you some advice, Omar. Never question an order. Just obey. What's your full name? I need it for my reports.'

'My name,' the Selessian said, 'is Omar Ebrahin.'

CHAPTER 4

The Spark

1

The fifteenth day of Hoj was a turning point. Hungry, relentlessly pursued by Sol-ket patrols, the ten companions made a fateful decision. With Sol-ket banners seeming to appear from every direction, they had gone two full days without food or rest. The close attentions of the Sons of Ra prevented even the resourceful Tanjurs from hunting. In the late afternoon the band took their rest in the shade of a tree while the horses drank from a stream. Shamana and Aaliya transformed into serpent eagles and flew away to search for food and pursuing troops.

'Did you see any Sol-ket patrols?' Oled asked on their return.

'You can't miss them,' Aaliya answered, anxiety crackling in her voice. 'They're everywhere. We have something of a lead on the nearest patrols but that is no reason for complacency.'

'I just wish the Four Winds would send us a sign,' Shamana said. 'Our wanderings are pointless. The Sol-ket are blocking our progress at every turn. We can't move north towards the Mountains of the Moon. There is no sign of revolt from the people. What is happening to our quest?'

Cusha felt the stirrings of unease. Shamana, usually so sure of herself, so steadfast, seemed to be losing hope.

'Maybe we should move on,' Vishtar suggested.

'I'm all for that,' Qintu said. 'I'd like to live to savour the delights of adulthood.'

Murima shook her head. 'You just want to savour the delights of good cooking,' she said.

'What's wrong with that?' Qintu asked. 'My stomach thinks my throat is cut.'

'The boy has a point,' Oled said. 'We've got to eat. We're bound to run into the Sol-ket again. If we cross swords with them while we are hungry and exhausted, we're finished anyway.'

Shamana shielded her eyes. 'The nearest patrols are still miles away,' she said. 'We've made good time. There's a village down there. Let's see if they can spare us some food.'

'Are you sure about this?' Cusha asked. 'For generations, the weaker of our people have sold runaways and insurgents to the Sol-ket simply to be able to live.'

'No,' Shamana said, 'I'm not sure at all. But does anybody have a better plan?'

A chorus of silence followed, deciding the discussion's outcome. On entering the village, the riders drew a small crowd of villagers. They looked apprehensive.

429

'Who is the village elder?' Shamana asked.

A tall, lean man of some sixty years stepped forward. 'I am Bulu. Who are you?'

There was some hesitation. How should they approach this? It was Murima who broke the silence. She was taking a great gamble. 'I am Murima-ul-Parcep,' she said. 'Everyone here has heard of my father. His name still echoes through the villages and towns. It was Shinar.'

Gasps erupted from the crowd. Even Shamana was taken aback by Murima's boldness.

'Is this true?' Bulu asked.

'What woman in her right mind would lay claim to his name?' Murima demanded. 'Who would choose to draw the wrath of the Sol-ket down upon their head? What I tell you is true. My father was the spirit of revolt in this land. The long night of oppression is coming to an end. I and my companions seek to stir the Helati once more.'

At that, several mothers hurried away with their children, as if mere words could put them in harm's way.

Bulu's eyes settled on Shamana. 'And you?'

Emboldened by Murima's example, Shamana slid from the saddle. Closing her eyes, she took the form of the She-wolf, the avatar she had assumed long ago as Queen of the Tanjurs. 'Do you know me now?'

'Your coming was prophesied,' Bulu said. 'I was at Dullah. As a young man, I fought for Shinar. I saw you ride by with him. Forgive me for not recognising you.'

Shamana smiled. 'Many years have passed since those days. Long servitude has withered me. My hair is grown grey. How has life treated you, Bulu?'

He raised the stump that had once been his right hand. 'This was my punishment at the hands of the Sol-ket. They let me keep the left so I could still work. I was one of the lucky ones.'

He caught Cusha's eye. Instantly, his face seemed to glow. He stepped forward and inspected her features. Then, very deliberately, he approached Vishtar.

'There is a resemblance here,' he said. 'Are they brother and sister?'

'You know them,' Shamana said. 'Any Helat who survived the horror of Dullah and the privations of the intervening years will recognise the Holy Children. Look at their eyes. Do you study the Book of Scales, Bulu?'

In the absence of his right hand, the elder raised his left to denote the symbol of the Scales. Some among the crowd gasped.

'I have dreamed of this day,' he said.

'Are there any Sol-ket here?' Shamana asked.

Bulu shook his head. 'The Lost Souls took the slave-master two weeks before the monsoon rains. We were able to hide from the demons in the granary cellars. We were lucky to survive.'

'I am aware that we are putting your lives in jeopardy again,' Murima said, taking over from Shamana, 'but we are hungry and exhausted. Do you have any food?'

Bulu cast his eyes round the expectant crowd. 'We will feed you,' he said.

The decision would have grave consequences. Before nightfall the next day, it would bring the swords of the Sol-ket down on his village.

2

Omar Ebrahin was brushing his fine Selessian mount in the garrison stables when he heard movement behind him. Two Sol-ket were watching him.

'Can I help you?' Omar asked.

'You can take your horse out of this stall,' one said.

Omar stopped brushing. 'I don't understand.'

'Auxiliary troops use those stables,' the second Sol-ket said.

Omar glanced through the open door at the neighbouring stables. 'It is identical to this one,' he said.

'Then there is no problem about moving your horse, desert rat.'

'There isn't room in there,' Omar said, choosing to ignore the insult. 'Every stall is occupied. That's why I brought my mount in here.'

'Well, you can take it out again,' he was told. 'These stables are Sol-ket only.'

'You use Selessian horses, just as we do,' Omar objected. 'All the animals come from the same stock.'

'But the riders don't,' came the answer.

Omar was considering his options when his second-in-command, Mehmet, appeared in the doorway. 'What's this,' he enquired, 'the famous Sol-ket hospitality?'

His arrival gave the Sons of Ra pause for thought. Then two more black-garbed Selessian warriors joined Mehmet.

'Do you still want me to move my horse?' Omar asked. The Sol-ket scowled and brushed past him. Omar addressed their backs. 'I'll keep the beast here then,' he said.

'Were they bothering you?' Mehmet asked.

'What do you think?' Omar said. 'You'd imagine they'd be grateful. It was our fathers and grandfathers who won the Battle of Dullah for them.'

'Gratitude isn't a Sol-ket quality,' Mehmet said. 'When do we ride north?'

'First light,' Omar said. 'I'll be glad to get away from this place.'

'Do you think the Sol-ket will treat us differently anywhere else?' Mehmet asked.

'I doubt it,' Omar said. 'They let us fight their wars. They let us die to protect their way of life. That doesn't mean they treat us as men.'

'Agreed,' Mehmet said. 'It makes you wonder why our ancestors fought for them at all.'

3

The next day, barely a mile from Bulu's village, a patrol was watering their horses. The Sol-ket officer filled his canteen from the stream and hung it from his saddle.

'Have the scouts returned?' he asked.

'Not yet.'

The officer cursed. 'It's like finding a grain of sand in the desert.' He cupped his hands and washed his face. 'Damn this Jingharan dust,' he said.

He was about to make another comment about the hardships of soldiering on the north Jingharan Plain when something caught his eye. A light was flashing.

'Did you see that?' he asked his squire.

'Yes, it's a signal.'

They both read the same message.

'Do you think it's a trick?' the officer said.

'I don't know, Master. Look, there it is again. It's coming from that village.'

'Who's going to know Sol-ket signalling code in a Helat village?'

The message was repeated twice more.

'Should we send scouts, Master?' the squire asked.

The officer shook his head. 'No, if there's any truth in the message, scouts would give the enemy a chance to escape. We will take the whole company.'

The message read: *The rebels are here. Give me time to*

433

get away. Come at noon. It was followed by a code word.

The officer smiled. 'We can trust the messenger. We will enter the village at the time he says.'

4

The Darkwing wanted some sport. 'You asked me to set you a challenge,' he told Jinghirza. 'Do you remember?'

'Yes, I remember.'

'I am ready to set you your first test.'

The Darkwing gave a gleeful cackle and seized her. As he flew with her over the snow-capped peaks, she looked down. The world seemed to swim around her, the vastness of its empty, fatal spaces menacing her. It would be so easy for the monster to let her fall to her death. She didn't pray for mercy. She hoped he was entertained.

'Where are we going?' she asked, her voice trembling.

'There.' He set her down on an exposed shelf of rock, scoured by ferocious winds.

'What must I do?' Jinghirza asked.

'Look to your left,' the Darkwing said.

Then she understood. There was a curving bridge. The far end of it vanished into mist. It was a fragile structure, carved by some ancient, superhuman craftsmanship from solid rock. It was barely broad enough to set your foot on it and it was covered with a sheen of ice. Jinghirza looked at the treacherous causeway and shuddered. Far beneath the jaws of a vast monster, made of mountain and mist, yawned open.

'Well,' the Darkwing asked, 'do you accept the challenge? If you don't, I will drain your blood here and now. I will make it quick.'

But Jinghirza shook her head. 'I will walk the bridge,'

she said. 'What is my reward for succeeding?'

'You get to live another day,' the Darkwing said.

'I want food for myself and the other prisoners,' Jinghirza said. 'I want you to promise not to feed on them.'

The Darkwing seemed fascinated by her defiance. 'Granted,' he said.

Biting her lip, Jinghirza took her first step. To either side of the narrow walkway there was a dizzy precipice. It looked impossible to negotiate the bridge. The thin ribbon of rock shrank almost to nothingness. But Jinghirza was a maiden of the Khut nation. Hers was a fierce, rugged people, stubborn as the most obstinate mule. In her soft, goatskin shoes, she made steady progress, always aware of the crags and faces thousands of feet below. On she walked, feeling out every inch of the icy surface with her feet, gasping when she slid. Already she was reaching the highest point of the bridge's arc; forcing herself to climb though it was like trying to grip on glass. The rock underfoot was more slippery than ever. Fear clawed at her with each uncertain step, with each heart-stopping slip.

'Please,' she said, her words flying up to her gods, 'don't let me fall. Don't give the monster the pleasure of seeing me fail.'

There was a wobble here, a half-slip there, but eventually she succeeded in reaching the far side. Taking a few rubbery steps away from the edge, she sucked in mouthfuls of air, grateful to be alive.

'You did well,' the Darkwing said, appearing out of the mist. But praise was followed by menace. 'Soon we will have better sport,' he said. 'The next trial will be more difficult.'

The prisoners ate that night. Grateful eyes turned towards Jinghirza. She didn't return the looks. Dread had her by the throat. She was already thinking about the next ordeal.

5

Murak was growing stronger by the day. He took the bowl of chickpeas spiced with garlic from one of the village women and thanked her. He was wiping the bowl with a piece of flatbread when Shamana appeared at the door to the mean hut in which he was sitting.

'You are recovered,' she said.

'The pain is easing,' Murak agreed.

'I came to thank you for what you did at the Demon Wall,' Shamana said. 'You saved my life.'

Murak shrugged. 'You and your comrades saved mine. It's a fair trade.'

Shamana offered her hand. 'Welcome to our fight for freedom, Murak.'

Murak took her hand. 'Will we tarry long in this village?'

'Why do you ask?'

'We are vulnerable here. It is only a matter of time before the Sol-ket follow.'

'You're right,' Shamana said. 'I have come to the same conclusion. We must not put this village in danger by our continued presence. We are about to leave.'

This seemed to satisfy Murak. They would be gone by noon. 'How have you kept your faith all these years, Shamana?' he asked.

'It is the nature of our cause,' Shamana answered. 'Throughout all the generations of mankind, kingdoms and empires have sought to conquer in the name of this or that tyrant. Udmanesh was the first man to claim the world for all mankind. Our long struggle is not to place the Helati or the Tanjurs above other mortal men, but to permit all men and women to hold the wealth of the land in common. All humanity will be free and equal before the Four Winds.'

'It is a great dream,' Murak said. 'Will we live to see it come true, do you think?'

'By the grace of Destiny, yes.'

Hearing footsteps, Shamana turned. 'Oh, it's you Oled.'

The giant seemed happy to see his mother and his friend talking together. 'The horses are ready,' he said. 'The villagers have given us provisions for our journey.'

'Then it is time to depart.'

Oled and Shamana left the hut. Murak followed a few moments later. The whole village gathered to bid farewell.

'May the Four Winds watch over you,' Bulu said.

'And you,' Shamana answered.

They exchanged the symbol of the Scales. Then, sending Aaliya to scout ahead, Shamana led the rebels north east out of the village.

6

A second signalled message had warned the Sol-ket patrol to expect a shape-shifter to go looking for them. The Warriors of Ra duly concealed themselves in a coppice half a mile to the west of the village.

'Do you think that's one of them?' the squire said, watching a hawk fluttering overhead.

'It's possible,' the officer said. 'We will remain out of sight for another few minutes.'

The time seemed to crawl by.

'Did you have any luck contacting the other patrols?' the officer said.

'Only one,' the squire said. 'They are going to teach the village a lesson for harbouring the rebels.'

'Good. We will have the glory of capturing the Holy Children.'

He was excited at the prospect of such an important mission. Only one thing troubled him. Why had their agent in the enemy camp asked them to wait until noon? Still, his orders were to follow the agent's instructions. He watched the sky. It was clear. He gave his men their battle orders.

'Our rules of engagement have been changed,' he told them, 'on the instructions of His Imperial Highness, Lord Muzal. The Holy Children we take prisoner.' He smiled, relishing the task ahead. 'The rest we kill.'

7

Shamana was concerned by Aaliya's report. She had discovered evidence of two Sol-ket patrols but she had only been able to locate one of them.

'Where?'

'South of the village.'

'We took care to leave nothing to implicate the villagers,' Oled said. 'They'll be quite safe. Bulu's a shrewd fellow. He'll know what to say.'

Shamana should have found her son's words reassuring. Nevertheless, she couldn't drive a nagging worry from her mind. Where was the missing patrol? She had trained her apprentice well. Aaliya was a meticulous scout, unlikely to miss a score of armed men. No, there was something wrong. Other forces were at work.

'I want you all to be quiet,' she said.

Glances were exchanged.

'What is it?' Murak asked.

Shamana pressed a finger to her lips and listened.

Untroubled by conversation, she allowed the sounds of Jinghara to float into her mind. At first there was nothing, then she heard something like the flutter of a tiny bird. The faint throbbing became clearer, a pulse, a repetitive drumming rhythm. Hoof beats.

'Prepare for battle!' Shamana yelled.

Murak drew his sword like the others. Nobody saw his puzzled expression. Why was the patrol attacking them when they should be punishing the villagers who had harboured the rebels? Why had they put him in such a difficult situation so early? He had no time to ponder further. The Warriors of the Sun came at the gallop, swords drawn. The scarlet tassels on their helmets rippled in the breeze. Gardep assessed the balance of forces.

'We need to break their charge,' he said. 'Can you do something, Shamana?'

Shamana winked. 'Elephants!' she roared.

Aaliya transformed, following her teacher's example. Two elephants thundered towards the advancing cavalry. They were followed by a rhinoceros, Oled's more modest contribution to the counter-charge. He noticed his mother's look of disgust. Would her son never master the fine points of metamorphosis? The three beasts broke the Sol-ket offensive, throwing the fine Selessian horses into panic. Racing in behind them, Gardep led the remaining fighters forward, falling upon the enemy with sword and bow, piercing flesh, cracking bones. His leadership inspired everyone. Even the youngest members of the group, Harad and Qintu, played their part, jabbing and parrying, covering the more seasoned fighters' backs. Hand to hand fighting followed. The three Tanjurs returned to human form and concentrated their attention on breaking the Sol-ket's formation. The Imperial charge stalled. The Sol-ket wavered.

'Bows!' Gardep ordered. 'Murima, Cusha, Qintu, Harad. You too, Murak. You've proved yourself a good shot.'

The five drew up a line, their shafts whispering through the air and thumping into the Warriors of Ra. Horses screamed and men fell. With the four remaining rebels returning to the fray, swords and battle-axes drawn, the Sol-ket officer broke off the attack. Just as he had done once before, Gardep set about destroying the remnants of the enemy force. His knight, the Lion of Inbacus, Rishal ax-Sol, had taught him well. Ruthlessness was the key to final victory. This time, however, Shamana prevented him embarking on a systematic extermination of the enemy.

'No, Gardep,' she cried. 'There is no time.'

She shouted to the archers. 'Gather as many arrows as you can. At this very moment a second patrol is approaching the village. I fear for our friends.'

8

The second company of Sol-ket swept into the village in battle formation, hurling lighted torches onto the thatched roofs to their right and left. They didn't care whether there was anyone inside the makeshift houses at the time. They too followed Rishal's code of total war. Terror-stricken by the onslaught, mothers, fathers, children spilled screaming from their homes, only to be cut down by the marauding Sol-ket. Half a dozen bodies littered the street in the first charge. Carrying on down the single dirt track between the blazing buildings, the Sol-ket wheeled round, ready to charge again.

'Defend yourselves!' Bulu roared.

The villagers stared at him in disbelief. Most of them

had lived their lives in fear of the Masters, never daring to even make eye contact. Now their elder was ordering resistance. Even as the Sol-ket swung their horses, nobody moved.

'Gather forks, hoes, spades, anything,' Bulu cried.

For the first time, some of the young men and women started running to the tool stores. Then, from Bulu's throat, there sprang an ancient war cry. With his surviving left hand, he swung a sledgehammer above his head and planted himself in the middle of the dirt road. 'Freedom or death!'

The Sol-ket came again, harness jangling, faces taut. Bulu stood his ground, the hammer in his left hand, leading by example. Armed with their hastily gathered implements, the young and the able-bodied ran to join him. In the mêlée that ensued ten of them fell, three dead, the rest wounded by sword cuts. But the slaves didn't run. More importantly, two of the Warriors of Ra fell too. One died, impaled on a pitchfork. Another writhed in the dust until a middle-aged matron finished him with a hoe.

'I never thought this day would come,' she howled with delight. 'We are a risen people once more. The Helati are fighting back, imagine that!'

The Sol-ket started their third pass through the village. This time the resistance was fierce. Where houses still stood, the young men and women clambered onto the roofs, hurling all manner of projectiles. More Imperial soldiers succumbed to the withering hail. A single act of courage had swung the skirmish in the villagers' favour. Bulu's grandson, Nikesh, gathered his friends and hauled a cart across the road, blocking the Sol-ket's escape. Inspired by his example, some of the women started to assemble an impromptu barricade. Within this cauldron of revolt, the wide-eyed Sol-ket stalled, met defeat, died.

9

The Ten entered the village some thirty minutes later. They found the buildings still blazing, the villagers massing around the funeral pyre of the dead. Shamana surveyed the scene with a practised eye. For long moments there was silence. The Ten gazed into the eyes of the villagers and the villagers looked back. Nothing in their expressions gave a clue to what they were thinking. Then Shamana did something that sent a murmur eddying around the crowd. Sliding from her saddle, she walked towards Bulu and fell on her knees before him.

'Forgive me,' she said. 'It was I who brought this catastrophe down on your heads. The blood of your murdered innocents stains my hands.'

Head bowed, she awaited Bulu's answer.

'Stand, Shamana,' he said. 'You should not apologise. You have our gratitude. Forty years we have grovelled in the dirt, abasing ourselves before the Muzals' assassins. This day we have won back our pride.'

'But what of your dead, your wounded?' Murima asked.

'We will mourn,' Bulu answered. 'Of course we will. But know this, bending the knee to the Sol-ket has not saved a single soul. All these years the Masters have killed and tortured to make us work harder, to ensure our obedience, sometimes simply for sport.'

The matron who had helped turn the battle stepped forward.

'One of my sons died in the fighting today,' she said, eyes welling with tears. 'Nobody has more right than I to speak on this matter.' She beat her chest with both fists. 'Though my heart breaks, I have no regrets. I would rather have my son enter the House of the Dead with a weapon in his hand, defending his people, than cowed and servile, regretting his wretched existence.'

Some of the other mothers nodded.

'This is the first day of our freedom,' one said.

'The long night of oppression is over,' her neighbour agreed.

Shamana looked around the massed villagers. 'Do you all feel this way?'

There was a powerful shout of agreement.

'And you realise what this means?'

Bulu answered for the whole village. 'We have made our choice, She-wolf. We will follow you. We will follow the daughter of Shinar and the Holy Children. The Masters have beaten our sons and daughters. They have sold them away from their families. They have tortured and killed our men and taken our women for their pleasure. Even if we die in this great undertaking, we will do so reaching for our freedom.'

The villagers brandished weapons, the hoes and spades with which they had fought, the swords and spears they had stripped from the bodies of the dead Sol-ket.

Oled looked at the two hundred or so Helati and murmured to Gardep. 'This is what we have been waiting for.'

Gardep nodded. 'Yes, it's Shamana's sign. The Four Winds have just given her their answer. What we have before us is the first company of the Army of the Free.'

CHAPTER 5

Fire and Ice

1

Rishal and Kulmat picked their way through the detritus of battle. The Helati had burned the dead of friend and foe alike on a single common pyre, something the Children of Ra found abhorrent. Whatever the villagers could use, they had taken: food supplies, weapons, horses.

'Two companies wiped out,' Rishal said, his eyes sweeping the charred remains of Bulu's village. 'The rebels have stripped our men of everything they could use. They now have weapons, horses, even Lyrian fire. By their idiocy, our own troops are turning the enemy into an army. By the holy face of Ra, is there no end to our troubles? The world is like a candle burning at both ends.'

'Surely the Darkwing is the greater danger, Master,'

Kulmat said. 'This is not the first slave revolt the Empire has faced. It won't be the last. It is in the nature of the Helati to resist their enslavement from time to time. It is a perennial danger, but one we can contain. Were the demon lord to prevail however, the whole world would perish.'

The squire chose his words carefully. Somewhere, somehow, he prayed there might be a happy outcome. If the Sol-ket were to capture the Holy Children, at least they would have to keep them alive. Dead, they were no use against the Darkwing. Kulmat tried to imagine a future in which he and Gardep could be friends, Gardep and his Cusha united. He was shocked at his own thoughts. Born and raised as a Sol-ket, he had started to think like a Helat. Though it was heresy to any Child of the Sun, he had even begun to conjure a world in which there was no struggle, no division between slave and slave-holder. Is it possible, he wondered, or will it be yet another broken dream?

Rishal sighed. 'You're right, you're right. But, if we move against the Darkwing, how can we ignore the fire at our back? No, there is a chance we could save the world only to hand it to the servile masses. We must fight on two fronts, Kulmat. There will be a council of war. Take a company of men. Tell Barath what has happened.'

Kulmat nodded and gave his bugler an order. At the signal, a score of horsemen climbed into the saddle.

'And Kulmat,' Rishal shouted, 'don't try to hide the gravity of the situation. You must let Barath know what we are dealing with here. There are fifty villages within a day's ride. News of a Helat victory will spread like fire in a tinder-dry forest.'

2

'It is beginning,' the Darkwing gloated. 'My scheme unfolds. Cruel winter begins to grip the land.' He had not intended the words to be heard. That didn't prevent Jinghirza interrupting him.

'Is this your doing, Lord?'

The creature's head snapped round. For a moment terror pinned her to the wall as his black eyes seared her mind. His jaws parted, exposing a mouthful of needle-sharp fangs. Then, to Jinghirza's relief, a sly smile spread over the demon lord's inhuman features. 'Do you wish to understand my intentions, Jinghirza?'

'As you see fit, my Lord,' Jinghirza answered, careful not to antagonise him.

The Darkwing released her from her chains. 'Come.'

Heart full of foreboding, Jinghirza followed him to the monastery's colonnaded entrance.

'What do you see?' he asked.

Jinghirza wondered what he was showing her. 'Snow. I see a world of snow.'

'Exactly,' the demon lord said, delighted by her answer. He seized her and flew south, settling on the lower slopes from which they could see the ancestral lands of the Khuts and the Obirs. 'Now tell me what you see.'

Jinghirza stared. Snowstorms were howling across the northern plains, blanketing the Khut villages and driving across the pastures of the Obirs.

'I don't understand,' she said. 'By now our crops should be sprouting. What has happened to the good light of the sun?'

Her answer made the Darkwing's eyes blaze with an intense joy. 'This is my great work, Jinghirza. At last, after all my setbacks, I will have my revenge. This world has taken everything from me: my youth, my lost love Kewara, my humanity. Now I am repaying it in full. You ask what has happened to the good light of the sun, Jinghirza? It is fading. The winter you see spreading across the north land will presently sweep south. The grasslands will wither and die. The cities will shiver. The southern ocean will ice over. Just imagine it. Karangpur will become a snowy confection. Golden Rinaghar will be coated in thick, silvery frost. Even humid Parcep will succumb, its palm-fringed boulevards covered with a sheen of ice. This is the end of things, my child. The age of reckoning is upon us.'

'No,' Jinghirza protested.

'Can you not feel it?' the Darkwing asked. 'Do you not sense the glacial fingers of eternal winter stealing through the marrow of your bones?'

'I don't believe it,' Jinghirza cried. 'I refuse to swallow your lies.'

'You believe it,' the Darkwing said. 'You just won't admit it yet.'

Turning away from her tormentor, Jinghirza watched the snow flurries scouring her native land. Tears stood in her eyes, slowly freezing to her lashes.

3

In the next four weeks, countless villages and hamlets followed the example of Bulu's community. Bulu's grandson Nikesh was the boldest and most respected of the younger generation. Once, when a Sol-ket insulted his sister, he had waited a week before tracking the offender down and killing him. He had made it look like an accident to prevent reprisals. The act had given him almost legendary status in the village. It came as no surprise when he was put in charge of a group of young men. They were given fast horses and told to raise Jinghara against the oppressors. The villages, bled dry for so long by demon and Master alike, feted the riders with garlands and songs. Everywhere they went, uprisings followed. The villagers looted stores, fired Sol-ket villas and dispossessed slave masters. Imperial patrols that had been hunting the Holy Children found themselves tangled in the complications of a string of riots.

Appointed Commander-in-Chief of the Army of the Free, Gardep set about training the thousands of raw recruits that Nikesh brought flocking to his banner. He did his work well. He organised his warriors into companies, platoons, regiments. He interviewed hundreds of eager fighters, selecting the most able and giving them command. All this was done with astonishing speed. The talents Rishal had once recognised were now being turned against the Empire. On a broad front across northern Jinghara, Gardep launched numerous attacks. There was nothing random about them, as he explained one night to an assembly of thirty of its leaders.

'We were nine,' he told them. 'At first recruiting a single man seemed beyond us. Now we are thousands. We are still too weak to meet the Grand Army in the field. As a result, we have had to turn our lack of training and equipment to our advantage. By constantly moving, by striking and running, we've got the enemy chasing us across hundreds of miles of empty grassland. Now is the time to make our move.'

'Meaning?' Murak asked.

'Oled Lonetread will take command of the Jingharan front,' Gardep explained. 'I will lead a northern expedition.

The aim of this force will be to reach Sangra Peak. There, the Holy Children will use their powers to destroy the Darkwing and restore the warmth of the sun.'

Atrakon was taken aback. 'You mean to divide our resources? This is madness.'

Oled found himself in agreement with the Selessian he distrusted so much. He stared at Shamana. 'Did you know anything about this?'

Shamana shook her head. 'You are Commander of the Army of the Free, Gardep. We can't spare you. Atrakon is right. We have had a few successes. That doesn't mean we can go splitting the army in half.'

'You entrusted me with command,' Gardep retorted. 'These are my orders.'

'I understand why you are doing this,' Murima said, trying to find a compromise. 'You want to be by Cusha's side. But Gardep, you mustn't let your personal feelings cloud your judgement. I was at Dullah. I know what division and intrigue can do. This plan of yours is a mistake for which we will pay with blood.'

Cusha and Vishtar watched the exchange of angry words in silence. Gardep's project was as much of a surprise to them as it was to any of the other leaders of the revolt.

'We are not the Sol-ket,' Oled growled. 'We have no absolute leaders to order us about. Our ways are set down in the Book of Scales. We seek a Republic of the Free where all have a voice and none are elevated to untrammelled power. Everyone here has been chosen by the casting of lots. No one man can take decisions for an entire people.'

'So why did you make me general?' Gardep demanded.

'You are a military man,' Shamana said. 'You know the way our enemy thinks. In battle, you are without compare.

449

But you must heed the advice of your brothers and sisters assembled here. Listen to Oled. This is the way of the Scales.'

'Then set out an alternative to what I propose,' Gardep said, eyes hard with anger.

'There is a way,' Vishtar said. All eyes turned in his direction. 'There is no need to divide our forces,' he said. 'Cusha and I need no protection from the Sol-ket. What are they going to do? We have their captured reports. They know the Darkwing's design. If the sun grows cold in the sky, they will die just as we will. Even if they were to capture us, they would not dare harm us. They need our powers to thwart the demon lord.'

Averting her eyes from Gardep, Cusha spoke in support of her brother. 'What Vishtar says is true. It is not an army we need, nor even a regiment. We will go alone. The Book of Scales prophesied this. It did not speak of an army, but of one heart. All we need is a single resourceful scout to accompany us.'

Atrakon seized on Cusha's words. 'The Holy Child is right. Three people can move quickly. They are more likely to evade our enemies. I volunteer to act as guide.'

'You?' Oled said with a scowl. 'Do you think we are complete fools? You fight with us now, Ebrahin, but there was a time you sold your soul to the priesthood. Do you think we have forgotten the years you spent in the service of the Hotec-Ra?' He shook his head. 'No, there has to be another candidate.'

'I have one,' Shamana said.

Oled looked around. 'Who? Who has the skills? Who can find their way north? Do you want me to go?'

'No, Oled,' Shamana said. 'Your talents are better suited to the battlefield. I mean my apprentice, Aaliya. She has perfected the arts of metamorphosis. She is a skilled swordswoman and archer. She can read the lie of the land as expertly as anyone I have ever known.'

Suddenly the thought of being parted from Aaliya made Oled's heart ache with loss. For all that, he raised no protest against Shamana. The same could not be said of Gardep.

'I will not permit it!' Gardep shouted. 'Do you really intend to send three against all the dangers in their way? They must cross the lands of the Khuts and the Obirs. Who knows what they will face when they reach the Mountains of the Moon?'

'The quest for the Black Tower began with five travellers,' Cusha said gently. 'Who travelled the road from Parcep to the Black Tower? I remember those who were with me then: Shamana and Murima, Harad and Qintu. We were women and boys. You took a different path from me then, Gardep. Sometimes the actions of a few single-minded pilgrims can change the face of the world.'

Her intervention cut the ground from under Gardep's feet. He could find no answer to her.

'Let's put it to the vote,' Bulu said, speaking for the villages that made up the vast majority of the army.

It was carried with only one vote against.

4

By the time Omar Ebrahin and his Selessians reached the Grand Army, the Imperial engineers had rebuilt the fortress of Zindhar. The new construction dwarfed the original. It had been extended to house many thousands of warriors. It was into this growing complex of buildings that the black-garbed desert warriors rode, their cloaks wrapped round them against the biting cold.

'By the Almighty,' Mehmet said. 'I had heard the north Jingharan Plain was windy. But this!'

Omar too wondered about the unnatural cold. Hostile eyes followed the Selessians. The words 'desert rat' were murmured more than once. Omar chose to ignore the insults of the surrounding Sol-ket. There was little choice. If his men threw the abuse back in the faces of the Imperial Army, what then? What could a few thousand do against an entire expeditionary force?

'You, Selessian,' a Sol-ket officer barked. 'Report to General Rishal's quarters.'

Omar looked around. All the buildings looked the same.

'Turn right at the canteen,' the officer said, pointing the building out. 'Carry on straight. You can't miss it. You'll see the sun standards.'

Omar nodded. 'Where are my soldiers' quarters?'

The officer chuckled. 'You're in those tents,' he said, 'outside the main stockade.'

'Tents,' Mehmet said, disgust in his voice, 'in this cold!'

'Get the men settled in,' Omar said. 'I'll see what the general wants.'

He found Rishal's quarters and explained his presence to the guards. After waiting outside for a few minutes, he was escorted to an ante-room. There was a strong smell of freshly hewn timbers. For the second time he was left waiting. Finally, the door swung open and he was brought before the Army Command. There were two-dozen men present. Most were senior officers. There was a single saffron-robed priest.

'You are five days late, Omar Ebrahin,' Rishal complained.

'We were delayed by frequent storms,' Omar answered. He had expected Rishal to dismiss his explanation as an excuse. Instead, Rishal introduced the members of the High Command.

'You are probably wondering why you have been transferred from Karangpur, Omar,' Rishal said.

Omar stood impassively. It was the Selessian way.

'The men of the desert kingdom have a reputation as expert trackers,' Rishal continued. 'We have need of your talents. I will allow Lord Timu of the Hotec-Ra to explain the mission.

Omar listened to Timu. Even his impassive features registered shock when the priest revealed the cause of the turbulent storms that were assaulting the northern plains.

'We believe the so-called Holy Children have already set off towards the Mountains of the Moon,' Timu concluded. 'Commander Rishal will suppress the Helat uprising and protect the Imperial heartland. General Barath and I will lead the pursuit of these infernal twins. We will make sure they reach the Darkwing and use their powers to overcome him.'

'Then?' Omar asked, already knowing the likely answer.

'Then they become expendable, of course.' Timu gave the inevitable humourless smile. 'By way of reward, we will sacrifice them to Holy Ra.'

When Omar reached the hundreds of tents raised to house his men, he took Mehmet aside and explained the situation.

'The Sol-ket have been swigging too much kinthi,' Mehmet said. 'It's driven them all mad.'

He was laughing at Omar's crazy story. Then he saw his leader's eyes and the good humour drained from his face. 'You're serious, aren't you?'

'Yes,' Omar replied. 'Insane as all this sounds, I could smell the reek of fear in that room. The Hell-fiend has the entire world by the throat, Mehmet.'

Mehmet looked at the sleet that was slanting across the usually sunlit grasslands. 'We're a long way from home, Omar, such a long way.'

Omar laid out his prayer mat. 'Which way is Juttah, Mehmet?'

Mehmet consulted his compass. 'The needle points that way.'

Omar removed his boots and knelt facing the Selessian holy city. When he had finished his prayers, he gave Mehmet an order to pass on to the men.

'There will be extra worship today,' he said. 'Instruct the men in their devotions. They will pray for the sun's golden light to return.'

5

Gardep and Cusha talked late into the night.

'You must not be afraid,' she told Gardep. 'I will return. I promise.'

Gardep took her hand and held it to his lips. She felt his tears on her skin. 'How can you possibly know?'

Cusha leaned her forehead against his and murmured her reply. 'I trust my brother.'

Gardep frowned. 'Vishtar? What do you mean?'

'We will not be alone in our quest,' Cusha said, earnestness oozing from every pore. 'He has communicated with the Lost Souls.'

Gardep stared at her. 'You trust the undead?'

'I trust Vishtar.'

'You say the Lost Souls speak to your brother?'

'The Book of Scales talks of *an innocent and generous heart.* It's Vishtar, I know it.'

'Lost Souls, redemption, prophecy . . . I am sick of such

talk,' Gardep said. 'I hate it all, the plotting, the sorcery, the endless shifting sands of Fate. I was born with a sword in my hand. I am a soldier, Cusha. I crave the simplicity of open battle. I want an enemy I can fight.'

'That is your strength and your weakness, my love,' Cusha said. 'That is why you need the wisdom of Shamana and the steadiness of Oled. We all fight the enemy in our own way.'

Gardep was stubborn. 'I should be with you.'

Cusha shook her head. 'The people need you. Your sword will lead them to victory against the Children of the Sun. This is the last time we will be apart, I promise.'

'Swear it,' Gardep said. 'Swear it by the Four Winds.'

Cusha put her arms round his neck and kissed him on the lips. 'I have sworn it a thousand times. What can I do to ease your torment?'

'Consent to betrothal,' he said.

By way of an answer, tears spilled from Cusha's eyes. A shaft of moonlight made them glisten on her cheeks. So it came to pass that, the following morning, the day of her departure, Cusha ul-Parcep stood before the Army of the Free to be betrothed to Gardep na-Vassyrian. Shamana conducted the ceremony.

'Take her hands,' she told Gardep.

When their hands were linked, she bound them with prayer scrolls, printed with verses from the Book of Scales. Finally, she poured water over their hands, symbolising their coming union.

'Are you ready to let me go?' Cusha asked.

'So long as you swear to return to be my wife,' Gardep said.

'Nothing,' Cusha said, 'not the demon lord, not the legions of the Sol-ket, not even the fires of hell will keep us apart.'

They embraced. Gardep whispered his love one last

time. Then Cusha said her farewells. She hugged Shamana then Harad and Qintu. She murmured something under her breath, first to Atrakon, then to Oled. She wondered if either of them would take notice. Finally, she threw her arms round Murima's neck and kissed her on the cheek.

'I will miss you so much, Mama-li,' she said.

'And I you, my dearest child,' Murima replied.

Within the hour Cusha had ridden out of the camp with Vishtar and Aaliya at her side.

6

Nobody noticed Murak's absence from the gathering. He slipped into the tent Shamana shared with Aaliya. Casting furtive looks through the flap now and then, he searched for the ingredients he needed. Soon he had them. Taking only the smallest quantities, so as not to be discovered, he left with the precious herbs and spices. He stole out of the camp as the Army of the Free gathered to witness Cusha and Gardep exchange their vows. Heart pounding, fearing discovery at every moment, he made his way to a venerable banyan tree. Under its spreading branches, he put together his mixture and lit it. Easing a thread from his tunic, he dropped it into the fire. The thread was taken from his sacred robes. The tiny flame danced for a moment then turned the saffron colour of the Hotec-Ra. Timu's face appeared.

'Murak,' Timu said, 'what has taken you so long? I was beginning to think you were dead.'

Murak scowled. You'd like that, wouldn't you? he thought. But, for now, the two priests were united in their search for the Holy Children.

'The rebels have been watching me every moment of

every day,' Murak said. 'It has taken me weeks to begin to gain their trust. I once managed to signal a patrol but only for a few moments. This is the first time I have been alone for any time.'

'Do you have any news?'

'Events are shifting in our favour,' Murak said. 'The Holy Children go north alone. They will have a single shape-shifter as their guide.'

Timu anticipated the name. 'The She-wolf?'

Murak shook his head. 'Not even the son, Lonetread. They have chosen the She-wolf's apprentice, Aaliya.'

'As you say,' Timu said, 'the wind has shifted in our direction. This is a less formidable opponent. We will assume the role of guide to Nandraghiri. That way, we will be in control of events. What is your present position?'

Murak gave Timu what information he could.

'I will take your news to General Rishal,' Timu said. 'The Imperial Army will throw a ring of steel around the Helat cockroaches.'

'I will do everything I can to make Rishal's task easier,' Murak said. 'It is time to annihilate them. With the rebel threat removed, we can concentrate on the Darkwing.'

'Consider this uprising strangled at birth,' Timu said. 'Rishal will kill them all.'

7

Cusha, Vishtar and Aaliya were riding towards the unrelenting storms.

'What day is it?' Cusha asked.

'Tomorrow is the first day of Buradish,' Aaliya said. 'I have brought incense. We will celebrate the birth of the scholar Udmanesh.'

Vishtar, always the gloomier of the twins, wondered whether they had anything to celebrate. They had one short month, just sixty days, to reach Nandraghiri and defeat the demon lord. Yes, one Jingharan lunar cycle, sixty fragile, all-too-fleeting days, to save their world from cold, darkness and oblivion.

'The horses are suffering,' Cusha said.

Aaliya nodded. 'I know. By the time we reach the Khut lands, we may have to go on without them.'

'Then how will we reach our destination?' Vishtar demanded.

'You forget,' Aaliya said, 'I am a shape-shifter.'

To prove her point, she transformed into a great snow bear. 'For now I need to preserve my strength. When the time comes I will take this form. Trust me. You will reach Nandraghiri.'

They pressed forward, bowing before the north wind like penitents. They could hear the howl of wolves, scavenging for food in the icy wastes that had only recently been fertile plains.

'I thought I despised the demon lord already,' Vishtar said. 'After all those years of imprisonment, I thought I couldn't loathe him any more. I was wrong.'

'I don't hate him,' Cusha said. 'I pity him. I have Gardep and I have you, Vishtar. After all the years when I had no memory, no knowledge of my previous life, I have something to fight for. What does the Darkwing have? He is consumed by hatred and despair.'

Vishtar was incredulous. 'You think you can persuade him to abandon this fatal scheme, don't you?'

'I think I can reach him, yes.'

'You are too soft-hearted, Cusha,' Vishtar told her. 'Do you still imagine you can find some fragment of humanity inside the creature? Don't you understand the depths of

458

his depravity? Sometimes the madness of hatred can fester so long, torture a soul so deeply that nothing is left.'

Cusha didn't answer. Still, she could not forget the Darkwing's story. He had been in love, just as she was with Gardep. It was love that had saved her. Could it not do the same for the demon lord?

'We can ride another ten miles before nightfall,' Aaliya said.

'It's hard to know day from night,' Vishtar grumbled. 'All we ever see is snow.'

'And it will get worse,' Aaliya said.

Much worse.

8

It was the first day of Buradish. At Zindhar, snowflakes drifted lazily on the icy gusts from the north. The fort was quiet under its light dusting of snow. There was only a skeleton garrison manning the now enormous military complex. A few days before, General Barath had ridden north-east at the head of a considerable force of Sol-ket and Selessian auxiliaries, in pursuit of the Holy Children. He was accompanied by Timu.

Commander Rishal was also on the move. Frustrated by weeks of fruitless skirmishing, he had decided to take the fight to the enemy and force them to fight in the open. With him, he took Linem's priests. They carried pots of red dust, promising to use it to make him a great weapon.

As they rode, Rishal glanced at Kulmat. He was suspicious of the cadet. Before leaving for the Mountains of the Moon, Timu had carried out an examination of the keep at the Demon Wall. It had revealed the cellar in which the rebels had concealed themselves to avoid detection.

But why hadn't Kulmat, a product of eight years of training in the Military Academy, discovered the hatch? It was time to put the boy to the test.

At sunrise, Kulmat was waiting outside General Rishal's tent, wondering why he had been summoned so early. The moment the commander appeared, Kulmat hurried towards him. 'Rishal-Ra, I have just received your message.'

'We have captured a Helat unit. We are going to interrogate them.'

Kulmat wondered why the Commander had taken control of such a minor operation.

'Come on, Kulmat,' Rishal said. 'You want to fight the enemy, don't you?'

'Yes, Rishal-Ra, more than anything.'

He climbed into the saddle and they rode west. By noon, they were approaching a village. Scrawny dogs fought over scraps with malnourished children. Kulmat became ever more concerned. After a few minutes they reached a stockade. Kulmat gave Rishal a questioning look.

'Bring them out,' Rishal commanded.

The gates swung open. From inside the stockade, a few dozen men appeared, some of them little more than boys. They were ill-kempt and many were bruised. They looked as if they hadn't eaten in days. Kulmat's sense of apprehension was growing. The blood was roaring in his ears.

'This is your mission.'

Kulmat surveyed the hungry, listless men. 'I don't understand, Rishal-Ra. You said we were going to interrogate them. They have already been beaten. Why are we here?'

One of the Helati seized on his words. 'It's true, my Lord, your men have beaten us and asked us many questions. We don't know anything. The people you see here are the ones who stayed. When the fighters left to join the daughter of Shinar, we would not go with them. We were afraid of the consequences. Have mercy, Masters, we are not rebels.'

'You are their kinsmen,' Rishal said. 'They will feel your pain.'

The Helat's eyes widened in horror.

Rishal nodded to the stockade guards. 'We are going to make an example of you.'

The Helati were forced to their knees.

'Bring some of your Fire Dust,' Rishal told the Hotec-Ra.

'Do you mean to butcher them in cold blood?' Kulmat asked. 'You're going to kill them, aren't you, Rishal-Ra?'

'No,' Rishal said, 'you are.'

9

The first day of Buradish dawned crisp and cold in the rebel camp. Though many had shivered in their blankets, the Army of the Free was in high spirits. The insurgents' numbers were growing and they now controlled a swathe of Jinghara. Word of the rebellion had travelled south to the towns and villages surrounding the fort of Karangpur and to the coastal settlements north of Rinaghar itself. In some districts they had turned the tables on the Sol-ket. In these pockets, where the resistance was at its strongest, the Warriors of the Sun no longer hunted the rebels. It was the risen Helati who pursued their former oppressors. They had no illusions that they were safe, of course. At Zindhar and in golden Rinaghar, great armies opposed them. But, for now, they were being held at bay.

There was music from veena, flute and tambourine.

Village girls in brightly-coloured costumes were going through their dance steps. For the first time in two generations the birth of great Udmanesh, prophet of the Scales was going to be celebrated in public. Though food was hardly plentiful, the Helati ate well that morning. Meat and vegetables sizzled in Balti dishes. Piles of flat-breads were heaped on plates. There were side orders of spiced onions and tomatoes, potatoes coated with yoghurt and various chutneys. Once they had eaten, they danced and sang. Plays were performed, telling tales of long ago, when the Helati were a free people. Towards evening, Shamana addressed the gathering.

'On this day we celebrate the birth of the scholar Udmanesh,' she said. 'When the Sol-ket sing of great men, it is warriors and priests they celebrate, men who have conquered cities or amassed great fortunes. Our holy man was born a poor flower-seller's son in the city of Inbacus. His greatness lay in his thirst for knowledge and his charitable heart. He left us the Book of Scales to guide us through our lives.'

She seemed to meet the eye of every man, woman and child. 'Most of all, he left us a light to show us the way to freedom. He predicted that two would come, twins, a girl and a boy, representing light and dark, the balance of all things. Even now, the Holy Children go north. This is the month of Buradish, the time of reckoning. By the time of its end, we will have entered a new golden age of peace and freedom or the world will have perished in darkness and chaos.' She lit incense and raised her arms, palms outstretched. 'I now call on the Four Winds to bless those who travel north, to give them wisdom and courage.'

She caught Gardep's eyes. 'Our new Army of the Free has had its first successes,' she said. 'For that we must thank our commanders: Oled, Murima, Atrakon, Bulu and Nikesh.'

'And you, Shamana,' one man shouted.

Shamana smiled. 'Yes, and the She-wolf. But, most of all, we should thank our General, great Gardep. With a heavy heart, he gave his blessing to Cusha. He confirmed what all the oppressed peoples of the land know only too well: great good will not come without great sacrifice.'

Even as her voice faded, rows of dancers burst upon the scene, finger cymbals tinkling as they weaved through the crowd. Shamana watched the bright eyes and smiling mouths of the multitude and her heart sang. There were many miles to go and formidable obstacles to overcome, but her soul throbbed with a rhythm of hope as powerful as the beat of the drums. She approached Murima and the boys Harad and Qintu.

'I sometimes wondered if a day such as this would ever come,' she said.

'I know what you mean,' Murima said. 'All those years I laboured in Rishal's kitchens, putting up with Mistress Serala's scolding, I thought I would die a slave.'

'Cusha will find Nandraghiri, won't she?' Harad asked.

'Of course she will,' Qintu said.

'She reached the Black Tower against much greater odds,' Shamana said. 'I believe in her.'

'I raised that wonderful child as a daughter,' Murima said. 'I know she will have the strength.' She was about to continue when she became aware of a hubbub over to her left. 'What's going on over there?'

Harad saw a horseman surrounded by crowds of people. 'It's Nikesh.' They hurried towards him.

'What is it?' Shamana asked.

The crowd parted to let her through.

'There's been a massacre,' Nikesh cried, eyes wide with

shock and outrage. 'I sent one of my men to persuade a village that had refused to join us. They found nothing but charred bodies. One lived, despite horrific burns. Just before he died, he told my rider what had happened.'

The jostling crowd listened to the news.

'How many?' Murima asked.

Nikesh lowered his eyes. 'Fifty, maybe sixty.'

Tears of rage and pity welled in Murima's eyes. 'There's more to tell, isn't there?'

'Yes,' Nikesh said. 'Some were no older than Harad or Qintu. These Sol-ket, they're killing boys.'

Some of the people turned to Gardep. Raised a Sol-ket himself, he became the object of their rage.

'You were one of them once,' Qintu accused him. 'Explain this outrage . . . if you can.'

But before Gardep could answer, Nikesh spoke again. 'I have the names of the men who commanded this mission. One was the commander-in-chief, Rishal himself.'

'And the other?' Murima asked.

'The officer in charge of the killing party was Kulmat na-Zamir.'

'Kulmat!' Gardep gasped. 'He would never do such a thing.'

'He is Sol-ket,' Qintu cried, 'as you are.'

It was as if he had struck Gardep in the face. 'Are you blaming me for this?' he asked.

'The butcher is your friend. What does that say about you?' Every ounce of good will Qintu had ever felt for Gardep had vanished in an instant. 'Once a Sol-ket, always a Sol-ket.'

Gardep's eyes welled with tears. 'I fought alongside you at the Black Tower. I have been with you every step of the way since. Does that count for nothing?'

Recovering from the shock of the news, Shamana shoved her way to the front of the crowd. Oled too had arrived.

'This is the work of Rishal,' Shamana said.

'The cadet Kulmat carried out the executions,' Qintu retorted, beside himself with anger and bitter humiliation. 'That's right, Gardep's friend ordered the massacre, the blood brother of whom he is so proud. Yet you make him general of the Army of the Free, Shamana. Oled should lead us, not this Sol-ket.'

Qintu's speech set off a chorus of agreement.

'Enough!' Oled roared. 'Cusha would tear out your tongues if she were here. Why do you insult our brother and comrade in arms? You were at the Black Tower, Qintu. You witnessed Gardep's courage. Without him, we would never have prevailed against the demon lord. I have fought alongside Gardep, as have you. He gave up everything to join our cause. His coming was prophesied. Who here will deny what is written in the Book of Scales?'

The giant looked at each of Gardep's accusers in turn. One by one, they lowered their eyes.

Shamana spoke more softly. 'We must not let our hearts be poisoned. By the Four Winds, have we learned nothing on our journey? Thus far we have marched together, united in our dream of freedom. Look at us: we are Helat and Tanjur.' She pointed out Gardep and Murak. 'These two were once Sol-ket. Now they are our brothers. We fight so that the world can have done with master and slave.' She threw out her arms in a gesture of disappointment and exasperation. 'Why do you think Rishal ordered this massacre? Do you not understand his intention? He wants to spread terror in the villages and despair in our hearts. Just imagine how happy he would be to see us at each other's throats. Rishal seeks to divide us in order to conquer us. This is the cruelty against which we fight.'

Her voice soared. 'I was at Dullah,' she cried, 'as were you, Murima. We have witnessed greater horrors than this brutal massacre. My people were hunted down and killed like rabbits. They were very nearly wiped off the face of the Earth. Did I turn against my own kind? Did I turn away from the cause of the Scales? You should be ashamed, my brothers and sisters. By blaming Gardep, you betray our cause and do the enemy's work for them.'

She drew her sword. 'We have no choice but to meet Sol-ket steel with burnished blades of our own,' she cried. 'But what do we fight for? To be like them, to find a people to enslave ourselves? Do you want to maim and torture the innocent? Can we achieve freedom through such actions? Have you learned nothing?' Her green eyes flashed. 'I don't fight the Sol-ket so I can rule over them as they have ruled over us. I want there to be no Sol-ket or Helat, no divisions between us, just women and men living side by side in peace. How, if the moment something goes wrong we seek scapegoats, will we ever achieve our freedom?'

Shaking her head in despair, she turned to Oled. 'Send these people away, my son. There will be no more recriminations.'

CHAPTER 6

North and South

I

From that day, the Sol-ket always maintained the upper
hand. Rishal's army, now fully recovered from the
mauling they had suffered at the hands of the Darkwing's
demon army, swung south and east, pushing the rebels
back into the endless grasslands of Jinghara. Time and time
again, Nikesh discovered that his raiding parties had been
intercepted and defeated. It was as if the Sol-ket now knew
the Army of the Free's every move. Every time Gardep
met with his commanders, he found the meetings ill-
tempered affairs.

'We have lost twenty fighters today,' Nikesh reported.
'Two of our patrols were ambushed this morning alone.
The Sol-ket anticipate our attacks. How can that be?'

'Isn't it obvious?' Oled said. 'There is a traitor in our midst. I say we expel the Selessian from this council.'

'Are you blind?' Atrakon retorted. 'Did you hear nothing Cusha said on my behalf? I hate the Empire and everything it stands for. If there is treachery, it doesn't come from me.'

'What about Murak?' Bulu asked. 'He was Sol-ket. Who vouches for him?'

Gardep shook his head. 'I too was Sol-ket, Bulu.'

'That's different, Gardep,' Bulu said. 'You have proved yourself. You crossed the land to protect the Holy Child. What do any of us know about you, Murak?'

Murak didn't speak. But Oled did.

'This man is my brother,' he growled. 'He was at my side at the siege of Karangpur. By the Four Winds, did he not save my mother's life in the skirmish at the Demon Wall?' He jabbed a finger at Atrakon. 'Just look at this desert rat. He was *an assassin*. Murak saved my mother's life. Atrakon tried to kill her. Your people were traitors at Dullah. I say you are traitors still.'

Oled's accusation was too much for Atrakon. Drawing his curved sabre, he leapt to his feet. Equally quickly, Oled drew his battle-axe. Before anyone could stop them, they were engaged in mortal combat, sword blade striking axe head.

'Enough!'

Shamana sprang between them, dashing their drawn weapons away with a spear. 'Are you mad, both of you?' she cried. 'We are meant to lead our people to freedom. Look at us. We have suffered setbacks, that is true. Is that any reason to go tearing out each other's throats?'

Atrakon and Oled faced each other, panting. At any moment the fight might break out again.

'I have a solution,' Shamana said. 'Suspicion has fallen

upon two of our brothers. Though I hold nothing against either of them, we cannot allow this contagion to poison our entire leadership. We must be even-handed. I say we relieve Murak and Atrakon of their posts as commanders and return them to the ranks. One day the truth will emerge. One or both of them will be cleared. Then they will return to the council.'

'This is a wise course of action,' Bulu said. 'I support Shamana.'

Atrakon sheathed his sword. 'The mother is wiser than the son,' he said, scowling at Oled. 'I too support Shamana. I am innocent. I have nothing to fear. When the accusations against me are proven false, I will rejoin this council and do my part in the fight for freedom. Until then, I am proud to be a common soldier.'

Murak wanted to argue against Shamana's proposal but Atrakon had made that impossible. 'I too will gladly return to the ranks,' he said.

'Does anyone oppose this decision?' Bulu asked.

Nobody did. Without another word, Atrakon and Murak withdrew.

'There is one more item on the agenda,' Shamana said. 'I call Nikesh again.'

'Not everything is bleak,' Nikesh said. He cast a glance in Gardep's direction.

'Go on,' Gardep said.

'With their superior numbers,' Nikesh said, 'the Sol-ket have us on the run here in the north. But to the south, in the Jingharan heartland, our Helat comrades are ready to rise in tens of thousands. Already Rinaghar has had to reinforce the garrisons at Durbai and Karangpur. There are even rumours of clashes in Parcep province though our lines of communication don't stretch that far south. We can't confirm the gossip.'

'You are talking of a general rising,' Murima said. 'Are you sure of this?'

'I can only go on the stories my riders bring back,' Nikesh said. 'But I trust the warriors under my command. They are not prone to exaggeration.'

'Nothing is certain in war,' Shamana said. 'There is only one way to test the resolve of the people. That is to march south.' She walked over to Gardep and took the seat next to him. 'I know this is a difficult decision for you to make,' she told him. 'You want to be as close to Cusha as you can. This will feel like a betrayal.'

Gardep had his elbows on his knees, his face buried in his hands. For long moments he said nothing. Finally, he raised his head. 'A hundred miles,' he said, 'five hundred miles, what does it matter now? There is nothing I can do for her. We must strike at the heart of the Empire and pray she succeeds in her quest. If we make our stand here, hungry and outnumbered, we will perish. There will be nothing for Cusha to return to. No, though it breaks my heart to say so, we must do what Nikesh asks. Give the order. Tomorrow, we march south.'

2

Only Vishtar was awake. Huddled in half a dozen thick blankets, he was still cold. Maybe it was all those years imprisoned in the Black Tower. He had never learned to cope with a biting wind. But it wasn't the cold that kept him from sleeping. It was the memories. The Darkwing seemed to fill his every waking moment. Vishtar remembered all those nights the fiend had appeared, as if from thin air, and drained him of his lifeblood. Would he have the courage to face the monster again? He looked at Cusha sleeping peacefully. In spite of his love for her, he actually thought of slipping away into the storm. He dismissed the idea just as quickly. No, he would face the demon lord once more, on a day that might be the end of time. He was still tossing and turning when, through the side of the tent, he saw a shadowy figure. He reached over to wake Aaliya, then stopped. He sat up and whispered a question.

'It's you, isn't it, Jackal?'

Scrambling into his boots, Vishtar slipped out into the bellowing wind. There before him stood Jackal, the night-strider with the blackened bones.

'Is it done?' Vishtar asked.

'Not yet,' the night-strider said.

'Then why did you come?'

Jackal looked south. 'The Sol-ket follow,' he said.

'We expected as much.'

'They won't kill you now,' Jackal said. 'They depend on your powers to defeat the demon lord. But they will slaughter you the moment you free them from the menace of the Darkwing.'

'Yes,' Vishtar said. 'I know.'

'There is terror to the north,' Jackal said. 'The Khuts are frightened. That makes them dangerous. There is no order in the north land.'

'Thank you for your warning,' Vishtar said.

'This is not a warning,'

'Then what?'

'I think I can solve both your problems in one fell swoop.'

Before Jackal could say a word there was the hiss of a sword leaving a scabbard.

'Step back from him,' Aaliya ordered.

'No, Aaliya,' Vishtar told her. 'It's not what you think. This is Jackal.'

He hesitated. 'A friend.'

Behind Aaliya, Cusha opened the tent flap. 'Invite him inside.'

Jackal shook his head. 'No mortal soul invites a night-strider into his home.'

'This isn't our home,' Cusha said brightly. 'That's one problem solved.'

Jackal found himself invited into a human dwelling for the first time in forty years. 'Tell me I am closer to the hour of my redemption,' he said. 'Tell me I will soon have peace.'

'You can trust me,' Vishtar said. 'Now tell me your plan.'

3

Gardep sat brooding for a long time, his back against a boulder, watching a stream rippling over a bed of small, polished stones. Faces floated through his mind, three more than any others. Cusha was foremost in his thoughts, of course. She was to be his bride. For a brief moment her image came to him so vividly, he thought he might be able to hold her, kiss her, smell the scent of her hair. Then she was gone. Kulmat appeared next.

'It's not true, is it?' Gardep murmured. 'You didn't kill those people, not in cold blood?'

An instant later, the face of his former knight Rishal appeared, giving him his answer. 'You were testing Kulmat, weren't you? You suspect him.'

Gardep pulled his fingers down over his face. He found himself looking back over his life. Much of it seemed to be lost in the mists of time. Sometimes he thought his life really began the day he met Rishal, a decade before. Rishal had carried the young Gardep out of the burning city of Inbacus, an orphan discovered wandering alone. Gardep wondered about his parents. But all this time he served as a squire to the great conqueror of Vassyria, Gardep had learned nothing of his past. *Forget what you were,* Rishal always said, *think only of what you will be, a Sol-ket master.* Sometimes spectral images of his family would steal into the depths of his mind. Just as he had done so many times before, he tried to recall them. He failed.

Before he could bring them into sharp focus they crumbled. His training had been thorough, making him more Sol-ket than Vassyrian, yet still there was some small part of him that yearned to know what he had been all those years ago, before the Warriors of the Sun fell like wolves on his home city. After a few moments, he remembered the tattoo Cusha had pointed out. Slipping off his jacket, he examined it, the lion with a bull's head. What did it mean? He shook his head. Here it was, the only direct link with his early years in Vassyria, and it was a mystery to him. He was still staring into the babbling water, remembering the past, when Oled found him.

'It's time to go, Gardep,' he said.

Instinctively, Gardep looked northwards.

'You will see her again,' Oled said.

Gardep smiled. 'Do you think of Aaliya?'

'I think of her all the time. Man's destiny is cruel.'

'Then we must make a new destiny,' Gardep said.

'There is only one problem,' Oled said. 'We have little more than fifty days to do it.'

They climbed the muddy embankment and joined the Army. It numbered many thousands now. Sleet was dancing in the clear blue sky. They knew the strange, all-covering winter was creeping southwards at an alarming rate. Some said even Rinaghar had had a light sprinkling of snow. If it were to come to Parcep then the whole Empire would understand what was happening. In a hundred generations, snow had never fallen on its terracotta-coloured walls and houses. Gardep and Oled joined Shamana, Murima, Nikesh and Parvin at the front of the column and the horses thudded towards central Jinghara. Within weeks they would face the fury of the Muzals.

4

Barath drove his men hard. In just ten days they crossed the Land of Four Rivers and entered Khut territory. They travelled on dirt tracks and logging paths, all now covered with drifting snow. He ordered his Selessians to make ever wider sweeps to the east in search of three travellers, two females and a male. They were under orders to take them alive if they found them. On the eleventh day they were taking their rest by a frozen waterfall, its normally gushing torrent suspended in midair, the ice hanging like inverted spears.

'This is madness,' Mehmet said. 'Any fool could pick up their trails in snow. What are we doing here?'

'I don't think they were expecting these blizzards when they summoned us,' Omar said. 'Could any of us have imagined the power of this Hotec-Ra spell? Besides, if they send us out to do their dirty work, we're the ones who will end up with our skulls split by some Khut hammer-warrior.'

They were turning the matter over when Mehmet's brother Uhmet appeared over the pure white horizon. He gave his report to Omar.

'Barath-Ra,' Omar called, 'Uhmet has some news of your quarry.'

Barath's eyes glinted eagerly.

'I picked up their trail due west of here,' Uhmet told the general.

'How far?'

'It will take us no more than two hours,' Uhmet said.

Barath ordered the men to saddle up.

'There is one other thing,' Uhmet said. 'I was told to look for three sets of tracks.'

'That's right.'

'For a short time they were joined by a fourth person. He walked with them a while and then left.' Uhmet scratched his scalp through the black headdress. 'There was something odd about the fourth set of tracks,' he said.

'Go on.'

'I will draw the print this one made in the snow.' Uhmet used the hilt of his sabre to draw what he had seen.

'It looks like it was made by bare bones, a skeleton,' Omar said.

'It's a night-strider,' Barath said. 'Take no notice. The things are wandering aimlessly across the land. Nobody knows why. We will escort them to their destiny.'

'Then you will kill them?' Omar asked.

Barath smiled. 'Of course.'

5

While Cusha, Vishtar and Aaliya trekked north, pursued by Barath, the Army of the Free went south. They had Rishal's army on their tail. When they reached the plateau of Dhurkhand, they gratefully plunged into its dense sal forests. The great timber-yielding tree gave them sumptuous cover. After many days journeying south, remaining in the saddle throughout the hours of daylight, their rough riders fighting a series of savage rearguard actions to slow the Sol-ket, the Army of the Free finally took a proper rest. From the plateau, a huge shelf rising abruptly from the plain, they would be able to see Rishal's approach.

'The flow of intelligence to the Sol-ket has dried up,' Gardep observed.

'Yes,' Shamana said, 'it looks like we removed our traitor when we asked Murak and Atrakon to leave the war council.'

'I'd have thought that was obvious,' Oled snarled. 'I don't know why you don't let me kill the assassin.'

'Under our laws,' Shamana reminded her son, 'all women and men are innocent until proven guilty by an assembly of their peers. Or do you forget the rule of law in your eagerness to prove yourself right?'

'Nikesh has news,' Murima said, joining the council.

'Is it good or bad?' Gardep asked.

'Ask him yourself,' Murima said.

Nikesh appeared in the clearing, coated with the dust of a day's ride.

'There's no snow to the south then?' Gardep asked.

'It's cold,' Nikesh answered, 'but the storms haven't started there yet.'

'That's good,' Oled said. 'We will make better time than the Grand Army. So what's this news of yours?'

'Inspired by our example,' Nikesh announced, 'a second rising has occurred.'

'Where?'

Nikesh glanced at Murima. 'They chose Gussorah to make their stand.'

Murima rose to her feet. 'Gussorah!'

'It seems they decided to emulate great Shinar,' Nikesh continued. 'As you, his daughter, know only too well,

Gussorah is where he lit the beacon of rebellion forty years ago. They thought it would bring the villages flocking to their standard.'

'Did it work?' Oled asked, leaning forward.

'After a fashion,' Nikesh said. 'Unfortunately, they were confronted by a substantial army sent from Rinaghar. Lacking armour, weapons and experienced leaders, they decided to retreat to the Dragon Mountains.'

'We have the weapons they need,' Bulu said, speaking for the first time. 'We have ransacked every store for hundreds of miles. We've got swords, shields, arrows, Lyrian fire.'

'Yes,' Nikesh said, 'and we have experienced leaders.'

'We are thinking along the same lines,' Gardep said. 'Can you get a message to them, Nikesh?'

Nikesh nodded. 'I think my scouts can find them.'

'Is it agreed?' Gardep said, looking round the council. He saw the approving nods. 'Good. Tell them we will meet them in the Dragon Mountains.'

Shamana counted the days remaining in the month of Buradish. 'I just pray Aaliya and the Holy Children are close to Nandraghiri.'

6

'There they are!' Barath roared.

At the far end of a carpet of pure white snow, broken by just three sets of hoof prints, the troops could see three riders.

'Selessians to the rear,' Barath ordered. 'This moment belongs to the Sons of Ra. Let's collect the Holy Children.'

'Selessians to the rear, indeed!' Mehmet snorted. 'We find them. They take the credit.'

The Sol-ket galloped eagerly.

'What's the hurry?' Omar wondered out loud. 'There are three of them, and two are children.'

But there were far more than three of them. As the Sol-ket thundered over the blanket of snow, hundreds of macabre figures exploded from beneath, creating a barrier between the Warriors of the Sun and their Selessian auxiliaries. At the sound, he swung his horse round.

'Night-striders!'

Omar stared at the triple row of skeletal figures, every one of them armed with a spear, a sword, a battle-axe.

'I thought Barath said these creatures were wandering aimlessly,' Uhmet said. 'This looks pretty purposeful to me.'

'What do we do?' Mehmet asked.

'You do nothing,' one of the night-striders said, stunning the Selessians. It was Jackal. 'This is not your fight, men of the desert.'

Even as the black-garbed warriors were recovering from the surprise of a Lost Soul who spoke, the night-striders engaged the Sol-ket in battle.

'Kill the barbarians!' Barath shouted. 'Selessians, charge!'

'*Now* he wants us with him,' Omar said.

'What are your orders?' Mehmet asked.

'I told you,' Jackal said. 'This is not your fight. The Warriors of the Sun abuse you. They call you desert rats. When are you going to stop doing their dirty work?'

'I didn't think I would ever say this, Omar,' Mehmet said, 'but that pile of bones is talking good sense.'

Omar made his decision. 'Stand down,' he ordered. 'Sheathe your weapons. The creature is right. This is not our fight.'

Seeing his auxiliary stepping away from the fight, Barath led his beleaguered troops in a brave but despairing charge. The Sol-ket fell in their tens, their scores, staining the snow red with their blood. Jackal met Barath in single combat. The first blow crushed Barath's shoulder. The general screamed but he would not surrender. The second blow was decisive. It split Barath's skull.

'Listen to me, Sol-ket,' Jackal roared into the faces of the surviving Warriors of the Sun. 'I know your intentions. You would have accompanied the Holy Children to Nandraghiri, allowed them to exterminate the monster for you, then casually cut their throats. Nobody dies, who doesn't have to. Do you understand?'

Some of the Sol-ket nodded.

'I give you a choice,' Jackal concluded. 'Ride away now and you can return to your quarters. If you choose to make a stand, you will die here.'

Reluctantly, the Sol-ket turned their horses and rode away. The Selessians were about to do the same when the night-strider spoke again.

'Come and meet the Holy Children,' he said. 'You may be interested by what they have to tell you.'

7

At the summit of Sangra Peak, the Darkwing was growing bored. At his approach, Jinghirza spat her defiance. 'Get away from me, monster.'

He looked more inhuman than ever. Serpent heads burst like boils from his flesh. Blue, venomous breath hung round his leathery lips.

'I do like your spirit,' the demon lord drawled. 'You remind me of the Holy Child.' That made Jinghirza stop. 'Ah, so you have heard of Cusha?'

'Of course,' Jinghirza said. 'Her name is written in the scriptures of great Udmanesh.'

'How interesting,' the Darkwing said. 'This Udmanesh certainly got around. Why, he seems to have infected half the world with the virus of rebellion. What would you say if I told you your Holy Child was coming here, to Nandraghiri?'

'I'd tell her to stay well away.'

'Now that would be rather stupid, wouldn't it? Of all the creatures of the Earth only two, Cusha and her snivelling brother Vishtar, have ever defeated me. They are coming to try again.'

Jinghirza stared at him. 'I hope they kill you!'

'Now is that any way to talk to your master?' the Darkwing said. 'I am about to set you a second challenge.'

At this, Jinghirza's heart stopped for a split second.

'You offered, remember?'

Her senses swam as she remembered the walk along the narrow stone bridge. 'What is my ordeal?'

The Darkwing leered. 'I will show you.'

Soon they were standing on an icy mountain path, in swirling snow.

'You look strong, yes, strong and quick.'

Jinghirza could feel the pulse throbbing in her throat. Her lungs were heaving. Terror seemed to be clawing at her insides.

'There is your test.'

Jinghirza stared into the white, howling void.

'The first time, I asked you to walk a narrow path to safety. This time you must jump.'

Jinghirza squinted against the driving snow.

'You will see the other side if you look carefully. It is there somewhere.'

At last Jinghirza saw it, a bare spur of rock on the far

side of a deep chasm. She looked at the narrow path. She would have to get every stride right. One slip, one stumble against the jagged rocks that bordered the path and she would lose momentum and miss the jump. Even so, even if she made the jump, she might miss her handhold and tumble to her death. Success seemed impossible.

'Of course, you can refuse,' the Darkwing said. 'But I would have to kill all your companions and drain every drop of your blood.'

'I will do it,' Jinghirza said, trying to disguise the shudder in her voice.

She walked to the edge of the precipice and waited for the snow to clear a little. For the second time, she glimpsed the spur. Retracing her steps, she crouched, testing the purchase her thin, goatskin shoes gave her on the icy path. Then, sucking in a deep breath, she ran. All her childhood, she had raced her brothers. But she had never tried anything like this.

Sure-footed, she caught the edge of the path, where it fell away, exposing the rocky abyss thousands of feet below. Her arms windmilled. Her legs pedalled. Finally, she thudded against the spur, gratefully grasping the cold granite. Blood trickled from a gashed knee and her upper arms were badly bruised. For all that, she was alive.

'Very impressive,' the Darkwing observed. 'Tonight, you and your friends will have a fire and two kinds of cooked meat. You never know, you may live to see the day the world ends.'

8

Jackal ushered Omar and Mehmet into his yurt. Cusha, Vishtar and Aaliya were already waiting for them.

481

'You are Omar Ebrahin,' Cusha said.

'How do you know my name?'

'Let me explain,' Vishtar said. 'Jackal here is our eyes and ears.'

Omar thought it would be impolite to mention that the creature had no ears so he said nothing.

'Your clan name is Ebrahin?'

'It is.'

'Where are you from, Omar Ebrahin?' Cusha asked.

'I am from Sahud, about fifty miles from our capital Juttah.'

Cusha and Vishtar exchanged knowing looks. 'Have you ever heard of a man called Atrakon Ebrahin?' Cusha asked.

'Of course I have,' Omar said. 'He was my uncle.'

'Tell me about him.'

Omar was agitated. 'Why do you ask about Atrakon?'

'Just tell the tale.'

'Atrakon was a kinsman,' Omar began.

'Please go on,' Cusha said.

Omar frowned and continued his story. 'A warlord took a fancy to Atrakon's wife, Leila. When Leila resisted him, the warlord killed her. Leila's unborn child died with her.'

'What did Atrakon do?' Cusha asked.

'I have a feeling you know,' Omar said.

'What did he do?'

'Atrakon took his revenge,' Omar concluded. 'But there was a heavy price. He sold himself to the governor and entered his service as an assassin. The Hotec-Ra hired him next and took him across the ocean to Parcep. Nobody has heard of Atrakon from that day to this.'

'Atrakon is an officer in the Army of the Free,' Cusha told them.

'I don't believe you!'

'There is proof.'

'What proof can there be?' Omar asked. 'We are in the middle of an icy wasteland. How can you possibly convince me that what you are saying is true?'

Cusha bowed her head. When she raised it again her face was transformed. In place of the pupils, the irises, the whites, her eyes were the purest black.

'By the Almighty!' cried Omar.

'Come forth, Leila Ebrahin,' Cusha intoned. 'Rise from the House of the Dead. Give witness that what I have told these men is true.'

Within seconds, the ghost of Leila Ebrahin was floating before their eyes.

CHAPTER 7

Attack

I

Sunrise brought terrifying news to the Army of the Free. They had been climbing into the Dragon Mountains for two days, searching for the masses who had marched from Gussorah to meet them. But the Dragon Mountains were a vast system of peaks and passes, valleys and ravines. For many centuries it had been a refuge for the fugitive and the hermit. At sunrise, Nikesh made a discovery.

'Look,' he cried from his vantage point at the edge of the camp. 'There in the foothills. I see scarlet banners.'

Shamana ran to his side. She could see the banners, like rivulets of flame, climbing through the dawn light. 'By the Four Winds!' she cried. 'It's true. Why were we not alerted before? Where are our scouts?'

'Dead,' Nikesh said, surveying the scene. 'If the Imperial troops have come this far unnoticed then you can be sure our outriders are already dead. To find them all, they must have had information from within the camp.'

Gardep joined the gathering crowd as they stood gazing through the mist at the ribbons of scarlet and gold. As yet they could not make out any soldiers, only distant splashes of colour. But they were all the proof the Army of the Free needed that an offensive was well underway. There were cries of dismay as the news spread. Mothers scooped up children and looked in vain for a hiding place. The elderly simply shook their heads and remembered other dawns like this, other beleaguered rebellions.

'It is not just the Sol-ket,' Murak said, running to join them. 'See the white standards. That's a Vassyrian regiment, probably sent from Parcep. There, to the left, you can see the Lukshmiris.'

He went on to point out Khuts, Obirs, Miridans and Ottoviths. Oled marvelled at his friend's composure. It was as if, in spite of his recent torture, the Imperial advance held no terrors for him.

'Sound the alarm,' Gardep ordered. 'Move those who can't fight up towards the snow line. Three valleys lead up to our position. They are narrow and the sides are sheer. We should be able to defend them for quite some time even with our inferior forces.' He called for his horse. 'We have to block the approaches. If they get through the passes, we have nowhere to run.'

Oled nodded. 'You're right, Gardep, but how do we spread our thin resources across three fronts?'

'Four,' Shamana said. 'We will need a reserve looking east in case they launch an attack from the rear. It would be hard to move a force over the mountains, but not impossible.'

Gardep considered the options. 'I will take the northern pass,' he said. 'That's where the Sol-ket are concentrated. I know the way they fight. Shamana, it is best if you take command of the central approach. It is the hardest to defend. I know you will find a way.'

The She-wolf nodded and took her leave immediately. Gardep continued with his battle orders. 'Oled, you hold the southern side. It suits your style of fighting best. You will be able to mount a charge down the gentler slope.'

Gardep ordered that the horns be sounded. It was time to fight.

2

Rishal oversaw the Imperial advance. 'Send forward the Vassyrians, the Miridans and the Khuts,' he ordered.

Kulmat issued the order. Horns sounded and drums beat.

'Climb quickly,' Rishal ordered. 'A rapid advance is the key to success.'

He permitted himself a smile. He had driven his troops hard, sometimes marching night and day to close the gap with the fleeing Helati. But it had been worth it. He had them in a trap and the jaws were closing. This time there would be no mistakes. The offensive had been many weeks in preparation. He had summoned reserves from Karangpur, Durbai and Parcep, leaving the army based in Rinaghar to pursue the Gussorah rebels. From the scraps of intelligence Murak had been able to smuggle out, he knew that the rebels were half-starved and squabbling among themselves. He marvelled that they weren't more disunited. Only the quality of the enemy leadership had prevented desertion and surrender on an enormous scale.

One man in Rishal's company was not of good heart, however. His squire Kulmat was staring up into the morning sun, searching for some sign of his blood brother, Gardep.

'May Ra keep us apart this day,' he prayed silently. 'May the Sun God preserve us both from harm.'

'My spear,' Rishal barked, breaking in on Kulmat's thoughts. 'Wake up, Kulmat. I want to watch the advance.'

'When do we go forward, Rishal-Ra?' Kulmat asked, his flesh crawling with dread.

'The Sol-ket will be the third wave,' Rishal said. 'Auxiliaries first and second to draw the enemy fire. Then, when the rebel arrows have been expended on barbarian flesh, the Warriors of the Sun will squash the cockroaches with their boots.' He slapped Kulmat's back. 'Why so stern, Kulmat? Is it battle hunger? Do you want some action?'

Kulmat forced a smile. It was only with the greatest difficulty that he uttered his reply. 'Yes, my lord, I am eager to cover myself with glory.'

3

The Vassyrians were thrown against the northern approaches. With their chequered scarves and open-faced helmets, they stood out on the battlefield. Gardep watched them advancing under their white banners and could not help but reflect on his own Vassyrian roots. What if Rishal had never come to Inbacus? What if he had never conquered great Vassyria? What course would Gardep's life have taken then?

'String your bows,' Gardep ordered, driving the uncomfortable thoughts to the back of his mind. 'Choose your targets well and show no mercy.'

He reviewed his archers. They held the high ground and were sheltering behind formidable defences. He rode along the line. He remembered the long evenings spent with Rishal, as squire to his master's knight. He recalled every principle the Lion of Inbacus had instilled in him: show no fear, lead by example, take firm decisions and never, ever reveal a single doubt to the troops under your command. They would be his watchwords. Yet nothing stopped the slamming of his heart and the twist of apprehension in his stomach. These were Vassyrians, his countrymen, not Sol-ket. He gave his order. 'Nock your arrows.'

He listened to the creak of the bows. Oled had taken on the role of armourer. He had done a good job, selecting some of the finest fletchers and steel-smiths from the surrounding villages and convincing them to join the Army of the Free. But, for all Oled's powers of persuasion, they remained few in number. The defenders were still poorly equipped compared with the professional regiments that faced them.

'Steady,' Gardep said, his sword raised. 'Don't shoot until I give the order.'

The Vassyrians were coming on, drums beating and cymbals clashing. The wail of horns echoed across the mountains. From behind the white favours, Vassyrian arrows flew but they clattered uselessly against the sheer walls of the canyon. Specially trained foragers scampered forward to collect the arrows. This was how they had learned to add to their weaponry, by taking from the enemy. The Vassyrians had now reached the narrowest part of the valley and were pressed together, able to proceed five abreast only. That's when Gardep gave the order.

'First cohort,' he shouted, 'loose your arrows. Aim true and choose your target well.'

The defenders emitted a murderous volley. The arrows buzzed as they fell. The deadly hail cut down the first rows of the attacking forces. Sol-ket commanders barked their orders. The second row of soldiers was made to climb over their dead comrades.

'Second cohort,' Gardep commanded, 'aim and shoot.' The second wave of Vassyrian soldiers found themselves looking into the rain of arrows. Each time one group fell, Gardep would order a halt. Then, the moment fresh troops struggled over the dying and the dead, his sword would fall and a new volley would hiss forth. To his relief, he heard the enemy trumpets sounding the retreat. Though he remembered little of his Vassyrian childhood, his heart ached that he had to fight his own kind and leave so many of them littering the slopes before him.

4

Shamana was being harder pressed in the centre. The climb towards her defensive position was less steep and offered the enemy more cover. The Miridan attackers were able to reduce the effect of the archers with a shield wall. Though less formidable fighters than the Vassyrians in the open field, these spearmen were expert skirmishers. They flitted from boulder to boulder, taking whatever cover they could find, taking care not to expose themselves to the defenders' arrows.

'Lower your bows!' Shamana ordered. They were wasting precious arrows. 'It's time to use our secret weapon.'

Shamana had had her troops working for days filling leather sacks with Lyrian fire. Transforming into an elephant, she braced herself against a wooden stockade packed with the primitively made containers.

'Light the charges,' she barked.

At her command, a dozen Helati set blazing torches to the fuses that were poking from the containers. At the first fizz of the fuses, Shamana put all her weight against the stockade. Balls of Lyrian flame leapt from the mountain-side. Black, sulphurous liquid roared into the approaching spearmen, roasting their flesh. Shamana watched as men rolled in agony, turned into living torches by her devices. When she spoke, there was no jubilation in her voice.

'How I curse mankind that we have to wage war.'

But even the hellish resort of Lyrian fire did not end the Miridan offensive. For all the terrible losses the makeshift bombs had inflicted, the Imperial Army had reserves aplenty, ready to return to the attack. The Miridan auxiliaries were set to overwhelm the defenders by sheer force of numbers. Shaman looked around desperately. She was reluctant to commit her ill-equipped and poorly-trained fighters to hand-to-hand fighting at this stage. A sudden reverse and the way would be open to the upper slopes, then on to the rebel camp itself. That's when she saw hundreds of Helati non-combatants streaming down the ravine from the snow line. At the head of them was Bulu, giving orders by gesturing with his mutilated right arm, and Murima, accompanied by Qintu and Harad.

'It looked like you needed help,' Bulu said.

'You can't fight,' Shamana protested, looking at the stump.

'I represent the northern villages on the war council,' Bulu answered. 'I can't wield a sword or shoot a bow to any great effect, but I can direct those who can.'

The new arrivals, mostly women and boys, were gathering what weapons they could from the fallen.

'Get the bows,' Shamana cried. 'Shoot their soldiers before they can reach you.'

The Miridans were no more than a few hundred yards from the defensive lines. There was no armour for these light infantrymen. They wore trousers tucked into their boots and thick jackets. Instead of helmets, they wore caps or turbans. Their protection lay in their speed and mobility.

'Murima, Bulu,' Shamana said. 'Try to inject some discipline into their bow work. They must choose their targets and shoot straight at them.'

She clenched her fist and repeated the key word. 'Discipline.'

Satisfied that the pair could slow the Miridan attack, Shamana looked around frantically. She surveyed the heights that overlooked the ravine. A plan started to form.

'You,' she shouted, addressing one of the men who had built the stockade for her fire devices. 'How did you get the timbers up here?'

'Ropes,' he said. 'Our elephants dragged the logs all the way from the sal forest.'

'Choose a team of your strongest men,' Shamana cried. 'I want them up there.'

The mahout got her drift. 'You can rely on me.'

The Miridans had almost reached the rebels. Shamana leapt onto her horse and rode between the lines. Standing upright in the stirrups, she emptied her quiver at the Miridans. Her example stiffened the rebel resistance.

'Support the She-wolf,' Murima ordered.

Flanked by Qintu and Harad, the daughter of Shinar showed deadly accuracy. From that moment, the Helati recovered their faith in themselves. Their every arrow seemed to tell. The Miridans wavered and fell back to raucous cheers from the Helati.

'Don't celebrate too soon,' Shamana warned. 'It will take them no more than a few moments to regroup and come again.'

Sure enough the Miridans surged forward once more, closing on the Helati. Long, expertly-honed javelins faced a motley collection of bamboo spears, scythes, hoes and clubs. Only the warriors Gardep had trained possessed swords. Hungry and ill-equipped, the risen slaves waited for the enemy to charge. The Miridans drummed their spears against their ox-hide shields and hurled their battle cries at their stubborn but anxious foes. But just as they were about to launch their assault, they heard a fearful rumble. Hundreds of boulders crashed down from the heights to either side. When the dust cleared from the unexpected avalanche, an impassable barricade blocked their way. High above, the mahout's team danced in wild celebration. This time Shamana didn't try to stop them. The pass was closed.

5

Rishal read the message and dismissed the rider who had delivered it. His face was hard with fury.

'What news, Rishal-Ra?' Kulmat asked.

'The rebels have closed the central approach,' the commander snarled. 'That's where I expected our first success. I sought to break through and outflank the enemy.'

Kulmat forced a show of outrage.

'But how could slaves hold the line against a regiment of Miridans?' he asked. 'It was a wide valley. They had plenty of cover. It was perfect for the spearmen. What went wrong?'

'This is the She-wolf's doing,' Rishal said. 'More of her shape-shifting tricks. She burned the Miridans' tails with Lyrian fire, the same stock they stole from our own troops.

Now a rock-fall has blocked the pass. The Miridans have suffered grievous losses. Where the hell is Murak? What's the point of a spy when he gives us no information?' He reached for his weapons. 'After this fiasco, I must enter the fray myself. I will destroy the traitor cadet and behead this rebellion. Gardep is mine. Sound the muster, Kulmat.'

Kulmat stood rooted to the spot.

'Now!' Rishal roared. 'Do I have to repeat every order twice?'

'No, Rishal-Ra.'

Kulmat's heart was pounding. The moment he had dreaded was at hand.

6

The defence of the southern valley lay in the balance. Their arrows and spears exhausted, Oled's tiny force would have no choice but to engage the Obirs in close combat. The Obirs were fierce tribesmen from the far north east, a land reputed to be without law or civilisation. Eking out a wretched existence on bleak, wind-swept plains almost devoid of plant growth, the Obirs sold themselves to the highest bidder, simply in order to live. The coffers of Rinaghar ensured their survival, hence their loyalty. But the Helati did not break before their wild onrush. When the slave troops got the signal to charge their battle cry was a simple one:

'Freedom!'

Attacking the Obirs head on was a risky undertaking. Should they fail, they would leave the camp vulnerable. Waiting there, less than five hundred armed fighters were available to defend the old, the young and the weak. Oled led his cavalry down the slope on stolen Selessian horses.

Their forward momentum carried them through the front row of the Obir warriors. A roar went up as the Obirs looked to close the line behind them but Oled had trained his horsemen well. When many cavalry units would have thundered on to pillage the enemy baggage train, Oled's riders refused the spoils of war and returned to the fray. Their cause was freedom, not loot. Wheeling about, they cut a swathe through the massing Obirs and prepared to charge again.

'Stay together,' Oled shouted. 'Keep your formation the way I showed you. Remain disciplined and you will triumph.' He looked around. 'Has anybody seen Murak?'

'Over there.'

Murak had his back to Oled. When Oled shouted to him he very nearly leapt out of his skin.

'What's the matter?' Oled laughed. 'Got a guilty secret?'

'No,' Murak answered, 'I was taking a rest. I am not fully recovered from my injuries.'

'Are you strong enough to fight?' Oled asked, concern in his green eyes.

'I'm ready,' Murak said, picking up his bow and sword and climbing into the saddle.

'Ride by my side,' Oled said. 'Good hunting.'

Murak laughed and they charged again. It was too much for the foot soldiers of Obiristan. Cut down in their dozens, the northmen fled back towards the Imperial camp. A triumphant roar rose from several hundred Helat throats. Then, just as quickly, it died.

'By the Four Winds,' Oled groaned, seeing a new threat emerging from the mist. 'That was but the first wave.'

Less than half a mile away he could see the scarlet and gold banners of the Sol-ket. They were marching up the slope on foot, preceded by the remnants of the Miridans that had attacked Shamana.

'They have to number at least five thousand,' Oled said. He could sense the tide of dismay eddying through his men.

'More like eight,' Murak said. 'See the cavalry being drawn up to either side of the infantry.'

Oled called over two of Nikesh's rough riders. 'You, take a message to the She-wolf. Ask if she can spare us any reinforcements. You, take the same message to Gardep.' He rubbed his whiskery jaw. 'It will be some time before reinforcements can reach us. That's if they come at all. Before then, we are in for a bitter fight.'

Murak nodded. 'At this very moment they will be discussing the reward for your head. They always put a price on the enemy commanders' heads.'

'Really?' Oled said. 'How much do you think I will bring?'

'Oh, a thousand dinar at least.'

'A thousand dinar!' Oled said. 'That's the most I've been worth in my whole life.' The giant gripped his battle-axe. 'Well, the dogs will have to earn their coins.'

Kicking his horse up the hill, Oled set about rallying his cavalry.

'We are facing a multitude many times our size,' he said. 'It isn't Obir tribesmen we're facing now. The backbone of the attacking force is made up of a crack Sol-ket regiment.'

A murmur rose from the ranks.

'Yes, you know the reputation of the Sol-ket. Some of you have been involved in skirmishes with their patrols. Well, this is the real thing, a pitched battle with the Imperial elite.' He could see the tension in hundreds of faces. 'But you know what that means,' he shouted above the battle cries of the enemy. 'They have had to send their best against us. Think about it. It means they're afraid of us. That's right, on Jinghara Plain you didn't run. You fought scores of rearguard actions against them. You drew Sol-ket blood. They are not invincible. They're men. They bleed, just like the rest of us. If they are all-powerful, why are they throwing a whole regiment against us?' He leaned forward in the saddle. By now, he was having to fight to be heard over the drums and horns of the Warriors of the Sun. 'Well, let's not disappoint them. Draw your swords and strike them down. Earn their respect with cold steel. We must hold this position until our comrades send reserves. Prevail against these battle-hardened soldiers and you can take the field against any fighters in the land. Have courage, brothers. Have hope, sisters. Fight for your freedom!'

But as Oled led the charge, he did not see a bow being bent and an arrow hissing through the air towards him.

7

On the northern front of the battle, Kulmat was reluctantly accompanying Rishal to the head of his regiment, doing his best to hide his true feelings. The remnants of the Vassyrian charge were limping past.

'It seems my young protégé has learned his lessons well,' Rishal said.

Oblivious to Kulmat's expression of dread, the commander shielded his eyes.

'He still has a lot to learn, however. He has more fighters than weapons. See, they are short of arrows. Let's test them a while longer with the infantry.'

The infantry moved in from the flanks. They formed a shield wall and started the climb towards the rebel lines. The cavalry advanced behind them, ready to begin their gallop.

'You're a lucky man, Kulmat,' Rishal said.

'How's that, Rishal-Ra?' Kulmat asked, feeling anything but lucky.

'Your first great battle was Jinghara Plain,' Rishal explained. 'There you witnessed the defeat of the Lost Souls. Now you will see the end of the servile threat. We are about to ensure further centuries of Imperial rule. How does it feel to be part of such a great undertaking?'

'I am very lucky,' Kulmat answered, trying to hide the flatness in his voice.

'Indeed you are,' Rishal said. 'Why, I must have been almost thirty years old before I participated in such a conflict.' He indicated the retreating Vassyrians. 'I feel sorry for these men. Once they were the proudest warriors on the continent. Now . . .' He sighed. 'Now we use them as pin cushions to exhaust the enemy's arrows.'

One passing Vassyrian overheard Rishal. His head snapped round and savage resentment lit his face.

'What's the matter?' Rishal demanded, noticing the reaction. 'Do my words offend you?'

The Vassyrian lowered his eyes. 'No, my lord.'

'No,' Rishal said. 'I didn't think so.'

Once he was out of Rishal's sight, the Vassyrian wiped a bitter tear away with his chequered scarf. One day, Rishal would have cause to remember the warrior's name. It was Adrius.

8

From his vantage point overlooking the battlefield, Gardep could see Shamana, Murima and Nikesh leading their troops to support Oled. He knew the Army of the Free was staring defeat in the face.

'This is bad,' he murmured, sensing the lonely burden of command.

Then, relegating his worries to the back of his mind, he went to examine the archers' quivers. They were almost empty.

'When there is nothing else to shoot,' Gardep told them, 'arm yourself any way you can and support our charge.'

The faces that looked back at him were grim. They had accepted that they were going to die. Turning his back on the archers, Gardep joined his cavalry. If Rishal could see their equipment, he would be laughing himself sick. The riders had little armour to protect their bodies and there were even fewer helmets to go round. Whereas every Sol-ket rode a thoroughbred Selessian mount, many of Gardep's cavalry had to make do with ponies, even mules. For all that, Gardep was happy to die alongside these fighters. They were defending a cause greater than them-selves: the belief that no man should hold another as a chattel. One thing alone gave him cause for regret. He might never see Cusha again. He imagined her trekking through the Khut lands, snowflakes landing on her hair and settling on her face. Closing his eyes, Gardep could imagine the scene. For a moment, in his mind's eye, he was there beside her, sharing the stark beauty of the Mountains of the Moon. But a shout dispersed his daydream.

'Here they come again!'

At the shouted warning, the archers planted their feet and drew their bows. Their contribution to the battle was almost over. Gardep watched the forward march of the Imperial infantry. Their shields were well made and strengthened with a boss that could club a man senseless. Maybe a third of the remaining arrows would bounce off them. It was time to try another tactic.

'Shoot into the air,' Gardep ordered. 'In this terrain,

they will be forced to bunch together as they attack. When they do, shoot over their shields.'

The archers raised their bows and waited. And waited. The Sol-ket heavy infantrymen were patient. The tramp, tramp, tramp of their boots made the ground shake.

'Steady,' Gardep said.

Officers started to bark commands along the line. The Sol-ket infantry began its charge.

'Now!'

Running at full tilt, the Sol-ket did not have time to raise their shields to protect their heads. The arrows fell like murderous, black rain. Half the attackers had breathed their last. Gardep's move had broken the first offensive. But it did not end the conflict. At that moment, Rishal appeared through the mist, followed by Kulmat.

9

Shamana hoisted herself into the saddle of a loose horse.

'What's he doing?' Murima said, noticing a solitary mounted archer. The man had covered his face. For some reason he had dropped back behind the rest of Oled's unit. He was taking aim not at the enemy but at his own general.

Shamana followed the direction of Murima's stare and cried out: 'Oled, my son!'

Hearing the warning shout, the giant of the Tanjurs reacted with great agility. Loosening the reins, he slipped down in the saddle. The archer's arrow whistled past. Re-seating himself, Oled continued the charge as if nothing had happened. The Army of the Free, a thinning band barely numerous enough to deserve that grand title, crashed into the enemy throwing their foremost ranks into disarray. Shamana and Nikesh followed Oled's men into battle. In the confusion, the mysterious archer made his escape.

The Sol-ket were shouting their battle cries. 'Destroy the cockroaches. Victory or death!'

The press of the enemy was becoming irresistible. Oled's cavalry was being hemmed in on every side.

'Cover each other's backs,' Oled ordered. 'You are a band of brothers and sisters. Live together or die together. For freedom!'

He looked around for Murak. 'Has anybody seen Murak?' he cried.

'I think I saw him fall,' one warrior said. 'It was back there.'

Oled beat his saddle with his fist. Murak fallen after having the courage to walk away from the Sol-ket . . . it was almost too much to bear. Another brave man lost in combat, and an exceptional one.

'Nobody runs,' he cried, raging at the injustice of conflict. 'Fight to the last man.'

Oled's beleaguered warriors followed their general's example. Though they were outnumbered and with no hope of relief, they fought furiously. Oled's chest swelled with pride to see slaves become heroes. As he swung his battle-axe to right and left, he wondered about the shout he had heard, warning him about a stray arrow. It had sounded like his mother, but how could that be?

The desperate struggle continued. Soon, such was the crush of the Sol-ket cavalry around the rebels that it was almost impossible to swing a weapon. Strangely, this was working to the advantage of the Army of the Free, preventing the Warriors of the Sun making their greater numbers tell. But Oled knew the stalemate would not last long.

'By the Four Winds,' he murmured. 'We need a miracle to come out of this alive.'

The miracle came in the form of a mighty war elephant thundering into the enemy, followed by a regiment of horses under the command of Nikesh. The power of the charge cut a wedge into the heaving, hacking mass and Oled was able to lead his battered cavalry back up the slope.

'Mother,' he said, seeing Shamana return to human form. 'That warning. I thought it was your voice.'

Shamana chuckled. 'Yes, big as you are, you still need your mother to take care of you!'

10

Amid the terrible clamour of battle, Rishal picked out Gardep. Seeing his former cadet just a few hundred yards away, he roared his challenge.

'Face me, Gardep na-Vassyrian,' he shouted.

Gardep forced his way to the front through the closely packed ranks of his warriors. He emerged from the meagre ranks of the defenders, bloodstained and weary from the long struggle.

'Face me, traitor,' Rishal shouted again.

Standing just behind Rishal's right shoulder, Kulmat willed Gardep to hide, to melt back into rebel ranks. You are not ready to face him, he thought. But he knew it was not in Gardep's character to hide.

'Is this your army?' Rishal cried, beating his way towards his former squire. 'All those years I prepared you for glory and renown in the eyes of Ra. But you gave it up . . . for this! Look around, you damned fool. Slaves these people were and slaves they will be again. That can never change. It is in their nature. Don't you understand that this is the immutable law of life, that some are born to rule and others to be ruled?'

The two men were just yards from each other now. The tide of battle was thinning, leaving a mere handful of exhausted warriors between them.

'Do you not have eyes, na-Vassyrian?' Rishal scoffed. 'You are outnumbered and outfought.'

A bold Helat warrior hurled himself at Rishal. He paid the ultimate price for his courage. Rishal cut him down and shoved his lifeless body away. Then he turned his horse to face Gardep.

'It's over,' Rishal declared. 'Here's a bargain. You know the way of the Sol-ket. Every warrior with a sword in his hand will die by sunset. Shinar had many times this number and he could not beat us. Walk away from this miserable rabble you call an army. Do that and I will let you live.'

Gardep's fighters turned to hear his answer. Their general didn't let them down. He hurled Rishal's offer back in his face. 'Even if I did take you at your word, what kind of life would I have? You say you would let me live. Where? How would I spend my days? Tell me that, Lion of Inbacus. You would throw me in some filthy dungeon, wouldn't you? You would make me suffer the way the Muzals made venerable Udmanesh suffer.'

Every warrior under his command was listening, hanging on his every word. The speech wasn't for Rishal. It was for them.

'Better to die with a sword in my hand and the sun on my face than to live in the gloom of a cell, hating myself for my craven surrender. Prepare yourself, Rishal. We, the Army of the Free, may be few in number but I swear, it will cost you dear to win your victory.'

Spurred by the heartened shouts of his fighters, Gardep joined swords with his former master.

11

'There was an assassin,' Murima said. 'At the same moment your mother cried out, I saw him. He wore a mask and concealed himself among the stragglers. It was no chance arrow. You were his target.'

'An assassin,' Oled said.

'Yes,' Murima said. 'He had his face covered, as I have said. One thing is certain. He did not come from enemy lines. This was a soldier in the Army of the Free. He would have shot you in the back.'

Oled's face clouded. 'Has anybody seen Atrakon?' he demanded.

'There you go again,' Shamana scolded, 'jumping to conclusions.'

'Who is more practised in the arts of assassination than the Selessian?' Oled demanded.

Shamana shook her head. 'There is no time to resolve this now. We have a battle to win.'

'It makes me sick at heart to think that we have a traitor in our ranks,' Oled said, 'and that we have allowed him to ride with us, break bread with us, fight alongside us.'

'Don't you think it hurts me too?' Shamana demanded. 'We share a dream, Oled, of a comradeship of the peoples. I heard Shinar's words all those years ago, before we faced the Warriors of the Sun on the field at Dullah. He reminded us of our aim, to create a Republic of the Free, without oppression or division. Now here, in our ranks, we have a man who reminds us of the old, cruel world. I want the traitor found, Oled. Unlike you, I believe in law. I want proof of his identity.'

At this point Nikesh reminded them of the proximity

503

of the enemy. Already, the Sol-ket were closing on them once more.

'We must retreat,' Shamana said. 'We can still hold the higher ground.'

Oled nodded. 'I will give the order.'

As Shamana turned to remount her horse, she stumbled.

'Are you all right?' Oled asked anxiously.

Shamana brushed him away. 'I'm getting too old for this,' she said. 'The effort of transformation drained me a little, that's all. I shall recover presently.' She wagged her finger under Oled's nose. 'If you'd learned your lessons better, you could take a weight off my shoulders. I remember when the three of us charged, you, Aaliya and me. Tell me the form you took then. Rhinoceros indeed! Now, let's fall back to those rocks. We must not let them pass.'

Oled nodded. Images burst into his mind, reminding him of the cost of defeat. He thought of the thousands of Helati who had left their villages to join the Army of the Free. They had marched across Jinghara in search of a refuge from lives of unremitting hardship. They had come to escape the casual cruelty of the Sol-ket. He saw the young people, the old, the women heavy with child. The sight of their faces, so bright with hope, so trusting, filled him with torment.

'We will protect our people,' he said defiantly. 'Whatever the cost, they will never return to slavery. Never!'

With that, the Tanjurs, mother and son, led their badly mauled cavalry up the slope towards the camp's final defences. What neither of them saw was the lone archer following at a safe distance.

12

Gardep wheeled round, barely escaping Rishal's lunge. The blade slid along his ribs, slicing open the skin. There was pain but it seemed far away, as if the wound belonged to somebody else. He became aware of a curious stillness, here at the heart of the battle. Though fighting continued in the distance, many warriors, both Helat and Sol-ket, had lowered their weapons. They were watching the furious duel between the opposing generals. Sensing his own deep exhaustion and the anxiety of his soldiers, Gardep forced himself to sit tall in the saddle, despite the blood that was oozing down his side. The wound made him groan. He sensed somebody by his side, guiding him away from Rishal. He recognised his rescuer. It was Atrakon Ebrahin.

'Is the hurt grave, my lord?' the Selessian asked.

Gardep stared at him then spoke.

'Listen to me, all of you,' he said. 'Don't ever call me or any other leader of the Army of the Free *lord.*'

Noticing Kulmat standing among the Sol-ket, listening to him, Gardep chose his words carefully.

'In this cause,' he cried, 'we are all brothers and sisters. We are equal before the sky and the Four Winds. Our loyalty to each other is worth all the coin in golden Rinaghar's treasury. There will be no Masters among us.'

Chastened, Atrakon smiled. 'It is a great dream, Gardep. But you are wounded. Let me take your place against Rishal.'

Gardep shook his head. 'I can't let you do that, Atrakon. I am the general of this army. It is my fight.'

Reluctantly, Atrakon stepped back. 'He comes again, brother Gardep.'

Gardep turned to face Rishal. 'No matter what happens to me,' he told the assembled Helati, 'I have been proud to lead you.'

Then he spurred his horse forward. He had an appointment with death.

CHAPTER 8

A Great Heart Stops Beating

I

While Gardep was preparing to face the man who had once been a second father to him, but now wished to destroy him, the Sol-ket were advancing on the southern front. The Army of the Free were fighting a rearguard action. For all their courage, they were being driven out of the valley. The Imperial infantry continued to press and the Sol-ket cavalry were making repeated charges against the rebel flanks, dispersing their opponents.

'If we do not hold them here,' Murima cried, 'Gardep will be caught in a pincer movement. Our fight for freedom will end on these slopes.'

'Yes,' Oled said, 'then the Sol-ket will have us all at their mercy. I have seen them at the point of conquest. They will make an example of every man, woman and child they can find.'

Everybody remembered the village massacre, when the ashes of fifty innocents were left to nourish the fields of Jinghara. It was impossible not to imagine the outrages the Sol-ket would visit on the Helati presently huddled in the camp. In his years at the fort of Zindhar, Oled in particular had witnessed at first hand the ruthlessness of the Warriors of the Sun. They would not care about the condition of their captives or their ability to fight. Be they old and frail, sick or infirm, they would face the same vengeful wrath. Be they women about to give birth or nursing mothers, they would suffer for the resistance of their fighters. The Sol-ket did not distinguish between their victims. They saw only rebels. They had been known to slaughter entire towns, dispatching every living soul to the House of the Dead. Sometimes they even butchered the animals, not for food, but to demonstrate how they dealt with resistance.

'Archers!' Oled shouted. 'To me. Murima, Bulu, I must prepare the cavalry. Take charge here.'

While Oled addressed the fighters on horseback, Murima reorganised them into three lines. She stood at the front, bow in hand, Bulu paced the lines, passing her instructions along.

'When I give the order, row by row you will keep up a steady stream of arrows. As the archers in the first row release their shafts, those in the second row will string theirs. Behind them, the third row will stand ready, waiting for Bulu to give the sign. In this way we will give the Sol-ket no respite. They must be weakened by the time Oled leads his charge.'

She didn't tell them what would happen if their quivers were empty before Oled was ready.

'On my signal,' Murima said.

The Sol-ket came again.

'First row,' Murima said. 'Now!'

She watched the foremost Imperial soldiers crumple to the ground.

'Second row,' Murima said. 'Now!'

Though they lost many men, the Sol-ket marched on, a remorseless line of red and gold. They were nothing if not courageous.

'Third row. Now!'

So it went on until the last arrow had been shot. Seeing the Sol-ket continuing their advance like an implacable juggernaut, Oled took over and roared his final command.

'Charge!'

He led the way back into the fray, battle-axe swinging. It was at this point, unseen by anyone, that the assassin emerged from the crowd. For a second time he bent his bow. Again, Oled was the target. But once more Shamana's keen ear heard the arrow's flight. With a cry she rode forward, using her mount to push her son out of harm's way. In so doing, she exposed herself to the danger. The arrowhead embedded itself in the flesh between throat and shoulder. Gasping for breath, Shamana crashed to the ground.

'Mother, no!' Oled cried, dismounting.

While he knelt to examine the wound, Nikesh stood over them, raising his shield. The assassin shot two more arrows. One missed its target, the other rebounded off the boss of Nikesh's shield. Then the traitor sought the only sanctuary available to him. He vanished into the welcoming ranks of the Sol-ket, who roared their congratulations.

'Is the wound deep?' Oled asked.

Shamana waved him away. Gritting her teeth, she snapped the shaft. 'It will take more than this to bring me down,' she growled. 'It is but a pinprick. Stop fussing, Oled. We have work to do.'

For all her brave words, pain was written into her features. A sheen of sweat covered her face. 'How goes the fight?' she demanded.

'Badly,' Nikesh said. 'When you went down, the cavalry broke off the charge. Our soldiers are wavering.'

Oled clung to Shamana, like the little boy he had once been. 'No,' he protested, 'you are wounded.'

Shamana squeezed his hand. 'Are you so blind?' she said, pointing to the blood that was soaking her tunic. 'I am worse than wounded. Oled, my son, darkness swims before my eyes. I am dying.'

'No,' Oled moaned. 'I refuse to believe it. Let me accompany you to the rear. I will get you medical attention.'

'Stop it, Oled,' Shamana told him. 'Stop deceiving yourself. How can you deny the evidence of your own eyes? At battle's end I will join my ancestors in the House of the Dead. You can read the signs as well as I.'

Oled continued to protest but with little effect. Shamana pushed him away and took her first stumbling steps towards the Sol-ket.

'Our warriors are on the verge of breaking,' she raged. 'I have to fight. I am the She-wolf, queen of the Tanjurs.'

The thunder of hooves made Shamana's mind up. The Imperial heavy cavalry was about to crash into the faltering rebel line.

'I have to keep alive the dream of liberation,' Shamana said. 'This is my final test.'

'Mother, no,' Oled protested. 'No heart is greater than yours, but you are old. You have suffered a grievous wound. Let me try.'

Shamana shook her head. 'How many times have I

scolded you for this?' she said. 'You have spent too much time with the Sol-ket. You have almost forgotten the ancient arts of your people. By the Four Winds, I wish Aaliya were here.'

The words wounded Oled, but there was no time to continue the exchange. By now the rebels had been forced so far back that they could see Gardep's regiment in the distance. Strangely, they seemed to be standing watching something. Nikesh wondered why there was no sign of battle.

'I have to break their charge,' Shamana said. 'It's our only chance.'

Oled was beside himself. 'No,' he cried. 'There has to be another way.'

Shamana whispered in her son's ear. 'Find it in your soul to achieve your destiny, and there will be.'

Then she started to run. As she did, her features began to change. A war elephant replaced the woman. But it was not as before. This time there was agony in her eyes. The transformation seemed to eddy across her body between the two states of being. The blood that had at first stained only her shoulder was now spilling down the grey hide of the elephant. Even as she covered the ground between her own lines and those of the Sol-ket, her pace was slowing. Still she fought to complete the transformation. She was part woman, part beast, staggering towards the onrushing horsemen. The elephant trumpeted. Shamana's voice followed. It was a mantra she had repeated many times: 'Damn me for growing old.'

'She can't do it,' Nikesh yelled, cutting down an attacking Sol-ket. 'It's too much for her.'

Oled rode after her, doing his best to shield her from the enemy arrows.

'No more,' he yelled. 'You're killing yourself.'

But there was a greater danger than the metamorphosis. As she fought to stabilise the transformation, the foremost Sol-ket rose in their stirrups intensifying the volleys of arrows into her throat and chest. Oled's efforts at protection were in vain. Shamana screamed in agony. The elephant's trunk rose pitifully then the beast shrank back into the woman. Scarlet blood burst from her mouth.

'Mother!'

A final arrow thudded into her. Oled saw the source of the arrow. His insides turned over as he recognised the bowman.

2

Far away, Cusha screamed at the very moment Shamana fell under the assassin's arrow.

'What is it?' Vishtar asked.

Cusha fell into her brother's arms.

'Is there nothing you can do to help her?' Omar asked.

Vishtar stared at her in horror. 'The pain is not Cusha's,' he said. 'She suffers another's death throes.'

'Whose?'

Vishtar shook his head.

'Traitor,' Cusha groaned, 'why did we not expose the traitor?' She clawed at her face. 'We tended his wounds. We treated him as our brother.'

She shuddered, as if a cold more intense, more numbing than the glacial wind outside, were stealing through the marrow of her bones.

'We obeyed what is written in the Book of Scales,' she whispered. 'We treated our poor suffering brother as we would be treated ourselves.' She seized Vishtar by the collar. 'Were we wrong?' she asked him. 'Should we have rejected him? In this barbarous world, is pity a crime?'

She released her brother. 'We have condemned the greatest of us to an agonising end,' she sobbed. 'Is there no justice in this land? Is there no goodness?'

She gave another shriek of misery and collapsed back into Vishtar's arms.

3

Gardep was riding towards Rishal. It was the third pass. Both men's armour and shields were dented and spattered with blood. The fight was nearing its end.

'Rishal has the advantage,' Atrakon murmured. 'He is fresh, while Gardep is exhausted from hours in the field.'

As yet, there seemed to be little evidence for this assessment. Master and pupil seemed evenly matched, trading blow for blow in the midst of a lethal struggle. Raising himself high in his stirrups, Gardep braced himself for Rishal's blow. His former master's blows had weakened him more than he cared to admit. When Rishal's sword crashed into the shield, Gardep felt the vibration run right down to the soles of his feet. Sagging back into the saddle, he had a sense of the world spinning around him. Still struggling to clear his head and regain control of his galloping mount, Gardep pointed his sword and gave the battle cry he had learned as a cadet: 'Victory or death!'

Swaying and rocking in the saddle, Gardep managed to gather the reins and turn his horse. Such was the speed of the fourth pass, the world seemed to blur as he swept towards Rishal. When the clash of steel against steel came again, with redoubled force, the shock of impact travelled through Gardep, rocking him backwards. His arm was on fire. His spine shuddered like a young sapling under the blow of the sword. But he was not unhorsed. Desperately twisting his hands through the reins, he clung on.

'This is it,' Atrakon said, 'Rishal is going to kill him.'

Hauling himself upright with his reins, a shaken Gardep struggled to wheel about. But he had no control over his panic-stricken mount. Before he could turn, Rishal was thundering towards him again, sword raised above his head. Gardep knew what that meant. He had thrown caution to the wind and was about to deliver the lethal blow. He had decided his former squire was in no state to defend himself. Pulling frantically at the reins, Gardep tried to steady himself. There was no time. With a roar, Rishal was upon him. This time the Sol-ket general's forward momentum was unstoppable. With a cry, Gardep crashed painfully to the ground. It was through sheer will power that he staggered to his feet. Even as he reeled, blinking sticky gobbets of blood out of his eyes, he saw Rishal striding towards him, confident and strong.

'So this is how it ends, na-Vassyrian. The master teaches the pupil. Then he kills him.'

He didn't waste another word. He scythed down at Gardep. These were not the subtle thrusts and parries Rishal had taught his squire at the Academy. They were brutal, clubbing blows, born out of pure fury. Under the force of one such blow, Gardep sank to the earth. Rishal grabbed his hair and displayed his weary opponent to the ranks of the Helati.

'Do you see, slaves?' Rishal bellowed. 'Do you witness this, you Helat dogs? This is the best man you have. But what is he now? Look at him; he is a boy to be beaten and whipped. I made him and I will destroy him.'

The insult put new strength into Gardep. Seeing his soldiers starting to bow their heads like the slaves they had always been, he tore himself free of Rishal. Incensed and determined to reignite the fire of revolt in their hearts, he summoned every ounce of strength into one last show of defiance.

'Raise your heads,' Gardep cried. 'Be proud, Warriors of the Free. Death will not conquer me. I will be avenged. My blood will nourish new revolts. I will be millions.'

Tossing his shield aside, he took his sword in a two-handed grip and drove at Rishal, rocking him back on his heels.

'You gloat too early, ax-Sol,' he panted.

For a moment, Rishal was himself being forced to retreat. Both men were exhausted and gasping for breath. Finally, Rishal recovered enough to speak. 'Well done, pupil. You're the first man to evade my death-thrust.' He searched for Kulmat in the crowd. 'Do you see, squire Kulmat?' he asked. 'Do you see the man I made? He learns his lessons well.'

Gardep followed the direction of Rishal's stare. He saw that Kulmat had his hand on the hilt of his sword. Was he about to intervene, taking a stand against his own knight? Gardep gave a brief shake of the head and his boyhood friend reluctantly slid the blade back into its scabbard. Straightening his back, Gardep hurled himself at Rishal. But the Lion of Inbacus deflected the blow with disconcerting ease.

'You have great courage,' Rishal told Gardep, 'but that does not make you my equal, Gardep. You will always be the pupil and I the master.'

With that, he swung his sword with such force it brushed Gardep's blade aside. Rishal slashed the younger man's side. Grunting with pain, Gardep clamped a hand to his ribs. He couldn't stop the blood oozing through his fingers. It was soon soaking his uniform. A roar went up from the Sol-ket lines. It was the decisive blow.

'First blood to Rishal-ax-Sol, Lion of Inbacus.'

But it was the last blood he would spill that day. Rishal would be the next to suffer. The wound would come from an unexpected quarter.

4

The Sol-ket fell upon Shamana like vultures, desperate to deliver the deathblow. Half a dozen men jostled to claim a coveted title that would earn him renown across the Empire. They all wanted to be known as the She-wolf's conqueror. Kicking and spitting at her tormentors, Shamana roared her defiance.

'Not one of you is worthy of striking the blow,' she told them. 'Rally, you Warriors of the Free. Don't be down-hearted. What do these dogs fight for but to spread misery and fear, to fill their villas with precious things? What kind of cause is that?'

The nearest warrior lunged at her but a blade crossed his. It belonged to the traitor, Murak. 'A pretty speech, witch,' he said. 'I'm going to make sure it's your last. You have found the man worthy of striking the deathblow. I outwitted you. I outwitted your fool of a son.'

'Kill me, then,' Shamana retorted. 'You will not kill my cause. It is written in the Book of Scales that to fight for one tortured and enslaved soul is to fight for all mankind.'

She twisted to call to the Helati. 'Don't give up. Throw them back into the valleys.'

Murak shook his head, almost in pity. But the triumphant smile was short-lived, erased by the vast shadow that had fallen over him. A bull elephant, covered in glittering armour, reared on its hind legs and trumpet-ed its war rage. Then, with earth-shattering force, it dropped its front legs on two of the soldiers who had encircled Shamana, stamping the life from them.

'Oled!' Pride shone through the She-wolf's pain. 'I prayed for this day to come,' she said. 'You have proven yourself a true son of the Tanjurs. Now destroy the oppressors and defend our people.'

Just as Oled dwarfed all mortal men, so the beast that he had become dwarfed any elephant the Sol-ket had ever seen. Some stood in helpless fascination. Others, with unsteady hands, tried to launch their spears. Still others threw down their weapons and ran. While Nikesh and his men formed a protective cordon, Murima, Qintu and Harad bore Shamana away to safety, and the war elephant drove its tusks through two Sol-ket before tossing them into their comrades.

'Kill him!' Murak howled as he turned to flee.

But the galloping horses of the Sol-ket had been thrown into panic and confusion by the beast's titanic onslaught. They unseated their riders and fled, crashing into the ranks behind them.

'For Ra's sake,' the warrior-priest shrieked at the awestruck Sol-ket, 'stop gawping and fight.'

But the forward rush of the Warriors of the Sun had been halted. Maddened by despair, the war-elephant rampaged through the screaming horses and their horrified riders. Only Murak seemed capable of rational thought. He stopped running and tried to rally the fleeing men. Even as Oled, in the form of the vengeance-intoxicated beast, sought him out, the infiltrator demanded a javelin.

'Javelin, damn you!' he bawled into the face of one wide-eyed young soldier. 'The creature has a heart. It is mortal. We can kill it.'

Spinning round, Murak prepared to hurl his weapon. But the war elephant was upon him, thrusting its mighty tusks at him and snatching the javelin away with its trunk. Disarmed, Murak could only flee, springing into the saddle of a riderless horse and vanishing into the confused maelstrom that was the disintegrating Sol-ket regiment.

5

Seeing Gardep tumble backwards, bleeding heavily, Atrakon ran to his aid, blocking Rishal's way.

'Do you have no sense of honour?' Rishal shouted, outraged that the Selessian had intervened. 'I am the victor. You have no right to intervene.'

'You dare talk of honour!' Atrakon snarled. 'Your infernal Hotec-Ra stole *my* honour. They made me hate myself. Back there in Jinghara, you butchered unarmed boys. You used the sorcery of the Hotec-Ra to burn them alive. Where is the honour in that? No, Rishal, I am a Selessian by birth and by every beat of my heart. Unlike Gardep, I am not bound by your criminal traditions. I will not obey your wretched Sol-ket code.'

'I have triumphed in single combat,' Rishal insisted. 'I demand that you hand over the boy.'

Atrakon drew his sabre. 'Demand all you like, ax-Sol,' he said. 'If you want to get to Gardep, you will have to go through me.' He laughed. 'That's right. War isn't a game. I have only one rule. I will do anything I can to protect my comrades and end the tyrants' rule.' He turned and shouted a new battle cry to the Helat ranks. 'Death to the Muzals!'

Rishal's eyes narrowed. 'You will pay for that, desert rat,' he said. 'I will cut you down and claim my kill.'

Atrakon could sense Gardep trying to get his attention.

'Rishal is right, Atrakon,' Gardep croaked. 'This is between him and me.'

Atrakon shook his head. 'You've got a lot to learn, Gardep. This isn't about two men. It isn't about individual pride or honour, or whatever fool idea drives you. It is about the cause of freedom.'

Rishal listened to the exchange then addressed Atrakon. 'I will make you grovel at my feet, Selessian,' he spat. He half-turned. 'Kulmat,' he said, 'give me a new sword.'

Even as Kulmat hesitated, a spear penetrated the general's thigh. Spinning round, Rishal fixed Atrakon with an accusing stare. 'Coward!' he yelled.

But it was not Atrakon who had thrown the spear. It was a young Vassyrian by the name of Adrius.

He taunted Rishal. 'Now who's a pin cushion, general?'

While the Vassyrians turned on their former masters, the Sol-ket carried Rishal to safety.

6

Sunset brought an uneasy peace to the Dragon Mountains. There was no sense of victory in either camp. In the foothills, Rishal was undergoing surgery. He refused the preparations that would dull the pain.

'Just tell me how long it will be before I can fight again,' he snapped.

The surgeon looked startled. 'Rishal-Ra, I have not even removed the spearhead. How can you think of battle?'

Rishal cursed him. 'You said there was no major damage. I will heal, won't I?'

'That is my best guess, yes.'

'So get the infernal thing out. I will be back in the saddle within weeks.'

He didn't tell the surgeon the reason. The sixty-day month of Buradish was half over. The world was dying.

'Well,' Rishal grumbled, 'what are you waiting for?'

The surgeon gave the general a leather strap to bite on. When he pulled the spearhead from Rishal's thigh, the scream could be heard in the rebel camp. There, Shamana was also receiving medical attention. But there would be no helping the She-wolf. 'What's that noise?' she asked, her voice no more than a frail whisper.

Outside the tent there was the sound of hammering and sawing. The Army of the Free were working on their defensive.

'Bulu is building a palisade,' Murima explained.

'That's good,' Shamana said. 'That's very good.'

Nobody shared her confidence. They all knew that, though the final blow had not been struck in the Battle of the Dragon Mountains, as sure as the winds blow, the Imperial Army would attack at dawn. Around the bed were gathered those who knew Shamana best: Murima, Gardep, Qintu, Harad and Atrakon. Recently returned from having his wounds dressed, Gardep was bandaged and propped up on a makeshift litter. Then, finally, there was her grieving son, Oled.

'You have something to say to Atrakon,' Shamana said.

Tears welled in Oled's green eyes. 'I have been a fool, brother Ebrahin,' he said. 'Do you have it in your heart to forgive me?'

'I bear you no ill will,' Atrakon said with a quiet dignity. 'I too bear the burden of my failings. We are mortal men. We make mistakes. Let the matter rest at that.'

'There must be something we can do,' Harad said, staring at Shamana. 'She can't die.'

Murima shook her head. 'The She-wolf is beyond our help.'

There was no consolation for Oled. He knelt at his mother's side, watching her fade from the world.

'Who's there?' she said, fighting back the darkness that had gathered around her.

'It's me, Oled.'

'You found your greatness today,' she said, patting his arm.

'The price was too great, mother.'

'Who else is here? Cusha?'

Oled, Gardep and Murima exchanged sorrowful glances.

'Cusha is at the end of the world, Shamana,' Gardep reminded her in her delirium. 'She goes to destroy the Darkwing.'

'Yes, of course,' Shamana said. 'I'm losing my wits.'

She heard the sound of the boys, Harad and Qintu, weeping.

'Is that you, Qintu?' she asked. 'You were always teasing me, remember. I didn't think you were so sentimental. As for you, Harad, well, you're soft-hearted by nature. That's not a bad thing.' She reached out and touched each of them. 'You must not mourn, any of you. I am happy. My life has not been in vain. I have lived to see our people rise again.'

She squeezed Oled's hand hard. Oled knew she was in terrible pain.

'Can't you give her something?' Oled asked Murima.

'She refuses everything.'

'Why?' Oled demanded. 'Why won't you take something to ease the pain?'

'I must be alert,' Shamana said. 'I want to see them before I die.'

'See them?' Murima asked. 'See who? Do you mean the Holy Children?'

Shamana shook her head. 'Do you not have ears? Can't you hear them? They're coming. It's our people. They gathered at Gussorah, you know.'

She hoisted herself up on one elbow.

'Dry your tears,' she said. 'Save your mourning for those who want it. I can't abide all this moaning, all these fine words. I want a world fit for future generations to live in. Sow my ashes and raise freedom from them. Many months ago I set you on the road to that world. You promised you would not sleep until we had attained it. I hold you to that promise, every one of you. Now, carry me outside.'

'What!'

'I want to see them. I want to see our brothers and sisters.'

Everybody thought the pain must have driven Shamana mad. That's when Nikesh burst into the tent.

'They're here!' he cried, eyes blazing with joy.

'Who?'

'Thousands of them, tens of thousands,' Nikesh cried. 'They've been wandering the mountains, trying to find us. It's the army that gathered at Gussorah.'

'There,' Shamana said. 'Didn't I tell you?' She frowned at Oled. 'You managed your elephant at last, my boy. Now you must perfect the hearing of a dog. Listen.'

At last Oled heard it: the tramp of thousands of feet, the lilt of flutes, the beat of drums, the sound of veena and sitar. They went outside the tent. Banners fluttered over the heads of the arriving masses. There were the symbols of the Four Winds and the Scales.

'The standards of Shinar,' Murima gasped.

There was even one banner inscribed with the dragon motif of the Tanjurs. The Helati remembered the sacrifice of the dragon-people.

'Carry my mother outside,' Oled ordered. 'Let her see the people.'

Shamana watched the procession of the Helat masses for several minutes, smiling as the endless column climbed the valleys towards them.

'Look at them,' she said, 'I told you they would come. Do you see the torches dancing in the night?'

'We see them,' Gardep said.

'That's your army, Gardep,' Shamana told him. 'Learn your lessons. Become the general we all want you to be.'

She gritted her teeth against the pain and forced out one last speech. Weak as she was, it carried across the multitude.

'I will be watching you all from the House of the Dead,' she said. 'Give the people their freedom. Do it, or I will haunt you to your graves.'

Suddenly her entire body was wracked with convulsions. She died without another word.

7

'She's gone.' Cusha sat staring at the yak-skin carpets that kept out the worst of the bitter cold. 'Shamana's dead.'

'And the others?' Vishtar asked.

Cusha shook her head. 'I felt the doors of the House of the Dead groaning open to admit her. Beyond that, I have no knowledge of the Army.'

'There is a terrible possibility,' Vishtar said. 'What if we defeat the Darkwing only to hand the world back to the Muzals?'

Cusha nodded wearily. 'The same thought has occurred to me. Maybe we should let the world die. At least all our suffering will be over.'

Omar rose abruptly to his feet. 'You don't mean that,' he said.

'How do you know?'

'I can see it in your eyes,' the Selessian said. 'You love life. It shines from your every smile. Yes, even from the intensity of your sorrow. Swear to me, Holy Child, you will not give up your quest while there is breath in you.'

Cusha seemed startled by Omar's words. 'Does this mean you have come to a conclusion yourself?'

'Yes, we Selessians will lend our sword arms to the cause of freedom. We will wash away the stain left on our nation's honour by the scoundrel, Ehut Haraddin.'

'Then let's swear a common oath,' Cusha said. 'I will continue to Nandraghiri with Vishtar and Aaliya. You will go south and join the Army of the Free.'

They embraced, kissing each other on both cheeks. Mehmet and Vishtar swore their oaths too.

8

Dawn saw heavy snow come to the Dragon Mountains. The Darkwing's winter was moving south. Gardep had his litter carried to a point high above the Sol-ket camp. He wanted to see the Grand Army's formation.

'If only these snowstorms would clear,' he said, blinking away the swirling flakes. 'What do the scouts report?'

'Visibility is poor,' Nikesh replied.

It was at this moment that a group of scouts galloped up the ravine.

'Infantry,' they reported. 'They're coming this way.'

Gardep seized the armrests of his chair. 'Are they Sol-ket?'

The head scout shook his head.

'To arms!' Gardep said. 'Rishal's sending his auxiliaries into attack first. I want every archer we can muster. Now!'

Within ten minutes hundreds of archers, most fresh from rallying at Gussorah, had their bows trained on the dense blizzard.

'Nock your arrows,' he said, seeing the first shadowy forms emerging from the snows.

Several hundred dark figures were now moving up the hill. Strangely, they did not raise their shields or form ranks. Their weapons were sheathed.

'What are they doing?' Bulu asked. 'Do they want us to mow them down like ears of corn?'

Gardep gave another order. 'Draw.'

But Murima interrupted him before he could tell his archers to shoot. 'Wait,' she said. 'Look. That's a flag of truce.'

'It's a trick,' Nikesh said.

'It's no trick,' Atrakon said. 'You only have to take a look at the way they're walking towards us. Hear them out.'

'Stay where you are,' Gardep ordered. 'You may send one man to talk for you.'

Without hesitation, one of the Vassyrians unbuckled his sword belt and handed his bow and quiver to his neighbour. Under the flag of truce, he approached the Helat lines.

'Who are you?' Gardep asked.

'My name is Adrius. I was the one who threw the spear at Rishal. I just wish I'd hit him in the heart rather than the leg. Did you not see us rise against the Sol-ket? We Vassyrians have come to a decision.'

'What do you want?'

'My men wish to join you.'

'Do you have proof of your intentions?' Gardep asked.

'Traitors have come to join us before. Your actions could be a ruse.'

Just along the line, Oled listened impassively.

'Is this enough proof?' Adrius asked. He raised his arm. Immediately, a score of buffalo lumbered forward, pulling heavy carts laden with weapons. 'All this was thrown away by the fleeing Sol-ket, or taken from their dead.'

'Fleeing?'

'Yes.' Adrius looked at the faces of the Army of the Free. 'By the gods,' he said, 'you don't know, do you? They've gone.'

'Gone?'

'That's right. At this very moment they're marching away from the field of battle. My guess is, they hope to skirt round to the north and link up with the garrison at Rinaghar.'

'I don't believe it,' Gardep said, his suspicions raised by the talk of sudden retreat. 'Rishal would never sanction it.'

'Of course not,' Adrius said. 'The Lion of Inbacus is a fanatic. He would never break off the fight. But he's delirious with a fever. In his absence, his junior generals decided to cut their losses and make an orderly withdrawal. It seems the arrival of tens of thousands of Helat reinforcements made their minds up.' He looked at the tense faces of those before him. 'Don't you understand?' he asked. 'You've earned a reprieve.'

9

The Army of the Free spent one more night in the Dragon Mountains. It was time to complete the valediction to their fallen. They gathered as a crimson sunset stained the snowy slopes. The storm had abated a little so the massed ranks assembled in drifting sleet. Many pyres were lit that night for the dead. Shamana's was the last to be fired. Her body was borne on an ox-cart, down an avenue of torch-bearers. All bowed their heads. All grieved for the She-wolf, the heart and soul of freedom. A funeral party made up of Murima, Qintu, Harad, Atrakon and Oled carried her to the summit of the pyre. Gardep, still recovering from his wounds, watched from his chair. The companions made a circle and hurled blazing torches onto the pyre. The firelight shone across the mountains, illuminating their stillness and their majesty.

'Look,' Nikesh said, pointing into the valleys below. 'It is as if our flames are lighting the whole of Jinghara. Did you ever see anything like it?'

'Give me your spyglass, Gardep,' Bulu said.

He stepped forward to examine the world below. It was true. Not only the valleys but also the foothills of the Dragon Mountains, the barren thorn forests and all the lands beyond seemed to glow in the night. Then he understood why. Everywhere he looked there were campfires. There were more banners bearing the symbols of the Four Winds and the Scales. The entire area was alive with activity.

'Word of what happened here is spreading,' Bulu said. 'The villagers have seen the Sol-ket crawling away with their tails between their legs. They are joining us in their many thousands.'

Even as Bulu spoke, Shamana's ghost rose from the pyre. The She-wolf looked upon the face of her son, Oled Lonetread, and there was joy in her eyes. Her cause was reborn in her son and in all the thousands gathered in and around the Dragon Mountains. As her ghost faded into the night, never to be seen again, a single sound echoed across the mountains, the howl of the wolf.

It was the thirty-second day of Buradish.

CHAPTER 9

Winter Deepens

1

The Darkwing had a new toy. The demon lord's captives shuddered as the creature slid out of the gloom. They saw the flickering tongues of the serpent heads, the floating night-black eyes. Then, wisely, they averted their gaze.

'Squeamish, are you?' the Darkwing gloated, casting a glance round the manacled prisoners. He stalked across the room and seized his new discovery by the throat. 'Do you know what we have here?' he said. He pulled back the newcomer's heavy winter cloak to reveal the saffron robes of the Hotec-Ra. 'That's right,' he chuckled, 'a priest of the Sun. I found him wandering in the storm. It seems he got separated from the Sol-ket. What's your name, priest?'

Timu kept his own counsel.

'You will tell me, you know,' the Darkwing said. 'Even Lord Linem spilled his guts eventually.' He saw the fear creep into Timu's eyes. 'What's this? You know your master's fate, don't you? Then you understand what might happen to you.'

A terrified answer shuddered from his captive's throat. 'My name is Timu.'

The Darkwing nodded slowly. 'I've heard of you. You're one of Linem's apprentices. Maybe you're hoping to step into his shoes. I'm sure I can arrange that, in more ways than one. What brings you to the Khut lands, Timu?'

The priest hesitated.

'Do you want me to take your eyes first,' the Darkwing asked, drawing a lethal-looking talon over Timu's face, 'or your tongue?' The threat was persuasive enough.

'I was to take possession of the Holy Children and guide them safely to your lair,' Timu said, fearing the consequences of his admission.

'To what end?'

Timu lowered his eyes. 'To destroy you and prevent the dying of the sun.'

The Darkwing's black eyes narrowed. Timu was seen to tremble visibly.

Then the demon lord leaned forward and roared into the priest's face. A swarm of flies buzzed from his open mouth.

'Now,' he said, 'what can you do to make amends?' His eyes settled on Jinghirza. 'This young woman is a Khut maiden,' he said. 'From time to time, in moments of boredom as I await the final going down of the sun, I set her various tests to pass the time. Would you like to take part in one?'

Timu stammered a reply. 'Yes, my lord.'

The Darkwing leered. 'I thought you would.'

2

Rishal ax-Sol surfaced from his fever. For some moments he listened. 'Why do I not hear the clamour of battle?' he demanded.

'We have left the Dragon Mountains, Rishal-Ra,' Kulmat said quietly.

Rishal's eyes sparkled greedily. 'A victory?'

Kulmat shook his head. 'A retreat.'

'What!'

'While you were lying ill, the Helat troops were joined by an army several tens of thousands strong. Your commanders thought the balance of forces was in the enemy's favour. They decided on an orderly withdrawal.'

'You mean the curs ran away! I want to see them all in an hour.'

Kulmat nodded. 'I will arrange it.'

As he walked to the tent flap, Rishal remembered something. 'You didn't hand me my sword when I demanded it. Why?'

'I feared that you had been weakened by the fight with Gardep,' Kulmat answered. 'I feared that, by fighting again so quickly, you might succumb to the Selessian.'

'That was the only reason?'

'It was.'

Through the open tent flap, Rishal could see the wide Jingharan Plain. 'Is that snow?'

'Yes, Rishal-Ra,' Kulmat replied. 'The flakes have been in the air since noon. Winter is moving south at a terrific pace. Soon golden Rinaghar and even Tiger-gated Parcep may be shuddering before its glacial blast.'

'That's it, then,' Rishal said. 'The demon's claims are more than idle boasts.'

'Yes, Rishal-Ra, this is the beginning of the Darkwing winter.'

He continued to stare after Kulmat long after the squire had gone. For all his ready answers, Kulmat had not allayed Rishal's suspicions. There was something flowery and evasive in his answers. Rishal vowed not to take his eyes off the boy.

3

Two days later, when Rishal was able to stand with the aid of crutches, he reviewed his troops. He could smell the reek of defeat. The previous afternoon he had raged at his officers, spewing his anger at them for the retreat from the Dragon Mountains. Now it was time to inject some much-needed morale into his dispirited troops.

'Warriors of Ra,' he began, 'since my recovery, I keep hearing the same word. That word is defeat. Let me say this as clearly as I can for you, we were not defeated. I vanquished their general in mortal combat. Is that defeat? But the rebel cockroaches refused to abide by the rules of battle. They have no honour. You all saw how a traitor's spear laid me low. The Vassyrian attacked without warning from our own ranks. It was the act of a coward.' He clenched his fist and roared his conclusion. 'They are craven curs. We are men. We were not defeated on the field of conflict!'

His eyes swept the listening soldiers. 'Then,' he continued, 'while I was incapacitated by a fever, some of your officers decided on an "orderly retreat."'

He let the words sink in. He had loaded them with bitter irony.

'What do these words mean?' he asked, weighing them in his open palms. '*Orderly* and *retreat*. I have a word for this strange idea. I call it cowardice. Some of your senior officers chose to run away.'

The objects of his scorn shuffled their feet.

'They are now standing with you in the ranks. They will fight their next battle as infantrymen. In their place, I have elevated new officers. Any repetition of such craven behaviour and I will kill any man who tries to step back from the cauldron of war.'

He could almost hear the sound of backbones being stiffened.

'But good did come out of the campaign,' he said. 'They have lost their chief sorcerer. Thanks to Murak here, the She-wolf is dead. Who is going to lead them now? Let's examine the candidates. Gardep na-Vassyrian? I whipped him in front of his troops. That's right, I had the fabled boy-warrior at my mercy. Oled Lonetread? He is still snivelling about his mother.' He saved his best joke till last. 'Murima ul-Parcep? She's a fat cook!'

The troops roared with laughter.

'This is our time,' Rishal told them. 'We will draw them onto open ground. Our heavy horse will grind them into the soil. This time we will meet them on the flat Jingharan Plain.'

Propping himself up on one crutch, he raised the other belligerently.

'I have sent envoys to Rinaghar and to Parcep. I have ordered reinforcements on a scale not seen in two generations. We are going to throw the full might of the Sons of Ra against the slaves. We will intercept them and chase them to the field of Dullah.'

A murmur ran through the mass of soldiers.

'That's right, Dullah. There, our forefathers crushed the revolt of the criminal Shinar. We showed them Sol-ket steel. We broke their bones. We broke their hearts too. We whipped them back into servitude. There, forty years on, we will drown the present uprising in blood. They will regret the day they took arms against the mightiest army on Earth!'

The troops had received Rishal politely at first, even sullenly. By the time he had finished speaking they were drumming their feet and bellowing their war cry. On and on it went, like rolling thunder.

'Victory or death!'

When the men had dispersed, Rishal drew Murak aside. Kulmat was the third man in attendance. 'Are you privy to the experiments of your fellow Hotec-Ra?' he asked.

'The Fire Dust?' Murak asked. 'Yes, I know all about it.'

'The priests have at last got the mixture right,' Rishal said, 'but they have not yet perfected a delivery system for the stuff.'

'What's the problem?'

'They've been trying to imitate the projectiles the She-wolf launched at our men during the battle. Unfortunately, Shamana's method would be no use to us. She used leather to enclose her Lyrian fire. This Fire Dust is far more volatile. It ignites when it touches anything made of animal skin. It simply consumes the container.'

'I see.'

'They tried using the pots in which they store it,' Rishal continued.

'More problems?'

Rishal nodded. 'The moment they left the catapult, the pots became uncorked and the dust sprayed everywhere. We lost five soldiers and two priests in the trials. It is very frustrating. We have a weapon that can turn the tide of any battle and we can't find a way to use it.'

Murak nodded. 'I'll give it some thought. We'll find a way to torch the rebels.'

Then general and priest sat down to share a meal.
Having heard their plans, Kulmat could only pick at his.

4

By the thirty-eighth day of Buradish, Rishal's intentions
were clear to the leaders of the Army of the Free. They met
in full council on the slopes above their growing army on
the Gussorah road. Atrakon had been reinstated. Gardep
summoned Nikesh to address his commanders.

'Tell them what you told me,' he said.

'It's the Sol-ket,' Nikesh said. 'They are on the move,
throwing a ring of steel around us. Two armies come from
the south. Another is on the road from Karangpur to the
north.'

'How many?' Oled asked.

'There are three huge columns. They are approaching in
battle formation. They come in full armour, standards
flying. Rishal leads one army. A new general, Ghushan,
commands the northern divisions.' He hesitated.

'And the final one?' Oled demanded.

'Oled,' Nikesh said, 'prepare yourself. Rishal has made
the murderer of your mother General.'

Oled's eyes hardened. So that's how it was. The Empire
had rewarded his mother's killer with promotion.

Nikesh continued to break the bad news. 'Murak has at
least twenty thousand men under his command.'

'Twenty thousand!' Gardep exclaimed. 'That alone
constitutes a Grand Army, and it is but one column. How
many do they number altogether?'

'The lowest estimate is fifty thousand.'

'And the highest?'

'Eighty thousand.'

Every listener stared at Nikesh. Their faces registered absolute shock.

'It's true,' Bulu confirmed. 'I witnessed it with my own eyes. I only saw the armies commanded by Rishal and Murak. But never did I see such a multitude.'

Murima interjected. 'That's not exactly true, is it, Bulu? You saw such a host once before. It was at Dullah, the most terrible of battles. By all the rivers that run, it is starting again.'

Determined not to give in to the mood of depression that was eddying through the assembly, Gardep chose to be decisive. He laid out a map.

'Come here, Nikesh,' he said. 'Show me how Rishal has set out his forces.'

Nikesh indicated the deployment of the Imperial Army. Three pincers: one from the south-west, one from the south-east and another from the north-west. Rinaghar lay due east, completing the encirclement. Gardep saw the pattern emerge.

'That's their strategy,' he said, tracing the direction of the three columns with his finger. 'They understand the symbolism of Dullah as well as we do. They mean to engage us there.'

'Of course,' Oled said, 'they have chosen the ground where Shinar's rebellion was destroyed. They know that we will be burdened by the nightmare of the past. If they win this second battle, no slave will ever dare fight for freedom again.'

'We're agreed then,' Murima said defiantly. 'We don't let the masters win.'

5

'We have to escape,' Jinghirza said.

Timu stared straight ahead, maintaining a stubborn silence.

'What's this?' Jinghirza demanded. 'Don't you talk to we lesser breeds?'

Still, Timu stared ahead impassively. She noticed that he was clinging tightly to a small object, enclosing it protectively in his palm.

'You think you're better than us, don't you?' Jinghirza asked. 'But we all breathe the same air and walk in the same sunlight. Believe me, when the sun dies, we will all die with it.'

'Don't you think I know that?' Timu said, breaking his silence.

'Then why don't we work together?' Jinghirza whispered.

Timu stared. 'What do you mean?'

'I've seen that package you've been hiding.'

Timu's face betrayed the surge of anxiety her words had caused. 'You won't give me away to him, will you?'

'Why would I?' Jinghirza asked. 'I have resisted the monster all the way. I want to walk away from this terrible place and return to my old life. The Khuts have many faults. Treachery isn't one of them. We don't crawl behind our enemy's backs. We meet them face to face and crack their heads. Well, what have you got in that precious little pouch of yours?'

'Fire Dust.'

Jinghirza was intrigued. 'Explain.'

Timu looked around the other prisoners. They were all either asleep or slumped in a kind of traumatised stupor. 'Kick that piece of meat over here.'

Jinghirza reached out and used her toe to punt the scrap of leftover food to Timu. The priest dropped a single, infinitesimal grain on the wallet-sized piece of meat. It immediately burst into flame. When the strange phosphorescence died, nothing was left but a minuscule cinder.

Jinghirza stared at the priest wide-eyed. 'This could change the face of warfare. How much damage could the whole package do?'

Timu smiled for the first time. 'I am hoping that it will destroy the demon.' Then the smile faded. 'You know what I can bring to our cooperation. What can you do?'

Jinghirza permitted herself a smile. 'I can get us out of these chains.'

Timu leant forward. 'How?' he whispered excitedly.

'You have already seen the reason,' Jinghirza said. 'The Darkwing gives me tests, ordeals. I remind him of someone. He likes to see me fight the terrors he throws against me.'

'I still don't see how this will help us escape.'

Shuddering from the searing cold, Jinghirza explained what she had in mind.

6

The first sighting of Sangra Peak came on the fortieth day of Buradish. For a few hours a day the blizzards would clear and they could see the Mountains of the Moon floating in a silvery haze. Until now, the other mountains in the chain had obscured Sangra Peak.

'That's it,' Aaliya said.

'How long will it take to get there?' Vishtar asked.

'Ten days,' Aaliya said, 'maybe fifteen if the snows get

worse.'

'That's too slow,' Cusha complained. 'The sun dies just twenty-one days from now.'

'It would help to know the Darkwing's whereabouts,' Vishtar said. 'It would help if we could penetrate Nandraghiri without his knowledge. Is there anything you can do, Aaliya?'

'I don't just transform into bears,' she said. 'It is dangerous but I will do it. Just keep going due north. I will find you on my return.'

Without further ado, she adopted the white plumage of the ptarmigan and set off across the grey sky.

'May the Four Winds watch over you,' Cusha murmured. 'Of your entire race, only two now remain.'

7

On the site of Shinar's fabled rising, in the open fields of Gussorah, Gardep addressed the Army of the Free. Oled and Murima, Nikesh and Bulu, Atrakon and Adrius flanked him. As he looked at the multitude, he imagined it as an endless sea. But they were farmers and boat-builders, carpenters and metalworkers, seamstresses and servants. They were not soldiers.

'I stand before you as your general,' he said. 'Some of you look at me and see only a Sol-ket.'

Qintu looked embarrassed and lowered his eyes.

'That was true once,' Gardep continued, 'not any more. This monstrous Empire killed many of our comrades, Shamana included. She was the finest woman I ever knew.'

He raised his voice. 'You are my brothers and sisters. We suffered together in the Dragon Mountains. We fought and died together. If you honour me with your trust, I will lead you. Do I have that trust?'

The question was met with a returning roar of acclamation. Qintu led the shout.

'The Sol-ket are coming,' Gardep continued. 'They are eighty-thousand strong. They think we will run to be hunted down like frightened deer. They're wrong. For good or for ill, we will meet them on the field of battle. They are trying to force us to take our stand at Dullah. They know this fateful spot is burned into the memory of our people. But we will not flinch from our destiny. Forty years ago, a great wrong was done there. We will right it.'

The roar of the crowd swelled once more. But Gardep wasn't finished. 'The Sol-ket think history will repeat itself. There is a difference. Forty years ago Shinar trusted his allies. The Selessian Erut Haraddin betrayed that trust. This time there will be no false friends. We will fight together, side by side, shoulder to shoulder. We will have freedom or we will have death.' He threw out a question to the throng. 'Which will you have: freedom or death?'

The reply came from thousands of throats. 'Freedom! Freedom!'

Gardep smiled. 'I expected no less. I am proud to have known you and led you in battle. Now put aside your fears. Set your faces towards the aim of liberation. On to Dullah!'

8

An hour after his speech, Gardep was wandering alone through the snow. He marvelled at the drifting whiteness. It was strange how the world sounded different in the snow. There was a great stillness about it, hinting at distant echoes. Standing there, he tried to imagine Cusha's face, so dark against all this whiteness. Conjuring her dark eyes, he smiled.

'Are you close to your destination, my love?' he murmured. 'Do you see Nandraghiri?'

But there was no reply. Only the sob of the wind could be heard over the open land.

At this moment, alone in the wind and the snow, Gardep felt weighed down by his destiny. To destroy the Darkwing at one end of the land, and defeat the Imperial Army at the other; was it possible? Kulmat's face swam in the drifting clouds of snow. Gardep remembered how he had drawn his sword, ready to fight his own knight.

'But I stopped you throwing your life away for nothing.'

Love, friendship, they were the only weapons he had against a gargantuan foe. The Sons of Ra possessed terror, cruelty, wealth, betrayal, torture and deceit. It seemed such an uneven struggle. Amid his musings, he heard movement. 'Who's there?'

'It's me, Adrius.'

Gardep turned to look at the Vassyrian. 'We have barely had time to talk. You took a great risk, throwing that javelin at Rishal. Did you know your Vassyrians would follow you?'

'Sometimes,' Adrius said, 'you have to take a gamble. That's how history is made.'

'That makes your action all the braver,' Gardep said. 'Do you have something to say?'

'I have something to ask. I have heard the soldiers call you na-Vassyrian. Why is that?'

'Do you not know the story?'

Adrius shook his head.

'I was born in Inbacus,' Gardep said.

Adrius seemed surprised.

'Rishal found me wandering the streets of Inbacus during the sacking of the city, an orphan of the war,' Gardep explained. 'He brought me back to Parcep to be raised in the Academy.'

'That doesn't sound like an ax-Sol,' Adrius said. 'Of all the orphans of that bitter war, why would he take pity on this particular boy? The Muzals are not known for their charity.'

Gardep stared. Why had he never asked this question himself?

'Do you remember nothing of your childhood?'

'Very little,' Gardep said. 'Oh, I have this.'

In spite of the biting cold, he slipped off his two heavy jackets and showed Adrius the tattoo on his bicep. It was Adrius's turn to look shocked.

'But this is the insignia of the royal family!' he cried, falling to one knee.

'Stand up,' Gardep said. 'What do you mean?'

'This lion with the bull's head,' Adrius answered. 'You are a prince of the royal line at the very least. But it can't be. Nobody survived the sack of the royal palace. Rishal killed them all.'

Suddenly, Gardep knew how Cusha must have felt just before she breathed in the vapours of the memory lamp. He was about to discover where he came from.

CHAPTER 10

A Gathering Storm

1

A pure white bird, perfectly suited to merge with the world of snow, would stand out in the chambers, tunnels and passages of Nandraghiri. Alighting on the thirty stone steps that led to the monastery entrance, Aaliya transformed into a mouse. For a few seconds she rose on her hind legs, staring with tiny, beady eyes at the vertiginous peaks and snow-scoured heights. Then, scurrying gratefully inside to escape the raw, northerly winds, she kept to the wall, fearful that she might be discovered at any moment. Scenting the Darkwing, the mouse's tiny heart beat even faster, an accelerated ripple of fear. Scampering on, she inspected every possible route through the complex. Particularly intriguing were several gloomy walkways that seemed to corkscrew downwards through the heart of the mountain.

Eventually, still wandering about the steep, winding steps, she entered the main sanctum. There she discovered eleven prisoners, one or two more dead than alive. Jinghirza drew her attention. She looked filthy and emaciated but otherwise well. Her resilience emanated from every pore. She was sturdy and brave, a born survivor. Timu too had some fight left in him. Hearing the scrape of steely claws on the stone floor, Aaliya squeezed into a crevice, willing herself to remain unseen and undiscovered.

'I am restless,' the Darkwing said, peering at Jinghirza. 'You are the only creature in this shivering, hostile world who entertains me. I am looking forward to your next trial.'

Jinghirza made her move. 'I have an idea.'

'*You* do!'

'My ordeals have always occurred in conditions of your choosing,' she said, doing her best to suppress her eagerness for the plan. 'I tire of your games.'

The Darkwing was intrigued. 'What do you have in mind?'

'Let me fight the Hotec-Ra,' Jinghirza demanded. 'His people oppress mine. They use us to fight their wars. He made an innocent boy suffer in one of your foul experiments. Is it too much to ask, a fight to the death with a mortal enemy?'

'I will tear you to shreds, girl,' Timu snarled. 'Don't insult me, master Darkwing. I, a senior priest of the Hotec-Ra, pitted against a mere girl? I won't do it.'

The Darkwing looked interested – more than interested, fascinated. 'This Khut maiden is a resourceful individual, Timu. You may have your work cut out.'

'She is beneath my contempt,' Timu said. 'I would

skewer her with the point of my sword. It would not even merit the title *combat*.'

The exchange sounded heartfelt enough. Yet something didn't ring true. Something aroused Aaliya's instincts. She watched Jinghirza's face, then Timu's. There wasn't a shred of doubt in her mind. It was all an act. But to what purpose? Aaliya thought of her companions waiting for news. But surely this took priority. Something was happening here. A spark was about to ignite a flame. She was going to stay.

2

Rishal stirred; his healing thigh wound made him restless and easily woken. Kulmat held his breath for a moment. Ever since the campaign in the Dragon Mountains, they had shared a tent, separated by a thin partition, in case Rishal needed attention during the night. Kulmat thought it was more likely to have something to do with his moment of resistance on the battlefield. He was standing on a splintering glass floor. Feeling vulnerable and exposed, he willed Rishal to slip back into a deep sleep.

After a few moments, he could hear the regular murmur of his master's breathing. Reassured that he was fast asleep, Kulmat slipped out of the tent. In the distance he saw the lights of the rebel camp. For the last few days, as both armies moved at an even pace, each acutely aware of the presence of the other, there had only been a few miles between them, the Sol-ket stalking their slave enemy ever closer to Dullah.

Kulmat stared at the inviting lights. How quickly their numbers had grown. They had been swollen tenfold by the outcome of the bitter struggle in the Dragon Mountains.

There would be no more prevarication. He had to warn them of the awesome weapon Rishal was developing.

Glancing back at the tent, Kulmat looked for the path he had seen earlier. He cursed inwardly that everything looked so different at night, especially now that there was a considerable dusting of snow. He paced up and down for a few moments, wincing at the crunch of his boots on the thickening white layer. Finally, he was able to make out the track. He was about to set off along it towards the Helat lines when he saw Rishal's shadow, silhouetted against the side of the tent by the lamp that hung from the roof. Fearing discovery, he knew he had to do something. Run now and Rishal would hear him. He planted his feet and waited for the general to appear.

'Kulmat, what are you doing?'

'I'm relieving myself, Rishal-Ra.'

Rishal listened for a moment before returning to bed. Resigned to serving him for another day, Kulmat walked back to the tent. Before retiring, he made Gardep a promise. *Tomorrow, my brother, I will be with you. Together, we will fight to bring down this evil dynasty.*

3

Far across the plain, Gardep was sitting with Oled and Atrakon.

'It seems strange to see you two breaking bread together,' Gardep said.

Atrakon shrugged. 'Oled didn't want to think ill of his friend. I can understand that.'

'There is a friend who is always in my thoughts,' Gardep said. 'In a few days, Kulmat and I could meet on the field of battle.'

'If he is a true friend, this is the time to turn his face from the Sol-ket,' Atrakon said.

'I think he wants to,' Gardep said.

He told them about Kulmat starting to draw his sword against Rishal.

'There is a change in the wind,' Oled said. 'The people don't fear the Sol-ket as they once did. Did any of us foresee Adrius and his Vassyrians coming over to us?'

'No,' Gardep said. 'Nobody did. But don't underestimate our foe.'

He pointed to the sea of lights far off in the night.

'Most of those men have been trained since their eighth year,' he said. 'They are disciplined and brave. Their only objective is to kill and eliminate any threat to the Empire.'

'It sounds as if you still admire them,' Oled said.

'I hate the power they serve,' Gardep said. 'That doesn't stop me respecting the individual fighters and their iron will. Rishal taught me everything I know.'

'Rishal is not your knight,' Oled said. 'You are no longer his squire. Don't think of yourself even as a former Sol-ket. Those days are long gone. You're a free man now, Gardep. Forget your past. Forget Rishal.'

'I wish it were that easy,' Gardep said.

'Very well,' Atrakon said. 'Remember what he taught you. But drive any affection you have left from your heart. Did you not learn from Shamana? To make a new world, you must make yourself anew.'

'As you have?' Oled asked.

'Yes Oled, as I have.'

Murima joined them. 'Are you unable to sleep, too?'

The three men nodded.

'Within days we will fight a battle that could decide our future,' Gardep said. 'So long as Cusha succeeds.'

Murima nodded. 'I think of her all the time.' She

watched the many figures, as sleepless as they, crouched around their campfires. 'It is a night for fears. Everywhere I walk among the people, they are whispering, wondering if we can overcome the Sol-ket, wondering if the Holy Children can prevail against the demon lord.'

'What do you say, Murima?' Oled asked.

Murima watched the campfires winking in the night. 'You may as well ask where the wind is born. I am proud that we have thrown off our oppressors' shackles. But if we were to be defeated again . . .'

'We will not be defeated,' Oled said fiercely. 'I would fight their entire army by myself, if I could avenge my mother's death. I would pursue this Murak into the depths of the House of the Dead. Let the dogs throw every man they have against us. We will overcome them all.'

4

Jinghirza struck the first blow. Timu stepped back, using the mannered, practised moves of the Hotec-Ra. He parried her axe with his sword, then stepped forward and thrust at the Khut maiden, making her skip back. Aaliya watched from her corner, taking in every attack and defence. There was something missing. There was no passion in their exchange, no hatred. Aaliya shot a look in the Darkwing's direction, wondering what he made of it. Surely he must notice that everything was just that tiny bit too slow, too predictable?

'I see no hatred,' the Darkwing yawned, confirming Aaliya's fears. 'Where is your fire, Jinghirza? I thought you wanted to avenge your oppressed people against this infernal priest.'

Jinghirza's eye caught Timu's. Yes, Aaliya thought,

recognising the look, you've got to make it more convincing. The thrusts, the feints, the parrying and slashing grew fiercer, more reckless. Their movements around the room became more rapid and dangerous. This pleased the Darkwing.

'That's more like it. This is a fight to the death, remember.'

He didn't appear to notice that the two fighters were edging ever closer to him, moving within striking distance of their tormentor. Aaliya craned forward. Was this it? Was this their plan, to strike at the monster as they fought? Jinghirza swung her axe at Timu. For once, her judgement failed her. The fabric tore and a small packet fell, unseen by the demon lord, a few paces from where Aaliya had concealed herself. Jinghirza saw the look of panic in Timu's eyes as he realised what had happened. Crashing the stock of the axe into his chest, she sent him sprawling to the floor in the desperate hope that he could recover the packet. To her horror, the Darkwing seized Timu and threw him back into the fray.

'Is this the girl you would cut to shreds, priest?' he chuckled.

Aaliya read the fighters' expressions and knew what they were going to do next. She felt indecision throbbing inside her. Should she join them and risk three deaths or should she bide her time? It was an agonising choice. In the end, she contented herself with dragging the package into a corner with her paws. It seemed important. She sniffed at it. Now she understood why. Her animal senses told her the sulphurous substance was combustible, a thing of fire.

Finally, having lost their weapon, the fighters moved against the demon lord. With a cry of hatred, Jinghirza turned her axe on the Darkwing. He fended off the blow easily, hurling her across the chamber. Timu attacked next. Lacking the same fondness for the priest that he had for the girl, the Darkwing drove his claws through Timu's heart in a single lethal thrust. Timu died with a startled look in his eyes, his life fading in an instant. Having finished with the priest, the Darkwing approached Jinghirza.

'You disappoint me,' he hissed. 'I expected something better than this. I allowed you to take the Holy Child's place in my heart. But the entertainment is over. You bore me now.'

Screaming, Jinghirza flung herself at him. But the Darkwing was too powerful. He raked a single claw across her forearm, causing a fiery pain to blaze through it. Jinghirza dropped the axe.

'I remember the fear in your eyes when I made you jump the mountain peaks,' he said. 'How I enjoyed it. Yes, that's where you will meet your end.'

He dragged Jinghirza away. A tiny mouse followed.

5

Rishal had a visitor. Kulmat saw Murak approaching and felt the first stirrings of unease.

'Well,' Rishal demanded, seeing Murak striding towards him, 'have you found a solution to our problem?'

'I have, Rishal-Ra. Would you like to see it? I have prepared a demonstration.'

Rishal grabbed his crutches, then hesitated and put them aside. Though he was limping, he could keep up with Murak. 'Show me.'

Murak took the knight and his squire to a secluded area, about a quarter of a mile from the camp. There, Murak's

Hotec-Ra had set up three lines of dummies. The straw figures had been made to represent an enemy regiment. In order to simulate human flesh, the dummies had been smeared with animal fat. Two hundred metres away, there was a catapult. Murak produced an object for the general to inspect. There were two pieces of metal, each like a soldier's helmet with a broad, circular brim. The brims clipped together. Holes were drilled through them. Rishal turned the sections of the container over in his hands.

'How does it work?' he asked.

'You fill the pan with the Fire Dust,' Murak explained. 'Next, you clip the brims together, taking care not to spark an explosion. We are trying to design special gloves to prevent the dust coming into contact with the operators' skin. Waxed paper seems to work best, like the first, small packets we made to carry the material. Once there is a good seal, you drive metal pegs through the holes. It can now be thrown by catapult without spilling the dust.'

'This is good, Murak,' Rishal said approvingly. 'Don't you think so, Kulmat?'

'Yes, Rishal-Ra,' Kulmat said. 'It's ingenious.'

'When the projectile hits the ground,' Murak continued, warming to his task, 'the impact drives the pegs from the holes. As a result, the two sections come apart and the Fire Dust spills over the enemy. Are you ready for the demonstration?'

Rishal's features were taut with excitement. 'Yes.'

Murak signalled to the catapult operators. They wound back the lever controlling the tension. Then, releasing the trigger, they sent a single projectile hurtling towards the dummies. They were in three lines of twenty-five each. When the projectile hit the ground in front of them, all seventy-five went up in flames.

'Well,' Murak said, 'what do you think?'

'Magnificent!' Rishal exclaimed. 'Truly magnificent. Within days, we will destroy the enemy.'

'The Helati have no chance,' Kulmat murmured.

Rishal clapped him on the back. 'You could be right, Kulmat. I can't wait to see the weapon in action.'

6

Aaliya followed the Darkwing, wondering what to do. She knew he was armed with an almost impenetrable carapace. He seemed even more powerful than the creature who had haunted the Black Tower. Should she attack now or wait for some unforeseen opportunity? She would have no help from Jinghirza. The girl was weak from loss of blood. Every few steps she would sag to the floor, only to be hauled back to her feet. The creature sniffed at Jinghirza for a moment. Seeing his hungry interest in the Khut maiden, Aaliya quietly transformed back to human form. Slipping her bow from her back, she strung it and eased an arrow from her quiver.

The Darkwing's tongue flickered over Jinghirza's face, his half-human, half-reptilian eyes seeming to savour the taste of her flesh. He lapped briefly at her fresh blood but seemed disappointed. Maybe she was too weak from lack of food to satisfy his appetite. Maybe she was the wrong prey. Jinghirza continued to struggle fitfully, but weakly. The Darkwing lifted her into the air. Then, almost casually, he tossed Jinghirza down the mountainside to die.

7

Kulmat was determined not to botch his second attempt at escape. Too much rested on the news he could bring to the Army of the Free. Even when they reached Dullah, they must not engage the Sol-ket. Armed with the incendiary weapon, the Imperial Army would be invincible. Giving a last furtive look round, Kulmat slipped out of the tent and started to run. This time there was no hesitation. He raced through the ankle-deep snow, keeping his eyes on the flickering lights of the Army of the Free. His face glowed. I should have done this long ago, he told himself. His faith in the Empire and holy Ra had been draining away from him ever since the Battle of Jinghara Plain. He should have gone with Gardep then. The memory of what he had been made to do to the fifty helpless prisoners haunted him. But soon he and Gardep would be together again, brothers in arms against the monstrous tyranny that had made him a cold-blooded killer.

Murak's weapon was the last straw. Armed with my information, Kulmat thought, we will turn the tables on the Imperial Army. His mind filled with thoughts of the future. I will see Gardep married to Cusha. Then I will find a wife of my own. We will raise a family somewhere by the sea, a little fishing village near Parcep maybe. But the usual tendrils of darkness soon coiled around the wonderful images. Was any of this really possible? It could only happen under certain conditions. *If* the Army of the Free vanquished Rishal's disciplined and ruthless force. *If* Cusha destroyed the foul demon in the northern mountains. Kulmat ran on, willing both dreams to come true.

But he never reached the rebel camp. Even as he stumbled through a waist-high drift, he heard the jangle of harness. Turning, he saw five horsemen. They were Rishal's own handpicked bodyguard. Kulmat felt a blinding pain shoot through his temple. Then all was darkness.

8

On the forty-fourth day of Buradish, a familiar, skeletal figure tramped into view.

'Jackal!' Vishtar shouted.

'I have news,' the night-strider announced.

'Of Aaliya?'

'Yes.'

'She's not dead?' Vishtar cried.

Jackal shook his head. 'Far from it. She is at Bhadra Zhoi. She is in the company of a Khut maiden. My comrades have just alerted me to the fact. I will point the way.'

'Will you come with us?' Vishtar asked.

Jackal shook his head. 'There is much for me to do. But I will not be far.'

The pair reached Bhadra Zhoi as a troubled, grey twilight gathered over the settlement. The snow was banked up to the eaves. Entry into the mean, wooden houses was only possible through the smoke hatches in the roof. In such a small village, it didn't take long to discover Aaliya and Jinghirza. Both were bruised and Jinghirza had her arm bandaged. Other than that, they were well.

'Why were you so long?' Cusha asked. 'How did you escape?'

Aaliya explained how she had discovered Jinghirza and Timu and the plot they had hatched.

'Do you think you could have trusted Timu?' Vishtar asked. 'He was a senior Hotec-Ra.'

Jinghirza shrugged. 'It was an alliance born out of

necessity. Once we had destroyed the Darkwing, we would have been enemies again. Even so, I regret his death.'

'But how did you escape?'

Jinghirza told the tale. 'I was barely conscious. I knew I was falling. As I tumbled through the air, I could feel myself floating away. I think it was dead. I'm not sure I thought about what was going to happen to me. I was in a kind of dream state. Then I saw a bird.' She glanced at Aaliya. 'It was a condor. I felt its talons grip my dress. It slowed my fall, but it could not halt it. Down and down we tumbled, slowing all the time. I wondered what was happening to me. I thought it might even be a predator, about to devour me. We started to spin. I could feel the bird straining to hold me. The wind was buffeting us. Then, as I slowly came to, I could see the snow rushing towards me. It was as if huge fists were pounding me. I rolled over and over, sensing the condor's feathers against my face. We seemed tangled, almost a single creature. The next thing I knew, I was lying beside a woman I had never seen before.'

She gave Aaliya a grateful look. 'I have heard many stories of you shape-shifters. I was raised on them. I always believed you were like the demons, unnatural. Now I know different.'

'You must tell us what you saw at Nandraghiri,' Vishtar said.

Cusha squeezed his hand. 'It will do tomorrow.'

Vishtar started to protest but Cusha shook her head. She said just one word. 'Tomorrow.'

9

'Bring him to me,' Rishal ordered.

He was speaking of Kulmat. Two squires had served him since his return from Inbacus, the scene of his greatest triumphs. Both had committed the basest treachery. Truly, he was cursed among men. Where did this ingratitude come from? Kulmat was brought into the commander's tent in chains. He had already suffered a beating. His face was swollen and his right eye was almost closed.

'Leave us.'

The Sol-ket who had delivered Kulmat exchanged glances.

'What, are you worried about me?' Rishal laughed. 'I may be recovering from a flesh wound but I can handle Kulmat. He has been beaten within an inch of his life and he is in chains. What more reassurance do you think I need?'

The soldiers left.

'Why?' Rishal asked. 'Why do you betray me? You had everything. Why throw your life away? What is it about these wretched Helati that you find so attractive?'

Kulmat remained stubbornly silent. He stood before his knight, having to draw on all his reserves of strength to remain upright; such was the punishment the Sol-ket had inflicted.

'Well, speak up, Kulmat. You have nothing to lose. Tomorrow is the last time you will see the sun. Nothing can alter that. Tell me the truth. It will be your last act in this world.'

It was some time before Kulmat could put his thoughts into words. When he did, they were simple.

'It is about . . . brotherhood.'

'Brotherhood!' Rishal scoffed. 'Do you put this brotherhood of yours before the Sol-ket code? Do you raise your great friend Gardep above your Emperor and your god? He is a mortal man. He could not even best me in arms. Why would you treasure his friendship above all things?'

Kulmat shook his head. 'You do not understand, Rishal-Ra.' His voice fell to a whisper. 'I hardly understand it myself.'

Rishal couldn't disguise his contempt. 'Go on. Let's hear it all. I want every heretic idea in that confused head of yours.'

'It is not just that Gardep is a brother to me,' Kulmat said uncertainly. 'There is a feeling among these slaves . . .'

'You're beginning to sound like one of them,' Rishal sneered, 'with their Book of Scales and their thoughts of heaven on Earth. Maybe you've been reading the forbidden texts of Udmanesh.'

'Maybe I do wish to be like them,' Kulmat retorted. 'Maybe I am not that different from Gardep. Maybe I want to live in a better world than this murderous chaos.'

'I would laugh if you were not such a sorry spectacle,' Rishal said. 'Just look at you, for Ra's sake. You are beaten and bloodied. Your bones ache. You can hardly see. This is where your soft heart and your even softer head have brought you. Tomorrow, we will break you on the sun wheel. It will be an example to the slaves and to any future renegades in the Imperial Army.'

Kulmat flinched at the thought of the sun wheel. It was one of the most terrible punishments man could inflict. He would be beaten until his bones broke. Then, kept from losing consciousness by the Hotec-Ra's potions, he would be bound to a great sun wheel and left to the buzzards and the vultures. He had seen men linger for days before they died.

'Beg for mercy,' Rishal said. 'Renounce Gardep and these ideas of brotherhood and I will spare you the agony of the wheel. I will give you a quick end.'

Kulmat shook his head. 'I am resigned to my punishment, Rishal-Ra. I will not beg.'

'Guards,' Rishal shouted.

'I have one question for you, master,' Kulmat said. 'Why are you afraid?'

'Afraid? Are you mad?'

'The slaves terrify you,' Kulmat said. 'Deny it. You see them in every household and every workshop, digging every canal and road, hoeing and seeding every field. They are the foundation on which Sol-ket power stands. I can see it in your eyes. You think they might do it, don't you? You think they might just topple an Empire.'

Rishal turned his back. 'Take him away,' he said. 'You know what to do.'

10

'Gardep!'

It was Harad's voice. Since before daybreak, he had been sitting at the edge of the camp, maintaining a lonely vigil, wondering where Cusha was now. Harad missed her terribly. Though they were not brother and sister by birth, their bond was every bit as close. In the greyish light of a sickly dawn, he saw the Sol-ket erecting a strange platform in the distance. They had ridden forward from their lines to carry out their gruesome work. It was some moments before he could work out what it was. When he did, he went running for the boy-general.

'Gardep, come quickly.'

Gardep reached Harad's side and cried out in anguish.

'Kulmat! What have they done to you?'

Commander Rishal had carried out his threat. His squire was displayed across a steel frame hoisted high above the Sol-ket lines. The rising sun showed the full horror of the punishment. A few hundred yards away, Kulmat was lying at an awkward angle, his body twisted unnaturally by the breaking of his bones.

'Is he alive?' Qintu asked, appalled by the sight.

'Oh yes,' Gardep said, 'they will have made sure of that. He's alive. That is the whole point of the punishment. They want you to experience a living death. This is the way of the Sol-ket, as it is with the Hotec-Ra. They wish to brand great dread into the minds of the living. They show you what it means to provoke their vengeance. That is how they maintain their rule.'

He was interrupted by Rishal's voice. 'Do you hear me, Gardep na-Vassyrian?'

Gardep shouted his reply. 'I hear you, ax-Sol. You are cursed among men. For this, I will find you on the battle field and I will kill you.'

Rishal gave a forced laugh. 'Do your worst, *boy*. You'll need to make a better job of it this time.'

With that, the Sol-ket rode the few miles back to their lines, leaving a small company to prevent the Helati attempting a rescue.

Oled arrived. 'Don't let him provoke you, Gardep.'

'Provoke me!' Gardep cried. 'Oled, this is my oldest friend. They have broken him on the wheel. How would you have me feel?'

'I would have you *think*,' Oled said, restraining his friend. 'You are our general. You will one day rule our people. You must have the interests of the people at heart. Begin by sparing Kulmat this anguish.'

'What are you asking?'

'Only what Kulmat will be asking himself. End his suffering.'

'Do you mean that I should kill him?'

'He will not recover from these injuries,' Oled said. 'It is the only thing to do.'

'I can't,' Gardep said. 'We were raised together. We learned our lessons together. We stole together. We even took beatings together.'

He took a scrap of bloodied bandage from his tunic. A tear spilled down his cheek.

'Oled, do you realise what you're saying?' Gardep thought for a long time. 'Can you take animal form and speak to Kulmat?'

Oled nodded. 'I managed a war elephant. A bird should be little problem.'

He chose the form of a songbird, tiny enough to escape the notice of the Sol-ket. Soon he was fluttering around Kulmat. The boy's face was caked with blood, his lips blistered, his eyes so swollen he could barely see.

'Kulmat.'

'Who's there?' Kulmat asked, trying to see through the blood and the darkness.

'Gardep sent me,' Oled said. 'He wants to know your wishes.'

Kulmat rocked his head. 'The pain.'

'Find your voice,' Oled said, his heart torn to see such suffering.

At long last, Kulmat summoned the strength, though it wracked his body with pain. 'Gar-dep!' His voice echoed across the snowy plain.

Gardep wept to hear it. 'I hear you, my brother.'

'End it,' Kulmat cried. 'End this agony.'

'Kulmat, how can I? You ask too much.'

But Kulmat's strength came back even more intensely.

'My body is broken. Don't let them break my spirit too. You have it in your power to release me. Do it.' Kulmat turned to the bird that was Oled. 'I have one last message. Listen carefully. It may save many lives.'

Once Kulmat had finished his story, Oled thanked him and returned to the Army of the Free.

'End it, Gardep,' the Tanjur said. 'For pity's sake, you must spare him this terrible agony.'

Gardep nodded grimly. 'I don't know if I have the strength.'

'It is a just act,' Oled said. 'The Four Winds will guide your arm.'

Gardep duly strung his bow and tested the tension. Then he nocked an arrow and bent the bow, looking along the flight of the arrow. Though tears were blurring his vision, he could see Kulmat's tormented form on the wheel.

'You are my brother, Kulmat,' he murmured as he drew the taut string to his eye. 'So you will be for all time.'

Then he let loose the string and watched the arrow on its way. It struck its target and the life went out of Kulmat. His suffering was over.

11

The Army of the Free discussed the threat posed by the Hotec-Ra's new weapon.

'A single projectile,' Gardep said, 'capable of killing seventy-five warriors. It is beyond belief.'

'It is worse than that,' Oled said. 'It was Kulmat's opinion that a single device could kill double that, especially in the press of battle.'

'You have flown over the Sol-ket lines,' Atrakon said. 'How many catapults did you see?'

The answer was disturbing. 'There were at least twenty-five,' Oled said.

'And how many of these projectiles to each catapult?'

'They were covered by tarpaulins,' Oled answered. 'I would guess at a score.'

The eyes of the war council were on him. The carnage would be unimaginable.

'This weapon could destroy an entire army without a sword being drawn,' Murima said.

'This is not warfare,' Gardep said. 'It is annihilation. We would be like animals led to the slaughter.'

Atrakon crashed his fist down on the table. 'We can't sit here and wait for them to burn us alive,' he said. 'We must destroy their artillery.'

'Do you have an idea?' Adrius demanded.

Atrakon nodded.

'How many warriors do you need?' Gardep asked. 'Fifty? One hundred?'

Atrakon shook his head.

'Then how many?'

Atrakon smiled. 'Just two.'

12

In the early hours of a frosty morning, a mongoose scampered across the snow. Oled concealed himself behind the catapults and waited, watching the guards struggling to stay awake. He imagined Atrakon, using his assassin's skills, moving through the encampment like a black ghost. For the plan to work, the Selessian would have to pick his way undetected through half the enemy camp. If there was a man who could do it, it was Atrakon.

'May the Four Winds protect you.'

His words came out as a tiny squeak. Nobody heard him. Satisfied that the guards were paying no attention to the small animal, Oled scurried over to the first pile of projectiles. Gripping the pegs with his paws, he eased them out. Having loosened two, he moved on. In this way, after three hours' painstaking labour, he had opened two or three projectiles in each heap. Finally, as he crouched, watching the guards, he saw one of them crumple to the ground. Within two minutes, three more had fallen to the unseen killer who had emerged from the darkness.

'You're good at your trade,' Oled observed.

'I am not proud of the fact,' Atrakon whispered. 'Let's get this done.'

Oled transformed and the two men gingerly ran trails of the red powder from pile to pile. Then, shrinking back into the gloom, Atrakon dipped the tip of an arrow into a sample of the Fire Dust.

'Do you think it is everything Kulmat said?' he asked.

Oled smiled. 'We are about to find out.'

Atrakon drew his bow and shot his arrow. The moment the arrowhead hit the canisters, a sheet of fire fifty metres tall exploded through the night, firing the catapults, their attendants and ten metres of earth to either side of the artillery positions. Its heat seared the faces of the two men, scorching their eyebrows.

'By the Almighty!' Atrakon gasped, watching the lurid flames licking the night sky.

'Don't just stand there gaping,' Oled said. 'They will be after us any moment.'

He transformed into a Selessian thoroughbred. 'We've got to go.'

Atrakon leapt into the saddle. In the confusion of the continuing explosions, the two men escaped. So ended the forty-fifth day of Buradish.

13

At dawn, Rishal and Murak inspected the damage to the artillery.

'A thousand men dead, all our catapults destroyed, virtually the entire stock of Fire Dust wasted,' Rishal groaned. 'How did this happen?'

'Do you have the names of the men who were attending Kulmat when he died?' Murak asked.

'I can find out,' Rishal said.

Half an hour later five anxious Sol-ket were standing before the commander and the lord-priest of the Hotec-Ra.

'Did anything unusual happen before Kulmat died?' Murak asked.

'We broke his bones,' one of the guards said.

'Are you trying to be funny?' Murak demanded angrily.

'No, Your Holiness.'

'I will repeat the question: was there anything unusual?'

'He cried out with great force,' another guard said. 'We were shocked. Where did he get the strength from?'

'Did he mention the Fire Dust?' Rishal asked.

All five shook their heads.

'No, Rishal-Ra.'

'So how did the rebels know of its existence?'

Murak thought for a few moments. 'Are you sure there was nothing else? Think, even the tiniest detail may be important.'

One man's face lit with understanding.

'What is it?' Rishal cried.

'I didn't think it was important at the time,' the guard said, 'but there was a tiny bird fluttering around him. He seemed to be talking to it. We were laughing at him, saying he had gone mad.'

Murak sighed. 'The She-wolf has had the last laugh on us. This is her son, Oled's work. Perhaps, Rishal, he is not quite the gullible fool I took him to be. It seems the mother's mantle has passed to the son.'

'He must suffer for what he has done,' Rishal said, looking at the plumes of smoke still hovering over the camp.

'Oh, he will,' Murak said. 'I will make sure of that.'

CHAPTER 11

Cat and Mouse

I

'The monster knows that you're coming,' Jinghirza said.

'I'm aware of that,' Cusha answered. 'I think he's looking forward to it.'

'When he watched me,' Jinghirza said, 'he saw you. In you he feels the life he has lost.'

Cusha said nothing.

'What are you thinking?' Jinghirza said, seeing the hooded expression in Cusha's face.

Their eyes met.

'No, tell me I'm wrong,' Jinghirza cried. 'You can't believe he is worth saving.'

'All the creatures of the Earth are worth saving,' Cusha said. 'So it is written in the Book of Scales. I have seen into his soul. I know his story. He loved a woman. He was loved in return.'

'I have heard this story,' Jinghirza said, wondering what bearing it could have.

'Then you know,' Cusha said. 'Once he was Sabray. He fought Lord Muzal, his father. Is there no way you can admit the possibility that there is something of the boy he was, some trace of goodness and humanity?'

'In all my days of captivity,' Jinghirza retorted, frustrated by Cusha's words, 'I was denied food. I was made to undergo terrifying ordeals. I was frightened and lonely and he mocked me in my misery.' Her eyes flashed with disbelief that Cusha could expect humanity from the Darkwing. 'You faced him, Cusha. He would have killed you. How can you think that he is anything but evil?'

'I have seen an assassin redeemed,' Cusha said, remembering Atrakon, 'and he was a man dedicated to killing. Is this so very different?'

'Yes,' Jinghirza insisted, 'an assassin is a mortal man. The Darkwing is the accumulation of all the world's despair and pain. Oh, Cusha, how can you be so blind? He is death!'

'Maybe you should return to your people,' Cusha said, stung by Jinghirza's words. 'Your family will be waiting for you.'

Jinghirza shook her head. 'You don't get rid of me so easily. First I will see the monster dead, then I will return home. It is a question of honour.'

They heard boots crunch through the snow. It was Vishtar and Aaliya. They sensed the tension between Cusha and Jinghirza.

'Cusha thinks she can reach the demon,' Jinghirza said. 'She thinks she can find some human quality in him and make him change his mind.'

'Is it not worth trying?' Cusha asked.

Neither Vishtar nor Aaliya spoke.

'Well,' Cusha said, 'will you not answer me?' She was to discover that, where it concerned the Darkwing, she was in a minority of one.

'I saw the monster,' Aaliya said. 'He must be destroyed.'

'I know him better than any other living being,' Vishtar said. 'I was his captive for eight summers and eight winters. Can you imagine how many times I tried to appeal to him? There is no power in heaven or in hell that will heal the wounds he has suffered. The fog of madness drifts through his mind. His entire being is ablaze with hatred. Pity him, sister, and he will destroy you.'

Cusha turned her back. The conversation was at an end. Riding off in silence, the three companions and their Khut ally continued north.

2

'I think you were impressed by the Holy Children, Omar,' Mehmet said, 'the girl especially.'

'I never dreamed that I would meet somebody with such powers,' Omar said. 'You saw the shade of Leila Ebrahin with your own eyes. Cusha raised her from the remotest regions of the House of the Dead. How is such a thing possible?'

Mehmet shrugged. He was a practical man, not given to easy enthusiasm.

'Sometimes,' Omar said, answering his own question, 'once in several generations, there comes a special person who changes the world. I swear, this Cusha is one such person.'

'But can a child really overcome such evil?' Mehmet asked.

'She did once.'

Mehmet was not convinced. 'For all the efforts of these Holy Children, the monster still lives. The girl won a battle. She did not win the war. The world is in greater peril than ever. There was no victory, Omar.'

The Selessians plodded on through the swirling snow, many wondering how they had come so far from the desert. Finally, they saw the towers and turrets of Karangpur in the distance.

'The Sol-ket gave us a hostile reception the last time we were here,' Mehmet said with a scowl.

Omar smiled. 'I wonder if their hospitality has improved.'

'Not if they know what we did when the night-striders attacked their column,' Mehmet reminded him.

Omar saw a Sol-ket patrol in the distance. 'We need fresh horses,' he said. 'Let's test the water.'

'What if they've had news from the north?' Mehmet asked.

'Then we fight.'

This satisfied Mehmet. Omar rode towards the Sol-ket and hailed their officer. There was no hint of suspicion. That was a good sign.

'We were reassigned to Karangpur,' Omar said. 'Our business is done in the north. Is General Ghushan still commanding the garrison here?'

'You've been gone a long time,' the officer said. 'Ghushan-Ra is now commanding a third of the Grand Army. He is leading his forces to Dullah. Our troops are about to destroy the Helat rising.'

'Is that right?' Mehmet said, encouraged by the news. 'So what's happening to the garrison here at Karangpur in the meantime?'

'There isn't much of it left,' the officer said. 'Just a

couple of hundred cadets. We're throwing all our efforts against the rebel cockroaches.'

'Really?' Omar said. He winked at Mehmet. They were going to get their fresh horses.

3

The Darkwing came after nightfall. Cusha was lying awake, going over her disagreement with Jinghirza, when she noticed Aaliya stiffen.

'What is it?' she whispered.

Aaliya pressed a finger to her lips and nodded at the wall of the tent. In the dying firelight a familiar silhouette had appeared: the unfurled wings, the reptilian form. Aaliya drew her bow and shot at the demon lord through the canvas. The arrow pinged off his carapace. A split-second after, his sinister head exploded through the material. Eyes blazed, fangs glistened, razor-sharp claws slashed.

'Raise the alarm!' Aaliya yelled, fending him off with her sword and axe.

While she struggled with the inhuman assailant, Cusha scrambled through the tent flap to summon Vishtar and Jinghirza.

'Help,' she screamed. 'We're under attack!'

Aaliya was barely holding the monstrous invader at bay. Then, as quickly as he had appeared out of the night, he shrank back into it. Vishtar and Jinghirza joined the panting Aaliya.

'I'm surprised we put him to flight so easily,' she said.

The words alerted Vishtar to a terrifying possibility. 'Where's Cusha?' he demanded.

'I don't know,' Aaliya said. 'She went to raise the alarm. I thought she'd be with you.'

Vishtar caught her eye.

'The Darkwing!' they said in unison.

They raced outside. There, just a few metres away, they saw the demon lord. He had his claws hooked through Cusha's cloak. In spite of her desperate struggles, he had succeeded in lifting her a couple of metres off the ground.

'Get away from her!' Vishtar shouted, hurling his sword at the demon lord.

'Ah,' the Darkwing said, 'there you are, Vishtar, the cup from which I drank all those years. What makes you hurry to face me, Vishtar? Are you so eager for me to feed on you again?'

Seeing Aaliya preparing fire arrows, the Darkwing rose rapidly into the sky. Cusha was trapped in his razor-sharp talons. She was kicking and screaming, her legs pedalling frantically in an attempt to break loose. The creature gave her a gloating look. But the eyes that met his were as dark as his own.

'Look into your past, demon,' Cusha cried, fixing him with a stare.

For a moment the shade of Princess Kewara of Banshu hovered round her features.

Mesmerised by the long-lost voice, the Darkwing flew lower. Encouraged, Cusha called on Kewara.

'Rise, sister,' she cried. 'Look into this creature's heart. Find Sabray the man.'

But before the ghost of Kewara could take form, the Darkwing dashed Cusha's hopes. 'You will not fool me with your party tricks,' he snarled. 'I know how you turned Atrakon's head. The Selessian is a sentimental fool. You will find me infinitely more difficult to hoodwink, Holy Child.'

He glanced at Jinghirza looking up from the earth below. 'I fed on her, you know,' he said. 'In your absence,

I made her my handmaiden, but she was almost tasteless. You're the one who will nourish me, Holy Child.'

At that moment, a sigh of dismay left Cusha's lips only to be followed, an instant later, by an agonised shriek from her abductor. With his attention held by Cusha, the demon lord had allowed himself to drift into range of Aaliya's fire arrows. Two tore through his wings. When a third hissed into his side, the monster released Cusha and started tearing the arrows from his flesh. A leaping tiger broke Cusha's fall. She fell with Aaliya into a snowdrift.

'You did well,' Aaliya said.

Cusha grinned. 'You did better.'

'I will see you all again soon,' the Darkwing said, snapping the final arrow in two. 'I will remember the pain you have just caused me. Believe me, it will be repaid in full. I will have you watch the black dawn of a new world, lightless and without the presence of mankind to sour the air. You should know, I have taken new captives. I now have fourteen, one for every day left of the sun's life. I will keep them alive until the day of my final victory. Then I will sacrifice them to celebrate the onset of eternal night. Remember me in your dreams . . . or your nightmares.'

With that, he was gone.

Jinghirza turned to a still-shaken Cusha. 'Do you still think you can find some conscience in this monster?'

Cusha did not evade the question. 'I will still try,' she said.

4

Mehmet found Omar in the Sol-ket stables, staring at the empty stalls as if each one held a memory.

'The men are ready,' he said.

'The Sons of Ra wouldn't let me stable my horse here,' Omar said. 'Do you remember?'

'I remember.'

'What did you do with the garrison?' Omar asked.

'The intelligent ones are locked in the dungeons with a two-week supply of food,' Mehmet told him. 'The stupid ones are dead.'

'You know your trade, Mehmet,' Omar said. 'You're a fine soldier.'

'When we get to Dullah, young master,' Mehmet replied, 'I'll show you what soldiering is.'

Omar strode out to review his warriors. They had eaten well, bathed and rested. They had fresh horses and supplies to last them on the journey. They were in high spirits.

'We ride on Dullah,' Omar shouted.

The Selessians roared their battle cries.

'By the time we get there,' Mehmet said, 'there had better be someone left to fight.'

Omar laughed. 'Who would deny a band of brothers such as this?' he said. 'You'll have your battle, Mehmet.' As he spurred his horse forward, he shouted, 'Men of Selessia, we have a hard ride ahead of us and a great battle at the end of it. Are you ready?' He listened to the cheers of his men. 'I never doubted it,' he said. 'On to Dullah!'

5

Buoyed by the success of the raid on the Sol-ket artillery, the Army of the Free were approaching Dullah. For days the pursuing Imperial Army seemed to have been preparing itself for imminent attack.

'They aren't chasing us at the same pace,' Nikesh reported.

'That's because we destroyed Rishal's fire weapon,' Gardep told the war council. 'I know the way the man thinks. If he still possessed it, he wouldn't have waited until we reached the sacred ground of Dullah. He would have exterminated us earlier. Now he will bide his time. He covets the symbolism a second battle of Dullah will have. He sees the coming conflict as a decisive moment. An Imperial victory would crush the spirit of rebellion for generations, maybe for ever.'

'We will arrive first,' Oled said. 'That will give us the high ground. We will have that advantage, at least.'

'It is an advantage,' Atrakon said. 'It will not be decisive.'

'Then what will?' Adrius asked, worried by the comment.

'The determination of the combatants,' Atrakon answered. 'Which of the two armies wants victory most. In the end, it always comes down to that.'

'Then we are bound to win,' Gardep said. 'Just rage fills our hearts. The Sol-ket cheat and deceive. They slaughter innocents. Our cause is righteous. We must sweep them from the field.'

He leaned on his battle-axe. 'There will be no mercy,' he said. 'I spoke of reconciliation once. I even befriended one of them, the murderer Murak. I was gullible, a soft-hearted fool. My actions led directly to my mother's death. I'm finished with foolish notions like forgiveness. It is time to break the enemy's power forever, even if it means slitting the throat of every Sol-ket in the land!'

His words were met with a deafening roar.

6

It was the morning after the war council in the rebel camp. The Helat masses would now be able to see Dullah on the horizon. Linem was gone and Timu lost, possibly also dead, far to the north. All the obstacles to Murak's power were falling one by one. On the morrow another, the slave rebellion, would go the way of the senior priests. Murak was now lord-priest of the Hotec-Ra and third man in the Empire behind Muzal and Rishal. With a resounding victory to point to, he would be within touching distance of the Sun Throne.

For all that, he felt hollow inside. Envisage the moment, he told himself. Picture yourself climbing the many steps of the Ziggurat of Ra. There you will stand before the exultant crowds of golden Rinaghar, master of the greatest Empire the world has seen. Still, the thought held no pleasure for him. It was not just that the fate of the world was in the balance. He was no longer sure that absolute power was what he wanted.

Instead, he kept thinking about the Army of the Free. Most of all, he thought about his friendship with Oled. Madness, Murak told himself. I betrayed Lonetread. I killed his mother. And what do I feel? Yes, I am jealous. He has the one thing I don't. There is comradeship among the enemy, whereas we Children of Ra cheat and deceive. We even turn our knives on one another in a desperate struggle for dominance. I am without friends or confidants. In my loneliness, I envy my foe. Utter madness.

'Murak.'

Hearing Rishal's voice, he looked up. 'What is it, Rishal-Ra?'

'I have just received a communication from General

Ghushan,' Rishal said. 'His troops have been held up by deep snowdrifts on the road from Karangpur. He will not arrive for two or three days. He suggests that we delay the attack until he is in place.'

Murak nodded. It suited his mood. 'That would make it the fiftieth day of Buradish.'

'Yes, a good round number,' Rishal said. 'A memorable date. If we are to write our names in the annals of glory, the fiftieth day of Buradish seems an auspicious date, don't you think?'

Murak smiled. 'Yes, Rishal-Ra.'

'That's settled then,' Rishal said. 'I will convene a meeting of the senior officers.'

Murak watched him go. The fiftieth day of Buradish, that's when it was all going to be decided. Strangely, only one word stuck in Murak's mind. It wasn't glory or victory. It was the word he had conjured earlier.

Madness.

7

'Look!'

Vishtar was pointing excitedly through the white veil that now cloaked the entire northland. At first, nobody could make out what he was showing them. Then Cusha saw, a hundred immobile forms etched against the blizzard. It was the Lost Souls.

'A hundred,' Vishtar said. 'Is this all you could muster?'

'It is all you need,' Jackal said. 'An army could not climb Sangra Peak. The rest of our doleful throng are needed elsewhere.'

'But where are the others?' Vishtar cried. 'Where are the thousands?'

'The servile masses need them more than you do,' Jackal said simply. 'On the morrow, the fiftieth day of Buradish, two colossal armies will collide and the future of mankind will be decided.' A thought lit his lidless, usually expressionless eyes. 'If, by the grace of the Four Winds, we succeed here at Nandraghiri and bequeath mankind a future.'

Jinghirza gazed at the foothills of Sangra Peak. 'At this time of year, the lower slopes are usually verdant and warm. How will we ever reach the top in just ten days?'

Jackal listened to the question in his usual emotionless fashion. 'There is a second route,' he said. He saw the light of recognition in Aaliya's face. 'You know something of this?'

'I have entered the demon's lair. I saw the passageways and wondered where they led.'

Jackal nodded. 'Come with me.'

He led them to a frozen waterfall. Immediately behind the jagged sheet of ice that now replaced the tumbling waters, there was a hidden cave mouth.

'Tens of thousands of steps climb within the mountain,' Jackal said. 'Sangra Peak is honeycombed with them. I have spent hours exploring the various passageways.'

'So that's why you had to leave us,' Vishtar said.

'It was one reason,' Jackal said. 'If we are to prevail, we need the element of surprise. You mortals will take this path. You will have a greater chance of success this way. Meanwhile, my people will follow the more arduous route up the mountain. The Darkwing will be expecting his enemy to approach from there.'

Jinghirza shielded her eyes and squinted against the dazzling whiteness. 'How can anyone, even the undead, climb such heights in these conditions?'

Jackal touched his chin with a bony finger.

'Many of us will fall,' he said, 'but some will get

through. All Commanders endure the suffering of those they lead.'

Vishtar heard something in Jackal's voice, a deep, abiding pain.

'You must lend us some of your clothing,' Jackal said. 'We will hide our true identities from the Darkwing for as long as possible. No matter what it costs to conduct the Holy Children to Nandraghiri, it must be done.'

Jinghirza shrugged off her outer robes. 'I would make any sacrifice to destroy the demon.'

'Cusha, Vishtar,' Jackal said, 'we need your cloaks most of all. This way we may distract the monster.'

8

Hearts slamming with the effort of climbing the snow-heaped slope that led to Dullah, the Army of the Free fell gratefully to their knees on the white-carpeted ground. Within the hour, they would set about clearing spaces for their tents and lighting fires. For the time being, they would gather their breath.

'So this is where our forefathers fell,' Nikesh said.

Dullah was a raised plateau, overlooking the rest of the plain.

'This is where they died,' Murima said. 'I was here, watching. My father led the final charge down that slope. You could see the enemy wavering.' A tear spilled down her cheek. 'That's when the Selessians came.'

She turned to point. 'Ehut Haraddin had his reserves lined up along that ridge,' she said. 'When the black-garbed horsemen streamed towards Shinar's fighters, we all cheered. That's when we saw the Selessians crash into the rearmost ranks of the Army of the Free. We had fed them. We had given them gold. It was the cruellest betrayal.' She fell on all fours and dug her fingers through the snow into the ochre dust of Dullah. 'I never thought the people would rise again after such a defeat. I did not dream that I would see this place again.'

It was Atrakon, bitterly aware of his Selessian identity, who helped her to her feet. 'It will be different this time,' he said. Then he made a joke of it. 'It will be colder, for a start.'

Gardep watched clouds of snow, like the crests of a tidal wave, approaching from the south-east. 'That's Rishal,' he said.

Oled saw similar patterns rising in the grey sky to the north-west. 'That is Ghushan, freshly arrived from Karangpur. Tomorrow we fight.' He looked around the others. 'It may be for the last time.'

Minute after long, silent minute the rebels stood or sat in the falling snow, letting it settle on them. Soon, the entire army resembled a mass of petrified, white statues. Then, without an order from anyone, the multitude stirred itself as one and started pitching their tents and preparing their battle lines.

9

Few slept that final night before the second Battle of Dullah. Tormented by the Darkwing winter, they huddled in their tents. But a deeper cold had them in its grip. Master and slave, Sol-ket and Helat, Hotec-Ra and Tanjur, the assembled thousands shivered at the icy touch of impending doom. Nobody, no matter how brave or carefree by nature, could keep the brush of mortal terror at bay. All felt the same foreboding. They might win the battle and still succumb to endless night.

Men like Atrakon and Adrius thought of their home-lands and wondered if they would ever see them again. Harad and Qintu feared that they might never reach man-hood. Nikesh trembled at the thought that he might give in to cowardice before his men. Bulu prayed that he had not been wrong to raise his people against the oppressor that day when the riders had fallen upon his village. Even Rishal stared bleak destiny in the face. What if, this time, Gardep were to turn the tables on him? What would happen to the Empire's golden cities? What would happen to his wife Serala and his daughter Julmira, the most pre-cious gemstones in the treasury of his heart?

Murima thought of her great father Shinar, so long in his grave, and her adopted daughter Cusha all those miles away, facing who knows what dangers. Cusha was at the forefront of Gardep's mind too. Even now, it felt as if he barely knew her. Their lips had barely touched to celebrate their love before events had torn them apart once more. The boy-general dwelt too on the fate of his dear friend Kulmat and he set his heart on vengeance. Vengeance, finally, was the emotion that stirred Oled to action. He saw Murak every waking moment of every day. He saw the assassin's arrow sink into his mother's throat and he beat his fists against his head in a vain attempt to drive the memory from his mind.

'Murak!' he bellowed into the snapping wind.

By some turn of chance or destiny, the Tanjur giant's cry was borne across the blizzard-swept plain. Murak heard its guilt-ridden accusation and bowed his head. Though he was afraid of no man, with every moment that passed, he dreaded Oled more. It wasn't that he feared his prowess in battle, though that was great. What he had begun to fear was having to explain a simple question. Why had he immersed himself so readily in the subterfuges of the Hotec-Ra? Why had he been so keen to stain his hands with blood?

Why?

CHAPTER 12

Dullah

I

Rishal was the first to send his men into battle.

'Today is the fiftieth day of Buradish,' he told them, his voice strong and confident. 'Let this date be seared into the mind of every living soul in the Empire. This is the day we finally, and for all time, crush the Helat threat.' He looked around his men. 'Some of your officers failed you in the Dragon Mountains. You will not find your general lacking in courage or leadership. The traitor Gardep is mine. None shall touch him but me. Warriors, we have unfinished business.'

His speech was greeted with deafening roars. Then, with pounding drums and braying horns, the Sol-ket quickened the pace.

'Javelins,' Rishal ordered.

The Sol-ket weighed their heavy spears, steadying themselves for the throw. Rishal had chosen spears above arrows. They were getting in close and the heavy steel spear points caused more carnage than any arrow head, as he knew from personal experience.

'Throw!' he ordered.

But Gardep had prepared for just this moment. His fighters broke their line briefly, then once the shafts had passed without inflicting serious damage, they closed the gaps once more.

'It is as I expected,' Gardep said. 'The battle will begin with an exchange of arrows and spears. Whoever has the strongest right arm will inflict the greater casualties. Then the auxiliaries will come at us. Rishal will use them to make us tire. But the real fighting will be done by the Sol-ket. When they charge, the earth will shake at their coming.'

'You still admire them, don't you?' Murima said. 'In spite of everything.'

'No,' Gardep answered, 'admiration is the wrong word for what I feel. I was raised to make war. I respect their prowess. It's different.'

For a while he did not speak again, only to speak a name. He felt the beat of another's heart, a mortal soul who had become his other half. Far from the beat of the drums and the shrill chorus of the horns, she was fighting a battle every bit as vital to the future of mankind.

'Cusha,' Gardep murmured.

Then, as he had predicted, the exchange of arrows started, a swarm of shafts that soon blackened the sky. The Army of the Free held the higher ground so their volleys told while those of the enemy fell short. In the short time he had had to train his regiments, Gardep had instilled an iron discipline in his fighters, drilling them to stand impassively while the juggernaut of the Imperial Army drove forward. Murima and Bulu commanded the archers. Again and again the urgent hiss of their arrows was heard. Each time many Imperial troops fell, reddening the snow with their blood.

The spearmen of Miridan and Lyria came next, rushing forward to hurl their shafts. But Gardep had selected his position well. In the lea of the hill on which the rebel fighters stood, there were several frozen streams and some boulder-strewn terrain. With the additional difficulty of thick snow, the spearmen were slow and vulnerable. The archers treated them to a withering hail of missiles. When the spearmen retreated, Rishal brought up what war engines he had left after the raid that had destroyed his catapults. The ballistae hurled immense bolts hundreds of yards. But Gardep had prepared for the enemy artillery. His regiments were mobile and responded with speed to every command, opening their ranks the moment a projectile arced through the air. In this way, though the Imperial officers had got their range, the Army of the Free avoided major losses.

'They'll try to get us down off this plateau,' Murima said. 'They will feign retreat to draw us out.'

'We don't move until I say,' Gardep answered.

He was no longer the boy who had wavered between love and duty. He was the general Rishal had trained him to be, the hero of the oppressed Shamana had foreseen. Rishal did as he had expected, launching his Obirs at the rebel lines. Forced to clamber over ramparts and palisades, they fell in their scores to the murderous hail of arrows from the Helat bows. Rishal had no regard for his auxiliary troops. By throwing them carelessly against the rebel defences, he was probing for a weak spot. It hardly mattered that the ground was littered with the dead and the dying.

'Selessians,' Nikesh reported, seeing a new danger.

The men in black belonged to the Haraddin clan, descendants of the notorious Ehut and for decades the ruling order in the desert kingdom. They duly thundered up the hill on their magnificent stallions, horses of such quality that the Sol-ket now bred thousands every year for their own cavalry.

'Light the ditches,' Gardep ordered.

Three ditches filled with Lyrian fire were soon blazing, forcing the cavalry to retreat. But the burning pitch wasn't the obstacle he had hoped. Hundreds of Obir infantry rushed forward. Wild and undisciplined they may have been, but they attacked with extraordinary boldness and courage. They carried wooden bridges to span the blazing trenches. Still the Helat archers shot their volleys but they were starting to run ominously short of arrows. The tribesmen had established a way over the ditches and the Selessians came again, thundering over the makeshift bridges.

'They were expecting us to use fire ditches,' Nikesh said, watching the Selessian tide sweeping towards them.

'Rishal taught me everything I know,' Gardep said. 'Is it any wonder we anticipate each other?' Then, raising his sword, he addressed his fighters. 'On my order.'

His ranks waited, and waited. On came the Selessians leaping over obstacles and evading arrows and spears. 'Now!'

Gardep signalled to Oled and the giant spurred his horse, leading his cavalry in a headlong gallop down the hill. With the advantage of the high ground, Oled's charge drove the attackers back. There was no wild pursuit of the retreating Selessians. Oled ordered his warriors to wheel around and return to the heights. The Selessians would come again, and behind them the mass of the Sol-ket. Battle was about to be joined in earnest.

2

It was at this point that Rishal played his hand. He sent an envoy to Murak, asking him to go forward. The moment Oled saw Murak's Hotec-Ra standard he was filled with rage. Giving a roar of hatred, he led his horsemen in a second charge. The sight sent a shudder through Gardep.

'This is a ruse,' he said: 'Rishal knew Oled would take the bait.'

He watched in horror as Oled's cavalry thundered forward, ignoring his express orders. Even as they engaged Murak's front rank, Rishal threw some of his own horsemen into the mélée, threatening to surround Oled.

'Why didn't he wait for my orders?' Gardep groaned.

'He saw his mother's killer,' Atrakon said. 'How did you expect him to react?'

Gardep shook his head. 'He is a leader of men. He must transcend his instinct for revenge.' He watched in an agony of indecision.

'What are you waiting for?' Murima demanded. 'Are you going to let the Sol-ket surround him?'

'If we leave the high ground,' Gardep said, 'we will lose our advantage.'

'And if we stay here,' Atrakon protested, 'Oled will lose his life.'

Gardep watched the furious struggle unfolding before him.

'Gardep,' Atrakon said, 'you must make a decision.'

Gardep sensed his dilemma keenly. If he attacked without a strategy, defeat was inevitable. If he left Oled's troops to be massacred, he would have betrayed every ideal Shamana had taught him. In the end, he let his heart triumph over his head.

'Nikesh, Atrakon, Adrius,' he cried, 'go to his aid.'

With Nikesh's rough riders to his right and Adrius' Vassyrians to his left, Atrakon spurred his horse forward. Thousands followed on horseback and on foot. The hastily assembled force crashed into the enemy. But soon came a sight that would steady the beleaguered Imperial troops. Tens of thousands of heavy Sol-ket infantry, held in reserve for just such a moment, were running towards them. It was Oled, cheered by the arrival of reinforce-ments, who rallied his troops. For all his recklessness, he was indeed a leader.

'Just look at them,' he laughed, brushing aside the murmurs of dismay that rose from his warriors, 'they rush onto our sword points.'

He swung his battle-axe and killed one of the foremost attackers. 'See, they bleed like any man. Their skulls split under a blade. What are you waiting for? Make them bleed some more.'

The Sol-ket were beating their shields and shouting their battle cries. But, heartened by Oled's example, the alliance of Tanjur general and Helat ranks did not waver. The battle song of blade and bow resounded loudly. There were curses, screams, shouts of rage, all the elemental fury of warfare. That's when Oled saw Murak's personal standard fluttering nearby.

'Murderer!' he bellowed, seeking out the enemy.

Even before Oled's eyes found him, Murak caught sight of the giant hurtling towards him, wild in his battle-rage, carving a path through the thinning ranks that separated them.

'Where are you, Murak?' Oled yelled.

Through all the swirling confusion of combat, there was only one face he wanted to see, that of the assassin who had killed Shamana. It seemed to hover in a scarlet mist, just like the Blood Moon. But by the time Oled had hacked his way through to Murak's battle-standard, the priest-general had gone.

3

It was at this point that Rishal's standard was seen for the first time. A long line of foot soldiers raced across the battlefield in front of the Sol-ket centre. These were the drummers, over a thousand strong, trained to beat fear into the hearts of the enemy. In perfect time, they began to climb the slope, hammering out the rhythm of war.

'Will you listen to that?' Harad said, his gaunt face tense with apprehension.

'I can feel the beat of those drums in the marrow of my bones,' Qintu said.

'Ignore it,' Gardep said. 'What is it but stick against hide? They will have as much effect on the outcome as waiting vultures.'

But his words did little to reassure those around him. The martial cannonade of the drums was unnerving many.

'Stand steady,' Gardep roared.

His command was passed down the line. Already however, many looked panic-stricken. There wasn't a soul present who was not haunted by the folk memory of past defeat. Seeing the effect of the drummers on the Helat ranks, Murima snatched up Shinar's ancient standard and set off at the gallop, riding the length of the rebel defences.

'Be scared if you want,' she told the Army of the Free, 'but don't take a single step back. Tremble if you want, but don't drop your weapons. Quake if you want, but don't forget to strike down your foe. We have not come here to retreat before mere drummers. What next? Are you going to falter before trumpeters?' She laughed out loud. 'And what would you do if they blew a whistle at you?'

At last the grim faces relaxed.

'We have come here to win our freedom,' Murima reminded them. 'So fight, damn you, fight!'

By the time she had ridden back to Gardep's side, the panic had subsided, replaced once more by battle-readiness.

'You truly are Shinar's daughter,' Gardep said, greeting her on her return.

'True enough,' Murima whispered, 'but, for all my brave words, I'm as scared as anyone here.'

Halfway up the slope, the drummers fell into a hundred lines of single file, allowing Rishal's cavalry to pass between them. The Sol-ket were now advancing at the trot.

'This is it,' Gardep said. 'Send the spear fighters forward.' The Sol-ket were beginning to canter. 'Throw your javelins,' he ordered.

The Sol-ket charged, galloping through the spears as if they were made of paper.

'Slingers,' Gardep ordered.

Replacing their bows with slingshots, Murima's archers took up slingshots. Soon the hum of stones and clay pellets filled the air and many riders fell. For all that, the Sol-ket charge had not been broken. Rishal had issued his riders with long shields and most had survived the rain of slingshot.

'They frustrate our efforts at every turn,' Gardep complained.

But worse was yet to come.

'Look!' Harad gasped.

Thousands of Sol-ket infantry had worked their way

round the hill and were racing forward to encircle the Helat army.

'Not again,' Murima murmured under her breath, crushed by the sight of the new menace. 'Please, not again.'

'Courage,' Gardep said. 'Remember your own words to the Army.' Then he raised his own voice to address his fighters. 'Listen to me, Oled has galloped into the heart of the foe. Brothers, sisters, will we do any less?'

He prepared to throw his own cavalry into the fight. They were his last reserves. He glanced at Harad and Qintu, then finally at Murima. 'Stay with me,' he told them. 'We live together or die together.'

As he led the charge, he appraised the situation. Everywhere slave and master were embroiled in hand-to-hand combat. The Army of the Free had lost the high ground and its warriors had been drawn into close fighting. In his heart of hearts, Gardep knew there could only be one outcome.

'We've lost, haven't we?' Murima whispered.

Gardep didn't answer. He couldn't. All around him, the Sol-ket were steadily driving forward. They were disciplined, ruthless, implacable.

'Rally!' Oled cried, beside himself with rage that the Army of the Free were starting to fall back.

'Fight for your freedom!' Murima shouted.

But the Helati were wavering. One more decisive blow and the Sol-ket would have them on the run. Then, just as all seemed lost, a shudder ran through the enemy ranks. There were cries of horror.

'What's happening there?' Gardep demanded, pointing to his right.

Nobody could furnish him with an explanation. That's when he saw with his own eyes what had thrown the enemy into such confusion. Everywhere, fleshless hands were breaking through the earth. Gardep looked around. Everyone was equally bewildered.

'This has got something to do with Cusha and Vishtar,' Murima said. 'It's got to be them. They talk to the undead.'

Even as she spoke, the soil exploded, showering the advancing Sol-ket. Horses reared and men tumbled as thousands of skeletal figures erupted from the swelling ground. Still the macabre beings poured from the fractured land, like so many insects swarming from a crack in the wall. Then their battle chorus could be heard echoing over and over again.

'Vishtar! Cusha! Shinar!'

'Didn't I tell you?' Murima cried, eyes gleaming to hear her father's name being chanted once again. 'They spoke to the undead. They have assembled an Army of the Lost Souls.'

The Army of the Free took up the chant. 'Vishtar! Cusha! Shinar!'

'The Lost Souls have their redemption,' Murima said.

The night breed, now a regiment of the Army of the Free, swarmed over the Sol-ket, slashing, cutting, beating and bludgeoning. Savage cries rose from them though they had no throats. They raced over the snowy ground like dancing puppets, things of bone and ripped flesh. They cared not whether they were run through or beaten down. They fought in a wild frenzy, abandoning themselves to the sheer exhilaration of engaging their ancient oppressors.

4

Rishal watched mesmerised. At the point of victory, an entire new army had risen against him, more terrible and more self-sacrificing than the first. Full of fury, he cut and cut again with his sword as the creatures threw themselves at him. But each time he severed a head the creature crumpled to the ground laughing in its death-throes. When he ran one through, its bony jaw gaped in gratitude. Each and every one of the Lost Souls relished its self-destruction, perishing as it was in the act of liberation. Rishal remembered the terror of conflict with the demon host. They fought without fear.

'Where is General Ghushan?' he cried.

At that moment, Murak appeared. Remembering the lessons Oled had once taught him he shouted to Rishal.

'We must pull back to stony ground,' he told him. 'That way, at least they won't be able to tunnel under us.'

Reluctantly, Rishal gave the command. The Sol-ket withdrew. Encouraged, the Lost Souls rushed forward in a frenzy of retribution, hurling themselves again and again onto the sword points of the Warriors of the Sun. That's when Murak noticed that the creatures were not attacking the auxiliaries. As a result, the Sol-ket's allies were simply standing and watching.

'Attack the demons!' Rishal cried.

Some of the auxiliaries responded to the appeal. Others remained rooted to the spot.

'You are our allies,' he screamed, lashing out left and right.

Then Rishal heard a sound he never thought to experience in this world. One of the hell-fiends was speaking to him.

'You have no allies,' it said. 'They fight for you because they fear you, or because you pay them. How many of them have you mocked or cursed? How many have you turned against you with your haughty contempt? Ask yourself this, ax-Sol, who will raise a hand to help you now?'

It was true. Rishal's army had broken in half. The auxiliaries, realising they were in no danger from the Lost Souls, simply fell back. Meanwhile the Sol-ket themselves, still many tens of thousands strong, were struggling to beat back the fevered assault of the night-creatures. Finally, with the battle still in the balance, Ghushan's northern army at last appeared on the horizon. Rishal met Murak's stare.

'It's not over,' Rishal yelled. 'We've got to steady the troops. We can still win.'

5

The Army of the Free was experiencing the same wild twisting and turning of emotion. Just as it seemed they had victory in their grasp, Ghushan's twenty-thousand-strong northern army was being thrown into the fray against them. Gardep and Oled rode back and forth across the battlefield, filling gaps in the line with any troops they could find.

'Don't tire now,' Gardep told them. 'Raise your standards. Grip your weapons. You are not slaves. You are free men and women. Fight on!'

The weary Helati stirred themselves and prepared to attack Ghushan's fresh troops. Even as they started to move forward a groan rose from hundreds of throats.

'What now?' Gardep demanded.

'There,' Oled said, 'that's what they've seen.'

Thousands of Selessian riders were pouring over a ridge to the northwest. Like a black tide, they swept down the slope, just as the men of Ehut Haraddin had come forty years before. Black silk banners fluttered at their head. Murima could only stare.

'Let me go to them,' Atrakon cried. 'Maybe there is still a chance to persuade them not to fight.'

'Do what you can,' Gardep said, turning to face Ghushan's advancing army. 'Just do it quickly.'

Atrakon kicked his mount up the hill, riding standing in the stirrups, waving his arms. He was still galloping towards the regiment in this way when he heard their battle cry. It was one word: 'Ebrahin!'

Atrakon stared in disbelief. Now he could read the slogans on the silk banners. Some mentioned him by name, proclaiming him Sultan. Others spoke of washing away the shame of the past. He met the looks of the lead riders.

'That's my name on your banners!' he cried, astonishment written in his eyes. 'I am Atrakon Ebrahin.'

'Then lead us,' Omar told him.

Turning his horse in a single, fluid movement, Atrakon drew his sabre. Aware of the Haraddin watching them across the battlefield, he changed the war cry. It was not the clan name Ebrahin he shouted. Instead he raised the cry of a unified country.

'This is our moment,' he roared. 'We can free our land from the oppressor. Men of the desert, let's wash away the stain of the past. For Selesssia!'

Immediately the Haraddin brandished their swords and added their voices to those of the Ebrahin.

'Selessia!'

The black streams came together in a single dark torrent and struck Ghushan's unsuspecting troops head on.

'Well,' Gardep shouted, 'what are you all waiting for? Charge!'

6

Even then, when it was obvious that the tide of battle had turned, the Sol-ket fought on. Reeling from the shock of the Lost Souls' appearance on the battlefield, demoralised by the intervention of the Selessians, the Warriors of the Sun fought a rearguard action without hope of victory. Oled, in particular, terrified them with his swinging battle-axe as he went looking for Murak. Rishal called his generals together.

'The best we can hope for,' he told Murak and Ghushan, 'is a strategic withdrawal. Rinaghar must be protected. This is my order to you both: retreat in good order. You may yet save the Empire.'

Murak noticed his use of the word *you*. 'Explain yourself, Rishal-Ra,' he said.

'I will hold them,' Rishal said. 'Break off the fight, both of you. My Parcep regiments will hold the line while you retreat towards Rinaghar. Well, don't just stand there gawping. I am Commander-in-Chief of the Grand Army. This is a direct order. No bugles, no horns. Organise it quietly. Just go.'

With that, he rode to the front of his troops and explained that the order to fall back was not meant for them. Their lot was to perish in order to salvage something from the defeat.

'Though we will fall,' he told them, 'the core of the army will withdraw to fight another day. You are my brother Sol-ket. We were together at Inbacus and at the Battle of Jinghara Plain. We have marched through the fires of Hell together. This is our final struggle. Let's acquit ourselves with courage. Victory or death!'

Hearts heavy, the regiments of Parcep waited for the

end. Oled and Atrakon broke in from the left, Murima, Nikesh and Adrius from the right. The end came when Gardep's cavalry outflanked Rishal and completed the encirclement of his troops.

'Give me Murak,' Oled demanded, as he careered through the ocean of humanity. 'Bring him to me.'

But Murak was gone. Rishal's rearguard action had bought the Imperial Army the time they needed. The reckoning would have to wait.

7

For Gardep, the reckoning was imminent. Just before sunset on the fiftieth day of Buradish, he received a messenger from his former mentor and knight, Commander Rishal ax-Sol. Sol-ket resistance was continuing. The battle would last into a second day.

'What does it say?' Murima asked.

'He challenges me to mortal combat,' Gardep said. 'He wants us to conclude our unfinished business.'

'So what are you smiling about?' Murima asked.

'It is the way he sets out his challenge,' Gardep explained, handing the note to her. 'See how he addresses me? He calls me squire Gardep, as if he still expects me to be his servant.'

'Don't do it,' Murima said.

'She's right,' Oled told him. 'You've no need to risk your life. The tide has turned, Gardep. We've got them on the run. Two-thirds of their army has fled towards Rinaghar. There is no need for this fight. Tomorrow we will finish the job here and pursue them along the Rinaghar road.'

Gardep was not to be persuaded. 'It is something I must

595

do. It is a matter of honour.'

'There is no honour in dying,' Murima retorted. 'Soon, by the grace of the Four Winds, my daughter will return to marry you, Gardep. Remember your promises to her. How could I explain that you had chosen to throw your life away . . . for honour?'

'Don't forget the fight in the Dragon Mountains,' Atrakon said. 'I watched an unequal battle. You are not ready to face him.'

Gardep ignored them all. 'He forced me to slay my own blood brother. This time I will kill him. I owe it to Kulmat.'

Some distance away, just out of earshot, Rishal's messenger was waiting patiently for a reply. Gardep summoned him.

'Tell Commander Rishal that I will meet him in battle on one condition. If I defeat him, his men will lay down their weapons and surrender. I want no further unnecessary bloodshed.'

The messenger returned an hour later. 'The commander agrees to your terms,' he said. 'Because this is a rite of mortal combat, as set down in the code of the Sol-ket, he requests that you wear this armour.'

Gardep looked at the Sol-ket uniform. 'I will not wear it,' he said quietly.

'You refuse! But it is the way of the Sol-ket.'

'That is the point,' Gardep replied. 'I am no longer Sol-ket. The last time we fought, deep in my soul, I think part of me still belonged to Ra. This time I will stand before your master as a free man, general of freed slaves, a servant of the Scales. I will not wear the uniform of the oppressor just to please the murderer of Kulmat. I will come dressed as I am now.'

The messenger scowled. 'You look like a Helat.'

'You think the word is an insult,' Gardep said. 'I consider it a great honour. I have surrendered every earthly possession and privilege I had so that my fellow man and woman could gain the world, to be held in common. Now go. Give the commander my answer. I will be waiting for him at first light.'

'You spoke well,' Oled said.

'Let's hope my blade speaks as eloquently tomorrow,' Gardep answered. 'Now leave me, all of you. I need some time alone.'

Gardep watched the light fading from the sky. Just for a moment the sun seemed to regain a little of its own strength, as if gladdened by the events of that day. The last of its rays stained the distant hills scarlet. It was an omen. Blood would stain the morrow.

8

There was a blare of trumpets, announcing General Rishal ax-Sol, commander-in-chief of the Grand Army. He marched between an honour guard of his men, acknowledging their battle cries. Gardep watched him in silence. The Army of the Free followed his example. He had ordered no ceremony, no show of ritual. In his mind, this was a private matter between two men.

'Show no emotion,' Atrakon advised Gardep.

The Selessian was acting as his second.

'You must be as cold as an assassin is cold,' Atrakon continued. 'I know killing.' He gripped Gardep by the wrist. 'Are you listening to me?'

Gardep nodded slowly but his gaze had drifted away to the approaching Rishal.

'Forget that you were once his squire,' Atrakon insisted.

'Forget that he slew Kulmat. Make the kill quick.'

Atrakon watched Gardep set off towards Rishal. Had he listened to a single word?

'Is this how you present yourself?' Rishal demanded. 'You look like a common footsoldier.'

'That is what I am,' Gardep said, breaking his silence. 'I serve a greater cause than myself.'

The words were meant for his troops' consumption as much as for Rishal's.

'What cause is that, in the name of Ra?' Rishal demanded. 'Freedom?' He glared at the Helat ranks. 'What do you think these cockroaches will do with their freedom? They are low born. They have no nobility.'

Gardep retorted immediately. 'And what nobility do you have, Rishal? You ordered your men to break Kulmat's bones. You had fifty innocents burned alive. You are not fit to kiss the feet of a single one of these men and women.'

Rishal scowled. 'We've talked enough,' he snarled, drawing his sword. 'Let's get to the matter in hand.'

Without another word, he stabbed at Gardep, aiming for the heart. Gardep side-stepped the lunge and countered with a sword-thrust of his own. Rishal raised his shield, emblazoned with an image of the rising sun, and parried it effortlessly. After that, steel clashed against steel. Both men sweated and grunted, struggling for purchase on the dry, dusty ground. Soon they were grimed with dirt and tiring. This was no repeat of the fight in the Dragon Mountains. They were evenly matched. Gardep noticed a slowness in his former master's movements, a legacy of Adrius' javelin. He recalled every lesson he had been taught. Don't strain for victory too early, he told himself. War is work, hard work. Victory must be earned. Gardep didn't go for the winning blow. He protected his head and his heart and resolved to use his youth to wear the older man down.

'It seems war has made you a man at last,' Rishal panted.

'Brotherhood did that,' Gardep retorted, remembering Kulmat's broken body displayed on the wheel. 'It is something you will never understand.'

Rishal slashed at his shins but Gardep skipped over the shining blade. His former master was tiring. His ribcage heaved with the effort and sweat dripped from his nose. What's more, blood had started to ooze from his thigh. The exertions of battle had reopened the wound. Gardep took advantage of Rishal's weariness to fire a question at him. 'Who am I?'

Rishal's eyes narrowed, as if trying to make sense of the question.

'I know that I am of royal blood,' Gardep said. 'Who am I? I want the truth.'

Hearing the yearning in Gardep's voice, Rishal unsheathed a new weapon. 'Yes,' he said, 'you used to ask me about Vassyria when you were a boy.'

Gardep waited.

'You want to know about your family, don't you?'

Their swords locked.

'I'll tell you about them,' Rishal hissed. 'I killed them all. That's right, *boy*, the day Inbacus fell I was first to reach the palace. Your father was called Imzal. He was the king's brother, a general who had sworn to protect him. He knew how to fight but I was always the stronger man. I killed him. Do you want to know how?' Rishal chuckled. 'I clubbed him to the ground and stuck him like a pig.'

Gardep's eyes burned with hatred.

'Yes,' Rishal gloated, seeing that he had struck a chord, 'then I watched his blood pool on the tiled floor of the palace. But that's not all.' He wagged the point of his sword under Gardep's nose. 'Do you want to know the rest?' he asked.

'Speak your mind, ax-Sol,' Gardep told him, 'before I kill you.'

Rishal jabbed. Gardep jumped back.

'Your father gave me a tougher fight than any man before or since,' the Commander said. 'While we fought, a project formed in my mind. Being without a male heir myself, I resolved to take his son and raise him to be the inheritor of my office. You came from fighting stock. I would fashion you into the greatest warrior the world had ever seen. There was only one obstacle to my plan. That was your mother, Nuqiba. You were sleeping in a side room. To protect you, she came at me with a knife.' He let this sink in, then continued. 'While you lay slumbering, dreaming sweet infant dreams, I killed her before your sisters' eyes.' He laughed. 'Then I dispatched them too. I was carrying you away to my quarters when you awoke in my arms. I remember the way you cried for your mother.'

He imitated the sound. '"Mummy, mummy," you wailed. Oh, I was so comforting. I told you that she was going to join us soon. In time you forgot my promise, of course, along with the faces of your family. What irony, Gardep! You clung to the man who sent your family to the House of the Dead. That's your story, the past you always wanted me to tell you about.'

It was too much for Gardep. With an animal roar, he set about Rishal. It was just what the commander had been hoping for. Rishal slashed Gardep across the chest. A groan rose from the Helat ranks as Gardep staggered back. His senses were swimming. As if through a fog, he saw Rishal moving in for the kill, slashing and stabbing. He felt another sharp buzz of pain. Then he saw Rishal smile. It cleared his mind. Gardep retreated, crouching, feeling the blood oozing from him. It was only with the greatest effort that he managed to parry Rishal's blows. He could hear the roars of the Sol-ket. Blinking the sour sweat from his eyes, he glimpsed the silent ranks of the Army of the Free. In that moment, like the cold heart of a flame, within Gardep's anger and despair, within the bitter fury he felt for Rishal, a cold, merciless core of determination formed. He went beyond anger, beyond battle-rage, to will. He felt the hands of his murdered ancestors steadying his sword. Rishal must die.

'What's that?' Rishal demanded. 'Speak up, *boy*. I want to hear your voice before I send you to the House of the Dead. At least you'll see Kulmat again.'

It was one jibe too many. Gardep launched himself at Rishal, stabbing through his armour. It was Rishal's turn to groan. His wound was grievous. His eyes dimmed. His heart faltered.

'You've learned your lessons well,' Rishal said, his legs buckling.

Gardep ripped off Rishal's helmet and pressed his sword point to his throat.

'Is it true?' he demanded. 'The story you just told me – is it all true?'

'You know it is,' Rishal said. 'I killed them all then I took you from your homeland. I made you in my image.'

Gardep gripped Rishal's hair just as the commander had once gripped his. 'I will never be like you, ax-Sol.'

Rishal sagged forward and clung to Gardep.

'The House of the Dead is opening to admit me,' Rishal said. 'I'm not going to beg for my life. What's the point? Finish it. Do it quickly.'

But Gardep had no mercy for the man who had killed

his family and had his best friend tortured and left to die. The lethal composure that had defeated Rishal hardened into a terrible alloy of cruelty and vengeance. Gardep sheathed his sword and shoved Rishal away to lie dying in the dust.

'You will have no mercy from me, ax-Sol,' he said. 'I am going to leave you here. You will die slowly, just as you planned for Kulmat. Each beat of your heart will pump your lifeblood into the earth. Spend your dying moments looking into the eyes of my murdered family. I hope you suffer greatly for your crimes.'

Rishal writhed on the ground. 'Do you have no honour?' he whined. 'I was a father to you, Gardep. For Ra's sake, don't leave me here like a dog. Kill me now.'

But Gardep simply walked away. When some of the commander's Sol-ket tried to go to him, the Helati closest to Gardep drew their arrows.

'Stand guard over the butcher,' Gardep ordered. 'Kill anyone who tries to help him.'

With that, he retired to his quarters.

CHAPTER 13

Into the Demon's Jaws

I

Gardep didn't look up when Oled entered his tent. Sitting cross-legged in one corner, he continued to brood on the day's events.

'If you have something to say to me, Oled,' he murmured finally, 'just speak your heart.'

'You have done our cause a great wrong,' Oled said. 'Your treatment of Rishal ax-Sol was an abomination.'

'I met him in mortal combat,' Gardep said. 'I prevailed. That's all there is to it.'

'You left one of nature's creatures dying in agony,' Oled retorted. 'How can you justify it? How can you live with yourself? It was left to me to restore the honour of our cause. Do you know what I did, Gardep? I countermanded your orders. That's right, I told your men to stand down. My battle-axe sang a song of mercy. I gave Rishal his wish.'

Gardep looked up for the first time. 'Are you telling me you delivered the death blow?'

'Exactly that.'

Gardep rose to his feet, trembling with fury. 'You had no right! He murdered my family. He tortured my friend. He deserved nothing.'

'He deserved a dignified end,' Oled answered. 'It is the right of all men. This is the way of the Scales.'

Gardep was beside himself.

'I am proud of my actions,' Oled said. 'Proud! How could I leave him writhing in pain? It would diminish me as a man. I understand your hatred for this Sol-ket but it is wrong to inflict such suffering.'

Gardep's eyes were cold. Still he said nothing.

'Even in war,' Oled said, 'there must be rules. We are not like the Sol-ket. Let them massacre the innocent. Let them torture their victims. Let them use deceit and treachery. We will conduct ourselves differently. How, if we behave just like them, can we make the world anew? When we rose against the Empire of the Sun, we swore to replace despotism with law and justice. What you did today was to inflict unnecessary pain. It was unforgivable.'

Gardep spoke at last. 'I don't need your forgiveness. I don't want it. I'll not have you judge me.'

He drew close to Oled and met his stare.

'What about you?' he demanded. 'I remember what you said on the eve of battle. No forgiveness, you said. Murak killed your mother. You sought him on the battlefield. What will you do when you meet him face to face? Before you stand here berating me, answer this question. Will you show mercy to Shamana's murderer? Well, will you?'

They continued to stare at each other.

'No,' Gardep said. 'I thought not.' He pointed to the tent flap. 'You're a hypocrite, Oled Lonetread. Get out of my sight.'

2

Cusha, Vishtar, Aaliya and Jinghirza had been climbing for hours. Their legs were heavy and their lungs were bursting.

'It is time to take a rest,' Jinghirza said. She used her torch to illuminate the ledge of rock before them. 'This will do.'

There was evidence of human habitation. The floor was littered with buckets and tools. The walls were covered with frescoes. But it was no scene of peace and harmony. Some were defaced and painted over with symbols of the sun.

'The Sol-ket were here,' Vishtar said. 'See, all the images of the god Sangra and the other deities have been chipped away or covered with their graffiti.'

Cusha got up and explored the gloom. 'You're right,' she said. 'The Sol-ket were here.'

Vishtar and Aaliya joined her. In a corner there were skeletons slumped against a wall. A sword blade was still lodged in the ribcage of one of them. A shield boss had smashed the skull of another. A ligature hung from the throat of a third.

'Now we know what happened to the monks of Nandraghiri,' Cusha said. 'The Sol-ket slaughtered them and destroyed the cult of Sangra.'

The deeper they penetrated into the cave, the more reminders there were of the massacre. Evidence of the monks' presence was everywhere. There were jute bags and conical bamboo baskets. In a wooden box, Vishtar discovered a scribe's tools: metal compasses, etching utensils and an ivory stylus. There were more wall paintings. They depicted Sangra and Ra as brothers. There was no sign of the fratricidal hatred between the two avatars as there was in the temples of Parcep and Rinaghar. The monastery had been built in an earlier age when the world was ruled by ideas of peace, not conflict. They were shown living in harmony, twin custodians of the land. But, once again, the images of Sangra had been defaced. The mottos painted underneath the frescoes had mostly been erased. Those that survived expressed a familiar message: *Through difference, unity. All things in balance.*

It was the message of their own faith, the way of the Scales.

3

To the east, in golden Rinaghar, Emperor Muzal ax-Sol, Light of the Sun, Conqueror of Shinar, was receiving the commanders who had survived the battle of Dullah. They had been riding hard for days. Their warriors were following, pursued by the Army of the Free.

'You swore it would never come to this!' he raged, spitting venomous recriminations at the men gathered in his throne room. 'The Empire is torn in half. All Jinghara is in the hands of the cockroaches.'

'Your Imperial Majesty,' Murak said. 'All is not lost. A great army will defend golden Rinaghar.'

Muzal's eyes narrowed. 'Yes, and by the time they get here the rebels' ranks will have swollen to many times their present size.' He waved a sheaf of reports. 'Look at these.

Lord Asun has just put them into my hands. Every province in the Empire reports Helat risings. The Vassyrian legions have risen against us, the Selessians too. The Miridans have deserted us. They have simply walked away from their officers. I have just had another message. The night-striders have crushed General Barath's forces. How do we turn back the tide of revolt?' His accusing stare swept the room. 'Well?'

The officers shifted their feet uneasily.

'We can promise you only this, Your Imperial Majesty,' Murak said. 'We will fight to the last drop of blood to defend the Imperial heartland.'

'I have heard all this before,' Muzal fumed. He jabbed a finger at his general. 'There were women in the Helat army, I hear. Is that true, Ghushan? Did you run from their painted fingernails?'

'Your Imperial Highness,' Ghushan protested, 'you insult my honour!'

'And you insult my intelligence!' Muzal bellowed into his face. 'What are you going to do to defend the city?'

'There is something I can do, Highness,' Murak said.

'Go on.'

'I slew the She-wolf. Her son, Oled Lonetread hates me more than any living man. I will challenge him to mortal combat.'

'Can you defeat him by force of arms?'

'I can try.'

'What if you do vanquish him?' Muzal snarled. 'Do you imagine that two hundred thousand slaves will then meekly walk from our walls?'

Asun intervened at this point. 'Your Imperial Majesty, Murak may have a point, though not the one he was trying to make.'

'Explain.'

'The slaves may appear a mighty throng. But they are new to war. It is only the quality of their leaders that has guaranteed their success thus far.'

For the first time, the Emperor sounded mollified. 'Go on.'

'We will tip Murak's sword with poison,' Asun said, warming to his theme. 'He only needs to scratch the giant and he will win the contest. Our assassins will target Gardep and the other leaders. Without their leaders, the Helat mob will disintegrate.'

'There,' Muzal said, 'at least somebody is talking sense. It is a good plan, Asun.'

Murak saw the delight in Asun's eyes, and the ambition. It begins again, he thought, the jockeying for position, the conspiring.

'Does anyone have an alternative to Asun's plan?' Muzal demanded.

Nobody did.

'Very well,' the Emperor said. 'Issue your challenge, Murak.'

4

The Darkwing attacked in the early hours of the morning, when he expected his human prey to be at their most vulnerable. Swooping down the cliffs, he fell upon the climbers with primal screeches that echoed eerily through the mountains. The clangour of steel reverberated from peak to peak. The Darkwing sent several of the hooded figures tumbling down steep crevasses. As the bitter struggle continued, the demon lord searched for two in particular.

'Where are you, Holy Children?'

Finally, he fastened on them, identifiable by their cloaks. They were several metres away from the others. Throwing himself into the searing winds, he plummeted towards them, only spreading his wings at the last moment as he opened his talons.

'This time,' he hissed, 'there will be no escape.'

He fell on the boy first, rounding on him with a low, phlegmy hiss. His mouth was close to his victim's, belching spite. Pulling back the familiar hood, he leered into the exposed figure's face. But it wasn't the expected Vishtar he saw. Staring back from a fleshless skull were the eyes of Jackal. Reeling from the shock, the Darkwing unmasked the creature beneath Cusha's cloak. For the second time, he felt a long tremor of disappointment. It was another night-strider. With a shriek of temper, the Darkwing broke off the attack.

Jackal watched the demon lord vanish into the darkness. 'He is coming, Holy Children,' he growled. 'May the Four Winds protect you.'

5

On the fifty-eighth day of Buradish, Emperor Muzal ax-Sol was plucked from his sleep by a cacophony of beating drums, alarm bells, gongs and shouts. For a moment, he lay in his bed, soaked in his own sweat. The noise fused with the nightmare he had just had. Millions strong, a slave army swarmed towards him, hands scrabbling at his puckered, ageing flesh while, over the whole scene, vast leathery wings spread outwards blocking the dying sun. Barely conscious, Muzal screamed in terror. His personal slave appeared at the door.

'What is it, Your Imperial Majesty?'

'It's nothing, Sanjay,' Muzal panted, 'just a dream, a stupid nightmare.'

Dismissing his night fears, the Emperor pulled on a gown. He was disgusted with himself for showing fear in front of a Helat.

'What is all the noise?' he asked, hearing a rising cacophony outside.

'Your Imperial Majesty,' Sanjay stammered. 'It is the rebel army. It masses before the city walls.'

Minutes later, Muzal was standing with Murak, Asun and Ghushan on the city walls.

'By the holy face of Ra,' he said. 'This is the sight all my ancestors have dreaded. Even that dog Shinar did not reach golden Rinaghar itself.'

For as far as the eye could see, the risen Helati filled the plain. Not only that, the rearguard were swarming down the hillsides beyond, carpeting the frosty slopes like ants.

'Have you issued your challenge?' Muzal asked Murak.

'A messenger left an hour ago,' Murak said.

'Is the poison prepared?' Muzal demanded.

'It is ready,' Asun said. 'My assassins are on the battlements.'

Minutes later, Murak's envoy returned.

'The barbarian accepts your challenge,' he told Murak.

'One scratch,' Muzal said. 'Don't fail me, Murak. We may yet snatch victory from the jaws of defeat.'

6

It didn't take the Darkwing long to discover his prey. Thrown into frenzy by the smell of human blood, he burst upon the four friends. But his real target was the Holy Children. Within moments, the silent cavern had become a wild maelstrom of sibilant screams. The clotted, predatory voice of the Darkwing reverberated through the winding tunnels. The shadows filled with his macabre form. The swords of the four friends glanced ineffectually off the armoured hide of their hell-born foe. As ever, it was Cusha the Darkwing wanted most.

'Stand back!' Aaliya yelled.

As Cusha, Vishtar and Jinghirza hurled themselves out of harm's way, the shape-shifter loosed her arrow. It embedded itself deep in the creature's throat. But he just laughed. A serpent head poked from a fold in his flesh and bit off the shaft.

'He's stronger than ever,' Vishtar cried. 'We can't hold him.'

Suddenly, everyone was stumbling back, fighting a panicky, stuttering rearguard action against the demon lord's ferocious onslaught. A moment later Cusha alerted her companions to a new horror.

'Look!' she screamed as more of the things welled up from the depths. 'His breath.'

Bluish vapour was spilling from the Darkwing's jaws. It was venom.

7

It was noon on the fifty-eighth day of Buradish when Murak took the poison-tipped sword from Asun.

'One scratch, Murak,' Asun reminded him.

Murak swung the blade, deftly positioning it just inches from Asun's throat. 'I know my business.' There was something playfully murderous about the look in his eye. 'Don't remind me again, Asun. My hand might just slip. The Hotec-Ra are making a habit of losing priests.

Do you want to add to the toll?'

The point wavered under Asun's chin. Seeing a single bead of perspiration work its way down his fellow priest's brow, Murak grinned. 'That's better,' he said.

'Are you ready, Murak?' the captain of guards asked.

'I'm ready.'

Murak looked up at the walls of Rinaghar. Two sets of standards fluttered there, the scarlet and gold flags of the Sol-ket and the saffron-fringed streamers of the Hotec-Ra. Murak waited behind the colossal Gates of Ra. Out of the corner of his eye, he glimpsed Emperor Muzal watching him. He didn't return the look. Instead, he waited for the gates to swing open. It took mere seconds, yet it felt like an age. Finally, the hinges creaked and he saw the Helat masses. The ranks of the Army of the Free were oddly silent, still and determined in the wind and the horizontal sleet. There was no drumming of sword hilt on shield. There were no battle cries. They watched Murak stride through the gates and every pair of eyes flashed an accusation. He was the man who had killed the She-wolf by stealth. He was a murderer. Even as these thoughts rippled through his mind, Murak saw the man he had avoided for so long. It was Oled.

'You fled from me before, Murak,' the giant said, his voice carrying over the silent plain.

'There will be no more running, priest. Face me here. Face me now.'

Murak weighed the sword in his hand, but it was his conscience that spoke. 'I'm ready, Lonetread. I'm weary of warfare. Let's be done with it.'

Two men who had once declared their friendship marched towards one another. Murak bore the great shield of Ra on his left arm and carried his sword in his right hand. Oled was content to use his battle-axe alone. He fought without a shield. He found the thing cumbersome. Oled was the first to attack, his axe striking Murak's sword and shield again and again with downward blows. Murak held his ground but failed to offer an offensive strike. Oled's power had reduced his muscles to water. From the battlements, Muzal watched, willing his man to jab, slash, anything to penetrate the Tanjur's skin and let the venom work.

'The shape-shifter is wide open,' he said. 'All it takes is a pin-prick. Why doesn't he strike?'

Asun said nothing. Instead, he glanced at the bowmen crouched behind the battlements. They nocked their arrows.

Oled continued to advance, crashing his axe repeatedly into Murak's shield.

'Look into my eyes,' he said. 'They are green, like my mother's. Do you remember her eyes, priest?'

He crashed the stock of the axe into Murak's face, forcing him to his knees. Murak was on all fours, spitting out gobbets of blood.

'What do you want me to say, Oled?' he panted.

'Get up, Murak,' Oled growled. 'I won't kill you while you crouch like a beaten animal. Face me.'

On the city walls, Muzal leaned forward.

'Strike now,' the Emperor hissed under his breath. 'Cut him. Stab the foot, the leg, anything.'

He saw Murak tightening his grip on the hilt.

'That's it,' Muzal murmured, 'do it now.'

Anticipating the fatal strike, Asun nodded to the archers. They drew their bows tight, ready to shoot.

'On my order,' he whispered.

Murak finally raised his head and looked into Oled's face. 'What are you waiting for?' he asked. 'You've won. Kill me. I betrayed you. Everything you say is true. By stealth I slew your mother. You have every right to take my life.'

'That's it,' Muzal said, 'get him off guard. Use your wits. Wheedle. Whine. Get him off guard, then strike.' He made an encouraging gesture, as if stabbing with a sword of his own. 'Strike hard.'

Oled raised his axe. Murak crouched in his shadow. One brief jab of his blade and the Tanjur was doomed.

'What's this I see?' he asked, gazing into Oled's eyes. 'Do you plan to deal a wounding blow, the way Gardep did? Do you want me writhing in agony like Commander Rishal?'

Oled gripped the axe with both hands until his muscles bulged and his eyes became like gemstones, hard as emeralds. Then, with a shudder almost like agony, he lowered his weapon and turned his back on Murak.

'I'm not going to kill you,' Oled said. 'Though you deserve to die a thousand times, there is a time to put aside the sword. You are a beaten man. It would be another pointless death.'

At that moment, seeing Oled walking away defenceless, the Emperor could contain himself no longer. He screamed at the top of his voice.

'Now, Murak! Kill him now!'

In response, Murak sprang to his feet. Sensing the movement, Oled spun round. But Murak didn't strike.

'The battlements, Oled,' he shouted. 'They mean treachery.'

Gardep saw the Sol-ket bowmen rising. 'Archers,' he cried. 'Look to the city walls.'

In the exchange of arrows, two shafts passed within a hair's breadth of the boy-general. But Gardep was too fast. Hurling himself to one side, he shot twice with his own bow, killing his would-be assassins. Hundreds of Helat arrows clattered against the city walls, sending the enemy archers scuttling for cover.

'What's this?' Oled demanded, turning to fix Murak with a stare.

'The sword they gave me is tipped with poison,' Murak said. 'Those archers were meant to slay your leaders.'

A frown creased Oled's brow. 'So why didn't you go through with it?'

'You spared me,' Murak croaked, his throat tight with emotion. 'In spite of everything I have done, you spared me. After that, I could not betray you again.'

As Muzal stamped away in disgust, followed by Asun, a murmur rippled through the multitude, Helat and Sol-ket alike. This had never been seen before. Both men, at different moments, had their opponent at their mercy. Neither had had the will to strike. What did it mean? Oled marched past Gardep on his way back to his quarters. Their eyes met and Gardep nodded his understanding of the Tanjur's actions. He stepped forward, standing alone beneath the walls. Five thousand Helat archers trained their bows on the battlements, lest there be more treachery.

'The war is over,' Gardep cried, his voice echoing across the plain. 'This is the meaning of Oled Lonetread's act of mercy. If you want it, the conflict ends this moment. Vengeance is easy. But it solves nothing. Listen to me, fighters on both sides. No man has suffered more than Oled Lonetread. By subterfuge, Murak slew his mother, Queen of Tanjurs. But Oled did not take the priest's life in return.'

He drew his sword. 'There has to be a time,' he said, 'when we put our weapons aside. He thrust the blade into the snow-dusted ground. 'The sword is not the answer to every question. You have until dawn tomorrow to decide.

Will you follow your corrupt and dishonourable Emperor and continue a war that can only end in your deaths?'

His eyes swept the listening Sol-ket. 'Or will you lay down your arms? I give you my word, there will be no reprisals. It is your decision, men of Rinaghar.'

Gardep's voice faded into the chill air. He would wait for the city's answer.

8

'Traitor!' the Emperor cried, storming into his apartments. 'Did you see him, Asun? Did you see what your brother-priest did out there?'

Asun bowed. 'I did, Your Imperial Majesty.'

'All it took was a scratch,' Muzal snarled. 'But what did he do? He threw down his sword. What madness possessed him?'

Asun made a show of bewilderment, though inwardly he was delighted by what his rival had done.

'The dog has gone over to the enemy,' Muzal bawled, sweeping plates and goblets from the table that dominated the room. 'He seeks peace with the cockroaches. It's over, Asun. That was our last chance to destroy their leadership. Even if we survive the Darkwing winter, the Empire will fall.'

Asun's eyes narrowed. 'Maybe not, Majesty.'

Muzal seized on the priest's words. 'What is it, Asun? Is there something you can do to save us yet?'

'I have been talking to Murak's priests,' Asun said. 'The rebels destroyed our artillery before Dullah. They destroyed our entire stock of Fire Dust.'

'I know this, priest!'

'Your Imperial Majesty,' Asun said patiently, 'what they

failed to do was destroy our *knowledge* of its properties. The firing of Commander Rishal's artillery was a setback. It was not the end of our hopes. My brother-priests think they can manufacture enough Fire Dust to defend the city.'

'So why are you standing here, talking to me?' Muzal demanded. 'Set them to work!'

Asun smiled. 'Majesty, I already have.'

9

In the cavernous passages of Sangra Peak, the Darkwing's black eyes fixed his victims.

'You'll not take me again,' Jinghirza cried. 'I would rather take my own life.'

'Then do it,' the Darkwing hissed, 'and good riddance. You were a poor plaything.'

Aaliya kept up a steady volley of arrows but most of the shafts glanced off her target's carapace. Her three comrades cut and slashed at the advancing demon without success. They could feel the paralysing vapours stealing into their lungs. They were weakening. The Darkwing's airborne venom was taking effect. Cusha swayed and crumpled to the floor.

'Protect her!' Vishtar yelled, stepping between her and the creature.

'Too late,' the Darkwing snarled, belching the fatal vapour into Vishtar's face. 'This time she is mine.'

But before the demon lord could collect his prize, there were newcomers in the heaving darkness. Scabrous fingers gripped all manner of weapons, rushing at the demon lord. Familiar skeletal figures were hurling themselves at the Darkwing.

'Jackal!' Vishtar cried gratefully.

The battle swept back and forth across the cave. The Darkwing cut great swathes through the ranks of the night-striders. Soon, piles of bones lay where they had fallen. Satisfied that he had broken their power, the demon lord melted back into the blackness of the tunnels. He would wait for the remainder of his enemy in his lair, where he was at his most powerful and deadly. Nandraghiri would be their tomb.

CHAPTER 14

The Ziggurat of Ra

I

Sanjay found his master, the Emperor, pacing his apartments.

'What time is it, Sanjay?'

'It is just before dawn, Your Imperial Majesty.'

Muzal dropped wearily into a chair. 'Draw the blinds, Sanjay.'

Sanjay let in the weak, weary light of dawn. It was the final day of Buradish, the eve of Kukhala-Ra.

'I wonder, Sanjay,' Muzal said, 'will we live to see many more dawns?'

Sanjay offered no answer.

'You have been a faithful servant to me,' Muzal said. 'How many years have you been in my service?'

Sanjay did not have to think long. 'It is thirty years, Your Imperial Majesty. I was a boy of fourteen when I entered the Imperial palace.'

'Yes,' Muzal said. 'I remember you. You always were the loyal one, Sanjay, unlike the vile cockroaches swarming around our walls. We have a wonderful life here in Rinaghar, do we not?' He gazed across the golden minarets and domes of the city. 'We live in a golden age. There is law, justice, art. Great academies teach the knowledge of the world. And what is it all based on?'

'I don't know, Your Imperial Majesty.'

'It is faith, Sanjay. We are the Children of Ra. The holy face of the sun is our truth.'

The steady pulsing of drums eddied through the morning air.

'Hear that, Sanjay?' Muzal said. 'That's the Helat war host. How dare they disturb the peace of golden Rinaghar?'

He patted Sanjay on the shoulder.

'You're not like them, are you Sanjay? Oh, you're from Helat stock, but you have enjoyed the privileges of a palace slave. You understand the greatness of our Empire.'

There was a knock at the door.

'Come in,' Muzal said. 'Ah, Asun. Is it ready?'

Asun glanced at Sanjay. Muzal read the look. 'Leave us, Sanjay,' he said. 'I have matters to discuss with Lord Asun.' He waited until Sanjay had closed the doors behind him. 'Well,' the Emperor demanded, 'how is production going?'

Asun heard how Muzal hungered for destruction. 'It will be ready by the dawn, Your Imperial Majesty.'

'Dawn! You mean we have to wait another day for the stuff?'

'What is twenty-four hours, master?' Asun asked. 'If Ra

favours us at all, by then the Darkwing's plan will have been thwarted. We can celebrate Kukhala-Ra by repelling the heretic enemy from our walls.'

'Is there no way we can do it sooner?' Muzal complained. He strode to the window, jabbing a finger at the vast multitude outside the city walls. 'Do you hear that?' he asked. 'Do you hear the way the vermin insult us? I want them annihilated. I want it now!' He railed against his misfortunes. 'The Hotec-Ra must not fail me again, Asun. First Shirep failed. Then it was Linem. Now Murak and Timu have gone the same way. Don't let me down, Asun. You're a dead man if you do.'

'I won't, Majesty.'

'And there's no chance of hurrying the process along?'

'Majesty,' Asun said with a sigh, 'you must be patient. It will be another twenty-four hours before we have sufficient quantities to demoralise the foe.'

The Emperor snorted his disgust. 'Very well. Tomorrow it is.'

2

At the same moment, but two miles across the plain, Murak was attending the war council of the Army of the Free. Like the accused going before a judge, he sat directly opposite Oled. Out of shame, he kept his eyes averted.

'You have slept on the issue at hand,' Oled said. 'Tell me, priest, what is your decision?'

Murak bowed his head. 'I will make the appeal. I will call on the Sol-ket and the Hotec-Ra to throw down their weapons. I will ask for the cessation of all resistance.'

He hesitated for just a moment. 'There is still a formidable army within the walls. The Emperor is greatly feared. I am but a general. Compared to him, I barely figure in the minds of the Sol-ket. My words may have little sway.'

'But you will make the appeal?' Gardep asked. 'You are a senior man. At worst, you are bound to make them think.'

'I will make the appeal,' Murak said.

He looked around the assembly, trying to read the impassive faces of the rebel leaders.

'But can it be true?' he wondered out loud. 'Are you truly offering me a share of power, after everything I have done?'

'You will have a sort of power,' Oled answered. 'I reprieved you out of a desire for peace. You will speak for your fellow Sol-ket in whatever government we create to rule this land.'

'I thought Gardep would be your king,' Murak said.

Oled shook his head. 'You will never understand us, will you, Murak? There will be no kings after this.' He rose to his feet. 'You will represent the Children of Ra, but only if you learn to share power with those you have tortured and oppressed. You will be one man among many, a servant of the people. That is the true meaning of reconciliation.'

He met Murak's eyes with a look that would reduce many men to stone.

'Oh, I will never be your friend, priest,' he said. 'Too much blood has been shed for that to be possible. Even now, my arm trembles with the urge to strike your head from your shoulders. But I will put aside my rage and sit down at the bargaining table with you. I am prepared to make this sacrifice in order to end long centuries of suffering. Can you put aside your dreams of absolute power and be one man among many, a small voice in a chorus of millions?'

Murak nodded. 'I will do everything in my power to help you bring peace, Oled Lonetread.'

'Then the war is over,' Oled said.

Within the hour, Murak was standing before the gates of Ra. He set out the terms of peace.

'There will be no retribution against the former masters,' he said. 'There will be no looting or destruction. You need not fear for the safety of your families. The Army of the Free ask only this of you, Children of Ra. You must give up your privileges and end the practice of slavery for all eternity. I trust this vast throng to keep their word. What say you to their proposal for peace?'

On the walls, Muzal wanted to throw the traitor's words back in his face. But he was not speaking from a position of strength. He had to play for time. Just twenty-four hours and he could settle accounts with this miserable priest. He would watch his flesh melt and hear his traitor's throat scream in agony.

'Tomorrow is the first day of Kukhala-Ra,' Muzal said. 'It may be the last day we have on this Earth. It may be the first day of a new world. Destiny will decide. But, if Ra grants that the good sun rises, we will sit down by first light, Sol-ket and Helat together, to draw up a peace settlement. I will send an envoy to make the arrangements.'

At that, there was a great roar of jubilation from the Helat masses. Muzal turned away and descended the steps. 'Let them have their moment of triumph, Asun,' he hissed. 'Tomorrow, the fools will burn in the fires of Hell.'

3

It was after dark when Asun was led into the tent erected for the following day's meeting. He was accompanied by three of the rebel leaders: Gardep, Oled and Atrakon.

'It stands halfway between the Army of the Free and the city walls,' Gardep told Asun.

Asun looked around then opened the tent flap and cast his gaze towards the city walls. 'Show me where your warriors will be standing,' he said.

Gardep pointed to a long row of fluttering standards. 'Nobody will step beyond that line.'

Asun examined the distances involved for some time then professed himself satisfied. 'All we have to discuss now is when the two sides will take their seats at the negotiating table,' he said.

Oled's eyes hardened. 'What's this?' he demanded. 'Are you planning some treachery, priest?'

Asun shook his head. 'Not at all. I was about to suggest that both sets of negotiators set off from their own lines simultaneously. If this war is finally to be settled, there must be mutual trust.' He looked at each of the rebel leaders in turn. 'Do you agree?'

Gardep exchanged glances with Oled and Atrakon. Each gave a slight, if wary, nod.

'His Imperial Majesty will be accompanied by Ghushan-Ra and three senior officers. I will be the final member of the negotiating team.'

'There will be five representatives of the Army of the Free,' Gardep said, 'the three men you see here, Murima ul-Parcep and the Vassyrian Adrius. In this way, every section of our alliance will be represented.'

'As you wish,' Asun said. 'That is decided then. We will meet an hour before dawn. We will set off at the same time. All we need now is an agreed signal.'

Atrakon smiled. He found all this slightly ridiculous. 'What about a bugler from each side?' he suggested. 'After all, everything has to be equal and fair, doesn't it?'

'On behalf of His Majesty, I agree to this arrangement,' Asun said. 'By the grace of Ra, the Darkwing will perish. Then sun will rise again over our deliberations. Good evening, gentlemen.'

With that, he turned his back on them and walked back towards the Gates of Ra. He permitted himself a smile of satisfaction. His fervent wish was that, Ra willing, the dawn would rise over a devastated and defeated foe.

4

Walking back towards their own lines, the leaders of the Army of the Free expressed astonishment at the priest's easy acquiescence. As they reached the city of tents, the remaining members of the war council hurried forward.

'Well?' Murima asked. 'What did he have to say?'

Oled explained the outcome of the discussions.

'Something's wrong,' Murima said. 'When did the Solket, and especially these Hotec-Ra, surrender anything easily?'

'I am beginning to have the same feeling,' Atrakon said.

Gardep frowned. 'Oled?'

'The enemy are treacherous,' he said, glancing in the direction of Murak, sitting alone by a campfire. 'But I can't see what they can do to alter the course of events. The tent is out of range of bowmen. Besides, their own emperor would be in the firing line if they attempted some skull-duggery.'

'What are you saying, Murima?' Gardep said. 'Should we call off the talks?'

Murima thought for a moment then shook her head. 'No,' she said, 'we owe it to Cusha, Vishtar and Aaliya to take the first step to peace. With the grace of the Four

Winds, they will rid the world of the Darkwing. It is up to us to secure an end to war and oppression. Like Oled, I can't see what they can do with Muzal if our negotiations are undertaken in the open before the city gates.'

'It is agreed then,' Gardep said. 'We will keep our wits about us and be on our guard. But we will go through with the talks. Does anyone oppose this course of action?' Nobody did. 'Very well,' he said. 'Tomorrow, we will meet the Emperor face to face. We will try to make the world anew.'

The assembled leaders accepted his words with a nod, more of resignation than enthusiasm. The closeness of freedom seemed to make them all numb, Gardep most of all. He walked away slowly, retreating into his own thoughts. Climbing into the saddle of his mount he rode up the winding path to the heights above the city. Finally, trotting through the chopping, snow-laden wind, he came to the spot from which he had first looked down on Rinaghar many months before. He recalled that day, when he was still a naïve cadet in the service of Rishal ax-Sol. Was it just a few months? He found it hard to believe. Since then, the entire universe seemed to have shifted on its axis. Dismounting, Gardep walked to a point from which he could see the vast, open plain. There, after watching the polar winds ravaging the city of gold for some minutes, he looked north, addressing a few simple words to his beloved Cusha.

'Can we do it, my love?' he wondered. 'Together, can we really make this world anew?'

The wind didn't answer. Instead, it roared, deaf to his questions, wild and unfathomable like some desolate beast. Gardep stood there until the driving snow blurred his vision. Then he climbed back into the saddle and rode back to his quarters.

5

Muzal couldn't sleep. He tossed and turned all night, again haunted by the many-millioned slave-demon that now pursued his thoughts through every troubled night. Eventually, he gave up any thought of rest and rose. He slipped out onto the balcony of his apartment, gazing at the vast servile throng that was washing around the walls of Ra like a human ocean.

'Soon,' he murmured, 'you will understand what fools you are to tweak this tiger's tail. You will burn on Earth, then you will burn in hell.'

The thought filled his heart with a burning stream of exhilaration. Then he remembered Sanjay sleeping in the antechamber, on hand to serve his master. Muzal decided to hold his tongue. Faithful as an old dog Sanjay may be, but he was still a Helat. Moving swiftly yet softly down the corridor, Muzal roused his bodyguards and went in search of Asun. He found him organising the recently rebuilt war machines. There were ten catapults, smelling of freshly cut timber.

'Only ten?' Muzal grumbled.

'There was not time to assemble more,' Asun informed his emperor. 'Even that meant the carpenters and engineers working round the clock.'

'And the ammunition?'

'There are five projectiles for each machine,' Asun said.

'That means, what, seven, eight thousand dead?' Muzal said. 'That is but a pinprick in the enemy multitude.'

'That depends on where we concentrate our fire,' Asun said. 'I have been observing our enemy. Hence the arrangement of our war machines. You will notice, Your Imperial Majesty that they are drawn up in a semi-circle. By pinpointing the enemy leadership, we can destroy their senior leadership and the entire cadre below them. It is a blow from which they will not recover. Trust me, Majesty, we are about to pluck victory from the ashes of defeat.'

'So many men have promised me victory,' Muzal sighed. 'Every one of them is dead.'

'I will not fail you, Majesty,' Asun said. 'The moment Gardep na-Vassyrian leads the negotiating party towards us, we will behead the rebel beast.'

'How many hours until we give the enemy the punishment they so richly deserve?' Muzal demanded.

'Four hours, Highness.'

'I can't wait for this moment of retribution,' Muzal said. 'I am going to relish every sweet, agonising moment.' He clenched his fists. 'I want you to kill them, Asun. Kill them all.'

6

Gardep didn't sleep either. The thought of Cusha facing the Darkwing without him by her side troubled him. Equally, Murima's warning words kept floating to the front of his thoughts: when did the masters ever surrender easily? By the time the Army of the Free finally gathered before Rinaghar, he had made a decision. Once they had assembled, he stepped forward to address them.

'Warriors of the Free,' he began, 'this is your victory. You have ended the tyranny of the Sol-ket. How many of you would have believed, even six months ago, that this day the Emperor would sit down with us to discuss the end of slavery? Before I speak to you about the importance of this day, I want you to bow your heads. Give a few moments to remember the fallen and to think of our comrades now entering the precincts of Nandraghiri to face the demon lord.'

Immediately, there was no sound but the snapping of the regimental banners. Some thought of a brother, a sister, a father, a mother, a fallen friend. Shamana was in many minds. Her example and her sacrifice had made this day possible. Murima thought of her dead father, Shinar, and Atrakon of his lost love, Leila. Gardep thought of Kulmat. But all, of course, thought of Cusha, Vishtar and Aaliya in their moment of peril. Finally, Gardep continued his address.

'The air grows cold,' he said. 'The Darkwing winter sweeps across the land.' He pointed to the far horizon. 'Who knows,' he continued, 'whether the sun will rise this day. By sunset we will have a new world or no world at all. But, in the hope that our comrades prevail, we must turn our thoughts to peace. It is said in the Book of Scales that there will be no king. But there must be a leader. Army of the Free, I can never be that man.'

A murmur ran through the great crowd.

'I was raised to know blood and fire, the song of the blade and the sweep of the cavalry charge. When I fought Rishal, to my eternal shame, I was without mercy. I would have allowed him to die in agony. It would have meant a wretched end. I must devote myself to the task of learning gentleness and sympathy. Over time, with Cusha's help, softer feelings will grow in me. Maybe one day I will learn wisdom. But I have not learned it yet. I will not lead you.'

He turned to the other leaders. 'I must pass that burden to another man, my friend Oled Lonetread.'

Oled looked thunderstruck.

'Yes, Oled, you are the man to lead us,' Gardep said. 'You spared Murak though he was responsible for the death of your own mother. This is the act of a man who can bring peace to this tortured and divided land. You know the arts of pity and fogiveness. Do not refuse this request, Oled. Look into your heart. You know I am right. You will look Muzal in the eye. You will be our voice.'

It took some time for Oled to speak. When he did, it was with strength and purpose. 'Gardep is right,' he said. 'The time of Kings is at an end. No man or woman was born to lead others. That right does not flow in our blood. It is not passed on from father to son or mother to daughter. It must be earned. If I am to conduct your affairs and administer justice, I must have your consent. Do I have that sacred trust?'

There was a roar of acclamation.

'Then, with humility, I will accept this honour,' Oled said. 'I will be your protector and your judge.'

'All hail Oled Lonetread,' Gardep cried, 'protector-general of the Free.'

'All hail!' came the answering chorus.

Oled smiled. 'Protector-general,' he said, 'it is a good title. I will not be king. I seek no permanence for my office. Each twelvemonth, let there be a casting of lots. The people will choose their leader anew. Yes, let the judge be judged.'

He gestured to the other four members of the negotiation team.

'Let's bring peace to this land,' he said.

7

Muzal nodded to the guards.

'There,' he said, 'twenty metres before these gates is the position from which we are meant to march towards the foe. But we will never enter their cursed tent of peace.

There will be only one road to peace in this land and that is through the crushing of all rebels and heretics.'

He glanced at Asun. 'When we reach that line,' he continued, 'the enemy leadership will be gathered facing the Gates of Ra. The moment we cross the line, you must unleash heaven's fire on the foe.'

He fired a warning glance at his soldiers. 'There must be no cheers,' he told them, 'no battle cries, nothing to warn the foe.' He winked at Ghushan. 'The moment fire begins to rain on them and spread dismay through their ranks, our brave Sol-ket will ride out and slaughter the leaderless herd. We will punish them for their impudence.'

He gave a smile of incipient triumph. 'They want freedom. We will give them death.'

As Muzal walked through the gates he noticed Sanjay in the crowd. Oddly, when he acknowledged his most faithful servant, Sanjay gave no sign of having noticed. Dismissing the curious moment, Muzal strode ahead of his fellow negotiators.

He was dressed in the Imperial white and gold, the crown of his ancestors on his head. As he walked briskly towards his line, he saw the rebel leadership set off.

'It's almost time, Asun,' he whispered. 'I'm going to enjoy watching this.'

Already, in his mind's eye, he could see the havoc the Fire Dust would wreak in the enemy ranks. He watched the insurgent leaders, focusing on each one in turn. He was surprised to see Oled walking at the head of the contingent. Behind him there were the warrior, Gardep, the slave Murima, the Vassyrian Adrius and the Selessian Atrakon. Every one of you will burn, Muzal thought. He just prayed the keen-eared Tanjur would not catch the creak of tension in the catapult ropes. He had no need to worry. The giant was too busy marching towards his place in history. Any minute now, Muzal thought. Any minute now. Finally, Muzal crossed the line. A split-second later the fire weapon exploded, engulfing thousands of men in flame.

8

Far to the north, Jinghirza led the way into the Darkwing's lair.

'Where is he?' Aaliya asked. She could see the chained prisoners but there was no sign of the Darkwing.

'He is here,' Cusha said. 'I sense his presence.'

'Stay close to me, sister,' Vishtar said. 'As always, our enemy will have murder in his heart.'

He was right. In a dark corner the Darkwing was waiting. He had forgotten Jinghirza, the girl he had tormented for so long. He could smell Cusha. He could see her. His bleak eyes hunted her through the gloom. The demon lord imagined the way her ribs would splinter, the way her flesh would tear, the way her heart would gush sweet, refreshing blood. Soon he would drain the Holy Child, leaving her as lifeless as the world would be by the end of day.

'I'm going to free the captives,' Jinghirza said.

She started to strike their manacles with her hammer. The freed prisoners barely moved. They were suffering the catatonic drowsiness of the demon lord's victims.

'He has fed on all of them,' Vishtar said, seeing the tell-tale signs. 'But where is he now?'

Nobody spoke. They listened to the squabbling cross-winds that were whipping round Sangra Peak. Outside, the gales wailed, yelped and shrieked. Filaments of trailing snow drifted across the entrance. In the tight, pulsating dark the demon lord waited. The intruders exchanged haunted looks. They couldn't hear him but they could smell him. The reek of evil permeated every atom of this terrible place. It crawled from every space, writhed and twisted from every crack and crevice. Even Jackal's night-striders were infected with the deep, numbing throb of fear.

'He's coming,' Cusha murmured.

All around her, her comrades sensed it, the intense coiling of snarling menace.

'He's coming.'

Then, with a vile, gut-wrenching screech, the Darkwing attacked.

9

The vast fireball climbed into the sky, like the black and crimson head of some ancient dragon. Men screamed as they writhed and twisted in agony, made living torches by the exploding projectiles of Fire Dust. One after another they detonated, spraying their victims with scarlet destruction. Cowering before the intense heat, those soldiers who had not been burned were thrown into confusion, their discipline and unity splintering before the searing conflagration.

'By the holy face of Ra!' Muzal exclaimed, watching the jaws of hell gape wide and swallow hundreds of cinder-black victims.

But there was no celebration in his voice. It was not the ranks of the Army of the Free that had been immolated, but his own Sol-ket.

'What happened?' he demanded.

Then, hearing loud roars behind him, he spun round to see the fury in the faces of the Army of the Free.

'Treachery!' Oled Lonetread roared. 'Why is it always treachery from these people?'

He looked at his companions.

'Whatever they had planned for us has misfired. We will not give them a second chance.' He caught Gardep's eye. 'The Gates of Ra are open. The Sol-ket planned to unleash war. We will impose peace by force of arms. I say we enter golden Rinaghar and subdue the foe.'

Gardep nodded. So did the other leaders. Taking up their weapons, they climbed into the saddle.

'For freedom!' Oled roared.

10

'Close the gates!' Muzal yelled as he re-entered the city.

'There are no gates to close,' Asun told him.

It was true. They were on fire and useless to resist the rebel throng. Muzal stared in disbelief at the firestorm that was consuming the heart of his army. 'In the name of Ra,' he demanded, 'what happened?'

Eventually, Ghushan fought his way through the screaming confusion. 'Fire arrows,' he panted. 'They were shot from within the city.'

'From *within*!' Muzal repeated. 'But how? It makes no sense.'

'It makes complete sense, tyrant,' a voice shouted.

Muzal searched for the speaker. When he located him, his face filled with rage and disbelief. 'Sanjay!'

Fifty or so Helati surrounded the house-slave. All were armed.

'I have been waiting for this day all my life,' Sanjay shouted. 'All these years I have had to put up with your tantrums and your punishments. Worst of all, I have had to swallow your mindless raving and ranting.'

'Ingrate!' Muzal yelled, drawing his sword. 'I fed you and gave you shelter.'

Sanjay shook his head. 'You gave me nothing. You worked me half to death. You treated me like a beast of burden. But I bided my time. My heart sang when my Helat brothers and sisters gathered outside the city walls. Then I heard you talking to Asun, preparing your weapon. I sought out any man or woman who wanted to strike against their oppressors. I found many Helati keen to fight. Then, ax-Sol, I struck.'

'You'll die for this, slave,' Muzal bawled.

'Do your worst,' Sanjay told him. 'I will be waiting for you at the Ziggurat of Ra.'

Even as this exchange was taking place, Gardep, Oled and Atrakon were leading the charge through the Gates of Ra. Leaping over the smouldering catapults they drove through the demoralised Sol-ket. But, even as the dogs of war were unleashed, there was a renewed appeal for peace. Murak had mounted the city walls and was shouting at the top of his voice.

'Listen to me, Sol-ket,' he cried, 'heed my words, Hotec-Ra. This is madness. You cannot resist the Army of the Free. Shrug off the influence of the Muzals. You cannot win. For Ra's sake, live to return to your families. At least then you can have some kind of future. Yes, you will have to share wealth and power. But what will you have if you're dead? Nothing!'

He threw out his arms. 'If I have learned anything from this war, it is this. Violence begets violence. Embrace the future, my brothers. We can have peace.'

Peace was the last word to leave his lips. At that moment an arrow pierced his throat. The bowman was Asun.

11

Murak's sacrifice was not in vain. His words made sense to the beleaguered Sol-ket. Defeated at the Dragon Mountains and again at Dullah, vastly outnumbered in the present conflict, they knew the war was over. Encircled everywhere by the Army of the Free, the Children of the Sun threw down their weapons.

'Disarm them,' Oled shouted. 'Stack their weapons and guard them well.'

He caught the eye of Gardep and Atrakon.

'Take over,' he said. 'I must go to Murak.'

With that, he raced to the priest's side. He found Murak dying.

'Is it over, Oled?' Murak croaked feebly.

'Yes, Murak, it is over. The Sol-ket are disarmed. There will be no more war.'

'Thank Ra,' Murak said.

Oled stared at him for a few moments, a tumult of emotions boiling in his breast. Then, making a decision, he knelt and cradled the dying man in his arms.

'Ours could have been a great friendship, Murak, but the ways of the Hotec-Ra were too strong in you.'

'I drew no pleasure from my treachery,' Murak said. 'With each act my mouth filled with a more bitter taste. If I could only run back the sands of time, Oled. If only . . .'

He spluttered blood. Oled stared at him. In spite of everything that Murak had done, he was overwhelmed with a great sense of pity. The scene reminded the giant of his own mother's death throes.

'The world is growing cold,' Murak said. 'Don't leave me, Oled.'

'I will be here to the end,' Oled said.

Murak managed a smile of gratitude. 'Tell me that I have discovered some shred of goodness in myself,' Murak pleaded.

'Yes,' Oled said, 'you did some good, Murak. You did some good at the end.'

Murak struggled with his breathing for a few moments longer, then he lost his fight for life and went limp in Oled's arms. A life devoted to treachery was over.

12

In the confused half light Muzal climbed the Ziggurat of Ra to face Sanjay. Behind him, even his Eternals had surrendered.

'You're looking old, Muzal,' Sanjay said, watching his master steadily climbing the steps.

'I'm not too old to kill you, Helat,' Muzal panted.

Sanjay waited between the unlit braziers at the summit of the Ziggurat. 'Then kill me, old man. What are you now, Muzal, an Emperor of cinders?' He pointed the tip of his sword at Muzal's chest. 'We are equals at last.'

'No Helat will ever be equal to a lord of the Sol-ket,' Muzal snarled. 'Imagine this, Sanjay. You think you have conquered. Maybe there will yet be a Sol-ket victory of sorts. I will kill you here, atop this monument to the power of Ra. With your dying eyes you will see darkness cover the world. Yes, look to the east. There is no dawn. What an irony! At the moment your Helat cockroaches are dancing in the street, celebrating their pointless victory, my monstrous son has triumphed in the Mountains of the Moon. All you have inherited, slave, is endless night.'

Then the talking was over. Their swords clashed. Up

and down the stairs they fought, striking and slashing, until the exhausted Muzal let his sword fall from his hands. With no reserves of strength or courage left, he sank to his knees. But, as Muzal awaited the deathblow, he glimpsed Asun approaching Sanjay from the rear. The priest was drawing a bow. The arrow was tipped with Fire Dust.

As the arrow left the bowstring there was a warning shout. 'Look out!'

Sanjay seized Muzal's shoulders and used him as a human shield. The moment Asun's arrow bit into the Imperial flesh, Muzal's body exploded into flames. He tumbled down the steps, burning as Shinar had burned forty years before. Appalled, Asun searched for the man who had shouted the warning. It was Gardep. With a single arrow, Gardep sent Asun to the House of the Dead. With their deaths, the Empire passed into memory. An hour later, the victorious Army of the Free gathered around the Ziggurat of Ra. Oled's words to them were simple.

'The war here is over. There is no more that we can do. It is up to the Holy Children now.'

As one, the vast throng turned to the north and prayed.

CHAPTER 15

An Innocent and Generous Heart

I

As they anticipated the demon lord's assault, the companions could feel his presence all around them, a tangible malevolence. The coldness and savagery of his soul seemed to coat every surface with evil. Cusha led the group. Hesitant, crouching, she edged forward. Sword in hand, she searched the gloom for some sign of movement. Every fibre of her being was buzzing with apprehension. The whole place reeked of menace. She found it hard to believe that, long ago, this monastery had been a refuge. She tried to imagine it. Once there had been order and tranquillity, each of the day's devotions announced by the dull boom of the bell. Now, those sacred routines were replaced by a silence that was heavy with danger. Aaliya and Vishtar followed, darting glances up at the vaulted ceiling, alert to every wheeze and moan of the wind. The few surviving night-striders came last, fanning out, weapons in hand, ready to strike when the time came.

Jinghirza shuddered. 'We must destroy this place,' she said, flesh creeping as she remembered her days of imprisonment. 'Brick by brick we must tear it down, burn what can be burned and sow the ground with salt.'

Such was the claustrophobic atmosphere of encroaching terror: few had any faith in their weapons. It would take more than weapons to defeat the Darkwing. If anything, Cusha and Vishtar were the most anxious of all. They knew the monster better than any living being, his ruthlessness, his disregard for human life. Even so, they didn't know what to expect. Then, just as the air itself seemed to be imploding with expectation, a primal, heart-melting scream drilled through the passages of Nandraghiri. Like a great, heavy blanket, the Darkwing dropped from concealed vents in the ceiling. Avalanching from the dark, he fell upon the intruders. Jackal was first to react but the demon lord hurled him out into the howling wind. It came as no surprise to anyone that the creature selected Cusha as his prey. In his lair, he was more powerful than ever. He tossed aside the rushing night-striders like so many toy soldiers; cast them aside as he had cast their leader Jackal into the glacial void outside.

He enveloped the Holy Child in his leathery wings, folding her in his black presence. In vain, the companions fought to free her, Vishtar more than anyone. He slashed at the monster, but the Darkwing seemed invulnerable. Strengthened by the foul brew in which he bathed every night, he felt their thrusts as pinpricks. Cusha struggled to get free, but the Darkwing refused to let her go. His talons closed round her waist. He was unnaturally strong. He sniffed at her throat and his lips parted revealing glistening fangs.

'Help me!' Vishtar cried as he stabbed and stabbed again without effect, his swordpoint deflected by the monster's carapace. 'He will kill her.'

'This is just too easy,' the Darkwing hissed, spearing Cusha with a fearsome gaze. 'Did you come all this way to succumb with so little resistance?'

With a desperate lunge, Vishtar succeeded in thrusting his sword up into the Darkwing's face. Gouts of black blood sprayed over the boy, making him recoil with disgust. Still grasping Cusha by the waist, the Darkwing snarled at the Holy Child. Cords of muscle stood out from his reptilian neck. The wound had barely even made him flinch. Vishtar stared into the raven-black eyes and his insides seemed to dissolve.

'Is that all you have?' the Darkwing demanded. 'Eight years I fed on you, boy. Eight years I filled your soul with torment. And what do you do? You give me a pinprick with *this*!'

Snatching the sword out of Vishtar's hand, he drove it into the ribcage of one of the last night-striders.

'Are the Helati mad?' he wondered out loud. 'Did they really think this pathetic band could triumph over me?'

Driving Aaliya and Jinghirza back with his poisonous breath, he dragged both Holy Children to the entrance, where the polar winds snapped and yelped.

'Look out there,' he roared. 'Soon it will be dawn. Tell me, where is your precious sun? Does it stain the hills yellow? Does it illuminate the valleys? No, not this day, or any other day in the future.'

The Holy Children gazed into the grey-black half-light and were dismayed at what they saw.

'Last night,' the Darkwing gloated, 'it set for the last

time. This is the day the world finally succumbs to the icy breath of the Darkwing winter.' He leered. 'Don't you think that's wonderful? Mankind has named its last days after me. This foul race's final act will be to curse *me*.'

He drew close to them, his putrid breath stinging their faces.

'How I have longed for this moment,' he grunted. 'Those who survive this battle – and I will make sure you two do – will die slowly of cold and despair. I will watch the colour drain from your flesh, leaving you grey like that sky. Next, I will see your limbs blacken and lose sensation. Then, finally, I will watch eternal night lay its black fingers on your eyelids and put you into the sleep from which no living soul recovers.'

Behind him Aaliya and Jinghirza were gagging at the effects of the venom. The Darkwing spread his wings and took to the air.

2

The Darkwing swept upwards.

'Where are you taking us?' Vishtar cried against the buffeting wind.

'Look to your left,' the Darkwing said, swooping between towering peaks. 'There are greater peaks than Mount Sangra. From the summit of the tallest of the Mountains of the Moon, you can see half the world. I wanted to show you what has happened to the land.'

Cusha stole a glance back at Nandraghiri.

'Oh, don't fret,' the demon lord said. 'I will return you to the monastery presently. First, you will witness my triumph.'

He set them down on the greatest of the range's many

cloud-raking summits. So deep and bone numbing was the cold, the Holy Children gasped like stranded fish. Their lungs heaved and their eyes blurred. Seized by the ferocious cold, their mouths sagged open, snatching wounded breaths. Oblivious to their distress, the Darkwing pointed to the south.

'Do you see?' he cried, though they were already unable to see anything. 'The Khut land shivers under endless snowdrifts.'

He spoke of things he could imagine rather than see.

'What do you think those dark clouds are that you see moving across the plain?' he asked the now senseless pair. 'They are animals. That's right, thousands of yaks, bears, wolves, deer and mountain goats are migrating towards Jinghara, searching for food. They will find none. Further south, the blizzards are swallowing up mile after mile of what was once hot, sultry farmland. Ice clings to the battlements of Karangpur, the minarets and temple roofs of golden Rinaghar, even the terracotta walls of Tiger-gated Parcep. The southern ocean has begun to freeze. Do you see, Holy Children? Do you see?'

He turned. Cusha and Vishtar were barely conscious. Overwhelmed by the glacial, penetrating wind, they lay groaning in a near coma.

'Oh no you don't,' the creature said. His face rumpled with a lethal intelligence. 'You must live to see the final darkness come.'

3

'Aaliya,' Jinghirza shouted, drawing her sword, 'they're coming back.'

Together, they stared at the demon lord. He was

carrying the limp forms of the Holy Children. To all intents and purposes, they were dead. He dropped them to the ground and swept on towards the two women fighters. Momentarily thrown into confusion and bitter dismay, Aaliya stood rooted to the spot while the demon lord closed on her. By the time she had recovered her wits enough to put up resistance, he was upon her, dashing her to the ground.

'Say your prayers to whatever gods you have,' the Darkwing told the cowering Jinghirza. 'It is time to die along with your world.'

'I may die,' Jinghirza said. 'All mankind may perish this day. But you will have no triumph. Your solitude will be your punishment. May you rot for all time in your dark coffin. This new world of yours will be your own private hell.'

Stung by Jinghirza's defiance, he came at her with primal force, spitting, snarling and stabbing. She saw his mutilated face. It was sweating dark bile. Jinghirza could only half-deflect the attack. She did her best to protect herself but the hell-creature fastened on her shoulder. With a cry of anguish, she succumbed to the torrent of agony that gushed through her veins.

'Who will be next?' the Darkwing bellowed, hurling his challenge at the remnants of the Lost Souls. 'Is there nobody worthy of my rage?'

He raised his claws to drive them through Jinghirza's heart. Lying dazed in one corner, Aaliya's eyes focused on the small packet she had concealed days earlier in a crevice in the wall. It was the Fire Dust. She drove an arrow into the packet and shot it at the demon lord. Instantly, he was engulfed in flames. For a few moments he staggered around the chamber, beating at his blistering flesh. Aaliya stabbed several more arrowheads into the Fire Dust and shot him again, intensifying the conflagration. To her horror, though he shrieked and howled in agony, when the flames burned down, he was still standing.

'No,' Aaliya gasped, 'it's impossible.'

The Darkwing lurched towards her. That's when a skeletal figure returned from the storm outside. Its legs were shattered and it was crawling across the stone floor. It was Jackal. He seized the demon lord by the ankle and momentarily slowed his progress. The Holy Children stirred.

'Return to the fight,' Jackal cried. 'No mercy, Cusha. He is beyond redemption. Help Vishtar rid the world of his evil. Do this and I will enter the House of the Dead happy.'

Even as the Darkwing mercilessly stamped him to dust, a familiar voice made him turn.

'Our business isn't done,' Cusha said, rising unsteadily to her feet.

Before Vishtar could struggle up, the Darkwing had swept across the room, enveloping Cusha in his wings. He shook her until her teeth rattled.

'I planned to let you live to see the end of things,' he said, taking her in his death-grip. 'But I grow impatient. Savour this moment, Holy Child. It will be your last.'

Seeing the razor-sharp claws glint before her eyes, Cusha screamed. The blades flashed, then a second scream, louder, more piercing, more riven with agony, blazed through her tormentor's corrupted flesh. Enraged by the destruction of Jackal, desperate to save Cusha, Vishtar had driven his sword clean through the Darkwing's body.

'Look,' the boy cried. 'The conflagration has weakened him.'

Shuddering and jolting with violent spasms of anguish, the Darkwing released Cusha from his juddering arms.

The demon lord's voice reverberated through the winding passages of Nandraghiri. 'Even weakened,' he snarled, 'I am too strong for you.'

Gripping Vishtar's weapon, the demon lord eased himself off the blade. It seemed to take an age before he slid the sword from his fractured carapace. When he did, gobbets of black gore squirmed from the wound.

'I will make you pay for that,' the Darkwing threatened.

In a final show of defiance, Cusha and Vishtar stood side by side and faced him. They were trembling. Then Aaliya's voice put strength back in their hearts.

'This is why you were destined to reach Nandraghiri, Holy Children,' she cried, 'not to redeem the creature, but to destroy him. Remember the prophecy. This is the final battle. On this feat of arms the fate of the world will rest.'

'Of course,' Cusha cried. 'Destiny was always going to lead us to this. Now I understand the prophecy.' She took Vishtar's hand. 'We are one flesh, brother. We are one heart.'

'An innocent and generous heart,' Vishtar said, understanding at last. 'I thought it meant you. You thought it meant me. All the time, it meant the two of us together.'

Vishtar nodded. Even Cusha knew Sabray was unreachable within the hideous form of the Darkwing. Supported by Aaliya, the Holy Children fought the demon lord.

The struggle was long. It raged back and forth across the inner sanctum of Nandraghiri. Sword struck claw. Enfeebled by the Fire Dust, the Darkwing was as vulnerable as he had once been as a mortal man. With a hacking blow, Vishtar struck the side of the Darkwing's head. A chunk of the creature's skull tore free. He swayed and fell to his knees.

'This is it,' Aaliya said, stamping her boot down on the

demon lord's throat. 'You must finish him now.' She gazed at Cusha. 'Can you do it?'

Vishtar twisted his sword and cracked open the demon lord's ribcage. While he lay struggling, Cusha reached into his chest cavity and tore out his still-beating heart. Black blood stippled her face. More of the stuff puddled on the floor. The Darkwing's still-wide eyes dilated and the black fire within them died. Then, behind the backs of the Holy Children, Aaliya saw a brilliant, golden dawn.

'By the Four Winds,' she gasped.

Across the room, warmed by the life-giving rays of the rising sun, Jinghirza began to stir. Aaliya helped her to her feet. 'The wound is not fatal,' she said, examing the Khut maiden's torn shoulder. 'You are young and strong. It will heal in time.'

Jinghirza smiled. 'Soon I will return to my family, and you to Jinghara.'

Together, the four turned. They saw the great, life-giving star as if for the first time.

'It's beautiful,' Cusha said.

The sun climbed steadily, burning away the greyness that had obscured the azure sky. For the world, a new age had dawned.

4

Far away, in the great city of a fallen Empire, Rinaghar was golden once more. A wondrous sun illuminated its roofs and walls, its minarets and temples, its broad boulevards and avenues. Flocks of birds, long absent from the skies, took flight and wheeled overhead in dense swarms. Most of all, the light of the dawn warmed the faces of Sol-ket and Tanjur, Helat and barbarian, freed slave and powerless master. The sumptuous light spread like a warm, welcome tide, washing away the cold and the dark, nourishing the trees and the plants, reviving the birds, the animals, the fish and the tiniest insects. The air pulsated with bright, irrepressible life.

'They've done it,' Gardep cried. 'They've conquered the monster.'

He thought of Cusha and his heart leapt with joy. Oled too laughed out loud as he dreamed of Aaliya's return. Around them, vast crowds cheered and danced. The Ziggurat of Ra, so long the site of barbarous oppression, became the epicentre of a lavish and unbridled celebration. Hour after hour, there was music and dancing. What food could be mustered was shared, no matter what the caste, creed or nationality of the person to whom it was offered. Only as sunset reddened the great Ziggurat did some realise that they were sharing their jubilation with someone who had, just hours earlier, been a bitter foe. True reconciliation would not come that day or even that year but, with the victory of life over death, light over eternal darkness, the process of healing had begun. It was Oled Lonetread, flanked by Murima and Gardep, Atrakon and Adrius, Harad, Qintu, Nikesh and Bulu, who climbed to the summit of the Ziggurat to bid the multitude good night.

'The threat of extinction has been lifted from the land,' Oled said. 'Soon, our heroes will return from the north and we will give thanks for what they have achieved. This is the first day of our freedom, my brothers, my sisters. From this moment on, we will look to grow a sturdy crop of peace from the ashes of the fallen. Take your rest. You have earned it. Tomorrow we begin the work of forging a new freedom in which all our children can live and grow in security and shared hope. By the grace of the Four

Winds, we will wake to another wondrous dawn.'

With that, the huge crowds drifted away to find a bed for the night. Rinaghar slept soundly.

5

The boulevards of golden Rinaghar were richly scented with flowering blossom on the day that a lone Khut rider reached the former Gates of Ra. Now renamed the Gates of Freedom, the charred wooden doors opened to admit him. The guards conducted a brief interview before leading him to the house where Murima lived with Harad and Qintu.

'She's on her way!' Murima squealed with delight. 'My daughter is less than an hour from the city.'

Qintu and Harad came running from the courtyard.

'Is it true?' Harad demanded.

Murima nodded. 'She'll be here before noon.' She clapped her hands. 'What are you waiting for? We've got to find Gardep.'

They discovered him in the cells of the Great Ziggurat interrogating Murak's priests, the men who had produced the fire weapon.

'How many of you were involved?' Gardep demanded.

'We are all here,' their leader said.

'You're lying!'

'We alone are privy to the secrets of Fire Dust.' The priest met Gardep's stare. 'I swear, it's true.'

'Knowledge of the material is a sin,' Gardep said. 'This is the mandate of the people.'

'Are you going to kill us?'

Gardep shook his head. 'There are some in the Army of the Free who demanded a death sentence,' he told them.

'You were responsible for a weapon which could obliterate human life. But we are not like the Hotec-Ra. You will live out your days in sealed apartments, attached to a temple. There will be gardens to walk in. You will have books and manuscripts. But you will not be allowed to speak to another living soul. The secret of this evil weapon must die with you.'

The priests lowered their heads. 'We thank you for your mercy.'

'And nobody else knows about the dust?' Gardep asked again.

'Nobody.'

Gardep exchanged glances with Oled and Atrakon. They had been listening in silence. Gardep was about to say something when he glimpsed Murima and the boys standing in the doorway. There was something in Murima's eyes that made his heart leap.

'Cusha?' he asked.

Murima nodded. 'She's here.'

Oled too had a question. 'Aaliya?'

'Yes,' Murima said. 'They all lived to tell the tale: Cusha, Aaliya, Vishtar, all of them.'

Atrakon looked at Oled and Gardep. 'Just go,' he said with a grin. 'I can handle things here.'

The thunder of five horses could be heard drumming towards the Karangpur road.

6

Atrakon oversaw the movement of the Hotec-Ra to their temple-prison. He was about to go when he saw a silhouetted figure waiting for him. 'Sanjay?'

The Emperor's former servant stepped forward.

'Don't believe them, Atrakon Ebrahin,' he said.

Atrakon frowned. 'What do you know, Sanjay?'

'When I spied upon Muzal, I learned many things,' Sanjay said. 'I counted the priests involved in the production of the Fire Dust. When I heard that you had captured the Hotec-Ra, I came to see if you had them all in custody. My heart sank when I saw them being led into the interrogation room. Two are missing.'

'Do you know their names?'

Sanjay nodded. 'I do.'

'And would you recognise them again?'

Once more, Sanjay nodded.

'Do you understand what this means?' Atrakon asked.

'Yes,' Sanjay sighed, 'for some men the task of guarding their fellow man goes on for ever. They must be eternally vigilant.'

'Are you ready for this sacrifice?' Atrakon demanded.

'My life has been one of hardship and enslavement,' Sanjay said. 'Nothing that destiny places in my path can be worse than that. I may face many dangers to pursue those who would put our freedom in danger but I will be a free man. If you are planning to arrange a party to hunt them down, I will go with you.'

Atrakon seized Sanjay by the hand.

'You are a good man. Be ready to leave at a moment's notice.'

Sanjay smiled. 'Will the fight for freedom ever be over?' he asked.

Atrakon shook his head. 'Maybe this is the meaning of the Book of Scales,' the Selessian said. 'All things are meant to exist in balance. But mortal men and women have to fight to maintain that equilibrium. There is nothing inevitable about the triumph of good over evil. Only one thing can safely be predicted: the contest will continue as long as some of nature's children seek power over others. Are you sure you are ready for that fight?'

Sanjay let the sun's rays fall on his face.

'Yes,' he said, 'I am ready.'

7

The moment Gardep saw the riders in the distance; he spurred his horse and galloped towards them. Cusha did likewise. They met on the spot where the tent of peace had been. Gardep swept his beloved from her saddle and they embraced, weeping.

'There were times,' Gardep said, 'that I was weak. I lost faith in your return.'

Cusha pressed her cheek against his. 'That is not weakness, my love,' she said. 'The same shadows often flitted across my soul. We dared to oppose the most sinister forces this cruel world has mustered. We are flesh and blood, not gods. Gardep, we are human, that's all, with human hopes and dreams, yes, and human fears.'

'I have something to tell you,' Gardep said. 'I have stepped back from the position Shamana gave me. Oled Lonetread is now protector-general of the Free. He will guide the people through the difficult first years of freedom. Are you disappointed in me?'

'Disappointed?' Cusha said. She laughed out loud. 'Oh, Gardep,' she said. 'These words fill my heart with great joy. I am coming home to a man, not a general. Let others conduct the affairs of government. Through all our trials we promised one another that, one day, there would be a time for love. This is that time.' She clung to him. 'In the darkest moments on the journey to Nandraghiri, at the most critical turning points in our struggle, it was the thought of your touch, your breath that enabled me to go on. I thank the Four Winds that you are free of the expectations of destiny.'

Gardep stroked wild wisps of raven hair from her face. 'By what miracle of Fate were you placed in my path?' he murmured.

'Why, by the providence of the Scales, of course,' Cusha said. 'Perhaps, in all the chaos of a troubled land, there is truly some sense of order, some trace of purpose.'

Gardep gazed at her. 'If I didn't know better,' he said, 'I would say that your eyes are even darker than when you left.'

Cusha shook her head and smiled. She didn't tell him that there was a reason for that deeper blackness. She had seen into a soul so cold, so lacking in mercy, so incapable of redemption, that an edge of irresistible foreboding had been added to her view of the world. The last trace of her childhood innocence had gone.

Murima, Aaliya and Vishtar joined them; Harad and Qintu hovering uncertainly at the edge of the group. Their time of great journeys and many hard struggles was over.

8

Cusha's marriage to Gardep took place at the summit of the Ziggurat of Ra. It would be their final appearance before the people as leaders. They met before a huge crowd beneath a canopy. Cusha's throat and midriff were bare and her hair dressed with fine jewellery. Their bodies had been anointed with turmeric, sandalwood paste and oils, making them pure and fragrant, ready to exchange their oaths. They swapped gifts and garlands and received the congratulations of the guests and the acclamation of the crowd. Cusha was an orphan, her parents long dead, so Murima and Oled performed the marriage duties instead, pouring water over Cusha's bare arms – the giving away of the bride to the groom.

Cusha glanced round at Oled. 'It will be you and Aaliya next,' she said.

Oled could only huff and rub his whiskers self-consciously.

'Step forward,' Aaliya said.

Then Cusha and Gardep faced each other. Aaliya, now the senior priestess of the Scales, tied the bride's sari to the groom's shirt in a knot, symbolising their union. After that, a sacred fire was lit and sprinkled with crushed sandalwood, herbs, sugar, rice, ghee and twigs. Gardep took Cusha's left hand in his right. After all this time, he started at her touch as if pricked by thorn bushes. In that precious moment, he knew he would never tire of her touch. Squeezing her hand tenderly, he faced west while Cusha sat facing east. She too marvelled that the warmth of his body behind her made her senses swim, that his presence made her blood race in her veins. With their free hands, they pointed to north and south. Overjoyed to be united for ever with his bride, Gardep's senses were swimming. He had made the right choice. What was duty and kingship compared to this?

'By the Four Winds and the secret ways of the Scales,' he said, struggling to speak through the tightness in his throat, 'I swear that I will do all in my power to make this marriage prosper.'

In response Cusha, smiling with joy, cupped her hands, receiving grain from Harad and Qintu before offering it as a sacrifice to the Four Winds.

'This grain I spill,' she said, the words ringing from

her lips like music. 'May it bring us both wellbeing and happiness.'

Bride and groom then stood before the ritual fire and closed their eyes, remembering their ancestors and their lost friends. Finally, after embracing, they took handfuls of flower petals from baskets held by Aaliya, Murima, Harad and Qintu and scattered them over the heads of the listening multitude. Their marriage ceremony was at an end. Immediately, old friend and new acquaintance alike engulfed them. Murima, Harad and Qintu were the first to offer their congratulations, their eyes glittering with tears.

'Just imagine,' Harad said, 'my beautiful sister married and the land free. Tell me it isn't all a dream.'

'If it is a dream,' Qintu said, 'then you've been asleep an awfully long time!'

Murima hugged Cusha, kissing her forehead. 'You are my heart, my life,' she said. 'By all that is holy in this world, I knew you were special the first day I saw you. For all that, I did not dream that these tiny hands would know how to turn the world upside down.'

Cusha blinked back her tears. 'It seems such a long time,' she said, 'since that sultry night in Parcep.'

The following morning, there was a parting of the ways for the companions who had crossed the great world to make it anew. Atrakon, Nikesh and Sanjay rode to Tiger-gated Parcep, there to embark on a ship for foreign parts. There was a rumour that the rebel priests were seeking refuge in distant Lukshmir. No matter what the cost, they would pursue the escaped Hotec-Ra to the end of the Earth and bring them to justice. They had to be stopped or the terrible secret of Fire Dust could yet cost mankind dear. Bulu departed for Zindhar, from which he would govern the northern provinces. With Adrius as their guide, Gardep and Cusha would set off on an expedition to

Inbacus, the city of the warrior's birth. Gardep wanted to discover the last secrets of his origins. Oled and Aaliya watched the departures from the Gates of Freedom.

'Do you think there will ever truly be peace?' Oled said, feeling the terrible weight of leadership on his shoulders. 'Will Shamana's dreams ever be fulfilled?'

'I fear that there is something destructive in the hearts of men,' Aaliya said, 'but we can be sure of this, my love. From this time on, no mortal man or woman will hold another human being in servitude. Nobody will have to endure a life being treated as a chattel to be bought and sold, flogged and denied freedom. From the moment you led the Army of the Free through the gates of golden Rinaghar, there has been an end to demons, an end to oppression.'

She took his hand. 'You are the son of the She-wolf,' she said, 'and a worthy successor to great Shamana. With you to lead us, there will be balance in the land, between male and female, light and dark.'

They watched the sun rising steadily over the Great Ziggurat.

'There will be justice.'

Also by Alan Gibbons

SHADOW OF THE MINOTAUR

'Real life' or the death defying adventures of the Greek myths, with their heroes and monsters, daring deeds and narrow escapes – which would you choose?

For Phoenix it's easy. He hates his new home and the new school where he is bullied. He's embarrassed by his computer geek dad. But when he logs on to the Legendeer, the game his dad is working on, he can be a hero. He is Theseus fighting the terrifying Minotaur, or Perseus battling with snake-haired Medusa.

The trouble is The Legendeer is more than just a game. Play it if you dare.

VAMPYR LEGION

What if there are real worlds where our nightmares live and wait for us?

Phoenix has found one and it's alive. Armies of blood-sucking vampyrs and terrifying werewolves, the creatures of our darkest dreams, are poised to invade our world.

But Phoenix has encountered the creator of *Vampyr Legion*, the evil Gamesmaster, before and knows that this deadly computer game is for real - he must win or never come back.

WARRIORS OF THE RAVEN

The game opens up the gateway between our world and the world of the myths.

The Gamesmaster almost has our world at his mercy. Twice before fourteen-year-old Phoenix has battled against him in *Shadow of the Minotaur* and *Vampyr Legion*, but Warriors of the Raven is the game at its most complex and deadly level. This time, Phoenix enters the arena for the final conflict, set in the world of Norse myth. Join Phoenix in Asgard to fight Loki, the Mischief-maker, the terrifying Valkyries, dragons and fire demons - and hope for victory. Our future depends on him.

SCARED TO DEATH

HELL'S UNDERGROUND BOOK 1

You sent me into eternal darkness.
I want nothing less for you.

Deep beneath the slick, sour city a dark heart stirs,
seeking chaos.

Deep inside an ordinary teenager a secret,
deadly power is emerging.

When Paul meets the enigmatic Redman, he begins a hell-raising journey that takes him from the streets and subways of London today back to the city's slums in the realm of Jack the Ripper . . . and into the horror of Hell's Underground.

A thriller and a horror story, *Scared to Death* is Alan Gibbons at his best.